Naked in the Rain

Naked in the Rain

Eowyn Wood

Copyright © 2007 by Eowyn Wood.

All rights reserved. No part of this book may be used or reproduced in any manner whatsoever without written permission from the publisher, except in the case of brief quotations embodied in critical articles and reviews; nor may any part of this book be reproduced, stored in a retrieval system, or transmitted in any form or by any means electronic, mechanical, photocopying, recording, or other, without written permission from the publisher.

The characters and events in this book are fictitious. Any similarity to real persons, living or dead, is coincidental and not intended by the author.

ISBN 0-9778738-0-3

Printed in the United States of America.

Publisher's Cataloging-in-Publication Data

Wood, Eowyn.
   Naked in the rain : a novel / by Eowyn Wood.
   p. cm.
   ISBN 0-9778738-0-3
   1. Male sexual abuse victims—Fiction. 2. Gay couples—Fiction. 3. Male prostitution—California—Los Angeles—Fiction. 4. Teenage prostitution—California—Los Angeles—Fiction. 5. Los Angeles (Calif.)—Fiction. I. Title.
PS3623.O6235N35 2007   813'.6
                        QBI06-600425

PO Box 83066
Portland, OR 97283
www.crookedhills.com

Grateful acknowledgment is made for permission to reprint lyrics from the following songs:

"Bionic"
Words and Music by Brian Molko, Stefan Olsdal and Robert Schultzbert
© 1996 by Famous Music LLC
International Copyright Secured. All Rights Reserved.

"Black-Dove" by Tori Amos
© 1998 Atlantic Recording Corporation and WEA International Inc.
All rights administered by Sword and Stone Publishing
Used by Permission. All Rights Reserved.

"Cowboys"
Words and Music by Beth Gibbons and Geoff Barrow
© 1997 Chrysalis Music Ltd.
All Rights in the U.S.A. and Canada Administered by Chrysalis Music
All Rights Reserved. Used by Permission.

"Cruel Sun"
Words and Music by MARK LINKOUS
© 1998 WB MUSIC CORP. and SPIRIT DITCH MUSIC
All Rights Administered by WB MUSIC CORP.
All Rights Reserved. Used by Permission.

"Disarm"
Words and Music by Billy Corgan
© 1993 Chrysalis Songs and Cinderful Music
All Rights for the U.S. and Canada Administered by Chrysalis Songs
All Rights Reserved. Used by Permission.

"Faith"
Written by: Robert J. Smith/Simon Gallup/Laurence Tolhurst
©1981 BMG Music Publishing Ltd. (PRS)/Fiction Songs Ltd. (PRS)
All rights for the World o/b/o Fiction Songs Ltd. (PRS) administered by BMG Music Publishing Ltd. (PRS)
All rights for the US o/b/o BMG Music Publishing Ltd. (PRS) and Fiction Songs Ltd. (PRS) administered by BMG Songs, Inc. (ASCAP) Used by permission
BMG Songs claims 100%

"Flood" written by Kristin Hersh
© 1995 THROWING MUSIC (BMI) Administered by BUG
All Rights Reserved. Used By Permission.

"Ghost Of His Smile"
Words and Music by MARK LINKOUS
© 1999 WB MUSIC CORP. and SPIRIT DITCH MUSIC
All Rights Administered by WB MUSIC CORP.
All Rights Reserved. Used by Permission.

"House Rent Boogie" by John Lee Hooker
© 1971 by ABC Dunhill Music, Inc.
All rights administered by Songs of Universal, Inc. / BMI
Used By Permission. All Rights Reserved.

"It's My Party"
Words and Music by HERB WIENER, JOHN GLUCK and WALLY GOLD
© 1963 (Renewed) WORLD SONG PUBLISHING, INC.
All Rights Administered by CHAPPELL & CO.
All Rights Reserved. Used by Permission.

"The Killing Moon"
Words and Music by PETE DE FREITAS, IAN MCCULLOCH, LES PATTINSON and WILL SERGEANT
© 1983 WARNER BROS. MUSIC LTD.
All Rights for WARNER BROS. MUSIC LTD. in the USA and Canada Administered by WB MUSIC CORP.
All Rights Reserved. Used by Permission.

"The Kiss"
Written by: Robert J. Smith/Simon Gallup/Laurence Tolhurst/Paul Thompson/ Boris Williams
©1987 BMG Music Publishing Ltd. (PRS)/Fiction Songs Ltd. (PRS)
All rights for the World o/b/o Fiction Songs Ltd. (PRS) administered by BMG Music Publishing Ltd. (PRS)
All rights for the US o/b/o BMG Music Publishing Ltd. (PRS) and Fiction Songs Ltd. (PRS) administered by BMG Songs, Inc. (ASCAP) Used by permission
BMG Songs claims 100%

"Ladies And Gentlemen, We Are Floating in Outer Space"
Words and Music by Jason Pierce
© 1993 Chrysalis Music Ltd.
All Rights for the U.S. and Canada Administered by Chrysalis Songs
All Rights Reserved. Used by Permission.

"Little Earthquakes" by Tori Amos
© 1991 Warner Music UK Ltd., a Time Warner Company
All rights administered by Sword and Stone Publishing
Used by Permission. All Rights Reserved.

"Lullaby"
Written by: Robert J. Smith/Simon Gallup/Laurence Tolhurst/Paul Thompson/Boris Williams/Roger O'Donnell
©1989 BMG Music Publishing Ltd. (PRS)/Fiction Songs Ltd. (PRS)
All rights for the World o/b/o Fiction Songs Ltd. (PRS) administered by BMG Music Publishing Ltd. (PRS)
All rights for the US o/b/o BMG Music Publishing Ltd. (PRS) and Fiction Songs Ltd. (PRS) administered by BMG Songs, Inc. (ASCAP) Used by permission
BMG Songs claims 100%

"Mystery of Love, The" by Polly Jean Harvey
© 2004 by Hot Head Music Ltd.
All rights in the United States adminstered by Universal–Polygram International Publishing, Inc. / ASCAP
Used By Permission. All Rights Reserved.

"Nancy Boy"
Words and Music by Brian Molko, Stefan Olsdal and Robert Schultzbert
© 1996 by Famous Music LLC
International Copyright Secured. All Rights Reserved.

"Pepper" by Butthole Surfers, lyrics by Gibby Haynes
© 1996 Capitol Records
All rights administered by Latino Buggerveil Music
Used by Permission. All Rights Reserved.

"Scared of Girls"
Words and Music by Brian Molko, Stefan Olsdal and Steven Hewitt
© 1998 by Famous Music LLC
International Copyright Secured. All Rights Reserved.

"Silent All These Years" by Tori Amos
© 1991 Warner Music UK Ltd., a Time Warner Company
All rights administered by Sword and Stone Publishing
Used by Permission. All Rights Reserved.

"The Sky Is A Poisonous Garden"
Words and Music by Johnette Napolitano and Bruce Moreland
© 1990 EMI LONGITUDE MUSIC, INTERNATIONAL VELVET MUSIC and DEAD LOS ANGELES MUSIC
All rights for INTERNATIONAL VELVET MUSIC Controlled and Administered by EMI LONGITUDE MUSIC
All Rights Reserved. International Copyright Secured. Used by Permission.

"Teenage Angst"
Words and Music by Brian Molko, Stefan Olsdal and Robert Schultzbert
© 1996 by Famous Music LLC
International Copyright Secured. All Rights Reserved.

"Teller" written by Kristin Hersh
© 1995 THROWING MUSIC (BMI) Administered by BUG
All Rights Reserved. Used By Permission.

"Who Killed Mr. Moonlight?" by Peter Murphy, Daniel Gaston Ash, David Jay, Kevin Haskins
© 1983 by Universal/Momentum Music 3 Ltd.
All rights in the United States administered by Universal–PolyGram International Publishing, Inc. / ASCAP
Used By Permission. All Rights Reserved.

"You Go To My Head"
By J. Fred Coots and Haven Gillespie
© 1938 (Renewed) Haven Gillespie Music and Toy Town Tunes, Inc.
Permission Secured. All Rights Reserved

"You're Sixteen"
Words and Music by RICHARD M. SHERMAN and ROBERT B. SHERMAN
© 1960 (Renewed) WARNER-TAMERLANE PUBLISHING CORP.
All Rights Reserved. Used by Permission.

PART 1

*"An introverted kind of soul
the earth did open
swallow whole"*

- Placebo, "Scared of Girls"

CHAPTER 1

River listened to the squeak of footsteps coming closer to his door. He hurried to hide his cigarettes under the mattress—they said he was too young to smoke. *Adults are stupid*, he thought.

He sat on the edge of his bed and scowled at the empty bunk across from him. He'd enjoyed having his own space since his roommate left the institution last week. But now some new idiot was about to disrupt his peace.

Fuck it, he thought and ran fingers through his messy dark blond hair. The door opened, and he glanced at the new boy—dark hair, pale. Young. River fixed his eyes on the blank wall straight ahead.

The nurse stood in the doorway. "River, your new roommate is here."

"Whoopee fuckin do." He folded his arms over his chest and kept his eyes on the wall.

She ignored his comment. "This is Brian. I trust you'll show him the ropes. Brian, dinner is in two hours in the cafeteria." She closed the door behind her and left them alone.

The new boy set his backpack on the empty bed, sank down beside it and leaned back against the wall. River took a better look at him. *He's just a kid.* He wondered what Brian had done to land in a mental institution.

River reached under the mattress for his cigarettes, and Brian sat up. "They let you smoke here?"

Their eyes met. *Whoa.* Brian had the most amazing eyes River had ever seen. Not just the way the vivid blue contrasted with his dark hair, but the unusual shape—so round on top.

Brian's eyes moved to stare at the cigarettes. River could tell he wanted one. *He's awful young to smoke.* He almost said it out loud, but he didn't want to sound like his stepdad. He frowned at the thought, and his mood darkened.

Brian turned to riffle through his backpack.

River craned his neck. "You got smokes in there?"

"I don't know. Probably not."

He sneered. "What, did your mommy pack your bag for you?"

"I guess so. I came here straight from the hospital."

River saw bandages around Brian's wrists and felt a twinge of guilt. He offered a cigarette from his own dwindling pack.

"Thanks."

River watched the way he smoked. Deep drags, fully inhaled. So the kid wasn't just trying to be cool; he really did smoke. Brian folded his arm across his stomach and rested his other elbow on it so the hand with the cigarette was propped up near his lips. Such a feminine pose. Disturbing. River noticed a tiny silver hoop in his left ear and said, "You smoke like a girl."

Brian looked hurt, and River actually felt bad for being mean. They smoked in silence until the cigarettes were stubs. River held out the empty pop can he used for an ashtray. Brian dropped it in without a word, then moved to unpack his few belongings—a digital clock, a dictionary, clothes. River watched him fold tee shirts and sweaters neatly and put them away in the nightstand. A piece of baby blue paint peeled off in Brian's hand as he pushed the drawer closed. Brian glanced around at bare, dull walls, then moved to stare out the window between the nightstands, his fingers hooked in the wire mesh that covered the glass, bandages around both small wrists.

River set the pack of smokes on his bedside table, and Brian helped himself to another cigarette. River frowned but found himself reluctant to complain. *What's wrong with me?*

Brian lay on his bed, stared at the ceiling and smoked until the cigarette was gone. River gave up waiting for him to speak first. "You gonna lay there all day?"

Brian seemed startled, as if he'd forgotten River was there. His eyes looked a little spacey.

"Are you on drugs?" River asked.

"No," he mumbled and rubbed his face. "I don't know. I'm tired, but I can't keep my eyes shut."

"Come on. I'll show you around."

"Okay." Brian stood up. "Thanks."

"Don't be thankin me yet. You haven't seen the place." He scrunched his face in disgust and laughed.

Brian responded with a slight smile.

On their way out River pointed to a second door. "That's our tiny-ass bathroom. Don't piss on the floor." *Like my last roommate.* River forced himself to glare.

Brian shook his head, eyes round, and followed him into the wide hallway. The walls were a dingy grey, made even uglier by bright fluorescents overhead. Their sneakers squeaked on the discolored linoleum.

Brian seemed nervous. River understood. *It's hard not to be scared here at first.* He commented on all the patients they passed. "Inmates," River called them. "Don't mess with that guy." He nodded toward an older teen standing by the wall. "He's a psycho. Violent tendencies. But this guy—" River pointed to another boy headed toward them. "He's hilarious. Hey, Jeff, seen any dogs lately?"

The boy's brow knit, and he answered in a high voice, "Where's my dog?" He glanced around as if he might find the dog here, then started bawling.

River laughed. "What a wimp."

Brian looked over his shoulder as a nurse tried to quiet the boy.

They reached the end of the hall and turned left to pass through heavy double doors. "These lock at eight. Don't get caught on the other side, or you'll be in trouble."

The short corridor opened onto a large room with a few couches, tables, an ancient console TV. Wire mesh covered all the windows. Teenagers and a few younger kids milled about, most of them clustered around the TV set. The mismatched furniture appeared to date from the seventies. Ugly orange couch, olive green chairs. At least the paint didn't seem as old as the furniture. The brick walls were cheery lemon yellow.

"This here's the common room, everybody's favorite—cos the chicks are here. We're in the boys' section," River explained. "The only place we can mix with girls is here and the cafeteria. And outside, if you got grounds privileges."

"Oh." Brian's eyes darted at all the people, and he fidgeted. "Do you have a cigarette?"

"No, dude. Not here. We ain't allowed to smoke. We're 'too young.' Bunch of bullshit." Though maybe true in Brian's case. "What are you, like twelve?"

A ghost of a smile touched Brian's face. "Almost. How old are you?"

"I'll be fourteen in a few months. January."

He whispered, "Aren't you afraid you'll get caught smoking?"

"Nah. I'm always in trouble anyway. What's the difference? Besides, I don't think they really care." River pulled up a chair, put his feet on the table and leaned back. "There ain't much else to see, except outside. But neither of us have grounds privileges just now."

Brian's brow furrowed as he took a seat. "We can't go outside? For how long?"

"Less than a week, if you're good." River gave a mischievous smile. "But I ain't always good."

"How long have you been here?"

"About a month. Two more to go. I'll be home in time for Thanksgiving. Whoopee." River rolled his eyes.

"You know when you're getting out?"

"Of course, same as everybody." River took his feet off the table and leaned forward. "Didn't they tell you?"

"No."

"Jesus Christ. This place is a fuckin joke." He shook his head. "It goes like this: everybody in the youth wing is here for three months. No matter what. Three months."

"What if you're not better?"

"Shit. They don't care. The program's for three months, so that's what we get. Besides, you can't expect these dumb asses to fix you." He shrugged. "I like the three-month thing, cos they can't hold it over my head. I'll get out no matter what."

"Three months." Brian stared at the table. "You know, I think they did say that. I remember my parents standing by the hospital bed talking about it, but it's so hazy.... I thought it was a dream. Don't you hate when you can't tell dreams from reality?" He gave a short laugh.

River quirked a smile at him. "Sure, Brian." *This guy's a nut.* "You were probably doped up. Speaking of, they're trying out a new program here—no meds. Except for the hopeless cases. Bummer." River shook his head. "Their way to save money, I bet."

"Hey, River-baby," a female voice called out. A pretty blond sauntered over, hips swinging.

"Hey, Sandra. This is my new roommate, Brian."

"Hi, Brian."

"Hello," he said softly. He glanced at her, then looked down.

She smiled. "Aw, isn't he cute?"

Brian blushed. He felt young and stupid and out of place. And tired. So tired.

River said, "He's too young for you, Sandra."

"Oh, no worries, hon." She squeezed River's arm, then walked away.

River's eyes followed her down the corridor. "That's one fine piece of ass."

Brian jerked awake that night and stared into darkness—but not as dark as it was before. Light shone dimly, outlining a figure in the doorway. His heart thumped. He pulled the covers up higher and stared at the silhouette.

After a moment the figure moved away into the hall and closed the door.

It was a long time before he slept again.

He asked River about it the next day during study hall.

"That's the duty nurse. They gotta do night checks on us. It's such a joke—they're supposed to be random, but they ain't. They always come between midnight and one. And again early in the morning, like at five." River grinned. "Did it scare ya?"

"Well . . . I wasn't sure if it was real," he mumbled and turned to his notebook.

River tipped his chair back, his feet braced against the table. Study hall bored him. They didn't even get real desks, just these long tables like in the cafeteria. The 'classrooms' were too big for staff to keep proper control. River didn't mind that.

He glanced at the dark-haired boy beside him. Brian had finished the homework sent by his school and seemed to be daydreaming, doodling on the piece of paper where he'd written the schedule in neat script: breakfast, then study hall all morning, lunch, 'assignments'—more like free labor—and finally the coveted free time. But only free when they didn't have group therapy or a private session. Or extra assignments for being bad.

River smiled at the memory of his latest adventure—his attempt to sneak into the girl's wing. He hadn't gotten far, but it was fun. His smile faded as he stared at the bare walls surrounding him like a prison. He glanced at the rows of kids goofing off, staff roaming around trying to keep order. The sweet kid beside him doodling.

He watched a dragon come to life from Brian's pencil, detailed and ornate. It breathed fire onto a human stick figure. River let all four legs of his chair drop to the floor. "You're left-handed? I didn't notice that before." He'd always thought left-handed people were a bit odd. *Brian is definitely odd.*

"I use my right hand for homework," Brian said. "I'm ambidextrous."

"Ammi-what?"

"Ambidextrous. It means I can use both hands."

"I never heard of that," he said, unconvinced.

"I think I was supposed to be left-handed, but my mom always moved the pencil to my right hand. So I used that hand when other people were around, in school and stuff. But I kept using my left in private. So it depends on what I'm doing." Brian shrugged. "I use my left hand when I'm writing in my journal or drawing. Stuff like that."

"Oh," River responded, nonplussed. *Weird.*

"Boys!" A staffer snapped her fingers at them. "Hush."

River laughed and tipped his chair back again.

ꙮꙮꙮ

"Hurry up," River said as Brian put on his shoes. "She's leaving any minute."

They rushed to the common room and arrived just in time. An older girl with spiky hair was heading down the hallway that led to the outside world. River yelled, "Hey, Kasey! Wait."

She turned around.

He caught up with her and whispered, "Can you pick up cigarettes for us?" He snuck folded money into her hand.

Her eyes lit up as she grinned. River knew it appealed to her nature to sneak stuff in here. She was a great source. She tucked the cash down her shirt and strode off.

"Yes!" River raised his fists in triumph and high-fived Brian.

"I'll pay you back, I swear," Brian said.

"No shit you will." He smiled. "Maybe you can do my chores for me."

"No, my sister promised to bring cash. The psychologist said I can have visitors soon."

River frowned. "We'll see. Let's get breakfast."

They walked to the cafeteria and stood in line with their trays. "Man, the food here sucks. I miss jalapeños."

Brian didn't seem to hear—daydreaming again. He said, "I've decided to become a vegetarian."

River snorted. "Why?"

"I've always felt guilty eating animals. If I can live without it, then I should."

River stared at him. "You're weird."

Their trays full, River led the way to sit beside Sandra. A younger girl with long braids sat across from Brian and smiled at him. "You're new, aren't you?"

"Yeah, I got here two days ago." Brian tried to focus as she introduced herself. Jenny. Heat rose in his face as she gazed at him, and he knew his cheeks were turning red. He hated that.

"What grade are you in?" she asked.

"I just started seventh. But only for a couple of weeks before . . . ." He stared at his tray, and his wrists itched under the bandages.

"I'm in seventh grade, too!" Jenny's smile broadened.

Brian managed to smile back.

A commotion broke out a few tables over—a couple of older boys arguing. Their voices grew louder, and they started pushing each other. River jumped up. "I gotta get in on this."

He hurried over, pushed one of the offenders hard and knocked him off balance. The other boy yelled at him. River threw a punch, and the three of them were in full battle. River picked up a tray and smashed it down on the boy's head.

"That's River for you," Sandra sighed. "Always loves a good fight."

ריריר

The psychologist put the Rorschach cards back in the drawer and folded his pudgy hands on the desk. Brian was a bit disappointed—he liked interpreting the crazy ink splotches. Much better than talking, anyway.

The man said, "You need to open up if we're going to help you."

Brian's eyes moved to the stacks of files and books that filled the small office. He didn't know why he couldn't talk about his problems. *Maybe cos I don't want to think about it. And what's the point? No one can help me.* But he didn't want to lose his pending grounds privileges. *Give him a little.* "My mom yells a lot."

The man nodded and seemed to think he'd won something. *You don't know anything,* Brian thought.

River rubbed the sting of his split lip as he walked back to his room, finally finished with today's assignments. He had extra chores for two weeks as punishment—he'd taken the work in exchange for grounds privileges. He remembered the satisfaction as his fists connected. *It was worth it,* he thought as he fell onto his bed.

He felt a tug on his arm. "Come on," Brian said. "I waited for you."

"In a minute." River smiled to himself. It was good to see Brian excited for once.

A few minutes later they stepped into warm afternoon sunshine. Brian took a deep breath and let it out with a grin. "I missed fresh air."

They wandered around the grounds, avoiding the guards who stood near the massive brick building. "Ain't much to see," River said. "Just trees and grass."

"That's enough. It's great to be outside again." Brian looked up at leaves just beginning to turn autumn gold and moved closer to touch a big maple. He ran his fingers down the trunk, his face aglow. "I love trees," he said softly.

River could see now that Brian's hair really was dark brown, not black like it seemed inside. It glinted in the sun with highlights he'd never noticed before. Brian looked down, and his long lashes made shadows on his flushed cheeks. *Pretty.* River shook himself. *Pretty? Guy's aren't pretty.*

Brian looked up at him, a smile on his full lips. "Your hair is pretty in the sun."

River blinked in surprise. It freaked him out for a second, like Brian had read his mind.

"Your hair looks blonder," Brian said. "With threads of gold running through it."

River smiled self-consciously and shrugged. If anyone else called his hair pretty, he would've slugged 'em. He glanced down, then bent to pick up a reddish-colored rock. "Look at this." He held it out.

Brian turned it over and rubbed his finger along the smooth surface. "It looks like jasper. Strange to see it here. Jasper comes from the desert."

"Huh. Like me. I'm from Arizona." River took the rock back. "Guess we're both a long way from home." He glanced at Brian. "How far is it?"

"Arizona to Connecticut?" He thought a moment. "Over 2,000 miles."

River tucked the jasper into his jeans pocket. "You're the kinda guy who does good in school, ain'tcha?"

Brian's cheeks turned redder. "Yeah, I guess. But I don't try. I hate school."

"But you still get A's."

"Yeah." Brian stared at the ground and thought, *Don't tell him you skipped a grade.* That did nothing to help his popularity and ensured he was always the smallest boy in class. He brightened and met River's eyes. "But not math—I'm really bad at that. I'm no good with numbers."

"Yeah?" River smiled. "That's about the only thing I am good at. And P.E." His smile broadened into a grin. "Bet I can beat you to the fence." He nodded toward the chain-link with barbed wire on top, then tapped Brian's arm and took off running.

"Hey!" Brian chased after him. He hit the fence long after River. "That wasn't fair," he panted. "You've got longer legs."

"But I still won." River grinned, his hair glowing golden like the leaves, grey-green eyes full of mischief.

Brian wanted to touch him. But he laughed instead and nodded. "You won."

The next day when River returned from his extra assignments, Brian was lying on his stomach writing in a leather-bound book.

"What's that?" River asked.

"My journal," he answered in a quiet voice.

"A diary?"

"Not exactly. I write feelings and stuff. Or words that repeat in my head until I write them down."

River frowned. *Weird.*

Brian closed the journal and put it away in his nightstand, his face sad and frail.

"Did you go outside today?" River asked.

"No, my sister visited."

Free time was also visiting time—though River wouldn't know. No one ever visited him. "I thought you wanted to see her."

"Yeah." Brian tucked up his knees and wrapped his arms around them. "I don't know why it upset me. I love my sister." He shrugged. "I guess it stirred up everything I've been trying to forget."

River met his eyes, the deep blue that reached right inside him. He wished he could take away Brian's pain. "Your parents suck, huh? Mine, too." River glanced away, and his fists clenched. "My stepdad's such a bastard. Beats the shit outta me all the time. And my mom's no help. She just drinks all day and lets everything around her turn to shit. She doesn't care." River stopped. He hadn't meant to say so much. He shook his head and stared at the floor.

Brian said softly, "I guess everyone has it bad."

"Does your old man beat you?"

"No. He's a nice guy. My mom's the problem."

"She hits you?"

"No. She . . . I guess she's pretty fucked up in the head. Which is unfortunate for those around her." His lips twisted down.

"Life's a bitch, and then you die." He gestured at Brian's wrists. "Or you can help it along."

Brian ducked his head.

"Sorry, man, you don't have to talk about it."

"I just . . . couldn't take it anymore." Brian bit his lip and looked like he might cry.

"Sure, I can dig that." River tried to lighten the mood. "Let's go outside and race. I'll let you win."

The next day they had lots of free time—Saturday. But the weather wasn't cooperating. They sat in overstuffed chairs in the common room and watched rain beat on the windows. Brian frowned and craved a cigarette. *It's not fair they don't let us smoke. It's our bodies.*

River said, "I forgot to tell you, there's optional religious service tomorrow in the chapel. Every Sunday."

Brian looked at him. "Chapel? I guess we missed that on our tour."

"Yeah." River shrugged. "I'm not sure where it is, actually."

Brian gazed out the window again and watched the pattern of rain on the glass. Like random notes of music. His fingers clenched. Music. His soul ached for it. *I need a piano.*

"Are you gonna go?" River asked.

"Go where?"

He rolled his eyes. "To the service tomorrow, smart ass."

"Oh." Brian laughed, glad for the distraction. "No, thanks."

"What religion are you?"

He shrugged. "I'm not any. I guess technically I'm an atheist."

River's eyebrows went up.

Brian said, "But people get the wrong idea if I say that. It's not that I don't believe in anything. I believe in afterlife and reincarnation and stuff. I just don't believe in god."

"How can you believe in that stuff without God?"

"Easy. I'm sure there's more than this physical world. I just don't believe there's an almighty 'god' controlling everything. We're all a part of it."

River grinned. "Like the Force?"

Brian laughed. "Sort of. What about you?"

"I dunno. I believe in God but not all the religious mumbo-jumbo. All the stupid rules and shit. My folks forced me to go to church when I was a kid, but I stopped a few years ago." River's eyes moved to the window. "What do you think the afterlife is like?"

"Something we can't imagine." He'd given the subject a lot of thought lately. "Or maybe it's just another plane of existence, like a parallel reality." The white

Naked in the Rain

place he'd glimpsed when he cut his wrists numbed him for a second.

River's voice brought him back. "You're way over my head, dude. Let's get lunch."

They stopped to check the assignment board on their way to the cafeteria. "Ooo, you're gonna have fun," River joked. "The worst chore in the whole place."

"'Mop bathrooms,'" Brian read.

"You pick up the mop and bleach from the nurse's station."

"Bleach?" Nausea rose in his throat. "I can't. I—I'm . . . allergic to bleach."

"Oh. So explain it to the duty nurse. They'll let you swap with somebody."

River was right. The nurse let him switch.

The boys walked on to the cafeteria, but Brian didn't feel like eating. He toyed with his rice and thought he could smell bleach beneath the food smell. Nauseating. He hurried away to kneel over the closest toilet.

That night River tossed and turned. He stared into darkness and heard Brian moving, restless, too. Brian started making strange noises. *Shit, he's not jacking off, is he?* River looked over, but it was too dark to see much. "Brian," he said in a loud whisper.

No reply. Brian thrashed around, whimpering. River padded over to the door and switched on the light.

Brian's head tossed from side to side, dark hair damp with sweat. River shook him gently. "Brian, wake up." He shook him again.

Brian's eyes flew open. He sat up and clutched his throat, his body shaking as he gasped for air.

River patted his shoulder. "Just a dream."

Brian nodded as tears streamed down his cheeks. He was finally able to mumble, "I'm okay." He wiped his face with trembling hands.

"What was that about?"

"Nothing. Just a dream I have sometimes where . . . I can't breathe."

"That sucks." River got up to dig through his nightstand drawer. "Here, have a smoke."

"Thanks." He was shaking too much, so River held up the lighter for him. Brian took a deep drag. And another. "Did I wake you?"

"Naw, I couldn't sleep." River lit another cigarette and sat on his own bed. "You should tell the Doc about that dream. It must mean something."

"I already know what it's about. I don't need a stupid shrink to tell me."

"You do? What?"

Brian shook his head. "I don't want to talk about it."

River let it drop, and they smoked in silence.

The boys sat around a table in the common room with Sandra and Jenny. Jenny giggled and hid her face behind her cards.

"Gin." Brian laid his cards down.

"Aw, shit." River's head fell back.

Sandra asked, "Are you cheating?"

Brian laughed and shook his head.

"River Deloy!" a voice called from the doorway. "Phone call in booth two."

River sat up straight. His first phone call. "Well, I guess I better get it." He hurried down the hall to the 'booth'—a bench with two wooden boards on either side that reached halfway to the ceiling. It provided only a token of privacy. He could hear the girl in the next booth crying as he sat down and picked up the receiver.

"River!" his sister's voice shouted in his ear. "How are you? Are you okay?"

"Yeah, yeah." He laughed a little to cover the sudden tightness in his throat. "I'm fine."

"I just found out where you are. They wouldn't tell me until now."

"Jackasses."

"How are they treating you?" she asked. "Is it horrible?"

"Naw, it ain't so bad. Food sucks. But there's some good people here."

"Mom won't tell me why they put you away. She was real vague . . . ."

"Drugs." Silence stretched until he added, "But it's not like I got a problem. You know how adults are. They freak over everything."

"Yeah."

He could see her nodding in his head. "I miss you," he said softly.

"Oh, River, I miss you, too. They said it'll be another two months."

"Yep, just about. What've you been up to?"

"Not much."

They chatted a few minutes, then the line crackled, and a nurse's voice cut in. "Thirty seconds left."

"What?" River bristled. "Shit. I guess there's a time limit. Shit." He suddenly didn't know what to say.

"River . . . ." She sounded sad.

"You okay over there, Dove?"

"Yeah, but . . . you know how it is."

He frowned. Dick never hit the girls, but he still treated them like crap. The nurse cut in again. "You have five seconds left. Say your goodbyes."

"River! I love you."

"I love you, too."

"I'll call again soon—"

The line went dead. He stared at the receiver a moment before he hung up. He cleared his throat and sat feeling numb, then walked back to the common room.

Brian was alone at the table reading *Spin*. He laid the magazine down and said, "Every time I read an interview with Robert Smith I have to get the dictionary out. Remind me to look up 'fatuous' later."

River laughed. "Yeah, right. I'll remember that." He took his seat, trying to act normal. "Where'd the girls go?"

"Group therapy." Brian nodded toward the kids in a circle of chairs at the far end of the room. He leaned forward. "So who was on the phone?"

"My sister."

"Must've been nice to talk to her."

"Yeah." River focused on anger to keep the lump in his throat away. "Fuckin parents wouldn't tell her where I am. She just found out or she would've called sooner."

"How is she?"

"Okay, I guess. Same ol'-same ol'. You know."

Brian nodded. "Is she your only sister?"

"No, I got two sisters and a brother. My brother and youngest sister are actually my half-brother and -sister. Different fathers. It's a complex family." River gave a short laugh.

"It must be nice to have that many siblings. Which sister just called?"

"Dove. She's a year younger than me. Our father was some kind of hippie, supposedly. That's why the two of us got such weird names. My brother Joe's a lot older. Ten years. Mom had him when she was real young. My other sister's only nine. Her dad's my stepdad, Richard." River frowned. "I call him Dick cos he hates it. Fits him, anyway, bastard."

"Are you all pretty close?" Brian asked. "Except Dick."

"Yeah, I guess. Not so much with Joe anymore. He's been outta the house a long time. But when I was younger we were close." He pushed away the sadness and forced a smile. "Me and Dove are real close. I guess cos we're only a year apart. And we both got such weird-ass names."

They laughed.

※ ※ ※

River plopped onto the common room sofa beside Brian.

Brian glanced away from the TV with a smile. "I love this show."

River shrugged. "It's okay."

"Okay? M*A*S*H is the best."

They watched a few minutes before Patricia called them over. "Damn," Brian said. "It's almost at the best part."

They made their way across the room to the circle of chairs where Patricia waited.

Ten minutes into group therapy Brian wanted to run away. He glanced at the other kids who formed their circle, then focused on the adult across from him as she spoke.

"You won't open up to the counselors; you won't talk to your parents. You've got to deal with your issues, Brian." Her voice was firm but gentle. "You can't refuse to see your parents forever. It's been almost a month. They really want to see you on your birthday next week."

Brian sighed and stared at the floor. *What a wonderful birthday that would be.*

"Promise me you'll think about it, okay? Brian?"

"Okay. I'll think about it." He shot her a look of resentment.

When the session ended he left the room in a hurry. *Group therapy is stupid.*

River ran to catch up with him. "Your birthday's next week? You'll be twelve?"

"Yeah."

He grinned. "Runt. What day is it?"

"October 12th. Saturday."

"Awesome. We'll do something special."

He shrugged and plodded on.

Brian sat in study hall and frowned at his math homework. He switched the pencil to his left hand to doodle instead.

River nudged him. "Your birthday's in two days. We're gonna par-ty!"

He gave a mirthless laugh. "Yeah, right."

"No, really. You need to loosen up." River pushed his shoulder gently. "Let off steam."

"I do."

"When bad shit happens, you gotta do something to get it out of you."

"I do."

River crossed his arms. "Like what?"

"I play the piano or write or something."

"You play piano?"

"Yeah. That's the worst thing about this place. No music. I really miss it." A constant ache deep inside.

"I don't like music."

"*What?*" Brian dropped his pencil. "How can you say that?"

A staff woman shushed them from a few rows away as she made her slow rounds through the room.

Brian lowered his voice. "Maybe you just haven't heard the right music."

"My folks listen to country-western. I hate it."

He grimaced. "Country sucks."

River laughed. "Everybody in that shit-town listens to country."

"I'll have to introduce you to *good* music."

"Yeah, okay. Anyways, I was saying, you gotta learn to have fun, cut loose."

"I have fun."

"No, you bottle everything up. And see what happens?" He grabbed Brian's arm and held it up.

Brian pulled away and rubbed the fresh scar on his wrist, then tucked his hands out of sight beneath the table.

"You ever been drunk?" River asked.

"No. But I tasted wine once."

"So you've never gotten stoned or tripped or anything?"

"No." He shook his head, eyes wide.

"Dude, you're missin out!"

The staffer headed down their row, a stern look on her face. Brian stood and walked toward her. "May I use the restroom?"

She seemed surprised by his politeness. "Come right back when you're done."

He made his way past her, out of the room filled with kids not doing their homework, into the wide, sterile hallway. Second door on his right. He said hello to the tall guard who always stood inside by the door. Brian felt sorry for him. Such a dirty place to have to stand all day. He didn't see why they needed a guard in here, anyway.

His nose wrinkled as he stood before a urinal. *This bathroom stinks.* Almost made him wish for home, but not really. He did miss his room and his sister. But he felt safer here.

The door opened, and he looked up expecting River, but a burly older boy walked in.

The boy caught him staring and sneered. "Whatcha doin, fag, jerking off?"

Brian's heart raced at the menace in his voice. "N-no."

The boy came closer. "Little faggot."

"Garrett." The guard's voice boomed and echoed off concrete walls.

Garrett veered away, snickering.

Brian's hands shook as he zipped up. He hurried at the sink and heard laughter as the door swung shut behind him. He frowned as he walked along the hall; the faint bleach smell made his head spin, and his fingers were drawn to the scar on his wrist. *Why should I be scared of him? I want to die.*

But he didn't really, not when he was away from his parents. Mother. His mind blanked out, and he found himself at River's side in study hall. Safe.

After dinner they went back to their room. River sat on the bed and flipped open the dictionary. "Check this out. 'Fuck' is in here. There's a whole bunch of em. 'Fucked-up,' 'fucker,' 'fuck off,' and 'fuck up.'"

They laughed as River read the definitions out loud. He spent the next twenty minutes looking up dirty words until they tired of the game. River tossed the dictionary aside.

Brian swung his legs. "So, if you live in Arizona, what are you doing in Connecticut?"

"That's a good question, my friend." He gestured at Brian with his cigarette. "I was visiting my grandpa in Southbury for a few weeks. I thought it would be great to get out of Arizona, see someplace new." River looked away with a frown. "But he's smarter than I thought. He nosed through my stuff and found coke and booze. I had to do *something* in that boring fuckin place."

"Why would you get in trouble for Coke?"

River laughed. "Coke-caine."

Brian's eyes got big. "Oh."

"My grandpa blew the whistle on me, fucker." River shook his head and took a long drag. "They tested me and found pot and blow in my system, so here I am."

"Wow, I've never done any of that stuff. What's it like?"

"It's great, but I can't really explain it." He leaned forward. "I'll show you sometime."

Brian nodded, both curious and nervous at the thought. But he didn't care what he was doing, as long as he was with River. *I'm glad you're here.*

River said, "Are you from here?"

"No. We moved to Connecticut about two years ago. My family moves around a lot."

"Is your dad in the military? Dick used to be."

"No. But I've lived in lots of places."

"Like where?"

"I was born in Indiana. That's where my parents are from; my grandma and the rest of my dad's family live there." Brian wished he could see them more. Then wondered if they knew he was in a mental institution. "We moved to Florida, Texas, Las Vegas, then Connecticut."

"Vegas! Cool."

"Not. Vegas sucks."

"Really? Well, I've lived in the same shit-town all my life. It must be cool to see all those places."

"I guess. But I hate leaving friends. The longest I lived anywhere was four years in Indiana, and I was a baby for most of that."

River grunted. "I've hardly been anywhere. Just here and Arizona. I wanna see the world!" River grinned and leaned forward, arms spread wide.

Brian woke with a start. He stared at the ceiling in the morning light, still caught in his dream. Sitting in the backseat, stuck in traffic with his dad and sister. A tidal wave was coming, and everyone had to get away. Suddenly he realized Mom wasn't with them. *Where is she? She shouldn't be on her own. She can't deal with an emergency. She'll panic.*

That's when Brian had wakened. *She could call Dad's pager. Where is she? Why doesn't she call?* Tears slid down the sides of his face.

"Are you crying again?" River was on his elbow looking across at him.

He laughed a little and wiped his eyes, then sat up. "I do love my parents."

River moved to sit beside him and put his arm around his shoulders. "I know," he said as Brian leaned against him. "That's why it hurts so much."

Brian let out a long sigh. "I think I should let my parents visit. It's important to them to see me on my birthday." He closed his eyes and felt safe for that moment, with River's warmth surrounding him.

*"she was a January girl
she never let on how insane it was
in that tiny kinda scary house
by the woods
by the woods . . .
she had a January world
so many storms not right somehow
how a lion becomes a mouse
by the woods
by the woods"*

- Tori Amos, "Black-Dove"

㋡㋡ CHAPTER 2 ㋡㋡

Brian's twelfth birthday dawned with a clear blue sky. Sunlight streamed through the trees, their red and orange leaves glowing as if on fire. "Beautiful," Brian murmured as he gazed through wire mesh out the window. His breath fogged the glass.

He glanced down and smoothed his black tee shirt with 'The Cure' written across it. The shirt was far too big and not warm enough for October, but he didn't care. It was his favorite, and he was determined to wear it on his birthday.

He turned as River got out of bed to hug him.

"Happy birthday, man. You're gettin old!"

Brian laughed and reached up to wrap his arms around River's neck. It felt wonderful to hold River, to be held by him. He wished the moment would never end.

River, on the other hand, realized suddenly he was hugging another guy. *What the hell's wrong with me? But it's Brian. He's sorta like a girl.* He pulled away and said, "Let's get breakfast."

The morning went by quickly, and River watched Brian head to the outside world. Brian's parents had permission to take him off-grounds for the entire afternoon, plus dinner. Brian had wilted at the idea of such a long visit, but he didn't argue. Like all the fight had gone out of him. River turned with a heavy sigh as Brian disappeared out the door. *Good luck, buddy.*

River's step lightened as he thought about his plans for the evening. It'd been a challenge to pull it together on such short notice, but he did it. He smiled and started to whistle. *No matter how things go with his family, I'll give him a night to remember.*

River stood at the window smoking another cigarette and stared at the night sky in agitation. *Shouldn't he be back by now?* He heard the door and turned to see Brian walk in with a large shopping bag.

Brian grinned. "Look what I got." He started pulling out boxes. "I think my parents feel guilty, so they got me a bunch of stuff. But here's the best gift, from my sister. Music!" He held up a small cassette player, then pointed to a black case. "And she brought all my tapes, too. Now you can hear good music."

"Cool." River picked up a small box. "A new watch. Nice. So . . . it went okay?"

"Yeah, I guess. Everyone was on their best behavior. And I got to play the piano—that was great." Brian sat on the edge of the bed. "It was weird seeing them again. Somehow I expected it to feel different, but it didn't." He shrugged. "I'm definitely glad to be back here."

"I got a surprise for you." River wiggled his eyebrows, then knelt to pull a brown paper bag from under his bed. "Ta da!" He whipped out a bottle of Bacardi rum.

Brian's eyes bugged. He jumped up to inspect the bottle. "Wow. How did you get that in here?"

"I have my ways."

Brian grinned. "Let's get started."

They sat side by side in the dark, leaning back against Brian's mattress. The blanket they'd spread over the linoleum made the floor only slightly more comfortable. But they didn't notice anymore.

"Here, I think you'll like this 'n." Brian struggled to operate the cassette player in the dim glow of the flashlight. He pushed in the tape marked The Cure, *Pornography*, and pressed play. Robert Smith's wailing guitar filled the room.

"Cool," River said.

Brian took a swig of the half-empty bottle. At first it had been difficult to drink, but now it tasted like water. "This is a really, really great album. Though the lyrics are depressing. Robert Smith is a genius."

River grunted and took the bottle for another gulp.

"My face is numb." Brian slapped his face lightly. "Weird." He lit a cigarette with difficulty.

"You smoke like a girl."

Brian looked at him. "You said that before. What the hell're you talking about?"

"The way you hold it, between your fingers insteada like this." River demonstrated with his own cigarette, held between thumb and index finger. "And the way you bend your elbow and hold up your hand while you smoke. That's weird. Feminine."

Brian shrugged. "That way it's closer to my mouth."

"And you move like a girl."

"No, I don't. I'm just . . . graceful." His sister had said that once.

"I think maybe you're gay."

"I am not!" Brian sat up straight, heart pounding.

"Don't freak out." River waved his hands. "It's okay. I mean, I might think you're a sick fuck, but I'll still be your friend."

"I'm not gay!"

"Oh, yeah? Have you ever kissed a girl?"

"Yes, I have," Brian said proudly.

"Really?" River's eyebrows went up. "Who?"

"Her name's Samantha." He leaned back against the bed. "She has the most beautiful red hair." He smiled at the memory of their one brief kiss. His only kiss. Except when he was six and those girls used to chase him around the playground. But he didn't think that counted.

"Is she your girlfriend? You never talked about her before."

"We used to be in school together. But this year when we started junior high her parents put her in a private school."

"So you never see her?"

"No." Brian sighed.

"Did you at least get somethin off her? Second base?"

"Uh . . . no." *I'm not even sure what second base is.*

"You kissed her, though, right? French kiss?"

He looked down. "Well . . . ."

"You had a girl and you didn' even slip her the tongue? Boy, I just don't understand you." River shook his head and glanced at the clock. "Bed check."

They hid the liquor, and River closed the window—difficult through the wire mesh, but he'd perfected the technique. The boys got under the covers and talked in loud whispers across the gap between them until footsteps squeaked in the corridor. "She's coming," River whispered.

Brian's heart pounded as the door opened, but it was hard not to smile with the world spinning around him. This was the best birthday ever. *River.* He almost opened his eyes to look at him; then the light went away, and the door shut.

They giggled in the darkness.

"Shh," River said. "Give her time to get back to the nurse's station."

Ten minutes later they sat on the floor again with River's flashlight. Brian put a different tape in the player. "Let's listen to somethin mellow. Cocteau Twins." Ethereal sounds emanated from the tape player.

River set the flashlight on the floor beside them with the beam pointed toward his bed. "You're into some weird music, dude."

"It's beautiful." Brian picked up the bottle, almost empty now. He set it down again without drinking. "D' you ever see your real dad?"

River glanced away. "Nope. Not since I was three. I don' remember him, really. Just a sense of him. Strong and . . . comforting." River took a swig of Bacardi and shook his head. "I can't believe your parents are still together."

"Yeah. But that isn't always a good thing."

"What d'ya mean?"

Brian gazed into the dark. "We'd be better off if they split up a long time ago. But Dad won't take us away from her, and he won't stand up to her. He doesn't protect us." Brian shook his head and listened to Liz Frazier's gorgeous voice. "I like it here."

River breathed a laugh. "You're crazy."

He smiled a little. "Maybe. But it's more peaceful here. I'm not always worried Mom's gonna freak out. I can relax. Think better. And I'm startin to realize some things."

"Like?"

"Instead of blaming everything on Mom, I'm startin to blame my dad, too.

That's progress, right?" He gave a little laugh, then felt like he would cry. He fought it down, but his voice shook. "I'm always trying to prove I'm not like my mother. Maybe that's part of why I did this." He looked at his wrists.

"I don't get it."

"Well, my mom . . . she, uh, gets crazy sometimes, totally hysterical and starts screaming and throwin things, and saying things. More than once she said she'd kill herself if she wasn't such a chicken shit." He whispered, "I wasn't chicken."

"That's not a good thing for a mother t' say to her kids."

Brian shook his head and bit his lip.

"Can I see?" River indicated Brian's wrists.

He shrugged. "If you want." Normally he was self-conscious about them, but right now he didn't care.

River staggered over to the light switch, then held Brian's offered wrists. "Wow. Looks evil." The purplish-red scars stood out stark against his white skin. "I can't believe you did that. I would never kill myself. I mean, I'm not afraid o' death, but I ain't helpin it along. But if I was gonna, I'd use pills or something." River shook his head as he traced one of the scars with his finger.

"That itches." Brian pulled his arms back. "Turn off the light."

River obeyed and sat beside him again.

Brian relaxed, more comfortable in the dim light. "I used what I could find. It didn' hurt."

River stared at him in disbelief.

"Really. I was numb. Well, not really numb, but separate from my body." He rubbed the scars, then sat on his hands and rocked.

River nodded. "I guess I can see that. Sometimes when my stepdad's hittin me, I don't feel a thing. Just go all numb, sorta like 'not-there.'"

"Yes! Exactly." Brian gazed into his eyes and met understanding and empathy he'd never felt before.

River said, "Tell me about that dream. The one where you can't breathe."

Brian glanced down, then sat back and let out a deep breath. "I don't really remember the dream, but I know why I have it. When I was six or seven, it was my job to clean the shower. My hands smelled like bleach for days."

"Didn't ya wear gloves?" River interrupted.

"No. Never occurred to me." He shrugged. "One time I was scrubbin the shower, and I could hear Mom in the living room, freaking out. Throwing stuff and screaming. She has quite a voice; you can hear her down the street when she gets goin'. Anyway, then she came into the bathroom." Brian paused, and his mouth twisted.

"She took one look at the shower and started screaming it was still dirty, and I did a shitty job. She started shaking me. 'Can't you do anything right? You stupid little shit.'" He breathed harder. Wanted to forget, but he forced the words out. "She . . . she shoved my face into the bucket of bleach. I tried to lift my head, but she was pushing me down. It burned. I couldn't breathe."

He broke off and leaned forward to cover his face. For a moment he couldn't get his breath; then sobs washed through him.

River took him in his arms and rocked him gently.

Naked in the Rain

. . .

River peeled his eyes open and blinked in morning sun that seemed too bright.

"Ugh," someone said.

He struggled to turn his head and saw Brian looking a bit green. Brian sat up suddenly and ran into the bathroom.

River lay still and pondered a spot on the wall. He felt nauseated, too, but it was a familiar sickness. He remembered the shock of his first hangover. *Poor Brian.*

Brian came back, his face ashen. He collapsed onto his bed and moaned. "Usually you feel better after you puke." A few minutes later he was breathing deeply, asleep again.

At least he's out of his misery for now. The thought jogged River's fuzzy memory of last night. His throat tightened as he gazed at Brian's angelic face. *How could anyone do that to him?*

Late afternoon sun slanted through the trees, and autumn leaves crunched beneath their feet as they wandered slowly through the grounds. "Feeling better?" River asked.

"Yeah. Still a little queasy." He'd never felt so sick as he had this morning. He smiled. "But it was worth it."

River grinned.

"About what I told you last night . . . ." Brian stopped walking and met River's eyes. "I've never told anyone about that before."

River put his arm around Brian's shoulders and gave him a squeeze. "Maybe the counselors are right. It helps to talk about stuff. That way it don't eat you up inside."

Brian nodded. But the truth was, he hadn't opened up to the counselors. Hadn't told them anything important. *I don't know why. I just can't.*

The boys sat together on a bench under the trees. River picked up pebbles and threw them at a puddle of water. "I got stuff I never told anybody, too." He glanced down.

Brian touched River's arm. "You can tell me if you want."

River's frown deepened as he sat in silence. Finally he spoke. "I used to baby sit my youngest sister, Janine. One time when she was three—" He broke off to stare up at the clear sky. "I was supposed to be watching her. But I went out back to try one of Dick's cigarettes. She must've climbed up on the kitchen counter." His mouth twitched. "When I came back, she was lying on the floor and . . . her head was bleeding."

He ground his jaw. "She had to go to the hospital. I lied and said she fell while I was in the bathroom. But it was my fault. My fault." He buried his face in his hands.

Brian put his arm around him and felt River's body trembling. He stroked his back. "It wasn't your fault." He did some quick math. "You were only eight. They shouldn't have left you alone to watch a three-year-old."

River sat up and wiped at his face.

"It wasn't your fault."

River stared for a moment at his hands clenched together. "It's weird. I told that lie so many times I started to believe it myself. If you lie long enough you almost forget the truth."

"But part of you remembers."

River nodded, then laughed suddenly. "You're funny. You're so much smarter than me, but you can't add for shit. Janine's four years younger. That means I was seven, not eight."

Brian gave a crooked smile. "Told you I suck at math." It was true. And he knew it made River feel good to be better at something.

River hugged him. "You're a good kid."

ൕൕൕ

The sound of violins filled the air as River walked into their room. Brian sat with his journal open on his lap.

"What's this music?" River asked.

Brian looked up with a smile that made his face glow. "Beethoven. Isn't it great?"

River shrugged. "Sure."

"Where have you been?" He closed the journal and set it beside him on the bed.

"Had to finish my assignment. I got everyone's favorite today, mopping the bathrooms." River made a face.

"Oh, shit!" Brian jumped up. "I forgot to do mine."

"You better run," he shouted as Brian bolted out the door.

River sat on the bed and glanced at his schoolbooks, but he'd be damned if he would study vocabulary after all those chores. His gaze wandered to Brian's side of the room. Always perfectly neat. Sometimes River would move something, just to see what Brian would do. Brian never said a word, just quietly moved it back. Everything had to be in its exact place.

Except this time he'd left his journal on his bed. River looked away. Looked back. The journal beckoned him.

River got up and started pacing. *He'll never know. I'll just take a little peek.* He picked it up.

"No!" He put it down and sat on his bed to flip through the *Travel and Leisure* magazine he snagged from the common room. But the photos of exotic places didn't hold his attention the way they usually did. His eyes kept straying to the journal. "Fuck it." He went over and picked it up.

He flipped through the pages. *So this is what his handwriting looks like when he uses his left hand. Real different. Freaky kid.* He stopped at the last entry.

> The other day River asked me if I was gay. I said no, and it's true. I like girls. But . . . I don't know. I do get funny feelings. Like when River holds me. The smell of him fills me up. I love the way he smells, and I want him to hold me forever, to touch me all over . . . .

River slammed the book shut and threw it back on the bed. "Holy shit." *I shouldn't have looked. I shouldn't have looked.* "God, what do I do?" He paced. "Brian can never know. I'm such a bastard." He sank onto the bed and slammed his fist into his thigh. "Bastard."

Brian's words echoed in his head. *'Touch me all over . . . .'*

*"One fluid gesture
like stepping back in time
trapped in amber
petrified"*

- Placebo, "Teenage Angst"

ᚱᚱ CHAPTER 3 ᚱᚱ

The next morning they undressed as usual to take turns in the shower. River had never been shy about his body, but the words in the journal haunted him as he passed Brian to go first into the bathroom.

He paused in the doorway and glanced back to catch him looking. But Brian was getting back in bed, pulling the covers up over his nakedness. *Kind of a big dick for such a little guy.* River glanced down at himself. *Well, I ain't too bad, neither.* He frowned. *Why isn't he looking?*

River shook his head and laughed at himself. *I've fuckin lost it.* He closed the door between them to jack off in the shower.

Patricia smiled across the group therapy circle at Brian and said gently, "You seem to have a lot of unresolved issues with your mother."

Brian's chest tightened. "I know."

"Have you tried family counseling?"

"Sort of."

"What do you mean?"

He glanced down. "We never got there."

"Why not?"

"Because she refused to go, okay?" he snapped. His pulse beat in his ears. "There's nothing wrong with our family, don't ya know?"

Her tone remained calm. "Whose idea was it to try counseling?"

"Mine." He frowned. "I went to the school counselor because . . . I had to do *something*. He called her. I didn't mean for him to do that. I just wanted to talk to him on my own. But he called her." He stared at his fists clenched in his lap.

"How did she respond?"

"I don't know."

"What did she say when you got home?"

"I don't know." He glanced at the yellow walls, the ugly orange couch, anywhere but the other people in the circle. Especially not River. He would lose it completely if he looked at River. His voice trembled. "I don't remember."

"How long ago did this happen?"

"About a week before I came here," he mumbled.

She leaned forward. "What happened that night, when you got home from school?"

"I don't know. Really. I don't remember anything, except . . . ."

"Except what?"

He whispered, "That it was one of the worst days of my life." He clenched his jaw and stared at the floor.

"You tried to get help, but you were thwarted. So you turned to suicide?"

He felt numb. He couldn't think, like his brain had frozen in panic.

"Brian?"

Her voice sounded far away, and his vision started turning white. He felt like he was floating away from the room; he couldn't quite see it through all the white.

River's voice said his name.

Brian jerked and blinked. He was back. Everything was too loud and too bright. He flinched at the sound of dice rolling on a table nearby.

"Let's go." River got up and pulled on Brian's arm. Brian wobbled a little as he stood.

Back in their room, River said, "Are you okay? Your eyes looked like you were on drugs."

"I'm fine. No big deal. It happens once in awhile."

"What happens?"

"You know." He shrugged. "Where you can't think, and you kinda float away. Can't remember where you are. You know."

"No, I don't. That ain't normal." River cocked his head. "Is that what it was like when you cut your wrists?"

"No. I knew what I was doing." He laid back on the bed. "I'm tired."

"You really don't remember what happened with your mom that night?"

Brian shook his head and closed his eyes.

He was awake when River returned a few hours later. Brian lay on his stomach, his homework unopened in front of him. Heavy, dreary sounds filled the room as the voice from the tape player sang in a monotone.

"Shit," River said. "Now there's a lively song. Fuckin depressing."

Brian turned the music down a notch. "He killed himself, you know."

"Who?"

"Ian Curtis, the singer. Joy Division."

"Joy Division?" River snorted. "What a misnomer."

Brian raised an eyebrow.

"My vocabulary word for the day." River grinned. "'Misnomer.' Thanks for givin me the chance to use it."

Brian laughed. "You're welcome." No one had ever been able to pull him out of depression the way River could, with a simple word or look. Brian smiled as longing tugged deep inside.

֍ ֍ ֍

Brian hummed to himself as he walked along the hallway, done with his assignment of straightening the common room. *Where's River?* A few older teens leaned against the wall nearby. Brian sucked in his breath as he recognized the boy who'd been mean to him in the restroom.

Garrett caught him looking and strode over to glare down at him. Brian felt very small. "You fuckin queer. Quit staring at me."

Brian glanced down quickly.

"Now you're staring at my dick. Faggot!"

Before Brian could react, Garrett's fist slammed into his nose. Pain blazed through his head as Brian hit the wall hard. Pinpoints of light sprinkled his vision and warm liquid ran over his mouth and down his chin. The boy grabbed Brian's shirt.

"Faggot!"

His fist reached back, but the blow never landed. In a blur, River tackled him. They landed on the floor with River on top. His fists pounded. "Motherfucker!" River got up and started kicking.

Brian saw blood smeared on River's knuckles. "River, stop."

River didn't seem to hear him. He grabbed Garrett's shirt and jerked him up. Punched him in the stomach, then the face again. Blood rained across the wall. The boy fell down, barely conscious.

"River. Stop!" Brian yelled.

Two orderlies rushed up as River kicked again. He fought the men as they tried to grab him. River caught one with a knee in the groin. The other man jabbed a syringe into River's arm. River's struggles slowed as his head lolled back, eyes half closed. They carried him away.

A nurse knelt to examine the bleeding boy. She looked up at Brian. "Carrie, check him out."

A large woman approached. He glanced down at his torn shirt splotched with blood and touched his chin. Warm and sticky. Like when he slit his wrists . . . .

Carrie jarred him back to the present by handing him a paper towel. "Here, hold this to your nose."

He didn't see River again until late the next day. River walked into their room, and Brian sat up quickly. "Where have you been?" Brian asked in a nasal voice. "Are you okay?"

River collapsed onto his bed. "Fuckers had me strapped down a whole fuckin day."

"Is that guy gonna be okay? He's in the infirmary."

"I don't care. Bastard deserved it." He stared at the ceiling. "I'm outta here soon, anyway." He sat up to peer at Brian's swollen nose. "You weren't hurt too bad?"

Brian shook his head. "What do you mean, you're out of here soon?"

"My three months are almost up. One more week and out."

Brian's mouth fell open.

"Don't be upset. You'll do fine without me. I gotta take a leak." River disappeared into the bathroom.

Naked in the Rain

Brian stared after him, his throat tight. He couldn't move.

River came out a few minutes later. "What's wrong?"

How can he not know? He met River's eyes, and his chin trembled. "You're leaving me?"

River squeezed his shoulder. "You'll be okay."

"Yeah, sure," Brian whispered, eyes averted.

River jerked awake in the middle of the night and listened to the silence. Silence. No sound of breathing. He squinted in the dark at Brian's rumpled, empty bed. *Must be in the bathroom.* River lay awake and refused to think about going home. Or how Dick might punish him. *I can take it.*

Ten minutes crept by and still no Brian. "That's weird." River got up to check the bathroom. Empty. His heart skipped. He pulled on socks and walked the length of the hall, eerie at this hour with the lights dimmed to almost nothing, absolutely silent. He called Brian's name in a loud whisper. Nothing.

He rounded the corner, and relief swept through him. Brian stood at the locked double doors in his pajamas and bare feet. River whispered, "What are you doing?"

No response. His eyes stared vacantly.

"Brian?"

Still nothing. "Dude, you're freakin me out."

Brian's face was calm and peaceful, forehead perfectly smooth. River had seen him sleep enough to recognize the look. "You're sleepwalking. Shit, you didn't tell me you do that. Come on."

He took Brian's arm and led him slowly back to their room.

Brian flopped his forehead down on his open book. "I hate this stuff." He pushed his math book away and reached for the tape player. The opening power chords of Bowie's "Moonage Daydream" blared.

River put down his homework as he got caught up in the music, surprised at how much he liked it. The guitar took over as the song reached its peak near the end. The music crescendoed, and bizarre sounds keened in the background. The result was abstract and eerie. River said, "This would be great stoned."

"Yeah?" Brian laughed. "Did I really sleepwalk last night?"

"Sure as hell did. You don't remember?"

"No." He met River's eyes. "Aren't you worried about going home?"

River glanced away. Impossible to stay hardened when he looked into those eyes. "Naw, it's no big deal."

Brian lay back and closed his eyes, quiet for the next few songs. River watched his sweet face and tried not to think about missing him. Brian's eyes opened; River looked away and pretended to be doing homework.

Brian leaned over to crank the music. "I can never get this song loud enough. It's my favorite Bowie. 'Ziggy Stardust.'"

River cocked his head. "I think I've heard this before. I like it."

The door opened suddenly, and Nurse Carrie stuck her head in. "Turn that music down."

Brian hurried to comply.

"This came for you." She handed an envelope to River, and her nose wrinkled. "Have you boys been smoking in here?"

"No!" they said in unison.

"You better not." She turned and left the room.

River opened the envelope. "A plane ticket to Tucson." Suddenly it was real. The ticket shook in his hand. He cleared his throat and shoved the envelope into the nightstand drawer. Out of sight.

Brian turned off the music, but River remained silent, so he opened his math book again and tried to study. The room grew dim as the sun got lost behind clouds. *I wish we could go outside.* But River lost his grounds privileges in that fight, and Brian wasn't about to go without him. Not when their time was so short.

"I don't want to go back," River whispered.

Brian looked at him across the space between their beds. "I don't want you to go, either."

River stared straight ahead, jaw clenched. A tear leaked out, and he brushed it away roughly.

"River." Brian moved to sit beside him and put his arm around his shoulders. "It'll be okay."

"Bullshit." River pulled away to face him. "Nothing's changed. Don't you get it? Nothing's gonna be okay."

Tears stung Brian's eyes. "I know," he whispered.

River shook his head and folded his arms across his chest. "It doesn't matter."

"Yes, it does." Brian's voice trembled. "They take us away for three months, then just shove us back home. How does that help?"

River looked at him. "You're not gonna do anything stupid, are you?"

"What do you mean?"

River put his hand on Brian's arm. "I think you know."

Brian met his eyes, and the tears came. "I don't know *what* I'll do." *I can't live like that. I can't make it.* His chin trembled.

River took him in his arms and held him tight. "Swear to me . . . ." His voice was thick. He pulled back and lifted Brian's chin, forced him to look him in the eye. "Swear you won't do that shit again."

Brian blinked. His mouth opened, but no words came out.

"*Swear.*" He gripped Brian's chin and choked out the words. "You won't kill yourself."

"River! Promise me I'll see you again." He searched River's eyes. *Give me something to live for.* "Then I'll promise."

He let go of Brian's face and said solemnly, "I promise we will see each other again."

"I want to believe you."

"We can make it happen."

"River, you live on the other side of the country."

"We can make it happen."

Brian smiled slightly. "You really think so?"

"I do." River smiled back. "I promise."

"Okay." Brian sniffled, then looked River in the eye. "I promise I won't try to kill myself."

River's last night came all too soon. Brian slid under the covers and tried not to think.

"I don't wanna go to bed yet," River said. "Let's stay up all night." He reached into the drawer to get his flashlight. It flickered. He shook it, then set it up on the nightstand. A small pool of light glowed on the ceiling.

The boys sat on the floor together and leaned back against Brian's bed, silent until River said, "Whatcha thinking about?"

"Trying to figure out how to get myself to Arizona."

He grinned. "So, you're coming to me?"

Brian shrugged. "I sure don't want to stay in Connecticut with my parents." He shivered at the thought.

"But you don't wanna meet my stepdad."

His eyes got big. "That's true." He bit his lip and thought. "You said you want to see the world."

"Yeah. You gonna take me on a tour?"

Brian laughed. "Something like that. Maybe we can meet up somewhere and just travel around."

"Sounds great."

Brian stifled a yawn. The red numbers of the clock glowed 1:15. River had been silent awhile, staring into space with a sad expression. "Are you okay?" Brian asked.

"Yeah." He looked down. "Just thinking . . . maybe I belong here. In a nuthouse."

"No, you don't."

River glanced at him sidelong. "You don't know the whole story. When they came to take me away, I kinda freaked. I was so fuckin mad and . . . scared. I fought em."

Brian nodded, not surprised.

"I guess I lost it. That happens sometimes when I fight. Grandpa was trying to calm me down, and I—I hit him." River leaned forward and hid his face in his hands, his voice muffled. "I didn't mean to."

Brian stroked his back.

"I hit my own grandpa. Punched him right in the face. What kind of freak would do that?" He sat back, jaw clenched. "I'm bad. They should put me away."

"River." Brian touched his shoulder, but River didn't look at him. He took River's face in his hands. "Everyone has a bad side. We all make mistakes. But you . . . you've helped me so much," he whispered, lost in his eyes. "You saved me. You make me want to live."

A tear rolled slowly down the curve of Brian's cheek, and River's throat tightened. His eyes stung as he took Brian in his arms and held him close, amazed how easily Brian cut through his defenses. River had never cried in front of anyone but his mom and sister. Except when he was little—he used to cry when Dick hit him. *Never again.* But here he was, bawling his head off with Brian all the time. He couldn't help it. Those eyes reached inside him like no one else ever had. So deeply and thoroughly. It scared him a little. He shook himself and pulled away.

Brian said, "I don't believe we're never going to see each other again. I really don't believe that. It's not right." He cocked his head, and a sweet smile touched his lips. "It's strange. I've only known you two months, but—" He put his hand on River's. "I feel so close to you, like I've known you forever."

River nodded and brushed Brian's tears away with his thumb. "I know what you mean," he whispered.

Brian turned his head to touch River's palm with his lips, then held it close against his cheek.

The room lightened as the dreaded morning arrived. River had fallen asleep around three o'clock, and Brian watched him sleep. He wanted to make every moment last. *I can't believe he's leaving me.* Brian swallowed his tears, determined not to make it harder for River.

The bed creaked as River sat up and ran fingers through his dark blond hair. He gave Brian a weak smile. "Well, today's the day." River swung his legs over the side of the bed. He ruffled Brian's hair on his way to the window. "What time is it?"

"7:25." Brian's stomach twisted. *Half an hour.* "Do you want breakfast?"

"Nah." River picked up his jeans. "I'm not hungry."

"Me, neither."

They dressed in silence, then sat across from each other. Brian said, "Will you be okay?"

"Of course. I'm tough, remember?"

Brian cocked an eyebrow, and a smile tugged at the corner of his mouth. It turned into a grimace as he ducked his head. "God, I hate this."

"Me, too," River said in a husky voice.

He looked up to see River staring at him, eyes filled with tears. "Oh, River."

They stood, and Brian wrapped his arms around River's neck. He breathed deeply of River's scent and refused to believe this was the last time.

River squeezed him tighter and picked him up off the floor, then set him down. He cupped Brian's cheek in his palm, his face serious. "Don't forget your promise."

Brian shook his head and smiled through his tears. "I won't."

"I'll call as soon as I can. Remember, don't talk about our plans over these phone lines. They're monitored."

"Got it." He stared into River's eyes. "I'll miss you." His voice caught.

River held him tight again. "I'll miss you, too."

A knock sounded, and a voice came through the door. "River, there's someone here to take you home."

He called out, "Just a minute." River wiped his face on his shirt.

The boys checked the clock. 7:43. It changed to 7:44 as they watched. "They're early," Brian said. "We still have fourteen minutes left."

River smiled a little. "Sixteen minutes. The cab can wait." He turned toward the door as the knock came again. "Okay, okay. Come in."

Nurse Carrie opened the door and said, "River, there's someone here to see you."

She stepped aside to let the woman behind her into the room. River's mouth fell open. His face crumbled as he squeaked, "Mom?"

"River." She rushed forward to enfold him in her arms. "My little boy, my baby." She stroked his hair and held him to her bosom.

River looked up at her. "I didn't think you would come."

"Oh, honey." She stroked his face, her cheeks wet. "Let's go home."

River turned to pick up his bag and met Brian's gaze. River strode over to him and rested his hands on Brian's shoulders. "Be strong. Take care of yourself, understand?" River shook him gently. "Or I'll kick your ass."

Brian breathed a laugh and nodded. He couldn't speak.

River touched his cheek, then walked away. His mother put her arm around him as they headed to the door. He glanced back. "I'll be seein' you, Brian." He winked and half-smiled.

They walked out, and Brian was alone.

*"I . . . feel my face
pulling me down
See the blood on the carpet
the blood on the door*

*you hold me tighter, till I can't breathe
you . . . smother me"*

   - Brian O'Kelly

෴ CHAPTER 4 ෴

"Poor Brian." Jenny gazed through the window and watched him wander the grounds. "He's been moping all week since River left."

"I miss him, too," Sandra said, then smiled. "Why don't you help Brian forget his troubles?"

Jenny blushed.

Sandra tugged on Jenny's braid. "Don't be embarrassed. He's a cutie."

She smiled wide. "Isn't he? I think he's beautiful." She looked out the window again and daydreamed.

That afternoon she found Brian in the common room and sat beside him on the couch. A commercial blared from the television. "What are you watching?" Jenny asked.

He didn't look at her. "M*A*S*H."

"I like that show." She bounced and tried to remember if she'd ever seen it.

"Yeah?" He turned to her with a slight smile.

She beamed at him. "So when do you get a new roommate?"

"I already did, a couple of days ago."

"Is he nice?"

Brian shrugged. "He's okay. Leaves me alone."

The commercials ended, and his attention returned to the TV. Jenny snuggled against him and laughed at all the jokes. His arm went around her. Her heart sped up, and warmth flushed through her.

"Brian O'Kelly! Phone call in booth one."

Jenny watched him hurry away. "I'll save your seat," she called.

But he didn't hear her. The waiting phone held his attention. He hoped, hoped . . . . He sat in the booth and picked up the receiver.

"Hey, dude," said the voice from the other end.

His throat constricted at the sound of River's voice.

"How ya holding up?"

Brian cleared his throat and tightened his grip on the receiver. *No crying.* "Okay,

I guess. But it's boring here without you."

River laughed.

Brian smiled at the sound. "You seem good. How are things with your folks?"

"So far so good. But Dick got his dumb ass fired while I was gone."

"Really?"

"Well, laid off. Same thing. Now he's home all the time. Totally sucks. But he just went outta town to visit his brother, so he's gone for awhile."

"That's good."

"Yeah. Sorry I didn't call sooner. I had to wait till he left. He don't like long distance phone calls. And the time difference screwed me up. It's fuckin annoying."

Brian grinned. It was so wonderful to talk to River again. He felt all full and happy. "How was the trip back?"

"Pretty boring. But it's good to see my sisters again. No news there? How's Jenny?"

"She's alright. I was just talking to her."

"Yeah? Any action?"

Brian laughed. "No."

"I'm telling you, that girl's hot for you. Get it while you can—that's my motto."

He laughed again. "We'll see."

They chatted a bit more; then a nurse cut in with a twenty-second warning. "Shit!" River said.

"Yeah." His eyes stung. "I miss you."

"Me, too." River cleared his throat. "You take care of yourself. I mean it."

"I will. You, too." He closed his eyes. "It's good to hear your voice."

"I'll call again tomorrow. I'll call every day till Dick comes back."

"River—" The line went dead. He managed to hold in the tears until he got to his room.

 papapa

Brian stepped outside and saw Jenny alone on a bench, frowning at the ground, her long hair loose over her shoulders. She shivered in the breeze and wrapped her coat tighter.

He walked over to sit beside her. "You look sad. Is something wrong?" he asked.

She stared at her hands in her lap. "Sandra left this morning."

"Oh. I'm sorry." He put his arm around her shoulders.

She leaned into him and sniffled. "I leave soon, too. Next week." She rested her hand on his leg.

Heat shot up his thigh. He swallowed and whispered her name.

She looked up at him. Her face was so close. Her delicate pink lips looked soft. He wanted to touch them. He bent slowly, slowly, and gently brushed his lips against hers. They were warm. She smiled, then touched his flushed cheek and leaned closer.

Their mouths stayed together this time. His arms moved on their own to stroke her back. Her hand snaked around his neck to pull him closer. He felt shaky and hot all over, felt her teeth as they kissed harder. Before he knew what he was doing, his tongue was in her mouth. She tasted sweet. Her head tilted back as he pushed against her.

A voice boomed out, "Brian O'Kelly. Get your hands off that girl."

He jumped. Nurse Carrie stood three feet away, hands on her wide hips. He blinked and tried to get his brain to work.

Jenny stood up and wiped her mouth. "I better go do my homework." She took a few steps, then turned to beam at him. "I'll see you around."

"Yeah." He grinned back.

Nurse Carrie loomed over him. He ignored her and watched Jenny wave as she stepped inside. The nurse shook her head and turned away quickly, but Brian saw the smile on her round face.

Hail clattered against the windows, the light outside so dim it seemed like evening instead of morning. Brian sat on the couch in the common room with his arm around Jenny. She made him warm and excited. So did the storm. But he felt bad for the kids who paced back and forth, cringing as hail beat the windows harder. The electricity flickered, and he stared up at the wavering lights. "I've got an idea. I'll be right back."

He returned a few minutes later with his tape player. "I don't think everyone would like my music, but this has a radio, too." He set it on a table and turned the dial. "If I can get a station in this weather . . . . Here we go." He stopped the dial on an oldies station.

A woman's voice sang through the static, "It's my party, and I'll cry if I want to, cry if I want to, cry if I want to. You would cry, too, if it happened to you . . . ."

He glanced around the room. Half the kids were already dancing. He offered his hand to Jenny. She giggled and bounced up. They danced together and sang along with the familiar words. He liked dancing, letting music inside his body in such a physical way. He didn't understand why some people were shy about it. He wasn't shy or self-conscious about anything related to music. Music made him forget all that.

He watched Jenny's body move. She didn't seem like the same girl who used to annoy him. Not since he kissed her yesterday. He wanted to do it again.

The song ended, and the DJ's voice cut in. "Now for all you romantics out there, here's a little Righteous Brothers to set the mood."

The smooth voice crooned about love. He took Jenny in his arms to dance to the slow music. "I love this song," he said. "It's so beautiful." A sudden longing for River swept through him, but the girl in his arms distracted him.

She put her arms around his neck and rested her cheek against his chest as they swayed. He felt her body warm against his and held her closer. His head spun, and his jeans felt too tight.

The music stopped suddenly mid-song. An orderly gave them a weak smile. "Sorry, but that's not allowed." A clamor of protests filled the room. He held up his hand. "Sorry. Rules are rules."

Brian frowned. But the hail had stopped, and the mood lightened. And Jenny's body still leaned against his.

"What time is it?" she asked.
He checked the watch that hung loose on his wrist. "9:55."
"We better hurry. The Sunday service." She tugged on his hand.
"What? I'm not going to that."
"Oh, come on, Brian. Please? For me?"
He shook his head.
She leaned closer. "Aren't you afraid you'll burn in Hell?"
He laughed. "No."
She dropped his hand and stepped back, horrified. "How can you laugh about that?" She turned and ran out of the room.

Brian sat in booth two.
"So you guys kissed?" River asked.
"Yeah."
"Tongue?"
Brian was silent a moment, then cleared his throat. "Uh huh."
"Alright! Score."
He laughed. "It was fun. But now she's mad cos I wouldn't go to the Sunday service, and I laughed at it."
"Yeah, dude, people get real touchy about religion. You gotta make up with her before she leaves."
"I'll try."
"Uh, Dick's coming back tomorrow."
His mood plunged. "I'm sorry, River."
"Yeah, well. Me, too. So I won't be able to call you so much."
"Will you be okay?"
"Aw sure. I've put up with his shit for ten years. I can handle it."

It snowed all morning Tuesday, but by free time the sky had cleared. Brian grabbed his jacket and hurried outside. The sun shone on glistening trees and reflected off the snow. The whole world was white. He bent to gather a handful and let the cold powder fall through his fingers. He laughed for the sheer joy of it.

He heard the door and turned to see Jenny walk outside. She pretended not to notice him and went the other way. "Jenny, wait. Please." He hurried to catch up with her. "Can we talk a minute?"

She frowned. "You've got one minute."

"I'm really sorry about the other day. I didn't realize how you felt." He reached out to stroke her cheek. "I didn't mean to offend you."

Her eyes closed.

"Please," he said. "I don't want it to end like this."

She looked up at him with a sad smile. "Me, neither."

Brian held her gloved hand. "Can we walk together?"

"Okay."

They strolled the length of the yard, then sat behind a snow drift, out of sight of the old brick building. He pulled off her glove to caress her cold fingers, then leaned closer to kiss her.

"Brian," she murmured and gazed into his eyes. "This is our last day together. I leave tomorrow."

Everyone leaves. He swallowed and looked down. She put her hand under his chin and brought her lips to his. His arms went around her as urgency filled him. He leaned into her, lost in her sweet taste. Wanting more.

He pushed her back against the snow. A thrill ran through him as he felt her body beneath him. He kissed her cheek, her throat, tugged at her sweater to kiss her collarbone. Her chest heaved, and his hand found her tiny round breast through the wool. He stroked it with his thumb. Her breath caught. He rubbed his cheek against her breast, and his groin tightened even more.

His body shook as he fumbled with her sweater. Wanted to touch her skin. Touch her. He glanced down—he'd pulled her sweater up to expose her stomach. His fingertips grazed the warm skin.

She put her hand on his. "No."

He stared at her as his sluggish brain struggled to process what she'd said. He let go of her sweater and lay back beside her, breathing hard. His body hummed as he gazed up at the blue sky. "Jesus," he whispered.

She smiled and snuggled against him as the snow melted through their clothes. He turned his head, and they kissed again.

ಐಐಐ

Brian walked slowly down the hall on his way to group therapy. He almost looked forward to it. He'd finished this week's homework in two days. Yesterday he spent all day in bed with one of his bad headaches. Now he was lonely and bored and depressed. River was gone. Jenny was gone. And soon he would be, too.

Patricia looked across the circle. "Brian, after your mother refused counseling, what did you do? I mean, in the days that led to your suicide attempt."

Why does she always pick on me? "I was depressed and upset, of course."

"Go on."

He shrugged. "I didn't know what to do. I felt trapped. Until . . . ."

"Until what?"

"Until the day I cut my wrists."

Clark turned to him. "What was it like?"

He stared at the floor. "It was easy."

Patricia asked, "At what point did you make that decision?"

"I didn't, not consciously. One day I felt really relieved all of a sudden. I went through school in a daze. When I got home . . . ."

His eyes closed as he relived the moment. *I walk over to the piano and touch it. It feels solid and real. Not like everything else. I play the first movement of* Moonlight Sonata. *Unbearably sad and beautiful. It feels right. I finish and stare at nothing. I am finished. I get up and mount the stairs. Time slows, like I'm in a trance.*

"What?" Clark prodded. "When you got home, what?"

"Huh? Oh." Brian blinked. "I went into my parents' bathroom and opened the medicine cabinet." Still not fully aware of what he intended to do. "I picked up a bottle of aspirin. But there were only two pills left." They rattled when he shook the bottle. A hollow, taunting sound. Disappointing. He spotted his mother's razor and picked it up. *How am I supposed to use this?* A disposable. He tossed it into the tub. It echoed as it hit the porcelain. He leaned against the wall, starting to panic. Then he remembered Dad's utility knife. *Yes!* He raced downstairs.

"Go on." Clark sounded impatient.

"I got a razor blade." *Excitement fills me as I pick a fresh razor blade out of the box. I check the clock over the stove. At least an hour before anyone comes home. I smile and sit cross-legged on the cold linoleum. I push my sleeves up but they keep falling down, getting in the way. I take off my sweater and toss it aside. I don't need it anymore.*

I pick up the razor blade, my heart pounding in my chest. I lick my lips and put the blade against my right wrist. As soon as the cool metal touches my skin, I know it is right. Calmness washes through me. I press. It stings a little at first, but then doesn't hurt at all. Warm blood runs down my arm. My whole body is filled with the warmth. Relief. Aah, such relief. I press the blade in farther. Suddenly the vein is cut. I don't know how I know; I just do.

My breath is fast and shallow. I switch hands to do my other wrist, but I have trouble holding the blade. It's slippery with blood. And my right hand is shaking violently. I'm surprised at this. I feel so calm and peaceful. I guess my body is not. I am separate from it. I cut into my wrist. It doesn't even sting this time. I finish quickly.

The blade slips out of my hand. There's blood all over. I shiver and lean back against the cabinet, cold and sleepy. So sleepy. From a great distance I feel my body sliding. My eyes are level with the floor. Dark blood spreads slowly outward like a lake. It's beautiful.

But I can barely see it through the mist. Everything is grey and sparkly. Soothing coolness wraps around me. I float away into a world of white, where there is no pain and no sadness.

"I'm afraid of meaning nothing again . . .

'I leave in the morning
I don't wanna go'
I said to the teller,
'if this is the future
I don't wanna know
I don't wanna know' . . .

After all this is over,
this is over after all
We cut a nice figure of a family"

- Kristin Hersh (Throwing Muses), "The Teller"

⁌⁌ CHAPTER 5 ⁌⁌

Brian's mother smiled at him from behind the steering wheel as they drove away from the institute. "You're awfully quiet," she said.

He glanced at her beside him. "Uh, well . . . ." His voice wasn't working right. He cleared his throat. *Think of something to say.* "How are Gracie and Cleo?"

"They're fine. Gracie still has fur balls, even in this weather!"

Her laugh sounded forced, and he realized she was nervous, too. He craved a cigarette as his fingers tapped his knee.

"Are you tired, honey?"

"Sort of." Actually, he was keyed up and tired at the same time. Didn't sleep much last night.

The scenery became more familiar. Almost there. He straightened as they turned onto their street. Huge oaks lined the pavement on either side, their bare limbs intertwining across the road. He loved the intricate pattern, how the branches stood out against the bright sky.

"It's good to see you smile again." Mom reached over to squeeze his knee.

He felt he should respond somehow, but he couldn't bring himself to do it. *I do love you.* But he was afraid of her, too.

They pulled into the driveway, and his mouth went dry as he got out of the car. He'd been home twice to visit—on his birthday and Thanksgiving—but it felt different now. *I guess cos I'm here for good.* Everything was quiet, most people at work or school. It felt surreal, as if the whole world held its breath. Cold wind blew against his face. He closed his eyes and took a lungful of crisp air.

"You coming, hon?" His mother smiled.

He followed her inside. The living room seemed dim after the brightness outside, but it smelled like home. His stomach twisted with mixed emotions. He moved to the upright piano against the far wall and rested his hand on it. Reassurance.

Mom went upstairs to put away his backpack, and his stomach loosened a little. It felt like he'd been gone for years instead of a few months. Something was different, but he couldn't place it. He wandered around and touched the couch, the curtains. He held his wrist up to the light from the window and rubbed the ugly scar, then glanced around the room again. *Nothing's changed here. It's me. I've changed.*

"Brian?" Tanya's long brown ponytail bounced as she raced downstairs. The room seemed brighter with her in it.

She ran to him and hugged him tight. Comforting and warm. He blinked back tears.

"Welcome home, baby brother." She held his face in her hands, then kissed his cheek and mussed his hair. "Why are you standing in the corner?" She tugged on his hand and led him into the dining room. "Gracie wants to say hi." Tanya nodded toward the long-haired grey cat asleep on one of the chairs.

Brian touched her soft fur. Gracie chirped as she woke, then sniffed his hand. He smiled. "I must smell pretty weird. Where have I been, huh?" he murmured as he stroked her. "Where have I been?"

He sat on the couch, a plate of pizza balanced on his lap. Dinner in front of the TV: family time. Pretty much the only time they were all in the same room. Brian ate in silence and watched the news. The pizza tasted good. Salty. He licked his fingers. His hands ached a little—he'd played the piano all afternoon, and his muscles weren't used to it anymore. But it was the best thing in the world.

A commercial break started, and his mother turned to him. "Are you ready to go back to school tomorrow?"

His heart stopped. "What? Tomorrow?"

"Yes, dear. The counselors say kids who . . . in your situation should get back to a normal routine right away."

"But it's almost Christmas break. Can't I wait until after vacation? Please!" He glanced around the room. His father's blue eyes stared down at his lap. No help there. Brian struggled to keep his voice level. He couldn't let them know how much it scared him. Didn't want to sound crazy. "That school's hardly a normal routine. I only went for a couple of weeks. Please. I want to be home for awhile."

She pursed her lips. "I don't know."

She didn't say no. Careful now . . . . "Christmas is less than two weeks away. I've got shopping to do." He aimed a smile at his mother.

"But we're not supposed to leave you alone. Maybe I could get more time off from work."

Oh, no—even worse. Shit.

Tanya jumped in. "Vicky's older brother is home from college. Maybe he could come over during the day."

"Well . . . ." Mom tapped her finger on her lips. "Alright. If Jeremy agrees, you can stay home, Brian."

He smiled for real this time. "Thanks."

Tanya hurried to the kitchen to make the phone call. She returned with good news.

Brian looked at her gratefully and mouthed, "Thank you."

His father finally spoke. "We'll get our Christmas tree tomorrow night. We waited so you could help pick it out, son."

Brian's smile broadened. He felt warm and fuzzy inside. He treasured the feeling; he knew it wouldn't last.

He bit into the pizza crust as the anchorman announced the next topic. "When our children take their own lives. A look at the increase in adolescent suicide."

He stopped chewing. His family sat like statues, their façade of normalcy suddenly broken. His mother covered her mouth as tears welled up. Her body shook with silent sobs.

"Mom." He moved to kneel before her.

She gathered him in her arms. "Oh, my sweet boy. My baby." She rocked him back and forth.

He held onto her as tears streamed down his face. He loved her so much it hurt. *Why do I have to hate her, too?*

Brian closed his bedroom door with relief. It was only 7:30, but he felt completely drained. He looked around his room, wandered over to the built-in shelves and traced his fingers along the spines of the books. They were like old friends.

He picked up the model horse who stood silently guarding them. Horsey wasn't a toy. He was special. Made before the new generation of model horse, his body was a thinner, hollow plastic, his brown and white pinto coat hand painted. Brian put him back on the shelf. *I wonder where he came from?* He didn't remember getting Horsey. He'd always been there. Brian smiled and patted him on the head, then slid under the covers. He gazed at the Cure posters covering the walls, at all his precious things.

It would be hard to leave them behind.

The clear voices of the Vienna Boys Choir filled the living room. Brian sang along as he helped his sister decorate the tree. Homemade ornaments vied for place with delicate red balls from the store. Brian laughed at the thing he made in kindergarten—dry macaroni glued onto cardboard, then sprayed with gold paint. Just lovely. But his mother insisted on using the ornaments he and Tanya made when they were younger. *She's so sentimental.*

They finished the tree, and he stood back to gaze at the lights. *Sometimes things are good.* He followed his sister into the kitchen to get more shortbread cookies. The shiny floor caught his eye. "You guys got a new floor."

Tanya gave him a strange look. "We had to replace the old linoleum because the bloodstains wouldn't come off."

He sucked in his breath. *The deep red spreads slowly outward from my body . . . .*

Tanya squeezed his shoulder and brought him back to the present. "Come on. Time for Christmas carols."

He sat at the piano as his family gathered round to sing. A traditional O'Kelly Christmas tree night. If only it would stay like this. He felt like he was holding his breath, waiting for the axe to fall. He shook his head, determined not to ruin the moment, and let his fingers wander over the keys.

Jeremy sat on the couch, eyes glued to ESPN. Brian frowned. *I don't need a babysitter. But at least Mom's not here.* He picked up the kitchen phone and tugged on the cord to get it around the corner and out the back door. He sat on the stoop to dial River's number.

"Hey—" River's voice came through loud and clear. "I was gettin worried. How ya doing?"

"Okay so far. But my family watches me like a hawk. They've got a neighbor here, like I need a babysitter." Brian shivered and pulled the sleeves of his sweater down over his hands.

"Dude, you're calling from home? Not good. You don't want them to see my number on the bill after you leave. That is, if you're still planning to . . . ."

"Oh, yeah. Absolutely. Things are fine now, but it won't last. Should we hang up?"

"Naw, but call from a payphone next time."

"Okay. Did you know Hartford had the first payphone in the United States?"

River laughed. "No, I didn't. Thank you. Now my life is complete."

"I'm full of useful facts." He grinned. So wonderful to hear River's laugh. *I can't wait to see you.* He reached into his jeans pocket for a piece of paper. "I called Greyhound and got some schedules." He glanced over his shoulder to make sure he was alone, then read the timetables out loud.

"No, dude. You can't take a bus straight from there. Your folks will be looking for you. They might go to the station with a photo. And trust me, people will remember you. Buy a ticket to somewhere big first, like New York City. That way they won't be able to track you."

"God, you're right. River, you're so smart. I never even thought of that."

"Yeah, yeah. I'm a genius. Are you gonna have enough money?"

"I think so. But it's pretty expensive to get all the way to Arizona. I'll sell some stuff, and I have lots of driveways to shovel—it's been snowing. But I won't have much left by the time I get there."

"That's okay. We'll pool our cash. I've got some money tucked away."

Brian heard sounds in the background. "Is someone yelling?"

"Fuckin Dick. *Just a minute!*" River shouted. "He's such a prick. I gotta go. He wants to use the phone."

The voice in the background grew closer. Menacing. Brian's words came out in a rush. "I'll call as soon as I can get to a payphone. River, I—I'll see you soon."

He felt River smile. "Okay, Brian. Call me."

He hung up, then with Jeremy's permission headed across the street to see if Mrs. Johnson needed her walkway shoveled. His boots crunched in the snow as he approached her small house.

The elderly woman's face lit up when she answered the door. She exclaimed over how healthy he looked and said she'd watched him go into the ambulance on a stretcher. That made him uncomfortable. Bizarre to know people had seen him like that. To him, life had stopped that afternoon in the kitchen, then started again when he woke in the hospital. There was no in between.

He thought about it as he shoveled snow. *I guess life goes on without me.* Though he couldn't imagine how it would be here when he was gone for good.

The next day he ate lunch quickly and escaped to his room—it was Saturday, so Mom was home, and Tanya was down the street with her best friend, Vicky. He sat on his bed, lonely, and thought about River.

His mother poked her head in. "Brian, honey, I thought you might want some dessert." She held a plate of brownies in her hand.

"Thanks."

She smiled and set the plate on his bed, then turned to leave. Something on the carpet caught her eye. She bent to pick up a penny. Her expression changed in an instant, contorting into rage. "What is this doing on the floor!"

His stomach twisted.

"What do I always tell you about being neat? Do I have to do everything?" Her voice rose to a shriek, and she started sobbing. "I'm sick of you all!" She pushed on Brian's dresser and knocked it repeatedly against the wall. Everything on it fell to the floor. She moved to his shelves, her voice a continual scream. "I can't take it anymore. What is wrong with you? Why can't you leave me alone?" She swiped her hand along the shelf, and books toppled to the floor.

Her hysterical tirade continued as she moved to the next shelf. She picked up books in both hands and threw them down. Threw them at the walls, at the bed. A few struck Brian and bounced off. He sat stone still and silent in the middle of the bed. Waiting for it to end. Bruised inside.

Tears ran down her face as she screamed, "It's you men. Stupid fucking men! You think you're so smart. You're all filthy dumbshit *pigs*." She picked up a book and threw it right at Brian. Horsey was next on the shelf. She slammed him onto the carpet, but he didn't break. She picked him up and threw him with all her strength against the closet door. Still he didn't break.

Brian thought his chest would cave in as his mother reached for Horsey again. She stood two feet from the closet door and hurled him against it. Again and again, until his plastic body finally broke.

A small sound escaped from Brian. He stared in horror at the pieces of Horsey. His mother continued to destroy his room, but he didn't notice. She wore herself out and left with a slam.

Brian made his way through the mess to pick up Horsey. He was in three pieces. Brian clutched them to his chest and struggled to breathe.

Tanya knocked on the bedroom door. No answer. She had to push stuff out of the way to get it open. "Brian?" No sign of him. Her heart skipped in panic.

She hurried through the debris and found him lying on the floor on the other side of the bed, his back squeezed tight against the box springs, hugging something to his chest. "Brian?"

He jerked.

She knelt beside him and recognized the horse in his hands. "Oh, no."

He looked at her without moving his head, his eyes swollen and dull. She scooped him up and held him tight.

He hung limp in her arms, all cried out. Empty and numb. He sat back against the bed with Tanya's arm around his shoulders. "Why did she do that to him?" His voice broke. *I wish she'd hit me instead.* He held up the pieces. "I'll fix him. He'll be alright. I'll glue him."

Tanya smiled and squeezed his arm. "I'll help you. We can make that our project tomorrow, okay?" She stood and held out her hand. "Come on. Let's clean up your room."

He set Horsey in a pile against the wall and took her hand.

He lay across the bed on his stomach. After several hours of work his room was back to normal. He put his head down, exhausted. But his eyes wouldn't stay shut. He couldn't let it go. Couldn't relax. He pulled out his journal and picked up a pen.

> *I hate her. I hate her. I hate her.*
> *Why would she do that, except to hurt me as much as she could? She tried to kill him. But I won't let her. I'll put him back together. He's not dead.*

Tears hit the page and blurred the ink. He nudged the paper out of the way and kept writing.

> *I wish she would hit me instead. I don't understand why she never hits me. She seems so out of control. She* must *be out of control. Otherwise how could she do the things she does?*

He laid his cheek on the bed and covered his face with his hand. Tried to shut those things out. But he couldn't. He clutched the bedspread and sobbed.

Nothing had changed with his mother and nothing ever would. *Thank god I'm leaving.* His mantra. *I'm leaving. I'm leaving.* The thought kept him sane. Kept him from the siren call of the peaceful place he found with the razor blade. *Maybe I can go there again. In my head.*

He focused on the memory, put himself back in that moment on the kitchen floor and found the peace inside his mind. The quiet white place. He stared blindly as white filled his vision. His breathing slowed and deepened as if he were asleep.

He didn't move until his bladder called him back to his body. He sat up slowly, disoriented. The room was dark. He tried to make sense of the glowing numbers on the clock. 6:22. Was that a.m. or p.m.?

He rose and headed to the bathroom. Just a short walk down the hall, but he was dizzy. He touched the wall to anchor himself. Made it. When he finished, he splashed cold water on his face and stared into the mirror. Strange that this pale little face was him. He felt so much older.

He went back out to the hall and heard the TV below. His fingers clutched the banister as he made his way downstairs.

His sister looked up from the couch. "Hi." She ruffled his hair as he sat beside her. "What'cha been doing? You look pale."

"I guess I fell asleep." Didn't seem quite right, though. He blinked and almost remembered a white place, but it was just out of reach.

Tanya's arm went around him. She pulled him to her and kissed his temple the way she used to. As he'd gotten older he wouldn't let her be so affectionate with him anymore. But he didn't mind now. He closed his eyes and let his head sink against her, safe and warm as she held him close.

ಒಒಒ

Tanya sat on the floor in Brian's room and opened the jar of chocolate brown paint. "Now Horsey will be good as new. It was nice of Jeremy to bring us to the mall—especially right before Christmas." She grinned. "I'll be sixteen next year. Then I can drive us around."

I won't be here. Brian frowned and refused to dwell on that or he'd cry. "I think Jeremy felt sorry for me." Jeremy had heard Mom yelling from two houses down. The thought made Brian's face hot. He shook his head. *Why should I be embarrassed? Mom's the one who should be embarrassed.*

He smoothed masking tape over Horsey's rump to reinforce the glue. So far he was holding together. Brian dipped the brush with his left hand and began to carefully paint. The color matched pretty well. Vicky had helped them find the paint at an art supply store in the mall. *Ugh, the mall.* It was super crowded. All those people. He shivered. But spending the day with his sister was great, even though he hated the holiday crowds.

He'd managed to buy a few gifts—a pair of gold sparkly earrings for his mom. He loved the 1928 brand, old fashioned and delicate. His fingers toyed with the silver hoop in his left ear. *I wish I could wear earrings like that.* But he couldn't, so he bought them for her. He picked out a book about sports cars for his dad—a long-standing love affair. *Maybe someday he can afford a real one.* For now, a book would have to do.

Tanya had gotten upset when he lit a cigarette as they headed back to the car. His family knew he smoked, but they didn't like it one bit. He never smoked around his parents. Usually Tanya was cool about it, but this time she freaked. Vicky sided with her, and they gave him a lecture about the evils of cigarettes.

"What do you want for Christmas, Brian?"

He blinked and realized he was sitting in his room. His fingers had continued their work. Horsey was almost done. "I know it's boring, but I really just want money. I'm saving up for . . . something."

"What?"

"It's a surprise." He looked away and changed the subject so she wouldn't get suspicious. "I hope you like your gift." He'd written her a song on the piano that was sweet and comforting, like her. He planned to write the score out on sheet music, then play it for her when she opened the envelope. He set down the paintbrush. "Ta da."

She smiled and squeezed Brian's leg. "Good as new."

Naked in the Rain

. . .

River's voice sounded funny, like he had food in his mouth. "My mouth's swollen," he explained. "Dick got the phone bill yesterday. At least he didn't knock out any teeth."

"God, River." Brian closed his eyes and leaned against the wall of the phone booth, his chest tight. "Are you okay?"

"Oh, sure. Same ol'-same ol'. It'll be over soon, anyway. I forgot to ask before, do you have an ID?"

"No. Should I?"

"No, that's good. It's better if you don't have one on you, unless you *want* to get sent home. And make up a couple of different last names. Get used to them."

"Okay." *I have to change my name?* Brian blew on his hands to warm them, then shielded his eyes from the sun reflecting off snow to glance across the street at the neighborhood market. Lots of people around. Last minute shoppers on Christmas Eve. "You're making me paranoid."

"Good. You should be."

"Aagh!" Brian almost dropped the phone as he spun around. "You scared the hell out of me."

Tanya stood with her hands on her hips. "What are you doing here?"

"Using the phone." He tried to keep his voice calm, but his heart thumped faster.

"What's wrong with the phone at the house? You walked here by yourself?"

He knew he was terrible at lying, especially to his sister. But he had to. "Mom's using it. I got tired of waiting." Inspiration hit as he remembered the redhead and his first kiss. "I want to see Samantha again, so I walked over here to call her."

"Oh. Okay." Tanya smiled. She patted his arm and walked away to wait for him on the corner.

Brian brought the receiver back to his ear. "That was close."

"Dude, I'm proud of you. Excellent lie. But would your sister try to stop you from leaving?"

"Absolutely."

"But she knows what it's like there. You don't think she'd understand?"

"It's not the same for her." *She doesn't really know. No one knows.* "Mom aims her shit at me. She doesn't like men. She said so again the other day."

"Did something happen?"

He shrugged. "She had one of her screaming fits, trashed my room. No biggie." He looked down. "You know. Same ol'-same ol'."

After they hung up, Brian walked back to the house with Tanya. He went into the kitchen to get a snack. Tanya joined him a moment later, eyes narrow. "You lied to me," she said. "Mom isn't using the phone. She isn't even here."

His pulse raced as his mind scrambled. "Maybe she just left."

Tanya looked unsure. "Oh, I don't know." She bit her lip and turned away, but not fast enough to hide the tears in her eyes.

He touched her arm. "What's wrong?"

She turned abruptly to face him. "What's wrong? You wanna know what's wrong?" She pointed at the floor a few feet away. "Three months ago I came home and found my little brother lying in a pool of blood." Her voice broke. "If I hadn't skipped practice that day you'd be dead. *Dead*." She sobbed.

"Tanya." He put his arms around her.

She held him tight. "How could you do that?"

He didn't answer. He felt awful. He hadn't known who found him. Hadn't thought about it.

"You were so white," she whispered. "At first I didn't realize what you'd done. I thought somebody stabbed you or something. There was so much blood. I couldn't tell where it was coming from." She pulled away to lean back against the counter. Her eyes glazed over as she remembered. "Vicky's the one who figured it out."

"Vicky was here?" He felt vaguely embarrassed.

"Not at first." Tanya took a deep breath. "I skipped basketball practice cos I didn't feel good. When I saw you lying there, I just . . . ." She looked at the ceiling. "I thought I would die. I remember holding you, screaming your name. Your eyes were open, but you weren't there. I kept shaking you. You were so limp and white. Even your lips were white." Her voice wavered. "Blood everywhere, slippery and sticky. I called 9-1-1. Then I called Vicky. I don't know why I called her instead of Mom or Dad. I guess I needed someone to be strong. And she's so close. She was here in, like, thirty seconds."

She stared at the linoleum, and her voice dropped. "Vicky saw the razor blade on the floor. She wiped off your wrists with a towel. Those gaping holes." Tanya shivered. "Blood was still oozing out. It was everywhere. On the phone, on my clothes, my hands." She whispered, "I'll never forget the blood." She focused on Brian. "Or the way your face looked."

His eyes filled. "I'm sorry," he breathed.

She took him in her arms and held him tight again.

"Tanya—" He looked up at her. "I promise I'll never do that again."

Her brow knit and fresh tears slid down her face. "You mean that?"

"Yes." So much easier to say now. Now that he knew he would end his life here in a different way. Because it had to end.

༄ ༄ ༄

Brian shoved coins into the slot with numb fingers.

"Hey!" River's voice shouted in his ear. "Good timing, dude, nobody's home."

"Good," Brian said quietly.

"What's wrong?"

"Nothing, really."

"Come on, Brian, you know you can't lie for shit. Especially to me. What's wrong? Are you having second thoughts?"

"No, no! Definitely not." He breathed a humorless laugh. "I wish I could leave today."

"What happened?"

"My mom, you know, she *is* trying." He lit a cigarette. "But nothing's really changed. Of course." He looked down as his sneaker kicked against the cement.

"Go on."

"This morning I was helping her clean up from Christmas dinner. She was washing dishes in the sink while I unloaded the dishwasher." He paused to take a drag on his cigarette and stared into the distance. "I picked up a glass and . . . I guess I didn't have a good grip. I watched it fall, but I couldn't move—isn't it weird how time slows down? It smashed all over." Broken glass sparkling on the kitchen floor. "Mom whirled around. She'd been washing a big butcher knife. She started screaming at me for being clumsy, and . . . well, I don't know if she *meant* to do it. Maybe she was only gesturing, but she was still holding the knife." He took a deep breath. "She poked at me with it. The big knife."

"Poked at you? Like how! Where?"

"In the stomach. I was backed up in the corner against the counter. I couldn't go anywhere."

"Did she actually touch you with the knife?"

"Yeah, a little," he said softly.

"Are you okay?" River sounded like he would explode.

"Yeah, yeah. It was just freaky. She didn't actually hurt me."

"She didn't break the skin?"

"Well . . . ."

"Brian!"

"Just a little."

"Holy shit. Holy shit. We've gotta get you outta there," he shouted into the phone.

"We will. I'll be gone in a few days."

"Maybe you should leave sooner."

"No, I've gotta earn more money and stuff." Brian flicked his cigarette ashes and shivered. "The holiday's over, so she'll be at work."

"Christ." River sounded like he was crying.

"I shouldn't have told you."

"Yes, you should have! Don't you keep stuff from me."

"Okay. I won't."

"Dude, I wish I was with you."

"Me, too. Let's go over our plans again. I think I can get there by New Year's."

༄༄༄

The day arrived. He'd lain awake half the night as his mind turned over the plan. He was worried. And scared. And guilty. He didn't want to hurt his family any more than he already had. But he knew he had to go.

He stared at the ceiling over his bed and refused to look at Horsey or his posters or books. This was no time to be sentimental. His parents were both at work. Now he just needed to get his sister out of the house. He'd laid the foundation last night when he suggested they go to a matinee with Vicky and Jeremy.

Tanya knocked and stuck her head in. "Time to leave for the movie. Why are you still in bed?"

Brian spoke softly. "I'm not going."

She moved to stand by him. "Do you have one of your headaches?"
He nodded.
Worry creased her brow. "I'll stay here with you."
"No, you go. I'll sleep better if no one's home."
She stroked his forehead. "You sleepwalked last night."
"I did?"
She nodded and bit her lip. "I worry about you, little brother."
"I'll be fine. I just need to sleep. You guys have fun at the movie."
Her voice trembled. "I'm not leaving you alone."

His heart skipped. *She means it.* He looked away. *What am I gonna do? I can't stay here. I can't.* His chest tightened.

"I'll get you some aspirin," she said and left the room.

He tried to reason past the panic. *What would River do? I could crawl through the window.* But if he got caught, he wouldn't get a second chance. Before he came up with anything better, Tanya appeared in the doorway. "We're out of aspirin. Will you be okay if I run to the store?"

Relief made him dizzy. "Sure." He hoped he didn't sound too happy.

"I'll be back soon."

The tears came as soon as he heard the front door close, and he realized that was it—he wouldn't see her again. Not for a long time, anyway. *Don't think about that. No time. No time.*

His hands shook as he threw on jeans and a sweater. He grabbed his jacket and the backpack he'd prepared last night, then glanced at his stereo. No time to haul it to the pawn shop as planned. *I'll barely have enough money for the bus ticket.* But it couldn't be helped. Tanya was walking to the store. Ten minutes there, ten minutes back.

He hurried downstairs and grabbed a piece of paper from the kitchen, then remembered the cassette tape—he'd recorded Tanya's song. He wouldn't be here to play it for her anymore. He found the cassette in his backpack and laid it beside the paper, then picked up a pencil with his left hand.

> *I love you all very much. But I have to leave. It may seem selfish, but I have to look out for myself. Protect my sanity. Please try not to worry. I'll be fine.*
>
> *I'm sorry.*
>
> Love,
Brian

He settled the backpack on his shoulders and peeked out the front door. Of course Tanya was nowhere to be seen. But his heart pounded in his ears as he stepped into the cold. Six minutes since Tanya left. Snow crunched under his feet as he ran down the sidewalk in the opposite direction.

He finally slowed when he got a stitch in his side after a few blocks. He glanced at his watch. Tanya would be home soon. What would she do first? Call Mom and Dad, probably. The police. *Shit.*

He cut through someone's yard and made it to a busy intersection, then hurried to the city bus stop and waited. Waited. He fidgeted and looked at his watch again. After what felt like an eternity, the bus appeared from around the corner and stopped before him.

It was a short ride to the Greyhound station. *They won't think to check here, will they? Not right away.* He bought a ticket to New York City. The next Greyhound was leaving in a few minutes, thank god.

He stood in line to board and glanced around at the holiday travelers returning home. He hoped no one noticed how nervous he was. *Hurry up.* The line finally moved forward.

He took a deep breath and stepped up into the bus without a backward glance.

Eowyn Wood

PART 2

Eowyn Wood

"Fly, you get high, right?
Fly, you get high, right?
Try, you get by alright
Try and you get by alright
Ryde, you're my bright light
you're my bright light
Oh god, I'm high
Waterfalls of light
flood my eyes with light
flood my eyes
my aching eyesight
my aching eyes"

- Kristin Hersh (Throwing Muses), "Flood"

ɯɾɯ CHAPTER 6 ɯɾɯ

Brian stared out the window as the bus pulled up to a huge building of steel girders—the New York City station. He wondered what his family was doing right now. He imagined Tanya reading the note, feeling guilty because she'd left him alone. *I'm sorry.*

His eyes filled, but he wiped them quickly. No time for that. People were getting off the bus, and now it was his turn to walk down the narrow aisle and out into the cold. He followed the crowd into the cavernous building, and his step faltered. The place was overwhelming.

River could do it. The thought made him feel better and worse. Brian missed him so much. *But I'll see him soon. I have to do this to see him.* He settled the backpack on his shoulders and walked through the crowds of people. He'd read somewhere that this was the world's busiest bus terminal. *I believe it.* But after a moment he noticed its beautiful art deco design, with mosaic floors, historic light fixtures, marble and granite. He bumped into an older lady and apologized. But she was nice and pointed him in the right direction.

He left the historic portion of the building behind and entered a modern area, shiny and metallic like an airport, and finally found the line for the ticket counter. The man behind the plexi-glass told a woman the bus she wanted was sold out. Brian's heart skipped. *What if mine is?* He glanced around the huge space. *If I stay here too long they might find me.*

He moved up as the lady walked away. His voice came out higher than usual. "Ticket to Tucson, Arizona. One-way." *One-way. I'm not coming back.*

The man typed on his computer. "The next bus leaves in a few hours. You got the last seat."

Relief made him dizzy. *River, I'm coming.*

He found the right terminal, then was afraid to leave it in case he got lost. The wait seemed to last forever. He kept looking over his shoulder, half expecting to see his mother bearing down on him in a fury. Or his sister running toward him.

He bit his lip but couldn't stop the tears this time. He hurried to the nearest bathroom to cry.

He felt safer once he boarded the bus. It pulled away, and his heart soared. *I did it. They'll never find me now.*

He was too excited to sleep at first, but soon the motion of the bus and his sleepless night caught up with him. He woke after dark, famished, and ate the first of four peanut butter and jelly sandwiches he'd brought, then fell asleep again.

The bus driver called out Toledo, Ohio, and Brian jerked awake. Morning already. He stretched stiff muscles and glanced out the window at a jumble of tall grey buildings. Toledo. The name seemed familiar. He checked his ticket. *I transfer here. Shit, what if I slept through it?* His heart thumped. *Gotta pay more attention.*

The Toledo station was so much smaller than the one in New York that it didn't seem scary. And no need to worry about his parents. He refilled his bottle at a water fountain, then found the next bus with no trouble and settled into the big seat.

They were soon underway. He stared out the window at endless cornfields rolling by, but that got old quickly. *Why didn't I bring a book? Because I'm running away. No books, no music. Only the necessities. I have to be tough now.*

But he was bored. He pulled out his journal and removed it from the plastic bag—in case of rain. He wrote and drew pictures until his hand got tired somewhere in Kentucky.

ಜಜಜ

He gazed out the bus window at the island of lights surrounded by blackness. Tucson. Finally. He was exhausted and hungry and sick of being on a bus. He'd eaten his last sandwich this morning, somewhere in Texas. *I never want peanut butter and jelly again.*

It was all he'd eaten the last two-and-a-half days, except for a candy bar in Dallas. He didn't want to waste money—he only had eight dollars left. *I hope River has enough money to keep us going awhile.* And then what? He refused to think about it.

Instead he stared at the lights of Tucson and remembered River's arms around him, remembered breathing in his scent. His pulse sped up. So hard to wait. He whispered, "Soon. I'll be with you soon."

River had told him where to catch the shuttle bus to the small mountain town of Sierra Blanca. Brian checked his watch. 9:30 on December 31st. *I hope I get there before midnight.* He wanted to be with River at the turn of the new year.

The Greyhound rolled to a stop at the Tucson station. He grabbed his backpack and tried not to breathe noxious fumes as he stepped out into the cold. Lights shone through the windows of the small station. But that's not where he needed to go. *The city bus.* He turned around to get his bearings but a tall building blocked his view.

"Brian!"

He whirled toward the sound of River's voice.

"Brian!"

He saw River through the small crowd. Brian breathed a laugh and hurried toward him. He dropped his pack as they collided and hugged each other tight. "River!" His voice caught. Safe and warm and wonderful in his arms, like they'd never been apart. And never would be again.

River held Brian's face in his hands. "You made it. You really made it."

Brian nodded, and his tears spilled over. River brushed them away gently, then held him close again.

Brian didn't want to ever move, but after a moment he picked up his backpack, and they headed away from the station. River said, "I figured, why make you come all the way to my dumb-fuck hometown? We're gonna leave tomorrow, anyway. Besides, it'll be more fun to party here tonight."

"Yeah." Brian grinned. He felt like he would burst. Had he ever been this happy?

River led him down a brick sidewalk with two-story buildings on either side of the road. Most of the shops were closed for the night, although one bar had people laughing and spilling onto the sidewalk, music blaring. The boys crossed the street to avoid them and passed a historic-looking building with a neon sign on the roof. The red letters glowed, 'Hotel Congress.'

River said, "I was hoping to spend New Year's Eve with Dove. Bein' my last night and all."

"Sure. I want to meet her."

"We gotta be careful not to let anything slip."

Brian nodded. They walked by an old fashioned streetlamp with globe lights, and he noticed a bruise on River's jaw. He wondered if Dick had put it there.

"Dove has a friend here in Tucson. Her mom's out of town."

They reached a covered walkway of brick with decorative green and terracotta tiles that surrounded the block-long city transit center. He followed River through an arch and saw several rows of well-lit platforms.

River bought Brian's ticket at a round booth, and they walked to the far end. River studied his face while they waited for the bus. "I was gettin worried when I didn't hear from you."

"Sorry. I tried to call from the road, but I got the machine."

"Oh." River nodded. "How was, uh, leavin and all?"

Tanya's face flashed through his mind, and his throat tightened. He pushed it away, but his voice trembled. "It was hard. But it's done now."

"Did you leave a note?"

"Yeah. A short one. Just so they'd know I wasn't kidnapped or anything." His lips twisted down.

River frowned. "I couldn't leave a note, since we're not leaving till tomorrow. But I won't be back to the house."

Brian touched River's arm. "We'll think of something."

A bus rumbled down their row and stopped before them. Brian sighed. *Another bus ride.*

Happily, it was a short trip. They jumped off the bus and walked along a dark residential street, then turned left at the corner. River pointed down the block. "It's that house there." Rectangular and squat, with a flat roof. Pueblo-style, like its neighbors, and small. Light glowed from square windows. "Remember, they think you're an old friend from school who moved away. You're just visiting. Be careful what you say."

He nodded. "Got it."

River knocked. An older teenage girl opened the door. "River, you're back."

He introduced them. Leanne was pretty and blond. Brian clutched his backpack and gave her a shy smile. The boys stepped into the smoky, bright living room full of teenagers and laughter. The radio blared Top 40 pop.

River led him to the couch where a girl with long, dark blond hair sat. "This is my sister, Dove."

She's beautiful. "You look just like River." Same grey-green eyes, same color hair. Same smile.

She arched an eyebrow.

He laughed. "No, in a good way."

The girl beside Dove was Leanne's younger sister. She used to go to school with Dove until her family moved to Tucson. *Like River and me,* he thought, remembering their cover story. Dove scooted over to make room for the boys. River grabbed a pack of cigarettes from the coffee table as he sat down and offered one to Brian.

"Thanks."

"Okay, final orders," a tall guy announced over the noise and moved to the front door.

"Bud!" several voices cried out.

River said, "Aw, we drink that all the time. Let's get somethin different."

Dove suggested Bacardi.

The thought made Brian queasy. River smiled and said, "I don't think Brian likes that anymore. How about vodka?"

They agreed and River called out, "A bottle of vodka for my friends here!" He turned to Brian. "It won't make you as sick cos it's more pure. That's what my brother told me."

"Okay," said the guy at the door. "We'll be back in a minute. Leanne, you coming?"

She grabbed her jacket and headed out the door.

They returned twenty minutes later empty handed. Frantic questions bombarded them. "Where is it? What happened!"

"Aw, don't panic. It's in the car. Let's go for a drive." Don held up his fist. "To the desert!"

"*Alright.* Yeah!" Everyone stood to go.

Brian picked up his backpack.

"You can leave it here," River said. "We'll be back."

They joined the group outside and eight people piled into Don's Chrysler. Brian squeezed onto River's lap. He rather liked being shoved in so close against him.

They headed toward Don's favorite spot and left the city behind. Brian watched the scenery as his eyes adjusted to the dark. Silhouettes of saguaro cactus rose thirty feet tall, their limbs like arms reaching toward the night sky, or sometimes twisting down, each one unique.

Naked in the Rain

The Chrysler finally pulled over onto a gravelly area and stopped. Brian spilled out of the cramped car, grateful to move his legs again. They stood a few hundred feet up the side of a mountain, surrounded by boulders and rocky sand. "Careful of the cactus," River said.

Brian skirted the prickly pear and gazed past hundreds of saguaros and short scrubby trees to the twinkling lights of Tucson, then up at the bright moon overhead. "It's amazing." His breath fogged in the cold, and he shivered.

River murmured, "I missed you."

Brian smiled up at him, and his eyes stung. So happy. River put his arm around his shoulders and squeezed.

"Here's the beer!" Don's voice boomed into the night. He handed out a few flashlights and water bottles, too.

They got the vodka out of the trunk. "What time is it?" River asked.

Brian checked the watch hanging loose on his wrist. "About eleven."

"We've got an hour to get good and ripped. *Woo hoo,*" River hollered. He took a swig from the bottle and grimaced, then gave it to Brian.

Brian wiped his mouth as warmth spread down his throat and into his stomach. "Better than Bacardi." He passed the bottle to Dove.

River grinned. "Guess what else we got." He reached inside his denim jacket to pull out a pipe and a small baggie of dried plant. "Come on."

Brian and Dove followed him to a pile of large boulders next to a two-hundred-year-old saguaro. River sat down and carefully stuffed weed into the bowl of the pipe. "Brian's never gotten stoned before."

"Oh." Dove's grey-green eyes grew big. She squeezed Brian's shoulder and grinned just like River.

He warmed at her touch, then looked down, afraid she would notice his flushed cheeks. But she was watching River pack the bowl.

"You ready?" River asked.

He nodded. But . . . .

"It's real easy," River said. "Just light it while you inhale. Hold the smoke in as long as you can—that's important. Should be easy for you, since you been smoking cigarettes awhile."

Dove asked, "How long?"

"Since my tenth birthday. So it's been . . . ." Brian's gaze rose to the night sky.

River shook his head and laughed. "Here we go with math again. Two years."

"Ooo, you're young," she said.

River closed the little plastic bag. "Only a year younger than you. Besides, he's older than his age. Dude." He slapped Brian's chest with the back of his hand. "Pay attention. Now watch me." He exhaled and put the pipe to his lips, then held the lighter sideways over the bowl and inhaled long and deep. "Here." He held his breath as he passed the pipe to Brian. "Want me to light it?" Wisps of smoke escaped from his mouth. He sucked in more air.

Brian nodded. He held up the pipe and inhaled as River ignited the pot. Harsh smoke filled his lungs. He struggled to hold it in, but it burned way more than cigarette smoke. Dove took the pipe as he coughed hard.

River exhaled and coughed, too. "It means you got a good hit if you cough."

"Oh." Brian laughed and coughed again, then glanced at the other group. They were passing a joint.

"Looks like there's plenty to go around." River took another hit and passed the pipe to Brian.

He held the smoke better this time, now that he knew what to expect. The pipe made the rounds a third time. Brian leaned back—but not too far—didn't want to get stuck with a cactus spine. Tons of vegetation grew out of the rocky sand. Not at all the sparse desert he'd expected. He stared at a dead-looking plant whose long skinny limbs grew in a cluster toward the sky. Ocatillo, River had told him. For a second he thought it moved. But no, of course not.

"I'm definitely feelin it now," River said. He looked at Brian.

"I don't know . . . ." His eyes moved to the other group of teens. He cocked his head as he tried to make sense of the image. A big black blob. It moved like it was spreading wings. Sorta like a cartoon. He watched in fascination, then laughed. "Yeah, I think so!" He turned his head to look at River and felt the weirdest sensation, like his head was still turning to catch up with him. "Whoa." He laughed again.

"Dude, what time is it?"

"Uh." Brian struggled to read his watch in the dim light. "11:15."

"We gotta remember to keep an eye on the time. Gettin stoned makes you forget stuff. Don't wanna miss midnight."

Dove said, "I'm gonna get some beer," and wandered off.

"This is so cool." Brian picked up the pipe for another hit.

"That's my man." River slapped him on the back. "But let me load it first. That's dust."

"Oh." Brian giggled and handed it over.

River tapped the ashes out onto the boulder. "What time is it?"

"11:17. No way. It's only been two minutes?"

River grinned. "Yeah, time slows down, too. Pretty cool, unless you're in class. But no more school for us!"

Brian's eyes widened. *That's right. No more school.* Suddenly it seemed very real and a little scary. He gazed at River and knew they stood on the cusp of some great adventure. Together.

"I'm so thirsty," Brian said.

"Cotton mouth." River handed him the vodka. "What the hell was I talking about?"

"I have no idea."

They laughed.

"Hey, guys," Dove called. "Come over here. It's almost midnight."

The boys joined the circle of teenagers. Green light glowed from Don's watch. "Okay, one minute!"

They all hooted and hollered and raised beer cans in salute. Brian raised the bottle of vodka. He laughed as River put his arm around his shoulders and shook him.

"Quiet!" Don commanded. "Okay, ten seconds."

"Ten, nine," everyone shouted. River took the bottle away from Brian and set it safely against a rock. "Four, three . . . ." He rested his hand on Brian's shoulder. "Two! One!" they shouted together.

"Wooh!"

"Happy New Year!"

Dove hugged River. Brian let out a whoop and looked up at the stars. He'd never felt so free.

River grabbed him in a bear hug and lifted him off the ground. Brian laughed, then almost fell when River set him down. River tried to help but lost his balance, too. They landed on the sand, laughing helplessly.

River turned his head to meet his gaze. "Brian . . . ."

He didn't need to finish. Brian stared into his eyes and understood. *Everything's okay now. We're together.*

They stopped at a twenty-four-hour diner on the way back. The room spun around him, and Brian felt a little sick. The smell of greasy food made him even dizzier.

"You hungry?" River asked. "Food's extra good when you're stoned. We shoulda brought munchies."

Hungry. Yes. He hadn't eaten since the disgusting peanut butter and jelly this morning. Seemed like a lifetime ago. He met River's eyes. *Before I was with you.*

River ordered a burger and coffee. Brian ordered grilled cheese and got coffee because River did. His face scrunched up when he tasted it. So bitter. It was better after he loaded it with milk and sugar. Almost good, even. And the food was wonderful.

He felt better afterward. Not so dizzy. "Eating is good."

River laughed, and they all headed back to the house.

Brian didn't last long once they got there. River set the half-full bottle of vodka on the dresser. He hadn't drunk that much, but the combination of alcohol and pot always fucked him up. *Brian must be wasted.* He looked so small lying in the middle of that big bed in his boxers and tee shirt. River stripped down to his briefs and slid under the sheet, then pulled the covers up over Brian. Brian's eyes opened a crack, and he smiled.

River hugged him, and his throat tightened. "I missed you so much. I'm so glad you're here."

"Me, too."

River pressed his lips against Brian's forehead. He felt him relax, unconscious in seconds, and he thought about what Brian's life must've been like the last few days. *Scary. And alone. Poor kid.*

River's life had been lonely, too. He just never noticed until he met Brian. *Guess I didn't know the difference.* He held him tighter and closed his eyes.

. . .

River wakened slowly and blinked in the light. They'd hardly moved all night, just enough to get their limbs tangled up. River glanced down and saw a wet spot on his briefs. *Aw, shit.* Must've had that dream again. The one he could never remember, except it was incredibly erotic. Full of touching.

Brian was still asleep, his face flushed, eyes moving behind his lids. *Hope it's not a nightmare.* River went to the bathroom to clean up.

Brian dug into his cereal, famished.

"You feel okay?" River asked.

"Yeah. A little shaky, but nothing like my birthday."

River nodded as he got another bowl from the cupboard. "We didn't drink as much this time, cos we had pot. Plus vodka don't make you as sick."

Brian's gaze wandered. River had jeans on, but no shirt yet. His tanned chest brought back the vivid dream Brian had this morning. Sliding his hand over River's smooth skin, their bodies rubbing—he blinked and stopped the memory as heat flooded his cheeks. *Don't think about him like that.*

The boys hoisted small backpacks onto their shoulders and left the house, their shoes crunching in the gravelly sand at the side of the road. Brian smiled up at the blue sky. Sunny and slightly warm. So different from Connecticut. The houses were different, too. Mostly pueblo-style, with flat roofs and no visible foundation. It made them look short.

He got out sunscreen to rub on his face. "Want some?" He glanced at River's clenched jaw and realized what this moment meant for him. Brian touched his arm.

"I didn't even get to say goodbye." Dove had already left for the mall by the time the boys woke up this morning.

"Maybe that's for the best," Brian said. "Saying goodbye is hard, especially when you're trying to act normal."

River sniffed and nodded. "I still gotta write that note." He led the way to a nearby park. They sat on a bench surrounded by dead grass shaded by short mesquite trees. "Shit," River said. "I don't have any paper."

Brian pulled the journal from his pack and tore out a piece.

"Thanks." River sighed and leaned back to stare at the clear sky. He sat for a long moment, then hunched forward and scribbled.

> *I'm outta here. Don't worry about me. You know I can take care of myself.*
>
> *Love you,*
> *River*
>
> *P.S. Tell Grandpa I'm sorry I hit him.*

"There." River folded the paper. "We'll mail it later."

Brian put his hand on River's, and River's composure started to crack. Brian said, "Please don't go if you don't want to. Don't do this for me. You have to be doing it for yourself."

"I am. It's hard, but . . . I hate that place. Mom picked Dick over us a long time ago. And I've had enough."

Brian's gaze lingered on the bruise on River's jaw. The bruises he'd seen this morning on his back. *I hate Dick, too.* He squeezed River's hand. River squeezed him back and let out a sigh that turned into a sob.

Brian wrapped his arms around him and held him tight. "We have to do what's right for us."

River nodded, then cleared his throat and stood up. "Come on. I wanna show you around Tucson before we go."

They took the bus to the transit center where they were last night and walked around downtown. The few skyscrapers weren't very tall. Most of the other buildings were older two-stories with shops on the first floor.

The boys approached a large sculpture formed by strips of flat red metal. The geometric design looked a bit like a dog, Brian thought, but mostly it was a jumble. A flock of pigeons scrounged for food beside it. "I don't get modern art."

River grinned. "You gotta be tripping."

A truck honked, and the pigeons took flight. Brian watched them move as a group, their dark wings in unison; then he followed River past the sculpture into a plaza. Across the street at the far end stood a large stucco building with a mosaic dome and scrolling façade. Graceful arches surrounded a courtyard with a fountain and the first truly green grass he'd seen here. "That's pretty."

"Pima County Courthouse. I try to keep away from there." River laughed. "Come on."

They walked several more blocks, past Saint Augustine's Cathedral, past the police station and around the corner. Farther on Brian read a sign posted on a building. "Cactus Counseling Associates? What's that?"

"They help cactus who're feeling depressed," River said with a straight face.

Brian laughed, and they turned another corner.

"Here it is."

Set back from the road, a wall of adobe bricks rose to an arch in the middle, then stepped down in levels on either side. It looked Spanish and very old. Candles stood in rows and clusters before it, but not many were lit. "El Tiradito." River rolled the 'r.' "The only shrine in the country dedicated to a sinner." He grinned. "That's why I like it. You're supposed to light a candle and make a wish. If it stays lit all night, your wish comes true."

"How do you know if it stays lit?"

River shrugged. "You just gotta believe." He knelt before a row of cylindrical glass holders with religious figures on them. "These are more likely not to blow out." He found one that wasn't lit and handed it to Brian, then got one for himself. River closed his eyes and gripped the candle tight while his lips moved to form his silent wish. He held his lighter to the wick until it caught.

Brian knelt beside him and closed his eyes. *Please let me be with River forever. Let him feel for me what I feel for him.* He lit his candle.

River nodded and stood. "We should get going now."

They wandered back toward downtown. Brian said, "Where should we go first?"

"How about L.A.? I wanna see the ocean."

Brian smiled, and his heart picked up. *We're really doing it.* "Okay. Should we take the bus somewhere else first? Just in case."

"Bus? No, dude. We're hitching."

"Hitchhiking?" Brian's eyes got big. "That's too dangerous."

"Naw. I've done it before, up to Phoenix."

"But what if we end up with someone bad?"

River shrugged. "I got a knife. And there's two of us."

"I wouldn't be much help in a fight."

"I can fight enough for both of us. Brian—" River held his gaze. "We can't afford to take the bus all the way to California."

Brian bit his lip. He couldn't argue with that. *We've got to make our money last.* "Okay."

River patted his shoulder, then turned to go into the post office. They walked up to the counter and River asked for an envelope, stuck his note inside and handed it over. He had his tough guy mask on, but Brian saw the slight tremor in his hands, his clenched jaw. Brian understood. This was it for River. No turning back.

They made it to Phoenix alright, though Brian was nervous the whole time. The man seemed nice enough, but still . . . .

The boys ate lunch, then stood at the on-ramp to the freeway and got picked up by an older lady heading to California. She seemed sweet, and Brian was glad for the free ride. River told her a long story about how they were going to visit their cousin in San Diego, but they lost their bus fare. Brian was impressed at how well River weaved the lie. She totally fell for it.

It was a long drive through desert and mountains into California. "Look at the hills," Brian said. "They look like M*A*S*H." Brown with tan-colored boulders tinted orange from the setting sun.

The woman smiled. "It was filmed here in Southern California."

"Really? Neat."

"I'm sorry I can't take you boys all the way to San Diego," she said as they entered San Bernardino. "Will you be okay?"

"Oh, sure," River said. "We're close enough now. Our cousin can probably come get us."

She dropped them off near a phone booth and waved goodbye. "Nice lady," River said.

"Didn't you feel bad lying to her?"

River shrugged. "Got us here, didn't it? We're real close to L.A. now." He dug through his backpack and pulled out a Youth Hostel booklet. "Let's check in. I'm beat."

The next day a man pulled over and said he could take them to Los Angeles. The stranger's gaze flicked over them and sent a shiver up Brian's spine. He grabbed River's arm in panic. "No." He pulled River backward, away from the car.

"What are you doing?" River said.

"I'm not going with him."

The man leaned over to open the passenger door and patted the leather seat beside him. "Hop in."

Brian's heart tripped. "No, River," he whispered. "He's bad. I'm not going."

River studied Brian's face a long moment. "Okay." He turned to the man. "Sorry, we forgot something. We'll catch a ride later."

They backed farther away.

"I can wait for you," the man called after them.

They shook their heads, turned and ran until they were out of breath. River leaned against a building. "That's weird," he panted. "Why would he want to wait for us?"

"He's bad."

"How did you know?"

Brian's voice shook. "I just know."

Brian refused to hitchhike after that. "We're almost there. It can't cost that much to take the bus."

River finally agreed, and they bought tickets at the Greyhound station. They couldn't even tell when they got to Los Angeles; the cities here all ran together. A world of pavement.

The boys got off when the driver announced the main L.A. terminal. "Guess we're here," River said.

They took a city bus almost all the way to the ocean. They stepped onto the sidewalk, and River took a deep breath. "What's that smell?"

"Besides the fumes?" Cars whizzed past them. "It's the ocean. Saltwater."

River's face lit up. "I didn't expect it to have a smell. Let's go."

They headed west along a wide street, surrounded by tall buildings under a cool grey sky. Brian asked, "You've really never seen the ocean?"

"Nope. I asked my grandpa to take me when I was in Connecticut, but he wouldn't. Prick." He adjusted his backpack. "I think he used to hit my mom when she was a kid."

Brian sucked in his breath. "That's terrible."

"Yeah. At least Dick doesn't do that. He don't hit girls." River shook his head, then smiled. "Bet I can beat you."

He took off running, and Brian chased after. It felt good to stretch his legs after so many days in buses and cars. The saltwater smell grew steadily stronger.

River slowed and Brian caught up with him. They crossed busy roads and passed a scattering of palm trees to finally stand on an overlook above the ocean. The endless ocean. They leaned against the fence, and River gaped.

Brian rested his hand on River's shoulder. River gave him a radiant smile and said, "Let's go."

They found stairs leading down and crossed another wide, busy road, then took off their shoes to feel the cool sand between their toes. Not many people around on a cloudy day in early January. Brian preferred it that way.

The waves got louder as they approached, until they stood on wet sand with the ocean lapping at their feet. The icy water hit their skin, and they both yelped.

"Shit, that's cold." River laughed and rolled his jeans to wade up to his knees. He stared out across the water.

Brian joined him. He could barely hear River's voice over the waves. "It's like eternity. Or something." River laughed again.

He'd never seen River so enchanted, his tough façade completely gone. River turned to him suddenly, picked him up and swung him around in circles. Brian laughed, thrilled by River's strength and joy.

River set him down with a splash and said, "Thanks."

"For what?"

"For helping me get my butt out of there. To here." He gazed out at the ocean again, and squeezed Brian's shoulder. "For being you."

Brian smiled and leaned against him. River's arm went around his shoulders, and they stood together looking out over the endless sea.

They checked into a youth hostel that night. But the lady behind the counter said the rest of the week was booked up. "You should have made reservations," she said.

"Shit," River muttered under his breath.

"You can try other hostels in the area, and there's an inexpensive motel down the street." She gave them the details.

Brian and River exchanged looks. If they had to stay at motels, their money wouldn't last long at all. Brian's gut twisted as reality sunk in. They would run out of money. Even in a best-case scenario, they would run out of money. It was just a matter of time. He bit his lip and tried not to wonder how they would manage.

River spent the rest of the evening calling other youth hostels. He made reservations for two nights during the week, but the rest of the time they were on their own. He tried a few hostels elsewhere. "Maybe L.A.'s just popular." But they were mostly booked, too. "Fuck." He sank down on the bench and stared at the floor. "I'm sorry."

"It's my fault as much as yours, River."

He shook his head. "I'm supposed to take care of you."

"No, you're not. You're my friend, not my mother." His voice caught. She never took care of him. He patted River's arm. "We'll be okay."

The next day the clouds burned off, and the boys decided to go to Hollywood. It was a long walk through the cement world—light-colored buildings everywhere, but not shoved up against each other like New York City. The tall ones were scattered among shorter two-stories and most of the streets were at least two lanes in each direction, so it felt open and bright. "Look." Brian pointed to a movie ad painted on the entire side of a tall building. "Weird."

He was about to give in to his aching feet when they saw the Hollywood sign perched on the side of a small brown mountain. "Just like the movies," Brian breathed, eyes wide.

They finally got to Hollywood Boulevard, and River grimaced. "This is Hollywood?"

"It's so dirty. Gross."

They walked over famous names carved into stars on the sidewalk, past ragged children and adults begging for money. Trash littered the sidewalk and gutter. The bright sun made the grime even more apparent.

They headed toward the pointed Asian architecture of the Chinese Theater, surrounded by tourists and beggars and more tourists. A homeless man with no shoes started yelling at pigeons.

"This place is weird," River said.

"Yeah. Let's go."

They took a bus to the beach. This time River stripped to his briefs and swam, despite the icy water. He emerged shivering but happy and sat in the sun. "I love swimming. I'm on the swim team. Or I was." A frown flicked across his face.

"Did you have a pool at home?"

River gave a short laugh. "Not even. We're poor. We can't afford that shit." He shrugged and stared out across the water. "Doesn't matter anymore."

When River was mostly dry, they took a long walk to the cheap motel and opened up their room. River grinned. "This is cool. Our own place."

"Yeah." Brian bounced on the bed. He felt very adult, staying in a motel without parents. *And only one bed*, he noted. Though he wasn't so pleased when he looked a little closer. "This place isn't very clean."

River shrugged. "What do you expect? It's cheap."

"I guess. So what should we do tomorrow? I wish we could go to Disneyland."

"Yeah. Maybe we could sneak in."

"No. I don't want to do that." He lay back, and his eyelids drooped. All the walking today made him tired.

The boys slept cuddled up in the middle of the bed. Brian rested his cheek against River's smooth chest and dreamed.

"Oh, River, that's gross." Brian pointed to the briefs soaking in the sink.

"I want clean underwear, damn it."

Brian laughed. "Okay. I'm all for that."

The underwear was still wet at checkout time. River put them in a plastic bag. "We'll hang em up to dry."

They found a small park with a few scraggly trees and worn grass. River hung his briefs on the lower limbs, then sat on the dirt beneath. He lit a cigarette and watched people look at his underwear as they walked by. "What are you staring at?" he said in a loud voice.

He and Brian laughed, but then River's face turned serious. "We can't afford to stay in motels all the time."

"I know." Brian glanced around the small park. "Maybe we should sleep here? Or somewhere like this."

River nodded slowly. "We'll have to be careful not to get caught."

. . .

They walked around the city and soaked in the atmosphere—tall palm trees, expensive shops, famous nightclubs. Everything cost money they didn't have. Brian wanted to see museums; River wanted to go into the clubs. "We're too young, anyway." Brian stared up at the giant Marlboro man. He bit his lip and wondered how many cigarettes they had left.

They kept going, scouting for a good place to spend the night—a park that would provide cover from police. They finally found one with a lot of shrubs and undergrowth. Next they went to a grocery store to buy a loaf of bread and peanut butter. Brian frowned at the peanut butter.

"It's cheaper than eating out all the time," River said.

They sat on the grass in their park and dipped bread into the jar. It was better than nothing.

When night fell and the air grew cooler, they crawled beneath hedges into a tiny clearing, barely big enough for the two of them. Wild vines formed a thick mat above, making them invisible from the outside. "This is perfect," River said.

They used their backpacks for pillows and curled against each other.

Brian woke as early morning light penetrated their bower. He shivered and pushed his face against River's warmth. River jerked awake. "God, it's fuckin freezing. I thought California was supposed to be warm."

"It *is* January." Brian's hair brushed against the vines as he sat up, and a denim jacket slid off him. River's jacket. "No wonder you're so cold. You shouldn't give me your jacket. You need it."

River shrugged and coughed. "It's cold no matter what. Let's go. It'll be warmer if we walk." He crawled out cautiously and gave the all clear.

The youth hostel seemed like real luxury after two nights in the park. Heat and a soft bed. Though he missed sleeping against River.

They went back to the park that night and counted out their money. Six dollars and fifty-two cents. Not even enough to stay at the youth hostel again. They stared at each other in silence.

They spent the last of their money two days later. *No more food.* Not that they ate much lately, anyway. Brian was always hungry. He put on a brave face and smiled. "Tomorrow's your birthday—today's January 9th." He'd seen the date on a newspaper.

"Awesome. We can—" River broke off in a fit of coughing. "We get a free meal at Denny's."

They woke early the next morning—always early. It was impossible to sleep through the cold. Brian kissed River's cheek. "Happy birthday."

They found a Denny's and washed off layers of grime in the bathroom. The boys settled into a torn orange booth that felt soft after the ground. River ordered a Denver omelet for his free meal and looked at the sweet, pale kid across from him who ordered water. *I can't do that to him.* He changed it to a veggie omelet.

The waitress asked for ID to prove it was his birthday. "No problem." River pulled out his wallet.

She smiled and wished him a happy birthday, then left. Brian looked kinda pissed. He leaned over the table and said in a loud whisper, "You told me not to bring an ID."

"It's fake. Look." River handed it over. "I ran into a guy before you came out, a friend of my brother's. I thought it might come in handy."

"'Reese Thompson,'" Brian read.

"I added two years to my age. According to that I'm sixteen today instead of fourteen." He shrugged. "Maybe it'll help down the line."

"Huh."

"Sorry I couldn't get you one, too. I didn't have a photo."

Brian shrugged and seemed okay with it. The food arrived, and all conversation ceased. River put the plate between them, and they wolfed it down, along with all the potatoes. River wanted to lick the plate, but he settled with licking his fingers instead. "Dude, I just had the greatest idea. We can visit every Denny's in town and get as many free meals today as we want."

Brian's eyes lit up beautifully. "Yes!"

And they did. They hadn't eaten so well in a week. They finished their final meal late that night, and River leaned back against the orange seat with a sigh. "A cigarette will make it perfect."

"What about our rule?" Only one a day—they were almost out.

"Fuck it. It's my birthday." He got two out of the pack and handed one to Brian.

River finished his first. "I'm going to the bathroom." *I never get to jack off anymore. That's why I have wet dreams all the time now. It's my birthday, dammit.* "I'll be awhile."

"Okay. I'll wait outside." Brian went out and leaned against the building to stare into the dark—though it was never truly dark here with the glow of city lights. A cool breeze hit his face, and the corner of his mouth quirked down. *River made my birthday so special. And what does he get? Denny's.* He stared at empty wrappers strewn along the pavement, took a final drag and added his cigarette butt to the litter.

A teenager came and stood against the wall nearby. He mumbled something.

"What?" Brian looked at him. Not much taller, brown skin.

"You wanna buy something?" He spoke quickly with a Hispanic accent.

"Like what?" The words spilled out of his mouth before he could think.

"What you looking for? I got speed, rock. Whatever you want."

Brian's eyes widened. *Drug dealer.* But another part of his brain remembered what River had talked about. *He deserves something fun on his birthday.* His mouth formed the word before he could think. "Acid."

"I got that."

"I don't have any money." His mind scrambled. "Would you take a trade?" He held up his wrist. He had no idea how much acid cost. He hoped the guy wouldn't get pissed. "It's a nice watch."

The Mexican boy pursed his lips. "I'll give you a few tabs for it."

"Okay." Brian started to take off his watch.

"Not here."

Brian followed him a few yards, into the shadow between streetlights. His pulse beat in his ears. *God, what am I doing?* He glanced around the deserted street. *Please don't hurt me.*

The teenager reached into his jacket and pulled out a small square of neatly folded tinfoil. They made the exchange. The guy slipped the watch into his pocket and walked away.

My god. I just bought drugs on the street in L.A. He looked at the shiny silver in his hand. *At least I hope I did.* He tucked it away and hurried back just as River emerged. Adrenalin flowed through him, and he couldn't stop his grin.

"What are you all smiley about?"

"I got you a present." He tugged on the sleeve of River's jacket. "Come on. Let's go to the park."

They sat on the ground in their park, and Brian handed over the square of tinfoil.

River's eyes got big. "Is this what I think it is?" He unfolded it carefully to reveal four small squares of yellow paper, about a quarter inch on each side.

Brian's heart fell. *We were ripped off.*

River laughed. "How the hell did you get acid?"

"That's acid?"

"Yeah. It's soaked into the paper."

"Oh." Brian grinned. "Happy birthday." He told him how he bought it.

River shook his head, eyes wide. "I can't believe you did that. For me. You're so brave." A warm smile touched his face. He hugged Brian, then laughed. "We're gonna have a blast. You ready?"

He nodded, but his heart pounded.

"You're nervous, ain'tcha?"

Brian shrugged.

"Don't worry. You'll love it." River picked up a square carefully between his fingers. "Try not to touch it too much. Put it on your tongue and let it dissolve." River set the first square on his own tongue.

Brian followed suit. It tasted like paper. "How long until it dissolves?"

"About twenty minutes. It's almost an hour before you feel anything. The peak hits in the middle, about four hours in."

"It lasts eight hours?" Brian asked. A long time if he didn't like it.

"Yeah, about. Though if you don't sleep afterward, you might start hallucinating again."

It sounded a bit scary. "What if I fall asleep during it?"

"You won't. You can't sleep on this shit." River picked up the third square. "Let's do two each. Make sure we get a good trip."

Brian wasn't too sure about that, but he took it anyway.

They waited, and the paper finally dissolved. "I guess it's been twenty minutes," Brian said. It felt strange not to be able to check the time. *But it really doesn't mat-*

ter—they had nothing to be late for. "That watch bugged me anyway. Rubbed on my scar and made it itch."

River picked up Brian's wrist to look at the purplish slash, then let go when a coughing fit shook him. Sounded worse, deeper. Brian tried not to worry.

It passed, and they sat in comfortable silence until River said, "It's startin to kick in. Feel it?"

"Uh . . . ." He felt pretty normal so far, except for the burning in his stomach. He stared at one of the park's scraggly trees for a long moment, and it started to move. Not like a tree might normally move in the wind but in slow undulations. As if he'd entered a slightly different dimension. He laughed. "Trippy."

As time passed, the strange undulations were everywhere he looked. And the noise of nearby traffic sounded completely different. Almost like raw music. He tried to describe it to River.

River laughed. "Dude, everybody's got their own trip. But that's one of the cool things about acid—it doesn't just affect your vision; it affects *all* your senses."

"It's like a whole new reality. Was all this here before?"

"Who knows?" River grinned wider than seemed possible, and his face rippled—but not unpleasantly. "Wanna go for a walk?"

Sounded like a wonderful idea. Usually the weight of his backpack bothered him, but not tonight. He couldn't feel it at all, like he was floating. Bouncing. As soon as he thought it, it became real. Like his imagination controlled reality. He laughed and grabbed onto River to steady himself.

"Careful of the cars," River said as he guided Brian across the street.

The world became stranger as they walked. They passed a homeless man sitting on the sidewalk, and his head started to expand like a balloon. Brian stopped to watch him. The man's mouth opened, but instead of words, colors poured out and floated through the air—orange, purple, red. They coalesced to form words, but Brian couldn't quite read them. The guy started to get up, and River pulled Brian away.

They wandered farther, and Brian said, "Wow, look at that tree." A huge oak stood apart from the buildings, its tangle of bare branches clear against the glow of the night sky. The limbs danced in waves, with an extra dimension like a 3-D movie. The tree dipped toward him, and Brian held out his hand. It touched him, warm and rough. He felt life flowing through it. It seemed to be talking to him. He could almost hear it, almost understand. But not with his ears. Some other sense had awakened.

He stood there a long time, until his attention moved to River sitting against the trunk, smoking. *That's what distracted me. The scent of a cigarette.* Brian joined him, and they shared the cigarette. It tasted different.

"This is amazing," Brian said. "I never imagined anything like this."

"I know. It's impossible to imagine till you try it."

"I think the tree was talking to me."

River looked slightly amused, then nodded. "Maybe so." He reached out to brush Brian's hair out of his face.

Brian pressed River's palm to his cheek and closed his eyes. He felt so close to River, like their skin had melted together. Their selves. *We are one.*

His eyes opened to see such a sweet, loving smile on River's face. River pressed his lips against Brian's forehead.

Brian leaned into him, and River's arms wrapped comfort around him. They sat like that a long time, as if they were lovers. But their touching wasn't sexual. Not tonight. *Is it ever?* Brian wondered. *Do I want it to be?*

The boys were back in their park when the world began to grow lighter. Brian hadn't been sure they could find it again, but he followed his instincts, and here they were. The hallucinations had faded, leaving him tired and refreshed at the same time. He watched darkness turn to different shades of grey, then a color here and there, and it seemed as if the colors were existing for the first time. More and more appeared as morning light touched the world. "This is amazing," Brian whispered.

"The afterglow. One of the best parts."

"Everything is beautiful. Even the trash."

River laughed and nodded. Beauty radiated from him. Brian smiled. *I love you.*

River hugged him. "Thank you, Brian. That's the best birthday I ever had."

He sat with his arm around Brian's shoulders. Brian leaned against him with a contented sigh. No matter what happened to them, he would never forget this time together.

ഇഇഇ

They sat on a curb in a residential area. Brian leaned his head against River's shoulder and stared at the houses. "I'm so hungry." He didn't mean to complain, but he couldn't think about anything else. He'd never been so hungry. They hadn't eaten since River's birthday the day before yesterday.

"Here, drink some water." River pulled a plastic bottle from his backpack and handed it over. "Think about something else." He proceeded to tell an extremely silly story about a cow and a bear.

Brian laughed and touched River's arm. *Love you.* But it was only a brief distraction from thoughts of food.

River tapped his leg. "It's time. Come on." He stood up. "We need to find a grocery store."

"But we don't have any money. That'll just be torture."

River cocked his head. "Trust me."

"I do."

They walked down the street lined with trees—real trees, not palms. Cute little houses. People with families. And food. Brian peered at the windows as they walked by. Couldn't see anything.

River pointed. "Looks like a main road up there. Hurry up, slow poke."

Brian increased his pace, but it was hard; he had no energy. They came to a busy street and slowed as they passed an Italian restaurant. The scent wafting from it made Brian dizzy. He grabbed River's arm.

"Steady now. Keep going. Or—" River stopped. "We could go in and eat, then skip out before the bill comes."

Brian's eyes widened. "What if we got caught?"

"We won't."

Brian looked at the door of the restaurant, propped open invitingly. But it seemed wrong. And dangerous. "No . . . I'm not that desperate." *But close.*

"What am I gonna do with you?" River shook his head. "But I didn't really think you'd do it. Come on. We've still got my other idea." River led him farther up the road, to the corner. "Yes!" He gestured triumphantly at the grocery store across the street.

"I still don't get it."

"Just follow my lead, okay? Trust me."

They went into the supermarket. River walked quickly along the front of the aisles, looking for something. "Aha! I was right." He headed toward a woman standing behind a table with a bunch of small plastic cups on it. Samples. River asked, "What have you got for us today?"

"We have two different types of cereal. Bran and whole grain. Which would you like to try?"

The boys picked up the cups eagerly. She offered them plastic spoons, but they'd already downed the milk and cereal.

"Hmm." River set down the empty cup. "That was quite tasty. I'd like to try the other one, please."

She handed him another cup.

"Me, too," Brian said.

"I don't know which one I like better. Maybe I should try that first one again."

The woman's eyes narrowed. She touched the pile of paper on the table. "We have coupons if you want to buy some."

River wasn't deterred. He kept at it until the woman finally told them they better leave. Brian tugged on River's sleeve. The manager was walking over.

They hurried away and squeezed past the line at the register. When they reached the door, River pulled on his arm. "Come on!" He started running.

Brian chased after him. They raced around the corner and down the street. River finally stopped when a coughing fit hit him, deep and harsh. He bent over until it passed, then straightened and wiped his mouth.

"You okay?" Brian panted. "Why'd we have to run?"

River grinned and reached inside his jacket. "The real prize." He pulled out three Snickers bars.

Brian's eyes widened as he grabbed one. "How'd you . . . the checkout stand?"

River winked and wiggled his fingers. "All in the touch, my friend. I woulda done it sooner, but I thought you'd get upset."

And he would have, if he weren't so hungry. Brian tore the wrapper with shaking hands.

River put the third candy bar back in his jacket. "We'll save that one for later." He bit into the chocolate. "God, this is good."

Brian nodded. He'd never tasted anything so wonderful.

"Look, a dime." River picked it up.

"Yeah, I found a nickel earlier. Let's look for more." They hunted for change, staring at the sidewalk as they wandered. "This is better than stealing."

River grunted. "Stealing's a lot faster."

Brian stopped and met his gaze. "Stealing is wrong. And what if you get caught and sent home? Unless . . . that's what you want."

River's eyes darkened. "No way. I'm never goin' back there."

"Me, neither."

"Okay. So we'll do it your way. For now." He picked up another penny.

After a few hours of scanning the sidewalks, River asked, "How much have you got?"

"I don't know."

"Aren't you keeping track as you go?"

Brian shook his head.

"I got about a dollar," said River. "Let's count yours."

They sat against a building and emptied out Brian's pockets. Mostly pennies, but those added up. River gathered up the change. "Enough for two burgers at McDonald's."

Brian bit his lip. He didn't want to eat meat, but he was so hungry . . . .

River looked around. "I don't see a McDonald's. Where are we?"

Brian took in their surroundings for the first time in hours. The sun sat low on the horizon. Paint peeled from graffitied buildings, and bars covered the windows. Tough-looking Hispanic teens clustered in groups on the sidewalk. *Gangs.* Brian swallowed hard.

River said in a low voice, "I think we wandered into the wrong part of town."

Brian nodded, his mouth dry.

"Let's get outta here."

They started back the way they came as night fell. A black man passed them and said, "Want some rock?"

They shook their heads and picked up the pace. "What's rock?" Brian whispered.

"Crack."

His eyes widened. *Do we really look like we want that?*

They walked for what felt like hours. River started coughing bad, had to stop and bend over until it passed. Brian rubbed his back and handed him the water. *You need medicine.* "We should rest. We walked all day." He didn't even feel hungry anymore. Just tired. So tired.

The area seemed slightly improved, but it was hard to tell—the streetlights were few and far between. River said, "Let's look for a park."

They found one a few blocks later and collapsed onto the ground. A group of teenagers entered the park from the other side and stood beyond the nearby bushes, laughing and being loud.

"Come on," River whispered.

The boys crawled to the other end of the park, past a homeless man asleep in the bushes. *Exactly what we're going to do,* Brian thought. *We're homeless, too.*

River found a spot where the hedges grew thicker. They crawled underneath and snuggled against each other for warmth. Brian flinched at the sound of voices, but they seemed far away. He longed for their park that felt so much safer—the closest thing they had to a home. And now they were lost.

He jerked awake at a sound and blinked in morning light. The sound came again. River coughing. River crawled out of the bushes, and Brian poked his head out.

The park was pitiful by daylight, strewn with trash, even a few tires. *Why would anyone do that to a park?* "Ugh!" He jerked his hand back from clear, oblong plastic. "Is that . . . ?"

"A used condom? Yes." River shook his head. "Gross."

Brian saw a few more and a pair of soiled panties. And a needle. A shiver went through him.

River helped him to his feet. "Let's get the hell out of here."

Brian nodded, so disgusted he couldn't speak.

But it was hard to keep up the pace once the adrenalin wore off. He had absolutely no energy. Just wanted to lie down and never move again. His head spun. "We've still got two dollars. If you see a McDonald's." He would eat a burger. He would eat anything.

The surroundings changed. The signs on all the buildings were in foreign characters, Chinese or something. No McDonald's.

River said, "We need a plan. Looking for change on the sidewalk takes too long, and look where it leads us."

"You need cough medicine."

"We need food. We've either gotta steal or get money somehow. Remember those kids asking for spare change on Hollywood Boulevard? I bet they make a bundle, especially with all the tourists."

"Yeah . . . ."

River stopped walking to face him. "We could make plenty; you're so young and cute. I know it's a lot to ask, but we don't have many choices. Or I can go into the corner store over there and steal some food."

Brian bit his lip. He didn't like the idea of begging, but it seemed the best option now. "I'll do it. I'll panhandle."

"*We'll* do it." River nodded. "So it's a plan. Now we just gotta find our way back to Hollywood Boulevard."

They walked all day under a cloudy sky. They glimpsed the Hollywood sign now and then between buildings, but never seemed to get any closer. They asked a few strangers who all pointed in different directions and said it was too far to walk.

Soon it was dark, and they were facing another night in unfamiliar territory. River sank onto a bench at a bus stop. "Maybe we should take the bus."

"That'll use all our money."

"I know. But I don't think we can walk anymore. We'll make more money when we get there. Then we can eat."

Brian nodded. A bus arrived a few minutes later, and River asked the driver if it went to Hollywood.

"Not exac'ly," the black man said. "You gotta transfer at Pico."

"Transfer at Pico." River handed over their hard-won change.

Brian sat down and watched the city lights go by. So much faster than walking. His eyelids drooped.

He jerked awake at the same time as River. They looked around in confusion. The bus was almost empty. River walked up the aisle to talk to the driver.

"Shit," Brian heard him say.

River came back. "We missed our transfer."

"What should we do?"

River thought a moment. "Let's get off at the next stop, then take the bus going back the other way. That should get us to Pico, right?"

Brian nodded uncertainly. He didn't have any better ideas.

They got off the bus. Brian looked up but couldn't see any stars. Still cloudy. He craned his neck at the skyscrapers surrounding them. The streets were deserted, except for a few loners with quick, furtive movements, and a scattering of homeless people lying against the buildings. Trash blew as the wind kicked up.

River said, "There should be a bus stop over here somewhere."

Brian followed him across the street and past an alley. Strange moans emanated from the darkness. A chill went up his spine as he stared into the black space between the tall buildings. This place scared him worse than where they were yesterday. Worse than anywhere ever.

The wind grew stronger, and a cold, wet drop hit his face. Within moments it was a full downpour. "Shit," River yelled. "Where's the bus stop?"

They were soaked almost instantly. And completely lost. Brian's eyes moved to the blackness of another alley, and the hair on the back of his neck stood up.

*"snow falls on my glittering hands
you found me hiding in the trees*

and I step blindly into the night"

- Brian O'Kelly

CHAPTER 7

"*Fuck*. This fucking sucks," River yelled as the rain poured down in sheets.

Brian shivered and held his hand up to shield his eyes. "Look, a diner." A neon sign shone dimly two blocks away. "We'll eat and . . . leave before the bill comes." He couldn't take it anymore. Had to eat. Had to get off this spooky street.

River stared at him a moment, then nodded. "Let's go."

They hurried toward the diner but paused as another coughing fit struck River. The rain let up a little, and Brian heard the crunch of gravel. A shiny black Mercedes slowed to a stop beside them. The tinted rear window rolled down and an older man's face appeared.

Brian met the man's amber eyes and felt heat rise in his cheeks. He couldn't look away; the man stared so intently. Icy water dripped from Brian's hair into his eyes. He blinked.

The man's gaze moved to River, and he spoke in a smooth, gentle voice. "Hello, boys. You look like you could use a ride."

Brian said, "No."

"Maybe." River moved closer to the car.

Brian followed reluctantly. The man asked, "Where are you headed?"

Brian answered quickly before River could say something crazy. "Just up there." He pointed to the restaurant.

The man smiled. "I'm headed there myself. You boys must be freezing. Would you like soup or a burger? My treat."

Brian shook his head slightly.

River said, "Let me talk to my friend a minute." They stepped back a few feet. "Why the hell not?"

It was hard to think, he was so hungry. He looked down at the pattern of raindrops hitting the puddles. "Okay. But we're not getting in his car—we'll walk."

Brian shivered and slid into the booth. The smell of food made him light-headed. He noticed a toaster perched on the end of their table. All the tables had them. He shrugged, too hungry and tired to comment on it, and scanned the menu. "I'm a vegetarian," he told the man—Grant.

Grant smiled. "That's a healthy choice. You poor boys are soaked through. What are you doing out in this weather?"

"We missed our bus," River said.

Brian's eyes stayed glued to the menu. "They've got garden burgers. God, I can't wait."

Grant waved the waitress over. After they ordered, Brian studied the man across from him. Late fifties. Amber eyes that matched his thinning ginger hair. He exuded wealth—well-mannered, well-dressed, well-manicured. Cultured. *So what is he doing here? Bullshit, he was on his way to Ships. He's probably never been in a crappy diner in his life.*

Grant excused himself and disappeared into the restroom. Brian listened in silence to River's enthusiasm about their luck.

"But he wants something from us," Brian said. "Can't you tell?"

"Nah. He's just lonely. And rich. I ain't gonna argue with a free meal."

No, Brian couldn't either.

Grant returned and took his seat across from them. "So what are you boys doing downtown at this hour?"

They shrugged and mumbled. River said, "We're just cruisin around, seeing the sights. We're on vacation."

"The Los Angeles area is filled with wonderful things to experience. But it's very spread out. Difficult to see much on foot." Grant smiled. "Especially at 10:30 at night in the pouring rain."

"Uh . . . ." The arrival of their food saved them from coming up with a response. Brian bit into his garden burger and could think of nothing else. He'd eaten half of it before anyone spoke.

Grant toyed with his salad. "My grandson, Trevor, is about your age. I wish he would visit more often. But he doesn't like sightseeing. He prefers to ride horses at my home or play the piano."

"You have a piano?" Brian leaned forward, distracted from his food.

"Several, actually. Trevor loves to play, though he's not very good." He lowered his voice. "But don't tell him I said so." He smiled. "Do you play?"

Brian nodded. "Not lately, though. I miss it." *So much.*

French fries distracted him from thoughts of music. When he and River had eaten everything on their plates—even the garnish—the waitress brought coffee. Brian loaded his with milk and sugar, then reached into his jacket pocket. "Oh, no." He fished out their last pack of cigarettes.

The box was dripping wet, like the boys.

"Not to worry." Grant pulled out a gold filigreed case with engraved initials 'GNH.' He opened it and presented the boys with perfectly dry cigarettes. After they each took one, Grant said, "I'm afraid you'll find the contents of your bags have experienced a similar catastrophe."

River peered into his backpack. "Everything's soaked. This is supposed to be waterproof!" He hit the pack.

Grant smiled. "Probably water resistant, not waterproof. You know—" He leaned forward. "Trevor keeps an entire wardrobe at my house. I'm sure he wouldn't mind if you borrowed some clothing until yours dries. Why don't you come home with me, and we'll get you sorted out."

Brian's heart pounded in his ears.

75

Naked in the Rain

"Uhhh . . . ." River said.

Grant spoke in a gentle voice. "You boys will catch pneumonia if you don't get out of the rain and those wet clothes. You need a place to dry off and warm up."

River turned to Brian. "Let's go to the bathroom."

Their shoes squished as they hurried to the privacy of the restroom. The door closed, and River said, "What else are we gonna do? Sleep outside in this weather? You gotta be shittin me." He ran a paper towel over his hair to soak up the water. "We're in more danger sleeping in a park around here than going home with this guy."

"River, god! Some stranger stops us on the street and wants to take us home? Are you crazy?"

"Is he bad? Is Grant bad like that man when we were hitchhiking?"

"No . . . I don't think so."

"We have seven cents between us. Our bus transfer has expired by now. In case you haven't noticed, we're fucked!" A sudden bout of harsh coughing shook him.

Brian watched him and imagined spending the night outside, wet and frozen to the bone. They'd both catch pneumonia; River was already halfway there. *What else can we do?* "You're right. It's our best option."

River grinned and slapped Brian on the back. "Don't worry. I'll protect you."

Brian and River slid into the back of the Mercedes. Padded leather seats. "We're getting them wet," Brian whispered.

"The seats will dry," Grant said over his shoulder. "Boys, this is my driver, Jeffrey."

"Hello, boys," a voice boomed out. A very large black man sat behind the wheel.

Brian tried to swallow, but his throat had gone dry. He glanced at River. River gave him a brave smile, but Brian could tell he was nervous, too.

Grant spoke as they drove. "Now we're entering the 101, which will take us home to the Hollywood Hills."

"We went to Hollywood," River said. "It's gross. I couldn't believe it."

Grant chuckled. "Yes, Hollywood the image and Hollywood the geographic point are two entirely different things. The Hollywood Hills are another matter. Harrison Ford has a house there."

"Really?"

"Cool!"

Grant smiled. "And to our left is the famous Capitol Records tower. The Hollywood sign is just up there, but it's difficult to make out in the rain. Have you been to Griffith Park yet?"

"Nope."

"It's lovely; you must see it. Ah, here's our exit. Excuse me a moment." Grant picked up a phone built into the dashboard. "Maria, please light a fire in the parlor. And put a few blankets near it. We have guests . . . . Thank you, dear." He hung up.

Brian noticed another built-in phone within reach. It comforted him at first, but who could he call if they got into trouble? The police? His parents? There was no one.

The Mercedes continued up a one-lane, curvy road. "Wow, look at that house." River pointed out the window at a huge monstrosity that loomed over the narrow road.

"And this one," said Brian.

They gawked at the mansions. The night grew darker as lights from the houses spread farther apart. They continued upward and made another turn. The boys peered into darkness on either side of the car and could just make out trees and vegetation through the rain. No houses. A final turn, and they slowed before a scrolling iron gate that slid open as they approached.

The Mercedes wound up a long driveway. The trees cleared, and the house finally came into view. "Holy shit," River swore under his breath.

It dwarfed the other homes they'd seen. Grant's house was actually two white Colonial-style mansions, set at an angle to each other. The car stopped in front of the far building. Jeffrey opened the door for the boys and held a large umbrella over them.

"Here we are, gentlemen." Grant ushered them up a short flight of marble stairs, past white columns to carved mahogany doors.

One of the doors swung silently inward. Brian's heart skipped. He was relieved to see a short, round Hispanic woman in the doorway. *Calm down. It's not haunted.*

"Good evening, Maria," Grant said.

"Good evening, sir," she replied in a thick accent.

She nodded to the boys and smiled as they stepped inside. Persian rugs covered creamy marble floors in the foyer and wide hall with a ceiling two stories high. The hall went straight back, all the way through the house. A fire burned toward the far end, and short columns stood against the walls, adorned with beautiful objects: antique vases; ferns; and closer, an ebony statue of a horse. Brian walked over to it.

"Do you like that?" Grant asked.

He nodded, afraid to touch it.

"Horses are such magnificent creatures."

He remembered Grant mentioned horses earlier. "You have a horse?"

"A whole stable full. Come along. A warm fire awaits."

They moved toward the marble staircase on their left and stood in the wide doorway to the parlor. The stairs broadened and curved at the base to open onto both the hall and the parlor; wine-colored carpet ran down the steps.

A fire blazed on the parlor's far wall. River went over to it immediately, but Brian was caught by the grand piano against the bay window on his left. He moved toward it and touched the shiny black surface.

Grant said, "Now, Brian, you must dry off and warm up first."

Brian forced himself away to join River by the fire.

"Blankets are warming on the hearth," said Grant. "Why don't you get out of those wet clothes while I fix hot chocolate. Maria will bring Trevor's clothing for you to wear while yours dry."

"Okay."

"Thank you."

Grant left them alone. The boys struggled out of their sodden clothing, then wrapped up in warm blankets and sat on the wood floor before the fireplace. They stared into the flames and shivered. Brian felt overwhelmed by this house, by the wealth. By Grant. But oh, the fire felt good.

Grant returned with a tray of steaming mugs. Brian wrapped his hands around the warm porcelain and sipped. Mmm. Hot and chocolaty. By the time Maria arrived with a pile of clothes, their hair was almost dry, and they'd stopped shivering.

"I hope something here will fit," she said with her accent. She laid the clothing on the couch that faced the fireplace, then picked up their wet clothes. She and Grant left the room.

Brian approached the cream-colored velvet couch. "This looks warm." He chose a fuzzy brown sweater and slipped it on over his head. It came to his knees.

River put on a red sweater and tweed pants. "These fit pretty good." He looked at Brian and laughed.

"These pants are so big they won't stay up!" Brian laughed and gave up. "I'll just wear the sweater until my jeans dry."

Brian wrapped up in the blanket again and looked around the room. The walls were painted a muted peach with cream trim. The ceiling was high, but not so high as in the hallway. Wide molding with classic egg and dart design edged it, and tall baseboards lined the floor. Reminded him of a book he'd read on historic architecture. "This place looks old. It's beautiful."

Grant returned and sat on the velvet couch. They smoked cigarettes and chatted awhile; then Brian asked if he could play the piano.

"Of course."

He kept the blanket wrapped around him and touched the keys gently. His fingers moved into Beethoven's *Moonlight Sonata*. The slow notes rang out, hauntingly sad and beautiful. He hadn't played this since the day he slashed his wrists. *That's over. I'm gone from there forever.*

The first movement came to an end. He skipped the second—never liked it much—and went straight into the fast, aggressive third movement. His fingers flew over the keys.

River moved so he could watch his hands. Brian's long fingers danced lightly over the keys, then pounded as the emotion crescendoed. Such emotion. River had never felt it so much from music. He stood entranced. The piece ended and Brian sat back, breathing deeply, cheeks flushed.

"Bravo." Grant clapped. "That was amazing. Truly."

Brian smiled at Grant, then met River's eyes.

River was speechless. He'd never seen anyone play like that, let alone his best friend. "Wow," he finally managed. He understood better now how playing the piano helped Brian get out his emotions.

Brian's gaze returned to Grant. "It's my favorite, but I have trouble remembering the second movement."

"It's one of my favorites, as well. I'm sure I have the sheet music somewhere. I'll look for it later."

Maria appeared with their dry clothes, and Brian retrieved his jeans.

"There's a small restroom under the stairs." Grant pointed to the corner.

Brian found the door partly hidden behind a tall plant and entered the half-bath. The large, ornate mirror reflected red tiles and a gold faucet. He wondered if it was real gold. *Probably. Everything here is amazing.*

When he came out Grant said, "Why don't I give you boys a tour?"

They walked across the hall, and Grant stopped in the kitchen doorway. "Maria, brew us some coffee. Decaffeinated, please."

"Sí, señor."

Grant moved down the hall past the kitchen. "On our right is the dining room." He opened the door.

The longest table Brian had ever seen stretched from one end of the room to the other. Three silver candelabras rested on the lace runner, and candles in sconces adorned the walls between windows. "Wow," he breathed. *Like in the movies.*

They walked the length of the table and out another door, back into the hall. "There's a bath here." Grant gestured to his right, then continued toward the back of the house, past the warm fire roaring in the hearth. The ceiling was lower here, almost normal height. Grant opened French doors at the end of the hall and stepped out into the night.

The boys followed him onto a well-lit deck. The rain was still coming down, but much lighter now. Water glistened a few yards away.

"A pool!" River said, then coughed.

"The grounds are lovely, but it's a bit wet to enjoy them properly now."

He led the boys through another set of French doors farther down. They entered a cozy room with a fire and a couch facing the glass doors. "This is the den. That's the same fireplace as the one in the hallway; it goes through the wall."

Grant led them through a door at the other end to the next room. Books lined all four walls floor to ceiling. "This is great," Brian said, eyes wide. He walked over to the shelves and traced his fingers over the spines of the books.

"You're welcome to borrow any you like." Grant smiled. "Now I think it's time for that coffee."

They followed him back through the den and into the hall. They passed a closed door as they walked toward the front of the house. "What's in there?" River asked.

"Nothing, really. Just an extra room I don't use."

Grant led them into the parlor and sat in an overstuffed chair near the fireplace. The boys settled on the couch as Maria brought in coffee and dessert. The chocolate cake melted in their mouths.

Brian curled up against the pillows as they chatted over coffee. He tried to focus on the conversation, but his eyes kept shutting. He heard River cough, but it sounded far away.

River set his cup down and looked at Brian, fast asleep. He and Grant exchanged smiles.

"I hate to wake him," Grant said as he stood. "Perhaps we should leave him there. River, why don't you sleep in one of the extra bedrooms? There are plenty upstairs."

"Okay."

Grant pulled a blanket over Brian, and River tried to move him into a more comfortable position. Brian's eyelids fluttered, but he didn't wake up. River realized suddenly how tired he was. Full and warm and utterly exhausted. His hand trailed on the smooth dark wooden banister as he followed Grant up the stairs.

*"All I want in life's a little bit of love
to take the pain away"*

- Spiritualized, "Ladies and gentlemen we are floating in space"

ರುರು CHAPTER 8 ರುರು

Brian woke up sweating. He pulled off the fuzzy sweater, let it drop to the floor and was asleep again with his arm hanging off the couch. Something soft brushed his hand. Feather light touches tickled his arm.

He woke with a start. A Himalayan cat was staring at him with dark blue eyes. Brian laughed and reached out to let it sniff his hand. The cat rubbed its cheek on his fingers, then ran its body against him. Brian stroked the long fur and glanced around the room. Morning light streamed in through lace curtains in the bay window behind the piano. *So it wasn't a dream.*

"I see you've met Sebastian."

Brian tilted his head to see Grant coming down the stairs. "He's beautiful."

"Do you like cats?"

"I love them. We have two." Brian looked away with a frown. *There is no 'we' anymore.* "Where's River?"

"I believe he's still asleep upstairs." Grant entered the parlor. "Did you sleep well? There are plenty of spare beds, but I didn't want to disturb you."

"It was the best sleep I've had in ages."

Grant smiled. "Ready for breakfast?"

River stumbled into the kitchen. Maria asked, "Would you like pancakes and eggs?"

"Sure. Gracias." He ran his fingers through tousled hair and tried to wake up. "Do you have coffee?"

Grant called, "River, there's coffee here at the table. Why don't you join us?"

River walked through the kitchen toward his voice. Brian and Grant sat at an oblong table in a small, sun-filled room that jutted out from the side of the house. Large windows took up all three walls, looking out onto lush green lawns and trees. A fountain sparkled off to the left.

"Wow," River said. "This room is great." He sat beside Brian, across from Grant, who picked up a silver coffee urn and poured into an empty mug. River added cream and sipped. He'd half-expected to wake up in the park this morning; this place seemed too good to be true.

Grant said, "Such a lovely, clear morning. It's always like this after a good rain—it washes away the smog." He leaned back and gazed through the window with a peaceful smile. "The view from Griffith Park is magnificent on a day like this. You can see the entire Los Angeles basin, all the way to the ocean." Grant poured himself more coffee. "If you boys don't mind my company, I would love to take you to the park. If you don't have other plans."

River looked at Brian, who gave a small shrug. River reached for a piece of bacon. "Okay."

Brian said, "But we don't want to be any trouble. I mean, if you've got important stuff to do . . . ."

Grant waved his hand. "Not to worry. My business runs quite smoothly without me most of the time. I'd love the opportunity to show off the city. And . . . I do get lonesome at times. I enjoy your company."

They smiled at each other as Maria came in with River's breakfast.

He wolfed it down in no time, and they stood up from the table. Grant said, "Why don't you give Maria the rest of the clothes from your backpacks? She'll have them clean by the time we return."

"Okay."

Brian walked to the parlor. "Where are they?" His heart thumped. They'd been so careful not to let the backpacks out of sight. Until now.

Maria said in her accent, "Here in the kitchen. I moved them so they would not get the wooden floor wet."

"Oh," Brian said, abashed. "Sorry."

"That's alright, little niño." She smiled a motherly smile, and he felt a rush of warmth toward her.

Showered and clean, the boys stood in the foyer waiting for Grant. It was too warm today for a sweater, so Brian had borrowed a long-sleeved black tee shirt from Trevor's wardrobe. He toyed with the ends of the sleeves that came almost to his fingertips.

River said in a loud whisper, "Can you believe this house? Holy crap."

"I know. Even the bathrooms are fancier than anything at home."

Grant appeared at the top of the stairs and headed down. "Jeffrey will meet us out front. I thought we'd take the limo today so we can all sit together."

Their eyes widened. A shiny black limo awaited when they stepped outside. Jeffrey, the big black man, opened the door for them, and Grant sat facing backward across from the boys. River said, "I never been in a limo before."

"Me, neither." Brian looked out the tinted window and wondered what was in the twin mansion set at an angle. Another, smaller building stood beyond it.

The limo headed down the long driveway and through the gate. River said, "Check this out." He opened a mini-bar filled with bottles of water, vodka and a bucket of ice. The limo had everything—a stereo built into the back, temperature controls, a phone. "Cool."

They drove a short way through the city, then turned left into Griffith Park. Lots of big trees, but they soon left those behind as they wound upward along a curvy road with sheer drop offs. A few trees blocked the view of the canyons below, but it was mostly scrub brush and dirt. No buildings in sight. It seemed impossible for the limo to make such sharp turns, but Jeffrey did it. A few minutes later they were parking near the white walls and black domes of the historic observatory.

Naked in the Rain

The boys jumped out and rushed to the railing at the edge of the cliff. "Wow!"

The view was breathtaking. The city stretched as far as they could see in all directions, stopped only by the ocean glistening on their right and a range of brown mountains in the distance to the left.

"That's downtown." Grant pointed to one of the clusters of skyscrapers. "And there's the Capitol Records building we saw last night."

"Check it out!" River pointed over his shoulder to the far right.

The Hollywood sign loomed, only a few miles away. They stood almost level with it.

"Wow," Brian breathed. "Weird to see it so close." Surreal. He stared for a moment, then turned back to the city view. "The lights must be incredible at night."

Grant nodded. "I love it here on a day like this." He closed his eyes and took a deep breath. He looked vulnerable for that moment. Old.

Of course he does, Brian thought. *He's old enough to be my grandfather.* Grant seemed a little sad as the breeze ruffled his thinning ginger hair. *He is lonely.*

Brian wanted to touch him but instead turned to look out toward the ocean. *Tanya would love this view.* He frowned and tried not to think about what he was putting her through. *How long has it been?* He gazed at the blue sky and tried to count the days since River's birthday on January 10th. But they were a blur of hunger and misery. "What's the date today?"

"January 15th. It's rather warm for January, don't you think?" Grant smiled down at him. "Although that would depend on where you're from."

Brian shrugged. "I'm not really 'from' anywhere. My family moves around a lot." He stopped himself from saying more. Didn't want Grant to know where his parents live.

The silence felt a bit strained until Grant said, "Come, boys. Let's go into the observatory."

Afterward the three of them sat on a bench outside to soak in the view before heading back. Jeffrey stationed himself a few yards away, his eyes on the many tourists wandering around. *He seems more like a bodyguard than a driver*, Brian thought.

Grant said, "Have you made it to Disneyland yet?"

"Oh, no." Brian shook his head. "It's super expensive."

"I haven't been in such a long time. Why don't we go tomorrow? During the week in winter is the best time. The lines are much shorter."

"Uh, well—" He glanced at River. River seemed eager, but . . . . "Thank you, but we can't. It's too expensive."

Grant smiled. "It's nothing to me, really. Not to be boastful, but I have so much money I don't know what to do with it. I'd love to show you boys the 'happiest place on Earth.'"

River said, "Sounds good to me."

Brian looked up at Grant's smiling face. "Okay. If you're sure."

"It's my pleasure. Oh, I found the sheet music you wanted, *Moonlight Sonata*."

"Really? Thanks." He was surprised Grant had remembered, let alone actually gone and found it. He didn't expect adults to keep their promises.

"Have you performed much?" Grant asked.

"At competitions, mostly."

"I imagine you did rather well."

Brian blushed and glanced down at the dirt. "First place."

Grant nodded. "Of course. Which competitions?"

He swung his legs. "The last one was the New England Youth Championship. After that I was supposed to go on to the national competition. . . . " He bit his lip.

Grant squeezed Brian's knee. "I'm sure you would do quite well."

They smiled at each other. Grant patted Brian's knee and excused himself to go to the restroom. Jeffrey positioned himself at the door to keep an eye on both Grant and the boys.

"January 15th," Brian said. "Two and a half weeks since I left."

River grunted. "Do you think about them a lot?"

He kicked the dirt. "I try not to, but yeah. They must be totally freaking out. I wish I could let them know I'm okay."

"We are now." River coughed, but it didn't sound as harsh as before—Grant had given him antibiotics. "Don't you think it's weird he never asks about our parents, or why we aren't in school?"

"I hadn't thought about it." Brian's brow furrowed. "Maybe he thinks it's none of his business."

River pursed his lips. "Maybe."

Lunch was ready when they got back to the house. So wonderful to eat when only just starting to be hungry. *I feel safe here.* Brian gazed across the table at Grant and wondered how long it would last.

Grant brought them out back after lunch. River said, "Can I swim?"

"After your food has digested." Grant sank onto a patio chair between the pool and the hot tub. "Why don't you two explore the grounds?"

Brian's eyes moved to the trees that lined the grassy space beyond the pool. Eucalyptus, alders, a few pines. To the left a stone bridge spanned a meandering stream; straight ahead a paved area was just visible through a break in the foliage, and lots of intriguing paths led away into the trees. Like something out of a fairytale. He grabbed River's arm. "Come on."

They went straight first, along a flagstone walkway through an opening in the trees, and entered a huge paved courtyard. A large fountain stood in the middle and a small one on either end. "Wow," River said. "Killer place for parties."

Trees surrounding the courtyard made it feel private even though it was near the house. Brian eyed all the paths leading off and wondered which to take first. He opted left in hopes of coming upon the stream. He and River ambled along the winding path, wide enough for three people across, with tall bushes and trees connecting overhead. Dappled sunlight shone onto the packed dirt before them. "Like magic," Brian breathed.

River smiled. "This is really cool."

And so quiet, the only sound the twittering of birds and wind in the trees. *I love it.* "I wish we could stay here."

"Maybe we can." River shrugged. "Take it one day at a time."

They reached a fork in the path, and Brian turned left. A few minutes later they heard the gurgle of water. "Here's the stream."

The bottom was visible, only about three feet deep and a few yards across. Brian knelt to reach into the clear, cool water, let it rush through his fingers and watched it swirl around rocks that jutted above the surface.

"Let's go this way." River started walking upstream.

Brian followed. They came upon a small wooden bridge, not the one they'd seen from the house. This one was surrounded by trees, invisible to everyone but them. Their own magical spot. They stood on the bridge, and Brian gazed up at the endless blue sky, then glanced at River, looking down at the water with a melancholy expression. Brian knew what he was thinking about—his family. "Do you regret leaving?"

"No!" River's head jerked, and he stared into Brian's eyes. "I feel bad, like you do. But that don't change things." He turned away abruptly.

Brian touched his arm and stared down into the swirling water.

They discovered two hidden courtyards much smaller than the first, then made their way back to the house. Still lots of grounds to explore, but Brian didn't want to be rude to their host, and River wanted to swim.

Grant still sat at the patio table, reading a newspaper and drinking coffee. He looked up and smiled as they approached. "Did you enjoy yourselves?"

"I love it." Brian grinned. "I could spend all day exploring."

Grant chuckled and nodded.

"What's in there?" Brian pointed to the almost identical building that sat at an angle close to the main house.

"Not much these days. The other wing is servants' quarters now, mostly empty. The building beyond is garages."

"Oh." Seemed a shame for such a large area to be empty. A second swimming pool lay deserted behind the other wing.

River said, "Can I swim now?"

"Certainly. Maria put swim trunks for you in the den." Grant gestured over his shoulder at the French doors. "You, too, Brian. If you like."

They changed in the den, then emerged and ran toward the pool.

"Wait, boys." Grant held up a bottle of sunscreen.

They went over to the table and slathered it onto their arms and legs. Brian's eyes flicked to River's hands smoothing the cream on his tanned chest. Erotic. His groin tightened, and he looked away quickly. *Stop it.* He glanced at Grant instead and noticed how intently he watched. Brian shook his head. *Why do I think everything is sexual? Stop it.*

"Don't forget your backs," Grant said.

River turned to let Brian do his back while Grant did Brian's. Brian tried not to have naughty thoughts as he rubbed the lotion on River's back, but the feelings crept in anyway. He finished quickly, but Grant was still at it, with slow, smooth strokes. It felt wonderful, like a massage. Brian closed his eyes and let himself enjoy it.

Grant finished and patted his butt. "All done. Go swim."

River was already in the pool. Brian walked toward it, flushed, and realized he had a hard on. He jumped into the water quickly to hide it.

He tired of swimming long before River. Brian showered in the bathroom off the hall, then came back outside and sat with Grant while his hair dried. "May I go play the piano?"

"Of course. Let me get that sheet music for you."

Grant stayed in the parlor while Brian played *Moonlight Sonata* again—all three movements this time, thanks to the sheet music. Next came Chopin; then Maria called them for dinner.

River dug into the cheese enchiladas. "Mmm. These are great."

Brian's eyes watered, and his nose ran.

"Here." Maria took away his plate and gave him a different one. "I make them not so spicy for Mr. Nesbit."

"Thank you." Much better. "Who's Mr. Nesbit?"

Grant smiled. "I am."

"Oh." Brian laughed. *Of course he has a last name. What's mine supposed to be again?*

He felt sleepy after dinner, and Grant suggested making it an early night. "We have a big day ahead of us tomorrow."

"Disneyland!" the boys shouted in unison.

Grant laughed. "Brian, let me show you your room."

All three of them went up the marble staircase, and Brian realized he hadn't been to the second floor yet. Grant turned left at the top of the stairs and went down the hall a few yards. He opened the first door on the right. "I think this will do for you."

"Wow." The king-sized bed and antique furniture took up only a small portion of the room. He walked across thick carpet to French doors that opened onto his own balcony overlooking the grounds behind the house. "Wow," he repeated.

"Look at this," River said.

A partial wall divided off a small area with a loveseat, TV, and mini-fridge. And next to that, his own bathroom.

Brian looked up at Grant. "Are you sure I should stay in this room?"

Grant's amber eyes studied him, and he smiled. "I'm sure."

Brian snuggled under the white down comforter in the giant bed, happy and full. Except he wished River were here snuggled up beside him. Touching him. He sighed and closed his eyes.

River's voice called his name. *Yes, River. I'm here. I'll always be here. I love you.*

"Brian. Dude, wake up. Disneyland."

85

Naked in the Rain

. . .

They hopped off the tram and made their way back to the Mercedes. Brian laughed and leaned on River's arm. "I know. You should've seen your face when that skeleton came out of the coffin!"

"I wasn't scared. Just surprised."

"If you say so." Brian grinned.

They piled into the car, and River said, "It was great when Jeffrey sang along with the pirates."

Jeffrey smiled, making his round face even rounder. They weren't afraid of the big black man anymore. Not after spending the day at Disneyland with him. His voice boomed from the front seat, "Yo ho yo—"

The boys joined in. "And a bottle of pink Pepto."

Grant laughed. "Those aren't the lyrics."

"They are now." Brian grinned.

"Space Mountain was awesome," River said as the car pulled out of the huge parking lot. "That was my favorite."

"Yeah," Brian agreed. "And the Matterhorn."

He gazed out the window at twinkling city lights. The Matterhorn, yes, and those bobsled seats. He'd sat between River's legs and leaned back against him. River's arms had wrapped around him, their bodies pressed against each other. The memory sent a thrill tingling through him.

He looked over and saw River's eyes were closed, his cheek against the backseat. Brian rested his cheek likewise and watched him. River's face was so different when he slept. Innocent. Brian couldn't look away, and he admitted to himself, *I want to be with you. I want to kiss you. Does that make me a freak?*

That night Brian lay in his big bed and dreamed he was wandering the grounds at night.

The trees glow silver in the moonlight, the moon so bright it casts shadows. There's magic here—I can feel it. I walk alone past a fountain, along a path. The round moon is reflected in the stream.

I turn and see a dark figure standing at the edge of the trees, watching me. My heart thumps. The moonlight does not penetrate his darkness. I turn to run but it's hard to move, like the figure is holding me somehow. I force myself forward, across the bridge and into the forest. But I'm lost. Trapped. River, where are you?

Tall marble stairs unfold before me. I climb on my hands and knees, higher and higher. I've almost reached the top. I look up and the dark figure is there, waiting for me. He opens his hand—he's holding something in his palm. Something I want.

Is he really evil, or am I just afraid of what I can't see? I want what he's holding. I want it.

Brian woke slowly and realized he was lying on something hard. He jerked his eyes open and saw a wooden floor. But not like the floor in the parlor. The wood was different shapes and sizes, fitted together to form a pattern.

He blinked and sat up. He was in a huge room with a high ceiling. Moonlight shone through windows near the ceiling onto the parquet floor. *Where am I?* He stood up and for a second thought he saw ghosts. But no, it was just furniture covered with sheets along the walls. The air smelled stale and dusty. *No one's been here for a long time.*

He moved toward a stage at one end of the room. Something large stood on it, covered in a sheet. He wanted to see what it was, but he was too nervous. He turned back and walked through the moonlight. *Am I really awake? Where am I?*

He remembered his dream, but only in fragments. Running through the grounds in the moonlight; a dark, frightening figure. And something he wanted very badly.

He shook his head. *I must have sleepwalked. Did I run through the grounds?* He looked down at the pajama shirt that went to his knees—the pants were far too big, so he didn't bother with them. No dirt or twigs. His feet were clean.

He moved to the double doors at the end of the room and pulled on the heavy door. It opened onto a short hallway that led to stairs going down. It was so dark he could barely see. He moved carefully down one long flight, then reached another door. He opened it onto a hallway. Doors lined both sides. It seemed impossibly long, like the hall in *The Shining.* He bit his lip and wished he hadn't seen that movie. *Am I really awake?*

He moved forward and decided to open one of the doors. His heart pounded, but he forced himself to do it. Just a bedroom. An empty bedroom. He tried a second door. Another bedroom, but this one wasn't empty. He heard breathing from the bed and saw a lump. He crept forward, eyes wide, and recognized the dark blond hair. "River!" His voice caught. Brian ran to the bed and slid under the covers against his warmth.

Grant smiled at them over breakfast. "You boys are on your own today. I have some business to attend to. But Maria will be here, and you can go horseback riding later, if the rain lets up."

"Okay. Thanks!"

As soon as Grant left, River said, "Let's explore the house."

Brian nodded. He wanted to see if the place he found last night was real. They started in the parlor—they'd noticed a door at the far end, near the bay window. But it was locked. "Damn," River said.

Next they tried the room Grant had skipped in his tour, behind the stairs. It was locked, too. "Why does he keep shit locked?"

Brian shrugged. "Maybe he has valuables in there."

They went upstairs and River turned right toward Grant's room. "No," Brian said. "That's his bedroom. It's not right."

"Aw, come on."

"There's plenty of other stuff to explore." Brian headed the other way, down the long hall, past the painting he liked so much that hung near his room. They checked out all the rooms. Nothing too exciting, just empty bedrooms with a few storage boxes, none as nice as Brian's.

But each room had an intercom like the one in Brian's room—rectangular metal on the wall near the bed, with a speaker and knobs and buttons. Neat. The speakers in the extra bedrooms didn't work, but the one in Brian's room did. The boys fooled around with it a few minutes; then River ran downstairs to the different intercoms—in the kitchen, the parlor, the den. River made gross noises into them and Brian laughed, alone in his room. He pressed the button and held it down while he spoke. "Come back upstairs."

"Okay."

Brian went out to the hall and started toward the stairs. Another short hallway branched off to the right, with a door at the end. River joined him, and they checked it out. The door was locked. Brian frowned. "Why is it locked? All the other rooms up here are open."

River shrugged. "Come on. Let's check that door at the other end."

Brian said, "I think it leads to more stairs."

They walked the length of the main hall. Yes, this was the same hall as last night. It looked so different in the dark after that dream he hadn't recognized it.

River opened the door at the end. Stairs. "How'd you know?"

Brian didn't answer, just went up. His heart pounded in excitement. *Is it really here?*

They reached the top and found heavy double doors. Brian grinned. "I was here last night."

They pushed on the doors and went in. It was as he remembered, except much brighter, even with the grey clouds. Carved burnished gold molding edged the ceiling around two dusty chandeliers. The paint on the walls had dulled to a faint cream.

River said, "This place is huge. You were here last night?"

"I sleepwalked and woke up here."

River wandered around the room. "Good thing you never did that when we were sleeping in the park."

Brian's breath caught. "That could've been bad."

River met his gaze. "No. I would've woke up right away. I'd find you."

Brian searched his eyes. "How long are we going to stay here?"

"I don't know."

"I feel like we're taking advantage of him. But I don't want to leave. This place is everything I ever dreamed of. And Grant is so good to us."

"He wants us here. He'll let us know if we wear out our welcome." He gripped Brian's shoulder. "Everything will be okay."

Grant took them shopping the next day. Brian's inner thigh muscles were still sore from horseback riding, but it was worth it. Amazing to feel so close to such a beautiful, powerful animal, to be a part of it. The stable hand had given them lessons, and Brian looked forward to more. But Grant wanted them to have proper riding clothes, so he insisted on a shopping trip.

Brian tried on riding pants. The stretchy material was awfully tight, but Grant said that's how they're supposed to fit. Grant's amber eyes warmed as he stared, and Brian felt special.

Grant bought them a lot more than riding clothes. Especially Brian, since Trevor's clothes didn't fit him. He had an entire wardrobe by the time they finished.

But all those clothes filled only a fraction of the walk-in closet in Brian's room. Grant smiled and touched Brian's back. "It's a start."

The next sunny day Grant took them out on his yacht. The ocean was calm and blue and infinite. Grant let them have alcohol—strawberry margaritas. Yummy. Brian felt lightheaded and giddy but got sleepy after the second one.

Grant sent him into the cabin to lie down, then came to check on him. He stroked Brian's cheek and leaned down to kiss his forehead. Twice, lingering.

Brian smiled at him and closed his eyes.

ﬡﬡﬡ

Is he ever coming in? Brian wondered. River was still outside in the pool, though it was getting dark.

Brian and Grant had just watched the sunset from the couch in the den. The room grew dim, the only other illumination from the fire to their right. Brian sipped blackberry sloe gin; it tasted like candy. He set down the glass and leaned his head against Grant's shoulder. So peaceful.

"Brian," Grant whispered and rested his hand on Brian's leg. Grant's fingers slid slowly up his thigh.

Brian's heart thumped, and his mouth went dry. Blood rushed to his groin.

"Brian," he whispered again and leaned closer. Grant moved his hand from Brian's leg to stroke his cheek. "May I share something with you?"

Brian nodded uncertainly. He was trembling, but from fear or excitement he wasn't sure.

Grant pressed his lips against Brian's forehead, his cheek, his jaw, his lips. His lips. Brian's heart pounded in his ears. *He's kissing me.* But it felt just like kissing a girl, except Grant was bigger. Bigger and stronger. That made it a little scary. And exciting.

Brian's body responded, and his arms went around Grant's neck. They kissed harder in sudden passion, their tongues stroking. Brian's head fell back as Grant's lips moved to his throat.

Grant pulled Brian's shirt up and kissed his chest. His mouth tugged at his nipples. The bite sent a bolt straight to Brian's penis. His breath caught, and he grabbed the back of Grant's head. *Touch me. Yes, touch me. Love me.*

Grant pulled Brian's shirt off and stroked his back. Kissed him again as his hand slid up the inside of Brian's thigh, brushed along the side of his groin. Brian moaned and clutched at him. Grant smiled a little as he unzipped Brian's jeans and pulled them down.

Brian's mind shot one final thought as his underwear followed. *God, what is he doing? What am I doing?* But he couldn't stop him. Didn't want to.

Grant knelt between his legs and kissed the inside of his naked thigh. Brian's legs shook as Grant's lips made their way closer. Painfully slowly. God, he couldn't stand it. And then Grant touched it. Took it into his mouth.

Brian arched and moaned, out of his mind with pleasure he never imagined. Grant went down again, faster. He cupped Brian's balls and squeezed ever so gently. Brian gasped, and his fingers tightened on Grant's arm. He cried out as his orgasm pulsed through him with an intensity he'd never come close to on his own.

Grant watched him, watched his face, his utter abandon. Brian lay against the couch breathing hard, bits of dark hair clinging to his flushed cheeks. Grant kissed all over his face, and Brian clung to him, gazed up at him with adoration in those incredible blue eyes. Grant smiled gently and touched his cheek. "You'll want to pull those back up," he said, indicating Brian's pants.

Brian looked down with round, innocent eyes, as if surprised to find himself nude. Or surprised his brain could still understand speech. He reached down to pull up his jeans.

Grant sat beside him on the couch, and Brian leaned against him with a sigh. Grant put his arm around him and rested his cheek against the top of Brian's head. Brian had done even better than he'd hoped. No hesitation or inhibitions at all.

Grant smiled. *Perfect.*

Brian frowned as he got out of bed and pulled on his clothes. Avoiding River last night was easy. Brian had fallen asleep on the couch, then gone up to bed. But today.... *How can I face River after what happened?* The memory made his cheeks hot and his groin tighten. He didn't feel bad or guilty, though the fact that Grant was old enough to be his grandfather made the whole thing stranger.

He forced himself downstairs. River stood in the parlor with his back turned, staring out the bay window. Morning light glowed golden in his hair. Brian moved closer. River's arms were folded tight across his chest, a scowl on his face. "Good morning," Brian ventured.

River grunted and didn't look at him.

His heart skipped. *Does he know?*

Maria's voice came from the doorway. "Good morning, niños. Would you like waffles for breakfast?"

River shrugged and said nothing. Not jumping at the mention of food. Yes, something was definitely wrong. He remembered River's words from the institute, when he thought Brian was gay. *'I'd think you're a sick fuck.'*

Brian grimaced. *I can't help it. And I can't keep secrets from him.* He called out, "In a few minutes, Maria," then lowered his voice. "River, we need to talk."

That earned him a sidelong glance. More silence.

"Upstairs?" Private.

River let out a long breath, looked down and nodded.

They went up to Brian's room without a word. River took up his same stance at the French doors.

Brian couldn't bear it any longer. "Do you hate me now?" he blurted out.

River turned in astonishment. "What are you talking about?"

"Grant... last night...."

River ducked his head as color flooded his cheeks—the first time Brian had seen him blush.

Their gaze met. A wall had gone up behind River's eyes. *God, I'm going to lose him. I can't take that.* Brian managed to hold back the tears, but his voice shook. "Grant and I—we . . . messed around." He looked away quickly.

"You did?" River sounded amazed, not disgusted. He sank onto the bed with wide eyes. Trembling slightly.

Brian sat beside him. "Are you okay?"

"I—I don't know. I thought it was just me. And Grant." He glanced at Brian, then away.

"You—" Brian sucked in his breath as it clicked. It made a weird sort of sense.

River stared down at his hands clenched tight in his lap. "I guess that's what he wanted all along."

Brian hadn't thought of it that way. "But is it wrong?"

River looked at him. "I don't know. I—" He blinked and broke eye contact. "I'm not gay," he said emphatically. "But . . . I let him do it."

"So did I." Trying to make him feel better.

"It felt so good. I couldn't tell him to stop."

Brian rested his hand on River's. "All he did was give us pleasure. And love. There's nothing wrong with that."

River's fingers closed around his and squeezed. "I was afraid of what you'd think."

"Me, too. I thought you might hate me."

River turned to face him, his brow furrowed. "I could never hate you." He gripped Brian's shoulders. "Nothing could ever make me hate you. I love you."

Brian made a small noise as tears streamed down his face. "I love you, too."

That afternoon when Brian took a break from the piano, Grant came closer to rest his hand on his shoulder. The touch sent warm shivers through him. His body remembered what Grant could do.

Grant leaned to murmur in his ear, "Would you like to see my bedroom?"

Grant's mouth was just as amazing as Brian remembered. Afterward he explored Grant's rooms. The door from the hall led not to the bedroom, but to a sitting room with a Victorian loveseat and a baby grand piano. Through the sitting room and another door was the bedroom with its extra large bed. And another door.

"That's my office," Grant said. "Don't try to open it or an alarm will go off."

"Oh." Brian yanked his hand back, glad the other locked doors didn't have alarms. "May I play the piano in your sitting room?" Whenever he saw a new piano he ached to bring it alive.

"I would love that." Grant kissed him gently.

₪₪₪

"No, don't plug it in yet," Brian said.

River put the wire down and folded his arms over his chest.

Brian finished hooking up the components of the brand new stereo for his bedroom. "I think I did it right this time. Plug it in."

"Okay, but if it don't work I'm gettin Jeffrey to help." River got down on his hands and knees to reach behind the dresser. "Okay. It's in."

Brian pushed the master power button. All the components lit up. "So far so good." He pressed play. The dissonant opening strains of Mozart's *Requiem* flowed softly through the speakers. "Yes!" He grinned.

River grinned back from where he knelt on the floor and raised his hand for a high-five. Brian slapped his hand, and their fingers intertwined. Brian said, "Look at your hair." He didn't usually see it from this angle. He leaned closer to run his fingers through it.

"What?" River sounded nervous.

Brian laughed. "Don't panic. It's just getting so light. You spend so much time in the sun, you've got all these gold streaks in it." Brian smiled, his hand still in River's hair. "Pretty."

River butted his head into Brian's stomach. Brian laughed as River pushed and forced him to back up until Brian almost fell over the boxes that littered the floor. River grabbed at him, and it became a wrestling match. River had Brian on his back in no time, wrists pinned to the floor over his head, both of them panting.

Brian laughed breathlessly and struggled a little, then gave up. He sobered as he gazed up into River's eyes, keenly aware of River's body lying on top of him. Touching him.

River's eyes broke away to stare at his lips—Brian could tell because Grant often did the same thing before he kissed him. *Do you want to kiss me? Please. Please kiss me.*

A loud rap sounded on the door. River jerked, then sprang to his feet. Brian sat up in a daze, his body throbbing as the door opened. Grant wanted to know if they managed to hook up the stereo.

River backed away and mumbled something about checking on dinner. He pushed past Grant out the door.

Grant smiled. "Mozart. I love your choice in music." He stroked Brian's cheek. "Why don't you come to my room?"

Brian writhed and clutched at the sheets. Arched back as he came.

Grant moved up to kiss him. Brian pressed his palm against Grant's shirt. He'd never seen Grant naked, even after a week of sex. He felt Grant's chest heaving through the cotton. Brian reached up to unbutton the shirt and kissed his chest. He pushed Grant onto his back and let his lips move down the curly grey hair to Grant's abdomen. Brian looked up at his face. "Teach me," he whispered.

Grant smiled and stroked Brian's hair.

Grant's penis tasted like regular skin at first, until it got all wet. Then it was really salty. Grant said it was natural lubrication. He gave Brian suggestions on where to touch him. "Now use your mouth on that spot."

"Like this?"

"*God, yes,*" he cried out and grasped Brian's head.

Brian kept at it, then pulled away as creamy fluid shot out the tip of Grant's penis. Brian's eyes widened. He'd never seen that before.

When Grant finished moaning, Brian asked, "How come nothing comes out of mine?"

"Because you're too young."

"Oh." He relaxed in Grant's arms. *That was fun.* He loved making Grant squirm like that and make noises.

"You're a natural. So perfect." Grant stroked his cheek and gazed into his eyes. "I love you, Brian."

A lump formed in his throat. "I love you, too," he choked out and his chin trembled. Brian clung to him as the tears came, his feelings for Grant twisted up with memories of his father.

༄ ༄ ༄

Brian stood in the doorway to River's bedroom. "Hey."

"Hey, what's up?"

"Maria's making a cake."

"Cool." River grinned. "Let's see if we can help eat it."

River brushed past him through the doorway, and blood rushed to Brian's groin. His body reacted to the slightest things these days.

He ignored it and followed River to the kitchen. Maria was gone, but a bowl of vanilla icing sat on the counter. River scooped some onto his finger and licked it off. "Mmm."

Brian stood beside him. He could feel heat from River's body pulling at him. His own body's response made him dizzy. *River, don't you feel it?*

River reached in again. Brian took River's hand and closed his mouth around his finger. He sucked the icing off slowly, sensuously.

River's breath sped up. "You missed a little," he whispered.

Brian licked the last bit of icing off, then traced his tongue up to the fingertip. He looked up at River, heart pounding, and their eyes locked. The moment stretched.

River blinked and pulled away abruptly, then turned and fumbled in the cabinet for a glass.

Brian's heart sank. He hurried out and raced down the hall to the bathroom at the far end. His eyes filled as he stared into the mirror. *Stupid! He doesn't want you. Just because he messes around with Grant doesn't mean he wants it with you. You'll ruin everything if you keep this up.*

"I swear I'll leave him alone," he whispered, and the tears spilled over.

Brian sat in the parlor with Grant, sipped red wine and gazed into the fire, drowsy after their love making.

Grant stood. "Why don't you find River and ask him to join us? I'll be right back." He unlocked the door at the far end of the parlor—his other office, he'd told them.

Brian rounded the corner to the hall and ran into River. "Come here." He tugged on River's hand, and they sat on the couch. "Have some wine." Brian poured a glass and handed it to him. It was comforting to sit so close to River now, with his desire satiated for the moment.

Grant emerged from his office with a wooden box. He set it on the coffee table in front of the boys, opened the lid and lifted out a smaller silver box with scrolls engraved on it. He opened it, and Brian saw white powder.

"Would you like a little cocaine?" Grant asked.

"Yeah!" River practically jumped out of his seat.

Grant picked up a razor blade and carefully prepared three small lines on the glass table. Brian's pulse sped. *I've done acid. This shouldn't be scary.*

"It's okay." River squeezed Brian's leg, then accepted a glass tube from Grant. "I never used a real tooter before. We always just rolled up a dollar bill." He turned to Brian. "It's real easy. Just close the other nostril while you inhale." River leaned over the table and snorted a line, then sat back. "Aaahh." He blinked rapidly and sniffed a little. "Good stuff." He offered the tooter to Brian.

Brian took it and hoped no one saw the trembling in his hand.

"Don't be nervous," River said. "It's fine."

Brian gave him a slight smile. *I trust you. It's fine.* He leaned over, trying to copy what River did, and inhaled a line through the tooter. It burned a little but not as much as he expected. He rubbed his nose and sniffed. The drug dripped down his throat, numbing it, and his scalp tingled.

A sense of confidence and pleasure filled him. He smiled wide. "It *is* good."

"That's my man." River patted his back.

Grant took his turn, and the boys started chatting. Brian suddenly had so much to say. It felt wonderful talking to the two people he was closest to in the world. They understood him. They loved him. And he trusted them.

Brian wandered alone in the gardens and stepped onto the stone bridge near the house. Cool, fresh air filled his lungs, and he smiled. Everything was perfect. Well, almost. *I have to accept our relationship as friends. I'm lucky to have River in my life.*

He caught a movement from the corner of his eye and turned to look up at a window in the Other Wing. He swore someone had been standing there, watching him. The curtain swayed.

A chill went up his spine. He ran to the main house, afraid to look back until he reached it. Nothing, of course. But he remembered the dark figure from his dream, and he shuddered.

ಐಐಐ

Grant took them shopping again. But this time they came home with very different clothes. Brian stared into the full-length mirror in his bedroom, the three panels angled so he could see how tight the pants stretched across his ass. *I look weird.*

The skintight white leather rode low on his hips. He pulled the laces of the matching half-vest and tied it tight. The leather hugged his torso as if it had been made for him. The vest stopped just below his ribs, leaving his lower stomach and bellybutton exposed. He felt a little uncomfortable with that, but Grant liked it.

He remembered how Grant had to help him get out of the pants. They were so tight they peeled off like a banana. His cheeks grew hot at the memory of what came next. But none of that now—Grant was out for the day on business.

He turned to find River.

The boys strolled through the grounds and paused on the wooden bridge—the private bridge surrounded by trees, not the one near the house. Brian didn't like that bridge anymore. He leaned back against the railing, his elbows on the wood. "I think this is my favorite spot." His eyes closed as he listened to the brook. But thoughts of sex strayed into his mind, as always.

He opened his eyes and caught River staring at his body. *It's the outfit. I know it looks weird.* "You're not wearing your new clothes."

"I don't really like them."

Brian shrugged. "They're strange. I'm trying to get used to it." The tight leather was uncomfortable. "I can't believe how warm it is today. I mean, it's barely February."

"Yeah." River shaded his eyes. "I'm kinda hot. Wanna swim?"

Brian got out of the pool and grabbed a towel. River got out, too. "You're done already?" Brian asked.

"Yeah, not really into it today."

They went inside and parted ways upstairs. Brian took his time in the shower. Dried off and wrapped his blue silk robe around him.

River was waiting on the bed, eased back against the pillows. "Took long enough in there. Jackin off?"

Brian flushed. "No." The flush reached his groin, and he hoped River didn't notice any change in the shape of his bathrobe.

But he couldn't help it when River looked the way he did right now. Leaning back cocky against the pillows, white button-down shirt clinging to his skin, still damp from the shower. And the way River was looking at him. Joking and teasing and—*I swear, flirting.* Brian frowned and sat near him on the edge of the bed. *Stop thinking you can be with him.*

River laughed a little and reached for the glass on the nightstand. His hand wobbled and water splashed onto his chest. "Crap," he said, and sat up.

Brian leaned forward. "It's just water." His hand reached out to touch the cotton, cold and wet against River's hot skin. His fist clutched the shirt in desperation. River was sitting up, their faces close. River's warm breath tickled his mouth. His heart skipped once, and then River's lips touched his.

The kiss grew instantly harder. Full of such passion, couldn't break away, couldn't breathe. Their mouths opened to each other, and no more thought. Just the beautiful sensation of River's tongue sliding over his, and around. It made him dizzy and full. And he never wanted to stop.

But eventually River's mouth moved away from his, to his cheek, his neck, and the robe was off his shoulder. *This is really happening* flitted across his mind as River pulled back to untie the robe. Brian watched his own hands reach to unfasten River's pants. Then up his stomach, fingertips reaching under the shirt as his lips touched the cotton. He had to taste him. Had to feel that smooth skin, that chest he'd longed to touch. He tried to rip open the shirt. River helped him with the buttons.

And their eyes met. He was afraid the walls would go up, and River would run away. But instead River's eyes sucked him in the way they could, into the depths of his soul. They fell toward each other and kissed as if they would never stop.

But his mouth left River's to taste his lovely chest, his navel, the stomach below. The little patch of hair. Ah, beautiful. Brian's mouth went to it, and River arched back. Clutched his head. God, he tasted good. Brian glanced up. River's eyes were closed, face unlined, almost the way he looked in his sleep. *I love you.*

Brian took him in again, swirled his tongue along the head. River's penis jerked. Brian rubbed his cheek against it, in love with it, with him. River's fingers tightened on his arm. Brian closed his mouth around him, felt it jerk again, and River cried out. Brian felt the pulse of semen move up the shaft and into his mouth.

River cried out again, long and throaty. Brian kept on until it was over, then moved up to kiss him. River kissed him back deeply, then glanced down. Brian was hard as a rock. He'd almost come when River did.

River spit on his palm. The touch was like an electric shock. Stroke. Oh, god. He clutched River. River moved down, reached his mouth toward Brian's cock, stroking, stroking. The waves flashed through him in an explosion of golden light beneath his eyelids, through his whole self. Stretching time.

River's arms wrapped around him, and Brian buried his face in his neck. Took in his scent as the pulses subsided. They lay back on the bed, legs and arms entwined. River took Brian's face in his hands and kissed him again. When they finally pulled away, River said, "Grant has taught you well, my son," in his best Darth Vader imitation.

They laughed, but Brian sobered. "Do you think he'll mind?"

"I don't know. I don't think so. But let's not tell him. In case." He stroked Brian's hair and gazed into his eyes. He whispered, "I love you."

Brian smiled, tears starting. "I love you, too."

That night River stood alone in his own bedroom and stripped down to his briefs. He frowned at himself in the mirror. *I'm not gay.* Yet he continued to let Grant touch him, and to his surprise, it didn't seem gross. River had even asked for instruction—he wanted to be good for Brian. Brian.

That was different. With Grant it just felt good. But Brian was the most wonderful person, the most wonderful thing that ever happened to him. River wanted to be with him all the time. In every way. He ground his jaw, and his eyes narrowed at the reflection in the mirror. *Faggot*, a voice in his head repeated. He turned away from those accusing eyes and shoved it down. Pushed it into the corner of his mind where he kept things he didn't want to think about.

He walked into the dim hallway and found his way through the dark to climb under the covers against Brian's naked back. The touch made him forget everything else. River caressed his soft skin, wrapped his arm around Brian's chest and pressed his lips against his shoulder.

Brian grunted and rolled onto his back, eyes still closed. River kissed his cheek, his hair. Brian's arms went around River's neck, and their lips locked together.

River was amazed every time they kissed. He'd never felt this before. As if it wasn't just their mouths kissing but something deeper. He didn't want to ever stop.

Brian woke in the morning with River's arms wrapped around him. He breathed in River's scent and smiled. The most wonderful way to wake up. Brian lay against him and felt River's heart pound against his cheek.

If I could wake up every morning in your arms, that's all I would ever ask for.

*"Harder, faster!
Forever after"*

- Placebo, "Bionic"

꙳꙳ CHAPTER 9 ꙳꙳

Grant stood by the bed and adjusted the cool washcloth on Brian's forehead. "You're sure you don't want us to stay home with you?"

"No," he said softly. "You go ahead and have fun. I just need to rest."

"Alright. Buzz Maria if you need anything."

Brian nodded, then winced and clutched his head.

Grant's frown deepened. "Do you want more aspirin?"

"No. It doesn't help. I just need to sleep."

Brian woke as afternoon sun slanted through the glass door. He gazed out at the blue sky and smiled. The headache seemed to be gone. He sat up carefully. So far so good. But no reading—he knew from experience that would bring the headache back. *There's plenty of other stuff to do.* He put on his sneakers and paused to look at the painting in the hall. *I miss snow.* His eyes wandered over the intricate patterns of tree limbs. He could stare at this for hours. But the real thing awaited him outside.

He made his way downstairs. Maria was dusting the parlor. "Brian, you're up. Are you feeling better?"

He nodded. "I'm going outside." He walked to the end of the hall and took a deep breath of warm air as he stepped onto the deck.

He wandered through the grounds and listened to the wind in the trees, watched birds and a squirrel. He entered a small courtyard surrounded by hedges taller than him. Two sparrows played in the fountain, throwing water over their backs to bathe. *So cute.*

He thought he heard a voice carried on the breeze. *Yes, there it is again.* He rounded the tall hedge, and it came clearer; someone was talking nearby, but he couldn't make out the words. He walked along the hedges where they grew beyond the courtyard. The voice was coming from the other side. He found a break in the greenery and poked his head through.

A young boy with brown hair was squatting down, arm outstretched toward a bush, his back to Brian. "Come on, Angel," the boy pleaded. "Come out."

Brian walked over and squatted beside him.

The boy jumped back with a yelp. "You scared me!"

"Sorry, I didn't mean to sneak up on you. Who are you talking to?"

The boy peered into the bush. "My rabbit, Angel. She got out of the pen. I know she's in there, but she won't come out."

"You have a rabbit? Neat."

They grinned at each other. Brian asked, "Did you try coaxing her out with a carrot or something?"

"I can't. If I leave she might move. Then I'll never find her."

"I'll go get one."

The boy's brown eyes lit up. "Thanks."

Brian raced off and returned a few minutes later, breathless, carrot in hand.

"Thanks!" The boy took the carrot and held it toward the bush. "Come on, Angel. Come and get it." He made smooching noises.

A white nose appeared, sniffing. The rabbit hopped out to nibble on the carrot. The boy laughed and held her in his lap while she ate her treat.

"Can I pet her?" Brian asked.

"Sure."

He reached out to touch the white fur. "Wow. She's so soft. Softer than a cat." He stroked her gently, then looked at the boy. "I'm Brian."

"David. You wanna hold her?" He carefully picked up the rabbit and set her on Brian's lap.

"Oh, she's so sweet. Little Angel." Brian crooned while he pet her. Angel sniffed his hand, then licked him. He laughed.

"She likes you."

"Her tongue's so soft. Not rough like a cat. Do you have any other pets?"

"No, but we have a whole pen of rabbits. They gave me Angel for my birthday—I just turned ten."

"Do you live here?" Brian asked.

"Yeah, on the third floor." He nodded toward the Other Wing looming above the trees behind them. "I'm new. I guess I haven't met everybody yet." David grinned. "I want to get a hamster."

"I had a hamster once, but they don't live very long. I love animals." He smiled and stroked Angel's ears. "I couldn't believe it when Grant said he has a whole stable of horses right here on his property."

David frowned. "*Grant* said . . . ." His eyes flew open wide, and he stood. "You're *that* Brian?"

Brian stood up, too, confused. "What do you mean?"

"I'm not supposed to talk to you! I'm gonna get in trouble."

"Wh—"

David took the rabbit from Brian's arms and backed up.

A lump rose in his throat. "I don't understand. What did I do wrong?" His mind raced. *Does he know what I do with Grant?*

"Uh . . . ." David stared at the ground. "Because . . . ." He looked up as if he just remembered. "Because my mom's one of the maids. We're not supposed to talk to you."

Brian was dumbfounded. "I still don't understand."

"Please don't tell anyone," David begged as he backed away. "I'll get in big trouble."

"Okay. I promise." He stared into David's warm brown eyes. "I guess I won't get to pet Angel anymore?" His voice caught. *Or see you.* He hadn't realized until now how much he longed for a friend. Grant and River made up his entire world.

David was quiet a moment. "Well, maybe sometime. But you have to swear you won't tell *anyone*."

"I swear."

"Okay." David took a few steps backward. "I gotta go."

"I'll see you then?"

David nodded and hurried back to the Other Wing. Brian watched him go, happy to have a new friend, but confused, too. Did Grant really not allow the servants' children to mingle with people in the Main House?

Brian frowned as he headed back. He couldn't believe Grant would be like that. *Maybe it's David's mother who made the rule.*

Brian helped himself to more pasta at dinner that night. He felt like he could eat the whole bowl.

Grant smiled. "I guess you *are* feeling better."

He nodded, his mouth full.

"Dude, we found this really cool store today." River leaned forward. "You'll love it."

Brian swallowed his food. "What is it?"

Grant said, "A music store, Phil's New and Used. They carry a great variety of imports and rare recordings. I'm sure you could find some gems there."

Brian grinned. "Can we go tomorrow?"

They stepped out of Phil's onto the busy sidewalk. Brian handed his heavy sack to Jeffrey to put in the trunk. "I love that place. I could spend hours there."

Grant smiled. "They get new arrivals daily. Perhaps you'll have to make a weekly pilgrimage."

They ambled along Melrose Avenue. Brian spotted a salon across the street as they waited for the light. He tugged on his hair with a frown. It was getting long and annoying.

Grant said, "Would you like a haircut?"

"Yeah. I don't know what I want, though. Something different."

River said, "I need one, too."

They walked into the salon, and the boys sat in the waiting area. Brian flipped through a magazine. River smirked and said, "Girlie magazine."

"I'm trying to find the right hair."

Grant sat across from them. "We're in luck. They have two openings shortly."

"Here." Brian pointed to the open page. "I want my hair to look like this."

River whispered in his ear, "That's a girlie haircut."

Brian laughed. "I don't care." He pushed his shoulder against River. "I think it's pretty." He turned the magazine around to show Grant.

Grant said, "That's an undercut bob. Are you sure that's what you want? It will take time to grow out. It won't look like that today."

"I know." Brian swung his legs. "I'm sure."

Grant smiled. "Whatever you want." He squeezed Brian's knee and winked.

ༀༀༀ

Brian answered the summons to Grant's room. He already had an erection as he entered the bedroom and slid under the sheets beside Grant, felt their naked bodies warm against each other. Comforting. Exciting.

Grant caressed his back, his ass, between his legs. "Brian," he whispered. "I want to try something new, alright?"

He nodded, barely listening.

"I want to really make love to you." Grant stroked Brian's penis. "It may hurt a little at first, but that will pass."

Brian's eyes widened as understanding hit him. His pulse beat faster as Grant's lips made their way down his stomach. Grant murmured, "Trust me."

Brian nodded, his throat dry.

"I can make it wonderful for you." Grant's mouth moved from his penis to his balls, then farther.

The hair stood up on Brian's arms as he squirmed and moaned. He forgot to be nervous.

Grant turned him gently onto his side so that Grant was behind him, then reached over to the nightstand to pick up a tube and condom. Brian's heart skipped as Grant put his knee between Brian's thighs. Grant kissed his shoulder. "Don't be nervous." His finger entered him, gentle and familiar, and it felt good. Grant reached around to Brian's penis with his other hand. Brian's eyes closed as Grant stroked everything at once, and all thought left him.

Then something much bigger nudged him. Pushed into him a little way. Brian gasped, and his eyes flew open. Impossibly big. His body tightened up in fear.

"Relax," Grant murmured. "I won't hurt you. I love you. I'll wait for your body to accept me."

After a moment Brian's muscles softened, and Grant slid in all the way. The feeling was so overwhelming he couldn't tell if it hurt. The penis seemed to fill his entire body, and he almost panicked. He clutched the sheets and heard Grant murmur soothing words, felt Grant's hand on his penis, Grant moving inside him. And realized it felt good.

Grant moaned as he pushed gently in and out, his slick hand stroking Brian in unison. Brian's fist tightened on the sheets, his breathing convulsive. It was almost too much, too much, *but don't stop!* The waves crashed through him hard, and Brian cried out, unaware of anything else in the world.

They collapsed together, gasping for breath. Grant rolled Brian onto his back and kissed his face, then gazed down into his eyes. "Are you alright?"

Brian couldn't speak. He breathed a laugh and pulled Grant closer to kiss him.

River snuck into Brian's room that night, as he did every night. Brian sat up and switched on the bedside lamp. "I'll show you what to do. And I've got this." Brian held up a tube of lubricant. "I found an extra one in Grant's drawer, so I . . . borrowed it."

River seemed unsure. "You've only done it once. It's not like you're an expert."

Brian arched a brow. "I know enough. The key—" He leaned closer, his voice low. "Is to make sure I'm *extremely* excited." He smiled. "I think you can do that."

River's breathing picked up, but he glanced away. "I'm afraid I'll hurt you."

"You won't. Please. I want to feel you inside me." He touched his fingertips to River's lips. "It's so intimate, like you're part of each other." He searched River's eyes. "I want to feel that with you. Please." To open himself up so completely. His lips brushed River's mouth. "Please," he whispered and kissed him again.

River's arms went around him, and they fell back onto the bed, kissing long and deep. Touching everywhere. Brian squeezed lubricant onto his hand and smeared it on River's penis, slid around, up and down. River shook.

Brian handed him the tube. "Your turn." He rolled onto his stomach, River's body pressed warm against his. Brian tilted his head back, and River leaned down to kiss him upside down.

Their mouths broke apart as River rubbed the lube in, then moved his hand forward to touch the other sensitive spots. Brian gasped and pushed back against him. He wanted River now. "Now!"

He felt River's cock sliding on his skin, pushing into him. That incredible sensation of being filled completely. River pushed in further and moaned.

"Yes!" Brian gasped. God, it felt so good to be together like this, their bodies connected as their souls were.

Brian's head rested on River's chest as they lay in the dark, limbs entwined. River whispered, "Are you awake?"

"Mmm."

"I'm starving. Let's get a snack."

They put on bathrobes and crept downstairs to the kitchen. River opened the refrigerator.

Brian leaned back against the counter and stifled a yawn. "You're always hungry."

"I'm a growin fourteen-year-old boy. Of course I'm hungry. Aren't you? Aha!" River snatched up a Tupperware container. "Leftover enchiladas."

Grant locked his downstairs office with a sigh. He hadn't meant to work so late, but several sculptures had arrived damaged, a disaster in the import business. *Careless handlers.* He turned toward the stairs but heard voices; the kitchen light was on. He moved closer and saw Brian leaning against the counter.

The microwave beeped, and he heard River's voice. "Want some?"

Brian shook his head. He tucked his hair behind his ear; it fell back into his face.

River walked over to him and stood close. "You're not really awake, are you?"

Brian put his arms around River's neck, and their lips met. The microwave beeped again. They jumped a little and laughed.

River moved out of Grant's line of sight. Grant turned and walked away into the dark.

🜲🜲🜲

They saw Grant in the parlor as they came downstairs. A stranger stood beside him, a tall man with brown hair in an Armani suit.

"Boys, this is my business partner, John Mackenzie."

He was much younger than Grant, probably late thirties. Brian shook his hand and met light blue eyes. Cold eyes. Brian tried to hide his immediate dislike.

The man turned to River as Grant introduced them. John smiled. "River, what an unusual name. Lovely." He stared intently.

Color rose in River's cheeks.

Grant said, "Now if you'll excuse us, boys, we have business to attend to." He ushered John out of the room.

"Oooo, I don't like him," Brian said as soon as they were gone.

"Why?"

"I don't know. Just something about him."

"He's suave. Classy." River shrugged. "Hot."

"I suppose. But he exudes something . . . a dangerous vibe."

River smiled. "That's what makes him exciting."

🜲🜲🜲

River showered and tied on his bathrobe; he saw no reason to get dressed for a 'lesson' with Grant. He smiled as he walked down the hall. *I'm never late when it's for sex.* He used to always be late, back home. Home. He frowned, and his step faltered. They could never accept his life as it was now. But he accepted it. It was easy. He just didn't think.

He opened the door to Grant's rooms and walked through the sitting area and into the bedroom. Afternoon sun slanted in through the French doors. River moved toward the bed and realized Grant was not alone. Brian lay naked beneath him. River's breath caught, and he started to back up.

Grant beckoned to him. "River, please join us."

Grant moved over and patted the bed next to Brian. The boys looked at each other with wide eyes.

River sat on the bed, his heart pounding. Grant leaned over to untie River's bathrobe. He pulled the robe off River's shoulder and ran his hand down his chest, then gently pushed him back to lie beside Brian.

"It's alright," Grant said. "I know you two have been sleeping together."

They looked at Grant in alarm.

"It's alright. I expected it." He whispered, "I want it."

Grant's lips brushed Brian's cheek while his hand stroked River's body. He leaned over to kiss River on the mouth, then Brian. River's gut twisted a little, seeing Grant kiss Brian. *But it's okay; it's Grant.*

Brian turned his head to touch his lips to River's, and it was hard to think of anything else. River pulled his mouth away, like pulling two magnets apart, and glanced at Grant. *If it's okay with Brian, I guess it's okay with me.* River's lips worked their way down Brian's body. A hand stroked River's ass, and he realized it was

Grant's. Grant was watching, touching here and there. Weird.

Brian moaned as River's mouth found his cock. Grant moved down to take River's penis into his mouth. River paused, then continued. *This ain't so bad.* It was great, actually.

After a few minutes River pulled away to turn Brian over. A small part of his brain noticed Grant watching, touching himself. But mostly he felt the tightness, the heat. The connection. He moaned.

When it was over the boys cleaned up quickly and headed for the door. "Brian," Grant called. "Wait a moment. I want to talk to you."

The boys exchanged looks, and Brian hung back. Grant patted the bed beside him. Brian sat dutifully and bit his lip. *Am I in trouble?*

Grant said, "I see you've done some teaching of your own."

Brian ducked his head. "I'm sorry," he whispered.

"No need to apologize." He lifted Brian's chin. "You and River don't need to hide things from me." Grant smiled. "You're obviously doing a good job with River. You seem to bring out the best in him, in a lot of ways. Just don't push him too fast. Be careful."

"Okay," he said softly; then his brow furrowed. "But he's older than me. I don't understand."

"Age isn't necessarily a factor. In fact, it can be a detriment. River has more barriers to overcome than you."

"Aah." He nodded. *River has a lot of barriers.* He'd never thought about that in terms of sex.

Grant patted his knee. "Alright, Brian. Run along now. Go be with River."

Brian lay in River's arms in the soft glow of morning light. He knew River had been awake for awhile; his breathing had changed. Brian finally said, "That was kinda weird with Grant yesterday, huh?"

River grunted. "Guess we don't need to sneak no more."

"Did it bother you? All three of us together."

River shrugged. "Nah. Not really."

"Me, neither."

River sat up and turned to face him but averted his eyes. Brian touched his cheek. "What is it?"

River met his gaze. "Are you in love with Grant?"

He blinked. "Well . . . I don't think I'm *in* love with him. I mean, I do love him." He searched River's eyes. "But it's not the same as the way I feel about you." He touched River's hand. "It's hard to explain. He's like a father to me."

River arched a brow. "Except for the sex."

Brian laughed. "Yeah, except for that." He sobered. "I feel like he's the father I never had. I know that doesn't make sense, cos I have a father." Brian lay back against the pillows and stared at the ceiling. "But it's like he was never really there."

River lay beside him. Brian turned to him and said, "Anyway, to answer you, jealous boy—" His lips quirked as he traced his fingertip up River's chest. "No, I'm not in love with Grant." He gazed deep into River's eyes. "I'm in love with you.

Only you." He brushed his mouth against River's.

"Good," River said against Brian's lips.

Their kisses deepened, and River murmured, "I want you to do it to me."

Brian pulled back. "Really?"

"I want to see what's it like."

"Are you sure? It might hurt a little . . . at first."

"I don't care."

"And—" Brian glanced down. "I've never done that before."

"Good. Then I'll be your first."

Brian met his eyes. *He is jealous of Grant.* "Yes. You'll be my first."

River used Brian's stomach for a pillow. Brian stared at the ceiling and stroked River's soft hair with one hand, a cigarette in the other.

Brian took a deep drag as he replayed the intense sensations, the incredible tightness beyond anything he'd imagined. But more than that, the feeling of control. Power. He tried to sort it out in his head. A very powerful feeling, to be the one doing it. Versus the absolute surrender of being 'the girl.' Not that power didn't exist there, too. Just a different sort. *Making someone want me, that's power. It doesn't matter who does what.*

River said, "Whatcha thinkin about?"

"Power."

River laughed. "That's the difference between me and you." He sat up. "I was thinking about how my stomach's growling."

"Hungry again?"

River nodded and grabbed Brian around the ribs, shook him a little. He growled, "You always make me hungry."

Brian giggled. "That tickles."

River grinned and let go, then started to get up.

"Wait." Brian put his hand on his arm. "Did I hurt you?"

"Nah." He kissed him. "Couldn't you tell I liked it? It was amazing. So different."

Brian smiled. "Let's go eat."

The boys relaxed on the couch in the parlor. Sebastian curled up on Brian's lap, purring. Brian stroked the long fur and leaned against River, his eyes heavy.

A chair creaked and startled Brian out of a light sleep. Sebastian was gone from his lap. Brian looked over to see Grant in a nearby chair, reaching down to pet the cat rubbing his legs. A tray of steaming coffee rested on the glass table.

"I didn't mean to wake you." Grant smiled as he caught Brian's eye. "But I do need to talk to you both."

Brian rubbed his face and took a mouthful of coffee. He was wide awake now; Grant looked serious.

Naked in the Rain

"I have a rule in my house," Grant said. "But not just here. It applies everywhere, always. Your lives could depend on it." He set down his cup and leaned forward. "You must always use condoms. Always. No exceptions. You know about AIDS, that it can be transmitted through intercourse?"

The boys nodded solemnly.

"The problem is, when you're in the moment, nothing will stop you. You won't care if you have a condom or not. I think you understand what I'm talking about."

They nodded again.

"So," Grant said. "The solution is to always have condoms with you. Always. Whether you think you'll be having sex or not. It's very simple. And while you're at it, you might as well carry lubricant as well." He set a handful of plastic packets on the coffee table. "Go ahead and take them."

Brian picked one up and read the packet. 'Mini Lube-Tube.' He smiled. "Little travel-sized lube. Cool." He picked up a few and put them in his pocket.

Grant smiled. "That's the idea. Now, more importantly, you need condoms."

He took a pewter box from the shelf beneath the coffee table. Brian knew what was in there—he'd peeked before. The boys grabbed a bunch of condoms and stuffed them in their pockets.

Grant chuckled. "You need only carry a few. A supply will be sent to your rooms. If you get low just let me know, or tell Maria." Grant turned serious again. "I hope you boys understand how important this is." He met Brian's eyes.

"I understand," Brian said solemnly.

Grant looked at River, who nodded. Grant's voice lightened. "Alright then. Who wants to watch a movie?"

River leaned forward. "Can we do some coke first?"

"Certainly." Grant smiled.

Brian came out of his bathroom to find River on the edge of the bed. River said, "Did you see John's tux?"

"John was here again?"

"Yeah." River glanced away. "He stopped by on his way to a party. He had on this great tuxedo. He looked so . . . I don't know. Suave and sophisticated." River lay back and folded his arms behind his head. "I wish I could be like that."

Brian frowned.

River looked over at him. "I don't know what you have against him. Maybe you're jealous."

Brian didn't think so. *I just don't like him. But it doesn't matter.* He crawled onto the bed to tickle River, reached under his shirt and tweaked his nipple. "I've been thinking about what Grant said."

"About condoms?"

He nodded. "Of course he's right. But—" He met River's eyes. "If we always use them with Grant and . . . whoever else we might ever sleep with, I don't see why we need to use them with each other."

River nodded. "I been thinking the same thing. But Grant would be super pissed."

"He won't find out. Just when we're alone." Brian kissed him. He murmured with his lips against River's, "I want to feel your skin against mine."

"Me, too." River clutched him tighter.

൲൲൲

Brian sat in the shade of the umbrella and watched River swim, but his thoughts were elsewhere. The last day of February. Two months since he left home.

River climbed out of the pool and sat in a nearby chair. "Why are you sad?"

Brian glanced down at his oversized black tee shirt with the words 'The Cure' across it. The shirt Tanya gave him last year. "It's been two months. They must be so worried."

"Yeah." River reached over to touch his hand.

"I've got to let them know I'm okay."

River's fingers tightened on his. "Don't do anything without talking to me. We have to be careful."

"I know. Don't you want to tell your family you're okay?"

River pulled his hand away and folded his arms over his chest. "No."

"Why not? At least Dove."

River's frown deepened. "It's better for them if it's a clean break. Let them forget about me."

"River, they'll never forget about you. Don't you think they deserve to know you're alive?"

River stood up. "No! Leave me alone." He stalked away and disappeared into the grounds.

Brian stared after him. "Sorry," he whispered.

He waited, but River didn't come back, so Brian went inside through the den. He intended to go play the piano, but turned instead into the library. So many books. For a moment he forgot his troubles in the excitement of choosing a new one.

Book in hand, he headed to the small courtyard between the house and wing, where the buildings angled and almost intercepted, creating a V-shaped area resplendent with flowers and greenery. And completely hidden from view. He wanted to get away for a little while.

He passed beneath an arbor covered in a vine of purple morning glories and stepped into the courtyard. Bell-shaped lavender flowers lined the pebbled path. He smiled. Spring had definitely arrived, if ever it had been winter in Southern California.

He settled onto a stone bench around a bend in the path and looked at the book in his hands. *Cry to Heaven* by Anne Rice. He turned to the first page and tucked his hair behind his ear. It fell back in his face. A sigh of irritation escaped him. He tried to focus on the words, but his eyes kept wandering off the page. *Is River still mad? I wonder what he's doing.*

"Hey!" came a loud whisper.

Brian jumped. He glanced around and saw brown hair poke around the corner, then a familiar face—the boy he met a few weeks ago with the rabbit. "David!" Brian grinned.

David ran over to stand before him, out of breath. "I saw you come in here, so I hurried before anyone could see me. I want to show you something." He reached into his shirt pocket and pulled out a white baby rabbit. It fit in the palm of his hand, its eyes still sealed shut.

"Oh, my god," Brian squeaked. He reached out to touch its soft fur. "It's so adorable!"

"I knew you'd like it." David grinned and sat beside him on the bench. "Angel had babies."

"Really? She's a mom?"

"Yeah. She gave birth about a week ago. I didn't even know she was pregnant." He shrugged. "Maybe that's why she ran off that day."

"Wow." Brian stroked the delicate creature.

"They were kinda ugly at first—didn't have any fur at all."

The bunny sniffed Brian's hand with its tiny nose, curious and unafraid. Brian grinned. "They're making up for it now. So cute!"

Brian heard the crunch of footsteps on the gravel path. David gasped. He shoved the bunny back into his pocket and practically fell off the bench, then dove behind a bush just as Grant appeared around the corner.

Brian smiled up at him, trying to look innocent. He didn't want to get David in trouble. Didn't want to lose his only other friend.

"Where's River?" Grant asked.

Brian glanced at the ground. "I don't know."

"Isn't he here with you? I heard you talking."

His heart pounded as he struggled to come up with a good lie. He grabbed the book lying on the bench. "I was reading out loud."

"Ah." Grant sat close beside him and took the book from his hands. "You'll enjoy this story. Later." He set it on the ground and put his arm around Brian's shoulders. Nuzzled into his hair and neck.

Brian's eyes widened. *David's watching! Shit.*

Grant caressed Brian's face and kissed him as his fingers slipped under the black tee shirt. Brian pushed him away.

Grant sat back, his eyebrows raised in shock. "What's wrong?"

His eyes darted. "I don't know, I just . . . ."

"No one can see us." Grant reached for him again but pulled away when Brian didn't respond. "Brian?"

"I . . . I don't feel comfortable here," he said lamely. He felt like crying.

"Making love outdoors is a wonderful experience." Grant studied him. "Alright. Why don't we go in?"

Grant picked up the book and stood. They walked slowly along the path toward the arbor. Grant stroked his back. "It's unlike you to be inhibited."

Brian ducked his head. "I'm sorry."

"Don't apologize. I'm just surprised."

Brian suppressed the urge to look back as they left the courtyard. He stared at the ground instead. *What does David think of me now? He'll probably never talk to me again.* He bit his lip to stop it from trembling.

He glanced up and saw River walking along the path, still in his swim trunks. River turned and went the other way.

Grant's brow furrowed. "Everyone's behaving oddly today."

Brian tucked his hands in his pockets and scuffed the ground. "We kinda had a fight."

"Aah. It all makes sense now." Grant smiled and squeezed his shoulder. "I'm sure everything will be fine."

River dried off and draped the towel over his shoulders as he entered the hallway. He rubbed his temple with a frown. He swam too long, trying to work out his anger. *I shoulda gone with them.* Brian and Grant left to go shopping, but River had refused to go. Now he was stuck here alone. He padded down the hall in his bare feet and turned toward the staircase.

"Hello, River," a man's voice said.

River jumped and looked toward the voice. John sat in the parlor reading a newspaper. He folded the paper and stood with a smile.

"Uh, hello," River stammered.

John was stunning as usual in his debonair way. A casual suit this time, but it looked expensive. River felt exposed in his swim trunks. The heat rose in his face as John approached.

"I've been waiting for Grant," John said. "But I just phoned him, and he'll be awhile longer."

"Oh." River's voice came out higher than usual. He wondered if John could see his heart pounding.

John stood close and gazed down at him. "I hate to waste a trip over here. Perhaps you could keep me company."

"Uh . . . ."

"Your hair is dripping." He brushed a wet strand back from River's face. His fingers grazed River's arm.

His body tingled from the touch. He glanced down. His trunks were beginning to change shape.

"That towel is wet, too," John said. He pulled it slowly from River's shoulders.

The friction made River's pulse speed up. *I can't help it. He's exciting.* As if danger and lust bubbled just beneath his cool surface.

John held the towel and looked River up and down. "Do you work out?"

"No." He struggled to keep his voice casual. "But I swim a lot."

"Swimming is the best exercise. Works the entire body," he said as he walked around River slowly. "Why don't you come sit on the couch with me?"

"Uh . . . I need to get some aspirin. I've got a headache."

"Oh, really? Let's see if I can help with that." He touched River's back to guide him toward the couch.

River balked. "My trunks are wet. I can't sit down."

"Of course. How thoughtful. Just relax. I'm sure we can get rid of that headache."

River's thighs pressed against the back of the couch. John stood behind him to massage his shoulders. It felt good. Really good.

John's warm hands moved to his neck, and River let his head fall back, both relaxed and aroused. John reached forward to massage his chest, then wrapped his arms around River's waist. Pressed his tall, hard body against him.

John's fingers moved to his nipples, tugged and twisted. River's breath caught, and he clutched the back of the sofa. John slid his hand down, along the material beside River's groin. He tugged on the bottom of the trunks, slowly pulled and sent shivers through River as the nylon slid against his skin. John yanked, and River's cock jumped out. John stroked it and scraped his teeth against River's shoulder. River gasped.

John let go to unfasten his own pants, and they fell around his ankles. He pushed on River's back to bend him over the couch, then used his tongue. River's body quivered, and he cried out, his voice muffled by the cushions.

John straightened and pushed into him. He gave River's body a moment to accept him, then thrust hard. Rougher than Grant had ever been. And bigger. River's fists tightened. It hurt, but *God* he wanted it. River's penis rubbed against the velvet cushions, his body rocked by John's powerful thrusts. John's hand pressed on his back, pushing him down. River had never felt so helpless, pinned like this. He couldn't move. *God!* River moaned, totally overwhelmed, and came into the cushions.

John thrust a few more times and uttered a long, guttural moan. After a moment he kissed River's back, then peeled off the condom and fastened his pants. He left the room without a word.

River pulled himself from the couch and looked around in a daze, his body throbbing. He felt guilty but excited, too. John was like an animal. *We didn't even kiss.*

River shook himself. *Grant and Brian could be home any minute. Brian.* His stomach twisted. He pushed the couch back into place and grimaced at the stain on the velvet. He turned the cushion over and ran up to his room.

Brian finally found him standing on the wooden bridge, throwing pebbles into the water. The sky had gone grey and gloomy; it matched the expression on River's face. Brian said his name softly.

But River wouldn't look at him.

Brian's throat tightened. "River, please talk to me." He put his hand on River's arm, but River shrugged it off. "I'm sorry." Brian's voice trembled.

"*You're* sorry?" River shook his head. Still didn't look at him. "You got nothing to be sorry for. I'm the one who—" His grip tightened on the wooden railing.

Brian put his hand over River's and whispered, "What is it?"

River didn't answer at first, then said softly, "John was here."

Brian's breath caught as it clicked. "You had sex with him."

River looked at him, and his eyes filled. He fell to his knees, wrapped his arms around Brian's legs and looked up at him. "I don't know what happened. I didn't mean to." Tears streamed down the sides of his face. "I'm so sorry." His voice broke.

He pressed his cheek against Brian's thighs and clutched him tight.

Brian stroked his hair. "It's okay." And it was. "It's just sex. It's okay." It surprised him that he didn't mind. But he wasn't jealous; it was just a physical act. Why should it matter?

River's body shook. Brian slid to his knees and took River's face in his hands.

"River," he said firmly. "I don't mind. I love you. Nothing's changed."

"You mean that?" he managed to say.

Brian nodded and kissed his forehead.

༄༄༄

Brian lay against River in the chair they shared by the pool, still tired from yesterday. Grant had taken them out on his yacht again. 'The Party Boat,' River dubbed it. But this time instead of margaritas, Grant presented them with white pills. Ecstasy. Brian smiled. *Now that is an excellent drug.* The music sounded so good. They danced a long time, until that one song. Brian giggled, remembering how he and River turned to each other in horror at the shrill singing. They raced to the stereo to turn it off.

The three of them ended up in the cabin. *That was pretty wild sex.* The 'sandwich.' Brian got the best position, between River and Grant. It was the most amazing feeling—fucking and being fucked at the same time. Brian sighed at the memory and stretched, a little sore. But he didn't mind.

River started tickling. Brian squirmed and laughed until Grant walked over. "Boys, listen up."

They stopped giggling and straightened immediately.

Grant sat across from them. "As a standard precaution, I get tested for HIV periodically. Dr. Griffin will be here tomorrow to take a blood sample. I'd like him to test you two as well, if you'll agree."

"Even though we're careful?" River glanced at Brian.

Brian knew what he was thinking. *Does Grant know we don't use condoms with each other?*

"It's just a standard precaution," Grant said. "A good habit to form now that you're in a high risk group."

He doesn't know. Brian said, "I got a blood transfusion once."

Grant looked surprised a moment, then nodded. "When you cut your wrists. How long ago was that?"

Brian frowned at the ugly scars that marred his skin. "It seems like forever ago, but I guess it hasn't been that long." He turned to River. "When did I go to the institute, in September? And now it's March, so that's . . . ." He started to count the months on his fingers.

River said, "About six months ago."

Grant asked, "Is that where you met? At an institution?"

They nodded. Brian said, "We were roommates." He added quietly, "I wouldn't have made it through without River."

River squeezed his hand and gave him a loving smile.

Grant stood. "Shall I tell Dr. Griffin there will be three of us to test?"

They nodded.

"Good boys." Grant kissed them both on the lips. "I'll go make that call."

၊၊၊

River found Brian in his bedroom writing in his journal. Brian looked up with a smile. "Where have you been?"

"John stopped by." He felt guilty talking about it, but Brian really didn't seem to mind.

"Did you have fun?"

"Yeah. He's not like Grant at all. I mean, they're both great, but real different." *At least we kissed this time.* He remembered John's aggressive mouth, his own absolute surrender. It felt freeing in a way, to give himself up so completely. He cleared his throat. "John's going away for a month."

"That's a long time. Where's he going?"

"Dallas and New York, on business. He's leaving in a few days."

"Huh." Brian was quiet a moment, then said, "I have an idea. You know I want to tell my family I'm okay . . . ." He bit his lip and hoped River wouldn't get upset.

"Yeah?" River raised an eyebrow.

"Maybe I could give John a note to mail to them. That way it would be postmarked from somewhere else."

River thought a moment. "Yeah, that should work. If it's what you want to do."

"It is. Except—I don't want John to see my parent's address." *I don't trust him.*

"You could send it to someone else. A friend or something."

Brian frowned. He couldn't think of anyone except his sister's friend, Vicky. But she lived on the same street as his family. Too close. "I know—my grandma in Indiana. She'll send it on."

"Be careful what you say. Let me see it first." He grinned. "I got a surprise for you in my room. Be right back." River returned a few seconds later with a small vial of cocaine.

"Where'd you get that?" Brian asked.

"Grant." River used a razor blade to form two lines on the nightstand. "I asked this morning, and he gave it to me. Said he'll get us whatever we want."

Brian picked up the tooter. "Really?" He tucked his hair behind his ear and leaned over.

"Yeah!" River grinned. "Is this paradise or what?"

Jeffrey took the boys with him into town the next day. They stopped at a drugstore to pick up a prescription for Grant. Brian spun the rack of postcards slowly, then laughed at one of a baby with an orange mohawk. "This is perfect." He showed River.

River examined it closely. "Yeah, this'll work. It don't say Los Angeles or anything."

Brian gave it to Jeffrey to buy and frowned. *Now what do I write?*

. . .

Brian lay on his stomach and tapped the pen against his teeth. He stared at the blank postcard on the bed before him.

March 14th

Dear Tanya and Mom and Dad,

First I want to say I'm sorry for all the pain I've caused you. But I had to leave. I won't try to explain that, but I hope you understand. Please don't worry about me—I'm not living on the street or anything. I'm staying with a wonderful man I met. He's really nice to me. And he has a beautiful grand piano!!

I'm sorry I took so long to write, but I had to wait for the right opportunity. I'm giving this to someone who is traveling to mail for me. I'm not in Dallas, so don't waste time trying to find me there. I promise I'll keep in touch.

Love you,
Brian

He addressed an envelope to his grandmother and scribbled a note. *'Grammy, please send this on to my family.'* Emotion hit him suddenly, and his chest constricted. He laid his head down as the tears came.

൩൩൩

Brian was sitting on his bed reading *The Tempest* when he heard a knock. "Come in."

Grant entered and shut the door, then sat close. Brian nuzzled into his neck. His head tilted back, and their lips met. The book fell to the floor as Grant pushed him onto his back.

They removed their clothes and were holding each other when another knock came. Brian looked toward the door, his arms still around Grant. But it wasn't River. His heart skipped as a stranger entered the room.

"Ah, Matthew," Grant said. "I want you to meet Brian."

But we're naked. Brian glanced at Grant, then back at the stranger.

"Hello, Brian." Matthew gave him a polite smile as if this were the most normal thing in the world. He was about forty, well-dressed and attractive, with sandy blond hair.

"Hello," Brian managed to squeak out as he clutched Grant.

Grant stroked him and spoke in soothing tones. "Brian, darling, Matthew is a dear friend of mine. I've been telling him how wonderful you are, and I'm hoping you'll do me a favor."

He nodded tentatively. *Anything for you. But . . . we're naked.* His eyes darted to the stranger again.

"You see, Matthew is a bit of a voyeur, and he'd love to watch us together. Would you do that? For me?"

He stared at Grant with wide eyes. "Uh . . . I—I guess, if you really want me to . . . ."

Grant beamed. "Brian, you're absolutely wonderful."

Grant kissed the side of his neck. Brian looked over to see Matthew seat himself on a chair opposite the bed. Grant's hand wandered to Brian's thigh, made its way up slowly. Brian gasped. Before long he completely forgot someone else was in the room.

Grant finally turned him to take him from behind, and Brian saw Matthew staring intently from the chair, his own penis in his hand. It felt surreal. Matthew seemed far away, as if he were watching a movie, while Grant's touches were immediate and close. A part of him.

Soon it was over. Matthew cleaned himself up quickly. With a pleasant smile and nod, he left the room.

"Are you alright?" Grant asked as Brian rolled onto his back. "Did that bother you?"

Brian shrugged and glanced away. "I don't know." It hadn't sunk in, really. "I guess it's okay. I mean, it was kind of strange, but—" He searched Grant's warm amber eyes and whispered, "I just want to make you happy."

Grant gave him a loving smile. "That you do, my boy, that you do."

The next evening Brian answered Grant's summons. Grant sat on the edge of his bed, Matthew in a chair nearby. Brian tried not to frown. He'd decided he didn't really mind; Matthew had only watched, after all. But he preferred to be alone with Grant.

I must be polite. He's Grant's friend. He nodded to Matthew, then smiled at Grant and sat beside him on the bed.

Brian took the vial from River and tried to sound nonchalant. "So—" He picked up the razor blade to prepare lines on the antique desk in his room. "Have you met Matthew?"

"No, who's that?" River asked.

He shrugged. "Just a friend of Grant's." Brian distracted him by handing him the tooter. "You first."

Grant and Brian clung to each other, Matthew sitting nearby as usual; Brian had learned to completely ignore his presence. Brian turned onto his side as Grant moved behind him. He felt Grant's erection against his leg as Grant held him close.

He closed his eyes and lost himself to the sensations, felt Grant's mouth on his penis. He moaned as his head fell back against Grant's chest. *Wait a minute.* His brain struggled to function. *Grant's behind me.*

He looked down. It was Matthew, not Grant, whose head was at his groin. Brian squeaked in alarm. Grant murmured soothing words and reached down to fondle him while Matthew's mouth continued its work. Brian's breath caught as his body arched. He was unable to protest.

ൟൟൟ

Brian stood on the stone bridge near the buildings and smiled at the reflection of clouds in the water. *Everything is good.* Even the strange sexual encounters didn't bother him anymore. They were fun, actually. *Grant knows best.*

The back of his neck prickled. He whirled toward the Other Wing and saw a figure in the nearest window.

David? Brian stepped closer and shaded his eyes from the sun. Not David. A man. He stared at Brian with an intense, hungry look. A chill ran up Brian's spine. The man looked like he was going to pounce. He pressed his hand suddenly against the glass and Brian jumped, then backed up, irrationally afraid to turn his back. His heart pounded in his ears to the rhythm of the word. Evil. Evil.

The man kept staring as Brian backed up. Brian reached a line of tall shrubs and ducked behind them, out of sight. He squeezed his eyes shut and hid his head. *Calm down. He's just a man. Probably a servant.* "Thank god he doesn't work in the Main House."

He finally screwed up the courage to peek around the greenery. The window was empty, the man gone. He let out his breath and ran back to the house.

He stepped inside and rubbed his arms, trying to shake the creeps. *I need River.* He hurried along the hallway and reached the staircase.

River came bounding down. "Hey, dude." He reached the bottom of the stairs. "What's wrong?"

"Nothing." He clutched River's shirt and laid his cheek against his chest, breathed in River's scent. *Safe.*

River held him close. "You okay?"

He felt the vibration of River's voice against his cheek. "I am now."

"I met Matthew."

Brian's eyes flew open, and he pulled back to look at River's face.

River's lips twisted in a wry smile. "Kinda weird."

He nodded and leaned closer to whisper, "I think our Grant's a little . . . perverted."

River laughed. "A little? Hello, you're twelve years old."

Brian smiled. "That doesn't bother you."

"Yeah, but I ain't old enough to be your grandfather." He grabbed Brian's waist and tickled.

Brian laughed and fell against him. Their arms went around each other once more. Enough to make him forget about the frightening figure in the window. Almost.

*"Does his makeup in his room
douse himself with cheap perfume
eyeholes in a paper bag
greatest lay I ever had*

*kind of guy who mates for life
gotta help him find a wife
we're a couple
when our bodies double*

*and it all comes down to the role reversal
got the muse in my head, she's universal
spinning me round, she's coming over me"*

- Brian Molko (Placebo), "Nancy Boy"

೧೪ CHAPTER 10 ೧೪

He watched in the mirror while the stylist shaped his hair, finally long enough for a proper bob. But it was hard to keep his thoughts away from sex. The other day Matthew had fucked him while Grant just watched. Brian frowned. He didn't understand the whole voyeur thing. *I can't imagine not wanting to participate.* It felt strange having someone inside him other than River or Grant, but exciting, too.

"All done," the woman said.

He blinked and came back to the salon. Stared into the mirror at thick dark hair that curled under slightly, just below his chin. Pretty. It did sort of make him look like a girl, but he didn't mind.

"It looks good," River said as they stepped outside.

Brian grinned and leaned into him. "It feels bouncy."

The sun glittered off the cement sidewalk and white buildings as they followed Grant. So clean here. Tall palm trees. No trash. Nothing like the places they saw before they met Grant. Everyone looked rich.

"I ain't changing my watch," River said.

"What?"

"How can the time change just cos someone says so?" He shook his head. "That's bullshit."

Brian laughed. They'd argued earlier when he told River to change his watch for daylight savings. Apparently they didn't do that in Arizona.

"You'll adapt," Grant said. "Here we are." The sign over the door read 'Andre's Stag.' They went in, and a flamboyantly gay man fawned over Grant. "Mr. Nesbit, so wonderful to see you. Oh!" he squealed as his eyes fell on Brian. "What have we here?" He touched Brian's hair.

Grant said, "Andre, meet Brian and River."

"Oh, my. Aren't you adorable?" he said, giving them each a limp handshake.

The boys glanced at each other in amusement. Andre turned the sign on the door to closed; they had the place to themselves. Brian wandered around, admiring the vivid colors, and let his fingers graze soft velvet dresses and satin shirts.

"Brian," Grant called. He held up a black leather miniskirt. "Would you try this on for me?"

Brian's eyebrows went up. "But it's a skirt."

"Who says men cannot wear skirts? They do in Scotland. Besides, since when are you one to follow rules?" He winked and smiled.

Brian smiled back and shrugged. "Okay."

"Andre, could you give Brian a hand? Let's make him up a bit."

"My pleasure, Mr. Nesbit," Andre oozed. He took the skirt from Grant. "This way, young sir."

Andre led him into a separate room. The light pink walls and white molding reminded Brian of cake icing. He smiled at his multiple reflections in the large mirrors that surrounded him.

Andre walked over to a four-panel screen painted with an Oriental motif of birds and flowers. "Here." He hung the skirt behind the screen. "You go ahead and get undressed. I'll pick out a top for you."

Brian went behind the screen to remove his clothes, then stepped into the skirt and pulled it up. "Strange," he murmured. Odd to feel his legs rub together with no clothing between them.

"Here we go!" Andre called out as he returned. A hand holding a black silk shirt appeared over the screen.

"Thanks." The shirt buttoned down the front, with a collar and half-sleeves. He slipped it on and felt the exquisite silk against his skin. The fitted sleeves stopped just above his elbows.

"Can I help you with that?" Andre's head poked around the screen.

"Sure." Brian walked out.

Andre fastened a few buttons but left the top two undone, as well as the ones on the bottom. "See, what we'll do is tie this like so, and voila!"

Brian looked at himself in the mirror. Andre had tied the black top so it revealed his pale lower stomach. The leather skirt rode low on his waist and came almost half-way down his thighs, tight. "Weird," he murmured.

"We're not done yet." Andre pulled black fishnet stockings out of a drawer. "Here, sit down. Now gather them up like so, okay, now stick out your leg and point your toe . . . pull them up . . . ."

Brian obeyed and stood to pull them up all the way. "Are they supposed to be so uncomfortable?"

Andre laughed. "You get used to them. Here, have a seat at this table."

Brian sat facing a mirror. Andre handed him a small, clear crystal bead hanging from a gold post. Brian exchanged it for his usual hoop with a smile. It sparkled and swayed when he moved. *I finally get to wear a pretty earring.*

Andre stood behind him. "I just love this hair." He ran his fingers through it and fluffed it up. "Don't need to do anything with that. How about if we put on just a touch of makeup?"

Brian shrugged. At this point makeup didn't sound so strange.

"We'll just highlight your features." He turned Brian around and picked up his tools. "A bit of dark eyeliner like so.... Look down. Just a touch of blue shadow to highlight those gorgeous eyes, mascara.... Look up. And a touch of rouge on those pouty lips. There. Now aren't you gorgeous!"

Andre took his hand and stood him up to look in the full-length mirror. Brian didn't recognize himself. "Wow," was all he could say. "I totally look like a girl." He wasn't sure how he felt about that.

Grant and River were perusing the leather pants when Brian emerged from the dressing room.

"Ta da!" Andre said.

Brian grinned, enjoying the attention and the look in Grant's eyes. He accentuated his natural grace as he strolled around.

"Bravo!" Grant moved closer. "Even better than I imagined. Let me look at you." Grant turned him around. "That black makes your skin look like porcelain."

Brian smiled up at him. "You like it?"

"Absolutely. You look absolutely perfect."

Brian beamed, then looked at River. River wasn't smiling. Brian walked over to him. "Do you hate it?"

River shook his head. "I thought I would. But it's real sexy." His eyes moved down.

Brian glanced at his stockinged feet. "I don't think my sneakers will go with this outfit."

Andre said, "Oh, sweetie, there's a *fabulous* shoe store right next door."

Grant said, "Why don't you boys walk over there while I finish up with Andre. I'll join you shortly."

Brian took River's arm as they walked out. Jeffrey got out of the limo parked in front of the shop. "Oh, my," he said, eyes bulging.

Brian walked up to him and stood close. "Do you like it?" His fingertip grazed Jeffrey's large chest.

"It's very nice, Mr. Brian."

"Shhh." He touched his finger to Jeffrey's lips, then stood on tiptoes to whisper, "I'm being River's girlfriend. Don't call me Mr. Brian." He laughed, then took River's arm and went into the shop next door.

Lots of fun shoes. River held up a pair of spike heels and wiggled his eyebrows.

"No way! Ooo, I like these." Black leather boots.

The clerk brought a few boxes out of the back. The second pair fit perfectly. Brian walked around and looked in the mirror. The boots hugged his calves almost to his knees. The two inch heels were chunky, so not too hard to walk in.

River picked out a few pairs, too—guy shoes. Brian smiled at the saleswoman while Grant paid. It was weird to know everyone thought he was a girl. Kind of fun to trick them all.

"Let's go see a movie or something," River said as they helped Jeffrey load up the car.

"Yeah," Brian agreed. "I don't feel like going home yet."

Grant smiled. "We'll see what's playing at the Century 14." He turned to Jeffrey. "Let's stop at the drugstore first. I need to pick up a prescription."

"Yessir, Mr. Grant."

There was a line at the prescription counter. Brian got bored and wandered over to the cosmetics, interested in them for the first time. He picked up a bottle of black nail polish. "I like this."

River followed him back to the chairs by the prescription counter, and they sat down—Brian's feet were getting tired from the heels. He held up the polish. "Will you paint my nails for me?"

River shrugged. "If you want me to."

He nodded, and River took the bottle.

A few minutes later River sat back to admire his handiwork. "Not too bad for my first time."

Brian blew on his black fingernails. "I like it. Thanks." He grinned and kissed River's cheek.

They got back in the limo and headed down Olympic Boulevard toward Century City. Brian stretched his legs out, smoothed the leather skirt and admired his black nails. "This makes me feel sexy."

"It is sexy," River agreed. "But I don't know why."

Grant said, "Brian appears to be a beautiful girl dressed in a provocative manner. However, that does not explain why I find it stimulating, since I do not find women to be so. I believe it's because we know he's a boy under there. No Adam's apple yet, but if you look closely, instead of breasts you see a bulge farther down, which I find highly exciting. I enjoy the juxtaposition of the feminine with the subtle yet obvious maleness." He smiled. "And of course, let's never underestimate the naughtiness factor."

River nodded. "Naughtiness factor. I like that."

Brian smiled and pulled out a cigarette; he immediately had two lights in front of him. He laughed and used both flames. "I could get used to this."

The next day Grant came to Brian's room. "Would you put on your new outfit again? Matthew would like to see it."

"Okay. Should I do the makeup, too?"

"Yes, let's try that." Grant helped him with the cosmetics. "Remember, less is better." When they finished he pressed the intercom button. "Matthew, could you please come to Brian's room?"

Matthew pulled away and Brian lay gasping, the silk shirt stuck to him with sweat. His eyes widened as he looked around the room. Grant was gone.

Brian threw on his jeans and hurried downstairs to find Grant in the parlor reading. Brian rushed to him and hugged him tight.

"Are you alright?" Grant asked. "I thought you and Matthew should have some time alone together. I'm sorry if I upset you."

I don't understand. I thought you were supposed to be a part of it. "It's okay."

A knock sounded at the door, and Brian sat up. Matthew lay beside him, spent. "Who is it?"

"River."

"Uh . . . just a minute!" Brian's heart sped. He pushed on Matthew and whispered, "You have to get up. It's River."

"So? He knows about me."

"But I don't want him to see us alone together. He'll be jealous." He felt sure of that, though he didn't understand it.

"Brian?" River's voice came through the door.

"Hold on a second." Brian pulled on his shirt.

Matthew dressed quickly. Brian tried to smooth the rumpled bed as Matthew opened the door.

"Oh," River said in surprise. "Hi."

"Hello, River." Matthew smiled and walked past him out the door.

River came into the bedroom, arms folded across his chest. "Gee, what were you two doing?" he asked sarcastically. "Without Grant?"

Brian avoided his gaze and reached into the nightstand drawer. "He just brought me something. Look." He pulled out a joint.

"Cool!"

They smoked half of it, then decided to go down to the stables. Brian headed to the stall of his favorite mare. "Hey, Glory, how are you?"

She nickered a greeting. He grinned and stroked her velvety muzzle. River handed him a brush, and they stood on either side of her. "I love grooming horses," Brian said. "Maybe even better than riding."

"Why?"

"I don't know. Maybe cos they like it so much." Glory's eyes closed halfway as the boys smoothed her brown coat with firm strokes. "And it makes them shiny."

Grant entered the stable and walked toward them through the corridor. "River, you might be interested to know John is back in town."

"Really?" He grinned and moved to the front of the stall. "When can I see him?"

"Now, if you like. He's waiting for you in the house."

River breathed a laugh. He tossed the brush down and climbed between the wood railings. "Shit, I smell like horse."

"I don't think he'll mind."

River's grin widened, and he raced off. Brian frowned and kept brushing Glory. Grant moved closer. "Are you alright?"

"Sure. It's just . . . ." *John's a bad person.*

Grant opened the gate and came into the stall. He squeezed Brian's shoulder and kissed the top of his head. "Why don't we go riding? Just the two of us."

Brian smiled up at him and nodded.

The next day River went off with John to go 'shopping,' supposedly. Grant came to Brian's room and said, "We've got the house to ourselves. Let's try something new."

Brian could tell he was talking about sex. He smiled and reached between the buttons of Grant's shirt to tug on the curly grey hair. "I can't wait," he said in a low voice. He stood on his toes to gently bite Grant's jaw.

Grant nuzzled into his hair. "Mmm, you are ready, aren't you?" He held Brian's hand to his mouth. His lips caressed the palm, then his wrist, traced the scar that cut across his skin.

Brian tingled all over. He couldn't wait to see what Grant had in mind. His surprises were always wonderful and exciting.

Grant pulled on his hand and led him out of the bedroom. They walked down the hall a few steps, past the painting of winter trees. Brian's breath caught as they turned down the short hallway that led to the Locked Room. Grant turned the knob.

It's not locked! He was disappointed by what lay behind the mysterious door. Just a large bed with an elaborate metal headboard that dominated the room. Not much other furniture, no windows. Recessed lights edged the ceiling with a soft, ambient glow. Grant adjusted the dimmer switch to make it a little brighter.

Brian admired the ornate medallion on the ceiling over the bed, then wandered around the room and noticed two other doors. He moved to the one at the far wall and opened it cautiously to find a bathroom with black and white tiles on the walls. He walked in to peer through the small window. It faced the front of the house, looking down onto the driveway. *Why was this room locked? It's just a bedroom.*

He went back to investigate the other door with a large full-length mirror beside it. A walk-in closet. The sharp scent of leather filled the small room. He pulled on the light cord and sucked in his breath. Black leather straps and silver studs. He'd never seen anything like these clothes. They scared him for some reason.

"Brian," Grant called.

He emerged from the closet. Grant walked over to him and stroked his face. "Those are just for fun; nothing to concern yourself with. Come over here."

Grant pulled him gently to the bed, sat on the edge and held Brian between his knees. He rubbed Brian's sides, stroked his buttocks through the denim, the back of his thighs.

Brian's tension ebbed away as he relaxed into Grant. Grant unfastened the jeans and pushed them down. Brian stepped out of them as Grant lifted off Brian's shirt.

"My beautiful boy," he breathed. "Here, sit down."

Grant kissed him. His hands roamed as he pushed Brian back, then reached up to fiddle with the headboard. "This is what I wanted to try." He held out cream-colored leather handcuffs.

Brian touched the supple leather, the inside lined with fleece. A chain with heavy links attached to the cuffs and connected to an opening in the headboard.

"This lever controls how long the chain is." Grant pulled the lever down, and the chain began to slide back into the wall. He put it in the middle position to stop it.

Grant nibbled Brian's neck and stroked his thigh. "Do you feel comfortable wearing these for me?" He held up the cuffs and ran the soft leather along Brian's arm.

Brian nodded. *Anything for you.* His heart skipped as Grant closed one of the cuffs around his wrist. "Wait!" he blurted out. "Just you and me, right?"

Grant smiled. "Just us, my love." He brushed his lips against Brian's mouth.

Brian couldn't wait to tell River they could have face-to-face sex.

River sat on the bed. "I don't get it."

Brian pulled River down on top of him. "I just put my legs up. Like this." He moved his legs up and wrapped them around River's back, pushed against him. "See?"

"Mmm...."

God, it was great. So intimate. They could kiss and stare into each other's eyes while River was inside him.

River lay on top of him as they caught their breath. He smoothed the damp hair from Brian's forehead and kissed it. Brian smiled. He felt so close to him, like they were one. *We complete each other.*

"I love you," River whispered.

ಜಜಜ

Brian gazed out the car window as the Mercedes entered the gate. Grant and Jeffrey chatted in the front seat about boring politics, and River dozed beside him. The buildings came into view as the car wound up the long driveway. The garage beside the Other Wing opened, and a shiny white BMW pulled out. Brian sat up. "What's that car doing here?"

"Oh, the servants live in the Other Wing." Grant waved his hand, dismissing the issue.

Brian's eyes narrowed. *Awfully expensive car for a servant....*

He sat at the piano, eyes half-closed. His fingers danced lightly over the keys without conscious thought, his mind wrapped in a fuzzy cloud, courtesy of the marijuana he smoked half an hour earlier. His fingers slowed as the piece came to end. He smiled to himself, slightly dazed.

"Brian," Grant said.

He jumped, startled he wasn't alone. He turned on the piano bench to look toward the doorway. An older man stood beside Grant. Skinny, with strands of grey hair combed over in a vain attempt to hide his bald head.

"I'd like you to meet a friend of mine," Grant said.

Brian stood for the introductions. Jean complimented him on his musical talent. *Nice accent,* Brian thought. *French.*

Maria entered with a tray of coffee.

"Brian, why don't you join us?" Grant said as he sat on the couch with Jean.

"Okay." He smiled, pleased to be included, and curled up on a nearby chair. He listened to the men and sipped coffee. He hoped the caffeine would counteract the effects of the pot. He wanted to follow the conversation about Grant's import business, since he was being included with the adults.

He was a bit lost as they discussed schedules and shipping, but he enjoyed the sound of Jean's voice. That lovely French accent and dry wit to go with it. Brian perked up as the topic moved to paintings and sculptures. He and Grant laughed at Jean's pointed observations on today's art scene.

"Oh—" Grant touched Jean's knee. "Have I shown you my new Cézanne?"

"No, you 'ave not. Please, I must see it right away."

The men stood and headed toward the stairs. "Come along, Brian."

Grant rested his hand on Jean's shoulder as they reached the second floor. *I bet they're lovers.* Brian smiled to himself and followed after them.

"Oh, here it is!" Jean clapped his hands together. "Lovely."

They stood before the painting of winter trees that hung in the hall near Brian's bedroom.

"Look how he uses shadow for contrast." Jean pointed. "And the blending of colors. Early 1880s, no?"

Grant nodded.

Brian smiled, glad someone who knew about art liked the painting, too. He hadn't realized it was so old.

"What else 'ave you been hiding from me?" Jean asked. "Show me more."

Grant laughed. "Alright. Come this way."

To Brian's surprise, Grant ushered them down the short hallway that branched off near the stairs. Brian followed, confused. He didn't remember any paintings in the Locked Room that wasn't locked anymore.

He glanced around as they stepped inside. His memory was correct. No paintings. Grant came up behind him and wrapped his arms around him, nibbled on his neck.

"Ah, Grant, my friend," Jean said. "I see where we are now."

Jean seemed suddenly nervous. Or excited. He paced a moment, then walked over to them and got down on his knees. He looked up at Brian's face and took his hand gently. "You're a good boy, aren't you?" The old man trembled slightly.

Brian reached out to stroke Jean's cheek. "Don't be nervous." He leaned forward and kissed his wrinkled forehead.

Jean laughed and patted Brian's hand. "Yes, definitely a good boy."

Jean came back the next day. The three of them soon ended up in the Room and Grant just watched again.

Whatever makes him happy. And anyway, he liked Jean. He was a bit old but kind and gentle. And that sexy voice. Brian closed his eyes and pretended it was a young, handsome Frenchman lying on top of him.

Brian checked himself in the large, long mirror that hung beside the closet in the Room; Grant had asked him to wear one of his sexy outfits. He smoothed the leather, and his eyes flicked to the closet. He knew why this room used to be locked. The weird leather clothes, the riding crop he'd seen when he looked in the closet a second time. He didn't understand what that was for.

He sat on the edge of the bed and swung his legs. The door finally opened. Grant entered, followed by a man Brian had never seen before. *Geez, how many lovers does Grant have?* Too bad none of them were attractive. But that was okay; he just used his imagination to pretend they were someone else.

When it was over he realized Grant had left them alone. But he'd ceased to be surprised by such things. He didn't understand, but that didn't matter.

The man dressed and left the room. Brian turned to get out of bed and saw a hundred dollar bill lying on the sheets. He picked up the money, his brow furrowed. *Did he drop it?*

He dressed quickly and found Grant in the parlor. His heart beat harder as he held up the money. "I found this on the bed."

Grant smiled. "Keep it. It's yours."

"No, it belongs to that man. He dropped it." *Tell me he dropped it.*

"He gave it to you as a sign of appreciation."

Brian looked at the money trembling in his hand, then back at Grant.

Grant rested his hands on Brian's shoulders and stared into his eyes. "You're a very special boy. People want to share in that." He caressed Brian's cheek. "So sometimes they pay for the privilege of sleeping with you."

His mind went blank. Grant's words floated around his head without landing.

Grant rubbed his arm. "Are you alright?"

Brian blinked and looked away. "I'm going to my room," he mumbled.

He walked slowly up the stairs in a daze, his eyes on the dark runner. *'They pay for the privilege of sleeping with you.' 'Pay to sleep with you.'* It finally sunk in. He gripped the banister as the world lurched beneath him. *They pay to have sex with me.* His breath grew rapid. He raced up the last few stairs to his room.

He stood at the French doors, arms folded tight across his chest. He thought he should feel something, but he was numb except for an undercurrent of panic. He didn't want his world here to end. *Does it really matter if they pay?* He looked up at the sky and thought of how much he loved Grant. That hadn't changed. His gaze fell as tears stung his eyes. *Maybe it doesn't have to matter.*

He wandered over to the bed and lay down, suddenly exhausted. But his eyes wouldn't close.

A knock sounded at the door. Brian blinked. He didn't know how long he'd been lying there, staring at the wall. He propped his head on his elbow. "Come in."

Grant entered and knelt on the floor before him, their eyes level. "Are you alright?"

He gave a small shrug and looked down.

"Brian." Grant touched his hand.

"I don't know," he said softly. He met Grant's gaze. "I don't know how I feel."

"Are you thinking about leaving?"

"No!" He sat up. The panic returned, and his voice trembled. "Do you want me to?"

"No, no." Grant squeezed his hand. "Of course not. I'd be devastated if you left me." Grant sat on the bed to gather him in his arms and held him close. "I love you," he whispered. "I don't want you to ever leave."

Me, neither. But he couldn't speak. He clutched Grant's shirt as sobs shook him. When the tears finally stopped, they lay back on the bed together. Brian's eyelids drooped.

He woke alone, rubbed his face and saw the crumpled hundred dollar bill on the floor where he dropped it. His chest tightened. *Grant, I love you.* He stared at the money a long moment, then picked it up and set it on his dresser.

He found Grant on the loveseat in his sitting room. Brian sat beside him and asked softly, "Does River know?"

"No. He hasn't had any clients yet. I'm not sure he's ready."

Brian looked up at him. "But you think I am?"

Grant smiled and brushed the hair out of his face. "I believe you are. What do you think?"

He didn't answer. He laid his head against Grant's chest and closed his eyes.

Brian sat staring into space with River beside him on the bed. "What's wrong?" River asked.

"Huh?" Brian jumped. His cigarette ashes fell onto the sheets. He brushed them off in disgust.

"You haven't moved in five minutes. Not even to smoke."

Brian stubbed out the cigarette and tried to think of what to say. "I'm just tired. I . . . haven't been feeling well."

"I'm sorry, babe." River kissed his cheek.

He felt like crying; he hated lying to River. But he couldn't tell the truth. River wasn't ready to hear it. And Brian wasn't ready to talk about it. *I need a distraction.* "Grant got his pictures developed." He reached into the nightstand to pull out a few photos. "I like this one." He showed River a picture of the two of them with Pluto at Disneyland. Seemed like such a long time ago. Made him a little sad.

"Yeah. This one's good, too." River held up a photo taken the day Brian got his leather skirt. "You totally look like a girl. A sexy girl. Can't see your bulge at all." He pushed his shoulder against Brian and grinned.

"You're sexy there, too." He smiled. "We look like such a normal couple."

They laughed. The photos fell to the floor as River lunged at him. Brian's arms went around him and held on tight.

ധധധ

Brian pulled the laces of the black leather half-vest and stared into his full-length mirror. Grant had given him a black outfit just like the white leather ensemble. But today Brian wore the miniskirt instead of pants. No stockings. No shoes. Nothing underneath. He'd painted his toenails black to match his fingers. He smoothed the skirt and frowned into the mirror. *I can do this.*

He let out a sigh and reached for a cigarette. But the lighter wouldn't work. "Damn it." He threw it across the room and used matches instead. He paced back and forth, kept checking the clock. Fifteen minutes before his first client. Or rather, the first client where he knew what was going on. That this man was paying for sex. That he, Brian O'Kelly, was being paid for sex.

He continued to pace, his fist pounding rhythmically on his leg. *A prostitute. If I go through with this, I'm a prostitute.* He looked up at the ceiling. *Or am I one already?*

He jumped at a knock on the door. "Yes?" He tried to sound calm.

Grant poked his head in. "May I come in?"

Brian nodded. He stopped pacing and folded his right arm across his chest, rested his other elbow on it to hold up his cigarette. It trembled in his fingers.

He looked up into Grant's eyes. He knew his emotions were displayed on his face loud and clear; he was never good at hiding them.

Grant's fingers brushed his cheek. "You'll do fine. I chose someone special for you. He'll make it easy." He caressed Brian's bare arms and whispered, "Do you want me to get you started?"

His heart beat hard in his chest. He glanced away and shook his head. "I . . . I think I want to be alone."

"Alright. He'll be waiting at the appointed time. Call me if you need anything. And don't worry; you'll be fine." Grant touched his face and kissed his forehead. "My sweet boy," he breathed. "I love you."

Grant turned and left him alone, staring at the pale face in the mirror. *Is it really me? Am I really doing this?* His gaze dropped to the cigarette, burned down to a stub. He took one last drag and crushed it in the ashtray, then popped a mint into his mouth. He went onto his balcony for fresh air, felt the warm breeze ruffle his hair. His eyes closed, and his mind went blank.

He stuck his head inside to check the clock. 2:57. He chewed the rest of the mint and made one last check in the mirror. Everything was in order.

He took a deep breath and reached for the doorknob.

*"I used to be a little boy
so old in my shoes
What I choose is my choice
What's a boy supposed to do?"*

- Smashing Pumpkins, *"Disarm"*

CHAPTER 11

Brian walked down the hall to the Room. His pulse beat in his throat as he pushed the door inward. A man leaned against the far wall. Brown hair with grey at the temples. Tailored suit. Like he belonged on Wall Street, or the cover of GQ.

Brian shut the door and leaned against it. The stranger smiled as he walked toward him. He spoke softly. "You're nervous."

Brian bit his lip and looked at the floor.

"It's alright." The man lifted Brian's chin, his hand warm and dry. "Grant wasn't exaggerating," he whispered. "So beautiful. So innocent." He caressed Brian's cheek.

The touch sent shivers through him. His breath caught, and he closed his eyes. The man ran his fingertips up Brian's arm, then leaned down to brush their lips together.

Brian's heart still pounded fiercely, but his body was coming alive. He clutched the lapels of the stranger's suit as their kiss deepened. The man's mouth moved to his throat, and he gripped Brian's ass through the leather. Brian's arms went around the man's neck. He breathed in the scent of expensive cologne mingled with underlying musk. Intoxicating. His mouth found the man's skin and tasted his scent.

Brian lay alone on the bed grinning. It had been so exciting, as if his nervousness increased his sensitivity. Even the fact that he never knew the man's name enhanced the erotic thrill. *'Never underestimate the naughtiness factor.'*

He breathed a laugh and glanced at the money on the bed beside him. "Grant knows best."

Grant unlocked the door off the main hallway downstairs and switched on the light. Brian frowned. It was nothing like the exotic place he and River had imagined. Just a rectangular room with no windows. A few chairs and a sofa lined the walls, magazines stacked neatly on tables. Nothing very interesting.

"This is the waiting area for your clients. Although sometimes they prefer to wait upstairs."

Brian nodded. *Like my first one.* He flushed at the memory.

"There's a restroom and shower through that door. That's really all there is to see here."

Brian laughed at River's comment about the smell of manure in Glory's stall.

"The stable hands need to get with it." River tossed the curry comb aside and smiled. "You must be feeling better."

"What?"

"You seem more yourself."

"Oh." Brian had forgotten about his lie. "Yeah, I'm fine now." *It's true—I feel great. I don't know why I thought it was a big deal.* He smiled at River over Glory's back.

Brian put down the newspaper at breakfast and glanced around. River had already gone out to the pool; he and Grant were alone. "Grant?"

"Hmm . . . ." His eyes didn't leave the business section. He sipped his coffee.

Brian bit his lip.

Grant glanced up and put aside the paper. "What is it, Brian?"

"How come . . . ." He took a deep breath. "How come some of my clients don't leave money? Don't they like me? Have they complained about me?"

"Oh, Brian. Of course they like you. They rave about you. Tipping is an individual choice. Some clients feel they've paid enough already, while others enjoy giving a tip directly to you. In no way does it indicate they don't like you if they don't tip you." He reached across the table to touch Brian's hand. "I've never received a complaint about you. They all love you."

He smiled in relief. "Really?"

"Really." Grant squeezed his hand.

Brian entered the Room clad in skintight black leather pants and vest. The client perched on the edge of the bed stood up.

Brian was taken aback for a moment, then grinned. *He must be in his twenties!* No need to use his imagination this time. The man's tousled light blond hair shone against tanned skin. He wore casual clothes, a tee shirt and loose pants. Totally different from the other clients. "You're so young," Brian said.

The man gave a nervous laugh. "So are you. My name's Brett." He took off his shirt.

Brian's gaze lingered over Brett's streamlined chest, then dropped to the baggy pants that hung below his waist. Brian walked around him. *Nice ass.* "You have a swimmer's build."

Brett turned to face him. "I surf a lot."

Brian moved closer and said in a low voice, "What else do you like to do?"

The man grasped Brian's bare waist and leaned down. Brett hesitated a moment; then their lips met and held.

Brian pulled away to taste the smooth, muscular chest. So nice to have someone young and in shape. His mouth toyed with the nipple as he unfastened Brett's pants and let them fall. He went down on his knees. Brett's cock was already hard. Brian kissed where his leg and body met, teased him a little before he took the shaft into his mouth. His fingers reached between Brett's shaking legs.

He tasted good, but Brian forced himself away—didn't want Brett to come just yet. They fell onto the bed together.

Brett fumbled with the leather pants in a frenzy. Brian helped peel them off. The man touched him everywhere, his belly, his legs, between them. Brett's hands shook as he rolled on a condom. Brian turned onto his stomach.

Brett stroked his buttocks, then pushed into him. Spread Brian's legs wide and thrust deeper. Brian's moans were muffled in the sheets, his breath restricted by the tight vest. Suddenly Brett stopped. He panted hard as he pulled out.

Brian turned over. "What's wrong?"

Brett's face was flushed. "I couldn't hold out."

Oh! "That's okay," he breathed. His stiff cock ached.

"You're just too perfect. So small and tight."

His warm fingers brushed Brian's body, cupped his balls. Brett bent to take him into his mouth. Brian groaned. It didn't take long.

They breathed hard as they lay beside each other. Brett untied the vest. "Let's take this off."

Brian helped him lift it over his head. Brett took him into his arms and held him close, then looked at the clock that hung on the wall across from the bed. "I've still got some time. Do you mind if we lay here till I'm ready again? I'll try to do better next time."

Brian smiled. "Sounds wonderful."

He filled with excitement as he zipped his skirt. Brett was back. Grant had explained he would have some repeat clients. Regulars. He was glad it wouldn't always be strangers. In fact, his third client had been Jean. Though technically Jean was really the first—he paid for that first visit. But Brian didn't think of it that way. He started count from when he knew what was going on.

He laughed and shook his head. Six months ago this would have been unthinkable. *Here I am counting clients. You just never know.* He popped a mint into his mouth and hurried down the hall to see the blond surfer again.

ಬಬಬ

Brian pulled his foot from the tangled sheets and reached for the stereo remote to turn up "Moonage Daydream." He and River passed a joint until the song ended. "You were right, that's great stoned."

River grunted and turned it down. "Grant keeps bringing in all these different men. He's doing that with you, too, isn't he?"

"Yeah," Brian answered slowly. *That's not a lie.* "How do you feel about it?"

"I don't know. It's weird, but . . . I guess I don't mind. I mean, it's kinda fun." He shrugged. "But it's weird to be with a stranger."

Brian didn't know what to say. He hated keeping things from River. *Grant will know when he's ready.*

"You okay?" River asked.

"Yeah, fine." He tossed his head and laughed. "I'm just really stoned."

River grinned and leaned over to kiss him.

Brian looked up from the piano, startled—no one ever interrupted in the middle of a piece. Grant squeezed his shoulder. "River just found out."

Brian sucked in his breath. He pushed back the piano bench and raced off. *Outside. He'll be outside.*

It didn't take long to find him. River leaned against the rail of their private wooden bridge and stared into the water. Brian stood beside him in silence.

River said softly, "I feel so stupid. It seems obvious now—all those different men. You already knew, didn't you?" It wasn't really a question.

He nodded, eyes downcast.

River sounded lost. "Why didn't you tell me?"

"I—" Brian met his eyes. "I didn't think you were ready to hear it. To know."

"How long have you been . . . you know . . . ."

"Just a couple of weeks."

"And it doesn't bother you?"

"No—but that's not what matters now." He touched River's arm. "How do *you* feel?"

River searched his eyes. "I don't know. It ain't exactly what I had in mind. 'Let's go to L.A. I'll protect you.'" River turned to stare down into the water. "What a fool."

Brian's hand reached for River and found rumpled sheets. He opened his eyes. River was sitting up in bed, staring into space as he brought a cigarette to his lips. Brian sat up to touch his shoulder.

River jumped a little, then turned to smile at him. "Good morning."

Brian's hand trailed down River's back. "What are you thinking about?"

"You." River met his eyes. "You're so young to be—" He looked away.

"River, stop worrying about me. I'm not your responsibility." He touched River's face, turned it toward him to look him in the eye. "I am *not* your responsibility. How do you feel about what's happening to *you*?"

River was silent a moment. "I still don't know."

"You need time to digest."

"It musta been hard for you not to talk about it."

He borrowed River's cigarette, leaned back against the pillows and took a long drag. "I guess. I didn't even make a real decision. Just, when the time came I went through with it." He smiled a little. "I think it's kinda fun."

River gave a short laugh and climbed on top of him. "Naughty boy."

. . .

The boys emerged simultaneously from their respective Sex Rooms. Brian walked up to him and looked into grey-green eyes. "Are you okay?"

River crooked a smile. "Yeah. I am." He sounded surprised.

He put his arms around River's neck. "I love you."

River held him tight. "Come on, let's eat." He entwined his fingers with Brian's, and they walked downstairs hand in hand.

Grant joined them as they sat at the table in the nook. "How are my boys this afternoon?"

"We're good." River smiled. "Real good."

Grant's smile broadened. "I'm glad."

Maria brought them homemade pizza. Brian picked up the newspaper and grimaced. "It's supposed to be almost ninety all week."

River said, "Good."

"But we never had winter." Brian gazed out the window at the green lawn. "I miss snow."

Grant's eyebrow went up. "Did someone say he misses snow? Hmm, where could we find that?" He stroked his chin. "Alaskan cruises start in mid-June. How would you like to be on the first one?"

"Oh, my god! Can we?" They grinned, eyes wide.

"We leave in two weeks."

Brian got up and ran around the table to hug Grant.

River gave out a whoop. "Watch out, world. Here I come!"

That night River was helping Brian decide what clothes to bring when Grant appeared in the doorway. Grant glanced at the Bauhaus tee shirt on the pile. "No tee shirts. They're too casual. Besides, it will be a bit chilly for that." He leaned against the desk. "We'll do plenty of shopping before we leave. But first I need to take care of a few details. Do either of you have an ID or passport?"

River nodded and ran off to find his ID.

Brian sat on the bed and swung his legs. "Why do we need passports to go to Alaska?"

"Because we'll board the ship in Vancouver."

River returned and handed over his ID.

Grant said, "You don't need passports for the cruise; you won't be listed on the ship's manifest. But you should have them for the flight to Canada." He paused to look at the ID in his hand and chuckled. "River, this is the worst fake ID I've ever seen."

River's face fell.

Grant smiled. "Don't worry. We'll get you set up in no time. I just need to know what names you'd like on your passports. Is this what you want to use, River? 'Reese Thompson'?"

"Yeah, if you think it's okay . . . ?"

"Oh, yes. It was smart of you to change your first name, since River is so unusual. Or is Reese your real name?"

"No, it's River."

Grant nodded. "What about a middle name?"

"I don't have one. Do I have to make one up?"

"Not if you don't want to. Brian, what about you?"

"Use the name Brian O'Dell." It felt weird to say it—the first time he'd used his fake surname. *Get used to it.* It was so close to O'Kelly, it shouldn't be too hard. "The kids at school used to tease me about my initials."

River laughed. "B. O."

He sighed. "I shouldn't have told you." He smiled and shook his head. "Oh, middle name. Maybe I shouldn't use Kieran."

"Kieran?" River asked.

"After my grandfather. But it's unusual. I probably shouldn't use it."

"Think of a name that don't mean anything to you."

"I don't know. Bob? Oh, no." He laughed. "Brian Bob."

River laughed, too. "Brian O'Brien."

Grant chuckled. "How about Michael?"

"Yeah, okay."

"It's settled then. Tomorrow we'll go shopping and get photos taken for your passports." Grant handed River his fake ID and kissed them both goodnight.

Brian went out to the balcony, River close behind, and leaned against the rail to stare up at the stars, brighter here than in the city below. "You know what that means, that we won't be listed on the ship's manifest? If, hypothetically, something happens and the ship goes down, no one would ever know we were on board. They'd never know what happened to us."

"We'd be a mystery. Vanished together without a trace." River stroked his back and kissed his shoulder. "Does that bother you?"

"I don't know." Brian searched the bright stars for an answer. "Yes."

༄༄༄

The boys followed Grant and John up the gangway and into the lobby of the *Emerald Seas*. Brian craned his neck to admire the stained glass ceiling two stories above. A waterfall spilled all the way down into a fountain on the ground level where a gold statue of a mermaid rose out of the water. Brian's ears perked up. He spotted a man in a tuxedo at a white Kawai grand piano.

So far this was nothing like the other ship he'd been on. His family took a three-day cruise when he was eight. He remembered the cramped, windowless cabin as the butler escorted them to the Penthouse Deck. *That's okay. I don't expect to spend a lot of time in the cabin.*

Grant said, "You and River will have your own room together. Mine is here, with Jeffrey in the next room. John will be directly across the hall. You two settle in before we leave port."

The butler opened their door. Brian stepped inside, and his mouth fell open. The spacious room had a couch and loveseat, its own bar and a kitchen. And best of all, a balcony. Brian gazed through the glass doors. "Wow."

"Where's the bed?" River asked.

The butler opened another door. "Right in here, sir."

Brian followed them in. The king-sized bed overlooked another set of glass doors that led to the same long balcony.

"Check this out."

Brian followed River's voice into the bathroom. A hot tub sat on a raised platform with a window that overlooked the sea. Brian shook his head slowly. "I had no idea they made ships like this. We don't even need to leave our room."

"Bein' rich is great, ain't it?"

Their clothes already hung neatly in the closet, thanks to the butler. Nothing left to do but relax. River discovered the bar was well stocked. He was about to pour drinks when they felt the ship's engines change pitch. The *Emerald Seas* was about to move out of port.

The boys found their way up to the deck to stand with the other passengers. Grant, John and Jeffrey joined them to gaze at the sunset and wave goodbye to Vancouver.

The next morning the boys lounged on their balcony—'veranda,' the butler called it. Brian wrapped the complimentary white terrycloth robe tighter and dug into his blueberry pancakes. Not blueberry topping, but blueberries cooked *into* the pancakes. Delicious. He warmed his hands on the coffee mug. "Let's do this every morning."

River nodded, but his eyes never left the scenery. Evergreens covered the nearby mountains. Two bald eagles soared overhead. He rested his feet on the rail with a smile.

They finally got dressed to explore the ship. And eat again—loads of scrumptious food was available at all times. They played ping pong in the enclosed court on the top deck. River beat him soundly, but it was fun.

Next they stopped in at the spa. Once the receptionist found out they were with Mr. Nesbit, the masseuse was suddenly available. They went into the sauna first to relax.

Brian eyed his naked body as River stood to pick up the ladle. His tanned skin glowed in the heat, glistening with sweat. Unfortunately, Brian was too hot to be horny. *What a waste.*

"I think this is what you're supposed to do." River spooned water onto the hot coals, and steam billowed out.

"Ugh." Brian held a towel up to his nose. "It's so hot I can barely breathe. How can people have sex in these things?"

"That must be BS." River leaned his head back against the wall. "This thing sucks the sex drive right outta you."

Brian stared at the clock. "Has it been long enough yet?"

"Six minutes. Yeah, sure."

They left the overwhelming heat behind and stepped into the cool shower together. Brian put his head under the stream. "God, this feels so good."

River laughed. "Maybe that's the point of the sauna. The relief when you get out."

They met in the dressing room after their massages. Brian leaned against the wall. "That was wonderful." He felt so relaxed he didn't want to move.

"Yeah. I never got a massage before. We should have one every day."

They went back to their room to nap, then joined Grant, Jeffrey and John in the Rose Court for teatime. The large room sat at the bow of the ship, with windows all the way around, almost 180 degrees. The view of tree-covered mountains and glistening water was spectacular. So were the scones and desserts. Brian leaned back with a contented sigh. "I could get used to this."

Grant smiled. "Go right ahead."

They walked out onto the deck after tea. The view had changed on this side of the ship. The mountain range was much farther away and clad in snow.

Grant pointed. "See where it looks like a smooth sheet? That's a glacier."

"Really? Wow," the boys exclaimed.

"Here." John handed his binoculars to River.

Grant said, "In a few days we won't need binoculars to see them so clearly." He put his arm around Brian's waist and gave him a squeeze.

The boys rested on their veranda, full from breakfast. Brian sipped coffee and read the ship's newsletter. "'The Misty Fjord National Monument is the southern gateway to the Inside Passage.' We're going there this morning on the way to Ketchikan." He skimmed the article. "Wow—it's over two million acres, with no roads into it; it's only accessible by plane or ship." He looked up. "Is this it?"

"Beats me. I'll ask Grant." River went inside and picked up the phone. He returned to say, "We'll be there in about ten minutes."

"Let's go up on deck to get a better view."

They made it to the deck just as the ship arrived. Pine-covered mountains enclosed the *Emerald Seas*. Miniature waterfalls ran down the rocky slopes. The ship floated in still water that reflected bits of snow and wispy clouds that clung to the mountainsides. Stillness. Silence.

"It's so peaceful." Brian pulled the sleeves of his sweater over his hands and leaned back as River wrapped his arms around him. A group of people stood against the rail and pointed down. The boys moved closer to see. "Look!" Three fins cruised near the ship, then the porpoises broke the water, their sleek bodies gleaming. They leaped and played as the passengers watched. Brian laughed in delight.

At Grant's suggestion they stopped in the ship's fine jewelry store. Jeffrey stood in the doorway while the four of them looked around the shop. "Oh." Brian gazed at a sapphire and diamond necklace beneath the glass countertop. "Sapphires are my favorite. I love that blue."

Grant smiled. "Why don't we take a look?"

Brian didn't see the point of looking at something he couldn't have, but the woman behind the counter unlocked the cabinet and positioned a mirror in front of him. Grant stepped behind him to place the choker around Brian's throat. It fit just right on the shortest link. Brian couldn't take his eyes from the large sapphires set off by clusters of small diamonds in between. Absolutely glorious.

Grant said, "The sapphires match your eyes, right down to the sparkle."

Brian tore his gaze from the choker to look at his face in the mirror. His eyes reflected the color.

Grant murmured in his ear, "It's lovely, so tight against your white throat." He straightened. "We'll take it."

Brian's mouth hung open. "Are you serious? But it's so—" He didn't know how much it cost. He couldn't imagine. Grant never even asked.

"Anything for you, my sweet." Grant squeezed his shoulder. "Why don't you show River before we wrap it up."

"Okay." Brian walked across the small shop in a daze to where River and John were looking at watches.

River turned, and his eyes popped. "Wow. That's gorgeous. *You're* gorgeous."

He gripped River's arm. "Grant's buying it for me."

River grinned. "Look what John's gettin me." A gold Rolex gleamed on his left wrist. "Waterproof."

"Wow."

"Yeah." River leaned closer. "I'm tellin you, man, we've hit the jackpot."

The boys stopped by John's suite on the way to dinner. John looked very dapper in his black tux. *But River looks better in his.*

John's eyes moved down Brian's body. "Don't you look lovely."

"Thank you." Brian gave his fake smile and hoped it appeared polite. *I do look good, though.* His new necklace matched the blue of his full-length silk dress, so he'd decided to do the 'girl thing' tonight. The low neckline cut tight across his chest, with delicate spaghetti straps. Long black satin gloves went past his elbows—the final touch. He felt very elegant as he took River's arm.

Jeffrey and Grant met them in the hall, and they made their way to the Captain's table for dinner. *I hope Nick's our wine waiter again.* Italian accent, dark skin, sparkly brown eyes. Brian was in deep lust. Nick was friendly with him, but Brian hadn't managed to attract the right kind of attention from him. *Maybe I stand a better chance as a girl.*

Nick did remark about the lovely new necklace. But he got an odd expression when he noticed the dress. He tried to cover it up, but Brian saw it. He sighed in frustration. *I need to corner him alone.*

. . .

Brian lifted his skirt and hurried along the corridor with a frown—he didn't want to miss the Cole Porter tribute. *Why do I have to get his stupid camera? He's the one who forgot it.* He stepped into John's suite and hurried to the bedroom to rummage through the nightstand.

The door clicked. He whirled, heart thumping, and saw John. "You scared me," Brian said. "I can't find the camera."

"Oh, really? I was sure it was there."

John stood beside him to glance into the open drawer, then pushed his body against him. Brian's eyes opened wide. Of course. He should've realized what John really wanted.

Brian shook his head and backed away. John gently took hold of his arm, pulled off his gloves and stroked the bare skin. Brian's breath sped up. But he didn't like John. Didn't like the way he looked or talked or smiled, or the way he felt when John touched him.

Brian pulled away and backed up again. "I'm sorry. I . . . I don't want to." He turned and walked toward the door.

John beat him to it and blocked the way. His ice blue eyes bored into Brian, intense and hungry. Brian's pulse hammered in his throat as he backed up. John advanced, slipped his arm around Brian's waist and held him tight. Brian could feel John's erection poke at him. He struggled, but the arm around him was like iron. Unmovable.

John's other hand brushed the bare skin of Brian's shoulder, pulled on a strap to reveal a nipple. John pinched it, then let go of him. Brian held still. He didn't know what to do.

John dropped to his knees and pulled the dress down farther. He reached beneath the skirt to slide his hands up the back of Brian's thighs. John grasped his bare buttocks and rubbed his face against Brian's chest. His rough cheek scraped the delicate skin. Brian's body was responding. He hated that. He hated John.

John yanked the dress down to his waist and in one swift motion picked him up as if he weighed nothing. He laid Brian on the bed with the dress bunched up around his waist. Brian inched away. He knew it was useless, but he couldn't help himself.

John watched a moment, then grabbed his bare leg. He pulled Brian down until his face was right below his crotch. John unzipped his pants to pull out his big cock. "You know you want it."

He cradled Brian's head with one hand and held his cock to his mouth with the other. Brian turned his face away. John laughed and forced his head back. Brian closed his eyes. *Get it over with.*

He relaxed his throat and managed not to gag.

John finally pulled away. He grabbed Brian's thighs and pushed them apart roughly. Brian's body tightened in fear.

But no, instead John brought his mouth to Brian's penis. Expertly worked him while his hands fondled everywhere. Brian squirmed. He fought it, but a long groan escaped his throat.

"That's right," John murmured as he reached for a condom and lube. "You know you like it."

Brian arched as John touched him in all the right spots. John sat up abruptly, pushed Brian's legs apart and thrust. Brian cried out as John penetrated him. Pleasure and pain. God, the mixture was overwhelming. John pinned his wrists over his head and pounded into him. Brian absolutely couldn't move. Oh, *god*. He felt dirty and disgusted and it *hurt* and—*god*—

Brian moaned deep in his throat as he came.

John walked over to the closet and took his camera off the shelf. Brian's eyes narrowed as he sat watching John from the bed. *Lying bastard.*

"Come on, Brian."

He didn't move. He felt slimy and disgusting and angry. The fact that he had an orgasm made it even worse. He felt like crying. But he didn't. He wouldn't, not in front of John.

John snapped a photo as Brian stared at him. He blinked, momentarily blinded by the flash.

"Brian, we're going back to the show now," he commanded. "Get up."

Brian obeyed.

"You've been quiet," River said as they undressed that night.

Brian shrugged. He avoided River's eyes and slipped under the covers.

River touched his arm. "What's wrong?"

He sat up. "I don't understand how you can like John." His voice quavered.

"Did something happen? You two were gone a long time getting his camera."

He toyed with the sheet and stared at his fingers. Sudden tears welled up.

"Brian! Did he hurt you?"

"No . . . not really." He whispered, "But I didn't want it."

River wrapped his arms around him, but Brian pushed him away to search River's eyes. "I want to know if you really like being with him. Tell me the truth."

"Yes. I do." He looked away. "He makes me helpless. I like that sometimes, to not be responsible for everything." He shrugged. "That sounds stupid."

"No, it doesn't." He touched River's leg.

River took him in his arms again. "I'm sorry he upset you."

Brian hugged him back. "It's okay."

The sun slanted across jumbled sheets and bare legs, young and old. Brian stared into space as he lay in Grant's arms, unable to relax.

"Is something troubling you?"

Brian sat up. "It's John." His heart sped at the memory. "He . . . had sex with me." He turned to look at Grant.

Grant's face betrayed no emotion. "And you enjoyed yourself?"

Brian glanced down. *Did I?* "I don't know if 'enjoy' is the right word. I mean, I—" He clenched his fist and looked at Grant again. "I don't like him. I don't want to do that with him again."

Grant frowned. "John is my business partner. You know that."

Brian's voice rose. "Are you saying I *have* to have sex with him?"

"You don't *have* to do anything. You always have the choice." Grant's eyes turned cold. "To stay or not."

Brian turned away quickly, grabbed his robe and headed for the door. *How can Grant be like this?* His hand shook as he reached for the doorknob.

"Brian, wait. I'm sorry. I'm angry with John, not you. I hope he didn't hurt you."

He stood still, his back to Grant, and shook his head.

Grant let out his breath. "I'll talk to him, alright?"

He glanced back at Grant and whispered, "Thank you," then hurried out so Grant wouldn't see the tears in his eyes.

פפפ

They stood in awe before Mendenhall Glacier. Brian was glad they'd driven straight here instead of exploring Juneau. He'd been dying to see a glacier close up. And here it was, with just a few pools of water between them. The size was difficult to comprehend; the ice sheet filled the gap between two pine-covered mountains. It was dirtier than he expected, with only a little white. The rest was brown or light turquoise.

He read the sign. "Look at this, River. 'Mendenhall Glacier is twelve miles long. It descends into the Mendenhall Valley from the 1500 mile Juneau Icefield.'"

"That's big."

Brian nodded, then shivered and wrapped his jacket tighter around him.

River smiled. "Cold enough for you?"

River put his arm around him as Jeffrey approached with a camera. Brian saw John out of the corner of his eye but ignored him. He refused to let John's presence ruin his time in Alaska with River. They grinned as Jeffrey snapped a photo, the glacier in the background.

The four of them sat in the Captain's quarters for pre-dinner drinks. Brian glanced around the room. The cabin was nice but no better than theirs. *I wish John weren't here.* Brian avoided eye contact with him. That wasn't hard—John ignored him completely.

Brian sipped his wine and tried to focus on the conversation. Stock devaluations and margins. *How boring can you get?* His gaze caught River's. Brian gave him a smile about sex and thought of what they did earlier in their hot tub. What they could be doing now if they weren't sitting here. He could tell River was thinking the same thing.

Their mutual fantasy was interrupted as everyone stood to go out to the veranda. The Captain held a pair of binoculars. The Inside Passage widened here; the snowy mountains were not so close to the ship as they had been this morning. Brian's ears perked up when he heard the word 'bears.'

"Ah, there they are." The Captain handed the binoculars to Grant and pointed.

"Lovely."

Grant passed the binoculars to Brian and slipped a hand around his waist as he helped locate the bears. Two dark blobs against the snow. Impossible to make out details even with binoculars, but he could see one was much larger than the other.

"A mother and cub," the Captain said.

"Wow," Brian breathed. Incredible to see them in their own habitat, undisturbed by humans. Something he'd never thought to see. He handed the binoculars to River and helped him find the bears.

Twenty minutes later they all headed out for dinner. Grant paused at the door to his suite. "Jeffrey, why don't you take the boys to the dining room? John and I will join you shortly."

Grant closed the door and gave John a cold stare. "What do you think you're doing? This trip is to cement the relationships, not push the boys away."

John raised his eyebrows.

"You will not touch Brian again until I say so."

John pursed his lips, eyes narrowed. He bowed. "Whatever you say, Mr. Nesbit."

"That's right. And don't you forget it."

The boys sat on a bench in Haines. River glanced around the small rustic town and lit a cigarette. "Man, I thought Sierra Blanca had nothin to do. Talk about the middle of nowhere."

"But look at the nature. The trees."

"I wouldn't wanna live here." River smiled. "But it's pretty cool. Never thought I'd see so many trees."

Brian rested his hand on River's leg and gave it a squeeze, then leaned up to kiss his cheek.

River took his hand. "Never thought I'd be in Alaska, either. Kissing you." He met Brian's lips.

They made it back to the ship in time for tea. Brian licked the jam off his finger as he finished his scone. "I love teatime."

River nodded, his mouth full.

Brian saw Nick the Luscious Wine Waiter serving tea on the other side of the Rose Court. "There he is."

River smiled. "Go for it, dude."

He made his move when Nick returned to the food bar. Brian walked over to lean back against the counter. "Hi."

Nick smiled his gorgeous smile. "Hello, Brian."

He remembers my name. Come on, you can do it. He moved closer and touched Nick's chest with his fingertip. "So, what are you doing after this?"

Nick gave him a funny look and hurried to refill his tray. "I have the first dinner shift."

"That's two hours away. Plenty of time . . . ." He leaned closer until their bodies almost touched.

Nick mumbled something and backed off, his tray still half-empty. Brian

frowned as Nick hurried away.
   He returned to his seat and plopped down.
   River said, "You scared him."
   He folded his arms over his chest. "I need a cigarette."

River held the ship's newsletter as they stood on deck before the glacier. "Hubbard Glacier is eighty miles long. *Eighty*."
   "Wow." It looked cleaner than the other glacier, the jagged ice light turquoise. Snow graced the slopes of the surrounding mountains. But the best thing was the seals. Striated ice floes dotted the water, with a seal on almost every one.
   "They're so cute." Brian leaned his elbows on the rail and gazed at the closest seal. "I wish I could pet them. I know, I know. But they look so squeezable."
   "They're fat."
   "You would be, too if you had to live in this climate. This is summer!"
   "No shit. It's fuckin freezing." River shivered and put his arm around Brian.

June 22nd

Dear Tanya, Mom and Dad,

   We're in Alaska! It's really amazing here. So different. The nature is stunning. And the wildlife—bald eagles, seals, porpoises; we even saw a mother bear and her cub. (Don't worry, they were far away.) Not to mention the glaciers. I didn't realize how much I miss trees until we came here. River says he's never seen so many trees.
   Hope you are all well. I'm doing great, though I do miss you. Take care.

Much love,
Brian

P.S. I'm in love!!! ♥ ♥ ♥

Brian frowned at the postcard in his hand. Maybe he shouldn't send it. *We'll be gone from Alaska by the time it's delivered, but still . . . .* "Damn." Depressing not to be able to share even this little bit with his family.
   He went to Grant's room to show him the postcard and ask if it was okay to send.
   Grant smiled and stroked his hair. "Certainly, my dear." He sat on the edge of the bed and set Brian on his lap. "You're safe with me; no one's going to get you. But of course you should still be careful. You're a good boy for checking with me." Grant kissed his cheek and murmured, "A good boy." His hand slipped beneath Brian's sweater.

. . .

Brian leaned against the pool's swim-up bar to sip his lemonade. River swam up beside him. "Man, I can't believe how much the weather's changed. It's so warm today."

"I know. I was actually hot this morning in Sitka. All those stairs."

"Great view, though."

Brian nodded. He waved when he saw Grant and Jeffrey enter the pool area, then frowned. John was right behind them. Of course.

Grant sat in a lounge chair beside the pool. "We found some marvelous pieces at the art auction."

"That's good." Brian glanced at John talking to River. *Ugh.*

He climbed out of the pool and grabbed a towel, dripping onto the deck as he headed to the shower. He rounded the corner and *boom*—collided right into Nick. Brian bounced back from the impact.

Nick reached for him. "I'm so sorry. Are you alright?"

Brian's blood rushed as Nick held onto his bare arms. Brian looked up at him and closed the gap between them. He plucked at Nick's white shirt. "I got you all wet. We'll have to fix that." He laid his palm against Nick's chest and reached between the buttons to touch the warm brown skin.

Nick's breath caught. He grabbed Brian's wrist and held it away.

"Relax. It's okay." His free hand felt Nick's crotch.

Nick grabbed that wrist, too. "Stop it."

Brian leaned closer and said in a low voice, "It'll feel good. I promise."

Nick let go of Brian's wrists and stepped back. "I do not do that with boys."

"How do you know you won't like it if you never try it?" Brian reached for him again.

Nick batted his hand away. "I don't care who you're with. I do not have to take this." He stalked off.

Brian stood with his mouth open. All along, Nick was only nice to him because of Grant. *It was all fake.*

"Is somethin wrong?" River slammed the ping pong ball over the net.

Brian didn't even try for it. He shrugged. "Nah."

"But you're playing worse than usual. I mean, you've been doin better till now."

Brian smiled a little and served the ball. "But you still always win."

"Yeah, well, I'm gettin better, too."

"I'll miss ping pong." The ship would dock in Vancouver soon.

River put down his paddle. "Brian, what is wrong?"

"It's the whole Nick thing. Not so much that he turned me down, but what he said."

"Guess that's the drawback to being rich. You don't know if people like you for who you are, or just for your money." He smiled. "But it's worth it."

Brian shrugged. "It doesn't matter. I've got you."

*"Did you feed us tales of deceit
Conceal the tongues for me to speak
subtle lies
and a soiled coin
the truth is sold
the deal is done*

*But don't despair
this day will be the damndest day
Oh, if you
take these things from me"*

- Portishead, "Cowboys"

CHAPTER 12

The boys lay back on Brian's bed with a sigh. It'd been a fun day off with no clients, but horseback riding was tiring. Miles of trails twisted through the forest behind Grant's property. *I wish he would let us ride alone. But I guess it could be dangerous. If anything ever happened to River, he would be very grateful someone was there to help.* Brian shook his head and cut off the train of thought.

At least Thomas had hung back and given them space. Especially when they stopped by the brook for lunch and made love. Brian smiled at the memory. It was great doing it outside, especially in some wild place he'd never been before.

He was about to go brush his teeth when Grant came into the bedroom with papers in his hand. "It will be easier if we write out your schedules like this," Grant said and gave a piece of paper to each of them. "What do you think?"

Brian read Grant's neat script. *'July 1st. Mr. Donaldson, 1 – 2 p.m. Brett, 6 – 9 p.m.'* A long session with Brett the surfer. Exciting. Brian folded the paper. He liked having it in writing. It would help him remember their names; sometimes they liked that. "This is good."

Grant smiled. "In the future I'll slip the schedules under your door so you'll have them first thing in the morning, unless you have an early client. Is that alright?"

They nodded.

"Goodnight then, my sweet boys. Sleep well."

Brian lay alone in the Room, exhausted. He finally moved his weak limbs to put away the handcuffs. He would've been nervous to let just any client use them, but not Brett.

He picked up the five hundred dollar bill with a smile and shook his head. *I would've done that for free.*

Naked in the Rain

ധധധ

Grant stood in the doorway. "Brian, River, get dressed. It's time to meet some important people."

They followed Grant out back. Brian noticed a line of people standing behind the Other Wing. He shielded his eyes against the sun and squinted. They looked short.

Grant squatted down in front of River and Brian and took their hands. "When I told you servants live in the Wing, that was true. But other people live there, too. Other boys."

Brian frowned and glanced at the distant line.

Grant said, "I take care of those boys, and they have clients, too. But don't worry, you're both still my special boys. You'll continue to live with me in the Main House. But I think it's time for you to meet the others."

Brian avoided his gaze.

"Are you alright?"

"I guess," Brian mumbled.

River gave a half shrug. "Whatever."

Grant winced as he stood and rubbed his knees with a little laugh. "I'm getting too old for this. Come along now." Grant put his arms around their shoulders and walked them over to the Other Wing.

About twenty boys stood quietly. Well dressed and neat. Disciplined. They didn't even turn their heads to look. The boys ranged in age from ten to seventeen or so.

Brian's eyes widened as he recognized the sandy-haired adult at the head of the line. Matthew. Brian flashed back to the beginning of it all, when he'd stared in shock at the stranger in his bedroom. It had seemed so odd to let him watch. *Now look at me.*

"Boys, you've already met Matthew. He takes care of the Wing so I can focus on other things. Like my special boys." Grant squeezed their shoulders.

Matthew smiled. "Nice to see you again."

They started down the line and stopped before the first boy. One of the older teens, tall, with brown hair and pretty green eyes. They focused on Brian and suddenly weren't so pretty anymore. The boy's lips smiled, but his eyes were like ice.

Grant said, "This is Trevor."

"Trevor?" Brian turned his head to look at Grant.

Grant leaned down to whisper, "I don't have a grandson. Surely you've realized that by now." He smiled and straightened. "I'm afraid Trevor may be a bit jealous. You've taken over his spot, Brian."

Trevor laughed, a bitter sound. "Not at all. You're both welcome here." His eyes flashed.

Brian was grateful to move on. He couldn't remember all the names; the faces blurred in his mind. Toby, Steven, Larry, Clint, David—David? Brian stifled a gasp. He stared into those sweet brown eyes and felt betrayed. Had *every*one lied to him? He continued down the line in a daze, guided by Grant's hand on his back until it was finally over.

The boys wandered around, released from the line. Most of them headed toward refreshments laid out on a white tablecloth. They laughed and chatted among themselves like regular kids. Brian stood in silence.

River touched his arm. "You okay?"

Brian looked down. "I guess I shouldn't be surprised. But . . . ." He shook his head, then spotted David alone under a shady tree. "I'll be right back."

"Okay. I'll get us some drinks."

Brian passed a cluster of boys but hardly noticed them. Until someone grabbed his arm. He whirled to look up at Trevor's face, lips drawn in a straight line, his grip tight on Brian's arm.

"Look, you little bastard. Don't bother trying to talk to anyone here. We all hate you. So fuck off." Trevor let go abruptly and turned his back.

The boys in his group laughed and turned away. Brian stared at their backs a moment. He shook with anger and hurt as he turned toward the lone boy under the tree.

He stepped into the cool shade, his face flushed. "David. You lied to me." He struggled to keep his voice level. "How could you all do that?"

David seemed offended. "What was I supposed to say? 'Look, I'm a prostitute, but we're not allowed to talk until you're one, too'?"

Brian felt like he'd been slapped. No one had used that word with him before. "Everyone here hates me. And I hate you, too!" He turned and walked back to the Main House, his fists clenched at his sides.

The next morning he leaned against his balcony rail as his gaze wandered over the grounds, full of boys enjoying the sun. He spotted David and felt guilty. He'd been upset and, he knew, unfair. He turned and hurried out.

He found David near the brook and called his name. Brian ran over, then shoved his hands in his jeans pockets and glanced away. "I'm sorry about what I said yesterday. I was upset and . . . I took it out on you." He met David's eyes. "I don't hate you. I'm sorry."

David smiled. "That's okay. It must be hard for you right now. Matthew says you're in an adjustment period."

"Oh. I guess that's true." He wasn't used to the idea that Matthew was in charge of the other boys. Wasn't used to any of this. He stared at the ground and felt numb.

"Come on." He pulled on Brian's arm. "I wanna show you something."

They walked along the path, and Brian thought about their earlier conversations. "You said you were new before. How long have you been here?"

"About six months. I came a week after you."

"How . . . how did you end up here? I don't want to pry, but I don't understand."

"I came here from another House." David grinned. "I was real happy about that."

"So you've been doing this awhile?"

"Yeah, about two years." David cocked his head and looked at him. "If you want to talk, I'm here."

"Thanks." They walked in silence a few minutes, then Brian said, "How, um...."

"Go ahead. Ask me whatever you want. I don't mind."

"Well, I'm wondering, uh, how you got to be... in this business."

David seemed eager to share. "Me and my mom ended up on the streets when I was eight. We slept at a shelter at night sometimes—when it wasn't full—and panhandled all day. On Hollywood Boulevard, mostly. Lots of tourists there, ya know.

"Sometimes Mom left me alone to beg. One day a rich-looking man came up and offered me fifty bucks to come with him for a few minutes. Fifty dollars! That was a fortune to me, you know?"

Brian nodded.

"So of course I went with him. That was my first sexual experience. It was okay. He didn't hurt me or nothin. I didn't tell my mom where I got the money, and she never asked. I guess she didn't want to know. That man came back a few times. Mom always took the money I made, no questions asked. It would be gone pretty quick. I didn't realize it then, but I guess she was buying drugs with it. Sure wasn't buying food." He frowned.

"One day the man offered her money to take me home. He said he could provide for me better than her. She started crying and didn't answer. He kept offering her more and more money, then said he'd come back the next day after she had time to think about it. That night she asked how I felt. Well, the man was always nice to me, and I was hungry."

David stopped walking and hugged his arms to his chest. "I said I wouldn't mind going with him. I didn't know that meant I would never see her again." His voice trembled, and tears welled up.

Brian held him while he cried. After a moment David pulled away and wiped his face. "Sorry. I didn't mean to do that."

Brian didn't know what to say.

David sniffled and walked on. "So, anyways, that man ran a House like this. Well, sorta like this. Not as nice. He traded me to another Provider after about a year. That place was pretty good. But Grant's is the best. It was a real honor to move here. This is the Number One House in L.A. The very top. It's unusual to start out here. You're lucky."

Brian's mouth opened, but nothing came out. He nodded instead.

David's face brightened. "Here we are. Look." He pointed.

Brian peered into the tall bush and saw a nest partly hidden in the foliage. Tiny beaks stuck out the top. "Wow," he breathed.

David grinned. "I knew you'd like it. Nobody else cares."

The boys stood quietly and listened to the baby birds' high-pitched squeaks. David pulled on his arm. "Come over here. If we sit real quiet the mother might come."

They sat on the ground a few feet away and waited in silence for the mother bird to feed her babies.

. . .

Brian stood waiting in the Room. He wandered into the bathroom and ran his fingers along the cool black and white tile wall, then went to the window to look down onto the driveway. The familiar mixture of excitement, nerves and a slight dread filled him as he waited for his new client.

A white BMW pulled up in front of the Main House. His heart picked up as a man emerged and passed out of sight beneath the window. A security guard moved the car into the garage. *That car.* Brian's lips tightened as he remembered the blasé wave of Grant's hand. '*Oh, the servants live there.*' Yeah, right.

River shook his head in frustration. He'd searched for Brian everywhere. No one had seen him outside, and he didn't answer the intercom. "Oh, I know."

River took the stairs two at a time up to the third floor, pushed on the heavy door and stepped into the ballroom. The sun cast pools of light through the high windows onto the patterned wood floor. Brian stood in the middle of the room, his head cocked to one side as he stared at nothing. He looked so forlorn; River was reminded of the desolate boy he met at the institute. "Brian?"

He jumped and looked at River with dazed eyes. "Oh, hi."

"What are you doing up here?"

"Nothing." Brian shrugged. "I just wanted to be alone."

"Oh." River turned to leave.

"No, wait." He reached out to grab River's arm. "Don't go." He laid his cheek against River's chest, the shirt clutched in his fist.

River held him and kissed the top of his head. "Are you okay?"

"I don't know. It's all so much." He pulled back to search River's eyes. "Grant lied to us."

"Only as much as he had to."

Brian let out his breath. "That's true. But doesn't it bother you?"

"No. What we do seems more normal now, cos there's a bunch of boys next door doing the same thing. It's kind of a relief."

"I never thought of it that way." He smiled a little and touched River's lips with his finger. "You always make me feel better when no one else can." He leaned up to kiss him, and his smile broadened. "I must be getting taller. I don't have to stand so far on my toes to kiss you now."

River arched a brow. "Maybe. But I'm growin, too."

"It's been almost a year since I was measured. Mom always did it before the new school year." His smile faltered.

River squeezed his waist. "I'm sure Maria's got a tape measure. I'll be right back." He raced off to find Maria and returned a few minutes later out of breath, tape measure and pencil in hand.

Brian looked up from where he knelt by a box against the wall. He grinned at River. "Look what I found." He gestured to an old Victorian couch, the sheets that had covered it in a heap on the floor. Delicate roses decorated the tapestry, the pink still vivid against a light background.

Brian tapped the cardboard box. "And look here. Old records. Check out the phonograph." He pointed to an ancient piece of machinery. "I wonder if it still works?" He pulled out a record with a bright purple cover and a woman's face in the center, her dark complexion set off against blond hair. "'Etta James, *At Last!*'" He stood to crank the arm of the phonograph, and the record spun. He set the needle down carefully.

It crackled; then the sound of strings emerged. A woman's throaty voice cried out and sang about the blues.

Brian grinned and threw his arms around River's neck. They moved slowly to the music and their lips touched, languid kisses. "Come on." He tugged on River's hand. "Let's measure."

They found an out-of-the-way spot and marked their heights on the wall. River wrote their names and the date next to the lines in pencil. "You're never gonna catch up with me," he teased.

Brian pinched his ass in response.

"Hey!"

River tried to do the same, but Brian kept turning away. They laughed as River chased him around the large, empty room. River held up the tape measure. "Your legs ain't the only thing that's been growin. I'm gonna measure you someplace else."

"River!" Color rose in his cheeks as the music ended. "Wait a second," he said breathlessly. He turned the record over, then squinted at the tiny print and laughed. "This song is called, 'I Just Want to Make Love to You.'" He cranked the arm again.

River crept up behind him and got him good. Brian jumped. "Hey! That's cheating." He slapped River's chest playfully, then grabbed his shirt and yanked it toward him. Their lips met as the voice on the record sang out.

River bent to scoop him up. Brian laughed and clung to his neck. River carried him easily to the Victorian couch and laid him down, kissed him deep and long. Brian stroked his hair as River's lips worked their way down his body.

Brian answered the summons. Grant was in his bedroom at the roll top desk. He looked up from his paperwork. "You've been avoiding me, Brian."

He stared at the carpet.

Grant walked over to him and gently lifted his chin. "Talk to me."

Brian searched his eyes. "I know you did what you had to, but . . . you lied to me."

"I'm sorry." Grant held him close, then led him to the bed. He sat on the edge with Brian between his legs and looked into his eyes. "Ultimately, what really matters is that you're happy here with me. Tell me the truth, Brian. Are you happy?"

He searched inside himself and couldn't deny it. "Yes. I am."

Grant smiled and rubbed Brian's arms. "I'm so glad."

Then what's the point of being upset? It was such a relief to let go of the hurt. Just let it go. He smiled and put his hands around Grant's neck. "I've grown two inches since last September."

"Really?" He reached under Brian's shirt with warm fingers.

Brian admired his new top in the mirror. He'd bought it especially for today: Grant's birthday. Or maybe not. David said nobody knew the exact date, just that Grant always celebrated his birthday with a special party during the first week of August. A private affair, just Grant's boys and a few handpicked guests. Brian was looking forward to it. *I don't know why. Hanging around a bunch of boys who hate me.* But it was Grant's day, and Brian wanted to make it special.

He straightened the collar of the black crocheted top, then held his arms out to his sides. The ends of the bell sleeves widened and hung down like a Renaissance shirt. He smiled and fastened the two middle buttons, then tied up the bottom the way Andre had. His pale skin showed through the crochet like misshapen white polka dots.

He zipped the black leather miniskirt, then picked up an earring from his dresser. Tiny diamonds sparkled in the gold filigree setting, reminded him of the old fashioned earrings he gave his mother for Christmas. Her face flashed through his mind, smiling and happy, and he fumbled as he reached for the sapphire necklace. He lit a cigarette instead and gazed through the glass doors as the sun disappeared behind the wooded hill.

He planted Grant firmly in his mind and fastened the choker around his neck, then sat to pull on his boots. They were new, too. Black suede with chunky heels. The supple leather hugged his calves to just above the knee. He swung his legs. Comfortable.

He stood before the mirror to inspect the end result. Stark black and white contrast, his bare thighs and stomach the focal points. "Oh, I almost forgot." He opened the dresser drawer and pulled out the final piece—a light blue garter belt. He stepped his left boot into it and pulled it up so the short skirt barely covered it. "There. Now I'm ready."

He wandered onto his balcony and leaned against the rail. The sky glowed a fierce purple where the sun had been. He watched servants light torches and lanterns in the main courtyard below. They'd spent all afternoon setting up—he felt sorry for them in the August heat, but now the air was cooling. White linen-covered round tables dotted the courtyard, and long tables brimmed with food.

The piano from the parlor had been brought outside for the event, and a man just finished tuning it. The stranger made his way through the courtyard quickly filling with boys. Brian watched him pass beneath the balcony on his way out. *Not bad.*

"Brian?"

He turned toward the sound of River's voice and stepped into the cool air conditioning.

River shook his head. "Damn, you're gorgeous."

Brian grinned. "Thanks. So are you." River wore brown leather pants and a pirate shirt.

Grant awaited them at the bottom of the stairs. Brian gave him a kiss on the cheek, then hooked his arm in Grant's. River took the other side, and they walked down the hall together and out the French doors.

. . .

Naked in the Rain

Brian leaned against River as they stood listening to Grant play the piano. Brian admired his elegant, easy style. The crowd applauded when the piece came to a close. Grant stood to take a bow, and someone in the audience caught his eye. Brian followed his gaze and saw John had finally arrived with a few of his boys.

Grant moved through the crowd toward Brian, and River slipped away to greet John. Brian watched them embrace. John kissed him a long time. Deep kisses. Brian frowned.

"Come along, Brian. It's your turn now." Grant led him over to the piano. "Dazzle them."

Brian sat on the bench and forgot everything else as his fingers touched the keys.

The string quartet began playing as David made his way over. "Wow, you're great on the piano. Way better than anyone else."

"Thanks."

"You look real nice, too. *Real* nice. I've never seen you all dressed up, ya know, in work clothes."

"Me, neither." It was strange to see David in sexy clothes. *He's too young.* Brian shook his head. *Don't be silly. He's been doing this for years.* He caught Trevor's glare from across the courtyard. "Why does he hate me so much?"

"Oh, don't worry about Trevor. He'd never actually do anything against you. Nobody would dare cross Grant."

Brian grimaced. "No, he'll just make sure all the other boys hate me."

"I don't hate you."

He smiled. "I know. I'm glad."

A waiter walked by with a tray of drinks. Brian grabbed two and handed one to David. They sipped the cranberry-colored liquid. It had a definite kick.

David made a face and set his glass on the table beside them. "The other boys aren't so bad. It's just easy for them to follow Trevor. Plus . . . ."

"What?"

"Well, none of us was allowed outside because of you. We couldn't use the grounds the whole time you've been here, up till you met us all a few weeks ago. Except when you went on that cruise. And sometimes when you went out, we got to use our pool for a little while."

"That's awful. I didn't realize." Brian bit his lip and glanced at the other boys. He felt terribly guilty. "I'm sorry."

"It's not your fault. That's the way it is when Grant trains a newbie. It's a small price to pay. They should be grateful to be at the Number One House."

"A newbie?"

"Yeah, you know, someone new to the business, who's in training but doesn't know it. Wouldn't wanna spoil it. That would be *big* trouble. That's why I kinda freaked when we first met. Thanks for not telling anybody."

Brian smiled. "You're my little secret. I didn't even tell River." He was surprised when he thought about it. "So don't let him know, or he'll be pissed I kept something from him."

"Everybody says you two are in love. Is that true?"

Brian smiled. He scanned the crowd and spotted River talking to the boys who came with John. "Yes, it's true." He breathed a laugh. "Does everyone know my business?"

"Boys talk. And all the clients are super excited about you. I mean, they're always excited when a new boy comes to a House. But a complete newbie *really* turns them on. Matthew says it's the 'innocence factor,' whatever that means." David shrugged. "But you're a newbie starting off as Grant's Number One. Matthew says that's almost . . . what was the word? Unpr- . . . unpresidented."

"Unprecedented?"

"Yeah. Trevor's just mad cos you knocked him off his seat at the top. You're the Number One boy in the Number One House. The top boy in all of L.A." He grinned. "The clients are super excited."

Brian's mouth went dry. "But I—I'm inexperienced."

"That's okay. Everyone says you're great. Grant knows what he's doing, putting you on top."

Grant does know what he's doing. But do I know what I'm doing? He finished his drink in one gulp and felt a little dizzy. Like he was in way over his head.

David held out his glass. "Want mine?"

Brian's loose sleeve slid back as he reached for it.

"Whoa." David's eyes got big. "What is that?" He grabbed Brian's wrist and turned it up toward the torchlight. "Wow. Gross, but kinda neat, too."

"Look, they match." He held up his other wrist and wavered as the alcohol hit.

"Is that—did you . . . ?" David looked at him with round eyes.

Brian gave him a half smile that turned into a grimace. He shrugged and pulled away. "Yeah," he whispered and stared at the ground. He felt stupid when he thought about what David's life had been. *But his pain doesn't negate mine.*

David touched his arm. "You must have been real unhappy."

Brian met his eyes, relieved to find understanding instead of accusation. He cleared his throat. "What happened to that drink?"

David handed him the glass. "Uh-oh."

Brian followed his gaze. Trevor. He walked up close and glowered down. "You think you're so great, showing off like that." Trevor nodded toward the piano. "But you'll come down someday." His finger poked Brian's chest. "The clients are just excited cos you're new. But you won't be Number One forever. One day they'll get tired of you. And *so will Grant.*" He spit out the words like venom and stalked away.

Brian swallowed his anger and a swirl of other emotions and turned to walk away into the trees. David followed, and they paid a visit to the bird nest. It was empty now.

They headed back to the courtyard. A boy ran up to them as they stepped onto the cement. "Grant wants you."

Grant sat at the far end near one of the smaller fountains. Pillared candles dotted the area and reflected on the shimmering water. Magical. Until he realized the boy perched on Grant's lap was Trevor. Brian stopped in his tracks. Grant waved him over. No going back now.

Trevor glanced at him from his seat on Grant's left thigh. The green velvet crop-top matched his eyes. *Too bad he's such an ass.*

Naked in the Rain

"Brian." Grant patted his other leg. "Hop on board."

Brian sat and did his best to ignore Trevor's proximity.

Grant turned his head toward John, who stood nearby. "Isn't this the life? Surrounded by beautiful, willing boys." He laughed.

Brian stared at him. He seemed a little off. Grant leaned to whisper loudly in Trevor's ear. Brian heard him say, "Trevor, darling, you know I still love you."

Grant's drunk. He'd never seen him like this before. *Well, if he can't cut loose on his birthday, when can he?*

Grant's arm went around Brian to pull him closer. The suede boots covering his knees rubbed against Trevor's leather pants. The candlelight glinted in Trevor's eyes as they stared at each other. Grant kissed Trevor's cheek and slipped his hand down the back of his pants. Trevor gave Brian a wicked smile.

Grant's touch on Brian's bare leg distracted him from the hateful gaze. Grant leaned closer to kiss his neck. His warm hand slid up Brian's thigh and tugged on the garter. The rough material scraped against his skin, and Grant's teeth clamped onto his neck. His hand moved further, gently squeezed the inner thigh, and a soft moan escaped Brian's lips. Grant's fingers were so close, so close. Brian clutched his arm.

Grant pulled away, and Brian opened his eyes. Trevor was kissing Grant's neck, his hand inside his shirt. Grant took a deep breath. "Alright boys, up. Time to go inside."

Justin, the cute party photographer, stopped them on their way. The three of them posed, then went into the house. When they reached the stairs, Grant said, "You boys go on. I'll be up in a moment." He patted their butts and sent them on their way.

They mounted the stairs in silence and walked through to Grant's dark bedroom. Brian tried to exude confidence as Trevor switched on the light. Their eyes caught, and Trevor took a step toward him. Brian intended to stand his ground, but his feet moved backward on their own. Trevor grinned.

Grant walked in with a silver tray. He hummed as he set it on the side table and poured wine into three pewter goblets. He handed one to Brian, then turned toward Trevor.

Brian knew he wouldn't have much time. He tilted his head back to down it all at once. If he was getting into bed with Trevor, he needed as much wine as possible. He wiped his mouth with the back of his hand as Grant turned to him.

Grant laughed when he saw the empty cup. "I guess you don't want to waste any time." He took the goblet from Brian's hand and moved closer, pushed his body against him gently. Back, back.

Brian sat when he felt the bed against his legs. He leaned back and looked up at Grant.

Grant brushed his cheek. "You look so incredible tonight. So beautiful."

Brian held Grant's fingers to his lips.

Grant closed his eyes. "Trevor. Come to bed."

Brian met his gaze over Grant's shoulder; then Trevor sat beside him on the edge of the bed. Grant backed off. "Now touch each other."

Brian avoided Trevor's eyes and reached out to rest his hand on his thigh.

Trevor pinched his arm hard.

"Ow."

Trevor grasped the back of Brian's neck and kissed him hard. Like he would devour him. Conquer him. Brian's body melted, and Trevor pushed him back against the bed. Trevor looked over his shoulder, and Brian felt a tug on his boots. Grant stroked his calf. He had stripped and was evidently enjoying the show.

He joined them on the bed, and the boys were all over him. Grant stroked and kissed and fondled. Brian's shirt hung open, but Trevor's clothes were off completely. Brian admired his body. Long, lean legs; stiff cock. Man-sized and dark with blood.

Brian reached across Grant to stroke Trevor's hip. Mmm, he wanted that cock. He didn't care who it was attached to. He lay across Grant's lap and grasped Trevor's ass to pull him closer. Gently tasted.

All three of them moaned.

An hour later they lay catching their breath, then Grant got up to go into the next room. Brian closed his eyes and stretched, content to lie here in this warm bed. He started to drift off when he felt a tickle in his ear. A breath.

Trevor pinched Brian's nipple and whispered, "By the way, I still hate you."

He jerked away and sat up. "That's good. Because I hate you, too." They exchanged cold smiles.

Grant returned with a wooden box. "I thought we could use a little wake up."

Brian leaned forward, eager. Grant smoothed Brian's hair, then lifted the lid to pull out the smaller silver box of cocaine.

The three of them went downstairs to rejoin the party, box in tow. Everyone cheered as they entered the courtyard and sang "Happy Birthday." Brian and Trevor escorted Grant to a huge, multi-tiered cake. Candles covered every inch, their light so bright it dazzled Brian's eyes.

Grant chuckled at the multitude of candles. "I'm not *that* old. Boys, help me blow these out."

Brian finally got River alone and handed him a drink. "Are you having fun?"

"Yeah. Kelsey and Rick are cool."

"Who?"

"Two of the boys who came here with John. It's nice to have someone my age to talk to."

"Oh." Brian looked down and tried to keep the hurt out of his face.

River brushed his fingertips along Brian's cheek. "I didn't mean it like that. I wasn't comparing them to you—no one compares to you. I just meant it's nice to have other people to talk to."

Brian nodded. "I know what you mean."

"I saw you talking to a boy earlier."

"David. He's sweet. The only nice one of the bunch. Want to meet him?"

"Sure. So how did it go in there with that jackass?" River nodded toward the house.

He shrugged. "It was okay, actually. Once we got started it didn't matter. You know how it is."

"He's telling everybody he showed you how it's done."

Brian rolled his eyes and laughed. "Whatever."

Brian woke slowly, confused about where he was. The afternoon sun was just beginning to break through French doors. He glanced around. *Oh, Grant's bed. How did I get here?* He craned his neck. River lay sound asleep on the other side of Grant. Brian grimaced.

Grant whispered, "Are you alright?"

Brian nodded and rubbed his stomach. "Just a little queasy."

"Did you have fun last night?"

He grinned. "Yeah. What I remember." Brian kissed his cheek. "Happy birthday. I love you, Grant."

೧೧೧

Brian lay alone in his empty bed. River had gone to spend the weekend at John's. *I hope he's having fun.* He sighed and glanced at the clock. Two in the morning and still wide awake. *I give up trying to sleep alone.*

He wrapped River's bathrobe around himself. It was too big, but he didn't care—it smelled like River. He padded down the hall to Grant's bedroom and slid under the covers.

The second night without River, Brian worked. His first All Night session—with Brett the surfer. Brian fluffed up the pillows and leaned back to smoke a cigarette. They'd already had sex twice, but he wasn't tired.

Brett was talkative. "I wanted to have all night to savor you." He stroked Brian's stomach. "Maybe get to know you a little. My birthday's this month, and Grant said this was a good time. So I decided to treat myself."

"Yeah? Happy birthday. How old will you be?"

"Twenty-eight."

"My birthday's coming up, too, in a couple of months."

"I'm not sure I want to know, but . . . how old are you, Brian?"

He flicked his ashes. "I'll be thirteen in October."

"Jesus." Brett closed his eyes. "I must be some kind of sick fuck."

"Why because you like me? Because we have great sex?"

"Well, yeah. I mean, you're just a kid."

Brian smirked. "At least you're not old enough to be my grandfather. Or my father. Are you?" His eyes rose to the ceiling. The math was too much for him at this hour. He shrugged. "Anyway, I like having sex with you. I *want* to have sex with you. You shouldn't feel bad about it." He leaned over to kiss him. "Can I ask you something?"

"Sure."

"How come you can afford to come here? You're so different from all the others."

"I'll answer, if you tell me how a sweet kid like you ends up in a place like this."

"Okay."

"Three years ago I inherited a shitload of money. I quit my stupid job, made a few good investments, and now I'm set for life. Never have to work again. Just surf all day. Surf and fuck."

Brian laughed.

"Your turn."

His face drew down. He watched his cigarette tap the ashtray while he ordered his thoughts. "I left home right after Christmas. Ended up in L.A. with no money. Grant picked me up and took me in." He shrugged. "That's all there was to it."

Brett took his hand and turned it over to kiss the scar on his wrist. "Guess it was pretty bad at home, huh?"

He frowned and looked away.

"I'm sorry." He grabbed Brian's waist and rolled on top of him, rubbed his hands up his chest and murmured in his ear, "I'm gonna fuck you all night."

Brian breathed a laugh and wrapped his legs around him.

൵൵൵

Brian sat up in bed and touched River's hand. "Did you have fun at John's?"

"Yeah, it was a blast. His place is a lot different. Real modern. He's got an indoor pool! I wish Grant had one."

"Wouldn't you rather swim outside?"

"Yeah, but John's got both. So you can choose." River shrugged. "Anyway, it's a nice house. The boys all live in the same building, but in a different part from John. He's got his own wing—don't share it with nobody." He put his hands behind his head and leaned back against the pillows. "The boys are real nice there. Way nicer than the bastards here."

"They don't have Trevor to poison them against us."

"I'd really love to kick his ass."

Brian grinned. "Yeah, that would be nice. But Grant wouldn't stand for it."

"I know. That's why I haven't done it." River cocked his head. "So, did you miss me?"

He slapped River's bare chest and leaned closer so his lips were inches from River's. "You know I did."

River closed the gap between their mouths. When he finally got a breath, he murmured, "Me, too."

൵൵൵

A knock sounded on the door. Brian looked up from his journal, hoping for River. Nope, Grant. His heart skipped when he saw the lack of emotion on Grant's face. Something was up. Something serious.

"What is it?" he asked, afraid of the answer.

Grant sat beside him and rested his hand on Brian's leg. "I don't know how to make this easier, so I'll just say it. River is going to move in with John."

"What?" Brian stood up as panic flooded him. "What are you talking about!"

Grant stood. "I know you're upset, but it's for the best."

"The best?" He shook and tears spilled down his face. "Whose best?"

"Brian—"

"Why? Why are you doing this?"

"You know John is my partner." His eyes grew cold. "This is business."

"*Business?*" Brian's fists clenched at his sides. "How can you do this?"

"River won't be far. John's House is only five minutes away."

"But it won't be the same, and you know it. I won't wake up every morning in River's arms—" His voice cracked. "Please!" He sank to his knees and sobbed.

"River is not everything."

"*Yes, he is.*" He clutched Grant's pants in his fists. "Please don't do this."

Grant's lips tightened. "It's already done. River was meant for John from the beginning. He was only here for training."

His mouth fell open. "How can you be so cold?" He stared into Grant's distant eyes. "Please. I'll never ask for anything again. Just let River stay here."

"Stop begging. It's pointless. Besides, are you so sure River doesn't want to go?"

Brian looked like he'd been slapped.

Grant regretted his words. "I'm sorry. But it must be." He touched Brian's wet cheek. "Go talk to River. John should be gone by now."

Brian left in silence, and Grant sank onto the bed, his head in his hands.

River stood at his bedroom window, jaw tight as he struggled to hold in his emotions. He turned as the door closed and saw Brian's pale, tear-stained face. They moved toward each other, and Brian's small body shook in his arms.

River's face twisted. He pulled back to stroke Brian's cheek as tears ran down his own. He didn't know what to say. What to do.

Brian searched his eyes. "You don't . . . you don't *want* to go, do you?"

"No, Brian, of course not! But—" He tore his gaze away. "Maybe it won't be so bad. John lives real close. I'll still see you a lot."

"But it won't be the same." His tears started again.

"I know," River whispered.

They clung to each other and cried a long time, then finally lay exhausted on the bed and held one another in silence. "River—" His voice caught. "We do have a choice. We could leave . . . if you want to."

He sat up. "You don't mean that, do you? You're happy here."

"Not without you." Brian took his hand. "I'll follow you anywhere. If you want to go." His heart beat hard as he waited for River to make the decision.

River squeezed his hand. "I think . . . we should see how it goes. Maybe it won't be so bad. We can always leave later if we want."

Brian nodded. His mouth twitched in both relief and disappointment.

"John said they'll work out our schedules so we get time off together. I can spend the night sometimes."

"Yeah?" Brian looked away. *Sometimes.* "I'll miss you," he choked out.

"God, I'll miss you, too."

*"I spend a lot of time
on my knees
begging to please
but that just leaves me bloody and worn
senses frayed and torn*

until I see you"

- Brian O'Kelly, "On My Knees"

ᕕᕗ CHAPTER 13 ᕕᕗ

The next morning Brian woke up painfully early. He'd hardly slept. His eyes felt like sandpaper. But he had to get up—he had a client at eight. He shut off the alarm before it sounded and gazed at River's face, so different when he slept. Innocent. Brian kissed his shoulder and forced himself to push back the covers.

He tried not to think as he stepped into the shower, but Grant's words kept repeating in his head. *'It's business.'* Tears mingled with the warm water.

Brian folded the hundred dollar bill and stuffed it into the blue ceramic box on his dresser. The bed was freshly made—Maria had been here. He showered again and went to look for River.

He didn't find him inside. He walked out to the pool. No River. But Grant sat near the hot tub, his face inscrutable behind dark glasses.

Brian squinted in the intense sun. "Have you seen River?"

"River is at John's." Grant took off the glasses. "We thought it would be easier if he moved while you were . . . otherwise engaged."

"What? You didn't even let me say goodbye?"

"Brian—"

He turned and ran into the house.

"He's just down the street," Grant called after him.

He raced up to his room to cry in peace.

He lay on his bed and stared out the open French doors at the hazy sky, breathed in warm air that flowed in to mix with the air conditioning. Maria had tried to get him to come down for lunch, but he refused. She brought it to him instead; it sat untouched beside the bed. The smell made him slightly ill.

The phone on the bedside table rang. *What now?* He picked it up to stop the noise.

"Brian, you okay?"

"River!" He closed his eyes and smiled through fresh tears.

"I'm sorry to leave like that. They packed my stuff and said it was time to go, so . . . ."

Brian whispered, "Yeah."

"John said I can come over tomorrow."

"Really? When?"

"After lunch. I can stay all afternoon."

He smiled wide. It felt so much better to have a concrete time to look forward to. "So how is it over there?"

"Okay so far. I'm all unpacked, and everybody's friendly."

"Do you have your own room?"

"Yeah. Not as big as my old room, but it's nice."

They chatted for forty minutes. Brian was amazed he could still laugh when his world had been so devastated. His left hand picked up a pen to doodle on a scrap of paper, drew hearts and rivers. As long as he was talking to River he was alright. But as soon as they hung up, loneliness crashed down.

He wrapped his arms around his knees, rested his cheek against them and stared outside. *Tomorrow. I'll see him tomorrow.*

Midnight came and went, and Brian stared at the ceiling over his head. He wanted so much to sleep—it would make tomorrow come faster. But the empty bed made him ache. No crawling into Grant's this time. *'Business.'* He forced his eyes shut and took a deep breath. *Guess I have to get used to sleeping alone.* He hugged the pillow to his chest.

He toyed with his eggs and tried to ignore Grant across the breakfast table.

"Brian, I thought you might enjoy piano lessons. I'll arrange it, if you're interested."

He looked up, his anger and hurt forgotten for a moment. "Yes—yes, I'm interested."

"I've found a different instructor for you. The man who teaches the other boys isn't up to your needs." Grant leaned forward. "This new instructor does not know what this House is, what we do here. Do you understand what I'm saying?"

He nodded.

"I want you to have someone worthy of your talent. It's my responsibility to make sure he never sees anything he shouldn't. It will be *your* responsibility to be careful of what you say, how you act, how you dress. I hope you understand how much trust I'm placing in you, Brian."

He nodded solemnly. "I won't let you down."

"I know you won't. You'll have two lessons a week, starting the day after tomorrow."

He grinned. It had been ages since he'd been taught anything new with the piano. He couldn't wait.

. . .

Grant slid under the sheets beside him, ran warm fingers along his skin. Brian's body responded instantly, heedless of his emotions. All he could think about was how fast River's visit had gone yesterday, how he wouldn't see him again until tomorrow. How he had to face his empty bed tonight—and tomorrow night and the next. And how it was Grant's fault. Grant, whose hand was slipping between his legs. He stopped thinking.

Afterward they lay still as their breathing slowed. Brian was normally so cuddly and loving after sex. But not this time. His body was rigid, face turned away. Grant waited for him to move, to soften.

He finally got up and left Brian alone.

Grant leaned against the back of the couch in the parlor and watched Brian struggle with the piece his new instructor, Quinn, gave him yesterday. Grant smiled to himself as he identified the problem—Brian's hands were too small for the reach. It was physically impossible for him to play the phrase as written. Brian sighed in irritation.

Grant sat beside him on the bench. "It will sound fine if you play an A there, instead."

Brian looked up at him in surprise.

"It's pointless to struggle with it. Your hands simply aren't big enough yet. Go on, try it with an A."

He did, and the phrase flowed smoothly. "You're right. It does sound fine." He rested his fingers on the keys, and his lips pressed together. "But it's not right that Bach wrote it like this, so I can't play it. It's not fair."

Grant's mouth twisted in a wry smile. "You'll find that's one of life's most difficult lessons. It's very hard to accept, that life . . . is not fair. I've always hated that one myself. Sometimes we must do things we don't want to do, things that hurt us, and hurt the people we love." He rested his hand on Brian's and met his eyes. "I miss you."

Brian frowned and looked away. His fist clenched beneath Grant's fingers.

Grant pulled his hand back and left in silence.

ಌಌಌ

Brian thought he heard a knock. He turned down the stereo as his bedroom door opened. River stuck his head in.

"River!" Brian jumped up and threw his arms around him.

River propped his head on his hand and smoothed damp hair away from Brian's face. "I guess there's one good thing about livin at John's. You always give me such an enthusiastic greeting."

Brian laughed and kissed him.

River glanced at the stereo. "I've heard this before."

"Led Zeppelin. Only one of the greatest rock bands of all time."

River smiled. "Yeah, it's pretty good." His eyes moved to the window. "Let's go outside."

They stopped in the kitchen on their way out—River wanted a snack, as usual. Brian felt a little hungry, too. He washed an apple in the sink as River scrounged the refrigerator. "Mmm." River pulled out a container of homemade pudding and dug in.

"You'll get fat eating stuff like that." Brian set the apple on a cutting board and started slicing.

"No, I won't. I'm a growing boy. It gives me energy." He leaned closer and wiggled his eyebrows. "Sexual energy."

He laughed. "I'll have to remember that. Aah!" Brian dropped the knife and held his finger.

River grabbed his hand. "What did you do? Let me see." Blood oozed from a small cut on his right index finger. "Brian!"

"It's just a little cut, no big deal." He tried to pull free, but River wouldn't let go.

"Did you do that on purpose?"

"Of course not, River. God. Don't freak out."

River wrapped a towel around his finger, then glanced into the hall. "Where's Maria? Come on." He tugged on Brian's arm.

They found her dusting the waiting room. "Let me see." She examined Brian's finger. "It is only a small cut. We'll fix you right up." She patted his cheek.

She led them back to the kitchen and pulled a first aid kit from the cabinet, cleaned his cut and put on a Band-Aid. "Now, you be more careful, Brian—" She rolled the 'r' in his name. "Or we won't let you near the knives anymore."

He smiled and nodded as River's lips pressed against the bandage.

The boys wandered along a secluded path. Tall bushes met overhead like a tunnel, their green leaves glowing as sunlight streamed through. River smiled and felt like he was home. "John's grounds are nothing like this. The bushes are all sculpted."

Brian cocked his head at the greenery. "I prefer it more natural."

River swept aside a small branch that angled across the path and held it as Brian passed through. "The gardeners missed one."

"Oh!" Brian backed up, eyes huge, and pointed at a large brown spider dangling before them at eye level.

River walked around it, then stopped and looked back. "What's the big deal? Come on."

Brian shook his head.

River rolled his eyes. "I'll take care of it." He held out his hand to the spider, and it crawled over his palm.

"Ugh!" Brian covered his face and stomped his foot. "That is *so* gross. How can you do that?"

River laughed. He resisted the urge to squash it—didn't think Brian would like that—and set the spider safely in the bushes.

They walked a little farther and left the trail to sit beside a tall hibiscus. Brian rubbed his arms and shivered. "I could've walked right into that spider. Aren't you

Naked in the Rain

afraid of anything, River?" He pulled a joint from his pocket and lit it.

"Nope. You know me. Mr. Tough Guy."

"Yeah, right." Brian passed it and sucked in air. "There's got to be something. Snakes? Bugs? Rodents?"

River made a face. "I ain't afraid of rats. I just don't like em. Give me the willies."

He smiled. "What about hamsters?"

"Hamsters are ugly."

He laughed. "They're adorable. But you're not *afraid* of them. You just don't like them."

"That's right." River exhaled smoke, then grew serious. "I'm afraid of losing you."

"River." Brian stroked his face. "Don't worry about that. I would never leave you."

River searched his deep eyes. "I've never known anyone with so much passion. I mean, passion for everything. For life. It's weird that you tried to kill yourself. It doesn't fit you." *And it scares me.*

"It seemed like the right thing at the time. I didn't know how else to escape." He put his hand on River's. "I had no hope at all. I didn't know you. Didn't know how wonderful life could be." He stared off, his eyes distant. "It was one of the most peaceful moments of my life." He was silent a few minutes, then carefully stubbed out the joint. "It's been almost a year."

"Is that all?"

"I know; it seems like a lifetime. So much has happened. My life has changed so completely, in every way. I feel like a different person. Like that old life is dead."

River nodded. "Deep thoughts."

"'By Jack Handy,'" they said in unison and laughed.

"What day is it?" River asked.

"Um . . . Monday?"

"Yep. Do you know what that means?"

He shook his head.

"It's a day you're gonna look forward to from now on. It's *our* day. And night." He grinned. "John and Grant worked it out. From now on we both get Mondays off. And Monday nights. All night."

Brian leaned forward. "You get to stay over?"

He nodded.

Brian breathed a laugh and wrapped his arms around him. "That's wonderful."

River kissed his forehead, then reached over to pluck a hibiscus flower from the bush. He examined it closely for bugs, then tucked the fuchsia-colored flower behind Brian's ear. The dappled sunlight made a pattern on his smooth skin. Brian seemed to glow. "You're so beautiful," River breathed.

"I'm so happy," he whispered.

Brian sat down to run through the Bach piece one more time before his instructor arrived. When he reached the phrase where Grant helped him, he sailed through it without a hitch. *Grant.* Familiar warmth filled him, but then his stomach twisted. He buried his face in his hands and cried.

Grant stood in the doorway while Brian played the piece for Quinn.

When he finished, Quinn said, "Very good, Brian, especially your dynamics and emotion. But I noticed you changed a note."

Brian sounded irritated. "I can't reach it as written." He demonstrated.

Grant nodded to himself. *The man pays attention. He's good.* He'd been concerned about Quinn's ability when he saw how young he was—thirty-five at the most. Grant was pleased to see his credentials were not exaggerated.

Quinn gave Brian a few suggestions before Grant reminded him their time was up. Brian's next client was due in half an hour. Plenty of time, but still, Grant didn't like to cut it too close. He ushered Quinn out the door.

"Grant," Brian said softly. "The phonograph in the ballroom isn't working. Do you think . . . maybe you could help me?" He hated to ask Grant, but Jeffrey wasn't around.

"Of course. I'll try." He smiled. "I'm not too mechanically inclined."

They went up to the ballroom, and Grant cranked the phonograph's arm. The record spun, but no sound came out. "Ah. See this piece here?" He pointed into the sound horn to a round pad mounted on a post. "It's in the mute position. It must have moved during the earthquake last night." He adjusted it, and Billie Holiday's voice crooned from the horn. "Good as new."

Last night's earthquake was the first Brian had felt. The whole room—the whole earth—had moved, but it was over before he had time to get too scared. Nothing broke. But he wished he hadn't been alone. "Thanks." Brian bit his lip and stared at the parquet floor.

Grant gripped his hands behind his back and looked around the room. "I haven't been up here in ages. I wonder how my old friend is doing?" He strode onto the stage and pulled off a sheet to reveal a cream-colored grand piano.

Brian followed him. "Wow. It's gorgeous." Carved scrolls surrounded the keyboard, white etching graced the music holder, and cabriole legs curved into ball and claw feet. Brian's left hand reached out to play a chord, and he grimaced. Grossly out of tune. He glanced at the high ceiling. "Good acoustics."

"Gregory, my predecessor, installed sound absorbers. We used to have wonderful, huge parties up here."

"Really?" He moved to the edge of the stage and looked out. He couldn't imagine his peaceful oasis filled with people.

Grant wandered off the stage and sank onto the Victorian couch. He ran his fingers along the cushion, a far away look in his eyes. "Gregory and Grant," he murmured.

Brian joined him on the sofa. "How come you stopped using it?"

"I don't know." Grant glanced around the room. "When Gregory died and I took over, I stopped having parties here and covered everything up. Too many memories, I guess." He sighed. "You know, Brian, this House and this business have been here a long time. Longer than you and me. This is not just some brothel. This is *the* House. It's a tradition. The business, it has to come first."

Brian rested his hand on Grant's leg. His voice trembled. "I don't want to be mad at you. But . . . I feel so betrayed."

Grant's face fell.

"Not necessarily by you." His gaze rose to the ceiling. "By life. River's the only one who makes that go away, makes me happy all the time. Now you've taken him away. How am I supposed to feel about that?" He searched Grant's eyes.

"You still see him. But when I said it was for the best, that wasn't just a cliché. Has it ever occurred to you perhaps you've grown too dependent on River?"

Brian's eyes widened. No, it hadn't. He sat in silence to absorb the new thought. Maybe it was true.

"Brian, this is not the end of the world. Please, don't—" He broke off and looked down. "I do love you. I never lied about that."

"Grant," he whispered and caressed his cheek.

Grant's eyes closed briefly, then met Brian's. Brian wrapped his arms around Grant's neck and held on tight.

꠶꠶꠶

He threw on jeans and his black Bauhaus tee shirt. His client had run over, and now he was late for his piano lesson. To make it worse, his client left him unsatiated, and now the jeans felt too tight across his crotch as he stood before the mirror. *Do I look like a regular boy?* He didn't feel like it.

He reached the bottom of the stairs and watched Quinn wander around the parlor admiring Grant's objets d'art. Quinn turned and jumped a little when he saw Brian, then laughed at himself with his perfect smile, tanned skin aglow, green eyes sparkling as he ran his fingers through tousled brown hair.

Brian felt dizzy. *My god, he's totally gorgeous. I must've been really upset before not to notice.* He bit his lip. *Behave yourself.* "Sorry I'm late."

They sat together on the bench. Quinn was so close Brian could feel the heat from his body. His fingers trembled as they touched the keys. He took a deep breath and tried to focus, but his body kept reminding him of its presence. He couldn't get lost in the music.

His arm brushed against Quinn as he reached for the higher notes, and a shiver ran through him. His fingers fumbled. He stopped and wrung his hands. "I'm sorry. I can't seem to concentrate today."

Quinn beamed a warm smile. "It's okay. Everybody has days like that. It's probably because you were running late and had to rush. Take a few minutes to relax, then try again."

But I can't relax next to you. He got up to pace the room and pulled out a cigarette. *Mmm.* It helped a little.

Quinn frowned but kept quiet.

Brian leaned against the back of the couch and closed his eyes, smoked in silence and tried to will his erection down. He finished his cigarette and popped a mint into his mouth. *Don't think about sex. Don't think about what he would taste like.* He shook his head and walked back to the piano.

It took all his self-control not to jump him before the lesson finally ended and Quinn left. *I hope he couldn't tell how I was looking at him.* He knew he was no good at hiding his emotions.

He wandered down the wide hallway. "Grant?" *Where is he? I need someone.* He pulled on his jeans to make them more comfortable, but it didn't help. He poked his head into the empty den and heard someone in the room beyond. He hurried through to the library. "Grant? Oh!" His heart pounded. "You scared me."

Trevor sneered.

Brian flashed back to the party, the way Trevor's cock filled his mouth. *God, I am horny. I hate him.* He took a deep breath and tried to put the image out of his mind. "Do you know where Grant is?"

"Hmm." Trevor looked up and pretended to think. "Gee, I wonder where Grant could be. Do you think he's in the Wing meeting with Matthew, like he does *every* Thursday? Oh, that's right, you wouldn't know. You just got here. You haven't been in the business for six years and worked your way up the hard way. Inexperienced little shit." His voice rose. "You waltz right in and take over, with your fancy little piano, your fancy little bedroom tricks—"

Brian walked out. He refused to be yelled at by anyone. He'd had enough of that in his life.

ריריר

He smoothed his leather skirt and opened the door to the Room. "River! What are you doing here?"

River was lying on the bed, completely nude. He cocked an eyebrow and smiled. "What does it look like I'm doing?"

Brian walked to the foot of the bed. "I've got a client all afternoon."

"Oh, yeah? Who?"

He recalled the name on the schedule. "Reese." It clicked. "You? What's going on?"

River grinned. "I wanted to surprise you on our special day."

His brow furrowed. September 17th. He couldn't figure out the day's significance.

River sat up on his knees at the edge of the bed to stare into Brian's eyes. "It's our anniversary. We met one year ago today."

"Oh," he breathed and hugged River tight. "River, you're so sweet."

ריריר

"I want you to wear this." Grant held up a dark velvet top with spaghetti straps. "Purple. For royalty."

Brian's stomach tightened. Tonight was Grant's annual end-of-summer bash.

Naked in the Rain

The Heads of all the Houses in L.A. would be in attendance. And this year they were all coming to see him.

Grant helped him slip into the cropped halter top and smoothed the delicate satin straps. "And I have a new skirt for you." Grant held it up.

Black leather, the same as his other skirt. Brian pulled it on. Now he saw the difference—it was even shorter, barely covered his ass. He gave a nervous laugh. "If it were any shorter I'd be hanging out."

Grant chuckled. "Just be careful when you sit. And don't bend over." He murmured in his ear, "Unless someone tells you to." He rubbed Brian's ass. "Mmm, that's lovely. But there's no time. I'm going downstairs to make sure everything's in order. Come down when you're finished." Grant let himself out.

Brian fastened the sapphire choker, then sat to pull on the suede boots that went over his knees. He tugged on the skirt, in danger of overexposure. *I have to remember not to sit.*

He stood to look in the mirror. The boots and micro skirt made his legs appear long. *That's because my entire thigh is showing. A real whore skirt.* His mouth quirked down as he pulled on the bottom of the skirt. He took a deep breath and headed out.

Grant was in the parlor. "Brian, I'd like you to meet Kristoff, Head of one of the top Houses in L.A."

Kristoff was a short, robust man with grey hair and a bushy beard. His blue eyes crinkled when he smiled. Brian liked him right away.

Grant stroked Brian's hair. "I asked Kristoff to come early so you could get acquainted. Why don't you take him upstairs?"

The skirt was certainly easy access. Kristoff's beard tickled his thighs. Brian wriggled. It was a turn on. So was his exotic accent. Kristoff was an excellent lover, took his time. His dick was short and thick, like his body. Felt good inside him.

By the time they finished, the parlor was full of men and boys—the Heads of Houses and their Number Ones for the pre-party dinner. A hush fell over the crowd as Brian and Kristoff appeared at the top of the staircase. A mixture of curiosity, jealousy and lust radiated from the parlor. Brian tugged on the skirt and plastered on his fake smile.

Grant greeted them at the bottom of the stairs and put his arm around Brian's waist. Brian felt better immediately. Grant exuded power; it gave Brian confidence when he stood so close.

John arrived as they were moving into the dining room. Strange to see some other boy by his side instead of River. Grant assured him River would be at the party. Later.

He'd never seen the formal dining room in use before. The candles were all lit—on the table, in sconces along the walls. Their light glowed on delicate china, crystal glasses, ornate silver. Like out of a fairy tale. Until all the men and boys sat down.

Grant took the head of the table, of course. Brian sat on his right, directly across from John. *Great. I get to look at him all through dinner.* But John ignored him utterly, spent the whole time talking to the adults. Grant was busy with the other men, too.

Brian glanced around the table. Most of the boys ate in silence. Brian recognized the older brown-skinned boy beside John from Grant's birthday party, but couldn't recall his name. *I wonder if he's friends with River?*

Kristoff was seated on Brian's right. He interrupted Brian's musings and made an effort to include him in the conversation. Brian looked past him to the silently accusing eyes of Kristoff's Number One. Brian set down his fork. He didn't feel like eating.

But dessert was another story. The crème brulée melted in his mouth, heavenly. He glanced up and caught John staring at him, eyes gone grey with a familiar, hungry look. Brian flushed and looked away.

John excused himself after dinner to take care of some business before the party. Grant shook his head and whispered to Brian, "John always has to be late. Make a grand entrance." He smiled. "I'm sure he does it just to irritate me."

Brian gazed at the cherub ice sculpture. *How do they keep it from melting?* It was warm out, even though the sun was long gone. He plucked a grape from the elaborate display and popped it into his mouth. Juicy. The drugs made everything extra good—Matthew was handing out special pills.

Brian glanced at the men and boys standing around in groups, filling up the big courtyard. Some of the men wore masks, like at a costume party—to hide their identities, Grant had told him. They added a festive and mysterious air to the party, along with the flickering torchlight.

He saw Jeffrey standing nearby, stern and silent. He would've looked frightening as shadows played on his dark face if Brian didn't know the sweet man underneath. Brian grabbed a glass of wine and walked over to give it to him. But Jeffrey wouldn't take it. Brian tugged on his shirt. "Come on. Loosen up."

"I can't, Mr. Brian. I'm on duty."

He noticed a wire hanging from Jeffrey's ear, like secret service stuff. Brian nodded solemnly. "Okay. But someday I'll catch you off duty, and we'll have fun."

Jeffrey smiled. "Sho' thing."

Brian turned away and glimpsed long golden hair disappearing into the crowd. A woman. A real woman. It seemed like forever since he'd seen one. Except Maria, but she didn't count. He tried to follow her, but couldn't find her through all the guests. Being short didn't help. He shook his head with a frown. Maybe she hadn't been there at all.

A boy ran up to him to tell him it was time, so he went to the piano. After he played the Chopin piece he wandered away from the party, tired of everyone looking at him.

His feet led him to his favorite little bridge. He leaned against the wooden rail and stared at the full moon reflected below. "Wow," he breathed. He went around the bridge to squat at the water's edge, low now at the end of summer, and still. He touched the surface and ripples spread out in all directions. He grinned and took off his boots.

He stood knee deep in the clear water, the smooth rocks slippery under his feet, and moved carefully to touch the reflection of the moon. He laughed and looked up at the real thing. This would be incredible even without the drugs. He grinned at the sky.

The first person he saw on his return to the courtyard was John. *Ugh*. His initial reaction changed when he realized River must be here, too. His feet left wet marks on the cement as he scampered around looking for him. He saw Trevor and veered the other way. *Look for the food. Aha.*

River sat on an armless chair of carved mahogany near the food, chatting with some boys Brian didn't know. Brian walked up behind him, close enough to smell his hair. Mmm. Vanilla. He reached around to slide his hands beneath River's suit jacket.

River looked up at him with a smile, and Brian slid around to straddle his lap. His mouth was higher than River's for a change. Exciting. He leaned down to kiss him, suddenly incredibly horny.

"Wait a second." River pushed him back. "You're on something. Where's mine?"

Brian's head tilted sideways as he laughed. He would've fallen if it weren't for River's arms around him. The strap dangled off his shoulder. "I saved one for you. But then I took it."

"Brian! No fair."

"There's more." He turned his head to scan the crowd. "Somewhere."

The boy in the next chair leaned closer. "Matthew's got em. You want one?"

"Yeah, thanks." River's attention returned to Brian. "Damn, if that ain't the shortest skirt I ever saw."

"Yeah?" Brian moved his body a little closer.

River caressed his thigh where the skirt ended. Brian squirmed and took River's face in his hands to kiss him long and deep. His arms went around River's back as their bodies pressed together.

"Hey. Here."

Brian blinked at the interruption. The boy had returned with an orange pill.

"Thanks." River popped it into his mouth and swallowed.

"I don't know how you do that without water. Let me see."

"Aaaahhh." He stuck his tongue out.

Brian licked it, then took it into his mouth to suck on it. River's hand slid around the skin at the edge of the leather until it was right against Brian's ass. His fingers moved closer.

Brian grabbed River's neck and pulled it toward him. It felt strange to tilt his head down to kiss him. Powerful. He yanked on River's tie to loosen it. Unbuttoned his shirt partway, then skipped to his pants. He could feel River's erection as he tugged the zipper down.

"Brian, shouldn't we—" He glanced around. "People are watching." The closest was pill boy, only two feet away. He stared.

"I don't care. I need you now." His hand disappeared down River's pants. He watched River's eyes close, his back arch. He loved the little sounds River made.

Brian pulled River's penis out to stroke it. River pushed the skirt up with shaking hands, his mouth on Brian's neck, and touched between his legs. Brian moaned and fell against him. He reached into River's suit pocket to pull out a pack of lube. A condom came out with it. *Oh, yeah.* God, he almost forgot—they had to use condoms around other people.

He put his feet on the chair on either side of River to lift himself up. Lowered onto him. They both gasped at the penetration. Brian pushed his body against him. Kissed him over and over as they moved together. Faster. God, it felt so good. He pressed River's face into his chest as they both came.

Brian held him tight, but not for long. He had too much energy to stay still. He pushed back and swung his leg.

River finished cleaning up and crumpled the wipes. "Good thing you're so young, or I'd have a big stain on my new suit."

"River." Brian's cheeks turned a darker shade of red.

River smiled to himself. Brian had just fucked him in front of all these people, and now he was blushing because of one little comment. He kissed his neck. "Silly boy."

"Am I next?" Pill boy leaned closer, his dick in his hand.

Brian made a face. "*No.* Come on, River." He got up and pulled on River's hand. "I want to show you the moon in the brook."

"Watch your skirt." River tugged on it.

Justin the party photographer with bright red spiky hair stood gaping nearby. He couldn't believe what he just saw. He'd been warned about Grant's parties, and the pay was more than worth it. But he wasn't prepared for *that*. Now he understood why some of the guests wore masks—who would want to be seen here? The boy met his gaze as he walked by. Hollow eyes. *The kid's definitely on something.* Justin began to realize his exorbitant pay was more hush money than salary. And discovered that he did, indeed, have a price. *I need a drink.*

When they returned to the party, Grant beckoned. Brian gave River a kiss. "See ya later."

River went to hang out with his friend Rick, and Brian moved toward Grant, Kristoff seated beside him. The world seemed a little slanty. Brian wobbled and went sideways for a moment. He smiled at the men as he approached.

Grant said, "Next time you decide to have sex with River in front of everyone, please let me know." He leaned forward. "I'm very sorry I missed it."

Brian laughed in relief. "I thought you were mad for a second."

"Oh, no. That's the sort of thing that makes these parties so . . . appealing."

At Grant's gesture Brian knelt at his feet. Grant stroked his hair while he chatted with Kristoff. Brian rested his cheek against Grant's leg and gazed at a flickering candle, mesmerized.

"Brian." Grant shook his arm gently. "Brian."

He jumped a little and looked up at him.

"See the group of people sitting on the other side of Kristoff? The man with the blue shirt. I'd like you to go to him and perform fellatio. Don't talk to him; don't kiss him. Can you do that?"

"Yes, Grant." He kissed his cheek and went to do his bidding.

Grant and Kristoff watched Brian kneel between the man's legs. Kristoff stroked his beard. "He certainly knows what he's doing. Yet he has such an air of innocence."

"Mm. He's only twelve; he *should* seem innocent, even if he isn't. I believe it's enhanced by the shape of his eyes, so round on top. Unusual."

Kristoff nodded. "A good selling point, in any case. And the perfect age. The boy has real talent."

"Yes. He's a true natural. He subconsciously reads his partner's body language to give what sometimes they don't even know they want. And he loves it." Grant smiled as the man in the blue shirt moaned and clutched Brian's head. "From the moment I saw him standing in the rain, I knew I had something special."

Brian left the courtyard again to wander the gardens, enjoying the feel of cool dirt beneath his bare feet. He looked up through thorny limbs of a tall rose bush at the moon. So round and bright—he found himself staring at it constantly. He forgot he was alone and turned to show River. *Oh.* The distant laughter of the party rode on the breeze. *I should go back and find him.*

He retraced his steps and entered the wooded path. Cool moonlight fell through the branches to light the way. A hand shot out from the bushes and grabbed him. Brian yelped in surprise as branches scraped his skin. A hand covered his mouth.

"Shhh," John's voice said in his ear. He took his hand away from Brian's mouth and held him tight against his body.

Anger surged. "Damn it, John. Why'd you have to scare me like that?" The magic of the moonlit woods was ruined.

"Because I like to feel your heart pound in your chest." His fingers slipped beneath the velvet halter.

"You like to scare little boys because it makes you feel powerful."

"I *am* powerful, Brian O'Dell." He pushed Brian down to his knees. "Or whatever your real name is."

"Yes, Mr. Mackenzie," he said in a snide tone.

John laughed, a low sound. He pushed on Brian's back until he was on all fours, then brushed his hand along the sensitive skin at the hem of the skirt. "Time to teach you a lesson." John gave his buttocks a light slap.

Brian's heart beat faster in a mixture of fear and arousal as John's hands roamed. But he knew John wouldn't really hurt him. *He just gets off acting this way.*

John called out, "Richard. Over here."

Brian's eyes flew open and saw River's friend, Rick, approaching on the path. *Shit.* He looked for River behind him, but there was no one. *Thank god.* He didn't want River involved in this.

At John's instruction Rick dropped his pants and stood in front of Brian. Rick's penis hardened in his mouth while John fondled Brian from behind. *Mmm . . . .*

John gestured Rick away and thrust. Brian gasped as his knees slid in the dirt.

His elbows bent as John filled him up and pushed him down. He laid his face on his hands to keep it out of the dirt.

Rick reached down to lift Brian's chest and supported him while he put his cock back in Brian's mouth. Rick's penis pushed in all the way with each of John's powerful thrusts. Filled him up at both ends. Too much. The choker tightened around his neck. He couldn't breathe.

John reached around to stroke Brian's cock. His throat relaxed as he eased into the rhythm. Suddenly it was fun. It gave his mouth something yummy to play with while he was getting fucked hard from behind. *Oh, yeah.* He wasn't going to last long. But neither was Rick. He shot into Brian's throat. Brian came hard, then John, and it was over.

John and Rick pulled up their pants and walked away without a word. Rick threw him a crooked smile over his shoulder as they rounded the corner. Brian sat quietly a moment, his arms wrapped around skinned knees, his body still throbbing. *I wonder if I could've handled that without the pills?* He closed his eyes and replayed the final moments. *That was good.*

Maybe John wasn't so bad. At least he always made sure his boys came. Unlike some clients who had no concern for the other person's pleasure. He couldn't understand that. *But John's still an asshole.* He grabbed a thick branch to pull himself up, wiped off the dirt and leaves and headed back to the party. He glanced down at his bare feet. *I wonder where my boots are?*

He woke up, surprised to find himself alone in his own bed. He struggled to remember how he got there. Instead, the memory of straddling River on the chair floated up.

Oh, god. He covered his eyes. *I can't believe I did that.* He laughed and shook his head. "I must've been really fucked up. I hope David didn't see." He shrugged and rolled over.

*"Consider green lakes
and the idiocy of clocks
Someone shot nostalgia in the back
Someone shot our innocence . . .
in the shadow of his smile . . .*

*All our dreams have melted down
We are hiding in the bushes
from dead men
doing Douglas Fairbanks stunts"*

- Bauhaus, "Who Killed Mr. Moonlight"

෴ CHAPTER 14 ෴

Brian reached the bottom of the stairs where Grant and an old man waited. *He wasn't on the schedule.* Irritation flitted through him; he'd been on the phone with River when Grant called him down. But he put on his sex smile and walked up close to say hello.

Grant said, "This is Mr. Wycliffe. He'll be your tutor."

He blinked. *My what?*

"He will be responsible for your schooling. English, mathematics, history. You'll have lessons three times a week. And homework. You're to do what Mr. Wycliffe says."

Math? "Yes, Grant."

The man spoke in a weak, nasal voice. "Let's go up to your room and get started. We'll begin with an evaluation so I can determine your level."

My bedroom? He shrugged to himself as they mounted the stairs. *Grant said do what he says, so that's what I'll do.*

He sat at the antique desk in his room, and the man handed him papers and booklets. Reading comprehension, vocabulary. Tests. *Is this for real?* Mr. Wycliffe settled on a chair and began to grade papers. Brian waited for the man to make some kind of move, to tell him to get on his knees. But he never did.

He finally accepted that Wycliffe really wasn't a client and focused on the tests. Strange to use his mind this way again. It annoyed him. But then again, he didn't want to go through life with a sixth grade education. He tapped the pencil against his teeth and tried to remember how to do fractions.

Brian turned the newspaper over to finish the article on global warming. "Do you have the rest of Section A?"

Grant handed it over. "Your birthday's coming soon. Is there anything in particular you want?"

"A kitten!"

Grant put down the paper with a frown. "No, Brian. I'm sorry. Ask me for something that isn't furry and won't mess the house."

"Please?"

"We already have Sebastian. One is plenty."

"But he hardly ever comes out of your room. I want one of my own who'll follow me around, sleep with me."

"On the bed?" Grant shook his head. "Think of something else. How would you like to celebrate?"

He frowned and shrugged. "It doesn't matter, as long as River's there."

"Come now, you can do better than that. Would you like a fancy party? A night on the town?"

He stared out the window at the peaceful lawns. "No. Just a quiet day with the people I love."

Grant smiled and reached across the table to caress his hand. "That we can do."

Jeffrey drove them to the coast in the limo. River sat with his arm around Brian's shoulders and whispered in his ear, "Happy birthday."

He grinned. "It seems weird it's my birthday—it's too warm for October. At least it's good weather for my favorite shirt." He smoothed the black Cure tee shirt.

Grant smiled from where he sat facing backwards. "That's Southern California for you."

"I love it," River said.

The limo parked at the beach house Grant had rented for Brian's birthday. A magnificent view greeted them as they stepped inside. Windows covered the entire back wall of the living room; waves beat against the sand a few hundred feet away, and a grand piano faced the ocean. "Great," he breathed.

"Hey, look in here," River called.

Brian followed his voice. A ping pong table dominated the small room. He grinned. "*Great*." Everything was perfect.

The four of them settled in the living room, and the boys sat cross-legged on the carpet. Brian reached for the present from River. He ripped open the box and gasped. A tour book from The Cure's *The Head Tour*. "Oh, my *god*. How'd you find this?"

"At Phil's. Look there." River pointed to a signature scrawled at the bottom.

Brian screamed and hugged him, then ran his fingertip over the ink. "Robert Smith *touched* this." He held it against his cheek.

River beamed.

After presents and cake, they lounged on the deck with drinks. Jeffrey didn't like fancy cocktails, so he had a beer instead. And once he started talking, watch out. He told the funniest stories, and they weren't even dirty.

Brian picked up the glass pitcher for a refill and stared into it. Empty. Jeffrey took it out of his hands. "I'll make more, Mr. B."

"I'll help." Brian bounced up to follow him into the kitchen.

Jeffrey poured tequila into the blender, and Brian reached out to poke his stomach. "Hey!" Jeffrey spilled.

Naked in the Rain

"Sorry." He grinned.

"Yeah, you look real sorry."

Brian laughed. He patted Jeffrey's wide chest with both hands and tugged on his shirt. "Come on, loosen up. Have another beer."

Jeffrey laughed. "Well, I just might do that."

Brian leaned into him. "You're so big." Jeffrey's chest dwarfed him. He glanced down. "Is it true what they say about black men?" His hand reached down to find out.

"Oh, no, you don't." He gripped Brian's wrist. "No, you don't. Not with me."

He squirmed in Jeffrey's grasp. "But I wanna see. Come on. It's my birthday."

"Too bad," he said in a stern voice. "You can't get everythin you want. Now don't be tryin that again." Jeffrey let go of him.

Brian looked down. "Okay."

Jeffrey turned back to the blender. Brian leaned against the counter and touched his bulging arm. "Are you mad at me?"

Jeffrey laughed and hugged Brian against him. "Of course not. Now help me with the strawberries."

A few hours later, Grant said, "It's time for you two to be alone." He kissed them both and lingered with Brian. "If you need anything, Jeffrey will be right next door."

"Okay. Thanks, Grant." Brian kissed his cheek. "See you tomorrow."

River brought the wine outside and joined Brian where he sat on the wooden deck instead of a chair. The sun hovered just above the horizon, a big orange ball that stretched and grew with its reflection on the water. River's gaze moved to deep blue eyes, and he clinked his glass against Brian's. "Happy birthday. I love you."

Their eyes held as they sipped. River leaned over to taste the wine on Brian's lips. Slow, gentle kisses. Suddenly more than that. River pushed him back against the wooden floor.

Brian tilted his head back as River's mouth worked down his body, stroked River's hair and stared upside down at the ocean, the sky. The sun was gone now. Purple and orange streaks bathed the clouds. He gazed at the glowing colors as the person he loved worshipped his body. A perfect moment forever locked in his mind.

They ordered pizza for dinner. Two pizzas, actually. River wanted to have plenty—and he wanted meat. River handed the delivery boy a hundred dollar bill. "Keep the change." He grinned at the teenager's expression, winked and closed the door.

He dug his finger into the icing as he walked by the leftover cake. He set the pizza boxes down and offered the icing to Brian.

Brian smiled and performed fellatio on his finger, long and slow. His tongue did the swirly thing on the tip that River liked so much. River moaned.

Brian dropped to his knees to do the real thing.

. . .

After midnight and more wine, they decided to play ping pong. "Let's make it interesting." River wiggled his eyebrows.

Brian missed the first serve. He laughed and pulled off his tee shirt. Next to go were his socks.

They decided River won when Brian had nothing left to take off. River had only missed one shot; his shirt lay in a heap with Brian's clothes. He stared at Brian as he unzipped his pants and threw them into the pile, then lunged at Brian's naked body. Brian squealed and ran around the table.

River caught him and carried him into the bedroom, then opened another bottle of wine. He brought it over to the bed, along with a can of whipped cream.

Brian's eyebrow quirked. "That looks like fun."

River smiled and set the whipped cream on the nightstand. "We'll play with that in a minute." He took a drink from the bottle and raised it in salute. "Congratulations, Brian. You're officially a teenager. Welcome."

Brian grinned and leaned back against the pillows. He waved the offered bottle away. "I don't want to get as drunk as I did on my last birthday." He laughed at the memory. "My first time getting drunk. I did a lot of things for the first time. Twelve was a big year."

"Yeah. Think of all the stuff you did. Drinking. Sex. Lots and lots of sex." He grabbed Brian's waist.

"And drugs—coke, ecstasy, a bunch of different ones. Oh, and I became a prostitute." He laughed at the ridiculous way it sounded.

River shook his head and climbed on top of him. "Only you would laugh at that." River gave him a soft kiss and stared into his eyes. "Brian O'Kelly, I love you more than anything else in this world."

"River." He wrapped his arms and legs around him and pulled him close. "I love you so much sometimes I can hardly stand it."

ꐕꐕꐕ

Brian walked into his bedroom and jumped, startled—Trevor was closing the closet door. "What are you doing in here?" Brian demanded.

Trevor's face darkened. "Fuck off. I'm just getting my stuff." He held up a menorah. "This is *mine*."

It suddenly made sense. "This was your room."

Trevor's eyes flicked down Brian's body. "Of course it was, idiot." His tone didn't fit the words; his gaze lingered.

Brian glanced down at himself and flushed. He still had on the leather bondage outfit John had told him to wear. Trevor moved toward the door and brushed past him, murmured, "Prick."

Brian stood alone in a daze. He knew this bedroom was for the Number One boy, but he'd never stopped to think about it. Never applied it to Trevor. *No wonder he hates me so much.*

He remembered his second night here. *Why did Grant put me in here, the one room* that was occupied? Did he already know I'd be his Number One? "How could he?" He shook his head and began the long process of unbuckling the leather straps.

That evening River came to spend the night. The boys undressed quickly and slid under the covers. River got on top of him as soon as Brian's head hit the pillow. Brian pulled his mouth away. "Just oral this time, okay?"

River looked puzzled.

"I'm a little sore."

River's brow furrowed, and a frantic glint lit his eyes. "Are you okay? Did someone hurt you?" He shook Brian's body a little.

Your buddy, John. He'd been rougher than usual, though it hadn't hurt much at the time. "I'm fine. Don't panic." He pushed against River's chest. "It's no big deal. It was fun at the time."

He didn't look convinced.

Brian stroked his face. "It's okay," he whispered. "It's okay." Brian kissed him softly, over and over. Pulled him closer and sucked on his tongue.

When River could speak he murmured, "Why don't you do me?"

River stretched and smiled, so relaxed. "I haven't listened to you play the piano in a long time. I miss it."

"You do?" Brian grinned.

They got dressed and went up to the third floor. "This was the best birthday present—besides yours," Brian said. "It was such a shame for this wonderful piano to be rotting away unused." He pushed on the door to the ballroom. "And I love it up here."

River positioned a wingchair in front of the stage so he had a good view. He loved watching Brian play, the emotions of the music so clear on his face.

"Any requests?" Brian smiled at him from behind the refurbished piano.

"Yeah. That thing you did the first time I ever heard you play, our first night here."

He breathed a laugh. "'That thing.' It's only Beethoven." He launched into *Moonlight Sonata*. Brian closed his eyes as the slow first movement took him over. But it didn't feel sad anymore. Just beautiful. Beautiful and loving. He met River's gaze, and they smiled.

ונוונ

Brian opened the French doors and stepped onto his balcony. It was damp out. He inhaled deeply, disappointed when he couldn't see his breath as he let it go. His lips curved in a wry smile. *People here probably think it's cold. I bet it's snowing in Connecticut.* His gaze rose to the billowing clouds. *I wonder if they have their tree yet? Their first Christmas without me.*

His mouth twitched, and he almost remembered his dream from last night. Dark and frightening. He couldn't get away, couldn't move. A shiver ran up his spine.

"Stop it." He shook himself and leaned inside to check the clock. Time. He popped a mint into his mouth and tightened the laces of his white leather vest, then stopped by the Room on his way downstairs. He pulled a condom and pack of lube from the wide mouth of the cobalt blue vase beside the bed, opened them with his teeth and set them on the edge of the nightstand. He fiddled with the headboard and stepped back. Everything was ready.

Alan admired the view as Brian led him upstairs. The curves of the white leather seemed to wink at him.

Brian turned to give him a seductive smile as he opened the door to the Room. The eagerness in the man's eyes was slightly distasteful, like a dog panting after food. The new client was a bit overweight and balding. Like someone you'd see at the grocery store or movies. An everyday Joe.

Yet something about him seemed a little off. Brian couldn't quite place it. The schedule noted that Alan wanted handcuffs. *It's always the normal-looking ones who want the kinky stuff.*

Brian sat on the edge of the bed. Alan approached and stood before him, his groin at face level. But Brian didn't touch it—he could tell the man didn't want that. Alan wanted to be in charge.

He pushed Brian back onto the bed and placed his fists on either side. The man loomed over him, breathing hard and sweating. *Ugh.* Brian noticed strange dots along the top of Alan's forehead, like someone had stuck a bunch of needles in. His eyes widened. *Hair plugs.* He glanced away as his stomach turned.

Alan's gaze moved to the headboard where the leather handcuffs dangled, waiting. A bead of sweat trickled down his face. Brian frowned at the thought of that sweat getting all over him. *That's what showers are for. Come on. You're a professional.* "Do you know how to work the chain?"

The man nodded—he had yet to speak. He untied the vest and pulled it off, then grasped Brian's waist to slide him up toward the cuffs. He fastened the leather around Brian's wrists and shortened the chain so his hands were together over his head. Then came the blindfold.

Brian heard fabric moving and knew the man was getting undressed. *At least I don't have to see him naked.* He suppressed a smile.

Alan touched Brian's stomach, his chest. He rubbed hard and grunted. Brian tried to wipe the image of a pig out of his mind. He felt the man's warm tongue on his nipple. Alan's teeth clamped down hard. Brian bit his lip to stifle a cry. Alan unzipped Brian's pants and practically ripped them off.

He started talking. "Oh, yeah, baby. Oh, baby. Beautiful." Alan's hands were all over him.

Brian was starting to get an erection, despite the man. He felt Alan's stiff cock against his leg. Alan stroked Brian's penis in a frenzy, then grabbed his balls and squeezed none too gently.

"Aaah." He squirmed in a mixture of pain and pleasure.

Alan let go. Brian could feel him looming over his face, then the man's wet mouth was on his. Alan kissed him hard and deep, bit at him. Brian didn't like the way he tasted. Sour.

Alan pulled away to straddle Brian's stomach and rested all his weight on him. Brian could barely breathe. Alan twisted his nipples hard. Brian's hands pulled involuntarily on the chain and a whimper rose from his throat.

Alan's weight lifted. Brian gasped for air. *You can breathe. It's okay.* A fist suddenly slammed into his stomach. The pain shocked him. No one had ever hit him like that before. He curled up on his side and struggled to breathe.

"You're going to bleed for me."

Oh, god! Adrenalin surged through him. His arms tugged frantically, uselessly on the chain.

The man rolled Brian onto his back. Grabbed his face, squeezed and shook it. A sideways blow landed across Brian's mouth. Pain exploded in his head. He felt dizzy and tasted copper. Blood. He squeezed his eyes shut beneath the blindfold. *This isn't happening.*

Alan hit his face again, then turned him over. His elbow bored into Brian's back as he pushed his thighs apart with his knee.

Brian's hands clenched as he fought the chain in panic. *Oh, god! Please help me!*

He cringed when he heard the man emerge from the bathroom, the rustle of clothing as Alan moved closer. Brian tried to hold still but couldn't quite do it. His hands tugged on the chain. He flinched as he felt the man reach toward him. Alan unfastened one handcuff and hummed as he left the room.

He's gone. He's gone. Brian's fingers struggled to undo the other cuff. They shook so much he couldn't do it. His body strained against the chain, and he heard a noise like an animal whimpering. The sound was coming from his own throat. He clamped his mouth shut and pulled off the blindfold. He saw blood on his fingers as he willed them to obey and unfastened the other cuff.

He wrapped the sheet around himself and curled into a ball. Drew ragged breaths while his body throbbed in hot pain. He had to get out of this room. Not safe. Not safe. He got to his feet, the sheet still wrapped around him, and reached for the wall as his legs wobbled. He was almost to the door when his legs gave out, and he fell to his knees. He grabbed the knob and pulled himself up to stumble down the hallway. His hand trailed along the wall to steady himself.

He made it to the refuge of his room, then raced to the toilet as dry heaves wracked him—the smell of that man made him sick. He finally leaned back against the wall. But the smell was still on his skin. Everywhere. He had to get it off.

He stepped into the tub, sank to his knees and scrubbed until his skin was raw. He ducked his head under the faucet to fill his mouth with water. But it didn't get the taste out. He stepped out of the tub and grabbed the mouthwash. Used half the bottle, then flinched from his reflection.

His mind went blank. His legs trembled violently as he stood dripping onto the tile. He lurched out of the bathroom and stumbled over the sheet that lay in a heap on the floor. He fell onto the bed and wrapped the white down comforter around himself. Curled up in a ball and rocked. His whole body throbbed in unbearable sharp pain radiating from his ass. His mind was numbing out; he had to do something but he couldn't think. *River.* He reached for the phone. It took three tries to dial the number.

River answered.

Thank god. "River?" His voice wobbled.

"Brian! What's wrong?"

The sound of River's voice was too much. He suddenly couldn't breathe, couldn't make a sound.

"Brian, are you there?" River's voice grew frantic. "What happened! Are you okay?"

Sobs broke out of him as he clutched the phone.

"I'll be there in two minutes! You wait for me, okay? Brian?"

He tried to answer, but only managed some kind of squeak.

"I'm coming now." River hung up.

River burst into the room. Brian lay facing the other way, the white comforter wrapped around him, his breathing harsh and erratic. He turned over as River climbed onto on the bed.

River's heart stopped. "Oh, my God." The side of his mouth and jaw were swollen and starting to turn purple. Blood oozed from a cut on his lip. "God!" Tears spilled down River's face. "Brian. Brian." He wrapped his arms around him and held on tight.

Brian clutched River's sweater in his fists.

"What happened? Who did this?"

He didn't answer, just buried his face in River's chest. River held onto him and rubbed his back. Brian winced. River's stomach dropped. He was afraid to look, but he pushed the comforter down. Ugly red marks covered Brian's back. River squeezed his eyes shut as nausea rose in his throat. "Does Grant know about this?" No response. "Does he?"

Brian's eyes looked scattered as he gazed up at River's face. River rested his palm on his cheek and asked gently, "Does Grant know about this?"

Brian shook his head slowly.

"Okay. Okay." River kissed his forehead.

Brian sank down onto his side and closed his eyes.

River stared blindly at the grey clouds. He couldn't handle this. Something on the floor caught his eye. A white sheet. With big dark splotches. His heart thumped.

He pulled the comforter back all the way. Blood smeared Brian's thighs and made gruesome patterns on the bedding.

Trembling started in River's chin, spread quickly through his whole body. He turned to punch the intercom button with his fist.

"Grant! Come to Brian's room." His voice cracked. "*Now!*"

*"Doesn't take much
to rip us into pieces"*

- Tori Amos, "Little Earthquakes"

ᚾᚾ CHAPTER 15 ᚾᚾ

River paced the hall, his stomach so twisted in knots he could barely breathe. He glanced at Grant's face, an inscrutable mask, and wondered how he could be so calm.

Dr. Griffin finally emerged from Brian's room with a cheery smile. "He'll be fine. The bleeding has stopped—there doesn't appear to be internal injuries. But he's out of commission for awhile."

River squeezed past him into the room. The doctor called after him, "He's asleep. I gave him a strong dose of pain meds."

River peered through the dim light at Brian's peaceful face. He looked even younger in his sleep, like an angel. Except for the bruises. The tightness in River's throat threatened to choke him.

Grant came in and put his arm around River's shoulders. River's fists clenched. "I want to kill that son of a bitch."

"We'll take care of him," Grant said in a monotone. "I'll tell John you'll be staying here awhile."

River's eyes never left Brian's face. He nodded.

Grant left him alone. River sat in a chair to watch Brian sleep and tried not to think. But he cried anyway.

When the room grew darker he undressed and climbed into bed. Brian murmured and stirred. He moved closer to lay his cheek against River's chest, then lifted his head and glanced around. "River?" His voice sounded fragile.

"I'm right here, babe. I'm right here." He stroked Brian's cheek—the unbruised one. "Does it hurt?"

He shook his head and laughed. "I feel . . . fuzzy."

River let out his breath. "Good."

"I'm so tired."

"You need to rest. Go back to sleep."

Brian looked at him with wide eyes.

"I'll be here when you wake up."

"I love you," he said as his eyes closed.

"I love you too," River managed to whisper.

. . .

Grant stepped silently into the man's living room. Alan sat in an armchair reading. He jerked and trembled as Grant moved closer.

"So we find you peacefully at home. Perhaps you understood it would be useless to run. You knew the rules; you chose to break them. Now you will pay the consequences." His eyes narrowed as he leaned closer, his voice like ice. "If Brian is ruined, you are *dead*."

Grant walked away, then paused in the doorway. "By the time my men are done with you, you'll wish you were." He glanced toward the dark shape looming in the shadows. "Jeffrey, take care of him."

Jeffrey moved in, followed by several equally large and menacing figures. But none so angry as he.

Alan closed his eyes and wished fleetingly that he hadn't lost control. But the boy had such perfection. *It was worth it.*

Brian soaked in the warm bathwater with River on a stool nearby, a constant presence. Brian wrapped his arms around his knees, careful to keep his left hand out of the water. Not supposed to get the bandage wet.

His brow furrowed at the gauze wrapped around his left index finger. Stitches underneath. He knew that. But he wasn't sure why the bandage was there. Why he was soaking in this tub for the second time today. His brain whited out in panic as his thoughts strayed too near.

He trembled, then felt River's warmth, kissing his temple, murmuring his love.

A long sigh escaped. *I love you, too.* Too much effort to say it aloud. So tired. And dizzy and numb. *Am I drugged?* He couldn't keep his scattered thoughts together.

"Time to come out, babe." River kissed his forehead, then scooped him up and lifted him easily. Water cascaded down to splash back into the tub. River was so strong. Brian wrapped his arms around him and buried his face in his neck.

River held him tight.

Maria knocked softly and opened the door. Brian was resting, of course, even though it was noon. But he wasn't asleep. She settled on the edge of the bed, and he sat up to stare at her with glazed eyes.

"Brian, I was cleaning up and—" She tried to block the memory of that bed. The bloodstains soaked through to the mattress. She cleared her throat and reached into her apron pocket. "I found this. It was meant for you." She held out a five hundred dollar bill. With dried blood on it.

His eyes widened. "I don't want it."

"But it is yours."

"No," he shouted and pushed her hand away. "I don't care what you do with it. Keep it. Burn it. But don't give it to me. I won't take it. I won't be paid for that." His voice cracked.

Her eyes filled. "My poor little niño. Come here." She enfolded him in her arms and pressed his face into her ample bosom. She felt the tremors run through his body and crumpled the money in her fist.

He jerked awake in the middle of the night and struggled to escape his dream. That man. He curled onto his side and sobbed. River touched his shoulder, but it just made him cry harder. And harder, until he couldn't breathe. He jumped up and raced to the bathroom. But there was nothing in his stomach.

When the heaves ended, he stood to splash cold water on his face and caught his reflection in the mirror. He almost didn't recognize himself. Not because of the swollen purple bruises by his mouth and spreading up from his jaw. It was his eyes. They seemed too big and shone with an odd gleam. His fingers gripped the edge of the counter. *I look crazy.* He blinked to clear the image, but it didn't change. He was caught in those horrified eyes.

He covered his face with his hands and turned away, then hurried back to bed. *Scared of my own reflection.* River's arms went around him.

Grant peeked into Brian's room in the morning.

Brian's eyes opened. "Come in," he said, his voice husky from sleep. He rubbed his face.

Grant stood near the door. "River, do you mind? I'd like to speak to Brian a moment." He sat on the bed as River left them alone. "I told Quinn you're ill. He sends his best. Brian—" He glanced down, for once unsure of himself. "I can't begin to tell you how . . . how sorry I am. He had good references. I don't—" He shook his head, his lips tight. "I should have been more careful." Tears stung his eyes as he stared at the innocent, bruised child beside him. He whispered, "Can you ever forgive me?"

Brian touched his leg, and Grant's control broke. He sobbed as Brian's arms wrapped around him. Grant buried his face in his neck and cried.

Brian stroked his hair and rocked him gently. "It's alright. It's alright." He kissed his shoulder. "I love you, Grant."

Grant clutched him tighter. "I'm so sorry, my baby boy. So sorry." The memory of his own father touching him flashed through Grant's mind. That old feeling—so filthy. Used. He held onto Brian tighter.

Brian sat up slowly, careful to settle a little to the side to avoid intense shooting pain. He was alone for a few minutes while River was in the shower. He stared at the wall with a frown, tired of feeling numb inside. *I used to be happy.* He could hardly remember what it was like.

The door opened and Grant came in with a breakfast tray. "Good morning. Feeling any better today?" He set the tray nearby and sat on the bed.

Brian shrugged and tried to ignore the nauseating food smell while Grant encouraged him to eat. Brian knew he wouldn't let up, so he picked up a strawberry. It tasted off.

When he'd eaten the whole thing, Grant said, "Would you like to go on a vacation? I thought you might want to get away for awhile. Or would you rather be at home now?"

He watched his hands wrap themselves in the sheet. Getting out of here sounded good. "Where would we go?"

"A Caribbean cruise starts in a few days—Jamaica, Grand Cayman, Mexico."

His eyes widened. Exotic-sounding places. He smiled a little and nodded. *River will be excited.*

Grant smiled back and patted Brian's knee. "Wonderful. I'll take care of it." He started to get up.

Brian grabbed his arm. "Is anyone else coming?" *Not John. Please.*

"Whoever you want, Brian. This trip is for you."

"No one else," he whispered. "Except—Jeffrey will come, won't he?"

"Yes. And Dr. Griffin, as well. We need to make sure you're properly cared for."

River emerged from the bathroom, a towel wrapped around his waist. Grant said, "I'll get started with the arrangements," and left them alone.

"Arrangements?" River sat on the bed.

Brian told him the news, and River's face lit up with a grin. "Alright!"

Brian smiled. He hadn't seen that grin in it seemed like forever. They chatted about how much they didn't know about the Caribbean, and things felt almost normal for a precious moment.

River leaned back against the headboard. "You seem pretty coherent for a change."

"The pills have worn off."

River took Brian's hand in his to examine the bandage on his left index finger. Brian tried to keep the pain out of his face. He didn't want River to know even that gentle touch hurt. Every inch of his body felt bruised, inside and out. It hurt everywhere his skin came into contact with anything. The bed. River's hand. He blinked and tried not to think about it.

"What happened to your finger?"

Brian looked at the bandage and felt like it belonged to someone else. "I don't know." He hadn't thought about it. Hadn't thought about— He swallowed and stared at the wall. "I guess . . . I must have cut it on the chain. I was yanking on it really hard. Really hard. I couldn't stop." Tears spilled over as his hand covered his mouth.

"Oh, God, Brian." River doubled over.

He stroked River's back, distracted from his own pain. "River," he whispered.

River pressed his face into the sheets, his voice muffled. "I want to protect you from everything. You should *never* get hurt. But I can't. I can't protect you." His fists pounded the bed. "It makes me crazy that I can't protect you." He hit his head with his fists.

"River." Brian put his hands over River's to stop him. "River." He kissed his back and rested his cheek against the warm skin. "I love you."

River sobbed.

֍ ֍ ֍

The ship's movement lulled him where he lay in a lounge chair against River's bare chest. The other passengers never seemed to come to this pool. He was glad. His eyes fluttered shut. Always so tired. The ship rocked him in River's arms, safe and warm.

He jerked awake when River moved.

"Sorry. My leg's fallin asleep."

Brian heard splashing and turned his head. Dr. Griffin's daughter, Andrea, sat at the edge of the pool with her feet in the water. He caught her staring, and she glanced away. She was about River's age, with shoulder-length wavy brown hair. Sort of pretty, except her nose was a little too big. *What does she think about me?* He knew the bruises looked bad against his pale skin, especially on his back.

She kicked her feet and leaned back so her boobs stuck up, well-developed for fifteen. "I'm bored. You guys wanna do something?"

"Yeah," River said. "Swim." He carefully extricated himself from Brian and stood. "You, too. The doc said you should get mild exercise."

Brian frowned as he settled in the chair. Pulled muscles all over his body cried out at the movement.

River tugged gently on his hand. "Come on."

He stifled a sigh and forced himself up. He knew once he started moving the muscles wouldn't hurt so much. And the warm water felt good, almost like a bathtub. "Does this count as a bath?" The doc made him take three a day. Said it would help him heal, but Brian was tired of it.

No roughhousing, of course. River splashed Andrea instead. She giggled and tossed her head. *She likes him,* Brian realized. He wasn't sure if he should care. *A girl?* But he was too tired to dwell on it. All he wanted was to lie down.

He stayed in the pool a few minutes more, then mounted the steps out. He heard Andrea gasp. She was staring again. She turned away abruptly, and he realized what she'd seen—the bruises on the inside of his upper thighs. His stomach twisted. *She knows. She knows what happened to me.*

It made him want to run and hide. But he didn't. River would follow, and Brian didn't want to ruin his fun at the pool. Besides, he didn't have the energy to run off.

He went over to the lounge chair and lay carefully on his stomach. He saw River watching him as his eyes closed. So sad. Always so sad. *River,* he sighed. But then he heard a splash and River's laugh. Andrea was a good distraction.

That night he lay beside River and fell into a dream.

It's dark outside my house. Nighttime. I step out into the big backyard. The fence runs all the way around and keeps us safe. A cat rubs against my legs. I stroke Gracie's soft fur and she purrs, then runs off toward a gap in the fence—the gate is wide open. My heart pounds. She might get out. It's dangerous outside the fence. I hurry over, but I can't get it shut. The gate opens onto a busy street. I can't close it! Gracie slips past me onto the sidewalk.

"No!" I run through the gate, pick her up and start walking along the sidewalk. I feel exposed out here. Motorcycles rev, their loud engines coming closer.

Suddenly I'm on the other side of the road, far away from the safety of the fence. A gang of motorcycles turns onto the street, heading my way. I clutch Gracie to my chest and huddle against the embankment, hold still as they roar past. They didn't see me. Thank god. But then they slow and stop.

The gang has stopped right by the gap in my fence. A young woman is there. She's afraid. So am I. The men get off their cycles and surround her. I see what they're doing to her. I shut my eyes, but I can still see. A sob wrenches my throat. They're raping her. My breath comes fast and shallow. I can't help her. God, what if I'm next?

I know they'll come this way when they're through with her. There's nowhere to hide. One of them pulls out a switchblade and cuts her. Down there. I'm paralyzed with fear and horror. He jabs the knife. She's dead. Oh, god. I couldn't help her!

They get on their bikes and start down the street, toward me.

He gasped convulsively, and his eyes flew open. His hands clutched the sheet to his chest as he struggled out of the dream. River's arms went around him, and Brian sobbed.

River watched from their veranda as the *Diamond Seas* approached her first port. He'd never seen water like this—so clear and light blue. *Brian should see this.* He glanced back and saw him still in bed. River went inside. "Come on. We're almost there. Get dressed."

Brian sighed and covered his face with his hands. "You go on. I'm staying here."

"Don't you wanna see Mexico?"

"Yeah." He stared up at the ceiling. "But I'm so tired. I can't—" He whispered, "I just want to stay in bed."

River sat beside him and put his hand on Brian's knee. "Okay. We'll stay here."

"No, you go. I'll be fine. I promise I won't even leave the room."

River folded his arms over his chest. "I ain't leaving you alone. If you're stayin here, so am I." He shrugged. "No biggie."

Brian closed his eyes a moment, then took a deep breath and swung his legs off the bed. "Alright, I'm coming."

"You don't have to. It's no big deal."

"River, don't lie. We're both going. Now come on."

They boarded a smaller, enclosed boat to reach the dock—the cruise ship stayed anchored out farther to sea. Normally it would've been fun, but Brian felt a bit nervous about the whole thing. He just wanted to crawl into bed and stay there forever. But the smell of the sea made him feel more awake, and the water was so lovely. Clear sparkling turquoise.

The movement of the boat made him slightly nauseated, but soon they reached the small wooden dock. One of the ship's crew helped them off the boat, and a personal guide escorted Grant's group past white sand into Playa del Carmen. Brian listened to the buzz of Spanish around him and wished Maria were here—she *was* in Mexico somewhere, visiting her family.

He sighed and leaned against River as they passed by white buildings with terracotta roofs and entered Quinta Avenida—a pedestrians-only street of shops and crafts and restaurants. His gaze moved to the pavement of interlocked bricks, each

Naked in the Rain

one an hourglass shape. He felt a little dizzy as he watched his feet. He looked instead at the shop windows filled with colorful clothes, silver jewelry, pottery. Any other time he would love it. But his body ached, and he couldn't shake the fatigue.

Even with River's arm around him and Jeffrey behind him, he didn't feel safe. He flinched as a man passed and almost brushed his shoulder. Too many people.

"Are you okay?" River gripped his shoulders. "You're pasty. Grant," River called.

They sat down at an outdoor café. Dr. Griffin held Brian's chin to look at his eyes. "He's just tired out. Needs a little break. Here, eat some sugar." He pushed a pastry toward Brian.

He blanched and reached for his juice instead. The glass shook in his hand, but he did feel a little better after a few sips. "Why am I so tired all the time?"

Dr. Griffin bit into the pastry and chewed thoughtfully. Bits of sugar stuck to his lips. "The medication can cause drowsiness, and you lost a fair amount of blood. Not to mention the emotional trauma."

"Did I have a transfusion?"

"No, but you are anemic. It'll take time for you to build up your strength, although mild exercise is good."

River said, "We need to take it slower."

Grant nodded. "We'll hire a car for the rest of the day. I believe it's time to visit the Mayan ruins, anyway."

Brian's eyes grew wide as he exchanged looks with River. *Mayan ruins.* Sounded intriguing and mysterious. He grinned, suddenly glad he hadn't stayed on board.

ശശശ

River flipped through the ship's four channels, bored. He glanced up as Brian came in from the veranda. "There's nothing on. I wanna see more ruins." He'd been amazed how much was left of the ancient buildings. A whole city.

Brian took the remote from River's hand and turned off the TV. "Reading is more entertaining."

River rolled his eyes.

Brian sat beside him on the bed and picked up the bottle of pain pills from the nightstand. "I'm tired of being sleepy. Maybe I'll try taking half."

"Whatcha doin' with the other half?"

"I was going to put it back in the bottle. Do you want it?" He held out half of the white pill.

River took it and popped it into his mouth.

"I guess that's a yes."

Twenty minutes later they were giggling and silly. River cocked his head. "This stuff makes me feel . . . fruity."

"Fruity like an apple or fruity like a banana?"

River grinned, suddenly horny. "Like a banana. A *big* banana." He growled and lunged.

Brian shoved him away, eyes huge and scared. That look cut into River's heart. "God, I'm so sorry. I didn't mean to do that." River's voice wobbled.

"No, no." Brian put his fingers over River's lips. His eyes filled. "I'm sorry. I didn't know where I was for a second. I didn't mean to push you away. I would never mean to push you away." He pulled River close and held him.

"Brian." River buried his face in his hair. *Please don't ever look at me like that again.*

Brian stared at the ceiling as the ship swayed and realized he was chewing his nails. *I never used to do that.* They looked terrible, the black polish mostly chipped off. He folded his hands on his stomach and tried to distract himself by watching River through the glass door. It was no use. Once the thought came to him he couldn't get it out of his head. His stomach tightened. *I have to talk to Grant.*

River followed him down the narrow corridor to Grant's room, but Brian went in alone. He paced and wrung his hands. "Grant . . . ."

"Go ahead."

"I—" He stopped and looked up at him. "I don't know if he . . . if Alan used a condom."

Grant took his hand. "He did."

"Are you sure?"

"I'm sure. I'm sorry I didn't tell you. It never occurred to me you didn't know."

"'s okay." Relief made him giddy. *I'm not contaminated.*

He left Grant's room and grinned at River, waiting in the hall. River looked worried. "Is everything okay?"

Brian nodded. He knew he ought to explain, but he didn't feel like talking about it. "Wanna walk around?"

They explored the ship and ended up in the spacious lobby, identical to the lobby on the other ship, except the statue in the fountain was a seahorse instead of a mermaid, and a Christmas tree two stories high filled a third of the space. He breathed in the pine scent and walked around the tree to the grand piano. He stroked it longingly, then glanced around. The area was almost deserted.

What the hell. He sat on the piano bench, and a great sigh escaped him. So wonderful to be able to play again. The bandage came off his finger a few days ago, along with the stitches. Though maybe he could have played with them, but he hadn't tried. Too busy hiding in his room.

His finger was a little stiff, but it loosened up as he played. A smattering of applause surprised him when he finished the piece. Several passengers had gathered to listen. He smiled and continued.

River glanced at a ship's officer moving closer. The man seemed like he was going to stop Brian but then changed his mind. *Good,* River thought. *Or I'd have to change it for him.*

His gaze returned to Brian as an elderly man went up to him with a request. Brian shook his head. "I'm sorry, I don't know that song."

"How about 'All of Me'?"

He shook his head again. "I guess my repertoire is pretty limited. I'm sorry."

"That's alright, sonny. You play whatever you want."

They grinned at each other, and River smiled. *Everyone loves Brian.* The man patted Brian's shoulder and turned away. He didn't see the way Brian flinched at the touch. But River did. His gut twisted. How could he stand this? How could he live with it? He hid his face in his hands.

When he looked up he saw the ship's officer return from a doorway behind the front desk and approach Brian. The man seemed shocked as he got closer, probably because of the yellowing bruises on Brian's face. He recovered and smiled. "I'm Philip, the Cruise Director. I have some of the music Mr. Glisan here was requesting." He handed him sheet music.

Brian studied it. "Jazz. I've never played that."

"You don't have to follow the music precisely, just get the rhythm down and take off with it. Improvise."

"Okay," he said, clearly excited, and began. It sounded great to River. The passengers seemed to think so, too. They clapped along, and a delighted grin lit Brian's face. The short piece ended. "That was fun."

Philip laughed. "We should hire you. That was better than our last pianist played it after a week of practice."

A hand landed on Philip's shoulder, and he turned to stare into Grant Nesbit's amber eyes.

"I see you've met Brian."

"Mr. Nesbit! It's an honor to have you on board." *Jesus,* Philip thought. *Thank God I didn't make the boy stop.* "You have quite a talented young man here. He's welcome to play anytime, of course."

Grant smiled. "Of course."

"This is one of my favorite places," Grant said as they stepped onto the dock. "Jamaica always feels like home. Time seems to move slower here."

Brian smiled up at him. It was wonderful to finally feel better. His body didn't ache anymore. He felt energetic. He'd never appreciated these things before. His gaze moved from the white sand and blue water to the mass of green jungle covering the hillside above Ocho Rios. "It's beautiful."

They took a car into town. He ambled along the sidewalk between River and Grant and felt safe, despite the honking cars that veered erratically over potholes. Until he heard an engine rev. He looked over his shoulder and saw a motorcycle winding its way through traffic. *Don't be stupid. It was just a dream.* His fingers clutched River's arm.

"You okay?"

"Yeah. Just . . . ." He shook his head. Too hard to explain. He took a deep breath of air so humid it felt thick.

Grant distracted him. "Look at this shop."

On the other side of the window stood the most beautiful guitar, with elaborate, colorful designs over dark wood. "Why don't we go in?" Grant led the way.

The guitar was handcrafted, one of a kind. Brian touched it reverently. Tiny figures of birds, flowers, and vines flowed around the neck and body. Red and green and gold. "Makes me wish I played guitar." He shrugged and forced himself away.

They walked back out to the crowded street. He soon forgot about the guitar as they perused a clothing shop. He loved the colors and native designs, especially the deep purple. The shopkeeper grinned as they heaped clothes onto the counter.

Brian stood waist deep in warm water and gazed up at Dunn's River Falls. "This is the most beautiful thing I've ever seen." Memories floated through his mind—the tree on acid, how River's face glowed when he smiled. "One of the most beautiful."

River nodded and put his arm around him. Lush green jungle surrounded clear water as it cascaded down layer upon layer of sand-colored rock. Grant had paid an exorbitant amount to temporarily close the site to other tourists. Even Dr. Griffin and Andrea weren't around. River smiled. *So romantic.* He hugged Brian close, brushed his cheek with his lips. *God, I miss sex,* he thought as he smelled Brian's hair, his skin. It was torture. He tried to think about something else. "We can climb up the falls, you know." He pointed to the limestone terraces that formed natural stairs.

Brian grinned. "Let's do it."

ධධධ

The boys watched a spectacular sunset from their veranda, orange clouds and glowing sky mirrored in the clear Caribbean water. When it was over, Brian opened the sliding glass door to walk into the living room of their suite, switched on the portable stereo and selected a gentle piano concerto. River carried in their empty wine glasses from the veranda, then came up behind him and put his arms around Brian's waist. Held him close. Brian sighed, content.

He turned to put his arms around River's neck, and they moved together to the music. His body pressed against River's as he rested his cheek on his chest. He felt River's groin harden against him, but River just stroked his hair. *Poor River must be dying.* He never left Brian's side, not even to visit Grant for sex. Brian kissed his chest through the thin linen and caressed River's ass. He smiled as he felt River's breath catch.

Their eyes locked, and he felt the intense sensation he always got when he gazed into River's eyes. Like River penetrated his soul. Made him feel so full he might burst. Brian clutched the back of River's neck to pull him down, and their lips met softly. Again. Weeks of pent up passion broke free as they clung to each other. He finally felt the urgency again, like it had never been gone.

He pulled his mouth away to move down River's chest, found his nipple through the thin linen and tugged on it with his teeth. River hissed and gripped Brian's arm. Brian tore River's shirt open. He had to have that luscious tanned chest. His mouth was all over it.

He dropped to his knees and rubbed his face against River's stiff crotch. River's legs shook. Brian unzipped the shorts and let them fall to the floor. River's cock sprang up, so ready.

Brian pushed him onto the couch, then knelt between River's legs. Took him in all the way, then toyed with the head. River was moaning nonstop. Brian pushed the penis down with his hand, watched it bounce back up. He had to taste it again. He felt River's hand in his hair. River moaned as he shot into Brian's throat.

River pulled him up to kiss him deeply. He lifted Brian's shirt off, brushed his chest with his hands. The bruises were almost completely gone now. His lips worked down Brian's body, along the crease between his leg and groin. Closer.

Brian writhed, lost in ecstasy once again.

Afterward they lay together on the couch as the room darkened, naked bodies entwined. River held Brian's cheek in his palm and gazed into his eyes. "I love you so much," he said, his voice thick.

Brian touched his lips to River's. The perfect moment stretched as they kissed. Brian smiled and rested his cheek on River's chest. It rumbled when River spoke.

"God, I missed that."

"Mmmm . . . ." His eyes closed. "I love you," he whispered and drifted into sleep, safe in River's arms.

He woke up in bed, turned onto his back and stared into darkness.

River mumbled, "Are you awake?"

"Yeah. Just remembering my dream."

River propped himself on his elbow and rubbed his face. "Another bad one?"

"Kind of. I lost my ticket to The Cure concert. It was about to start, and I couldn't find it anywhere!"

River laughed.

"What's so funny?"

"Nothin." He stroked Brian's arm. "It's just nice to hear you talk about a normal dream."

River leaned over to kiss him. Brian's arms wrapped around him, and they made love again.

River snuggled against his back, his arm around Brian's waist. Brian smiled and rested his hand on River's as sleep came again.

I hear voices in a meadow. It's bright. Light glows from all around, from the shimmery air. River's hair shines like gold, glowing around him. The voices come again. The words turn to silver, like the trees. Liquid silver dances as it hangs in the air, then coalesces into a word, 'Brian.'

He awoke. It was morning. River still held him close, his arm wrapped around him. Grant stood in the doorway talking softly with River. The voices in his dream. Brian smiled and rolled onto his back to stretch. "I was having the most wonderful dream."

River smiled and pressed his lips against Brian's forehead.

༄༄༄

Christmas morning. The room was still dark, but the ship's gentle sway couldn't lull him back to sleep today. River snored softly beside him. Brian kissed his shoulder and climbed out of bed.

He grabbed two bottles of nail polish from the medicine cabinet and went out to the living room. He thought about yesterday's conversation with Dr. Griffin while he painted his nails red and green. Brian had a clean bill of health, fully recovered. Physically. He smiled and held up his fingers. A nice Christmas present.

Yes, he definitely felt fine physically. His breath sped up when he remembered last night. He'd never done 69 with River before, cos they normally jumped right into anal sex. But since they weren't doing that now, they had more opportunity for other things. *God, it was great.* He heard River stir as he blew on his nails. *We should do it again before we head out.*

Brian crawled onto the bed and murmured, "Merry Christmas."

Grant led them to his room. "Brian, I have something for you." A large, rectangular box almost as tall as Brian leaned against the wall. Grant laid it gently on the floor.

"What is it?" He knelt to rip off the paper, lifted the lid and gasped. The lovely classical guitar from Ocho Rios. "Grant!" His eyes filled, and he got up to hug him.

"Merry Christmas, Brian." He kissed the top of his head.

"Thank you. Thank you so much! I wished I bought it ever since we left Jamaica." He sat on the floor and held the guitar on his lap, tentatively strummed the strings. A soft, mellow sound resonated. "Beautiful," he breathed.

He finally left the guitar long enough to join everyone in the lobby. The smell of pine filled the room. Christmas. He gazed at the presents piled under the giant tree and wondered if any were for him.

Andrea came running up to give him a hug. "Merry Christmas." She moved to River, gave him an extra long embrace and a kiss on the cheek.

Grant led Brian over to the Cruise Director. "I'm sure Philip can give you a few pointers on your new guitar."

"Really?"

Philip smiled. "I'd be delighted."

They chatted a few minutes about guitars; then Brian made his way to the piano. Time for Christmas carols.

Brian climbed over River's hot, naked body to get behind him. Bit his shoulder while his hand ran down River's chest and gripped the inside of his thigh. He rubbed River's firm, round buttocks, so white against the tanned flesh.

Brian grabbed the lube with shaking hands. Had to have him *now*. His penis slid inside the tight warmth. They moaned together. He thrust harder, pushed River down. *Harder.* Strands of hair clung to his face as he fucked River harder than he'd ever fucked anyone. He was powerful. In control. And no one could hurt him.

Brian sat on the cement between the pool and hot tub, his arms wrapped around his knees. He turned toward Grant in the hot tub. "You can play the same note in all these different places on the neck. There's an endless variation of ways to play stuff." He shook his head in wonder. "It's so different from the piano. Exciting."

Grant smiled. "I'm glad you're enjoying it. Could you get River's attention, please?"

Brian turned to wave him over. River gave Andrea a parting splash, then swam over to rest his arms on the edge of the pool. "What's up?"

Grant said, "As this is the last day of the cruise, I'm wondering, Brian, if you feel ready to go home yet?"

He frowned and stared at his finger tracing patterns on the wet cement.

"Or—" Grant continued. "We could spend more time on one of the islands. If you like."

He perked up. "Could we?"

Grant smiled. "Pick a spot."

He turned to River. "You choose. I didn't pay much attention to the different places."

River wiggled his eyebrows. "Jamaica, mon."

"Give me life
Give me pain
Give me myself again"

- Tori Amos, "Little Earthquakes"

CHAPTER 16

The boys had the best room in the house Grant rented near Ocho Rios. The sliding glass door of their bedroom opened right onto the beach. Brian put on sunscreen while they sat in the doorway, their feet in warm white sand.

River passed him their new pipe. 'Chalice,' the Jamaicans called it. "Damn fine weed. Ganja. We gotta stock up before we leave."

Brian nodded and looked out at the ocean. A lone figure stood at the water's edge. "Is that Andrea?"

River shrugged.

"Do you like her?" He didn't mind if River did. *It's no different than a guy.*

"She's okay."

"No, I mean *like* her like her. You know."

River looked him in the eye. "Brian, I don't like girls."

"Huh?" His brain felt slow. "But what about—what was her name? That girl at the institute." Memory flash of Jenny's warmth beneath him in the snow. His first true moment of passion. "Sandra. What about Sandra?"

"We never did much. And it never felt like it does with a guy." He took the forgotten pipe from Brian's hand. "I was forcing it with girls. Overcompensating. John says that's real common."

"Are you sure?"

"Yeah. I tried it once. John wanted to see if I should have female clients."

"And?"

"Didn't go so good." River frowned. "She didn't turn me on."

"Are you sure you weren't just scared?"

"I'm sure. It's a fact. I am not attracted to women."

Brian blinked. "Huh."

After a few more rounds of the pipe, the boys decided to walk over to the ocean.

Andrea watched them from up the beach. They were being silly. Laughing and splashing each other. It was good to see Brian having fun. Poor guy. But he seemed better lately. He looked so happy this morning when he played the piano. Weird to see a kid play like that. Amazing. She dug her toes into the wet sand and waited for them to notice her.

They didn't. River bent to scoop Brian up. Andrea admired his muscular back and shoulders. Tanned and glistening. She sighed. *I wish he liked me.* She knew she looked good in her new bathing suit. *If he would just turn around.* She folded her arms and kept staring.

What are they doing? Her breath caught. Kissing. They were kissing. River turned and carried Brian to the house.

Andrea's mouth hung open as she stared after them. *Oh. My. God.* "I'm so stupid." She slapped her head. "I should have known, the way they act together." She sank down on the sand. "Oh, my God."

River laid him on the bed and pulled off their swim trunks. Brian's head fell back as River's hand went between his legs. His fingers tightened on River's solid arm.

River's lips made their way down his body, kissed his hip while his fingers wandered, touching him everywhere, everywhere except where no one had touched him since—

"Aaah," Brian cried out. "Touch it—you can touch it. I want you to."

River's mouth worked up his thigh to the sensitive spot behind his balls, then back further. His tongue traced around and around.

Brian writhed. "*God.*" He almost couldn't stand it, it was so good.

River finally stopped and brought his head up to meet Brian's eyes. Brian gripped his arm and slid his hand down to River's. "I want you." He grabbed lube from the nightstand and squeezed it onto River's finger. "Please."

He put River's hand between his legs. River gently slipped a finger in just a little.

Brian made a sound deep in his throat and pushed against River's hand, took him in all the way. Aah, it was so good. Sweet. Oh, he missed that. He was going to come soon. But he wanted more. He pushed on River's arm, pushed it away.

River looked confused. Brian wrapped his legs around River's back. "I need you inside me."

"What?"

"Please." Brian clutched at him, desperate.

"Are you sure?"

"Yes, River. *God.*" He held River's cock against him. Pushed against it as River hesitated.

River slid in gently. As gently as he ever could, ever had.

Brian's head fell back. "Aaahh. . . . " His fingers dug into River's back as his body pushed against him. In and out. Filling him up. So sweet, so . . . *oh* . . . .

Brian cried out as the orgasm pulsed through his entire body. River collapsed on top of him. They held each other, breathing hard. Connected, body and soul.

Brian rested his hand in River's soft hair as River kissed his neck, his jaw, his lips. "River," he breathed. Brian stroked his cheek as they stared into each other's eyes. "My life."

The afterglow finally started to fade, and they settled back to earth. River glanced down and touched his own stomach. "Hey, look." He held up wet fingers. He grinned and nudged Brian's arm. "You're growin up."

"What?"

"When you came, something came out."

"Really?" Brian raised himself on his elbows to take a closer look at the wet spot on River's stomach. "Huh. Weird."

"Why?"

"I don't know, just is." He reached over to the nightstand for the wipes.

. . .

The clouds cleared, and the boys left the shop they'd ducked into when the daily afternoon rain hit. They wandered along the crowded streets of Ocho Rios, the air filled with the sharp scent of ozone and the honking of cars that splashed through potholes. The humidity was so high Brian's sunglasses fogged up when he tried to wear them. He took them off and wiped sweat from his brow. Everything was warm here—the ocean, too. Yesterday they snorkeled in clear water as warm as a bathtub. Fun and amazing—sea fans sprouting from coral, colorful fish everywhere. Like another planet. He wanted to do it again.

They dodged street peddlers and begging children as they walked by a whitewashed church. The young boys even tried to sell them baggies of water. Brian remembered their days on the streets of L.A. and frowned. He wanted to give the children money, but Grant had warned him not to. *'You'll have a horde of them around you.'*

He glanced over his shoulder at Grant and Jeffrey a few steps behind. Jeffrey made a face, and Brian laughed.

He turned forward again and almost ran into a tall woman with long dreadlocks. She smiled down at him, white teeth bright against her dark skin. "Where are you going, little one?" she asked in her rolling Jamaican accent.

He shrugged. "Nowhere, really."

"Ooh, I doubt that." She took his hand and studied his palm, traced her fingertip along the lines. "You have a lot of pain in your life. But a lot of joy, too."

He stared at her in surprise.

She touched his hair and let his hand go. River gave her money. She wanted to read his palm, too, but he hid his hands behind his back with a frown. "Come on, Brian."

He followed River away from her, then glanced back and saw her watching them. Almost glowing with some secret magical power.

Brian stared into the bonfire dancing before him and thought about their romantic horseback ride earlier today—the last day of the year. At sunset the horse had taken them into the calm bay. Amazing to feel her swim beneath them. Like galloping through the air.

River stroked his arm and brought him back to the present. "Two hours till midnight."

I wonder what this new year will bring? His mind couldn't wrap itself around all that happened this past year. Life had changed so unpredictably and so completely. "Remember last New Year's?"

They smiled at each other. Andrea poked her head around River to look at Brian and asked, "What did you do last New Year's?"

He felt Grant's attention turn toward them, away from the local boy who sat at his feet. "It was my first night with River after we'd been apart . . . six weeks?" He gazed into River's eyes. "It felt like an eternity. I wasn't sure I'd ever see you again."

River brushed his lips against Brian's and whispered, "It was meant to be."

Naked in the Rain

Andrea looked away. She wished River would kiss *her* like that. At least she understood now why he didn't like her. But she couldn't help being jealous. And curious. She watched as they stood to walk around the bonfire hand in hand. Brian stopped by Grant's chair and gave him a kiss on the lips, then went into the house with River.

Andrea's brow furrowed. After a moment Grant got up to go inside, too. The little black boy tagged along. She crossed her arms and turned to her father. "Does Brian kiss *every*one around here?"

He gave her a strange look and muttered, "I shouldn't have brought you." Then louder, "You saw nothing, Andrea. You hear me? *Nothing.*"

Her eyes stung. "It's your turn to have me at Christmas, and you don't even want me here? Mom's right. You are a bastard." She stormed off to walk on the beach alone.

A cluster of shimmering green lights brightened the dark sky, then faded as they fell toward the ocean. Brian leaned back against River, his hand on River's arm as it tightened around him. The fireworks had started a few minutes ago, when the clock struck midnight. He could hear people farther down the beach yelling and celebrating. Their voices mixed with the distant sound of a reggae band.

But his own small group watched the display in silence. Except Jeffrey. He was laughing, as usual, his arm around the waist of a lovely Jamaican woman. Nice to see him have that kind of fun for a change. Andrea stood alone off to the side looking sad. *Poor girl.* He looked back at the sky and smiled. "I've never seen fireworks on New Year's before."

"Mmm," River said into his hair.

"I heard they have good ones at Disneyland. We missed them when we went."

"I wanna go back. That place is a blast. Maybe we should go to Disneyland for my birthday."

Brian leaned his head back to smile up at him. "Yeah."

River kissed him upside down and squeezed him tighter.

🌀🌀🌀

River floated half-asleep listening to the night frogs, until he became aware of another sound. He turned over in bed to peer through the dim light. Brian's small fists clutched the sheet. Tears seeped from beneath his eyelids.

River shook him awake and held him a long time.

When River woke again the sun had risen. *We're leaving soon,* was his first thought. It made him sad. He turned his head and saw Brian lying on his back, hands covering his face. "Are you okay?"

"Headache. Bad." His fingers pressed against his skull.

"Should I get your pain pills?"

"They're gone. Doc won't give me more. Said they're addictive."

"I'll talk to him."

River returned a few minutes later and stroked Brian's hair back from his pale face. "I got your pills." He opened the prescription bottle and gave Brian water. Watched his face slowly relax.

An hour later River stared at the ocean from where he sat in the open sliding glass door, his feet in the warm sand. A loud knock made him jump. It woke Brian.

Grant stepped inside. "I'm sorry, dear."

Brian smiled and sat up a little, his hair mussed. "It's okay," he mumbled. "The headache's better."

River moved closer. "That's good, babe."

"Boys, Thomas has flown here especially to take back whatever we don't want to carry onto the plane ourselves." Grant's eyebrows lifted. "If you take my meaning."

River caught on first. "Oooh. You mean like this." He picked up a bulging baggie of marijuana from the nightstand.

Grant smiled. "Precisely. Don't carry anything yourselves tomorrow. We don't want any incidents at customs. Clear?"

"Clear."

River followed Brian down the street that afternoon during their final trip into Ocho Rios. Past a small reggae band playing on the sidewalk into a seedier area of town—he worried a little, since they'd left Jeffrey behind. But they finally found what they sought. They crossed a dirt road to the dilapidated phone booth. "Are you sure you want to do this?" River asked.

"Yes." He pulled a handful of change from his pocket. "It's not like they'll trace the call. And we'll be long gone, anyway."

"That's not what I mean."

Brian looked him in the eye. "I just want to hear her voice." *I need to hear it.* He turned to shove coins into the slot before he lost his nerve. He listened to the rings. *Please let Tanya answer.* He'd have to hang up if it was his mother.

"Hello?"

He closed his eyes. "Tanya."

She screamed. "Oh, my God, Brian! Oh, my God, it's Brian. Are you okay?"

"Yeah, yeah. I'm fine." Tears sprang to his eyes at the sound of her voice. "I just . . . wanted to wish you a happy new year. And Merry Christmas. I wanted to hear your voice."

"Brian. Oh, my God." He could tell she was crying. "Are you really okay?"

"Yeah. Did you get my postcards?"

"Yes—oh, Brian, please come home."

"No, Tanya. Don't. We don't have long—I'm at a payphone. Very long distance. Don't waste time with that."

"Where are you? Do you need money?"

He gave a short laugh. "No. Trust me."

"You sound different."

"Do I?" He slipped more coins in.

"You said you're in love. Anyone I know?"

"River. I'm in love with River. And he's in love with me."

Brief silence. "Oh."

"Are you shocked?"

"Uh, no, not really. I always knew you were different. But . . . how old is this guy?"

"Almost fifteen."

"Good. Adults could take advantage of you. You have to be careful. Not everyone has your best interests at heart, Brian. There are bad people out there."

He laughed again, bitter this time. "Really. Thanks for the tip."

"Are you okay?"

"Sure. What's going on with you?"

"Nothing."

"You're sixteen now. Did you get your driver's license?"

"Oh, yeah."

"Congratulations. And happy birthday. A little late."

"You, too. You're a teenager now. Two teenage boys . . . . Brian, are you having sex?"

"No, I'm on the phone with you."

"You know what I mean!"

He saw her stamp her foot in his mind. "Don't worry, Tanya. We're careful."

"Oh, Brian. Don't grow up so fast."

Too late. "Look, I gotta go. I'm out of change."

"Brian! God. We miss you so much. *Please* take care of yourself. And call again."

"I will."

"Send us a picture of you and River."

"Okay. I love you, Tanya. Tell Mom and Dad I love them, too."

"I love you." She could barely get the words out.

"Goodbye," he whispered and hung up the phone. Then it hit him. He leaned against the wall and sobbed.

River held him in his arms their last night in Jamaica. "You okay? You're so quiet." He stroked Brian's cheek. "It was that phone call, wasn't it?"

Brian frowned. "Why does Mom . . . . " He closed his eyes and tears leaked out. "Why does she do those things?"

"I don't know." River's throat constricted, and he held Brian tighter. *I wish I could take away your pain.*

Brian shook as he pressed his face into River's chest and cried.

River held him a long time. Finally Brian spoke again. "She almost left me at a grocery store once. According to Tanya. I don't remember—I was only two."

"What happened?"

Brian sat up against the pillows. He reached over to the nightstand for a cigarette and smoked in silence. River thought he wasn't going to answer.

"Mom started to drive away from the grocery store. Tanya pointed out the window and started crying. Mom's like, 'What?' Tanya goes, 'Brian, Brian.' I was still sitting in the cart in the middle of the parking lot."

"Jesus."

"If Tanya hadn't been there . . . ." He shrugged. "I always wondered if she did it on purpose." He paused to flick his ashes. "Probably not consciously. I think she just really didn't want a boy. Really, really didn't want a boy."

"Come here." River held him close. "I love you so much. I want my love to make up for what she did. All the things she did. Our love is better than that. It's more real than anything else."

Brian smiled and hugged him tighter. "It is."

"I'm glad you're a boy."

"Me, too. I'm rather fond of my penis."

River chuckled. "Me, too."

"Drown myself in something else
Take me down to the well
Rest in the waters that are you...

The river is burning"

- Brian O'Kelly

CHAPTER 17

Brian walked into his bedroom and breathed a sigh. It was good to be home. He and River collapsed onto the bed, tired from the long trip back. Rain dripped down the window, with darkness beyond. River frowned. "I miss Jamaica already." He rested his head on Brian's thighs.

"I like the rain."

"You're weird."

Brian laughed and gazed out at the night sky. *I wonder how long he'll be allowed to stay here with me? Probably not much longer.* He stroked River's hair. *Enjoy it while you can.* He sat up to kiss River's hair, his cheek, his lips. Suddenly they weren't so tired anymore.

Brian sat up and pulled on his pants.

"Where you going?"

"There's something I have to do."

River followed him out of the bedroom to the short hallway that led to the Room. Brian's heart raced as he steadied himself against the wall.

River said, "You don't have to do this."

"Yes, I do." He moved forward and reached for the doorknob. He almost hoped it was locked. No such luck. He opened the door, and there it was. Same as always. Bed made neat and ready for him. Waiting. His pulse pounded in his throat.

He forced his feet forward and sat on the edge of the bed. It felt different. A new mattress, he realized. His hand toyed with the coverlet as he stared blindly at the floor. A sob broke out of him.

River sat beside him and took him in his arms.

Brian clung to him. "Just hold me."

"I am. And I'll never let go."

Brian finally lay back on the bed, drained from crying, and stared up at the medallion on the ceiling. "I need a cigarette."

River lit one and handed it to him. They smoked in silence. Brian felt better. It was right to come here and face it, to let it out. He felt cleansed.

But River didn't look too happy. "I think we should leave."

"What?" Brian sat up.

"How can you go back to it now, after what happened? What if—" He couldn't say it, but Brian knew what he was thinking.

What if it happens again? He touched River's hand. "Who's to say what would happen if we leave? It doesn't mean you or I would be any safer." Too true. He turned to tap his cigarette in the ashtray—an excuse to look away and compose his thoughts. "I don't want to let what he did change my life. I don't want to give it that power over me." His voice trembled. "I won't let it." He shook his head and took a deep breath. "If we decide to leave, it will be on our own terms because we want to. Not because someone's forced us to it." He searched River's eyes. "Do you understand?"

River whispered, "I think so."

Brian woke up in the middle of the night. He'd been dreaming about Grant, and now he felt an overwhelming urge to touch him, to be held by him. River was sound asleep. Brian crept out of bed.

He slipped silently down the hall, into Grant's bedroom and under the covers. Grant stirred and held him tight, whispered, "I've missed you."

༄ ༄ ༄

He walked into the parlor and saw Quinn standing at the bay window. Quinn turned to give him a warm smile. It was great to see him again. *He's such a good, kind person.* He appreciated that more now. But seeing him stirred up emotions. He felt jittery—happy and freaked out at the same time.

They sat at the piano to get to work. *Everything's back to normal,* he told himself. But his hands shook as he reached for the keys.

Quinn noticed. "Are you okay?"

He tossed his head and smiled. "Sure." But a lump formed in his throat when Quinn touched his arm.

"Did something happen? You disappeared so suddenly."

Brian turned away. *'Did something happen?'* God. He was losing it. Couldn't help it with this sweet person touching him. He bit his lip and tried to hold it in. Tears quivered in his eyes and slid silently down his cheeks. He sniffed and wiped them away. "Sorry."

"What is it?" Quinn's grip tightened on his arm. "Is something wrong with you? Grant said you were sick . . . ."

He breathed a laugh, relieved Quinn had no idea. "No, it's nothing like that. I'll be fine." He took a deep breath and ran his fingers through his hair. "Let's get started."

The boys hugged a long time when River returned from John's. He'd only been gone a few hours, but it felt lonely without Brian, even with all of John's boys around. It had been a little awkward with them. Kelsey finally asked how Brian was doing. Kelsey knew. They all did. Their concern only reminded him of what he was always trying to forget. But never could. Never.

River shook his head. He'd worried the whole time he was gone. He took Brian's hand and squeezed. *At least I'm still here part-time.*

Brian said, "I've got new music I need to work on."

"Piano or guitar?"

"Piano. I haven't started my guitar lessons yet. That's tomorrow."

They went up to the ballroom, and Brian sat on the bench. "I missed this piano." He smiled at River, in his usual chair right in front of the stage. "I'll warm up with a short piece called 'Rustle of Spring,' and it really does sound like that. There's this great background behind the melody that sounds like water."

River never ceased to be amazed when Brian played. His fingers moved lightly over the keys, one hand always going fast. Like tinkling water of a brook. Or rain. River smiled as he finally understood what Brian had been saying, what he was always trying to explain. River had never grasped how music could portray such sounds before.

The short piece was over just as River was getting into it. *Gotta remember that one so he can play it again.*

"This next one I need to practice. It's hard cos it's new. I don't like the beginning, but it gets better."

"What is it?"

Brian seemed pleased he wanted to know. "Tchaikovsky's *Piano Concerto No. 1*. Well, not the whole thing. That's too long." He launched into the chords. "This part's kind of pompous and boring. But it gets better. Quinn says I'd like it more if I heard the orchestra playing along." He stopped talking as it got faster.

River watched his face grow intense. Brian leaned over the piano, staring at the sheet music while his fingers flew in intricate patterns. A bead of sweat rolled down the side of his face.

When it was over, Brian sat back and took a deep breath. "I'm tired." He got up to sit with River in the wingchair. He cuddled against him, and River's arm slipped around his waist. "That one part is so intense. My fingers are in it, and they won't let me stop. The music takes over completely." His eyes closed. "I'm just tired today. Bad dreams last night," he mumbled.

"What about that Moonlight one? It's real fast. Does it make you tired, too?"

"The last movement's fast . . . but exhilarating at the same time. And I've played it a million times, so it doesn't seem hard anymore. Just intense."

"Hmm." River wished he understood better. He kissed Brian's hair. His eyes grew heavy as they sat quietly, Brian's breathing slow and even.

River jerked awake. Grant leaned against the stage watching them. Brian raised his head and rubbed his face.

"I'm sorry to wake you," Grant said. "But I want to show you something."

They went with him downstairs, down the hall. To the Room. River glanced at Brian's pale face as they followed Grant to stand near the headboard.

Grant said, "We've installed an emergency button. It's here, hidden in this groove."

Brian moved closer to run his finger along the spot.

"Go ahead and press it. I want you to be familiar with it. If you ever need help, press that button. It will ring myself, Jeffrey, and the main security station."

Brian pressed it and murmured, "A panic button."

"Something I should have done long ago. I never thought I'd need it here." Grant took a deep breath. "It's disconnected now. We'll activate it tomorrow morning." He touched Brian's shoulder. "Are you alright?"

Brian nodded, but his eyes never left the button.

"Well, then. I have business to attend to. River . . . ."

They exchanged looks. River forced his voice through a tight throat. "I'll take care of him."

Brian sat on the bed and reached to find the button. He faced away from it. Reached back and struggled to find it. He had to turn around and look.

He lay down, and his hand went right to the button. He smiled. "This is good." He did it over and over. Sat in different positions. Lay sideways. Every position he could think of.

Watching him reach for the button repeatedly, obsessively, made River want to cry. Or kill someone. How could he possibly bear this? How could he stand here helpless to change the past? Always helpless.

"River." Brian's hands shook as he opened the slot in the headboard and pulled out the handcuffs. "I need you to put these on me so I can practice."

"Brian—"

"Please." He blinked rapidly and held out his wrists. "Do it."

River obeyed, kissed his clenched fists while Brian trembled and sweat beaded on his upper lip. River stroked and kissed and murmured his love until Brian could breathe again. "Okay. I'm okay."

He practiced until he could go right to the panic button from any position. With his eyes closed. In his sleep. By then he was used to the cuffs again, too. Though he wouldn't have let anyone put them on except River. And maybe Grant.

He finally gave in to River's pleas to stop and get something to eat. They went downstairs and saw it was dark out. Brian had no idea they'd spent so long in there. He felt strange. He knew the day was coming when he would see clients again. It didn't seem possible he could do it. But he would. They sat at the table as Maria brought out her homemade cheese enchiladas. He smiled and dug in.

roroi

The face of his guitar instructor floated up in his mind as he headed downstairs. A woman. An actual woman. Young and pretty. He'd been nervous and made a stupid comment when she showed him the proper way to sit, with one foot up on the stool. He looked down at his spread legs and said, "You wouldn't want to wear a miniskirt." Then he worried. *I shouldn't have said that.* But she just laughed and agreed.

She's nice. He paused at the bottom of the stairs and wondered what he was doing. *Oh, yeah. Looking for Grant.* He glanced around the parlor and saw the door to Grant's office ajar. He walked over, but paused when he heard Grant's voice. On the phone.

"He's doing well, thank you for your concern. I believe he'll be back to normal soon enough. Brian is very resilient. And tougher than he looks."

His eyes widened. Strange to hear himself talked about like that. But he was pleased by what Grant said. He tiptoed away. *I'll ask about Disneyland later.*

He lay exhausted in their suite at the Disneyland Hotel, waiting for River to come out of the bathroom. They had a wonderful day. Just the two of them, plus Jeffrey. But he hung back most of the time. Gave them space. They made out on Pirates of the Caribbean and the Haunted House. Brian smiled. A lot different than their last visit to Disneyland.

River finally emerged from the bathroom and crawled into bed. Brian snuggled against his warmth. "Happy birthday." He stroked River's face and kissed him, then pulled back. "Something's different." The skin beside River's mouth felt smoother than normal. And up near his ears. Brian sat up. "You shaved!"

River smiled and ducked his head. "Yeah."

Brian breathed a laugh and kissed him again. "Exciting." He stroked the smooth spots. "Fifteen. You're so grown up."

River smiled and gave him a squeeze. "You know what my best present is? Holding you. Knowing you're safe and happy."

Brian took advantage of the unusually warm January day, grabbed a sweater and beach towel and went out to the grounds, in search of a quiet place to get away. He needed a break from all the pity and worry surrounding him. He hated that everyone at Grant's knew what Alan did to him. Hell, all of John's boys surely knew, too.

But no one really knew what it had been like. For someone to hurt you so bad on purpose, just because he wanted to. That was the most disturbing thing about it. To know firsthand people like that were out there.

He shook his head and took a deep breath tinged with pine scent. He touched the soft needles as he moved through the gardens. He wasn't sure he wanted to talk about it, anyway. And who would he tell? David looked at him with such sad eyes. And River . . . poor River. It hurt him so bad.

He left the paths behind, where the grounds grew wilder, and made his way up the wooded hill at the edge of Grant's property. He finally found the perfect place—a shady spot with a view of the grounds and house. He spread the towel on the dirt, hugged his knees and absorbed the view. *I know—my journal. I'll tell my journal.* He took a deep breath. *Next time I'll bring it with me and write it all down.*

He lay down on his side. So peaceful. He jerked when Sebastian's wet nose touched his hand. He laughed. "Did you follow me? That's nice for a change." The cat curled up against his chest. Brian smiled and stroked him slowly. Stared into space. His mouth twitched, and sobs suddenly overwhelmed him. He cried until there was nothing left, then lay exhausted. But the knot inside his belly felt looser. He needed to let it out, to let down his brave face. A long sigh escaped him.

He set his guitar in its stand with a frown. He'd put it off long enough. Time to talk to Grant. He found him on the couch in the den. Brian paced. "Grant, I . . . I think I'm ready to start seeing clients again." As soon as the words were out of his mouth, panic tightened his chest. *God, am I? Maybe I shouldn't have said that.*

Grant's eyebrows went up. "Are you sure?"

Brian sank to his knees and looked up at Grant's face. "No," he whispered.

Grant smiled and stroked his cheek. "Perhaps you could start with one client, of your own choosing. See how it goes and take it from there."

He nodded, relieved, and knew right away who he would pick. *I can't imagine being afraid of Brett.* He put his arms around Grant's neck and hugged him. "Thank you."

Grant laughed a little and kissed his hair. "I don't know why you're thanking me."

Brian just held on tighter.

"River, I know this is gonna bum you out, but I need to have sex with you."

He laughed. "Oh, darn."

Brian tugged on his hand and led him down the hall. "In here." He opened the door to the Room.

"Oooh. I get it."

He still felt a little scared in there, but it passed when River caressed him.

Afterward River held him. "You okay?"

He smiled and snuggled against River's chest. "I never feel safer than when I'm in your arms. Doesn't matter where we are."

Okay, this is it. He paced his bedroom. *Why am I nervous?* He glanced at himself in the mirror, the sexy leather he hadn't worn in so long. As if nothing had happened. He frowned and shook his head. He just wanted it over with.

But as soon as he walked into the Room and saw his surfer Brett, everything was okay. Brett hugged him and said, "My God, I'm so sorry about what happened. It's so awful—I can't even think about it."

Brian looked up at him. "You know?"

"Grant told me so I'd understand if you . . . get upset. So I'd be gentle with you."

"Oh." He blinked, disconcerted.

Awkward silence fell until Brett said, "I got a tattoo." He pulled off his shirt. A thin line scrolled around his chest and stomach. The color changed from blue to green to gold to red as it wound over his muscles. "Friend of mine designed it."

"Wow." Brian touched it with the tip of his finger. The scroll circled partway around a nipple, then ended. "Mmmm." He traced it with his tongue.

"*Oh.*" Brett clutched Brian's arm. "God, I missed you."

. . .

Brian propped his head up with his elbow. "So what have you been up to? Besides getting that tattoo." He touched Brett's chest.

"Um . . . I met some of Grant's other boys."

He raised an eyebrow. "Yeah?"

"I've got these urges, you know? I figure it's better to take care of them here than bottle em up." He folded his arms beneath his head and stared up at the ceiling. "I guess I've had the feelings a long time, but I first realized it a few years ago at the beach. Watching young boys frolic in their trunks. I always had to hide my hard on." He shook his head. "I know it's sick, but there it is."

"Hmm. So who'd you see in the Other Wing?"

"Trevor mostly, and a few others."

"Oh." His lips pressed together.

Brett kissed his hand. "You're *so* much better."

Brian grinned.

"You were my first, you know. My first boy."

"Really?"

"Yeah. Once I admitted to myself what I wanted, I did some investigating. Someone pointed me to the top House in L.A. Since I can afford the best, that's what I wanted. And that's what I got."

Brian's smile widened. He reached under the sheets. "Let's do it again."

"a knife flashes in the sun
I cannot breathe
until he is done"

- River Deloy

௸௸ CHAPTER 18 ௸௸

Tinkling notes of the piano greeted River when he pushed open the door to the ballroom. The notes grew louder as they descended. Pounded. He moved closer and watched Brian's face. So intense. A tear slid down Brian's cheek as he played a final chord. It faded, and he sat staring straight ahead.

River leaned against the stage. "That was great. What was it?"

Brian turned. "Oh, I didn't hear you." He took a deep breath and wiped his face. "Nothing. I just made it up."

"Really?" He couldn't find the words. *You're amazing.* "I hope you wrote it down or somethin."

"Even better." He held up a small tape recorder and clicked it off. "Quinn told me to tape myself. When I finished the piece we've been working on, I just kept playing." He stood up and stretched. Time for a break. "I'll transcribe it later." He stepped off the stage and walked over to River.

River held him tight and murmured into his hair. "Are you okay? You were crying."

"Yeah. Just—" *It was about being raped.* "It got really intense."

River kissed his temple.

"Don't you cry sometimes?" Brian asked. "For no reason, just to let it out?"

"No."

You should. He touched River's face and leaned against him. "I've seen four clients now."

"Yeah? Is it okay?"

He nodded and counted on his fingers. "Brett, Maurice, Jean, and Mr. Clayton. They're all easy. Have you been with Brett?"

"I don't think so."

"You'd remember. He's a young surfer dude."

River laughed. "Nope, guess I haven't met him."

He reminds me a little bit of you. He didn't say it out loud. Didn't want to make River jealous. Brian reached up to kiss him.

He sat alone on his bed and picked up a photo. River and him on Christmas. That would be good to send Tanya, except. . . . He frowned. Couldn't use a picture from that trip. He'd have to get one from before the bruises.

He opened the bottom dresser drawer to pull out photos from the Alaskan cruise. He flipped through them, stopped and grinned. "This is it." The photo in front of Mendenhall Glacier. River's arm was around him, his cheek against Brian's hair. Big grins lit up their faces. And they had on regular clothes.

Now the hard part. He sat cross-legged on the bed and picked up a pen to write on the back. He stared at the blank space and tapped the pen against his teeth.

February 25th

Isn't he gorgeous? He's so sweet and wonderful to me. Makes me happy in a way I've never felt before. You can tell from the picture, can't you? That's River and me last summer in Alaska. Yes, that's a glacier behind us.

We've traveled to other wonderful places, too, like Jamaica. And I've started playing classical guitar. I love it! Grant gave me a beautiful guitar for Christmas. I'm taking lessons. Running out of room—Love you!

- Brian ♪

He addressed an envelope to his grandmother in Indiana and enclosed a short note for her to send it on to his family. Someone here was always traveling—it would get mailed soon. He set the photo up on his nightstand in the meantime, stared at the picture and leaned back against the pillows with a sigh. He picked up the phone to call River.

No answer. *Damn.*

He hung up and glanced through his English homework, but he couldn't focus. A warm breeze wafted through the open French doors. He took a deep breath of spring air. And suddenly knew what he needed to do.

He slung his backpack over his shoulder, grabbed his guitar case and made his way through the woods up to the secluded spot that overlooked Grant's property. He sat down to unload—journal, guitar music, a bottle of water, and box of tissues. He knew it would be painful to go back to that moment. But he had to relieve the burden of being the only one who knew all that happened. His guitar would cheer him up afterward. He touched it and smiled, grateful it was portable.

His eyes moved to the journal. *Let's get it over with.* He bit his lip and began.

Life is slowly returning to normal. But I can't truly get there until I get this out. I can't pretend it didn't happen. I have to tell someone. So it's you.

He wrote everything he could remember. All the little details, still so vivid. Alan's acrid smell, his sour taste. He shivered and felt sick but forced himself to continue. The pain. The incredible pain. Like a white-hot knife stabbing through his insides, through his entire body. His hand shook as he wrote.

I'm sure he hurt me on purpose. That was the point. How can anyone be like that? I've never known such physical pain. Being hit was nothing compared to it. Nothing.

I tried to escape to the peaceful white place. But what was happening to my body was too intense. I couldn't separate from it. I waited to go numb, but that didn't happen either. Time slowed and stretched—weird how that happens. Sometimes it's not a good thing. Definitely not a good thing. It seemed to go on forever. But . . . it did end. And Alan left.

He reached for the tissue box, half gone already. His head felt like it would burst. He rubbed his face and tried to remember the rest. The act itself burned excruciatingly vivid in his memory. But afterward was hazy. He didn't remember getting to his room. Something about the bathtub. Then River was there. He shook his head and wrote what he could. *'Thank god for River. I never would've made it through without him.'*

He ended the journal entry with lyrics from one of his favorite Cure songs.

'rape me like a child
christened in blood'

He hadn't been able to listen to it because of that line. *But now I can. I will.* He wouldn't let Alan ruin it for him. He closed the journal and lay on his side, grateful to be done. *Done.*

John stroked River's smooth chest as he thrust one final time. "Aahhh." His other hand milked River's last drops. John kissed his shoulder. *Incredible. River's a wild one.* Taming him was one of John's favorite pastimes. He eased away, and they lay beside each other to catch their breath.

River started to get up, but John touched his arm and said, "Stay here a minute." River lay back down.

John asked, "So . . . how is Brian these days?"

River's defenses bristled immediately. He tried to sound casual. "He's doing pretty good."

"I understand he's seeing clients again."

River shrugged. "A few."

John's finger traced a line on River's chest. "Which ones?"

Maurice, Jean, that surfer dude. "I don't know."

John met his eyes. "You don't know, or you don't want to tell me?"

River feigned innocence. "Why wouldn't I tell you? We haven't talked about it, that's all."

"What *do* you talk about? Do you tell him what goes on in this House?"

"No." River's heart beat harder. *What is he driving at?* He tried to keep his breathing even. "You and Brian are separate in my head. You're a completely different part of my life, and I want to keep it that way. I don't talk about Brian with you, and I don't talk about you with Brian." *Please drop it now.*

John studied him. "You spent a lot of time in Grant's House. And you still do.

Sometimes I wonder where your true loyalty lies."

He didn't miss a beat. "With you, of course. Grant's a nice old man—" He leaned closer and said in a low voice, "But you're much more exciting." River touched his lips to that spot he knew John liked.

John chuckled and pulled away. "Alright." He got out of bed and looked down at him, his face serious again. "Just remember, River, you're part of *this* House now."

River nodded, relieved when John broke eye contact to get dressed. *Jesus. What the hell was that about?* He hated to admit it, but John scared him sometimes. River kept searching for a crack in that cold exterior for a glimpse of what lay beneath. Sometimes he feared there was nothing at all.

He didn't trust John one bit. But he could use him. Time to deal with the obsession that kept him awake long nights, eating him up with impotent rage. He sat up as John reached for the doorknob. "John, wait. I . . . I need a favor. It's serious." His voice shook slightly.

"Go on."

"First . . . I want to know what happened to Alan."

"He was punished."

"But what does that mean exactly?"

"I don't know. Honestly, River. I don't know the details. It's better that way."

River squared his jaw. "Whatever it was, it's not enough." He searched John's ice blue eyes and said the words. "I want him dead."

John's eyebrows shot up. "Are you serious?"

"Absolutely."

"That's a big favor you're asking, River. Grant would not be pleased if I interfere."

"He doesn't have to find out. I'm sure you know how to make it look like an accident."

John pursed his lips, quiet a moment. "Have you given this thought? Do you truly want to be responsible for that?"

"Yes, I've thought about it. I can't think about anything else. I *want* to be responsible for it." His fist tightened on the sheets.

"If I agree to this, you must tell *no* one. Especially Brian. Understood?"

"Yes." *I would never tell Brian.* For a lot of reasons.

John nodded slightly. "I'll think about it."

River knew him well enough to realize if John didn't say 'no' outright, he would probably agree. River's mouth went dry.

ഇഇഇ

Quinn sat beside Brian on the piano bench. "Did you learn anything from listening to yourself on tape?"

"Yeah, I think so. I'm rushing this part—" He found it in the sheet music and pointed. He ignored the way his head throbbed when he focused on the tiny notes. "This part with the runs."

"That's right. Were you able to fix it?"

"Uh, not really. It's hard not to play them faster." He played the phrase.

"Try again, but this time bring out the melody—it's hidden in that run. When you find the notes of the melody, picture your hand heavier."

He tried it. "Wow. It sounds so different like that."

"And you're not rushing anymore."

Brian grinned at him. *You're so great.* His attention returned to the sheet music. "But how do I know to play it that way? It's not marked."

"It's a matter of interpretation. Have your previous instructors talked about that?"

"No."

"Well, here for example." He pointed to a downward run on another page. "You can play the same run different ways. First play it like a tinkling stream running down a slope."

Brian obeyed.

"Now without playing louder, picture it as a powerful waterfall."

He did. "Wow, that's cool! I mean, it's the same thing, but it sounds totally different."

"Yeah, it's cool." Quinn laughed. "That's interpretation. You can play the same phrase lots of different ways, then pick your favorite. Or mix it up, play it different every time."

Brian grinned and touched Quinn's arm. So exciting to have someone who actually taught him new stuff. His fingers stroked the firm bicep. *Oops.* He took his hand away. *Can't touch him. I can't behave when I touch him.* He turned back to the piano and lost himself in interpretation.

Half an hour later, he closed the door behind Quinn with a sigh. *Such a nice ass.* He turned around and jumped—Trevor stood a few yards away. "Jesus, you scared me."

Trevor looked away, his jaw tight. "Sorry."

What? 'Sorry?' No. I will not take pity from you. He let his voice grow sharp. "What are you doing here? Did Quinn see you?"

Trevor took the bait. "No, your *special* little teacher didn't see me. I'm not an idiot."

That's more like it. He folded his arms across his chest. "Why are you here?"

"Fuck you. I don't need your permission to be in the Main House."

Brian smirked. He felt oddly as if he'd won. His tone softened. "But of course not, Trevor."

Trevor made a face.

Brian said, "If you're looking for Grant, he was in the library earlier."

"Fine." Trevor turned and went down the hall.

Brian shook his head at Trevor's receding figure. *Oh, wrong thing to do.* He closed his eyes and rubbed his temple. It was getting bad. He'd had a headache since last night, when he woke up standing in the kitchen. His head had gotten progressively worse all day but he'd managed to ignore it. Until now. A wave of nausea hit him.

He clutched the banister with one hand, his head with the other. Time for a pill. At least he didn't have any more clients today. But River was coming to spend the night. *Shit. It's not fair to have a headache when River's here.*

River poked his head in and saw Brian lying on the comforter facing the other way. River crawled onto the bed. Nuzzled into Brian's neck and let himself forget everything else.

Brian giggled and turned onto his back. River tried to meet his gaze, but Brian's eyes were slits. "Brian, hey." They opened wider. Looked dazed. "What are you on?"

He smiled a little and massaged his head. "I had a bad headache." It was hard to enunciate the words. He sat up and clutched River's arm as the world spun. "Sometimes the pills don't work so good. So I decided to try something different."

"What'd you take?"

"Just a pill and this." He held up the pipe they got in Jamaica. "Want some?"

"Cool."

Brian handed him the pipe, then fell back onto the bed and stretched his arms overhead. He forced his eyes to stay open. "I'm really fucked up. But not in pain anymore, and I'm conscious. Sort of." He laughed.

River stroked his stomach where the tee shirt rode up. Brian touched his hand. "I don't think I'm up for sex. I'm barely here."

River reached for the prescription bottle. "Give me one. Then we can be barely here together."

A few minutes later they settled onto the loveseat in Brian's sitting area, on the other side of the partial wall. River picked up a video from the end table. "*Yoga for Beginners*. What's this?"

"I found it in Grant's stuff. He said I could keep it."

"Weird."

"No, it's not—I do it every day. It's good exercise, and it's peaceful. You should try it."

River grunted and picked up the remote to surf channels until he found a movie. They stared at the TV with glazed eyes. "Bill Murray's great," River said. "Me and Dove used to call this fat kid at school Mr. Stay Puft."

"That wasn't nice."

"Well, not to his face. Okay, Dove didn't say it to his face." He stared at his lap. "I hope she's okay."

Brian touched his leg. "I'm sure she's fine. She's tough, too."

River smiled a little. "Yeah, I guess you're right." He turned back to the screen.

Brian cuddled against him. The pain of the headache started to make its way through the fog. He closed his eyes and laid his cheek on River's chest. Focused his awareness above his head, away from his body, until he didn't feel the pain anymore.

Brian woke with a stiff neck, but the headache was gone. He blinked and looked around. They'd fallen asleep on the loveseat. The room was turning grey as the sun rose. He stood up to turn off the TV and tugged on River's hand. Whispered his name and pulled harder.

River's head jerked. "Hey."

"Come on. Let's get in bed."

River followed him. By the time they reached the bed, he was awake enough to be horny. Brian laughed as River tickled him.

"River, wait. I want you to do something for me." He pulled leather handcuffs from the nightstand, looped the chain around the headboard and handed the cuffs to River. "Put them on me."

"What?"

"Please. I want to be able to do it again. I know it'll be okay with you." He touched River's chest. "I could never be afraid of you."

River's hands trembled as he stared at the cuffs. Flashed on a faceless man fastening them around those sweet, small wrists. River's breath came harder. *He'll never hurt you again.*

"River? Please."

River shook himself. Tried to stuff Alan into the corner of his mind where he kept things he didn't want to think about and focused on the blue eyes staring into his soul. He kissed Brian's forehead while he fastened the cuffs around his wrists. Brian's face remained at peace. No sign of fear.

River took his time, and it was wonderful.

Grant set down his toast. "Now, Brian, don't let me push you too fast. But I'd like to declare you officially back to part-time."

He smiled and nodded. "Okay. Good."

"I'll continue to schedule only carefully chosen clients you know well. You be sure to tell me if you're uncomfortable with any of them. I know it's against the Rules to decline a client, but this is an exception. Let me know if there's a problem. Alright?"

"Okay." He sipped his juice, and his mind wandered. "Grant, when I first came here, why did you put me in Trevor's room? Did you already know I would replace him? How could you?"

Grant smiled and rested his chin on his hand. "I *hoped*. From the moment I first saw you standing in the rain, I knew you were special." He reached across the table to stroke his cheek. "You've surpassed my wildest expectations. I'm so very proud of you."

Brian beamed a smile past the lump in his throat.

ʣʣʣ

"David's rabbit had babies again. They're *so* adorable."

River leaned against the pillows with a smile. "They must fuck almost as much as we do."

Brian laughed and hit River's chest. "Oh, damn it." He held a hand up to his eye.

"What? What's wrong?"

"Just my eye twitching again. It drives me crazy!"

"Let me see." He pulled Brian's hand away. "Where?"

Brian pointed to the lower lid. "Ugh, it feels so gross."

He squinted. "Oh, yeah. I see it. But it's small."

"It feels huge." He shook his head. "Distract me."

River obliged. Brian didn't notice when it stopped twitching.

He woke with River's arms around him. Breathed in his scent and remembered his dream. Very erotic, starring River and Grant. He wanted to act it out and woke River with a few well-placed touches. "Come with me."

They found Grant and crawled onto his bed. Grant gently fastened the cuffs, as Brian had requested. He loved giving up all responsibility. *I'm so glad it wasn't ruined for me.*

Grant got out the blindfold and whispered in his ear, "Are you sure you want this?"

He nodded. It had been so perfect in his dream. River's tongue touched his nipple as Grant put the leather strip around his eyes. Brian's breath caught. His hands clenched and pulled. *Oh, god. No.* "No—take it off!" His heart raced in panic and his body bucked. "Take it off, please," he begged.

Grant pulled the blindfold off while River hurried to unfasten the cuffs. Brian curled into a ball and sobbed. River and Grant held him tight.

Brian slipped off his shirt and boxers and climbed into bed. River sat facing the window, away from him. It had been a strained evening. Brian felt terrible. He'd truly thought he was ready. But he was wrong and ended up hurting the people he loved.

He touched his palm to River's smooth back, and River let out his breath. Brian sat up behind him to run his hands over his shoulders, down onto his chest. Held him tight and whispered, "I'm so sorry."

River turned around. "What are you sorry for?"

"For putting you through that. I . . . I thought I was ready. But it was too much." He stroked River's face. "I never meant to hurt you."

"Brian. I can't believe you're apologizing for that." He put his fingers over Brian's lips, and his voice trembled. "Don't. Don't do that." River kissed him softly.

River blinked in morning light and forced himself awake. He stroked Brian's arm. "I have to go. I got a client this morning."

"Can you stay over again tonight?"

"No. I wasn't even supposed to last night. John doesn't like me to stay here when I got a client in the morning. But Grant said I should cos . . . you know." River sat up with a sigh. "John thinks I spend too much time here. He's made a Rule. I'm only allowed to stay over three nights a week, at the most. He said otherwise I might as well be living here."

Brian's lips twisted. "I wish you were."

"Me, too. But John's weird about this. Paranoid. He worries about my loyalty." River snorted. "It's stupid, but that's adults for you."

"Hmm. But there's no particular limit on you, say, coming over for the afternoon . . . ?" He traced a line up River's chest.

He smiled. "Maybe I can come back for a few hours. Okay?" River gave him a kiss, then forced himself out of bed. God knows his visits would be *very* limited if he was late.

Brian wandered into the stables, lonely and bored. Grant was playing golf somewhere. River was at John's, of course. Even Maria was away on her weekly trip into town. *Glory will keep me company.*

His mood lifted as he inhaled the aroma of hay and horses. Particles of dust glinted in morning light that slanted across the corridor. He stopped at Glory's gate to call her. She whinnied a greeting and trotted up.

"Hello, girl." He stroked her long nose and velvet muzzle.

She lipped playfully at his hand.

"Hey!" He laughed, then picked up a curry comb and squeezed through the wooden slats. Glory grunted in pleasure as he swept the comb firmly downward. He reached under her mane to scratch her favorite spot and rested his fingers against her warm neck.

A loud snort and thrashing sounds broke the peace. He hurried toward the noise, back along Glory's outside run. Two stalls away a horse lay on the ground, wracked by violent convulsions.

Carl and another stable hand stood in the empty stall between them. He turned to Brian. "She's been sick awhile; it was just a matter of time. You shouldn't watch this."

But he couldn't turn away. The convulsions continued. Her tongue lolled out, and she moaned. Her struggles finally slowed. Her head shook as she made a few final whimpers, then lay still.

Tears flowed down Brian's face. Glory came up behind him and nuzzled his back. He buried his face in her mane, then glanced at the dead mare. Dust covered her dull eyes and tongue. He shivered and suddenly had to get away.

He hurried out of the stable and left the path to walk through the trees. His feet carried him downhill toward the front edge of Grant's property.

By the time he reached the fence he had stopped crying, numb, yet deeply sad. He opened the smaller, human-sized gate and walked out to wander along the side of the road. He paused to lean against a tree and stared into the forest.

Why did that have to happen? He glanced at the ground. Sitting calmly a few feet before him was an orange and white kitten, its eyes crusted shut. Brian blinked. It was still there.

He crouched down, held out his hand and spoke softly. The kitten turned away to take a few blind steps, then turned back toward Brian and sat down again. He breathed a laugh and reached over to pick it up. The kitten didn't struggle at all. Poor thing was skin and bones. He stroked and crooned to it in a low voice, then headed back to the house with the kitten cradled in his arm.

. . .

After a brief search, he located Sebastian's supply of food. He dumped the can onto a plate and set it in front of the kitten with a bowl of water. The kitten had no trouble finding the plate even though it couldn't see. It wolfed down the food. "How long since you've eaten?" He kept his tone soothing. "Poor little thing." Its long fur was dull and dirty, but through the mess it was mostly orange stripes, with a white nose, chest and feet, its front paws stained with blood and ooze from its eyes.

When the kitten finished eating, Brian got a damp towel to clean off its eyes. It didn't struggle—didn't seem to be afraid at all. Puss bubbled out as he wiped away the crusty mess. His stomach turned. "Poor thing." He reached over to press the intercom button.

"Yes?" A voice blared out—Thomas, head of security for the Other Wing.

"I need you to take me somewhere." Silence. "It's important."

"Grant hasn't approve that."

"How can he if he's not here? I'll call a taxi if I have to."

"No, no. Grant definitely wouldn't approve of that. I'll be right there."

Thomas stayed in the waiting area while Brian went into the exam room. He explained to the vet how he found the kitten.

She opened its mouth to examine the teeth and gums. "This little guy's about three weeks old. Should still be getting milk from its mother." She lifted the tail to insert a thermometer. "It's a male."

The kitten cried and struggled a little. "Shh, it's okay," the vet said softly. "Obviously he's malnourished and has an eye infection. But he's also extremely anemic. In his weakened condition, the fleas have almost finished him off. He'd have been dead in another day or two, if you hadn't found him." She smiled at Brian. "We'll test him for diseases, and he'll need a blood transfusion. It could get expensive . . . ."

"That's okay! Do whatever he needs."

Brian lay on his bed with the kitten and murmured, "Sweet little schnookie."

A voice said his name through the intercom, and they both jumped.

"It's okay." He stroked the kitten and reached to answer Maria. "Grant's back?"

"Si."

"Thanks, Maria." His heart sped up.

He slid off the bed and walked toward the door. The kitten followed, tail up. "No. You have to stay here for now." Brian slipped through the door and shut it quickly behind him.

High-pitched kitten cries came from the other side of the door. He closed his eyes and squeezed his fists. So hard to ignore that sound. "I'll be right back," he said in a loud whisper.

He headed downstairs, and Maria pointed toward the parlor. The room was empty, but the door to Grant's office was ajar. Brian knocked softly and poked his head in.

Grant stood behind a mahogany desk in the small room, the phone to his ear. He waved Brian in with a frown. Brian sat down and looked around. He'd never been in here before. The smooth desk top shone—there was nothing on it except the phone, not even a pen. His gaze flicked to the walls. No windows. Just a few paintings, a cherub sculpture in the corner, and a door on the wall behind the desk. He wondered where that went.

Grant hung up the receiver, his face serious. "I understand you were in the stables today."

He nodded. His eyes filled as the memory flooded back.

Grant held out his arms. Hugged him close and kissed the top of his head. "My sweet boy. I'm sorry you had to see that." Grant stroked his hair. "Are you alright?"

He nodded. "But there's something else." Brian pulled away to stand behind the chair on the other side of the desk. He faced Grant and gripped the chair back. "Afterward I went for a walk."

Grant nodded, lines of worry etched deep on his face.

"I—I found something." He glanced away. "A kitten."

Grant let out his breath. "Brian, you scared me."

"I took him to the vet. They gave him some transfusions and said he'll be okay. He doesn't have any diseases."

"And where is this kitten now?"

He looked at the floor and mumbled, "In my room."

"I see." Grant rested his knuckles on the desktop and leaned forward. "And how did you get to the vet?"

"Thomas took me."

Grant pursed his lips.

"I made him."

Grant's mouth twisted as he nodded.

Brian's control broke. "Please let me keep him! He's clean—the vet gave him a bath. He can stay in my room if you want. *Please.* He needs me."

Grant smiled. "Of course you can keep him."

He laughed in relief and rushed over to hug him. Couldn't speak for a moment.

"Now run upstairs and take care of that kitten."

He sat cross-legged on his bed, the kitten in his lap. The special milk formula dribbled down the kitten's chin as Brian held a dropper to his mouth.

River stroked the kitten's back. "Why is his throat shaved?"

"That's where they gave him the transfusions. He needed two. Fleas almost killed him, can you believe it? I have medicine for his eyes. He'll be able to see okay once they clear up." He murmured, "Sweet little schnookie."

"What are you gonna call him?"

"I don't know. I'm not good at picking names." The dropper was finally empty. Brian stroked the rounded belly, and the kitten purred, eyes closed. "His mother would normally wash his stomach after he nursed. It helps him digest."

"I wonder what happened to her," River said.

"I don't know. I didn't look around." He frowned, then squished the kitten gently and smiled. He leaned down to kiss his soft belly, and the kitten purred louder.

"Maybe we should go back and look."

He smiled at River and nodded.

"This is where I found him." He touched the rough bark of a tree. "Or he found me."

"You sure?" River asked.

"Yeah, I remember this tree. See the limbs? They're all twisted weird."

They walked around for the better part of an hour. Called and looked in holes for kittens or the mother. River got bored and went back to the twisty tree, pulled out his pocketknife and carved 'River + Brian ∞' into the trunk. "What d'ya think?"

Brian took his hand. "You're sweet. But what's that sideways eight?"

"It's a math symbol. It means infinity."

"Forever." He squeezed River's hand and smiled. "But you're supposed to be helping me look for kittens." He reached up to kiss his cheek.

"Yeah, yeah. I'm lookin."

But they found nothing. They gave up and walked back to the gate. Brian punched the code to get in. "Kinda weird. Where did he come from?"

"He must've known you were coming." He twined his fingers with Brian's. "He knew you have a good soul."

Brian hugged his guitar case as he walked into the music studio with Thomas. Usually it was fun to get away from Grant's for his weekly lesson, but this time it was hard to leave his little kitten. Thomas took a seat in the empty waiting room, and the inner door opened. Julia walked out with a warm smile. "Good morning, Brian."

"Your hair—"

She touched it. "What?"

"You usually wear it up." But today it was loose, in brown waves all the way down her back. Like his sister's. *I wonder how long her hair is now? Or maybe she's cut it.* The thought disturbed him—that she might have changed, that he wasn't sure what she looked like anymore.

He shook his head and followed Julia down the hall. She seemed younger with her hair down. "How old are you?" he asked.

"I'm thirty."

"Oh. You look so young."

She laughed and opened the door to the practice room. "Thirty *is* young."

"I didn't mean it like that. It's just . . . you remind me of my sister."

"Really? How old is she?"

"Uh . . . ." He added three years to his own age. "Sixteen. She just got her license." It felt strange to talk about her like this. As if they lived together and knew about each other's lives.

She smiled. "How exciting for her. Tell her to drive carefully."

He tried to smile back. "I will."

River's fists clenched in the handcuffs as he writhed beneath John's touch. John paused. River opened his eyes in time to see John's hand come down toward his thigh. Something long and black flashed.

River jumped as leather stung his leg. Instant fury raged through him. He strained against the cuffs. "Don't you fuckin hit me!" The veins bulged in his neck. "Don't you hit me!"

John threw the riding crop onto the floor. "River, calm down." He reached to unfasten the cuffs. "Calm down."

River jerked his hands free. "If you ever hit me again, I'll be outta here so fast—"

"I won't do it again. I didn't mean to upset you. Calm down." John lay on his back. "Okay, don't calm down. Take it out on me. Focus that anger and fuck me."

River slammed his hands against John's chest.

"That's right. I can take it. Give it to me."

He did. River focused all his anger and hate into the most aggressive sex he'd ever had. He lay panting when it was over, completely empty. All that strong emotion gone in a quick fuck.

John turned his head to look at him. "I won't hit you again. But you can fuck me like that anytime. Understand? Anytime."

Brian sat cross-legged on the grass watching the sky turn orange and purple. Schnookie stared off, too. *I wonder if he can see the beauty of the sky?* But the kitten seemed more interested in the bugs flying around.

David walked over holding a young white rabbit. "We're headed to the fountain. I think Oliver's thirsty."

Brian joined him, and they walked past spring flowers to the courtyard. He set Schnookie on the wide edge of the fountain. The kitten's tail went up as he sniffed the rabbit's nose in greeting. Brian grinned. "How adorable is that?"

David nodded enthusiastically. "Your kitten is *so* cute. I'm glad they're friends." He grinned at Brian.

"Me, too." He looked over at a sound.

Grant smiled as he approached, took Brian's hands and kissed his forehead. "Hello, Brian. David." Grant continued on.

"Wow," David said with wide eyes. "He knows my name."

"Of course. What do you mean? Don't you know him?" Brian glanced at Grant's receding figure as it disappeared into the trees.

"Oh, no. I've never even talked to him."

"But you live here. Haven't you . . . haven't you had sex with him?"

David frowned. He watched his sneaker plow through a pile of twigs to scatter them on the concrete. "Normally he tries out the new boys, but he was real busy when I came. You'd just gotten here an' all."

"That's no excuse. He's had plenty of time." Brian folded his arms across his chest. "I'm sure he's just forgotten. Seems like he's always busy." *Too busy to ever take me into town.* He stared into the darkening trees, suddenly lonely. He turned to watch the bunny and kitten lap water from the fountain. So cute.

His smile faded. "I've got my first new client tomorrow. I've been full-time for a few weeks, but only with clients I already know. He'll be my first *new* one since . . . since we got back from Jamaica."

David touched his arm. "That's good."

"Grant says he's a nice guy, and he's been a client at this House longer than I've been alive."

"Who is it?"

"Jimmy. Grant said all the boys like him."

"Yeah, he *is* nice. Old and gentle."

He smiled in relief. Of course he trusted Grant's judgment, but David's words were reassuring. "Grant said if I'm nervous I could use poppers. Have you used those before?"

"Yeah, sure. Haven't you?"

He shook his head.

"Oh. They're cool. Except they can give you a headache. But they relax you, ya know, in that key place. And the head rush is fun."

"I dunno." He was reluctant to do something that might give him a headache. But then again, he drank too much sometimes. *Maybe I'll try one on my own first.* "And you sniff it right there in front of the client? Doesn't it make them think you don't like them? That you're not turned on?"

"Naw, lots of people do poppers for fun. And the clients don't care. They're not allowed to. It's a Rule—they can't complain about that. Besides, some of them *like* it if you're nervous. Or they don't give a crap one way or the other."

"I don't understand how people can be like that. Their sole purpose is to get off. Like the other person doesn't even exist. Isn't even a real person." He hadn't had any of those clients in a long time. But he knew they'd be back on the schedule soon enough. "It makes me mad."

David smiled slightly and touched his arm. "You're cute."

Brian smiled and slapped River's hand lightly. "Stop that." He retied the lace of his white leather vest and sat up to look out the window of the limousine. He ignored River's tug on the fringe that hung from his faded cut offs. He'd made his jeans into shorts—better for this weather.

"Hey, look." He pointed to a Ships diner up ahead. "Is that the same one where we met Grant?"

"Naw, that was a scary-ass part of town. This here's nice."

Brian leaned forward. "Jeffrey, can we stop there?"

"Sho' thing."

The diner's air conditioning felt good as they stepped inside. Brian smiled at the waitress, an aging woman with bouffant hairdo, her stained yellow dress too tight and her makeup too loud. But she was sweet and called him hon. He looked around the diner as she led them to a table. The place was almost empty. *That's right; it's*

Monday. Most people are at school. Or work.

She seated them by a window. Brian slid into the booth first so he could look out, and Jeffrey sat beside him. The street that turned off La Cienega looked pretty, with a small grassy park on the corner. *I've lived in L.A. almost a year-and-a-half and hardly seen any of it.* He turned to River in the seat across from him. "We should come to town more often."

"Yeah." River reached for the toaster—all the tables had them. He fiddled with the knobs. "Wonder if this thing works? I should order something with toast."

Brian leaned forward. "Did you feel the earthquake yesterday?"

"Yeah. I was with Dogman. It was hilarious—he got scared."

"Who?"

"Dogman, you know."

"Oh!" Brian covered his mouth with his hand and laughed until he was almost crying. "You call him Dogman?"

"Yeah, all the boys do. Cos he barks."

He laughed again and nodded. "Like a dog. He really does."

They laughed harder. River said, "The earthquake was so funny—he got all scared and made me hold him."

"How sad! I kinda like him. I mean, I don't *like* him, but . . . you know, he's one of those clients who doesn't like to actually fuck. It's nice for a change."

"Yeah."

The waitress interrupted to take their order. When she was gone Brian said, "I had my first new client."

"Yeah? How'd it go?"

"Fine. It was fun."

River let out his breath. "That's great."

"Jimmy. Have you had him?"

Jeffrey put his hand up. "No names, please, boys."

"Sorry."

The waitress brought their drinks.

River smiled and sipped his Coke. "Yeah, I know him. He's nice."

Brian made sure the waitress was gone. "Do you ever use poppers?"

"Sure. Don't you?"

"No. I did one the other day to see what it was like. But I've never done it with a client."

"Why not?"

"Grant only just told me about them last week." Brian fiddled with the toaster. "It gave me a little headache but not too bad."

"Oh, that's why he didn't give em to you sooner—cos of your headaches."

"It was nothing compared to those, so I guess it's okay for me to use them. I'm good at relaxing on my own, but it'll be nice to have something to help once in awhile." *When the unfun clients come.*

The waitress seated an older couple in a nearby booth. Jeffrey leaned closer. "Boys, time to change the subject. Remember, we're in public. You got to be careful what you say."

Brian's eyes widened. "Sorry," he whispered.

Naked in the Rain

River let out a little bark that sounded just like Dogman. Brian laughed until his stomach hurt. Jeffrey smiled and shook his head.

Brian was still giggling when the waitress set a plate of eggs in front of him with two slices of bread. Untoasted. "So we *are* supposed to use the toaster."

The waitress smiled wide. "That's right, sugar."

The toaster worked.

He finished his omelette and pushed the plate away, then got out the postcard he'd bought at the pharmacy. He loved the swirling, soothing colors of Monet. He turned it over to stare at the blank paper. "Let's write to Tanya. I want to tell her about Schnookie."

May 1st

> *I got a kitten! He's so adorable. I found him when he was only three weeks old. He was malnourished and anemic. The vet said he would've died if I hadn't found him. Poor thing! He's six weeks old now and really healthy. It's wonderful to have my own kitten to love. Schnookie sleeps with me every night. He's orange and white and fluffy. And super sweet—though Grant's cat doesn't like him. But he'll come around, I'm sure.*
>
> *I'll write again soon.*
>
> *Love, Brian*

He remembered his talk with Julia and added a note at the bottom. '*P.S. Tanya, drive carefully!*' He sat back with satisfaction. "See? I can write to them without lying."

River frowned and looked away. "Yeah."

Brian touched his hand. "I told them how wonderful you are in the last one."

Jeffrey picked up the bill. "Let's go, boys."

Warmth radiated from the asphalt parking lot. "Hey, Jeffrey—" Brian tugged on his sleeve and pointed down the street. "Can we walk down there? I want to walk around." He tugged again. "Please?"

Jeffrey laughed. "Alright, Mr. Brian. Just a few blocks."

They crossed the busy street at the light and walked along the sidewalk as cars whizzed by. It was loud here compared to the silence at Grant's. But he liked it. Brian smiled up at a magnolia tree, its dark leaves swaying as the warm breeze touched his face. The houses seemed small and close together compared to Grant's, but they had their own character. One even had little decorative turrets, like a castle. *Nice.* He wondered what it would be like to live here, in the middle of everything.

River pointed. "Look how the road just changed." The pavement was suddenly smoother.

Jeffrey said, "That's cos we just entered Beverly Hills. The street names changed, too."

Not only the names, but the street signs were different, too—white with black letters and a fancy hump on top. The shape reminded him of the shrine in Tucson, and he realized his wish had come true. *River loves me.* He grabbed River's hand and squeezed.

River pointed again. "Ice cream."

Brian's gaze moved to a small complex on the corner. A woman came out of one of the shops as they approached. She spoke quietly to the little girl with her as she passed by.

"Did you see that?" River's eyes were round.

"Yeah—that was Jamie Lee Curtis! Oh, my god!"

"Wow." Their first real celebrity. "How cool."

Jeffrey said, "You boys got to hang around Beverly Hills more often. There's lots of famous folks."

River smiled. "I love it."

Their ice cream was gone by the time they got back to the car. Brian gazed out the window as they drove down Olympic where they had just walked. It went by so much faster in the car. They passed the ice cream shop and kept going. It seemed familiar.

River looked past him through the window. "Hey, isn't that the store? Yeah, Albertson's—where we stole those Snickers."

He laughed. "We stole? You stole. But they were *good*."

"Best damn thing I ever ate." River shook his head and patted the leather seat of the limo. "Man, times have changed."

Brian touched River's hand and smiled.

They finally arrived at the coast. Jeffrey knew the best spots, deserted and private. The air was filled with salt and the cries of seagulls. The boys took off their shoes to walk in the sand. Kicked water at each other when the waves came close.

Jeffrey approached. "You better put this on." He handed Brian a bottle of sunscreen.

River turned to stare out at the sea, and the ocean water splashed a scratch on his leg. The sting reminded him of the leather riding crop. A lot like a belt.

"River? Is something wrong?"

He started, then looked down and pushed the wet sand with his toes. "Kelsey says John likes to test people's boundaries." *He found mine.*

Brian touched his arm. "Did something happen?"

He smiled and shrugged it off. "Nah."

"Who's Kelsey?"

"John's Number One. You met him at Grant's party last summer, remember? Dark-skinned. He's from South America. Speaking of—" River pulled his shirt off over his head. "Gotta work on my tan."

Brian touched the golden skin. "Beautiful," he breathed.

ಬಬಬ

He strolled along behind his kitten. Schnookie stopped to sniff every flower, every blade of grass. After only a month he'd already doubled his weight. His coat shone, and his ears glowed pink in the sun. Brian smiled as the breeze hit his face, and he gazed up at the clear sky.

Naked in the Rain

His heart skipped when he looked down again. *Where is he?* His eyes skimmed the ground. "Oh, thank god."

Schnookie was a few yards away, jumping after a butterfly. The kitten chased it and led Brian all the way to the far side of the house. Schnookie lost the butterfly but kept going. He rounded the corner and started toward the front of the house.

"Oh, no, you don't." Brian increased his pace to pick him up. He buried his face in the soft fur. Schnookie smelled good, like fresh air with a hint of sweetness. Brian held him against his chest, and the kitten purred.

Music drifted to him on the wind. It grew louder as he moved toward the front of the house. An acoustic guitar, slow and rhythmic. And a deep, familiar voice.

He looked up. Jeffrey sat on a balcony that jutted out from the side of the house. *On top of the eating nook*, he realized. He'd never noticed it before. Never came over to this side of the house. He moved closer to stand below the balcony and listened in rapt silence.

"And then he said, Mr. Brian, holding your kitty so sweet, come on up, and get somethin to eat."

He laughed.

Jeffrey ended the song. "Come on up, Mr. B." He indicated a white staircase.

Brian mounted the wooden steps, and Jeffrey opened the gate at the top. "Wow," he breathed. "You've got the best balcony. Even better than Grant's." It had a great view—he could even see a bit of the front yard. And private. The only balcony on this side, oblong instead of a narrow rectangle like the others.

"Welcome to my porch." Jeffrey gestured to an empty chair and a bowl of peanuts, then strummed a chord and began another song. His big shoe tapped the rhythm and became part of the music.

Brian set Schnookie on the floor. The kitten played with Brian's foot, which had started tapping along on its own. He watched Jeffrey's large fingers glide up and down the neck with ease, telling a story as surely as his rich, deep voice.

Brian clapped when the song ended. "That was great! I didn't know you play guitar."

"Oh, sho. This here guitar's been with me for almost twenty years."

His eyes widened. *It's older than me.*

"Would you like to hold her?" Jeffrey passed the guitar over. "Go ahead and play with her. She don't mind."

He grinned and picked a few notes. "It sounds so different from mine, not as mellow." He played around with it. It felt weird. Bigger than his classical and harder to play. The steel strings hurt his fingers a little.

"Don't just pluck at it. This ain't no classical guitar. Give it some force."

Jeffrey gave him a pick to use and showed him how to play the rhythms with his right hand. It was hard to grasp at first—he wasn't used to strumming. But then he got it. He laughed in delight.

Schnookie scratched at the door. Jeffrey opened it, and the kitten went inside. Brian peered after him. Jeffrey said, "Wanna see?"

Brian followed him in. The room was large but cozy. A bed, big stuffed armchairs. Framed black and white photos hung on one wall. A black man holding a trumpet. Another of a man with a guitar. That one had writing on it. An autograph.

"Who is that?"

"John Lee Hooker, of course."

"Who?"

Jeffrey put his hands on his hips. "Boy, you don't know who John Lee Hooker is? And you lovin music the way you do. That's just a crime." He grinned. "We gotta fix that."

He turned to a record player and set the needle down carefully. Static spit out, mixed in with a guitar lick, then a voice. Brian stared at the spinning record. "Isn't that what you were just playing?"

Jeffrey smiled and ruffled Brian's hair. "That's right." Jeffrey reclaimed his guitar and sat on the bed to play along with the record.

Brian made himself at home on the floor to watch and listen, mesmerized. The fast songs were fun and made his body move. The slow songs were even better. Hypnotic when the heavy beats combined with Jeffrey's low voice.

Hey, there's piano, too. Sounds like fun. Such a different style, the way all the pieces fit together. He sang along when the chorus became familiar.

They were interrupted by Grant's voice through the intercom. "Jeffrey, do you know where Brian is?"

He leaned over to press the button on the wall. "Sho' thing. He's here with me."

"Oh, hello, Brian. I thought you might want to know River's here."

"Oh—thanks!" He bounced up to give Jeffrey a hug and kiss on the cheek. "I gotta go."

"You come back, and we'll do it again. Okay?"

He grinned and nodded, then picked up Schnookie to head down the unfamiliar long hall, back to the rest of the house.

He knelt on the edge of the bed where River stood and ran his palm up the smooth chest. River leaned forward to meet his lips. Pushed against him as they kissed harder.

"Wait. I want to try something." Brian leaned over to the get a leather blindfold from the nightstand. "It's been a long time now. It should be okay."

"Oh, no, Brian."

He rested his hand on River's chest, felt his heartbeat and stared into his eyes. "Please. I need to do it. No cuffs—just this. If I'm wrong, I'm sorry. Really sorry. But I've got to try."

River frowned. "Okay." River slowly raised the blindfold.

Brian's hands moved to River's shoulders as his vision was cut off and rested against his warm neck. He smiled wide. He could feel River. Smell River. Touch him. He felt no fear or panic. He stroked River's chest. Without his eyes, his fingertips felt more alive. He didn't need to see River's body—he had it memorized. He wanted to explore every inch of it.

River whispered, "I love you."

Brian found his mouth.

*"Boys are like velvet
girls are like silk"*

- Brian O'Kelly

೧೧ CHAPTER 19 ೧೧

"Now, Brian." Grant set him on his knee. "Remember, we'll be in public, so you must behave properly—as if I'm your grandfather or guardian."

"Guardian." He didn't want to pretend they were related. That would be icky.

"Don't touch me sexually. Not in public. You and I . . . that's illegal. Understand?"

He nodded as the words sunk in. He'd never thought of it that way. *A lot of things are illegal.*

"However, when we're at the nightclub it will be different—it's a private club. It's alright for you to touch or kiss me when we're there. But not the rest of the time."

"Okay. Just at the club." Brian leaned in to kiss the side of his mouth.

Grant smiled and pushed him back a little. "Now, Brian, pay attention. You may see people you recognize at the club. Clients. Under no circumstances are you to indicate you know them. *Never* acknowledge a client outside of this House. Don't even give them a look. That's very important. Do you understand?"

That would be hard. "What if they come up to me?"

"It's alright if they initiate conversation with you. But no sexual touching." He stroked Brian's back. "That was a very good question. Have I answered it for you?"

He nodded and rested his body against Grant's, excited about this evening. *'Night on the town with John and River,'* the schedule said. He didn't mind that John would be there, since it meant River would be, too. Besides, John ignored him unless he wanted sex, and that hadn't happened in a long time, not since— He cut off the thought.

His mouth moved to Grant's neck. This time Grant didn't push him away.

Brian spent an hour deciding what to wear. He finally settled on his original white leather ensemble—the low cut pants with matching vest. Well, not the *original* set. He'd outgrown that. But this looked exactly the same. A man came to measure him, and he had a new outfit the next day, although the man had to come back a week later to take in the leather where it stretched. Now the pants fit perfectly. Brian liked that he could keep the same clothes even though he got bigger, but he would rather go shopping. Grant never seemed to have time anymore. He shrugged. *Tonight will make up for it.*

He headed downstairs and arrived as Maria opened the front door. John's black

Jaguar slid to a stop outside, and a man rushed over to open the driver's door. River emerged simultaneously from the other side. Brian grinned. He looked great—casually elegant in a grey suit. River saw him through the open doorway and returned his smile.

The limo pulled up in front of Shutters in Santa Monica. Brian put on the navy blue blazer Grant insisted he wear during dinner. Grant said the leather outfit was too risqué for a thirteen-year-old at Shutters. Probably wouldn't pass the dress code, anyway.

They walked through the hotel lobby, past gleaming dark wood with a matching grand piano and a bar area overlooking the beach. They stepped into the restaurant and saw a row of windows that faced the ocean and light sand just beyond the glass. The four of them sat by the windows, with Jeffrey and one of John's men at a nearby table. Brian glanced around the small restaurant and recognized more security scattered about. He leaned toward Grant. "They didn't ride with us."

"No, they arrived separately—ahead of us. You're very observant." He smiled at Brian but didn't touch him like he normally would. A subtle reminder to behave.

Brian met River's eyes. Heat smoldered between them. Normally sex was the first thing they did, but not this time. They made out in the car on the way over, but that only made it harder. *Literally.* Brian flushed and broke eye contact.

John and Grant were talking about boring business stuff. Grant turned to them. "Boys, you should pay attention. You might learn something."

River said, "But you're not even talking about the *real* business."

Grant raised a brow. "On the contrary. It's important to have a legitimate business, completely above board and legal. Something for the auditors to look at. Plus it allows us to indulge our other passions. With Nesbit Collections I pursue my love of art. John's business allows him to pursue—" He gave John a little smile. "His love of money."

River perked up. "I don't understand what that is. A brokerage firm."

John proceeded to explain it in excruciating detail. River was into it, but Brian reeled from boredom. Grant rescued him with a side conversation about sculpture.

After dinner they strolled along the cement boardwalk that stretched across the sand. It was a warm June night, so the boys let Jeffrey carry their jackets. They walked ahead, toward the Santa Monica pier and the distant lights of the Ferris wheel, then stopped to stare out at the dark water. He felt River's hand on his ass and turned to kiss him. They pressed against each other as their mouths melted together.

He pulled on River's tie and flashed back to the party last summer. Straddling him and tugging on his tie and fucking him right then and there. *God.* It was so hard not to keep going—he wasn't used to stopping. He murmured in a shaky voice, "River, I want you so bad."

"You can have me." River kissed his eyelid, his forehead. Pulled him closer to slip his fingers down the back of Brian's pants.

Brian laughed and pushed him away. "River! Not here." He took his hand and walked back toward John and Grant.

Naked in the Rain

Grant suppressed a smile. "I must say we enjoyed the show. And so did everyone else walking along the beach tonight."

Brian blushed.

River looked at John. "You said not to touch you in public, but it's okay if *we* do, right?" He gripped Brian's hand.

John shrugged. "If you don't mind people staring. It's not illegal for the two of you, just . . . not socially acceptable."

River snorted. "I don't give a shit about that."

Brian said, "But people see what they expect to see. I'm sure they just think I'm a girl."

River's eyes dropped down Brian's body. "Not in *those* pants."

"Oh." Brian covered his mouth and flushed redder. He turned away.

River leaned closer. "Sorry, babe. I never know what will embarrass you." He kissed his neck.

Grant said, "Come along, boys. Time to go to The Lily."

A short drive later, the limo rolled to a stop in a well-lit area. The brick building had no sign and no windows, just a single door painted black. A man in a suit stood beside it. He nodded as they approached and opened the door. "Mr. Nesbit, so wonderful to see you again. Would you like your usual table?"

They entered the club, the hum of conversation noisy, but not overpowering. A soft beat played in the background, and muted light glowed from green glass shaped like lilies on the walls and tables. Art deco designs edged the ceiling and made Brian think of the twenties.

He felt like everyone was staring at him. *Don't be paranoid.* Grant put his arm around Brian's waist as they moved toward the back to a circular booth in an alcove. Private, but with a good view of the club. Brian and River slid in first, with Grant and John on either end. Two bottles of red wine waited on the table.

A man poured the wine, then moved out of earshot but remained nearby, ready to refill their glasses. Brian looked the other way to where Jeffrey stood against the wall beside their booth. "Can't Jeffrey sit with us?"

"No. He's working."

Brian sipped his wine and glanced around the club. Mostly men, with a few male couples on the dance floor. He noticed a stage beyond it with a baby grand piano and drum kit. "There's live music here?"

"Yes, soon."

His eyes swept the club, searching for clients. He didn't want to be caught off guard. He spotted a familiar man across the room but couldn't place him until a teenage boy sat beside him. *Oh, right.* Grant's big party last summer. The man had been at the dinner table—Head of a House.

"What if I see people from other Houses? Should I pretend I don't know them?"

"No, you may speak with them if you wish. But remember you're representing our House so . . . good behavior, please."

River's hand on his leg distracted him. River nuzzled into his hair. They gave each other gentle touches while Grant and John talked. Soft kisses. It was maddening. He wanted to climb onto River's lap and grab him. But he managed not to.

"Here comes the music." Grant nodded toward the stage.

Men sat at the drum kit and piano as the lights dimmed. A black woman walked across the stage in a sleeveless blue sequin dress, a blue spotlight centered on her. She sang in a low, smoky voice. Songs about moonlight and love. Old songs. The light cast a moving shadow behind her as she swayed. Brian sat back, spellbound and transported to another age.

The lights came up when her set ended. "That was great." Brian grinned. And he had an excellent buzz going. The wine was yummy.

Grant turned to him and stroked his thigh. "The dance music will start soon. I thought you boys might like a little coke first."

River leaned forward. "Yeah!"

At a signal from Grant, Jeffrey and two other security guards stood in front of the table. Their large bodies effectively blocked the view. Jeffrey handed Grant a black vial and a tooter, then turned around to face out into the club.

Brian's eyes opened wide. *Here? Now?* Yes. Grant tapped the cocaine out onto a small mirror, then set it in front of Brian. It seemed weird to do it in public, but Grant nodded and smiled, so Brian snorted it.

River, John and Grant took their turns. "Ah, lovely." Grant wiped his nose and handed the vial back to Jeffrey.

A loud beat pulsed through the club, and the dance floor began to fill up. Brian's fingers tapped the table. It was hard to hold still after the cocaine.

Grant said, "They play a variety of music here. The Lily caters to its younger crowd, as well."

The next song began with a familiar beat pattern. Brian bounced. "I *love* this song—'Blue Monday.'" He grabbed River's hand. "Let's dance."

They hurried to the dance floor, filling up with boys from other Houses. Brian closed his eyes and let the beat take him over. Moved his hips and tossed his head. His eyes opened at River's touch on his waist. He shifted closer, and they moved their hips together. Like sex. Mmm.

The music changed and River glanced up. "I know this song. What is it?"

"'When Doves Cry.'"

River's eyes widened, and Brian wished he'd stopped to think before he spoke. *Sorry.* He wrapped his arms around River's neck and leaned against him. After a moment River let out a long sigh, and his warm breath tickled Brian's ear.

River rubbed his back as they moved to the slow rhythm. Brian could feel River's erection against his stomach. God, his own pants felt like they would burst. He couldn't stand it. He pulled away to put a little distance between them and reached his hands over his head as his body moved to the grind.

Grant watched River sink to his knees to touch Brian's stomach with his lips. River held his ass and ran his tongue down the muscle to the top of his pants. Pushed them down a little farther.

Grant leaned forward and glanced at Jeffrey, on his way to the dance floor. Grant signaled him to wait. He hoped they would stop on their own. But River didn't look like he was about to stop. He rubbed his cheek against the bulge, then reached for the zipper.

Brian laughed and hugged River's head against his stomach. Broke the tension. He tugged on River's arm, pulled him off his knees and led him away from the

Naked in the Rain

dance floor, back to the booth.

Grant let out his breath; Brian was in control of the situation. He couldn't blame River—he was under Brian's spell. Grant could understand that. He was, too. *I'm not entirely in control of our relationship anymore.* He put aside the discomfort that aroused. *It's a good thing. Brian is wonderful. And strong.* He leaned back. *It's a good thing.*

ൡൡൡ

David put the rabbit back into the hutch and latched the door. He smiled at Brian, who looked wonderful as always in long-sleeved purple silk. David gazed up at his incredible eyes. "Are you wearing contacts?"

"No."

"Your eyes look like they're glowing."

Brian laughed. "It's this shirt. Purple makes them look darker."

They strolled along a wooded path, and David said, "You talked to Grant about me, didn't you?"

"Yeah. I hope you don't mind."

"Mind? It's great! I mean, *he's* great—already taught me some new stuff. Plus it's good for my career. I'm excited."

Career? Brian thought. "Uh . . . that's good."

David stopped walking and touched his sleeve. Stroked it and looked up at him. "Thank you so much."

Brian smiled at his earnest look. "You're welcome, David."

He grinned and ran his fingers down Brian's arm. "I love silk. It's so soft."

"Me, too."

They walked on, and Brian led them toward the side of the house. He was always hoping to catch Jeffrey on the porch with his guitar again, but he hadn't had much luck. This time he heard music as they rounded the corner.

Jeffrey nodded to them, and they climbed the stairs. The boys made themselves comfortable on the wooden floor and listened to him play. Brian's voice joined in when he remembered the words.

Jeffrey held out the guitar. "Yo' turn, Mr. Brian."

"Thanks." He took the guitar reverently and held it on his lap. "It would be great if we could both play at the same time. I should get a guitar like this. An acoustic."

"That you could do, yessir."

Brian grinned. "I will."

The sound of Schnookie scratching on the door penetrated his sleep. *Damn.* He forced his eyes open and glanced at the clock. Midnight. He'd only been in bed an hour, but he was already in a dream. Something pleasant. His eyes closed.

The kitten scratched again. Brian shook his head and sat up. Wouldn't want Schnookie to have an accident on the carpet cos he was too lazy to get up. "Alright, I'm coming." He pushed the covers back.

Schnookie ran out as soon as Brian swung the door open. A figure loomed out of the dim hallway. Brian jumped, suddenly wide awake. The figure came closer. John.

John's eyes flicked down his naked body as he closed the door behind him. He touched Brian's arm—the first time John had touched him since Alan—then bent to brush his lips against Brian's. *He's never kissed me before.*

John was more gentle with him than he'd ever been. Brian was surprised to admit it was actually quite nice. He didn't know John could be like that. John kissed his shoulder, then pulled away. "I see you're growing up." He indicated the wet spot on the sheets.

"Oh." Brian blushed.

John smiled and stroked his cheek before he stood to get dressed. Brian marveled at this new gentle side. Wondered if it was real.

John paused in the doorway. "Welcome back, Brian."

He tied on his bathrobe and bent to pick up today's schedule. '*June 28th, Mr. Parks, 11:00 a.m. – noon.*' Brian glanced at the clock. *Better hurry.* His eyes returned to the paper. '*3 p.m. – ?*' There was an 'X' instead of a name; some men preferred it that way. It was the question mark that caught Brian's eye. "An open-ended session?" It didn't make sense.

He hurried through his shower so he could ask Grant but then couldn't find him. Maria was in the kitchen. "Good morning, sleepyhead. I thought I would have to wake you. Are you ready for breakfast?"

"Not yet." It wasn't good to eat a big meal right before a session. And Mr. Parks wasn't exactly a fun client. His stomach growled. He snagged a piece of Maria's fresh pumpkin bread. "Mmm." He savored the warmth as it melted in his mouth. "Do you know where Grant is?"

"Mr. Nesbit went out. He'll be back in a few hours."

"Oh." He frowned.

Grant still wasn't around by 2:50. Brian zipped his black leather pants. *What am I supposed to do with an open-ended session?* His lips tightened in irritation.

But then Grant stuck his head in. "Let's talk a moment."

They sat on the bed, and Grant took his hand. "There comes a time in a boy's life when he needs to find out about himself and his sexuality."

Brian's eyes widened.

Grant smiled. "I'm not trying to scare you. It's nothing bad. Just . . . it's time for you to find out if you're attracted to women."

His heart skipped. "What?"

"A woman is waiting for you in that room. Don't look so frightened. Nothing will be forced on you. If it doesn't work out, you don't have to go through with it."

Brian blinked as it sank in, and he remembered his conversation with River when they sat with their feet in the sands of Jamaica. '*John wanted to see if I should have female clients.*' Brian had never thought to apply that to himself. But why not? If

John's House did that sometimes, then surely Grant's did, too. It just never occurred to him to picture himself with a woman. Not since he came here, anyway.

"Are you alright?"

He shrugged and answered in a small voice. "I guess. It's just . . . so sudden."

"I'm sorry to spring it on you like this, but I've found it's better if you don't have time to dwell on it."

"If I don't like it, I don't have to do it?"

"That's right. Trust me, I will understand completely if you're not attracted to women." He squeezed Brian's hand. "I expect you to give it your best, but she is *not* a client. So you are not obligated to complete the act. Alright? Come along now, Brian."

They stood. *What if she looks like Tanya?*

He left Grant behind and walked down the side hall to stare at the closed door. His pulse hammered in his throat. He was so nervous he almost felt sick. *It's no big deal. I don't have to go through with it.* The memory of Jenny lying beneath him in the snow flashed through his mind. Maybe he *did* want to. *Don't think; just do.* He took a deep breath and opened the door.

He did a double take when he saw the young woman sitting on the edge of the bed. He'd only caught one glimpse of her almost a year ago, but he had no doubt. Hair cascaded over her shoulders like burnished gold. "You were at Grant's party."

She smiled and spoke softly. "That's right."

She had a Southern accent. He loved that. "I lived in Florida a few years," he said and moved closer.

"Really? Ever been to Baton Rouge?"

He shook his head and noticed how her chest heaved every time she breathed. She wore a sleeveless dress with a black ribbon laced up the bodice, tight across her breasts. Pushing them up.

"That's where I'm from," she said in her sexy drawl.

"Yeah?" He sat beside her on the bed. She was taller, even sitting down.

"Brian—that's your name, isn't it?" She put her hand on his.

He nodded, unable to form words with her touching him.

"I'm Michelle. Now, remember, we'll only do as much as you want. I know you're good at being with men. So if it turns out you like girls, too, it should be easy for you."

He tried to swallow and managed to whisper, "I don't know why I'm so nervous."

She smiled. "It's just new, that's all."

He caught her scent as her hand moved to touch his cheek. He leaned closer. She evoked different feelings than he was used to. Like he wanted to protect her and dominate her at the same time.

His gaze fell to her bosom, and his groin tightened. Oh, yes. He wanted her. No doubt about it. Her body was so close. He could feel her warm breath against his face. Her fingers ran through his hair, and their lips touched. Soft. Sweet.

They kissed harder. She tasted good. His mouth moved to her throat, down, down to the swelling above the tight bodice. Her skin was so soft. Smooth and rounded. *God.* It was almost too much. She was breathing harder now—made her breasts even more exciting.

His hands shook as he pulled the ribbon that kept the material snug. Her breasts moved as the tension was released, and the shape of her nipple showed through the cotton. He felt it with his fingers. *Oh. God. Don't come in your pants.* He strove for control. Pulled the dress back to reveal the dark pink nipple against her pale skin. He moaned and touched it with his finger. It grew harder. *God.* He pinched it, and she sucked in her breath.

"Girls like softer touches than men."

He lightened his touch. Reached for it with his tongue and pushed her back against the bed. Oh, her breast felt so good in his mouth. Fit so perfectly. And the nipple. . . . He stroked it with his tongue, sucked.

"Aahh . . . softer, Brian."

He let up a little. Her body moved beneath him. "Mmm, that's right," she said. "Just like that."

Her hips pushed against him. God, he wasn't going to last long. Next thing he knew his hand was under her dress, moving up her thigh. He looked down at her legs. Long and thin and smooth. He backed off, his entire body shaking. Time to get undressed. And slow down, slow down.

He stepped out of his pants and heard Michelle's dress fall to the floor. He turned to look, and his mind went blank. She lay back on the bed and stretched her arms over her head. Her body was so incredibly beautiful. The way her breasts stood up; the way her waist curved in and her hips curved out; her stomach so smooth; how it ran down, down, to a mysterious patch of brown. Almost like fur. He wanted her but didn't know what to do with *that*.

"Brian." She reached for him and pulled him closer. "I'll help you. Don't be scared." Her hand slid down his back, his ass, slipped between his thighs.

His nervousness vanished. Their mouths met again, and he was on top of her. His fingers played with her nipple, then trailed down her stomach. Hesitated.

"Go ahead and explore. I'll guide you."

He took her breast into his mouth. Her hips pushed against him as her legs spread. Suddenly his hand was between her thighs, and he touched her. "Oh." His penis jerked. He wasn't prepared for the wetness. *Oh*, yes. His fingers slid around in it as he explored the mysterious folds. Her body arched, and she gasped. He touched the spot again. A thick button of flesh.

She gripped his arm. "That's the clitoris."

He watched her reactions as he played with it. Her body writhed beneath him, and she made the most beautiful sounds. Oh, *god*. He was so hard. He wanted to be inside her. But he still didn't know where to put it.

"Now—" She panted, "Slide your hand back, straight back."

He obeyed, and his finger slipped inside. He groaned. *God.* There it was. So incredibly soft and warm. And wet. Jesus, he better hurry. He pulled away to slip on a condom. Tore open a pack of lube with his teeth.

"No." She touched his arm. "We don't need that."

Right. All that wetness—natural lubricant. He felt it again and touched her nipple with his tongue while his fingers slipped in and out. *Now.* He moved on top of her as her legs spread wider. She helped guide him in.

They both moaned. It wasn't as tight as he was used to, but her body fit him perfectly. Beautifully. Her legs wrapped around his back as he pushed into her. The way her breasts bounced when he thrust—*god*, he couldn't hold out. He cried out and fell against her.

"I'm sorry," he finally managed.

"What for?"

"You didn't come. Or did you?" *How do I know?*

She laughed a little. "You're a sweetheart. I don't expect to have an orgasm when it's your first time. But it was real nice."

"Can you stay? I'll last longer next time, I promise."

She touched his cheek. "We've got all afternoon. Next time I'll teach you to go down on me."

Yes. They cleaned up, then lay side by side to rest. He stared at the medallion on the ceiling. "Is it true women can have more than one orgasm?"

She smiled. "Yes, it's true."

He turned to look at her and grinned. "Let's try it."

"You ready already?"

"I will be."

"Alright. Why don't you start by running your finger up my arm, as light as you can. Barely touch it." She sucked in her breath. "Ooo, yeah. You just sent goose bumps through my whole body."

He noticed her nipples were standing up more.

"That's a good way to get a girl's attention. Get her thinking about sex."

He leaned toward her, and they kissed. Gentle. Sweet. He made his way down her body like he would if she were a man, except he paid more attention to her breasts. They both seemed to like that. He finally moved down her gorgeous, smooth stomach, then paused to look up at her.

"That's right, Brian. Keep going."

He moved down, brushed his lips along her inner thigh. Her legs spread wider, and he took a look at where he was going. It looked confusing, but the scent was intoxicating. His mouth went to it on its own. Her taste wasn't much different than a man, but mustier. Reminded him somehow of a teddy bear. *Maybe it's the fur.*

His tongue found the right spot, and her body writhed. He loved the sounds she made. Almost like a bird.

She told him to hum. He thought he heard her wrong at first. The vibration, she explained. He tried it, and her thighs trembled. He changed pitch to see her reaction. She gripped his arm, crying out loudly now, and her hips lifted off the bed. *She's coming*, he realized and kept doing what he was doing. *Oh, my god.* It went on and on. He was totally blown away. He'd never seen anything like it. So intense. And long. She lay panting. He looked down at himself. He'd come, too.

But he wanted to be inside her. *Well, she said a woman can have more than one.* He dove in again. *This is great. She could go on all day.* She told him to put his finger inside her when she came so he could feel it. He did. Mmm . . . so warm and soft, like velvet. She gripped the headboard as her body bucked. And he felt it—the flesh pulsed around his finger. *God.* Incredible. He was amazed again. Even after she lay still, a stray pulse gripped his finger now and then.

He finally pulled away. Her second orgasm had done the trick to get him hard again. She looked down and saw he was ready. "You want to come inside me, Brian?" she breathed.

He nodded.

"Go down on me a little longer to get me going again. Then put that lovely thing—" She gripped his penis and stroked a few times. "Inside me."

He kissed her body on the way down.

His eyes kept closing as he lay beside her. Michelle got out of bed. "It's gettin late. I better go now."

He sat up, wide awake. "Will you be back?"

She smiled at him. "Yeah. We get to do it all again tomorrow."

He had a wonderful afternoon the second day, too. But now it was time for her to leave again. He watched her slip into her dress and asked, "Will I see you again?"

"I don't know, Brian." She headed for the door, gave him a little smile over her shoulder, and she was gone.

He dressed quickly, walked through the parlor and found Grant sitting behind his desk in his office. Brian asked, "Will Michelle be back?"

"No."

His heart dropped. "But—" *I want to see her again.* "Don't I need to learn?"

"You know enough. Brian, listen to me." Grant stood to take his hands and stared into his eyes. "Women are not to be trusted."

"What?" He blinked, so amazed and appalled he could scarcely think. "Are *men* to be trusted?"

"Good point." He chuckled and squeezed Brian's hands. "You're too smart for me. But I'm serious. Women are different from men. Don't trust them."

Of course they're different. That's the point!

Grant kissed his forehead. "Now run along. I've got work to do."

Brian left the room in a daze. He couldn't believe Grant. He condemned half the world's population just because it was female? 'Not to be trusted.' His sister's smile flashed through his mind. *How dare he say that? I never would've made it through childhood without her.* He shook his head as he mounted the stairs. *I shouldn't be mad. I feel sorry for him.*

Brian knocked on Jeffrey's door, new acoustic guitar in hand. "Hi!" He grinned.

"I see you got yo'self a *proper* guitar. Come on in."

They settled on the porch with their guitars and played a long time. It was one of the greatest experiences of his life, jamming with Jeffrey to old blues tunes. The way they could play off each other, improvise and turn it into something new. Their voices, too, so they each had two instruments.

They finally took a break. Jeffrey's mouth broadened in a wide smile. "Well, Mr. B, you givin me a workout today. Been a long time since I played with somebody."

He grinned. "I've never played anything like that. It's *great!*" He leaned back in the chair, and they sat in peaceful silence. "Jeffrey . . . you like women, don't you?"

"Like women? I love women."

"I mean, not just for sex."

"Yeah, not just for sex. Some of the wisest, kindest people I've known are women."

"Grant—"

Jeffrey put his hand up. "Oh, I know. Mr. Grant has a thing against women. But it don't mean *you* can't like em." He poked Brian's chest.

He grinned. "I do. A lot."

Jeffrey laughed. "That's good."

Brian's smile faded at the memory of her soft Southern drawl. "He said I won't see Michelle again."

Jeffrey squeezed his knee. "Sho' you will. Maybe you won't get no more *special* visits, but she usually comes to the big summer party."

"Oh, yeah, I saw her last year. You think she'll be there again?"

"Sho' she will. You'll see her again. That party's only a few months away."

A few months seemed like a long time. But better than never. *Much* better.

He opened the waiting room door to greet his client and gasped. A woman. His heart pounded. 'Pat,' the schedule had said. Not a man. A woman. Her breasts poked out against grey silk.

His eyes moved to her face; she seemed amused. He found his voice. "Pat?"

She said in a gravelly voice, "Patricia, really, but I prefer Pat."

A woman. A real woman. His mouth went dry. The *Saturday Night Live* 'Pat' flashed through his mind and almost made him giggle—nervous craziness. But she looked nothing like that, thank goodness. Very short, frosted hair. Tailored clothes, jeweled rings. She exuded wealth and sophistication. *And she's here to see me?*

She was much older than Michelle but not *old* old. Forty? He stepped closer and looked up into her carefully painted face. More like fifty. "I'm Brian."

"Yes, aren't you though." She stroked his bare arm.

A thrill ran through him. He took her hand and led her out of the waiting room.

Her breasts were different from Michelle's. Saggier. But still fun. Pat was very enthusiastic once they got started. That cold exterior melted right off. She said odd things while he was inside her. "Oh, yes, my little boy. Come to Mama. That's right. Give it to me."

He didn't like the 'mama' comment, but he'd learned to ignore the things people said during sex. He had to use all the tricks Grant had shown him to hold out until she came—luckily that didn't take too long. Her manicured nails scratched his back. It felt good. He bit her neck, and it was over.

They lay side by side to catch their breath. She sat up against the pillows and lit a cigarette. He lit one of his own, propped his head on his hand and watched her.

She watched him back. "Brian." She said his name like she was trying it out. "I'm glad we finally met. I've been waiting."

"I'm glad, too." *I hope she comes often.* He smiled at the double entendre. *She will if I have anything to say about it.* "Will you be a regular client?"

"Yes, I believe so." She tapped her cigarette and stared at him. "Being with boys makes me feel young again. But you probably hear that all the time."

"No." *No one tries to justify why they come here. Most of them don't even think of me as a human being. But that's alright.* He didn't really think of them as human, either. That was their role. And his.

He stubbed out his cigarette. "Ready for more?"

🌀🌀🌀

River handed him the pipe, then pointed the remote to turn down the TV in Brian's sitting room. "You're not supposed to work when you're sick. You don't wanna get the clients sick."

"It was a headache. That's not catchy. I didn't know it would get so bad—it wasn't that bad beforehand." Brian held the lighter up and inhaled deeply. *I wonder if it would've been different with a nicer client, like Brett.* "The doc finally came cos I couldn't keep any pills down. He gave me a shot."

"Did that help?"

"Yeah. It knocked me out." He sighed and leaned back against the cushion. "What a relief. That was a bad one."

River brushed a strand of hair from Brian's face and kissed his cheek. "Do you feel okay today?"

"Yeah, just tired." His eyes moved to the TV. "It's back on." He loved underwater documentaries. The octopus was so different from any land creature, like it came from another world. The sea creatures were *all* amazing. It reminded him of Jamaica.

River said, "Reminds me of Jamaica."

Brian laughed. "Me, too." They watched in fascination until commercials came on again. "Oh, I like this one." Victoria's Secret. Women in underwear. "Look at them. The one on the left. Don't you want to run your tongue down her stomach?"

River gave a little laugh. "No."

"I don't understand how you can not be attracted to that."

"Not everybody's the same as you."

"Yeah, I guess. I wish I had more female clients. Just the one, so far. Every two weeks." He frowned and thought of Michelle. *Two more months.* "I guess there aren't many women who want to have sex with a thirteen-year-old."

River grunted. "Seem to be plenty of men." The credits rolled for *Life of the Octopus*. "Aw, man. That was good. Now there's nothing on."

He knew what River had in mind when he turned it to the Weather Channel. Harmless background noise. River pulled him onto his lap.

Afterward they relaxed on the loveseat and stared at a graphic of the globe with cloud patterns moving over it. Brian said, "Whoa. That looks really cool."

River agreed, then laughed. "We must be really stoned if we think the Weather Channel's cool."

"Yeah." He picked up the pipe. "Look, there's still some in here. I hate to leave just a little bit."

"Yeah. That's so annoying later." River finished it and packed more in. "Gotta have a fresh bowl." He said it like a toilet commercial, and they laughed.

The local forecast came on. Brian reached for the bag of corn chips and said, "Let me guess. Sunny and 90. Oh, this music's awful. It's the Beatles—they turned the Beatles into Muzak! That's sick." He grabbed River's hand for the remote.

River laughed and flipped channels. "I love cable. So much crap to choose from."

"There. Keep it there." News. Something about cancer research. "My grandpa died from that," Brian said softly.

"Really? Sorry."

"He's the one I was named after—my middle name, I mean. Kieran O'Kelly."

"How old were you when he died?"

"Ten. It's the only time I've seen Dad cry. That was awful."

"I've never lost anybody. Not from death, anyhow." He looked away.

Brian rested his hand on River's. "It's sad for your father that he doesn't know you. His life is less because of it. I bet he thinks about you a lot."

River made a face. "Naw. Twelve years. I think he woulda called."

"He never wrote or anything?"

"Nope. Never. When I was a kid I used to pretend sometimes—" His voice caught. "Pretend he was trying to contact me but Dick wouldn't let him." He ground his jaw. "Stupid kid."

"River." He leaned closer, his lips inches from River's cheek. "I'm sure your father regrets leaving you, very much." He squeezed River's hand. "And I'm sure I love you, *very much*." He pulled River's head against his chest and held it. "You can let it out. It's okay." He stroked River's hair. "Let it out."

River cried.

*"Alcoholic kind of mood
lose my clothes
lose my lube
cruising for a piece of fun
looking out for number one
different partner every night
so narcotic outta sight
what a gas
what a beautiful ass"*

- Placebo, "Nancy Boy"

༜༜ CHAPTER 20 ༜༜

Grant surveyed the crowd. He'd invited more guests this year. Another birthday—a big one this time. But he didn't feel old. Not tonight, with this young boy on his lap. "Now, David, sit up straight."

He stiffened.

Grant stroked his back. "You can be relaxed and still have good posture. Look at Brian." Brian stood twenty feet away, laughing and flirting with a guest. "See how he stands? Straight but relaxed. See his natural grace? You should emulate Brian."

"Okay."

"Do you know what emulate means?"

David looked down. "No."

"If you don't know what a word means, just ask. That's how you learn. To emulate Brian means to try to be like him. Look up to him."

"I do."

Grant kissed his cheek. "Good boy. But not in *every* way. Brian smokes too much. I don't want you to smoke cigarettes."

"Okay."

Grant beckoned to Brian and watched the skirt move with his slow strides to reveal flashes of white skin and garters above the fishnets. "He looks magnificent, doesn't he," Grant murmured to himself.

"Yes," David answered.

Brian stopped an inch away from Grant's knee and said hello to David. David wore a tiny leather top and skirt. Brian hadn't seen him dressed like that in a long time. Seemed weird.

Grant said, "I never thanked you for bringing David to my attention. He's a clever little boy."

David beamed.

Grant looked at David's glowing face and said softly, "And very eager to please." They kissed.

Brian glanced away with a frown. *What's wrong with me? I'm the one who got them together.* He shook his head. *Guess it's weird cos David's a friend. And . . . he seems so young.*

He was grateful when they stopped kissing. Grant turned to Brian and patted his knee. "Hop up."

His heart pounded as he obeyed. *Shit.* He gave a tentative smile to David, perched across from him. So close. Their knees brushed. *Shit. Shit.*

Brian closed his eyes. He felt sick, even with Grant nibbling on his neck. Grant's hand moved to his thigh, to the top of the stocking and the delicate skin above it. Brian sucked in his breath. *God, what am I gonna do?* His fingers tightened on Grant's arm. *Please don't take us upstairs.* But he knew that was exactly what Grant intended.

I really, really don't want to do that with David. Please don't make me do that with David. He felt like he might cry.

Justin the cute photographer approached. Grant put his arms around the two boys and hugged them close. Brian tried to smile for the camera. Couldn't do it.

The flash blinded him a moment, but he felt Grant's arm around him, David's leg touching his. *I've got to get out of this.* When his vision cleared he saw Kristoff standing nearby. *Yes! God, please let it work.* He touched Grant's chest and tried to sound casual. "May I go say hello to Kristoff?"

"Of course."

The relief made him dizzy. *Don't cry.* "Thank you, Grant." He kissed his cheek and hurried away.

River saw Brian and Kristoff walking along the flagstone path from the house to rejoin the party. Brian left Kristoff and made his way over. "Have you seen Grant?"

"He went inside with David. And Trevor." River watched closely for a reaction. Didn't get the one he expected.

Brian's eyes closed. "Good."

"You're not mad?"

"No. I don't want to do that with David. I don't feel sexual with him. He's my friend."

"Oh." River had slept with most of his friends—didn't bother him.

"Besides, David's too young."

"Isn't he the same age as you when you first came here?"

"Almost, but I mean he's too young for me. I like men. Or guys who are older than me, anyway."

River nodded. The boys at John's tended to be older. There were only a few really young ones. He hadn't realized that before. *I guess each House is a little different.* "Grant likes em young."

൹൹൹

Brian chewed on his black painted fingernail and stared out the car window at city lights. *Going* to see a client. Weird. Grant had assured him the man was safe. He'd been Grant's friend and client for over thirty years. The man was recovering from a hospital stay, so Grant thought it would be easier on Mr. Padrea if Brian went to him.

An All Night session away from home. No matter what Grant said, it still made Brian nervous. He glanced toward the front of the Mercedes. At least Jeffrey was here. Grant had offered to come along, but Brian said no. He didn't want to be a baby.

He looked down at himself. *And I hate this top.* Couldn't even really call it a top. Just strips of black leather. Two ran across his chest just above and below his nipples. Another strap went around the bottom of his rib cage. Plus two over his shoulders. *Why'd they put the buckles where I can't reach them? So stupid.* He needed help to get in or out of it. And it made him look weird. But Grant said Mr. Padrea would like it.

The streetlights flew by as they sped down Wilshire Boulevard. Jeffrey told him it was time, so he slipped into his black blazer and buttoned it as the Mercedes stopped before a cluster of tall buildings. He peered up through the darkness as he got out of the car and practically bent over backwards trying to see the top of the skyscraper. "He lives in there?"

"Yessir, Mr. Brian." Jeffrey gave the keys to the valet, rested a comforting hand on Brian's shoulder, and nodded to the man who opened the large glass door for them.

Brian glanced around the lobby. Chandeliers, shiny wood, a uniformed clerk behind the counter. Like an expensive hotel. He felt conspicuous in leather miniskirt and boots. At least the blazer covered the tightest parts. Besides, the place was almost deserted. *I guess it is pretty late.* Almost midnight on a Tuesday.

He stepped into the elevator with Jeffrey, empty except for a man who pressed the buttons for them. *What do we need him for? We can press buttons. Button. Panic button. There's no panic button.* He clenched his fists. *Don't freak out. Grant wouldn't send you to someone like that.* He stared straight ahead and ignored his twitching eye. Focused instead on the distorted image reflected on the wall. *I look so short and tiny next to Jeffrey.*

If things went well, Mr. Padrea would become a regular client—every other week. *Why does it have to be all night?* He sighed, quite sure he wouldn't be able to sleep in a strange place.

The elevator opened, and Jeffrey led him down a long hallway. They stopped at a set of double doors near the end. Jeffrey said, "Now remember, I'll be right out here if you need anything. So don't worry." He squeezed Brian's shoulder. "You'll be fine, Mr. B."

Jeffrey knocked softly on the door, answered immediately by an old man in a bathrobe. Mr. Padrea's eyes opened wide as he stared at Brian. He looked a bit like a chicken, with wispy white hair sticking straight up. He whispered, "Come in. Come in."

Brian smiled and went in. He wasn't scared anymore.

He stifled a yawn and opened the door that led out to the hallway. Jeffrey stood leaning against the wall nearby, arms folded across his chest. Brian closed the door softly behind him. *Don't know why I was nervous.* Mr. Padrea was totally harmless.

But Brian was right about not being able to sleep. And not because the man wanted to have sex all night, either. They only did it twice. Once upon arrival, of course; then Mr. Padrea slept. They had sex again in the early morning, right before it was time to leave.

He didn't mind the break, although the man wasn't a bad lover—mostly because Brian had learned how to make it pleasurable for himself if his partner was halfway decent. But it had been terribly boring to lie there all night. And lonely. He missed Schnookie. Poor kitten spent the night all alone. *Oh, well. Just once every two weeks. We'll get used to it.*

He walked up to Jeffrey with a smile. "Have you been standing here all night?"

"Yep, that's right, Mr. Brian."

"Geez. You must be as tired as I am."

Jeffrey laughed and put his arm around him as they walked toward the elevator.

"Practice this for our next lesson." Quinn pulled sheet music out of his bag and set it on the piano, then turned on the bench to face him. "I don't know much about your background. Have you played with other musicians?"

"Not much. I played a duet with my piano teacher once, but—" He leaned closer to whisper, "He wasn't very good."

Quinn smiled and nodded.

"And when I was a kid my mom and I used to play little songs together. You know, on the same piano." He looked down, his chest tight, and took a deep breath.

Quinn touched his arm and gave it a little squeeze.

Brian jolted back to the present as tingles spread up his arm and through his body. He wondered if Quinn could feel it, too. *God, I want you so bad.* He bit his lip.

"Have you performed much?" Quinn asked.

Performed? It took a moment to realize he meant with the piano. He cleared his throat. "I used to, in competitions."

"Which ones?"

"The biggest were the Texas All-State Youth Competition and the New England Youth Championship."

"Does it make you nervous to play in front of a crowd?"

"No. Not once I start playing."

"Hmm." Quinn glanced at the clock. "Oh, geez. We've got just enough time to run through that piece I gave you last week."

Brian opened the music and played it through.

"That was good, but pay more attention to the dynamics. Remember, this is a trio. In the introduction the violin and cello are dominant. You're providing a backdrop for them. Here, where you crescendo—" He pointed to the spot on the music. "The piano becomes an equal member of the trio."

Brian nodded.

"Obviously at the solos you can let loose more. But the rest of the time you're blending with the other instruments. If it's marked pianissimo play it *very* quiet. The piano can barely be heard, but you're actually providing the foundation."

Quinn turned the page. "The second movement starts out with a piano solo. This whole movement is slow and dreamy. The violin and cello join here. It's marked. It sounds incredible when you hear it with the other instruments. You'll understand better when you play along with this."

Quinn reached into his bag to pull out a CD. "This is a recording of the trio, minus the piano—that's for you to fill in. You need to get used to playing with other instruments. It's such a rewarding experience, but it's hard at first. Don't be lazy about counting the rests." He handed over the CD. "And don't get frustrated. Okay?"

"Oh, no. I won't." He grinned. "Thank you."

"I meant to start it with you today, but we're out of time. Why don't you work on the first two movements, and we'll go over them Thursday. Okay?" He stood and ruffled Brian's hair. "Have fun."

As soon as Quinn was out the door, Brian grabbed the portable player and hurried up to the ballroom. He sat on the bench and looked at the disc in his hand. Mendelssohn, *Trio No. 1, op. 49*. He put it in the player, then opened the sheet music.

Deep, long notes of a cello filled the air, joined in a moment by violin. Oh, lovely. Then quiet. "Oh. Woops." *I'm supposed to be playing.* He started it again and played along softly for the first few measures. It felt strange to play with other instruments, to not be totally focused on what he was doing, but instead part of a larger whole.

He listened as the different parts weaved together, heard the blending of the rhythms. *Oh, yes.* Wonderful. Then a piano solo. When the other instruments joined in he paused, caught off guard and distracted by them. He shook his head and skipped the CD backward.

Forgot to count the rests and had to go back again. He finally got to the second movement. Slow and dreamy, Quinn had said. And it was. Brian started it alone. A few lines later the other instruments joined. The tone was so beautiful, the way they all blended together. He closed his eyes and smiled. Didn't feel the wetness on his cheeks as the music filled him with beauty.

He jumped when he opened his eyes. Grant was standing by the stage, arms folded across his chest. "Do you know what time it is, Brian?"

His eyes widened. Grant was pissed. "No."

"It's eight minutes after two. You are *late* for your client."

He stood up. "Oh, my god, I'm so sorry!" He hurried off the stage. "I had no idea how late it is. I'm sorry."

"I'm glad you're sorry, Brian, but that doesn't fix anything." He glanced around the room as they walked toward the door. "Perhaps it's time to reconnect the intercom system up here."

"Oh, no." He didn't want his magic oasis invaded. "Please, Grant. I promise I won't let it happen again."

"You're not even changed or showered yet. We'll have to apologize and give Mr. Parks extra time at no charge." He paused with his hand on the door and turned to Brian. "We must treat our clients better than anyone else. Do you understand how this makes us look?" He stared at Brian with cold eyes. "I thought you were a professional."

He felt like he'd been slapped. He gripped Grant's arm. "I'm sorry. I know—" His voice caught. "I know I have a responsibility to my clients. I'm terribly sorry I messed up. I feel awful." It was true. He knew Grant could see it in his face.

Grant shook his head, lips tight. "This behavior is really not acceptable. If it happens again I'll . . . I won't let you come up here anymore. Understood?"

His heart skipped. He said softly, "Yes, Grant."

He practiced yoga as he waited for one o'clock. Jeffrey had promised to take him to the mall to buy an alarm clock for the ballroom. Brian insisted on getting it himself. It was *his* problem, and he would solve it. Besides, he hadn't been to a mall in ages. He'd put on a fresh coat of black nail polish for the occasion and 'regular' clothes— jeans and his black Bauhaus tee shirt.

Jeans weren't so great for yoga, though. Not flexible enough. He was balancing on one hand and one foot when a head poked through the open door. But not Jeffrey's. It was Justin the photographer's spiky red hair and unshaven face.

"Hi," Brian said in surprise. He put both feet on the floor and straightened up.

"Hey. I'm lookin for Grant to give him more photos from the party. Maria said he's in his sitting room, but I don't know where that is." He glanced down the hall. "There's a lot of doors."

"Those rooms are all empty." He pointed toward Grant's side of the house. "It's the other way, past the stairs. Wait—can I see the pictures?"

"Naw, sorry. Grant's the only one who gets to see em." He glanced around the room. "So this is where you live."

"It's really nice. There's a mini-fridge and look—a great balcony."

Justin followed him outside, his ever-present camera cradled in his hand. "Mind if I take a few photos?"

"Go ahead. It's a great view of the grounds." The warm breeze ruffled his hair. He took a deep breath and stared off into the hills.

Justin snapped a picture of him. Brian laughed and grinned at him.

Justin took another, then stepped back inside. He glanced around and nodded. "Nice."

"Can I take a picture of you?" It occurred to him that no one ever did. And Justin was so cute. There should be lots of pictures of him.

"Sure. Here's what you do." He came closer to show him the light meter and focus.

His arm brushed Brian's shoulder, and Brian caught his musky scent. He felt that familiar, almost dizzy sensation. And he was *on*. Like a snap of the fingers, it was that quick. He walked away to take a few photos. "Pose for me." Click. "Come on. Show me some skin."

Justin tugged on the top button of his shirt and laughed.

Mmm. Light hair curled on his chest. Brian closed the door on his way and started to hand over the camera. "Wait." He set it on the dresser instead, then leaned in to run his palm up Justin's chest. Tweaked the nipple through the cotton.

"Whoa-ho—wait a minute." Justin put up his hands as if to fend off an invisible foe. "I don't go that way."

"What way is that?" He traced his fingertip down the bare V of his chest and tugged on a bit of the curly hair. He liked that Justin was short. Their mouths were not so far away.

"I'm straight, Brian." He backed away but didn't get far. His shoulders pressed against the wall.

"Oh, of course you are. But there's nothing wrong with a little experimentation." He closed the gap between them. "I just want to touch you." He brushed his hand along Justin's thigh, just short of his crotch. "Taste you." He pulled the shirt to lick the skin showing between the buttons. "Mmm. . . . "

"Brian—"

"Shh . . . ." He put his finger on Justin's lips. "You don't need to talk. You don't need to do anything." He dropped to his knees and rubbed his bottom lip up Justin's crotch. It moved beneath his touch.

"Uh . . . ."

"That's right." He unzipped Justin's pants and let them fall. Touched his lips to his thigh, then pulled down the underwear. *Lovely.* He reached in to caress his balls, the delicate skin behind them. Stroked and pressed. Justin's legs trembled.

Brian directed him to the bed and pushed him down. Justin was completely erect. Looked delicious. Brian sucked on his nipple while he twisted the other. Justin's hand went under Brian's tee shirt and up his back.

Brian nibbled on his ear. Let his fingers finally graze his cock as his lips sought Justin's. They kissed long and deep. *Straight, huh? There's no such thing.*

Brian smiled and moved down to run his tongue up the length of the shaft, then moved away. Made him wait. His mouth toyed with everything else. Justin writhed and gripped the bedding. Desperate. Brian took the cock into his mouth, all the way. His nose bumped into Justin's body. The musty scent filled him, intoxicating. Back up, then in again. It wasn't long before Justin stiffened and sent a pulse of semen into his mouth.

Justin gasped for breath. Brian lay on his back beside him, panting, too. He unzipped his jeans to relieve the pressure. Justin propped himself up to look down at Brian's flushed face. He shook his head, then his gaze wandered to Brian's unfastened pants. "You must be pretty hard now." He reached over to feel.

Brian sucked in his breath at the touch. Nodded.

"Let's see about that." He pulled out Brian's penis. "Yep, you got something going on." He licked his hand and began to stroke him.

It was so much more fun when someone else did it. Brian arched back.

"Gotta help you out." Justin went on spouting inanities. Brian wasn't listening. He gripped the tight muscular arm as Justin jacked him harder.

"Oh—" Brian's eyes closed as he came.

Justin left in a hurry, and Brian went to the bathroom to clean up.

Jeffrey was standing in his room when he came out. "Ready to go, Mr. B?"

He took a deep breath and nodded. That was close with Justin. *Be more careful.*

They took the Mercedes. He sat up front beside Jeffrey for a change. Brian was totally lost as they wound their way through the parking garage of the Beverly Center. "How confusing. I'm glad I don't have to drive."

They finally parked and walked over to the escalators at the side of the garage. Brian looked through the glass at the countless buildings and cars below. *So many people in this city.* He didn't feel a part of it.

They walked out into the wide mall corridor. He stuck close to Jeffrey's side as they headed for the electronics store. He felt like everyone was looking at him. *Maybe it's just the two of us together. I'm so small and pale, and he's so big and dark.* He smiled up at Jeffrey.

The store only had a few alarm clocks to choose from. He picked one with a battery backup. Didn't want to risk being late again. He broke a hundred dollar bill to pay for it and pocketed the change, then handed Jeffrey the bag as they headed back out to the mall. "Can we walk around? I want to buy another yoga video."

It felt weird to be around all these normal, everyday people. He didn't belong. He was just floating through their world. "Jeffrey, I love you, but . . . I'd really like to be alone right now."

"Say no more, Mr. B." Jeffrey dropped back to put a little distance between them.

Brian wandered slowly. Looked at the people more than the shops. He still felt like everyone was watching him. He shook his head. *You're paranoid.*

He saw a piano store, gazed through the window and thought about what made him late yesterday. It had been so incredible to play with other instruments. And if it was that great with a recording, how much better would it be with actual musicians?

He heaved a sigh and moved on. He didn't see that happening. *Maybe someday. At least I get to play guitar with Jeffrey.*

A glass vase in a display window caught his eye. *I wonder if I should get River a present?* Their second anniversary was only a few days away. He went into the shop.

Jeffrey waited by the doorway and watched all the people in the store react to Brian. The clerk with mistrust. The old woman with a smile. Everyone noticed him. It was the same out in the mall. Something about the boy got people's attention. Jeffrey felt sure it was more than his striking looks.

Brian wandered past him back out into the mall and walked up to the Mrs. Fields counter. He looked back at Jeffrey and made a slight movement of his head. Just like Mr. Grant. *Boy's learnin.* Jeffrey went over to him and breathed in the intoxicating aroma.

Brian smiled up at him. "Want a cookie?"

They each got a cookie and milk. Brian pulled out money to pay.

The teenager behind the counter looked nervous. "Uh, I can't take that."

A hundred dollar bill. "Oh, sorry." He reached into the other pocket and found a twenty.

They sat on a bench to eat their yummy snack. "I decided not to get River a gift—it's more important that we spend time together." Brian swung his legs. "But maybe a surprise. Is there a store here that does piercings?"

It was a perfect anniversary. Grant had easily agreed to the afternoon *and* night off for both of them. They decided to go to the same beach house where they spent

Brian's thirteenth birthday. That had been so wonderful. And this was, too. River loved the water, and Brian loved staring at the water. And at River. They watched the sunset, then got naked and chased each other around the deserted beach.

Later Brian stared at the ceiling and listened to River's steady breathing. He'd told River if he didn't like it, he would take out the new piercing—a small silver hoop in his bellybutton. But River thought it was sexy. Brian did, too. He turned to watch River's sleeping face. It was hard to believe they met only two years ago. It felt like they'd known each other forever. "Forever," he whispered and snuggled against River's chest.

༄ ༄ ༄

Brian played with his hair in the bathroom, ready early. Grant's All Houses party fell on a Monday this year, which quite frankly sucked. *Grant knows Mondays are for River. 'We're accommodating the needs of others,'* Grant had said. *Oh, well.* Maybe he could guilt Grant into an extra night with River later. He could usually sway Grant when he put his mind to it. Besides, it was only fair.

River came into the bathroom and dug in the cabinet for his aftershave.

"I think I should wear my hair up sometime." Brian held it back, out of his face. "What do you think?"

River looked at him. The hairstyle brought focus more sharply to Brian's bone structure. The shape of his face. Incredibly beautiful. River's eyes moved to the white satin halter, nipples visible through the thin fabric. The satin stopped at the bottom of his ribcage. River's gaze traveled down Brian's smooth white stomach. Past his perfect bellybutton with the delicate silver hoop, to the black leather mini-skirt and fishnets.

"River. What do you think?"

"Yeah."

"But not tonight. It would fall down for sure. David said we always get those pills for the big party. That'll be fun—last year was a blast."

River moved behind him, nuzzled Brian's hair and wrapped his arms around him. "You're so gorgeous. Sexy." He touched Brian's bare shoulder with his lips. Moved the satin strap to kiss the skin underneath. "Turn around." He grasped Brian's bare waist and lifted him onto the tile counter.

Brian giggled and wrapped his legs around him. The skirt moved to reveal bare skin above the thigh high fishnets. River touched it and felt the blood rush to his groin. Their mouths met.

He always loved that precious moment when Brian hooked his leg over River's shoulder. That moment right before penetration.

Brian's fingers dug into his arm. "Now, River *Now*."

A few minutes later, River helped him off the counter, then glanced down at his shirt. "Oops. Good thing I didn't put on my tie yet. You got me." He took off his shirt.

The color in Brian's cheeks deepened. But he smiled and kissed River's chest on his way out of the bathroom. "We better hurry. Grant wants us there for cocktails."

River went into the closet to pick out another white dress shirt. "Hey, where are all my clean shirts? There's only one here."

"Well . . . I like to wear them sometimes."

"They're way too big for you."

"I know, but—" He walked over to help with the buttons. "They smell like you."

River kissed him, then reached for his tie.

Brian moved to the mirror to put on his sapphire choker. He had to use the third link now instead of the first one. His neck had gotten that much bigger in one year. *Wish I would get taller.* He shrugged and sat down to pull on his new boots. Exactly like the old ones, except bigger. He stood and smiled at River. "Ready?"

Brian saw a flash of golden hair and hurried to intercept her. "Michelle. Hi." He grinned.

She smiled back and greeted him in her delightful Southern accent, then glanced at his outfit. "You're lookin lovely tonight."

"Oh." He glanced down at himself. It felt weird to wear a skirt in front of her. He shrugged. "The men like it."

"Yeah, I know how that is. You got your bellybutton pierced. I like it."

"Thanks." They walked together. She was still taller, but he didn't mind. He felt bubbly and excited. The drugs were kicking in. "Did you get a pill?" he asked.

"Half a pill. I like to just get a little bit."

"Yeah?" He'd convinced Matthew to let him take two. "They're fun." He couldn't stop grinning. Between the drugs and being near this gorgeous woman, he was flying. Michelle looked innocently seductive in a low-cut yellow sundress. He watched her breasts bounce as she moved.

They walked along the flagstones, away from the noise of the courtyard, and he said, "I have a regular female client now. It's great, but I wish I saw her more often. Or someone. You." He stopped and turned toward her, his gaze locked on the thin fabric covering her breasts, the top button undone and open in the breeze.

"Brian," she whispered and took his hand.

He looked up at her face, brushed his lips against hers and squeezed her hand. "Can we go upstairs?"

She nodded.

He grinned and pulled her around the side of the house, past Jeffrey's porch. He didn't want Grant to see them go inside. Besides, it was more fun to sneak. They went around to the front door and upstairs to his bedroom.

"Oh, this is lovely." She wandered around and admired the antique desk and dresser, glanced at the framed photos of him and River.

He showed her the balcony. The lights of the party, the distant laughter. He moved behind her and touched his lips to her neck. Ran his fingers lightly up her bare arm. She leaned back against him, and his hand moved to her nipple. He felt it harden through the thin material. He couldn't stop playing with it. Her breath sped up, and she made a little sound.

He pulled her inside.

. . .

Grant led Brian away from the party and into the house. A man with grey hair stood in the parlor, a black party mask covering the top half of his face. Brian hadn't seen him outside with the other guests. *Is he hiding in here?*

Grant said, "I'd like you to meet Mr. Jones."

Brian grinned and moved closer to touch his chest. "Hi."

"He's a very important new client. Why don't you take him upstairs?"

"'kay." He tugged on the man's hand. The pills were in full swing now. *I wish Grant would let us have them more often.* But just once a year, at the big party. According to David, the drug was some special concoction Grant and the Doc cooked up years ago. Brian wasn't sure he believed that. But whatever it was, he loved it.

He smiled at the man as they reached the top of the stairs. Mr. Jones. Didn't matter what he was like in bed. The pills ensured a good time.

Justin watched Brian and snapped his camera. The kid was all over the place tonight. And all over everyone. Justin couldn't believe that mouth had been on his penis. And even worse, he wanted it there again. He couldn't stop thinking about it. *Best damn blow job I ever had.* Brian looked truly sexy in that miniskirt with garters and pale skin peeking out every time he moved. Justin shook his head. *What am I thinking? He's a he. And he's a kid.*

Brian glanced over his shoulder and caught Justin staring. Winked and gave him a slow smile. The guest next to Brian goosed him. Brian squealed and laughed, then reached up to give the old man a long kiss.

Justin tried not to think and kept taking pictures—not of the guests, just the boys, per his instructions. The tall man who worked closely with Grant approached Brian. Justin didn't like him—but then again, did he like any adults here? *Am I any better?* The man said something into Brian's ear. Justin frowned as Brian dutifully trailed after him toward the house.

Brian followed John upstairs to his bedroom. He touched John's arm. "Wait." His bedroom was for people he liked—people he *chose* to have sex with. He took John's hand and pulled him down the hall, into the Room. "Let's do it in here."

John raised a brow. "If that's the way you want it." He pushed Brian onto the bed and knelt over him. "Why don't we use these, since we're here?" He held up the leather handcuffs. Brian's heart skipped, and John smiled. "That's right," he said as he fastened the cuffs around Brian's wrists. "A little scary, isn't it?"

But there was nothing to be scared about. John was uncharacteristically gentle again—at first. Got rougher as they went along. But it was fun. Would've been even without the pills. Brian hated to admit it, but John was a great lay. *He's still an asshole.*

Brian rolled out of bed at two o'clock the next day. Just enough time to shower before Quinn arrived. Thank goodness Grant had moved it to afternoon. He couldn't have made a lesson at ten in the morning. *I wonder what time I got to bed?* He had no memory of it.

He moved slowly down the stairs. The shower hadn't helped him wake up. His body felt heavy. And sore. He headed to the kitchen for coffee.

It didn't help much. Quinn's first words were, "Are you sick? You look terrible."

Brian gave him a weak smile. "No, just tired."

"You're hoarse, too. Are you sure you're not coming down with something?"

"I'm sure," he said as they headed to the piano. "Grant had a big party last night. I was up late. I'm just tired."

"Alright." Quinn squeezed Brian's shoulder. "If you say so."

He closed his eyes and let himself enjoy the brief touch.

Quinn settled on the bench. "Did you listen to that radio program I told you about?"

"Yeah. It was neat." A youth show with performers under eighteen.

"It's on every Sunday night. That sixteen-year-old pianist who played Chopin's *Impromptu*, what did you think of her?"

"She was really good."

"Yes, she is. And you know what? You play that piece just as well, if not better." He turned sideways on the bench to face him. "Have you thought about what you want to do when you grow up?"

"Not really."

"You have a gift. You could become a professional concert pianist. Or you could teach, like me. Or do both." He took Brian's hand. "What I'm trying to say is, you can take this places. If that's what you want."

He blinked. He'd never thought about it before.

"I want you to audition for that radio program. I know you could make it. It's a wonderful experience and a great step toward a career. Would you be interested?"

He nodded emphatically, and a grin spread across his face. *I could play the piano for a career. I could be on the radio. Maybe I'll be famous!* "Yes, yes!"

Next thing he knew they were hugging. But for once it wasn't sexual. He was so excited by the prospect of the radio show he wasn't thinking about sex.

Quinn was like an excited school kid. "We'll need to prepare two pieces. One for the first audition, and I know you'll be called back for a second. I think your first piece should be *Moonlight Sonata*. Normally I would choose something less well known, but you play it with such emotion and passion. I don't think there's anything I can teach you with that one."

"I don't think I could change. It's ingrained—I've been playing it since I was six. Except I couldn't reach all the keys then."

Quinn breathed a laugh and murmured, "Amazing. Your age will help, too—not that you need help. But the judges tend to be more impressed the younger the kids are. You're thirteen, right?"

"Yeah, but only for a couple more weeks. My birthday's October 12th."

"Oh, happy birthday a little early!" He squeezed Brian's knee.

He's touching me a lot today. I wonder if he wants me?

"We need to decide on a piece for the second round." Quinn tapped his finger on his lips. "I'll have to think about that. Dig around for something obscure and challenging." He grinned at Brian. "This is gonna be great."

Brian sipped his orange juice and studied Grant across the table. He'd noticed something odd on the schedule. Could Grant have made a mistake? "Mr. Jones is on the schedule again today, but I just saw him a few days ago." No response. "I thought the Rule is no more than once a week. I don't understand . . . ."

Grant smiled. "Most rules have an exception. Mr. Jones is that exception. He's a very important client who spends most of his time out of town. So when he's here, we accommodate him."

"Oh." So it *wasn't* a mistake. An Exception.

"Speaking of business, I think you might be ready to use the handcuffs again—with select clients only, of course."

Brian swallowed his toast.

"Only regular clients with whom you're comfortable. Brett, for example."

"Oh! Yes, okay."

"That's my boy." Grant reached across the table to squeeze his hand. "Seems to me you have another birthday coming up. What would you like to do?"

He toyed with his scrambled eggs. "It's on a Tuesday this year, so I'll be at Mr. Padrea's." He was trying to be mature, but he'd been depressed about it since he realized it fell on Padrea's night.

"No, Brian, I would never make you work on your birthday. Mr. Padrea will have to be rescheduled."

Brian stared at him. He'd had no expectation Grant would do that. "Really?"

"Really. In fact, perhaps we could coordinate your birthday with a trip I need to make, to San Francisco."

"Yeah!"

He smiled. "Just a few days. I have some business to take care of. I thought you and River would enjoy it. Have you been there?"

He shook his head and listened to Grant talk about the city's unique character and beauty.

"Sounds great." Brian turned to Maria when she brought more juice. "¿Más pan, por favor?"

She smiled and squeezed his shoulder. "Claro. Muy bien, Brian." She'd been teaching him Spanish.

He grinned at her, and his mind skipped to the other thing he was excited about. He turned to Grant. "I'm gonna audition to be on the radio! That youth show. Quinn's sure I'll win. He hasn't picked a second piece for me yet, but I know he'll come up with something great—"

"Brian." Grant shook his head. "My dear boy, you can't do that. If you win that competition, your photograph will be in *The L.A. Times*. Think about the circulation of that paper."

Brian's face fell as it sunk in.

"That radio program is played in markets across the country. I don't think you or I want that much publicity, now do we?"

He looked down at his plate and whispered, "No." His parents. His clients. *I'm so stupid. I should've thought of that.* He felt the tears coming, excused himself and ran up to his room.

. . .

He watched Quinn pace the parlor, fists clenched. Quinn turned to face him, and Brian took a step back. He'd never seen him angry before.

"I don't understand. I don't understand why Grant won't let you be in the competition."

Shit. "He's right, though. I should've realized before. I'm sorry." He struggled to come up with something. "I can't do it. It's just . . . too much right now."

"Yeah, that's about as good an explanation as I got from Grant. You know what he said? 'I don't pay you to ask questions.'" Quinn's frown deepened. He pulled sheet music out of his bag and shook it. "And I found the perfect piece." His eyes pleaded, and he said quietly, "I don't understand."

Brian pulled on his arm and led him over to sit on the piano bench. "Quinn." *What do I say?* His fingers stroked Quinn's arm. *That would distract him. No, no. Making a pass at him is not the answer.* His gaze moved to Quinn's face, so full of concern and passion, and their eyes met. *If it weren't for River, I'd think I was in love with you.* He bit his lip and looked away. "You found a good piece?"

"Yeah." He handed it over.

Brian turned the pages. The notes had a different pattern than he was used to, a different rhythm. "This looks neat."

"It's by an obscure South American composer."

He looked up into Quinn's green eyes. "Can we work on it anyway? Please? I'd love to hear how it goes." *Please can we not talk about it anymore?*

"Sure. Of course."

He turned to the piano and dove in. He had fun working on it—it *was* a great piece. Different from anything he'd played before. But his enjoyment was dampened by Quinn's demeanor. He was quieter than usual. Subdued. Brian hoped he would let it go. *He will. He has to.*

ꙮꙮꙮ

He sat on the large bed in the Room and waited impatiently for the man to come out of the bathroom. He wanted it over with; Mr. Nolan was definitely an unfun client. Besides, afterward River was coming over to go shopping. He chewed his nail and brushed an orange cat hair off his bare thigh. *What's that?* He pushed the skirt up to look at his thigh. Welts. On both of them.

He blinked and flashed back to yesterday afternoon. John's voice saying, *'I'm going to teach you a lesson today: how much pleasure you can get from pain.'* Of course that scared him, as it was supposed to. But John didn't say it just for effect. When things got heavy he brought out a riding crop.

The black leather came down on the back of his thighs, and he jumped. But it didn't hurt. He was even more surprised to feel his erection grow. It wasn't that he liked the pain—there truly was no pain. *Bizarre.*

Grant explained to him later about chemical changes, how when a man is aroused, the endorphins make something that would normally hurt feel like nothing. Or even feel good. But still, he had no idea John hit him hard enough to leave marks.

He stared at the welts in fascination and touched them. It stung. The bathroom door opened, and Brian sat up. He put on his fake smile and focused on the job at hand.

The man approached the bed, naked, fat and already fully erect. Mr. Nolan never wasted time. Brian reached for a popper, though he knew it wouldn't help much. *God forbid he should take a few minutes to arouse me so it won't hurt.*

Brian lay on his back and glanced at the large mirror that hung beside the closet. For a detached moment he watched the fat man pounding into the boy. His gaze rose to the ceiling. Mr. Nolan grunted and pushed Brian's leg up farther, penetrated deeper. His breath caught at a hot flash of pain, and his fingers dug into the flabby arm. Mr. Nolan was going hard now. It hurt more, but at least that meant it would be over soon.

He squeezed his eyes shut. "Aah." He breathed hard as he fought to ignore the pain. *Stay relaxed.* A bead of sweat ran down the side of his face. *Soon now, soon.*

Mr. Nolan collapsed on top of him. It was over.

Phil stood at his post behind the counter and smiled at the boy with electric eyes and an armful of CDs. He came into Phil's all the time and spent tons of money. *Spoiled little rich kid.* Phil looked at his beaming face. *But sweet.* He started ringing him up.

The older boy came to stand behind him, put his hands on his waist and kissed his shoulder. Phil watched through the corner of his eye. Unusual for teenagers to be so openly gay in public. *Good for them. Hope it doesn't get them beat up.* He glanced at the hulking figure by the door. *Not while they've got their own personal bodyguard. They must be really loaded. Must be nice not to work for a living.*

The boy tucked his dark hair behind his ear and picked up a CD from the pile. "River, look. I've been trying to find this for ages."

River read over his shoulder. "*Nocturne.* Siouxsie and the Banshees? I don't remember you talking about them."

"This is a live album while Robert Smith was their guitarist. I didn't think I'd ever find it!" He beamed that sweet smile at Phil again. "This place is great. Do you have the video?"

Phil shook his head. "Sorry."

"If you get it, will you hold it for me?"

Couldn't say no to that face. "Sure." Phil decided to help out his neighbor. "Have you seen the new shop down the street? Music store. Specializes in guitars."

"Really?"

"Yep. Just down the street." He pointed.

Brian handed the heavy sack to Thomas and walked along the sidewalk in the direction Phil had pointed. Even though these weren't his tight pants, the leather still rubbed against his thighs and stung. Thank goodness River hadn't noticed the welts. Brian didn't want to deal with that.

"Here it is." They walked into the guitar shop. "Look at them all. Oh, this one. And this one."

River trailed behind him. "Uh huh."

Brian grinned. "I'm going to buy myself an electric guitar for my birthday." He smiled at the salesman who walked over. "I don't know anything about electric guitars. Which one should I get?"

The eager salesman showed him around, talked about action and bridges and stuff River didn't have a clue about. Seemed like they would look at every guitar in the store. River wandered over to the magazines and flipped through them. Boring music stuff. But some cute guys.

"Hey, River. I like this one. What do you think?"

He walked over to where Brian sat cradling a shiny black guitar. Brian strummed a few chords. "Sounds good," River said. *Like all the others.* He smiled at Brian's excited face. "Sounds great."

The salesman reminded him he would also need an amplifier. "Maybe you'd like to look at pedals, too."

River reached over to read the tag on the guitar and spoke in Brian's ear. "Do you have this much cash on you?"

"Huh? Oh, no. I didn't think about that."

River smiled and patted his arm. "I'll get Thomas."

Brian stood in the parlor holding out cash.

Grant didn't take it. "What's this?"

"For the guitar. I'm paying you back."

"Oh, Brian, that's not necessary. You keep the money."

"No! I want to pay for it. It's my present to myself. I'll pay for it." He forced the money into Grant's hand.

Grant chuckled. "Alright, dear. Just remember, anything you want. All you need to do is ask."

Brian headed up to his room. No more clients tonight—too bad River had one. But at least that gave him plenty of time to play with his new guitar. He'd spent the evening messing around and figuring out the different knobs on the amp. Now he wanted to share it with someone. He lugged the heavy equipment down the hall to Jeffrey's room.

"What've we got here?"

Jeffrey tried out the shiny black guitar and showed him some tricks. By the time they finished playing a few blues tunes, Brian was at ease with his new instrument. They took a John Lee Hooker song and made it their own, improvised and jammed on it for twenty minutes.

Jeffrey stopped playing and cocked his head. He put down his acoustic. "'scuse me a minute."

He got up and went through the door on the east wall, the door that was always closed. Brian craned his neck. He could hear Jeffrey's voice but couldn't make out the words. *What's in there?*

He asked as soon as Jeffrey came back. "Oh, just a security station."

"Can I see?"

"Sho'. Come on in."

Brian followed him into a small room lined with monitors. Their black and white screens glowed in the dim light. He studied the image on the first one. "That's the front door!" And the gate. "Wow." The others he didn't recognize—mostly views of the Other Wing.

"Course I ain't here to watch all the time. They got more equipment over in the main security station next door."

"In the Other Wing?"

"Yep." He pointed to a monitor. "Sensors in the ground near the gate detect the weight of a car. Sets off a buzzer in the security station so we know when somebody's comin. And we can let em in from here, too." Jeffrey sat down and clicked the computer mouse. "See, I control the camera angle with this."

"Cool!" He watched a moment, then glanced around the small room. Not much else to see. They were in the corner of the house, with windows facing the front and side. But it was too dark to see anything through those. He looked at the monitors again. The front door. He tried to remember if he'd done anything naughty at the front door. *The party*—*Michelle*. That wasn't really naughty, but still, he thought they were sneaking. *Michelle*. He couldn't believe it would be a whole year before he saw her again. A fucking eternity.

"What's wrong with you, boy? You lookin all sad all of a sudden."

He shrugged and glanced down. "Just thinking about Michelle. I won't see her again. Not for a long time."

"Well, that's only if you don't go to the party at Jasmine Lane."

"The what? Where?"

"Jasmine Lane. That's the House where Michelle lives. They throw a costume party every year on Halloween."

"They do?" He leaned forward.

Jeffrey grinned. "Yep. Mr. Grant don't ever go. You know how he is bout women. Wouldn't go to a House full of em."

A house full of Michelles.

"But there's a standing invitation to him and his House, of course."

"Really?" He gripped Jeffrey's arm. "Can I go?"

He laughed. "You gotta ask Mr. Grant. But I don't see why not."

Brian hugged him. "Thank you."

*"On candystripe legs the spiderman comes
softly through the shadows of the evening sun
stealing past the windows of the blissfully dead
looking for the victim shivering in bed
searching out fear in the gathering gloom and
suddenly! a movement in the corner of the room!
and there is nothing I can do as I realize with fright that
the spiderman is having me for dinner tonight!
quietly he laughs and shaking his head creeps
closer now closer to the foot of the bed and
softer than shadow and quicker than flies
his arms are all around me and his tongue in my eyes
'be still be calm be quiet now my precious boy
don't struggle like that or I will only love you more
for it's much too late to get away or turn on the light
the spiderman is having you for dinner tonight!'
and I feel like I'm being eaten by a thousand million shivering furry holes
and I know that in the morning I will wake up in the shivering cold
and the spiderman is always hungry . . . ."*

- Robert Smith (The Cure), "Lullaby"

༄༅ CHAPTER 21 ༄༅

Brian, River and Grant relaxed at an outdoor table at a café near Pacific Heights. It was unusually warm for October in San Francisco. *October 11th. Tomorrow I'll be fourteen.* Brian smiled and stirred his iced tea. Fourteen sounded so mature. *I'm older than River was when we first met. How weird.*

He glanced around and noted the security guards stationed at tables nearby, standing against the wall, even across the street—the smaller guards who blended in. Grant had hired a private jet for the trip and filled it with security. *'We're entering someone else's territory,'* he'd explained.

San Francisco intimidated Brian. So many tall buildings clustered together. So much a 'city' city. Sounded odd from someone who lived in L.A., but it was more wide open and spread out there. He glanced at the shops lining the street. But this neighborhood was different. Quieter and slower paced, with gorgeous huge Victorian homes. He sipped his iced tea and smiled. An exciting place to turn fourteen, anyway.

Grant stood up, his eyes on a dapper man with smooth brown hair and a big moustache walking toward their table. This must be the man they were here to meet. Head of the top House in San Francisco. River stood up, so Brian did, too.

Grant held out his hand. "Jim, good to see you again. This is Brian."

He could tell Jim wanted him from the intensity of his stare, the way he touched his hand. Brian's cheeks flushed.

Jim greeted River, then took a seat. "It's been a long time since you visited,

Grant."

"Yes, well—" His eyes flicked toward Brian, and he said with a slight smile, "I've been busy."

Jim's gaze moved to Brian. "Yes, I'm sure you have. The whole west coast is abuzz about Grant's new Number One. Not just the west coast, actually." Jim's dark eyes burned into him. "I've been eager to meet you. Find out firsthand what all the fuss is about."

His pulse picked up. He gave Jim a coy smile and wondered if they would have sex right after lunch or later. *After lunch, I bet.*

"Perhaps you could accompany me to my House." Jim leaned forward. "There are so many things I could show you."

His heart skipped. Jim's House specialized in bondage. Adults worked there, too. Grant had also told him in San Francisco, the Houses were not entirely voluntary. In L.A. the Voluntary Rule was the number one Rule—absolutely *no* exceptions. It was Grant's duty as Head of the top House to enforce it. But not here. Not at Jim's House. Jim's Bondage House. Brian didn't want to go there. The thought of people working at a place like that against their will made him sick.

Grant raised a brow. "I don't think so, Jim. I don't trust you *that* much."

Jim leaned back with a little smile. "Touché."

Grant set his coffee cup in the saucer. "But of course we'd love you to come to the hotel with us. We'll be heading back after lunch."

Ah. I was right—sex after lunch.

Brian turned off the TV and undressed while River brushed his teeth. He crawled onto the bed, exhausted, and his mind went over the day's events. Their morning tour of Alcatraz. That place gave him the creeps. He didn't understand everyone's fascination with a prison. *Alcatraz in the morning and Jim in the afternoon.* Made for a weird day, overall.

River came out of the bathroom and did a double take. "What the hell are those marks on you?" River grabbed him.

Brian looked down at himself. *Shit.* He hadn't realized how bad it looked. "Nothing. Just . . . a little bondage. You know—"

"*What?*" River's eyes were huge.

"You know Jim's House is into that stuff. Of course that's what he wanted to do. It's no big deal."

"But . . . ." He sank onto the bed with tears in his eyes. "You let him hit you?"

"Oh, River." He held River's face in his hands. "Please don't be upset. It didn't hurt."

Tears fell down River's cheeks.

He pulled River's head against his chest and held him. In truth, he *was* sore from his afternoon with Jim. It was more bondage gear than he'd ever seen. Made him nervous, but he had a good time. Like all Providers, Jim was an expert at what he did. Never really hurt him. Pushed him farther than John had, though.

Left a lot of marks.

Naked in the Rain

. . .

River followed him down the crowded street to a phone booth near the hotel. "You think she'll be there?"

"I hope so. It's three hours later there. She should be home from school, and my parents should still be at work." He stuck quarters into the slot and dialed the old, familiar number.

"Hello?"

"Tanya!"

She squealed. "Brian, it *is* you! I knew it when the phone rang—it's your birthday! God, I should shut up so I know if you're okay. Are you okay?"

He laughed. "Yeah, I'm fine. Everything's great. I just wanted to say hello."

"Happy birthday, little brother. I miss you so much. Your voice is lower."

"It is?"

"A little bit, yeah." He could hear the tears in her voice. "I'm missing you grow up."

"Oh, Tanya." His throat tightened. "I'm missing you, too. Do you still look the same? I mean, did you cut your hair or anything?"

"No. I'm still the same. We got the photo you sent—it's wonderful! You and River are beautiful."

"Oh." He'd forgotten about that picture. Alaska. It seemed like forever ago.

"*Your* hair's different," she said. "Longer."

"Yeah, I guess it is." *I've probably changed more than she has.* A lot more. "Hold on. River, could you put in more quarters?"

"Sure, babe." He stuck a handful into the slot.

Tanya said, "Was that River? I heard his voice! He sounds sweet."

Brian smiled wide. "He's wonderful. I wish you could meet him."

"Me, too. Hey, maybe I could. We could arrange a place away from here. Wherever you want. Just you and me. And River. No parents, no one else."

"Tanya—"

"Please, Brian, I've got to see you."

"Stop it. I know you better than that." She'd have the place surrounded with cops or something. She always thought she knew what was best for him. "You have OSS," he said. Older Sibling Syndrome—their joke growing up together.

"*Brian,*" she sobbed.

"Tanya, calm down. Come on. I've got lots of quarters. Let's talk."

She sniffled and pulled herself together. "Okay. I wanted to tell you, Mom's going to therapy."

"Really?"

"Yeah. She's different. Better." Tanya lowered her voice. "She's on medication."

"What?" *My mom is on drugs.* "What is she taking?"

"I don't know, but it seems to help. She's not so moody now."

"She's going to therapy? I don't believe it."

"Yeah, really. Your psychologist from the institute's been pushing her since you ran away. She finally agreed about six months ago."

"Wow. She's seeing Dr. Monroe?"

"No, somebody else."

River tapped his shoulder and pointed down the street. Thomas stood with arms folded, watching them. "Oh, shit," popped out of Brian's mouth.

"What?" Tanya asked.

"Nothing . . . just, I've gotta go. I'm sorry."

"Oh, Brian, God. I hate this."

"Me, too."

"Call more often, damn it! It's been almost a year."

"I'll try."

"Happy birthday, baby brother."

"Thanks. I love you."

"Love you, too," she whispered.

"Bye." He hung up the phone and bit his lip. No time to cry now. Thomas stood glaring at them.

He wiped his face as they hurried back to the hotel and rode up in the elevator with Thomas. He didn't say a word. No one did. The three of them went to Grant's room. Grant and Jeffrey were at the table. Grant was saying, "I don't want to train a new boy now. He should go to Kristoff."

Thomas approached and spoke into Grant's ear. River took Brian's hand and held it as Grant walked over to them. "Brian, were you using a payphone?"

"Yes, Grant." His voice came out in a whisper.

He folded his arms. "And whom did you call?"

"My sister."

Grant's eyebrows shot up.

He let go of River's hand and moved closer to Grant. "I just wanted to say hello, let her know I'm okay. I didn't tell her anything. I didn't think there was any harm in it . . . ."

"Perhaps not. But sometimes small things say more than you realize."

River said, "I was there. He didn't say anything."

Grant pursed his lips, silent a moment. "Alright, Brian. No harm done. But next time check with me first. I don't like you sneaking off behind my back."

"Oh, no. I didn't mean it like that."

Grant smiled and touched Brian's cheek. "I'm not angry. Just talk to me first next time. We must be careful."

ריריר

Mr. Padrea fastened his robe and walked him to the condo door early in the morning. Brian smiled at him. "Thank you for letting me come on a different night."

"No problem at all, my sweet. Happy belated birthday." He kissed Brian's forehead, then his lips.

Brian heard a noise like a cough or gasp. He turned to see a woman standing on the other side of the room. Her mouth hung open.

He glanced down at himself. Black skintight pants and strappy leather 'top' that wasn't really a top. His blazer lay folded over his arm—he hadn't bothered to put it on yet. *Huh. This must be an interesting sight.* She was in her robe. *Must live here. Is she his daughter?* He studied her across the room. Late twenties? *Maybe his granddaughter.*

"Oh, dear." Mr. Padrea broke the silence.

She sputtered, "What—what—"

"It's nothing." Padrea closed his robe tighter. "It's not what it looks like."

Yeah, right. You just kissed me. And look at me. What else could I be?

Mr. Padrea got his wallet from the side table and handed him an extra hundred dollar bill. "Let's not mention this to Grant."

Brian looked at the woman. "*I* won't tell anyone."

"Don't worry, neither will she. Right, Leah? You did not see this."

She looked lost. "Mr. Padrea!"

"We'll talk about this later."

'*Mr. Padrea.*' *So not his granddaughter.* Brian folded the money and slipped it into the waist of his leather pants. "Nice to meet you, Leah." He winked at her, then put on his jacket and walked out the door. Kept up his professional face for the security escort. *Shit.*

ריריר

He sat on the bench beside Grant in the private courtyard between the Main House and the Wing and stared at Justin behind the camera. Grant wanted portrait photos of the two of them, like family photos. He'd asked Brian to wear the white leather outfit.

Grant slipped his arm around Brian's waist, toyed with the belly ring and the bare skin beneath it. His lips touched the side of Brian's neck. So much for 'family' photos. Brian aimed a slow smile at Justin. *You taste good.* Brian was getting turned on. So was Grant. Good time to ask for something. "May I go to the party at Jasmine Lane?"

Grant pulled back, and the lines on his forehead deepened. "No one from this House ever goes there. Remember what I told you about women. I don't want you around them."

"Grant—" *That's ridiculous.* "I really want to go. Please? You don't have to come. Jeffrey can take me. Or Matthew."

"It would seem odd for a boy to go without the Head of his House."

"They don't have to know who I am."

He chuckled. "Oh, they'll know."

'*They'll know*'—sounded positive. He touched his finger to Grant's chest and leaned forward so their mouths were almost touching. "Please." He brushed his lips against Grant's. "Please."

"I don't know, Brian. . . . "

He kissed the sensitive spot on Grant's ear and murmured, "Please. I'll be good. I'll be really, really good." He caressed Grant's neck with his mouth and reached for the spot that really got Grant going.

Grant's body moved. "*Brian.*"

"Say yes. Please. Say yes."

"Yes," Grant breathed.

Yes! He laughed and kissed him deeply. His head fell back as Grant's lips trailed down his throat. Brian turned his head. "Is he going to keep taking pictures?"

Grant's mouth didn't leave Brian's body. He loosened the vest. "Do you want him to?"

"No," Brian said firmly. The thought disturbed him. "I don't."

Grant waved a hand at Justin, dismissing him without even looking up.

Justin walked away in a daze. He glanced back as he reached the corner. Brian's pants were coming off. Justin pulled himself away with reluctance. *What is wrong with me?*

He left them alone to wander through the grounds. *This place is like a maze. It's gorgeous.* He used the rest of his film taking photos of birds and flowers and trees, until a sound caught his attention. He turned and saw Brian approaching, a wide grin on his face.

"There you are." Brian walked up close and touched his leg. "I've been looking for you."

"I, uh—"

"Shhh." He held his finger against Justin's lips. "Remember, you don't have to talk. It's okay." He rubbed Justin's crotch through his pants.

He backed away. "No, I—I shouldn't."

"Yes, you should. You want it. I know you do."

He glanced around. "Someone might see us."

"No, they won't."

"Really, Brian. Grant would—" He didn't know what Grant would do, and he didn't want to find out.

"Come with me." Brian took his hand and led him through a wooded area. They turned off the path, up a slope and down again. Brian whispered, "No one can see us here." He dropped to his knees.

"Wait." Justin sank down before him. Suddenly needed to touch him. He fumbled with the leather clothes. Brian helped.

There was something really hot about jacking another guy off. *Who'd have thought?* The lube made it nice and slippery. A real turn on. Got them both hard quick. Justin gripped Brian's thin little arm. Like a woman's. The part of his brain that kept saying, *What are you doing? What are you doing?* faded until he couldn't hear it anymore.

Brian picked up the schedule. Just one client today—unusual. An unfamiliar name. '*Mr. Reynolds, 11 a.m. – noon. See me.*' Grant had never left a message like that before. Sometimes there would be notes—'*be submissive*' or '*wear your skirt.*' But never '*See me.*' Made him curious. And a little nervous.

Grant was waiting for him on the Victorian loveseat in his sitting room. "Good morning, dear. Come sit by me. I have a special outfit for you to wear for your client."

Oh, is that all? He sat down, relieved.

Grant handed him a small pile of clothing. Brian held up the soft cotton. Blue pajamas with little Superman figures all over them. He blinked. Not what he expected.

Naked in the Rain

"Be passive. He likes to do all the work. And . . . you know how some clients enjoy word games. Mr. Reynolds likes his boys to ask him to stop. Throughout the session you should do that. Beg, even. The more the better. Alright?"

He nodded slowly. Beg him to stop. That might be hard to remember once they got going. Didn't sound very nice. *I don't think I like Mr. Reynolds.*

"Don't worry. He won't hurt you." He smoothed Brian's hair. "He'll be waiting for you in the Room at eleven."

"Okay." He clutched the pajamas and headed for the door.

"And Brian, I'll be downstairs in my office if . . . you need me."

He walked down the hall to the Room. This outfit was much more comfortable than his regular clothes. He hadn't worn pajamas in ages. He opened the door and saw a tall, thin man perched on the bed facing the other way. *Remember to beg him to stop.* He closed the door with a soft click.

Mr. Reynolds stood and turned toward him. Brian's heart skipped. He'd seen this gaunt face before, long ago. The figure in the Other Wing's window who scared him so badly just by staring at him. Those dark eyes were boring into him again, but this time from only a few feet away. And coming closer. Creeping toward him like a spider. Brian backed up against the door. The man smiled.

It was an evil smile. Everything in Brian told him to turn and run. He stood shaking as the man approached and brushed his cheek. The touch sent a creepy feeling through him, made him flinch. He whispered, "Please don't." And he meant it.

When it finally ended Brian ran to his room, straight through to the bathroom. He thought he would be sick. The words 'please stop' kept repeating in his mind. He sank to the floor with a shiver, wrapped his arms around himself and cried.

Eventually he pulled himself together enough to take a long hot shower, then went to talk to Grant. He clutched the banister as he moved slowly down the stairs to Grant's office.

Grant looked up from his paperwork. "Are you alright? You look pale."

He glanced down. "I'm fine. I just want to know, is he . . . is Mr. Reynolds going to be a regular client? How often?" His heart pounded as he waited for the answer.

"He is a regular client of this House, but he likes to make the rounds of all the boys and dips into other Houses as well. It works out to once every two or three months."

He let go his breath. Two months sounded far away. *Thank god. I don't know what I'd do if he came every week.* The thought made him want to cry.

Grant said, "Some of the boys are afraid of him. I waited until I thought you were ready. Was I wrong?"

"No, no. I'm fine." He forced a smile and told himself it was no big deal. Really, the man hadn't hurt him. *I don't know why I'm so upset.* Just something about that man . . . gave him the creeps.

. . .

He stared at the dark ceiling and listened to the harsh sound of Mr. Padrea's breathing. Almost three months coming here, and Brian still couldn't fall asleep. Boring. And lonely. He didn't like where his thoughts kept going. He shivered and sat up, then grabbed his pack of smokes and got out of bed. *Why not? He never wakes up. And I'm not a secret here anymore.* He found a black silk robe in the closet and slipped it on.

He'd never explored the condo before. City lights illuminated the living room with a soft glow through a window almost as big as the wall. He moved to the grand piano that stood before the window and touched the shiny black with a wistful sigh. The lights drew his gaze again, and he noticed a door leading to a balcony.

He stepped out, careful to leave the door open behind him. Although the days were still warm in October, at two o'clock in the morning the cement chilled his bare feet. But he hardly noticed. The entire city stretched out before him, as far as he could see in every direction. "Incredible," he whispered as the cold wind whipped his hair. He felt suspended in mid-air. He laughed for the sheer joy of it, then moved forward to lean against the rail and look for landmarks. The Hollywood sign. Below it, the round violet neon of the Capitol Records tower. *And there's downtown.* He couldn't pick out much else. Didn't know the city very well.

He glanced down. It was so far he couldn't comprehend it. He clutched the rail, dizzy. Maybe looking down wasn't a good idea. He moved away from the edge and got out a cigarette. The wind made it hard to light, but he finally managed. He stared at the city and smoked.

When there was nothing left but the filter, he stubbed it out on the cement, then wondered what to do with the butt. A naughty idea came to him—what River would do if he were here. Brian walked to the edge of the balcony, leaned over and let go of the cigarette. He tried to watch it fall, but it disappeared too fast. He rested his chin on the rail and frowned. *I wish River were here.* "I seem to wish that a lot." He shook his head and decided it was time for a snack.

He went back inside and found the light switch for the big, modern kitchen. The refrigerator door squeaked. Nothing fun in there. But the freezer was a different story. He settled at the kitchen table, tightened the silk robe and dug into rocky road ice cream. "Mmm."

"Is it good?"

He jumped a foot and turned to see a woman emerge from the shadowed doorway. The woman he'd seen here before, in her bathrobe again. He scowled. "How long have you been standing there?"

"Not long. I heard a noise so I got up."

He turned away and stabbed his spoon at the ice cream.

She wandered over to the freezer. "That looks good. Think I'll have some."

He watched her while his heart settled back to normal. *Sneaking up on me.*

She sat across from him, and her hazel eyes met his. "My God, you look even younger close up. How old are you?"

He glared at her and didn't answer.

She tasted her ice cream. "I'm thirty-three."

"That's great." He started eating again.

"When I first saw you, I thought I should call child welfare or something."

His eyes widened.

"But I didn't."

His voice came out steadier than he felt. "A wise choice, I'm sure." *I sound like Grant.*

"Mr. Padrea was very convincing. Very adamant. I thought he would have a heart attack." She shook her head. "He's a good guy beneath all the bluster."

"I know."

She raised a brow. "I suppose you do."

He lit a cigarette.

"You're not allowed to smoke in here."

He took a deep drag and flicked ashes into his bowl. Watched her as he blew smoke in a stream toward the ceiling. "Mr. Padrea lets me."

She shook her head, and her bushy, light ash brown hair fell around her face. She murmured, "I can't believe he does this," then focused on Brian again. "How long have you been coming here?"

He stood up, the cigarette dangling from his lips as he pushed in his chair. "Awhile." He put his bowl in the sink and headed out of the kitchen. "Goodnight, Leah."

ཀཀཀ

He pulled on the phone cord and laughed as he listened to River on the other end, barking like Dogman. Brian said, "Have you spanked him with the riding crop? Isn't that weird?"

"Yeah. It's fun—I like to give him a good whack. 'You've been a bad boy.'"

Brian shook his head. *I don't like hitting people.* He had to totally psych himself up for it. Made him feel weird, like someone else. He much preferred this morning's client. "One of my clients said the funniest thing. After we fucked I turned over, and he's got this dreamy look. Stares into my eyes and calls me his 'Reservoir of Love.' It was hard to keep a straight face."

River was laughing so hard he couldn't comment.

Brian lay back on the bed. He stared out the window and sobered as he remembered the dreams that haunted him all week. "Have you had that creepy guy?"

"Who?"

"The guy who wants you to beg him to stop."

"Oh, yeah. He's kinda weird."

Brian tried to keep his voice level. "I don't like him."

"Aw, he ain't that bad."

He shook his head. River didn't understand. *Change the subject.* He thought of that woman at Padrea's—Leah. *No. Don't tell anyone about that.* "Are you going to the party at Michelle's?"

"Who?"

"Michelle. The woman who tested me out."

"Oh, right. I remember her."

"So you *did* get her. And you didn't want her?"
"That's right. So what about her party?"
"I'm going. Are you?"
River snorted. "Why would I wanna go to a House full of women? That's no fun."
He closed his eyes and smiled. "Sounds wonderful to me."
"You're weird."
Brian laughed. "*You* are."
"Oh, hey—I can stay longer than usual tomorrow, cos I don't have a client Tuesday morning. My first one's at two o'clock."
He sat up. "Really? That's great." He was sure John always scheduled a morning client on purpose to cut off their time together. "I have my piano lesson in the morning."
"Good. I finally get to meet this Quinn guy."
"Yeah." Seemed weird. Mixing two of his worlds together. "I can't wait to see you."
"Me, neither, my Reservoir of Love."
Brian fell back against the bed laughing.

River snuck into Brian's room. He'd decided to come over early to surprise him—it was barely light out. He stopped short. The bed was rumpled but empty. "Damn." He looked in the bathroom. Nothing. *Maybe he's with Grant.* But that would be odd for a Monday morning; Grant usually left them alone.
River stopped in front of the closet and obeyed the impulse to open it. Brian lay curled up naked on the floor, fast asleep. "Brian." River shook him gently. "What are you doing in here?"
"Huh?" Brian rubbed his face. "What?" He looked up at River.
"Why are you in the closet?" River helped him to his feet.
"I don't know. I . . . guess I was sleepwalking."
"The closet? Is that some Freudian thing?"
"No, I just like closets."
River led him back to the bed.
Brian kept mumbling about closets. "She didn't realize I like em. I always thought it was kinda funny."
"What are you talking about?"
"My mom used to lock me in the closet sometimes." He yawned and lay back on the bed. "But I liked it. Except when she left me in there too long . . . ." His voice trailed off, and he was asleep.
River stared at his innocent face and held onto him tight.

River sat sideways with his feet on the couch and watched Brian and Quinn on the piano bench. *Gorgeous. I can't believe Brian's not doing him.* Brian clearly adored him. River's gut twisted.
Brian finished the new Beethoven sonata he'd gotten last week. Quinn said,

"That's a difficult piece. You play it very well, but you never even looked at the music. It seems like the harder a piece is, the more you memorize it."

"Oh." Brian hadn't noticed. *I guess it's true.* The harder music was, the more his hands took over. "I don't do it on purpose."

He caught River's eye over Quinn's shoulder, and they smiled at each other. He'd been a little nervous about them meeting, though he wasn't sure why. He'd debated about how to introduce them. *'This is my boyfriend, River. My friend. My best friend.'* They all sounded stupid and inadequate. He finally just settled on, *'This is River.'* That had worked fine.

River was about the only thing that could distract him from Quinn, as it turned out. "What? I'm sorry." He had no idea what Quinn just said. Whenever his eyes met River's there was always a sudden connection. Like no one else existed in the world. *Oh, I did it again.* He caught the end of Quinn's sentence.

"—see new things in it, so you should look at the sheet music sometimes, even if it's memorized. We'll work on the Chopin next time, okay? See you Thursday." Quinn stood up. "Nice to meet you, River."

Brian closed the door behind Quinn. "Isn't he dreamy?"

"Dreamy? He's fucking gorgeous. I can't believe you two aren't doing it. Are you sure you're not sneaking a little—" He made an obscene gesture. "Activity under the piano?"

He laughed. "I wish. But Quinn doesn't know about this place. Grant was very clear I'm to behave like a regular boy."

"*Regular* boy. What's that?'

"I don't know. But I don't think it includes jumping Quinn. Besides, I wouldn't want to ruin things with him. He's such a great guy." He let out a big sigh. "Isn't he great?"

River frowned.

ΩΩΩ

Brian paused at the edge of the lawn to absorb the view lit by hanging lanterns. A house full of Michelles, indeed. The theme at this year's Halloween party was the early 1800s. The women wore Empire dresses, their chests accentuated by low necklines and high waists—right beneath their breasts.

The men were nice, too, but he wasn't interested in them tonight. He got plenty of those. He straightened his black waistcoat and moved in. A waiter offered him a glass of red wine. He sipped it and looked around for Michelle.

He spotted two boys from another House. *Good. I'm not the only one here.* Matthew and Thomas were already engaged in conversation with someone he didn't know. His own security guard hovered nearby. Brian didn't even know his name. *Should've asked.*

He perused the food tables and nibbled on a sliced pear. A child's laughter floated over the murmur of conversations, and he turned to see a toddler running through the crowd.

The child saw Brian watching and slowed down. They grinned at each other. The toddler had bright blue eyes and wispy blond hair. He waddled over, and Brian squatted down. "Hi. I'm Brian."

The child touched his arm, laughed and scampered off again. Brian watched him veer to the left and clamber onto a woman's lap. Michelle. Embroidered gold vines cascaded from the high waist of her white Empire dress. Lovely. But not as lovely as she was.

She cooed to the baby, then looked up. "Brian! Well, don't you look handsome in your suit. But I didn't expect to see you here."

He smiled shyly. "I convinced Grant to let me come."

"Good for you. He's not here, is he?"

"No." Brian made silly talk with the child in Michelle's lap. The toddler grinned and waved his arms.

Michelle kissed the chubby cheek. "Tyler likes you."

Brian held out his hand. Tyler gripped it with strong little fingers. It felt amazing. "How old is he?"

"Two and a half." She gave him a squeeze. "He's my joy."

Brian looked at her with wide eyes. "He's yours?"

"Yeah, that's right."

"Wow." *Michelle is a mother.* He wasn't sure he could feel sexual with her anymore.

Tyler struggled to get off her lap. She let him down gently. "Alright, Ty, but stay by Mama." She set a stuffed giraffe on the cement by her feet.

Tyler sat down and waved the giraffe in the air. Brian sat beside him to talk to Michelle while he played with the baby. "Has he lived here all his life?"

"Yeah. I came here when I was pregnant," she said with a little frown. "Grace took me in, gave us a home." She was silent a moment. "Can I ask you a question? How old are you?"

"I turned fourteen two weeks ago."

"And how long have you been at Grant's?"

"Almost two years." He thought he detected some reaction in her face, but then it was gone.

"They start you boys real young."

He didn't know what to say to that. "How old are you?"

"I'll be twenty soon." She scooped Tyler up and set him on her lap. Kissed his cheek and smoothed his hair.

Brian felt a lump in his throat as he watched them together. His voice came out in a whisper. "You're a good mother." He had to look away, or he might cry.

"Brian."

He turned toward her. She touched his cheek, and the tears spilled over.

"Oh, honey. Come here." She scooted over.

He squeezed into the chair beside her. She held him tight and kissed his forehead. "You're such a sweetheart."

He lay against her and tried not to think about his mother, how he missed her sometimes. Or rather, missed that feeling. But it was gone long before he left home.

After a few minutes he noticed his face was against Michelle's soft breasts. And suddenly he tingled everywhere his body touched hers. He lifted his head to kiss her throat, and she met his lips. God, she tasted so sweet. He wanted her. Needed her.

She stood up, set her son on her hip and held out her hand. "Come on." She dropped Tyler off with the servants on the way to her bedroom.

Michelle left him to mingle with the other guests. He gave his waistcoat to the security guard—it was a warm night, and he was still flushed from sex. He smoothed his white shirt and wandered around, snacked on desserts, drank red wine. So many gorgeous women everywhere. He wondered if he could have sex with them. *Worth a try. But which one?* He didn't know how to choose; he wanted them all.

Then he saw her. A lovely girl with dark hair piled on her head, not much older than him—sixteen, maybe. A delicate chain circled her pale throat and dropped down between her breasts. He wanted to know what was on the end of that chain.

He put a few petit fours on a plate and walked over to sit beside her. "I thought you might like some chocolate." He held out the plate.

"Thank you." Her brown eyes smiled as she took a little cake.

He offered to get her a drink, but she already had one, so he asked her name. Beth. She seemed shy, but he managed to chat with her a few minutes. The wine helped. Then the string quartet started up again. "Would you like to dance, Beth?"

They were the same height. Great not to be shorter than the woman for a change. He held her close, felt her small breasts against his chest, and breathed in her delicate scent. He finally whispered the question. "Can we go upstairs?"

She smiled. "Sure."

It was a tiny cross that hung on the end of the chain.

He watched the lights of Jasmine Lane grow distant through the rear window. What a perfect night. He'd doubled the number of women he'd slept with. The last one had propositioned *him*, said, "You're Grant's boy, aren't you? I heard you were here. Let's go upstairs." No argument from him.

But now it was over. The limo rounded the corner, and the House was gone. Now it really *would* be almost a year before he saw Michelle again. He hadn't even been able to find her to say goodbye. So he'd said goodbye to her darling Tyler instead. Held him and told him to take care of his sweet mama. Brian closed his eyes and rested his cheek against the seat. Tears slid down the leather upholstery.

༄༄༄

River sat up in bed and lit a cigarette. He seemed agitated. Brian asked, "You okay?"

"Sure, it's just—uh . . . ." River flicked his cigarette, then turned to face him. His words came out in a rush. "John's going to New York City for two weeks. He wants me to go with him."

Brian's heart fell. He tried to hide it.

River said, "I'm not going."

"What? Don't you want to?"

"Yeah, but Grant won't let you go; John already talked to him. Kelsey can't go either. I guess being Number One has drawbacks."

Brian glanced away. "Yeah." He wasn't surprised Grant said no—client obligations and all. *Not sure I'd want to go with John anyway.* He looked at River again, with his tough guy mask on. Brian touched his leg. "Of course you should go. I'm not a baby. I can survive two weeks without you."

River avoided his gaze. "Naw, I'll stay here. It's no big deal."

"Yes, it is. You want to see the world."

"Yeah, but . . . ." River met his eyes. "What if something happens? I should be here."

"River. I'll be fine. Besides, we'll be in contact. You damn well better call me!"

River laughed. "I will."

His heart beat harder. "When are you going?"

"Next week."

"Will you miss Christmas?"

"No. We'll be back Christmas Eve."

Brian nodded and bit his lip.

"It's just two weeks."

"Yeah." *Two weeks.* The longest they'd been apart was what, three days? But River deserved to go. Brian smiled and gave him a squeeze. "You'll have so much fun."

He wandered through the grounds, almost cold enough for the sweater he'd put on. The dreary sky matched his mood. So very sad—Monday morning and no River. The whole day stretched before him, empty. He almost wished he had clients.

His mind returned to what River said right before he left. *'If . . . you know, the plane crashes or something, I want you to tell my family I love them and . . . I'm sorry.'* Of course Brian was appalled and spouted statistics about planes being much safer than cars. River stopped him. *'Just promise, okay? I want them to know.'*

But the plane didn't crash—River called upon arrival as Brian made him promise in return. His first words were, *'It's fuckin freezing here!'* Brian smiled as he passed by the fountain. At least River had finally admitted he still cared about his family—he didn't even say to leave out Dick.

Brian heaved a sigh. *I'm sure he's having fun.* He stared up at the slate sky. *No, I bet he's missing me right now, too. New York must be beautiful this time of year.* He glanced around. *But it's beautiful here, too.* White lights draped along the bushes and trees that surrounded the courtyard. Their soft light glowed in the misty air.

He left the courtyard behind and heard voices. *David?* He moved closer, up the path through the trees and around the corner. Not David. *Shit. I just want some peace.*

Trevor gave him a fake smile.

Brian didn't know the other boy. Trevor spoke quietly to him, and the boy hurried away. Trevor folded his arms in a cocky stance. "So, just the two of us now. Alone out here where no one can see us."

"Yeah, so?"

"Aren't you scared?"

"I'm not scared of you." It was true.

"You're right. It's not me you should worry about. It's the young ones who'll get ya."

He frowned and refused to let Trevor's words penetrate.

"It's already happening. Can't you tell? Your voice is getting lower. You'll grow so fast you won't know what hit you. And here's the real catch—" He poked his finger into Brian's chest. "When you're not a little boy anymore, Grant won't want you. That is a fact."

His heart pounded. "Fuck off."

Trevor grabbed his sweater and shook him. "Don't you talk to me like that!"

For an instant he was sure Trevor would hit him. But instead Trevor's mouth pressed hard against his. Brian's arms went around him, his leg, too, and they fell to the ground. Trevor slipped his hand down the front of Brian's jeans.

Brian arched against him. Pulled on his arms, his back. *Got to have him. Now.*

Next thing he knew his pants were off. Trevor unzipped, and there it was, that gorgeous cock. Brian sat up to take it in his mouth. Oh, it was so good, so hard. He wanted to taste it forever. But that wasn't all he wanted. He looked up and Trevor pushed on his shoulder, pushed him back onto the ground. Brian pulled him closer and whispered, "Fuck me."

He did. *Oh, god. Hard. Hard.* It was over all too soon.

Trevor stood to peel off the condom. Brian watched in a daze from the ground. *Oh, yeah. Condom.* Good thing they always carried them. This was one of those times he would've done it anyway.

Trevor left without a word. Brian pulled leaves out of his hair and gathered his clothes.

He went back inside. Spent most of the day playing the piano, then took another stroll after dinner. Hoping to run into Trevor again—that was hot—but no luck. He gave up and went back in, reached the top of the stairs and paused. He didn't want to face his empty bed. He was used to sleeping alone with Schnookie, but not on a Monday. Not after what Trevor had said. He turned toward Grant's rooms and found him reading in bed. Grant welcomed him with open arms.

Brian sat up against the pillows. "I've never noticed this before." He switched on the lamp and picked up a silver frame from Grant's bedside table. An old black and white photo of a boy with a flute in his hand, standing beside a man seated at a grand piano. The piano in the ballroom. The boy seemed familiar somehow. Something in the eyes. . . . He turned to Grant. "That's you!"

Grant chuckled. "Yes. And Gregory at the piano. We played duets together. A long time ago." He was silent a moment, then said, "I've lived in this House since I was twelve years old—just like you. It's been my home for most of my life. And now it's yours." He kissed Brian's forehead.

"Did you run away, too?"

"Technically, yes. But not in the same manner as you. You were very brave. I already had a place here. I chose to come live with Gregory instead of my father."

"You already knew him? He was Head of this House?"

"Yes. We met a few months earlier at a party. Got to know each other. Fell in love." Grant lay back against the pillow and gazed at his memories. "It was a wonderful time. Exciting and full of promise."

Brian studied the photo. Young Grant had one hand on the piano; Gregory's hand rested on top of it. Grant had a slight smile on his face. He looked happy. And so young. "Did you miss your father? Did you see him again?"

Grant's voice turned cold. "No. To both questions."

Brian touched his arm to soften him. "You play the flute?"

"I used to. I don't think I remember how anymore. I still have it somewhere."

"You do?"

Grant smiled. "Would you like to borrow it?"

Brian grinned. A new instrument would be fun. But more importantly, he happened to know Quinn also taught flute. One of those useless bits of Quinn information he had tucked away in his brain. Not so useless now. *Maybe I can see him three times a week.* "Yes, please."

"I'm sure it's in one of the empty bedrooms I use for storage. I'll look for it tomorrow."

"Thank you!" He was too excited to sleep now. He got up to wander around the room and stopped before a closed door—the one with the alarm. "What's in here?"

"My office."

"But your office is downstairs."

Grant's gaze lingered on Brian's body. "I have two offices. This one is off limits to everyone but myself and Jeffrey."

"Oh." Brian was disappointed. He wanted to explore. *Why can't I go in there?*

Grant moved his legs over the edge of the bed. "But there *is* something I'd like to show you. Let's get dressed first. Shoes, too."

Brian threw on his clothes and waited while Grant dressed more slowly.

"It's time you learned a House secret. Follow me."

He was surprised when Grant opened the closet door, switched on the light and went in. The scent of cedar filled the long room. They walked the length to a row of tuxedos that hung against the back. Grant pulled on the rod. It swung aside to reveal a blank wall.

"Now pay attention." He reached into a corner shelf and moved a book to reveal a small lever. "This is how you open the hidden door. Remember, it's behind *Moby Dick.*"

A door. A secret door at the back of the closet. Like Narnia.

Grant pulled the lever down, and the back wall slid aside without a sound. A musty scent emanated from the blackness. "This is an escape route. In case of emergency."

Brian's mouth was dry. "What kind of emergency?"

"It's unlikely anyone will ever use this tunnel. But it could theoretically save us in case of a disaster such as a fire. Or the FBI."

Brian's eyes got huge.

Grant smiled and touched his arm. "I'm not trying to scare you, my dear. We have very powerful allies; the possibility of something like that is miniscule. This House was built with the tunnel incorporated into the design as a precaution only. Most likely all Houses have them. Now let me show you a bit."

Grant reached around the edge of the opening into darkness. "There's a shelf here with a flashlight." He picked it up and showed Brian. "We'll use electric lights today, but in an emergency it's better not to. Here, you carry the flashlight."

Grant found the switch in the darkness and flipped it, the sound loud in the still air. Brian saw a wall straight ahead. Plain wood, like the floor.

"Come along." Grant stepped over the threshold. "I hope you're not claustrophobic. It's only about nine feet wide."

"I'm not." His voice sounded small. He followed Grant into a wooden tunnel that stretched to his left. A row of bare bulbs along the ceiling provided light.

"Aesthetics are not of interest here, as you can see."

Their footsteps creaked on the wood floor. Everything was plain wood—the walls, the ceiling. No visible doors. The tunnel ended about fifty feet away. Grant stopped halfway. He pointed to the blank wall at the end of the tunnel. "That leads to Jeffrey's bedroom. In theory it would be best to meet here and escape together. But in a worse case scenario, any of us could go alone. I'll show you the escape hatch."

He turned to walk back, all the way to the closet entrance at the end, then looked down into Brian's eyes. "You mustn't tell anyone about this. Not even River. This is a House secret. We don't want to advertise it. Alright?"

He nodded.

"You have the flashlight?"

He held it up in a tight grip.

"Shine it here." Grant indicated the wall opposite the closet. "It's the fourth beam in from the corner." He counted the beams out loud. "See, it has this dark swirl pattern."

Brian shone the light on it and saw the pattern.

Grant touched his fingers to the top of the plank. "Feel this. Can you reach it?"

He gave Grant the flashlight and reached up to feel the crack between the two pieces of wood.

"Now push down."

The wood moved. Then a whole section of the wall was sliding aside with a loud grinding noise. Darkness. He sensed a space there. A hole. The scent of earth wafted up.

Grant shone the flashlight onto wooden stairs that disappeared into pitch black. "They go down through the bottom of the house to an underground tunnel. It's a long way. There's a door at the other end, just a regular door, that leads to a garage with a car and supplies."

Wow. "Can we see it?"

Grant smiled. "I'm sorry, Brian. But I'm too old to make that trip unnecessarily. Gregory showed me when I was a boy. It's a long way." He put a hand on Brian's shoulder. "That's enough for tonight. It's getting late."

Grant went through the doorway to the closet. Brian took one last look down the wooden tunnel. He wanted to go though the hidden door on the other end, to Jeffrey's room. Wanted to go down those stairs to where the earthen smell originated.

He stepped into Grant's closet. Grant put the flashlight back and shut off the lights. He pushed the lever up, and the inner wall to the stairs slid back into place. Then the closet wall slid closed.

They went back to bed. Grant fell asleep immediately, but Brian lay awake a long time. He finally fell into a dream about caves and tunnels and secret places.

౫౫౫

Brian picked up the schedule and gasped. 'Mr. Reynolds.' The creepy guy. Had it been two months already? *It's okay. He's just another client. No reason to freak out.* He tried to believe it, but he felt nauseated.

He didn't leave his room for breakfast. He chewed his nails and felt sicker as the minutes passed. The waiting was so bad he was almost relieved when it was finally time. But not really. He forced himself down the hall. It took all his courage to go into the Room. Where Creepy Guy waited.

Two days later Brian still had the creeps. No River to comfort him. But he had other distractions. He smiled as Quinn followed him into his bedroom for his first flute lesson. If anyone could take his mind off Creepy Guy, Quinn could.

Quinn in my bedroom. It felt like a special occasion, so he wore his black leather vest. Might be a little cold, but he didn't care. He wanted to look sexy for Quinn. But not *too* obvious—so he chose faded jeans instead of leather pants. Only part of his stomach showed.

They stepped onto the balcony into the grey world. A heavy mist hung over the grounds and made the air wet. White Christmas lights glowed faintly from the trees lining the courtyard. He smiled and remembered when he showed Justin the same view. And what happened afterward.

He turned to show Quinn his belly ring.

"That's nice, Brian. Aren't you cold?" Quinn touched his arm and sent jolts running through him.

He wants me. Please want me.

They went back inside to get to work, but he had trouble keeping his mind on music. *Quinn's in my bedroom, and I'm wearing something sexy. Maybe he'll make a move.* Brian sat on the edge of the bed while Quinn showed him how to put the flute together—it was in three pieces. Brian struggled to get a sound out of it, but he couldn't do it.

"Like this." Quinn took the flute. "Do you mind? I don't have too many terrible germs."

He laughed. "Go ahead." *Please touch it with your mouth.*

"Hold it up to your lips like this and blow *across* the hole. Not into it." He demonstrated. A lovely clear note sounded.

Brian was too busy watching Quinn's mouth to really notice. *I wonder what kind of kisser he is?*

"It's easier to make a sound with just the mouthpiece." He pulled out the mouthpiece and handed it to Brian. "Cover the end with your hand. Now blow across."

Naked in the Rain

Brian finally managed to get a sound out of it.

"There you go!"

He grinned. Then couldn't get a second sound.

Quinn said, "It's hard to play when you're smiling. You must be serious." He put his hands on his hips and glowered a mock stern look.

Brian giggled and stared up into his twinkling eyes. But Quinn made him get back to business, and he finally got another sound from it. Then it was easy. "Neat."

"Now try it with the whole thing." Quinn put the flute back together and explained how to hold it. "No, turn your hand the other way. Here."

Quinn sat on the bed. Brian felt body heat behind him as Quinn guided his arms, his hands, his fingers. The touches on his bare skin sent shivers through his entire body. He couldn't hear a word Quinn was saying. He leaned back a little and connected with Quinn's body. Felt it against his back. Like he'd fantasized so many times.

Before he knew what he was doing, he'd turned around and was moving toward that perfect jaw line. Took it between his teeth and bit gently, tasted the rough skin. He pulled Quinn's face toward him to bring their lips together. Soft and yummy. He felt Quinn stiffen, but Brian couldn't stop. He kissed him again, harder.

Quinn stood up. "What are you doing?"

He stood, too, and moved closer. "Please. I just want to touch you."

Quinn backed up against the wall.

"I've wanted you since I was twelve years old." He caressed the spot next to Quinn's penis.

"Brian! Stop it."

But he couldn't. "You like guys, don't you?"

"That doesn't mean I like children."

"I'm not a kid anymore. Please!" He dropped to his knees in desperation. "You don't have to do anything. I just want to touch you. Just fellatio." His fingers felt Quinn's penis through the cotton, slid back between his legs. "The best you've ever had. Please." He touched it with his mouth.

Quinn pushed past him and walked out.

Brian moaned. *Oh, my god. What have I done? Shit, shit.* He curled up on the floor and covered his head with his hands. *Oh, god.* All these years, come to nothing. Worse than nothing. *And you had to beg, didn't you? But I thought I had a chance. I had to try.* He sat up. "Fuck."

He got to his feet and started pacing, then opened the nightstand drawer and dug around until he found Quinn's business card. He tried to compose himself, then picked up the phone. *He won't be home yet.*

He closed his eyes at the sound of the recorded voice on the answering machine *Oh, Quinn, I'm so sorry.* It beeped. His eyes opened in alarm. Should've rehearsed. "Uh, Quinn? It's Brian. I . . . I'm sorry. I'm really, *really* sorry. I didn't mean to do that. I . . . shit," he said under his breath. "It won't happen again. I *promise.* I really value you as a teacher. I hope you'll come back." He said softly, "Please come back." He was about to hang up, then brought the phone back to his ear. "And please don't tell Grant! *Please.*" *Or I'll never see you again.*

274

. . .

The next two days dragged in a heavy blur. He counted down the hours until his next piano lesson. No word from Quinn. *What if he doesn't come back?*

He bit his lip as he stared through the parlor's lace curtains, waiting for Quinn's car to come up the driveway. He glanced at the clock. *Should be here any time now. Any time. Come on, Quinn. Ah!* His heart leapt as Quinn's Honda pulled up.

"Oh, thank god." He laughed and covered his mouth. *Don't cry.*

Maria went to get the door, and he suddenly realized how awkward this would be. Quinn walked into the parlor. Brian stood by the bay window and gave him a tentative smile.

Quinn answered with a slight smile. A sad smile. He walked over to sit on the piano bench.

Brian joined him, and they went straight to business, as if nothing happened. Well, not nothing. There was no silly banter, no friendly touches. No warmth. He tried not to notice and focus on the music. *It's my fault. Just be grateful he's here at all.*

It was an excruciating ninety minutes. Quinn looked at the clock. "About time to wrap up. I'll be away for awhile." He stood to gather his things without looking at Brian. "Visiting my parents in Michigan for the holidays. So . . . I'll see you in a few weeks." He paused in the doorway and met his eyes. "Have a Merry Christmas, Brian."

He answered softly, "You, too."

Quinn turned and walked out.

He put away his flute and closed the music book. He'd been teaching himself, since he spoiled his only lesson—wanted Quinn to be impressed when he came back. If he came back. Quinn had told Grant the next piano lesson would be January 9th. *He wouldn't give Grant a date if he weren't coming back.*

The phone rang, and he grabbed it. River. His eyes closed. "God, it's so good to hear your voice. Did you go to the Statue of Liberty yet?"

"Yeah. It's totally giant up close. I took lots of pictures."

"Good. Hey, did you know Jeffrey grew up there?"

"In the Statue of Liberty?"

Brian giggled. "No, New York City."

"Really? That's cool. Too bad he ain't here to show me around. Too bad you're not here. Whatcha been up to?"

"I was just practicing the flute."

"How's that going?"

"It's fun, but weird to only play one note at a time. Quinn's away visiting his family, so I've only had one lesson." He didn't want to say more. The phone was not the place.

"I'll be home in three days, my Reservoir of Love."

*"under the blue moon I saw you
so soon you'll take me
up in your arms too late to beg you . . .*

*in starlit nights I saw you
so cruelly you kissed me
your lips a magic world
your sky all hung with jewels"*

  - Echo & the Bunnymen, "The Killing Moon"

൰൰ CHAPTER 22 ൰൰

The door to Brian's bedroom swung open silently. River stood still while his eyes adjusted to darkness. The moon appeared from behind clouds to shine through the window. Cool light illuminated the bed, Brian asleep on his back with his arm around Schnookie. River gazed at his innocent face. *Like an angel.*

He wanted to hold this perfect moment forever. But the desire to touch won out. He climbed onto the bed, careful not to jostle him, then smiled to himself. *But I want him to wake up.*

The cat woke with a surprised chirp, so River patted its head. Brian stirred and whispered his name. Their arms went around each other and held on tight.

He lay in River's arms, his gaze fixed out the window. "The moon looks like magic. That's why I leave my curtains open, so I can see it." He stroked River's chest. "I thought you wouldn't be back until tomorrow."

"John decided to come back early." He shrugged. "I don't know why. But I'm glad. I mean, I had a great time—it was excellent to see New York. But—" He kissed Brian's forehead and whispered, "I missed you."

They spent all morning in the bedroom and ate snacks out of the mini-fridge. But hunger for a bigger meal sent them downstairs eventually. Brian took River's hand and pulled him down the hall, away from the kitchen. "I thought it would be fun to eat in here."

He led River into the formal dining room set for two, candles lit on the table and along the walls.

"Brian, this is beautiful."

He smiled. "I wanted something special for your homecoming. Plus it's Christmas Eve day. Maria did all the work."

The boys sat across from each other, and Maria served enchiladas. River finally slowed down enough to talk. "I never thought I'd get to New York City. I flew into

New Jersey once to visit my grandpa, but he wouldn't go into New York. I could see it just across the water. I wanted to go so bad. Pissed me off." He frowned and shook his head. "Anyway, it was awesome! So many skyscrapers and people."

"L.A.'s got that, too."

"Yeah, but it's different there. L.A.'s spread out. New York's got all these people and tall buildings jammed onto an island. Everything crammed together. Kind of claustrophobic, actually. I know that sounds stupid, but . . . ."

"Nothing you feel is stupid."

River gave him half a smile. "Well, it's a cool place to visit, but I don't think I'd wanna live there." He shivered. "Too cold, anyway. Give me Southern California any day. But you woulda loved the Christmas decorations in Times Square."

Brian rested his chin on his hand. "I wish I could've been there."

"Me, too. Next time."

"Yeah." He sighed and toyed with his food.

"What about you? What's been going on here?"

"Not too much." Brian told him about decorating with Maria, Christmas shopping on Rodeo Drive, how hard it was to get a sound out of the flute. But he omitted a few small details. Like the tunnel. His encounter with Trevor. And Quinn.

He didn't want to talk about Quinn. He had two full days with River. He didn't want to spoil it by thinking about that. He pushed his plate away, still heaped with food.

River frowned. "Are you sick?"

"No."

"You hardly ate. Is something wrong? Did something happen while I was gone?" His voice went up with a hint of panic.

"No, I'm fine. I'm just trying to watch what I eat. But dessert—" He grinned. "Maria made chocolate pudding especially for you."

"Hold on, back up. What do you mean, watching what you eat? Are you getting enough protein? Maybe you shouldn't be a vegetarian anymore."

"What? No, I get plenty of protein. I'm just trying not to eat too much, that's all."

"Are you joking? You're tiny—you eat any less you'll disappear."

"I'm not tiny. And I'm getting bigger. It's just . . . ." He shifted in his chair and looked down at his plate. "I don't want to grow too fast. It'll be harder to do the girl thing, and, you know. It's . . . bad for business."

"What the fuck are you talking about? Did Grant say that?"

"No."

"Jesus, Brian, you can't avoid growing up." He leaned forward and took Brian's hand, forced him to meet his eyes. "Do not be on a diet. Please. You're fourteen years old. You're *supposed* to eat a lot. Boys grow fast. You can't avoid it—and you shouldn't want to."

A slight smile crossed his lips. "You're right. I know that in my head, it's just . . . ." His shoulder twitched in a shrug. "I worry sometimes. Grant told me a long time ago he never wanted me to leave. But . . . things change. And he'll always put the business first."

"Don't worry about it, Brian. God, that's forever away. You don't need to think about it now."

He smiled. "You're right again." He shook his head. "It's silly."

River pushed Brian's plate toward him. "Now eat."

"Yes, sir." He picked up his fork.

The boys lounged in front of the fire with Grant and sipped eggnog with amaretto. The firelight glinted on ornaments, and the scent of pine filled the parlor. Brian stroked Schnookie, curled up on his lap. The cat was tired after helping them decorate the tree.

River's arm went around Brian as they stared into the flames and listened to the wood crackle. Soon Grant said it was time for him to turn in. He kissed them goodnight and left them alone.

After they made love again, River followed him up to the ballroom. Brian and Maria had strung white lights around the stage and in swags along the ceiling, all the way around the room. "Wow. You guys did a good job."

Brian smiled and led him through the dim light toward the stage. River took his usual seat, and Brian lit two candles on the piano. "This is my favorite Christmas music—Vienna Boys Choir. I always play it on Christmas Eve. It's a tradition."

He sat on the bench and turned on the CD player. Sweet, ethereal voices soared. Brian sang along and played the organ part on piano.

River felt like he'd been swept into a magical realm. The sheer beauty of the voices, of the soft white lights, of the boy before him. Brian's face glowed in the flickering candlelight.

He turned to smile at River and sang, "Amen, amen," as the song ended.

"Amen? You're singing 'amen'? Never thought I'd hear that."

Brian laughed. "I don't care that it's religious. The music is so beautiful. Besides, it's in another language so I can't tell what they're saying."

"I never heard you sing like that before. You sound just like em."

"Thanks." He glanced away. "But not much longer. This is probably my last year." He hadn't realized it until now, but he could hear the change in his voice.

"Then make it count."

"Yeah." He turned back to the piano and couldn't resist saying, "You know, they used to castrate boys to keep their voices like that."

"God, Brian! That's sick."

"I know." He laughed, proud to have grossed out River—not an easy task. He turned the CD back on.

When he'd finally played enough, he glanced at the clock. After midnight. He got down from the stage to sit on River's lap in the wingchair. He touched River's face and whispered, "Merry Christmas."

ﭼﭼﭼ

Brian pulled on his black leather pants and vest and left Mr. Padrea's room. He'd been avoiding the kitchen, but not tonight. He didn't care about that woman—River was back, and nothing else mattered.

He helped himself to rocky road and sat at the kitchen table. He'd barely tasted his ice cream before Leah showed up. "Did I wake you?" he asked. "I'm sorry."

She smiled. "That's alright. I'm a light sleeper. And it's fun to get up for a midnight snack." She lifted tinfoil from a platter on the counter. "Want some cookies?"

"Yes! Please."

She set the cookies on the table and handed him a glass of milk. He saw her gaze move to the scar on his wrist. He ignored that and let the shortbread cookie melt in his mouth. "Mmm. Did you make these?"

"Yep. For Christmas."

"They're good. Is that what you do here? Cook and stuff?"

"That's part of it." She sat across from him. "I help keep up the house for Mr. Padrea. He can't manage on his own anymore. But the main thing I do for him is physical therapy."

"Oh. Me, too." He laughed. "I help relieve stress, anyway."

"Hmm . . . ." She frowned, and her hazel eyes met his. "Brian, why do you . . . do what you do?"

He shrugged. "Why not? It's fun." *Sometimes.* He reached for another cookie.

"I don't understand that."

He thought for a moment. "Well, I'm a guy, see. You know how guys are. We like to have sex." He licked his fingers. "All the time."

"But that should be with a partner you choose, not someone who pays you."

"Or I can have both." He lit a cigarette. She looked like she would say more, so he leaned forward to cut her off. "You don't know anything about it. I have a good life. I don't need to hear your judgments." He sat back and took a drag. "So. Did you have a nice Christmas?"

"It was alright. But I missed my family in Iowa."

"You didn't visit them?"

"Not this year, with Mr. Padrea needing me here. What about you? I bet you miss your family."

He shot her an angry look and stood up. "Not really."

"Brian, wait—" But he was already gone.

Brian held onto Grant's arm, excited. He'd never seen *The Nutcracker* performed live. And he couldn't remember the last time he'd seen such a huge crowd. Orderly masses of people in fancy clothes filed into the Dorothy Chandler Pavilion.

He picked up his long dress as they mounted the stairs. He'd decided to go as River's girlfriend tonight. Maria helped him put up his hair. They used lots of hairspray. Grant liked it very much—said it showed off his throat and face. And the sapphire choker, of course. Then Grant commented that his Adam's apple wasn't very prominent yet. Brian hadn't even noticed it before. His body kept changing; it was hard to keep up.

He put those concerns out of his mind and looked for River as they took their seats. Not here yet, of course. John was never early. He kept an eye out and finally saw John's head above the crowd. But it was Kelsey at John's side, not River. The sudden disappointment made him feel like crying. He ground his jaw. *Damn it, John, why didn't you bring him?* They hadn't seen each other since Christmas.

The lights dimmed. Kelsey took the seat beside Brian and told him he looked nice. Brian tried to be polite, reminded himself Kelsey was River's friend. *I wonder if they've had sex? Probably.* He pictured Kelsey's dark complexion against River's lighter skin and frowned—jealous not of the sex, but of the time they had together, being in the same House.

Grant touched his arm and whispered, "This is a wonderful production."

Brian focused on the stage. He finally managed to get lost in the magic and forget about River for a little while.

The next evening was another big night out. Grant picked up the strappy 'top' and said, "This is not like the parties you're used to. It's a gathering of very powerful people, but not other boys or Houses. You'll see some clients tonight, but you must give *no* indication you know them. Can you do that?"

He nodded and held out his arms as Grant fastened the buckles. Brian frowned into the mirror at the black strips of leather tight across his chest.

"You may touch me," Grant said. "But don't overdo it. This party is business, not recreation. You're not to have any alcohol or drugs."

No fun. "Yes, Grant."

Grant held up a tailored black blazer, and Brian slipped it on. "Keep your jacket on unless I tell you otherwise. We'll meet a few potential clients tonight—one in particular I've been after for some time, waiting for the right opportunity. The right boy. I've been unable to get him to any of our parties, so we'll go to his instead."

Grant stood behind him, hands on his shoulders, and they looked at each other in the mirror. Brian's eyes moved to his own reflection. The jacket came to a nice V down his chest. Couldn't see the ugly strappy thing at all. He smoothed the satin lapels. "Will River be there?"

"Oh, I don't think so. I'm sure John will bring Kelsey."

His forehead creased. "But I've hardly seen him since they got back. He wasn't even at the show last night. Can't you tell John to bring him? Please?" Brian turned to run his hand up Grant's tuxedo shirt. Brushed his lips against his jaw, his ear. "Please?"

"We'll see." Grant cleared his throat and stepped toward the door. "Meet me downstairs in fifteen minutes."

They waited outside while Jeffrey pulled the car forward. *The car.* Brian had never seen this one before. The black Rolls-Royce looked like an antique. "It's beautiful," he breathed. The glow of the setting sun reflected off its polished surface as he walked around it. The license plate read, '# 1.'

Grant ran his fingers along the gleaming surface. "Gregory loved this car. It's one of only 491 Wraiths built. He bought it new in 1939. We've put in a new engine since then, of course. But the interior is original."

Jeffrey opened the door for them. Brian took off his blazer so it wouldn't get wrinkled, then sat on soft leather upholstery. *Wonderful.* He gazed up at the clouds as they got on the freeway, watched the light fade and darkness take over. He leaned against Grant and stared at the city lights. Grant's hand strayed on his bare skin. Tweaked a nipple. They kissed.

The car suddenly slowed. Jeffrey said, "Sorry, Mr. Grant," and pulled onto the wide shoulder.

Brian looked back at blue and red flashing lights behind them. His heart skipped. Grant took his arm from around him and moved away a little as the cop walked over.

The young policeman spoke to Jeffrey through the open window. "Are you aware of the speed you were going?"

"Sorry bout that, officer."

The cop glanced into the back. The glow from his headlights illuminated the car, and Brian knew the man could see him, half naked with a few leather straps across his chest. They stared at each other with wide eyes.

Grant leaned forward and handed over his ID. "Why don't you run this through your little machine?"

"Uh, yes, I—I will." He stepped away.

Oh, my god. Oh, my god. He knows what I am. He reached for the blazer with shaking hands. Grant helped him put it on. *He's going to take me away.* A small sound escaped from his throat.

Grant patted his knee. "It's alright, Brian. Stay calm."

The cop stuck his head back in and handed the ID to Grant. "I'm terribly sorry for the inconvenience, Mr. Nesbit."

"No harm done—" Grant glanced at his badge. "Officer Stevens."

Within seconds they were on their way again. Brian couldn't think. Grant hugged him close. "It's alright, my dear boy. You're safe with me."

He still had adrenalin shakes by the time they reached the party. They stood outside by the Rolls for a few minutes while he smoked a cigarette and stared up at the stone façade. The mansion was built to look like a castle. *Neat.* It helped distract him, and he focused on his professional responsibilities. "Okay. I'm okay."

It looked like a castle on the inside, too—tapestries warmed the stone walls of the entryway. He held onto Grant's arm as they walked into the main room. Not as many people as he expected, but everyone looked very elegant.

At first he felt insulted when he was continually passed over during introductions. Then he found it amusing. Everyone tried so hard to pretend he didn't exist, when in fact they couldn't stop noticing him. He glanced around and saw a few clients, but they stood across the room by the Christmas tree, so it was easy to ignore them. He sipped his lemonade, bored with the conversation about manipulating oil prices. *I hope River comes.*

One of the men talking to Grant pulled out a pewter cigarette case. Early forties. Dark, wavy hair. *And he's really good at not seeing me.* Brian focused his energy on him as the man offered cigarettes to everyone in their group. *Look at me. Look at me.* The man looked. Their eyes held. After what seemed an eternity, the man extended the cigarette case toward him.

"Thank you," Brian said ever so politely. *It's about time. People are so rude.* Grant held up a lighter for him. The man was nervous now. Kept glancing at him, back and forth between him and Grant.

Yes, I exist. I'm a human being. He couldn't resist being a little bad. Gave the man a slow look up and down, a sex smile. The man almost dropped his cigarette. He looked away and soon excused himself from the group.

Too easy. He glanced around the room and caught several men staring. They pretended not to be. But a few kept looking. Brian imagined having sex with them. *I'd love to find out if I'm right about him—he likes it rough.* The waiter with an athletic build approached a group of people. A woman took a glass from the tray and sipped. Brian's eyes followed the motion, dropped down her throat and cleavage to her white sequin dress. The curve of her hips. Then slowly back up to her face. She was watching him.

The pity in her eyes jarred him from his fantasy. This time he was the one who glanced away. Anger coursed through him. He focused it and stared back at her. It worked. Made the pity vanish. She seemed surprised and turned away.

He waited until Grant stopped talking, then touched his chest and leaned up to whisper in his ear. "I need to use the restroom."

Grant stroked his hair and pointed it out to him. "Come straight back to me, alright?"

He took his time in the luxurious bathroom. Played with his hair in the mirror until someone knocked. He opened the door to leave and practically ran into the woman in the white sequin dress. They stared at each other for a surprised moment.

She searched his face. "How old are you?"

"Eighteen." A blatant lie, and they both knew it.

"You can't be more than fifteen."

He smiled a little, pleased she guessed older than his real age. Or maybe that wasn't a good thing. He glanced at Thomas standing against the far wall, watching. "I'm not supposed to talk to you."

"Does your mother know where you are?"

He raised an eyebrow. "Of course not." He walked away and noticed one of John's security guards near Thomas. He glanced around the room. Found John. And River. *Yes!*

River looked stunningly handsome in a black tuxedo. Brian hurried over to give him a big hug but refrained from *too* much enthusiasm. "I need to talk to you. Let me just tell Grant first."

He made his way to where Grant stood with several people and waited for a lull in the conversation. "River's here. Thank you!" He reached up to kiss his cheek. "May I go talk to him? Please?"

"Yes, but stay within sight. And no necking. Behave yourselves."

Brian led River over to a couple of chairs against the wall. "Oh, my god, you won't believe what happened!" Brian told him about the cop who pulled them over.

River listened intently and muttered, "Holy shit," a few times. He leaned back when Brian finished. "Man, Grant's one powerful dude. And so are you. Otherwise I wouldn't be here tonight—John wasn't gonna bring me. But you made him, didn't you?"

"Yeah, I guess I did." He loved the idea that he had power over John—as long as he could get Grant to do what he wanted. But that wasn't important right now.

"River, listen. When that cop saw me in the car, I thought he would take me away. I thought . . . what if I never see you again?" His voice caught.

"Brian." River's fingertips brushed his cheek. "That won't happen."

"But what if we get separated somehow? How would we ever find each other?" The thought sent shocks of panic through him.

"We won't."

"You don't know that."

"I'd find you."

That's not good enough. "We need a plan. A place." He lowered his voice. "A place to meet up . . . just in case."

River nodded slowly. "A backup plan. That's good. Where?"

"I don't know. Pick a city."

"Uh . . . Boston."

"No. That's too close to Connecticut."

River rested his chin on his hand and stared at the party. "Fort Worth."

Brian had lived in Texas briefly but not in that area. He had no connections there. "Yeah, okay. Fort Worth."

"Meet you downtown."

"Okay." He laughed with relief and hugged him.

"But it won't happen. I'll never let you go." River stroked his back and finally pulled away. "I'll get us some drinks. I think you could use one."

He shook his head. "Grant said no alcohol tonight. I'll stick with lemonade." But damn, he wanted that drink. "Something else happened while you were away. I made a pass at Quinn. It didn't go well. He left."

"How far did you get?"

He sighed and looked down. "Nowhere. I tried, but . . . he thinks I'm too young. I ruined everything. He said he was going away for the holidays, but I'm afraid he won't come back."

"Sure he will, Brian. Relax." He squeezed his leg. "I'm surprised it didn't happen sooner. The guy's a babe. And you know how you are."

Brian pushed at him and grinned. "I have a *little* self-control. I'm not on your lap right now, am I?"

River leaned closer. "I wish you were."

"Mmm. You're coming over tomorrow night for New Year's, right?"

"Just try and stop me." He stroked Brian's hand.

Brian glanced at Thomas. Thomas moved his head slightly. "Grant wants me. I'll see you later, River." Brian gave him a lingering kiss and got up.

Grant was chatting with a small group in the foyer. His eyes never left the man he was talking to as his arm snaked around Brian's waist. Brian saw one of his clients approach. The Exception who got to visit more than once a week.

The man across from Grant said, "I believe you've met Senator Jones and his wife."

Senator Jones? *Holy shit.* An important client indeed. Mr. Jones didn't even glance at him. Brian looked at the woman beside him. *Pat!* Brian gasped. He turned it into a cough and looked away. His heart pounded. *Jesus Christ, I'm doing a Senator and his wife?*

Pat gave him a little smile. He couldn't return it.

Senator Jones said, "Grant, I'd like you to meet our host, a close friend of mine." He gestured to a silver-haired man who was suddenly beside him, dressed in black with a white collar. "Cardinal Richards."

Cardinal. Wow. Brian didn't know exactly what that meant, but he knew it was someone important. He wasn't introduced, of course, but he was looked at. Most definitely looked at. Heat rose in his cheeks as the Cardinal's eyes bored into him. *Holy shit.*

Senator Jones and Pat faded away and left them alone as Grant and the Cardinal talked about their art collections. Cardinal Richards' eyes kept flicking toward Brian. He finally suggested that Grant might like to see a special piece he acquired recently. Grant smiled.

The Cardinal led them down the hall, farther away from the party. The stone façade was everywhere, with tapestries on the walls. *Someday I'll see a real castle.* Brian glanced over his shoulder and saw Jeffrey following at a discreet distance. The Cardinal guided them up a flight of stairs and down another hallway.

They finally came to a halt when they entered a library. Jeffrey waited outside, and Grant closed the door. "It's a bit warm after that climb, isn't it, Brian?" He gave him a look.

Brian understood. He gave the Cardinal a little smile while he unbuttoned his jacket, then slipped it off his shoulders like Grant had taught him and let it fall to the floor. The cool air hit his bare skin, and he shivered. The Cardinal seemed to like that. His cold blue eyes heated up as they raked his body.

Grant said, "I understand you're pursuing a new interest, Your Grace."

His gaze never strayed. "I wouldn't call it *new*."

Grant smiled. "If you'll excuse me a moment, I need a word with Jeffrey." He paused by Brian on his way out to whisper, "Let him touch you a little, but nothing more. I'll be back in a moment."

Brian responded with an almost imperceptible nod, and Grant left them alone.

Brian leaned back against the large ebony desk and looked at the Cardinal through his lashes. The Cardinal approached, and Brian moved away from the desk to stand close. Almost touching. Round eyes that made him look innocent stared up into the Cardinal's pale blue irises. The man's pupils grew, and his breath picked up, but they still hadn't touched.

He whispered, "I'm Brian," and at the same moment brought his hand to the Cardinal's. The touch was like an electric shock, so much tension had built between them. Brian drew circles on the palm.

The Cardinal made a noise deep in his throat and seemed about to pounce. But instead he stepped back abruptly, then turned and walked out of the room without a word. Brian heard him say, "What's your price?" as the door closed.

Brian hurried over to press his ear against the wood but couldn't hear anything. He backed off to wait. After a moment the door opened, and Grant walked in.

He beamed a proud smile. "Not only have you convinced him, but he wants you *now*. He'll be back in a moment. When he comes in, go down on your knees and kiss his ring. Jeffrey and I will be right outside the door. Call my name if you have any problems."

"But you can't hear anything through that door."

Grant chuckled and brushed the hair out of Brian's face. "I see. Alright, we'll leave the door ajar."

Grant left as the Cardinal returned, resplendent in a long red robe with a matching red cap. Brian went to his knees as the man approached and kissed his ring, the gold warm against his lips.

He stroked Brian's hair. "Put your hands behind your back. Now see what you can find."

Brian felt like he was bobbing for apples. His mouth had no trouble locating the hardness beneath the robes. He rubbed his face against it. The Cardinal lifted the red fabric, naked underneath. Brian resisted the urge to bring his hands forward. Gripped them behind his back and let his mouth do all the work. Until he realized that's what the Cardinal wanted. *So he can punish me.* He brought his hand forward to stroke him.

"Bad boy, I said no hands." The Cardinal slapped it away after a moment, then gripped his wrist and brought Brian's arm up behind his back. Not enough to hurt him, just enough so Brian couldn't move. The Cardinal pushed on his back to bend him over and commanded him to lower his pants to receive punishment.

Brian obeyed, then returned to position on all fours, his back curved toward the floor. The Cardinal ran his fingers along the sensitive spots, then slapped his ass. The man lifted his robes and fucked him hard, pulled on the leather straps that ran across Brian's back. Grunted and groaned. It was over in minutes. The man gave him a final slap and left without a word.

Brian stood to pull his pants back up. He had trouble zipping over his erection. Grant came in and kissed his forehead. "My wonderful boy."

"Grant." Brian ran his hand up his chest.

He could tell Grant almost said no. His gaze flicked over Brian's flushed cheeks to his chest heaving against the leather straps. Grant dropped to his knees. Brian leaned back against the desk and gripped the edge. It didn't take long.

They left the library behind. Jeffrey led them through another hallway, down a different set of stairs and out a side door. The servant's entrance, Grant said. He explained it was better if no one saw them leave—that way people would think they'd left earlier.

Thomas had the Rolls waiting. They piled into the car. Brian couldn't stop his grin, even though he was sorry not to say goodbye to River. He felt like some kind of spy. James Bond, sneaking out the secret entrance. He laughed as the car sped away.

*"excuse me but can I be you for awhile
my dog won't bite if you sit real still
I got the anti-Christ in the kitchen yellin' at me again
yeah I can hear that . . .
my scream got lost in a paper cup
you think there's a heaven where some screams have gone . . .
sometimes I hear my voice and it's been
here
silent all these years"*

- Tori Amos, "Silent All These Years"

CHAPTER 23

Brian lay alone in the semi-dark of his room. Last night with River was wonderful—another New Year's Eve together. They'd gotten drunk and looked for shooting stars from Brian's balcony. But now he was alone. He stared into space as he listened to the radio youth program. The violin sounded sad. Lonely. So lonely. Even though River was back, somehow it hadn't changed. It didn't make it better.

He stripped and put on one of River's dress shirts. It smelled good. Made him feel even more alone. He lay down again and squeezed his eyes shut. Jumped at the knock on the door. "Come in."

He swung his legs over the edge of the bed and sat up, expecting Grant. Not Grant. His breath caught as Trevor approached slowly. His spandex crop top showed off lean muscles. And riding pants showed off the rest of him.

Trevor gave him a soft pinch and stood to get dressed. He paused at the door with a slight smile, then walked out.

Brian stared up at the ceiling. So relaxed. *That's just what I needed.* He could never get enough of Trevor's penis in his mouth. He didn't know why, but it was extra delicious. He'd have to take his time with it someday. If they could ever manage to slow down. God, it was so intense. And quick.

And now he was alone again. He almost wished Trevor stayed to cuddle. *Well, maybe not. But if he stayed longer we could do it again.* He sighed and rolled onto his side, saw something shiny on the carpet. A shirt button. *Oops.*

He stared at it until his eyes lost focus. The loneliness filled him up again as the radio host's voice filled the room. Sounded like his father. He pulled the comforter around him and fell asleep to the tones of a fourteen-year-old cellist.

He's back. He's really back. Brian bounded downstairs to greet Quinn, but stopped himself from hugging him. *Don't push it.* They grinned at each other.

"Did you have a good Christmas, Brian?"

"Yeah." He asked about Quinn's vacation, his family. Found out he was an only child. *How sad.*

"We need to talk." Quinn glanced around the parlor. "Somewhere private. Maybe out front?"

"No, there's a security camera." He frowned and ignored his sudden nerves. "We can use the courtyard between the two buildings. We'll see if anyone comes in."

They walked down the long hall and stepped out into cool dampness beneath a slate grey sky. Quinn paused to take in the grounds. "Gorgeous."

"I'd love to show you around sometime," Brian said softly. *Oh, it'll be bad if we run into other boys. Shit. Be careful.*

They moved on and passed beneath the arbor into the V-shaped courtyard. Brian led him to a small willow tree where they could see the entrance.

"Brian—" Quinn seemed nervous. He licked his lips and blurted out, "What is your relationship with Grant?"

He sucked in his breath, unprepared for that line of questioning. "He's my guardian."

Quinn took a deep breath and paced. "Something's been bothering me since that day. Of course a lot of things bothered me, but there was something else. It took awhile to figure it out." He stopped walking and faced him. "It's the word you used. 'Fellatio.' That's not the sort of word fourteen-year-olds use. It's the sort of word—" He searched Brian's eyes. "Grant would use."

Brian stifled a gasp.

"Has Grant molested you?"

His mouth fell open. He finally found his tongue, but his voice shook. "No, no, of course not. He's good to me."

"And the other things you said—and did. Like you're experienced."

"I am." Brian clung to an idea. "I have had sex. With River. He's my boyfriend. My love." *Yes, this will work.* "I'm sorry about what happened. River went to New York for two weeks. I've never been without him for so long and I. . . . " He stared up into Quinn's eyes. "I didn't mean to do that. I was afraid you wouldn't come back."

"No, Brian. I would never hold that against you." He gripped Brain's shoulders. "I care about you. You're a talented student and a wonderful person."

It was all he could do not to cry. "Thank you." *For being you. And for being distracted from Grant.*

River wanted to try something new on his birthday, so he'd asked John to get them mushrooms. John had it made into tea—said it was more palatable that way.

The boys lounged on the deck of the beach house. *Their* beach house, they called it now. Their special place. They sipped mushroom tea and watched the sun go down. Brian leaned against River with a sigh. His body felt so satiated. Now that they'd had plenty of sex, it was time for drugs.

The effects were similar to acid, but more visual. And no burning in the stom-

Naked in the Rain

ach, no shakes. Less freaky. "I like this." Brian stared up at the stars, barely visible above the dark ocean. "It's mellow."

"Yeah."

He turned to River. "I can't believe you're sixteen. My sweet sixteen." He grinned as the old Johnny Burnette melody entered his mind. He pulled River to his feet. They danced and Brian sang, "We fell in love on the night we met. You touched my hand, my heart went pop. Ooo, when we kissed, I could not stop."

River gave him a long kiss.

"Lips like strawberry wine. You're sixteen, you're beautiful and you're mine."

"All yours." River picked him up and swung him around.

Their laughter filled the night.

༄༄༄

Brian woke early and picked up his schedule. Cardinal Richards at ten, then Roger at one, and a note. *'See me.'* His stomach twisted. *Oh, please, not another Creepy Guy.* He threw on his robe and hurried down the hall.

Grant lounged in his sitting room with coffee and newspaper. He smiled at Brian. "Come sit with me. What's wrong, dear?"

"Nothing, just. . . . " He held up the crumpled paper in his hand. "It says 'See me.'"

"Oh, yes. I need to explain about Roger. Although he's a new client, you may recognize him. He's a successful actor who's been in many films. But when you meet him, behave as if you don't know who he is. As if he were not a celebrity."

"A celebrity," Brian repeated. He sat back and laughed in relief. "Okay. No special stuff for him?"

"Just that you don't acknowledge his fame."

He smiled. "I can do that."

Grant lifted the silver urn from the coffee table to pour a cup for Brian. "And wear one of your bondage outfits."

"'kay." He wrapped his fingers around the warm porcelain. "I'm surprised the Cardinal comes here. He's such an important client. I thought I would go to him."

"You don't go to clients. They come to you. That's a Rule. It doesn't matter how important they are. You're important, too."

"But Mr. Padrea . . . oh—he's the Exception."

Grant smiled. "That's right. Bernie and I go back a long way. We've been friends for over thirty years. He deserves that exception."

He couldn't imagine that length of time. But he was pleased Grant would bend a rule out of friendship—it wasn't always purely business.

"Remember, Brian, the identity of your clients is confidential. We are in the information business."

He nodded as it all clicked into place. He finally understood the true root of Grant's power. It had nothing to do with money and everything to do with knowing people's darkest secrets. *Important* people's secrets. Information.

. . .

Afternoon sunlight streamed in the window and warmed the bed where Brian sat. Having a movie star for a client was weird. But fun. Surreal to walk into the Room and see him in person. He looked exactly the same as in the movies—only shorter.

But having a celebrity client wasn't much fun when he couldn't tell anyone. Grant and Jeffrey were gone at some meeting and wouldn't be back until late. He picked up the phone to call River. No answer. He hung up without leaving a message.

He thought about his conversation this morning with Grant. *Yeah, we're powerful. But so what? It doesn't change the fact that I'm sitting here alone with no one to talk to. Nothing to do.* Well, that wasn't true—he had homework. But he didn't want to do it. Didn't feel like playing any of his instruments. Didn't feel like doing anything. He frowned at the blue sky.

Schnookie jumped onto the bed. Brian smiled and petted him while the cat basked in the sun, purring. He kissed the soft pink pad of Schnookie's paw. Schnookie purred louder and licked his hand. Brian said, "I love you, too."

He lay beside the cat and admired his long fur. The sunlight illuminated each hair. They glowed, almost iridescent. He murmured, "My shiny rainbow boy."

His breath caught as he was overwhelmed by the *mommy* feeling. Remembered his mother saying those exact words to him when he was very small. Her voice, her smile filled him. *'My shiny rainbow boy.'* It hurt. He missed it so much. Hadn't had that feeling in ages—not since long before he ran away. *Mommy.* He couldn't breathe for a moment. He hugged his chest and sobbed.

A long time later he got up to splash cold water on his face, then stood at the glass doors and stared out. A long time. He lost track. Jumped when Schnookie rubbed his leg. He patted him absentmindedly, then went to take another shower. Just wanted to feel the water on his body. He lost track again. Stared blindly at the tile wall with water running onto his chest. He jerked back when it got too hot and turned it off.

The air felt good on his bare skin. He wandered over to the closet to put on one of River's dress shirts, buttoned a few buttons and sat down at the desk. He opened the wooden box from Jamaica, loaded marijuana into the pipe and sat and smoked. Stared out the window. He got up to put the *Disintegration* CD into the stereo. He hadn't listened to The Cure in awhile.

He sat at the desk again as waves of sound crashed over him and found where he'd left off in his journal. Didn't read what else was on the page. That was his rule—so it wouldn't influence where he was now. When he wrote something, it was done. Out of him. He didn't go back and read it again.

He doodled with his left hand. Listened to the sad music, Robert Smith's sad voice.

> *I do love them. That's what makes it hurt so much. River was right about that. He's so smart about things. He's so much more than he gives himself credit for. I wish he were here. I miss him.*

He held his fist against his mouth to stop himself from crying again. He'd had enough of that. He sniffed and reached for a cigarette. Then remembered the pot. Switched back and forth between them.

I wish anyone *was here. Anyone.* He stared at the door. Willed someone to knock. But no one did. He pushed his journal away and glanced at the lines he'd drawn. His doodle had come out ugly. Just the way he felt inside. He laid his head on the desk and stared at the door. But no one came.

He didn't see or talk to anyone the rest of the day. Except when Maria called on the intercom to ask if he was coming down for dinner. He told her he had food in his fridge, and he would eat in his room. But he didn't. Wasn't hungry. He finally crawled into bed. But it was a long time before he slept.

ഇഇഇ

He tried to focus on his tutor's voice and the political differences between the Union and the Confederates. But the Civil War was much more interesting in *Gone With the Wind.*

Mr. Wycliffe's voice droned on, background noise. All Brian could think about was how Trevor snuck into his room again this morning. So hot.

"Brian."

He jumped.

"What did I just say?"

"Uh. . . ." His brain wasn't working. All the blood was someplace else. He shifted in his chair and rested his elbows on the desk.

"You must pay attention."

They'd never really gotten along. Not since Wycliffe accused him of cheating on his first creative writing assignment. Asked him who had written it—that left-handed scrawl had thrown him off. *But he shouldn't have assumed I was cheating.* He swallowed his irritation. Mr. Wycliffe was right this time. "Yes, sir."

"Perhaps this will catch your interest." He dug through his briefcase. "This was made during the Civil War." He pulled out a cloth and unfolded it onto the bed.

Brian got up to take a closer look and touched it with his fingertips. "Wow," he breathed. The cloth was faded and blotched with stains, but the embroidered design was clear. Two figures stood in the center, surrounded by scrolling vines and flowers. "It's beautiful."

"My great grandmother made this. It's been handed down through my family." He folded it carefully and put it back into his briefcase.

Brian stared at him. He'd never thought of his having a family, or parents. Hadn't ever really looked at him properly. The old man's eyes were a faded, watery blue. *Must have been beautiful once.* Brian's fingers grazed Mr. Wycliffe's cheek. He leaned closer to touch his lips to the wrinkled throat.

"No, no, no." Mr. Wycliffe grabbed his wrist and led him out of the room.

"What? Where are we going?"

He didn't answer, just pulled Brian along behind him, down the hall to Grant's rooms. *Uh oh.* Brian had the feeling he was in trouble, though he didn't understand why.

Grant answered the knock.

"Your boy here just made a pass at me."

Grant looked him. "Is this true?"

"Uh...."

Grant's lips tightened. "I see. Brian, I'd like a word with you."

Brian entered, and Grant closed the door behind him. "You may fool around with the other boys all you like, as long as it doesn't interfere with your work. But not the help. That's a Rule." Grant shook his head and took a deep breath. "However, I neglected to tell you that. So I'm not angry with you. But from now on remember—" He pointed his finger. "You are not to have sex with the help. They are beneath you. Do you understand?"

He blinked. *Beneath me? What the hell does that mean?* "Yes, Grant."

Grant smiled and rubbed Brian's shoulder. "That's my boy. Now go apologize to Mr. Wycliffe and continue your studies." His hand trailed down Brian's back, and he murmured, "They could never afford you, anyway."

Brian turned away to hide his anger and walked back to his room. *Couldn't afford me? What if I want to have sex with them? For free? I can fuck whoever I want.*

He put on a contrite smile and apologized to Mr. Wycliffe. But he still couldn't focus on the lecture. *'They're beneath you.'* Carl the stable hand, and Justin and Maria. And Jeffrey. *Jeffrey*. How could Grant say that about them?

It was one thing to have a Rule. But a rule based on prejudice .... He would not follow rules he didn't believe in. He certainly wasn't about to stop messing around with Justin. But he had to be careful. He didn't want Grant to limit his access to these people. They were the only people he had.

He shivered and tightened the black silk robe as he searched Mr. Padrea's freezer. No rocky road. He picked up vanilla with a frown.

"Would you like chocolate sauce with that?" Leah said from the doorway.

He grinned. Didn't mind her showing up like this if she was going to offer him chocolate.

"I'll show you how to make it."

"Make it?" He thought chocolate sauce came out of a bottle.

"Sure. It's easy."

She got out the ingredients and told him his job was to stir. She handed him a wooden spoon, then dropped chocolate squares and butter into a pan. He watched them melt as he stirred, surprised the chocolate went first. Soon it was smooth and steamy. He snuck a little onto his finger. Hot. He licked it off, and the bitter taste made his face scrunch. "Oh, this is terrible."

She laughed. "That's *unsweetened* chocolate. It'll taste good once we add this." She poured in sugar while he stirred. "So what have you been up to?"

"Uh...." He tried to think of something he could tell her. Not about his exciting new clients. "River just turned sixteen. That was fun."

"Who's River?"

"He's my ... the love of my life."

She smiled. "What'd you do for his birthday?"

"Went to a beach house we rent sometimes. We hung out—just the two of us. Had sex on the beach." *Did drugs.* "It's private there."

Her eyes widened slightly, but she smiled. "That sounds nice."

"It was. We always have a great time there."

"Do you go often?"

"No, just for special occasions. Birthdays, anniversaries."

"Anniversaries?"

"Yeah. We went there for our second anniversary."

"You and River? Two years is a long time for someone your age."

"It was two years in September—the anniversary of the day we met." He smiled at the memory. River had tried to be so hostile at first. He remembered how they sat close together on the floor between their beds, how River held him when he cried. *I can't believe I never kissed him. But it wouldn't have been a good idea. River wasn't ready then.* Bubbling chocolate brought him out of his reverie. "It's really hot in there."

She seemed surprised by his comment, and he realized she'd been watching him. She glanced at the sauce and turned down the burner, then picked up a small bottle of dark glass. "This is an important ingredient. Always use real vanilla, not imitation. Real ingredients are what make things taste good." She poured a small amount into a measuring spoon.

"Shouldn't we use more then?"

"No. It'll be ruined if we use too much."

"But if it tastes good, then more would make it taste better."

"It doesn't always work that way, Brian. More of a good thing isn't necessarily better. Some things are best in small amounts." She smiled at his obvious disbelief. "Maybe when you're older you'll understand."

I doubt it. He couldn't comprehend how more of something good wasn't better—it didn't ring true with anything in his life. Sex. Love. Sex. He shrugged and chalked it up to adult weirdness, then gazed into the swirling chocolate and lifted the spoon out. "Ow." The chocolate on his finger burned.

"Yeah, something cooking over an open flame tends to be hot," she teased.

"Oh, my god, that's good!"

They poured the sauce over ice cream and sat at the table. He tasted the warmth and cold together. "Mmm. This is *so* good. Way better than regular chocolate sauce. River would love this."

She gave him a warm smile. "It's wonderful you have someone like that."

"Yes."

🌿🌿🌿

They walked out of The Lily and into the warm evening air. Spring was here already. Grant and John stopped to talk to someone near the entrance, so the boys took the opportunity to be alone. They walked a short distance and stood near the road. Brian took River's hand as he watched a car pass by—not many on this deserted street. "You're still spending the night?"

"Yeah."

A cop drove by slowly and slid to a stop. The policeman got out. His eyes flicked over Brian's black leather pants and vest. "How's business tonight?"

Brian felt insulted. *These aren't even my tight pants.* He played it innocent. "What?"

"Let me see your ID."

"I'm just standing here. What do I need an ID for?" He was irritated but kept his voice reasonable.

"Loitering's not allowed."

"I'm not loitering. I was just in there." He indicated the club behind him. "I'm waiting for . . . ." He paused, unsure how to finish the sentence. *Grant and Jeffrey.* "My family."

Grant appeared beside him and rested a hand on his shoulder. "What seems to be the problem?"

"No problem, sir. I just wanted to make sure the boys here were alright. Have a nice evening." The cop made a quick exit.

Grant gave him a squeeze. "You handled that well."

He shrugged. He hadn't felt nervous at all. Quite a contrast from his last encounter with a cop. "He was stupid."

Grant chuckled and guided them to the limo. John and Kelsey followed. River announced he was hungry as they climbed in. "How can you be hungry?" Brian asked. "We ate a big dinner before The Lily."

"So? I want dessert. Ice cream or something."

Brian grinned. "Yeah! Grant, can we get ice cream?"

River poked Brian's stomach. "Thought you weren't hungry."

"I'm not. But like my grandpa used to say, there's always room for ice cream. It slides down easy."

Everyone seemed to agree with that. Within moments the limo stopped in front of Swensen's. They walked into the empty, tiny ice cream shop with only a few booths, and River said, "We got one of these in Tucson."

Brian looked at him quickly, and River's eyes widened. River only missed a beat. "When I was passin' through one time."

Brian glanced around. Grant and John weren't paying attention. Kelsey was the only one who'd heard. But he didn't seem to catch the slip, only said, "I love this place. There used to be one closer, but it closed."

Brian's heart calmed down, and they ordered. He couldn't resist the flavor called sticky chewy chocolate. It really *was* chewy. Delicious. He watched Kelsey across the table as he licked his ice cream cone and wondered how old he was. Older than River, he was sure. Dark brown hair and eyes and skin. Brian wondered if his skin was that dark everywhere. *From South America,* he remembered. But Kelsey didn't have an accent. "How long have you been in this country?"

"Since I was five. I don't really remember anything before I came to San Francisco. Not even my real name." He laughed a little and glanced down.

River said, "He's been at John's for almost ten years."

"Wow."

Kelsey's eyes met his. Brian gave him a little smile and caught a drip with his tongue. Kelsey smiled back. His foot rubbed Brian's leg under the table. A promise for another day.

When they got home, River sat on the bed and put a tab of paper on each of their tongues. "Doing 'shrooms made me want to do acid again. It's been a long time."

"Yeah. Remember that homeless guy?"

"He was yelling at you."

"I know, but I couldn't hear him. Not with my ears, anyway."

They laughed and waited for the paper to dissolve. Brian looked out the window at the dark grounds. "Let's go outside."

They stayed out all night. Stared at trees and bushes and weird, morphing shapes. Brian leaned against the edge of the fountain and ran his hand through the water. The sensation was like nothing he'd ever felt. He could swear the bubbling water was talking. It felt alive on his fingers. "I'm not shaky like when we dropped acid before, in the park. And my stomach doesn't burn."

"Yeah. This stuff must be better quality. Grant only gets the best, right?"

For some reason that made Brian think of his clients. "Did you see those gross stitches on Dogman's leg?"

"Nah. I don't see him anymore."

"Why not?"

River shrugged. "Guess I'm too old for him now."

"Oh." The thought sent a shiver of panic through him. But River didn't seem upset. "Doesn't that bother you?"

"Why should it? There's plenty of other clients."

"I guess." He thought about Dogman and his bondage fetish, which reminded him of another client. "Hey! I never told you about my famous client. But you have to promise not to tell. Not even John."

"Brian, I don't tell John *anything*. But I swear I won't tell a soul."

He grinned. "He's a movie star."

River's eyes got big. "Who?"

Brian made him guess a few times before he finally said the name.

"You're shittin me!"

He laughed. "Nope. He likes bondage stuff."

"No way! I used to watch his movies all the time."

"Me, too. It was weird to see him in person." He sighed and lay down to watch the stars form different shapes overhead.

Hours later colors emerged as the sun rose. Brian decided this was his favorite part of tripping—the afterglow, when the hallucinations had worn off and blissful peace enveloped him. Beauty radiated from everything. The pebbles. The dirt. River.

Especially River, as if the beauty of his soul shone through his skin. Brian took his hand and kissed his fingers one by one. The afterglow was the perfect time for sex. They lay in the damp grass and made love. Long and slow and beautiful.

But then it was time to go inside. River had to get back to John's soon; he went upstairs to shower. Brian detoured to the kitchen to see Maria. He leaned against the doorway and said, "Buenos días."

She turned around, startled. "You're up early. Or is it late?"

"Late." He walked closer to stand before her. It felt strange to look down at her round face. "I'm finally taller than you. A little."

She held his chin and looked into his eyes. "You should not do drugs, little niño. They fry your brain."

He loved the way she rolled the 'r' in 'fry.' He could never quite get that. He smiled and hugged her. "I love you, Maria."

She stroked his hair. "I love you, too, mi pequeño niño." She pushed him back to hold him at arm's length. "I should say nothing, but . . . I do not like what you do here. It is not right. Little boys doing things with nasty old men. They take advantage of you."

"Maria, don't say that. They're not all 'nasty old men.' Besides, I love Grant. This is my home."

She shook her head. "I should not speak these things." She held him close again.

River left half an hour before Brian's piano lesson. Brian paced the parlor. Damn, he was tired. *We shouldn't have done it so late.* It hadn't occurred to him he wouldn't get a chance to sleep. Two nights in a row—he still didn't sleep much at Padrea's.

He sat at the piano. *This'll keep me awake.* Especially if he tried something new. He remembered the way the pianist at The Lily played, but his first attempt to duplicate the sound was frustrating.

He closed his eyes and put himself back in the club. He felt light-headed from drugs and lack of sleep, but it helped him visualize. He kept his eyes closed and reached for the keys as it came to him. *Yes!* Now he had it. He laughed and played on, added to it. Finally brought it to a close.

"I've never heard you play jazz before."

He jumped at the unexpected voice.

Quinn stood leaning against the couch. "That was great. Maybe we should study jazz today."

"Yeah." Brian avoided his eyes—he wasn't sure if his pupils were still dilated.

He tried to act normal, but it was hard. Quinn asked once if he was okay. "Sure. Just tired."

After the lesson Quinn and Brian walked to the door, past Grant in the foyer. Quinn watched Grant's gaze flick down and up. *He's looking at Brian's body.* Quinn clenched his fists. *Or maybe he's noticing the dirt on his jeans. I don't have any proof. I could be totally wrong.*

Quinn opened the door and almost ran into a man coming in. A tall man with cold eyes. Grant introduced him as his business partner, John. They shook hands perfunctorily. Quinn stepped outside, then glanced back and saw Brian through the open door, leaning against the wall. He was watching John, emotions plain on his face. Intense dislike. And maybe a hint of fear.

Quinn's heart beat harder. "Brian, can I talk to you a minute?"

Brian came onto the porch, and Quinn remembered about the cameras. "Let's walk."

They went down the marble stairs and walked along the driveway. Brian wondered what Quinn wanted. Brian just wanted sleep. He felt miserable.

Quinn stopped and turned to him. "That man, John, did he molest you? Is that why you took off suddenly to Jamaica?"

His eye started twitching. "*No.*"

"I saw the way you looked at him. With hatred and fear."

"John's a bad person. But that doesn't mean he molested me. Quinn, nobody molested me." *It's not like that.* "Stop looking for something that isn't there. I'm sorry about what happened between us. I was lonely without River. Out of control."

Quinn sighed and looked up at the sky a moment, then leaned down to Brian's eye level. "Alright. If you say so. But if you ever want to talk—about *anything*—I'm here. You don't have to be embarrassed or afraid I'll tell Grant. Is that a deal?"

Brian smiled sadly. *You're such a good person. But I can't tell you anything.* "Deal."

He watched Quinn drive away in his little Honda. Quinn's concern made him feel warm, but guilty, too. He frowned and went back inside to take a nap before his first client.

ממם

River said, "You shouldn't call from L.A. It's too risky."

"Grant told me it's okay as long as I don't use a phone near where we normally go."

"Oh." River kicked the ground. "Well, I guess. . . . "

Jeffrey drove them. Drove for a long time. Brian had no idea where they were. He didn't recognize anything as they sat stuck in a sea of cars. He glanced at the clock. "It's getting late there. Damn it." He bit his nail. Didn't want his parents to be home from work.

Jeffrey finally pulled into a parking lot at a 7-Eleven. He stayed at a polite distance while the boys went into the phone booth. Brian's hand shook as he put in the quarters.

Tanya's voice greeted him with her usual enthusiasm and concern.

"Yeah, I'm fine," he said. "Hey, I called sooner this time. It's only been like six months."

"Good. That's good. I've been wanting to tell you—" Her voice broke, and she was suddenly crying so hard she could barely talk. "I'm so sorry for all the things Mom did to you. I didn't know, I swear. I would've done something."

"I know, Tanya."

"We've been to family counseling. Found out stuff. I can't believe what she did to you." She couldn't talk anymore.

"Tanya, stop thinking about it. Come on, pull yourself together."

She took a deep breath. Her voice trembled. "I understand better now. Why you left. I *hate* Mom for what she did to you. For making you run away. I will *never* forgive her."

He'd never heard such venom from his sister.

"I'm moving out as soon as I turn eighteen." She sniffed. "I'll get a place with Vicky."

"How can you afford that? What about school?"

"I've got a job. I'll up my hours. I can handle it."

He knew she could. "What job?"

"I'm a waitress at Friendly's."

"Neat. But you *better* finish school."

"I will. And look who's talking! Are *you* in school?"

"Well, no. But I have a tutor."

"A tutor? Trips to Alaska and Jamaica? You found yourself a rich guy, didn't you? No matter what you keep saying, I cannot believe you're in a good situation. This man who's taken you in, spent his money on you, what does he get out of it? What does he get in return?"

Don't panic. He tried to sound innocent. "What do you mean?"

"Are you having sex with him?"

"What? Tanya! I can't believe you would say that. Grant is like a father to me." *Didn't lie—I didn't lie.* But she knew him well enough, she might catch that.

"Come home and live at Vicky's house. They've already said yes. *Please!*" Such desperation in her voice.

"Don't make me go through this every time. I'm not coming home."

"You wouldn't have to live with Mom."

But she'd be just down the street. "I'm happy here. You shouldn't want me go back to that life. That misery." Now he was the one crying. "I *can't* go back. I can't live with that."

"Brian, I'm so sorry," she sobbed.

His mother's voice loomed in the background. "Don't let him turn you against me! Give me that." Her voice shouted in his ear. "Brian! You come home *this instant.*"

He jerked the phone away like it was poison. Couldn't hang it up fast enough. He covered his ears and slid down to the cement floor.

"Brian! What happened?" River held onto him as he trembled.

After a moment he leaned back and wiped his face with shaking hands. "Sorry," he managed to get out.

"What is it? Is she alright?"

"Yeah. Just—Mom grabbed the phone. Her voice—"

"Oh, babe." River held him close.

River had to leave as soon as they got back to the house. His brow furrowed. "I don't want to leave you alone now, but I've got a client."

"It's okay. I'm alright."

"Maybe John'll let me come back afterward. I've got another session in the morning, but I'll try to convince him."

He took River's hand. "Don't get into an argument with John over this. Just go. I'll see you tomorrow afternoon."

"You sure? Okay." River kissed him on his way out. "Call me if you need me. Love you." He hurried away.

Brian let go his brave face. Hot tears spilled down his cheeks as his mother's voice filled his head. He curled into a ball on the bed and cried. Lay there a long time.

His father's face flashed through his mind. A silly face he used to make. Brian laughed. Then cried again. *I miss him so much.* He didn't usually feel it. Didn't usually miss his parents at all. But it was there. It was always there.

He stood to stare through the French doors, his gaze drawn to purple irises that lined a wooded area. *Schnookie must be out there somewhere. He loves the grounds. So do I.* It was dusk—his favorite time to be outside. But he didn't feel like going out now.

The intercom buzzed, and he jumped. Maria asking him to come down for dinner. But he didn't. Instead he watched darkness descend over the grounds and stared into the black night, then finally undressed and crawled into bed. Last night's dream came back to him. About Alan. He shivered and suddenly didn't want to sleep.

He put on his robe and padded silently down the hall into Grant's dark bedroom. He moved closer and realized two figures were asleep in the bed. *David.* He backed away quickly—before Grant could wake up and invite him to join them.

He headed back to his empty bed. But it wasn't empty. Schnookie sat there waiting for him. Brian laughed and hugged him as tears rolled down his face.

*"he don't get out much these days
but I wouldn't call him lazy
he sees the dawn sneak into the room
and knows the dogs will be up soon*

*and we thought that he was doing alright
as the sun chased down another night
and days green
like the waters
of a river rushing
to the sea . . .*

and we thought that he was doing alright"

- Mark Linkous (Sparklehorse), "Ghost of His Smile"

༄༄ CHAPTER 24 ༄༄

He listened to the familiar sound of Mr. Padrea's breathing deepen into sleep. Brian sat up to put on his leather skirt and tiny halter top, then his boots. He picked up his jacket and headed for the door, but not to go visit with Leah. To go home. This wasn't his regular night. Padrea had been begging to see him more, but Grant couldn't spare him for another All Nighter. So instead he scheduled an additional session. Just an hour. And now they were done, and Mr. Padrea was asleep. Brian paused to glance at the clock. It'd only been forty-five minutes, but Padrea wouldn't wake up. No point in staying.

He stepped into the hall and looked toward the kitchen. Toward Leah's room. It seemed strange to come here and not see her. Sad. *Maybe I'll just say hello.* His boots were silent on the thick carpet. He stopped before her door and bit his lip.

He couldn't bring himself to knock. It felt wrong to wake her, to seek her out. This was not his normal night to be here. She wasn't expecting to see him—maybe she didn't want to.

He turned and walked slowly to the front door. He felt like crying. *That's stupid. Cry over what?* He reached for the knob and paused with his hand on it.

"Brian? What are you doing here? Why are you leaving?"

He turned to see her tying her robe, and his throat tightened.

"Why are you leaving without talking to me?"

He glanced down. "I didn't want to bother you."

"Bother me? What are you talking about?" She came closer.

He was almost as tall as her with these boots on. "You were in your room, and . . . it's not my normal night to be here. I . . . didn't feel I had the right."

"The right? Brian—" She touched his face and made him look at her. "You're my friend. I care about you. I want to see you when I can."

He lost the battle with his tears. They slid slowly down his cheeks. She made a little noise and hugged him tight, her breasts soft against him, then took his hand. "Come here." She led him to her bedroom and turned on the light. "This is my room. Mr. Padrea lets me decorate it however I want."

"Oh, it's *beautiful*." She'd painted the walls a soft terra cotta, but the most striking thing was the flowers. Flowers everywhere. Delicate bouquets, wreaths on the walls, white roses. In fact, most of them were white. Their sweet scent filled the room.

"I love white flowers." She touched the daisies.

"Me, too." He hadn't realized it until now. "You've created your own little world."

She smiled. "It's the only part of the house that's mine, so I make the most of it." She sat on the edge of the rumpled bed. "There's a great flower shop I visit almost every day. You should go sometime. You'd like it."

He leaned back against a small side table and crossed his boots. "What's it called?" He didn't expect to ever go, he just wanted to keep her talking.

"Petals on the Wind, on the corner of Melrose and Highland. A bit of a drive from here, but it's a great shop. And it's nice to get out for awhile."

I can understand that. He stared at the oriental rug she'd laid on top of the carpet.

"Maybe I'll see you there sometime," she said.

He gave her a little smile. *I don't think so.*

"You don't think so?"

He laughed. "Is it that obvious what I'm thinking? I don't go into town much."

"But you have to get out to see your clients, right? Stop by sometime. I'm there in the mornings."

"No, I don't go see clients, except for Padrea. All the rest come to the House."

"Oh." Her eyes flicked over his scanty clothing—he knew she'd been trying not to look. "Why?" she asked.

"It's a Rule. I don't go to clients. They come to me. Mr. Padrea's the Exception."

"Why is he an exception?"

"Cos he's Grant's friend."

"Oh."

She seemed a little shocked, and he hoped he hadn't said too much.

"You come here every other week," she said. "Surely that's not the only time you leave your house?"

He shrugged. "Shopping. But I haven't done much of that lately." Hadn't gone to Phil's in months. He wasn't sure when he stopped, or why. *Maybe I finally have enough CDs.*

"So when was the last time you went into the city? Besides coming here."

"Uh. . . ." That was a tough question. *Oh, yeah.* He answered in a quiet voice. "A few days ago, when I called my sister."

Leah leaned forward. "You called your sister?"

"Yeah." He avoided her eyes. "I do that once in awhile. Just to let her know I'm okay. And make sure she is."

"You miss her a lot, don't you?"

He nodded. Swallowed hard.

"Is she your only sibling? Younger or older? Tell me about her."

He gave her a slight smile. "She's my only sister, three years older than me. She said she's gonna move out when she turns eighteen in September." *Oops*. He caught himself too late. *Oh well, she already knew I'm underage.*

Leah looked disturbed. *Because now she knows I'm fourteen.* Time to steer the conversation away from himself. "Do you have any brothers or sisters?"

"I had a sister. But she died."

His heart skipped. "My god, I'm sorry."

Her face twisted. "Me, too. It's been a long time. But I still miss her."

He moved to sit by her and touched her hand. "That's terrible."

Leah ignored the ache deep inside that she'd learned to live with. Brian looked like he might cry again. "I didn't mean to upset you. You really love your sister, don't you?"

He nodded and bit his lip.

"It's good that you call her." She smiled and squeezed his leg, then looked down at her hand. She hadn't expected to touch bare skin. She tried to remove her hand without seeming in *too* much of a hurry. She forgot sometimes what this sweet boy did for a living. Forgot a lot of the time. She had to—how else could she stand it?

He glanced at the clock. "I have to go. I'm only here for a regular session. It was supposed to be over already." He smiled at her. "Thank you for sharing your room with me. I feel honored."

"I'm glad you came." But she thought of what that meant—that he'd just had sex with Padrea. "I mean, it's always good to see you. I really enjoy our talks." She added as they stood, "And Mr. Padrea is always in a better mood after your visits. He's much easier to get along with the next day."

He laughed and took her hands. "Goodnight, Leah."

༄༄༄

Justin arrived early for the photo shoot in the third floor ballroom. He'd already hauled most of the equipment up there. Then thought it wouldn't hurt to stop in and say hello to Brian. Just say hello.

Brian lay on his stomach on his bed, doing homework like a regular boy. Except for the skintight white leather pants and no shirt. Justin's gaze wandered over the firm round buttocks.

Brian grinned and seemed genuinely happy to see him, then got up partway, onto all fours. His back curved toward the bed like a woman's when they did it doggie style. Justin shook his head. *That's not why I came here. Why did I come here?* "Just wanted to say hi." It sounded weak even to him.

Brian beckoned, and Justin found himself by the bed. Brian tugged on the waist of Justin's pants to bring him closer, then pulled him down beside him. It wasn't long before they were both naked.

Brian's head sank. Justin couldn't get enough of that. He wished his girlfriend could give head like that. Brian stopped before Justin came, worked his mouth up his body to his lips.

Justin stroked his ass. So smooth and round. Brian bit Justin's lower lip gently and whispered, "I want you inside me."

Justin's heart beat faster. That would be too weird. And God, if Grant found out. *People pay thousands of dollars for this.* But it was so hard to say no to Brian. Justin could never quite bring himself to stop him.

It was over quickly, and Justin hurried out. Brian rinsed off in the shower, smiling as he replayed the last few minutes. He'd hoped to catch Justin alone, but hadn't expected Justin to seek him out. A nice surprise. He dried off and picked up his pants—Grant wanted him to wear the white leather outfit for the photo.

Grant had decided they would play a flute-piano duet for the parties this year. *I can't believe it's summer already.* The last six months were a grey blur of loneliness. He shook his head and focused on the present, picked up his flute case and headed upstairs to the ballroom.

Grant was already there. He greeted Brian with a kiss and sat at the piano. Brian got out his flute. The lights Justin set up reflected off the shiny silver.

Grant wanted to play the piece first—the same duet he and Gregory used to play. Brian loved it. It was so much better to play with a live person than a recording. When they finished, Grant said, "Now lay your hand on the piano and smile at the camera." Grant rested his hand on Brian's.

Brian recognized the pose from the old photo in Grant's room. He turned with a smile and saw tears in Grant's eyes. Brian gave him a hug and held on a long time.

ɷɷɷ

Brian ignored the shiver deep inside and focused instead on the tanned body lying beside him. Ran his fingers up the tattooed chest and through sun-bleached hair.

Brett propped his head up with a smile but avoided Brian's eyes. "It's hard for me to only see you once a week. But Grant won't allow more than that."

"Sorry. That's a Rule."

"So I thought maybe I'd see other boys, too." He glanced at Brian's face as if he expected a reaction. "I'd totally rather be with you, but since I can't . . . I hope you don't mind. I don't want you to feel bad."

Brian gave him a slight smile. "It's okay, Brett. I don't mind if you see other boys."

"Really? Good." His smile faded. "Are you sure? You look upset."

The shiver got stronger. "It's nothing. Nothing to do with you."

"What? You can tell me." He paused, but Brian didn't respond. "I've had a bad day, too. A fight with my girlfriend. She's getting suspicious. Thinks I lie about where I go. Which I do, of course."

"Are you two serious? Do you live together?"

"We don't live together. I don't know if we're serious or not. I can't exactly tell her the truth about me—can't tell anyone."

"No, I guess not." *That would be tough.* "I bet you live on the beach."

He grinned. "Yep."

Brian's head fell back against the pillow. "River would love that."

"Who?"

He was amazed that in over two years he'd never mentioned River. *And I never* knew he had a girlfriend. We don't really know each other. Brett's a client. We can never truly be close. It made him sad.

"Brian, what's wrong? Please tell me."

"Nothing, just . . . a client I had this morning." He'd sort of gotten used to Creepy Guy. Went kind of numb. But he hated the way he felt for a long time after. "I—don't like him." His heart beat hard. He shouldn't talk about a client to another client. It wasn't appropriate. But it was hard to keep it all inside.

"Is he mean to you?"

"No, he just . . . gives me the creeps." The shiver reached the surface and swept through him. He suddenly felt like crying. He turned away and sat on the edge of the bed with his back to Brett. *Get ahold of yourself. You can't cry in front of a client.* He fumbled with a pack of cigarettes.

"Can't you ask Grant not to see him anymore?"

Brian spoke without turning around; his voice shook slightly. "No. It's a Rule." He took a few calming drags, then cleared his throat and changed the subject. "How come I never see you at Grant's parties? Will you be there this year?"

"Nah. I think I'd feel uncomfortable. Out of place."

"Yeah, you're probably right."

"I don't like seeing you sad."

"I'm fine, really." He ground out the cigarette. Didn't want it anymore.

Brett's warm hands touched his waist. He murmured, "I know how to make you feel better."

Brian lay back on the bed and gripped the headboard as Brett went down on him. "*Aaah.*" God. His body moved against the blond head.

Brett kissed his stomach. "I love the feel of you in my mouth. So much bigger now. It's exciting to watch you grow." He moved up to enter him, slow and sweet.

Brian gasped and wrapped his arms around him, and he was not alone.

ಬಬಬ

Grant smiled. It felt wonderful to give Brian the news. John was making another trip to New York, and River would stay at Grant's for the duration. The look on Brian's glowing face was priceless. Brian was so grateful—that was quite memorable, as well.

Grant hoped it helped; Brian seemed depressed lately. Grant wasn't sure why or what to do about it. But this would certainly help. At least for the week River was here.

River sat on the edge of the bed, notebook open on his lap. "I thought you said you have homework."

"I'll do it later." Brian strummed a chord while his foot pushed the pedal on the floor. "See how it distorts the sound?"

"Cool. Turn it up."

Brian adjusted the knob on the amp and played a long riff. "Do you recognize that? It's from a Cure song." It felt so great to play something Robert Smith wrote.

He played a different riff, experimented with it.

"Was that The Cure again?"

"No. I made it up."

"Really? That was great."

Brian smiled. "Thanks." He lifted the strap over his head and set the guitar on its stand. "Listen to this song, 'Voodoo Dolly.' *Then* I'll do my homework." He picked up the *Nocturne* CD. "I can't figure out how Robert Smith makes his guitar sound like that live."

He sat beside River to listen. The guitar built slowly until its roaring mass of sound filled the room. Finally faded away. "Wow," River said.

He stared wistfully at the speakers. "I wish I could play like that."

River touched his leg. "You will."

He smiled and glanced at the notebook in River's lap. "What's that?"

"Stupid creative writing. I'm almost done."

Brian caught a few words that leaped off the page. *'Blood spurted,' 'his knife flashed in the sun.'* He shook his head. *River* would *come up with something like that. We're so different.*

Brian pulled his algebra book over. "I hate this stuff." He opened it to his assignment and read the first word problem. "Mumbo jumbo bullshit."

River read over his shoulder. "That's as far as you've gotten in math? Geez, Brian."

"It's stupid!"

River tried to explain it.

Brian interrupted. "I don't understand why X means that."

"It just does. Just because."

"What do you mean, 'because'? That's not a reason."

"It's a Rule. Just accept it."

He frowned.

"Brian, you're so smart. You're only bad at math because you don't like it. You don't *want* to be good at it. Now look—" He pointed to the word problem and went through it step by step. "X is the unknown. Think of it like a puzzle. Take it piece by piece and build an equation out of it. That's the solution."

"So . . . ." Brian wrote some figures. "X is 52."

"Right!"

He grinned. "You always make me see things differently. You're good at explaining. Way better than Mr. Wycliffe." He laughed a little. "Did I ever tell you I made a pass at him?"

"Who?"

"My tutor. Don't you have him?"

"Naw, we got a different guy. Is he hot? Did you guys fuck?"

"No—he turned me in! And he's *not* hot."

"Why'd you do it, then?"

Brian shrugged. "I dunno . . . ."

"Was Grant mad?"

"A little. He said—" *'They're beneath you.'* "Not to do it again." He shook his head and touched River's arm. "I'll have to ask you all my math questions." He knew it made River feel good to help him.

"Sure. Math's always been my best subject, besides sports. I liked science, too, back at school. Me and my lab partner used to set stuff on fire with the bunson burner."

Brian laughed. River with a chemistry set was a frightening thought.

River lit a cigarette. "My science teacher was cool. Mr. Franklin. He didn't like me, though. Always lecturing about how I could get good grades if I applied myself. But he was a nice guy." He took a long drag. "He was a babe. I had the hots for him. Course I didn't realize it then. But I think he was my first crush." He thought a moment and nodded. "Who was yours?"

"Robert Smith. I've been into him since I first saw 'The Love Cats' video when I was nine."

"Yeah? I was thirteen when I had Mr. Franklin." He frowned. "I wonder what he thinks about me now? Probably doesn't," he murmured and flicked his ashes toward the ashtray. "I kinda miss school."

"What?"

"Well, not really. I just miss blowin up shit."

Brian and River lay side by side in the Sex Room while their client dressed and left. It had felt weird at first to be in there with River. A 'shared' client. He'd done that a few times with boys from the Other Wing but never with River. He rolled over to touch River's stomach. "That was fun."

River sat up abruptly and faced away. "It wasn't fun. It was awful!" River turned to him, his face twisted. "Seeing that man's hands all over you. His mouth—" He looked away.

"River." Brian stroked his back. "You know it happens all the time."

"Yeah, but I don't have to see it."

"We've been together with Grant before."

"That's different." He folded his arms over his chest, silent a moment. His voice shook. "I know it's stupid, but I can't help it."

Brian leaned against his arm. Kissed it. "It's not stupid." Though it hadn't bothered him when the man touched River. *I don't have to understand. What matters is that River's upset.*

Normally he would never say anything to Grant about a client—he knew better than that. But for River's sake, he had to try. He waited until River went for a swim, then found Grant in his downstairs office. He tried to broach the subject casually. "I've never shared a client with River before."

"Mmm." Grant looked up from his paperwork.

Brian's voice came out in a whisper. "River didn't like it."

Grant's eyebrows went up. "Why not?"

"I don't know. He said he didn't like seeing the man touch me. He was pretty upset."

Grant leaned back in his chair. "I've already scheduled another client for you to share."

"Oh." Brian bit his lip and looked away.

"But this man likes to watch, mostly. So perhaps it won't bother River."

I hope not.

Grant stood and moved closer. "And there's nothing better than the two of you together." Grant kissed him. "We should practice our duet once more before the party." He pulled Brian closer and nuzzled into his neck. Murmured, "In a few minutes."

Brian wasn't in the mood. But his body soon changed his mind.

༺༺༺

"Brian!" David called through the crowd of people celebrating Grant's birthday. "Look, I'm wearing your pants."

"What?"

David stopped before him and touched the black leather on his hips. "These were yours. Grant said you hardly wore them cos you grew so fast—"

Brian's stomach twisted.

"So he gave em to me. They fit, see?"

He forced a smile and nodded. He hadn't so much grown taller as grown thicker. Less like a child every day. He pulled his mind away from that abyss and focused on the present. He didn't understand why David was excited to wear hand-me-downs, but it was sweet. He touched David's arm. David beamed and started chatting.

Brian's mind wandered to the client he and River shared yesterday. It was better this time—the man hardly touched them, and River didn't seem upset. *Maybe it's good that he'll be back at John's soon.*

I can't believe I just thought that. He dreaded River leaving. But at least they wouldn't share any more clients.

David moved closer to whisper a secret in his ear about one of the boys. Brian didn't even know who he was talking about. David's hand ran along the silk camisole covering Brian's chest, grazed his nipple and came to rest on his bare stomach. Stroked it. *Shit, David, no.* He was relieved to see Trevor and his entourage headed toward them.

David backed away as Trevor started spouting about how he was better than Brian. "Grant only made you Number One cos he likes *young* boys. You didn't earn it."

Brian's eyes narrowed, but he refused to be baited. He saw River approach. *Uh oh.* One of these days he feared River would punch the bastard.

River arrived as Trevor said, "My dick is bigger than yours."

Brian blinked at his crudeness. *He's getting desperate.* Brian raised an eyebrow. "At least I'm still growing."

They glared at each other and started thinking about sex. Brian turned away. He couldn't quite suppress his smile.

River followed Brian as he walked away. "He's right—he *is* a big dick."

Brian laughed. "Don't take him seriously. He's full of it." He glanced back at

Trevor, caught him staring. "I don't mind him, really. He can be amusing."

"He's still a dick."

Brian laughed again. "Yes." He picked up a cigarette from the selection on the table and held it up to River's lighter. He glanced over his shoulder again. Met Trevor's gaze and held it.

"Brian." River touched his arm.

"What? Oh." He had no idea what River had been saying. "Sorry. Do you have any cigarettes? I don't like these."

"No. I'm gonna go hang out with Kelsey and Rick."

"Okay." Brian's eyes wandered over the cigarette selection, and he frowned. His brand wasn't there. *I'm not gonna smoke these.* He crushed out the nasty tasting thing and headed inside to get his own, up to his room.

He opened the nightstand drawer and heard the door latch. Trevor moved closer. Brian pushed him onto the bed, then joined him. Trevor moved so he was on top, but not for long. Brian rolled out from under him and pushed Trevor onto his back.

Brian's head sank. Trevor groaned and thought, *Don't come yet. Don't come yet.* Trevor could no longer fool himself into believing he was in control in any way. Brian had it all. Got him so close, then backed off. And again—so close. Over and over. Trevor was completely lost.

Then Brian was inside him. Nailing him hard. Trevor couldn't hold out. "God!" Brian collapsed on top of him.

Trevor dressed and left without a word, as usual. Brian lay back on the bed with a contented sigh and heard voices in the hallway. *River?* He sat up, his heart pounding. No, just some people walking by. *God, what if River had come in? He would've flipped.*

"Shit." He gathered up his clothes. "Gotta be more careful." Nobody was supposed to know about this. *Some things ought to be secret. We're supposed to be enemies.* "We *are* enemies. We just like to fuck." He smiled and zipped his skirt. "*Really* like to fuck."

He went downstairs and returned to the courtyard. Kristoff and Grant sat chatting, a boy on each lap. Brian noted the absence of John with pleasure. John hadn't missed one of Grant's parties in a long time. He was barely missing it, though. *He'll be back tomorrow. And River—* He bit his lip and refused to think about it.

He helped himself to another drink and wandered around as he sipped it. *I wish Grant would let us have the special pills for this party, too, instead of just coke.* Especially since there were fewer clients at the smaller party, and lots of boys. Brian eyed a few older ones. The group moved, and he was suddenly staring into Kelsey's dark eyes.

Brian gave him a slow smile and moved toward the edge of the courtyard. Kelsey paralleled him through the crowd. Brian's blood rushed. He sprinted the last few yards into the woods and ran up the path laughing. He turned as Kelsey caught up with him.

They were on each other immediately. He wondered why he'd waited so long to try out John's Number One. *God!*

Afterward Kelsey helped him up and kissed him a long time. Didn't run off like Trevor always did. They walked back to the courtyard together.

Naked in the Rain

. . .

Brian undressed after the party and climbed into bed with River. Their last night before River went back to John's.

River leaned back against the pillows. "I heard you and Kelsey went off together. Did you have a good time?"

He grinned. "Yeah."

River's jaw tightened as his fingers shredded yesterday's schedule into tiny pieces.

"What's wrong?"

"Why'd you have to do that? Kelsey's my friend."

He sat back in shock. "I had no idea you'd be upset. Haven't you had sex with him?"

"Well, yeah. So?" River frowned and sat in angry silence. Finally said, "I just . . . I'm gonna miss you. Being with you every day."

"I know." Brian hugged him. Having River around all the time was so wonderful. And now it was over. Brian squeezed him tighter, but he couldn't stop the tears. They turned into sobs.

River pulled back to looked at his sweet, wet face. "Are you okay? Is something else wrong?"

"No, just . . . ." He sniffled and wiped his cheek. "I'm so lonely without you. So lonely." He closed his eyes and whispered, "Sometimes I can hardly stand it."

River pulled him close again and stroked his hair. It had never occurred to him how alone Brian was here. River had tons of friends at John's. *But Brian doesn't have anyone. The boys next door are all assholes.* He kissed the top of his head. "I'll try to come over more often, okay?"

"Can you?"

"Yeah, I think so. Even if it's just for a little while. Does that sound good?"

Brian nodded against River's chest and held him tight.

Brian walked along the path with David and picked up a rose from a pile left by the gardeners. The petals were still a soft cream flushed with pink around the edges. They fell from the stem as he walked and left a trail behind them.

David rattled on, gossiping. Brian smiled at him. *Such a sweetheart, but I hope he doesn't try to touch me again.* He had no idea what David was talking about. He wasn't interested in the Other Wing's power struggles. But it didn't matter what David was saying—he just wanted company.

"So he thinks he should be the leader, now that Trevor's gone."

Brian stopped short. "What?"

"I said Larry wants—"

"Trevor's gone?"

"You didn't hear?" David grinned, clearly thrilled to bear such important news. "He moved to another House a couple days ago. Right after the party."

His mouth hung open. *I can't believe he didn't tell me. Didn't say goodbye.* His hands curled into fists. *Damn him.*

"I thought you'd be happy."

"Sure, I'm just . . . just surprised." His eye started twitching.

He couldn't pretend he didn't care. He mumbled an excuse and hurried off, back upstairs to sit alone on his bed. He tucked up his knees and felt very small in this big house. *It's not as if I saw Trevor much.* Brian had never visited the Other Wing. But still, he'd known Trevor was there. He felt like they had some kind of connection. A mutual understanding of what it was like to be over here. To be Number One. Alone in this house.

And he left without saying a word. Tears stung his eyes. *Was it to be mean, or did he not even give me a thought?* Brian shook his head. Ground his jaw and wiped his eyes. *I'm not going to cry over that bastard.*

Trevor's words came back to him from long ago. 'When you don't look like a boy anymore, Grant won't want you. That is a fact.'

He found Grant reading in the den and sat on the couch beside him. He asked quietly, "How come you made Trevor leave? Is it because he got too old?"

"Trevor went of his own choosing. He knew it was time to move to a House that caters to clients who like older boys."

Older boys. I'm almost fifteen.

Grant looked into his eyes and seemed to suddenly understand. He set the book aside and pulled Brian onto his lap. "My dear, you are the Exception. Intelligent, compassionate, beautiful. Gifted in many ways." He brushed the hair out of Brian's face. "I never want you to leave. As you get older your clientele will change, but we can accommodate that. There is no age limit for you." Their gaze held. "There will always be a place for you in this House."

༄༄༄

He stood on Mr. Padrea's balcony, smoked and stared out at the lights. The warm breeze ruffled his hair, but he didn't feel the usual elation. He'd gotten spoiled when River stayed at Grant's, and now he felt even worse than before. Couldn't seem to get past it.

He sighed and wiped ashes from his leather pants. *Don't think about it.* Not now. Not when he had his time with Leah. He went inside to make noise in the kitchen.

She arrived right on cue. He smiled at her. "I can't find the ice cream."

"Sorry. I didn't get to the store. I wasn't feeling well."

"Are you okay? If you're sick you should be in bed."

She smiled. "No, Brian, it's nothing like that. It was . . . a female thing. I'm better now."

His eyes grew round. "Oh." One of those mysterious woman things.

"Let's see what can we dig up." She opened the refrigerator. "We've still got strawberries."

"Oh—strawberries dipped in chocolate. Grant had those at his birthday party. They're the best!"

She smiled. "We could try it with our regular chocolate sauce." She got out the ingredients. "Did Grant have a big birthday party?"

"Kinda. Not as big as his other party. This one's mostly boys." He leaned against the counter while she dropped chocolate squares into the pan.

Mostly boys. She tried not to visualize. Tried not to notice she could see Brian's nipples through the black netting of his spandex top. "How old is Grant now?"

"Nobody knows. Except him, I guess."

She handed him the spoon to stir. "Well, if you had to guess, what would you say?"

He shrugged and looked at her. "Older. But not as old as Mr. Padrea."

She recognized the wariness in his eyes. The wall was starting to come up. "Here, why don't you put in the sugar? I'll stir."

When the sauce was done they washed strawberries together. She dipped the first one into the chocolate and set it on a plate. Brian did the next strawberry, then insisted on tasting before they made anymore.

"Mmm! This is so good."

She had to agree. They made a few more and giggled when sauce dripped onto her foot.

An angry voice broke through their laughter. "Brian! What are you doing out here?"

Brian gasped, blind for a moment with panic. *Don't take her away.* But logic quickly returned. *He won't want Grant to know we're friends, either.* No need to worry about Grant—just Padrea. And he was easily dealt with.

Brian switched into sex mode. He moved toward the old man who stood angry in his robe, white hair sticking up in wisps like a mad chicken. Brian gave him a slow smile and traced his finger down the exposed skin in the center of Padrea's chest. Slipped his hand under the robe to tug on his nipple and brushed his lips against his ear. "We're making a surprise for you."

"A surprise?" All traces of anger had disappeared.

"Let me just get it." He pulled away to go back to the stove.

Leah stared with her mouth agape and watched him carry the pan of chocolate over to Padrea. "I thought we could have fun with this."

He put his free hand around Padrea's neck and whispered something in his ear. Mr. Padrea grabbed onto Brian's waist with an excited glint in his eye she'd never seen before. Lust. Her stomach turned. She watched the old man paw the lovely boy, touch his nipple through the sheer fabric. Not just any boy. Brian. Her wonderful, sweet Brian. She felt like crying.

Brian led Padrea off toward the bedroom. She heard him say, "We'll have to let it cool first." He glanced back to throw her a smile and a wink.

She stared down the hall after they disappeared and tried to cope with what she'd just witnessed. She was amazed how Brian changed so fast. When Padrea first caught them, he looked terrified. But in a heartbeat it melted away, and he became this sexual creature. He'd played Padrea so easily. By far the youngest person in the room and absolutely in control.

She couldn't get the image out of her head—the old man pawing him. It hit her, what they were doing right now. Right now as she slumped into a chair and hid her face in her hands.

He leaned against River in their booth at The Lily and listened to the blues band. He loved how the muted trumpet sounded old and mellow. The woman sang, "You go to my head, with a smile that makes my temperature rise. Like a summer with a thousand Julys. You intoxicate my soul with your eyes."

Brian murmured, "What a great line. I wish I'd written it." He turned to River and repeated, "You intoxicate my soul with your eyes."

River's smile faltered, and he glanced down. Brian's heart sank. "You're going away again, aren't you?"

River looked at him in surprise. "Yeah."

He pulled his hand away, though he didn't mean to. River looked hurt. Brian clenched his fists beneath the table, barely under control. "When? How long?"

"We leave in a few days. For about two weeks."

He stared at the table and nodded.

"Brian . . . ."

He kept his eyes down and forced a shrug. "It's okay. Where are you going?"

"Hawaii. I'm gonna learn to surf."

He couldn't help but smile. "How perfect for you."

River touched his arm. "I wish you could come."

He nodded. Bit his lip and forced back the tears. *I'm not going to cry. Not here.* "Let's dance." *Distract me.*

"I gotta piss first."

Brian waited near the dance floor and watched people. Mostly gay men, except for two lovely women kissing each other. Incredible turn on. He forgot all about River and Hawaii.

River joined him and said something.

"What?" He couldn't quite tear his gaze from the women.

River glanced over and smiled. "Stop staring. It's rude."

As if on cue, the women left the floor and moved away, out of sight in the crowd. *Damn.*

River held up a closed fist. "Look what I got." He opened his hand. Two white pills lay on his palm. "E."

"How'd you get that?"

"In the bathroom. A guy was selling em. Here."

Brian popped one into his mouth—he'd finally mastered the trick of swallowing pills without water. "Let's dance."

But they didn't feel like dancing for long, so they sat in the booth again with Grant and listened to the band. Disturbing lyrics about bodies hanging from trees. It gave Brian the creeps. His hand shook as he reached for his water. He felt a little sick. He whispered to River, "Are you sure that was ecstasy?"

"That's what he said. Don't feel like it though, does it? Maybe it's not as good quality as we're used to."

He nodded. The world was too loud, and his heart was too fast. He was glad when Grant said they should call it a night, even though it meant parting with River.

He hurried up to his room as soon as they got home. Grant followed. He stood in the doorway with arms folded, his face drawn in a deep frown. "If you think you fooled me, think again. I know you and River took something at the club. It's quite obvious."

Brian's eyes dropped to the carpet.

Grant's voice rose. "Do you have any idea how dangerous that is? You don't know what was in that." He shook his head. "I know you love River. So do I. But he's a bad influence sometimes."

Brian's head snapped up. "How dare you? River's the best thing that ever happened to me! I wouldn't be here without him—in more ways than one. I *never* would've gotten into the car with you that first night if it weren't for him." His tone turned vicious. "I guess he *is* a bad influence."

Grant's lips tightened. "Point taken. Goodnight, Brian." Anger seethed behind his eyes as Grant closed the door.

Brian moved to the French doors to stare out at the darkness. He rested his forehead against the cool glass, and his fist hit the wall. He felt dizzy and sick.

It took forever to fall asleep, and he woke in the early morning before dawn. He felt better but—*my god, I can't believe I said that to Grant.* "I can't leave it like that."

He slipped into his robe and went to Grant's room. Deep breathing sounded loud in the dark. He peered at the bed to make sure Grant was alone, then dropped his robe and slid under the sheets.

Afterward they held each other. Brian watched the room turn grey in predawn light. "I'm sorry, Grant. I never should have spoken to you like that. And you're right. It was a stupid thing to do. It's just . . . ." He met Grant's eyes. "When you said that about River, I snapped."

"I know. I was angry, too. I shouldn't have spoken against him."

"He helped me understand the joy in life." He smiled and touched Grant's lips. "But so have you, in your way."

Grant kissed his fingertips, then gripped his hand. "Just don't do it again. Buying drugs like that is dangerous. You know I'll get anything you want, of safe and good quality. No reason to go elsewhere."

He was in Grant's bed again a few nights later. Monday night and no River. It was more bearable if he didn't spend it alone.

Grant leaned back against the pillows. "How would you like to go on a trip? Not to Hawaii, don't get too excited. But some business has come up. I thought it would be a nice diversion for you, with River out of town. We'll be gone a week, maybe more."

He grinned and sat up. It seemed like ages since he'd traveled. "Where are we going?"

"Boston."

His heart skipped. "I can't go there! My parents—" His eyes stung, and his fists clutched the sheets. "My parents go there a lot."

Grant's eyebrows drew down. "I don't want to leave you here alone."

His voice wobbled. "I can't go there."

"I can protect you from your parents. You're safe with me."

Brian didn't want to be left alone. But he couldn't stand the idea that he might run into them. *I could stay in the hotel the whole time.* He imagined looking out the window and seeing his parents walk down the street. A shiver went through him. "No." He couldn't be that close. Couldn't even be on the same coast. "Please. I can't."

Grant leaned back with a sigh. "Alright, Brian. I'll arrange for you to stay in the Other Wing."

"*No!* Please, don't make me."

"I don't want you here alone."

"Maria will be here."

"True . . . . You'd rather stay in the Main House with just Maria?"

He nodded emphatically.

"Alright. I'll talk to security." He stroked Brian's cheek. "I'm sorry, my sweet boy. I had no idea this would be a problem. I'll take care of my business as quickly as I can."

Brian lay beside him a long time before he finally fell asleep and into a familiar nightmare. He chased the cat through the gap in the fence, but this time it was his precious Schnookie. The roar of motorcycles made him tremble. Time slowed as they rounded the corner. He knew what would happen, and he was helpless to stop it. He saw the woman down the street as the motorcycles surrounded her.

He sat up with a gasp, tears streaming down his face. He wrapped his arms around his knees and rocked.

Grant didn't wake up.

Hours later Brian slept again, drifted lightly until a noise tugged at him. He swam up and opened his eyes to see Grant get something out of the dresser. Something shiny, like a key. Sleep reclaimed him, and he dreamed about keys and pumpkins.

He was alone when he woke again. He didn't like that. He went downstairs and saw the office door ajar. Grant's voice came from inside. "I want security here whenever he has a client." Pause. "No, he wants to stay in the Main House. Why don't you come to my office, Matthew, and we'll discuss the details."

His pulse raced as it sunk in. *I'm going to be alone.*

*"I try to shake the creeps
But they keep following me"*

- Brian O'Kelly

೫೫ CHAPTER 25 ೫೫

Brian watched from the bathroom window as his client drove away in a red Porsche. He rested his fingers against the glass and stared out at the trees and bright sky. Nothing else to see. Nothing but Grant's grounds. Seemed like that's all he ever saw.

A movement caught his attention. Maria was leaving, too. Her weekly trip into town for groceries. She always went at the same time. Actually, she was a little late today. His lips quirked when he realized why. *She didn't want to leave when I'm with a client.* He filled with warmth.

I should go with her next time. How long since he'd been in a supermarket? It would be fun. He laughed, delighted with the idea. "Yes, I'll do it. Next time."

He tied his hair back into a short ponytail—he kept it slightly longer these days so he could do that—and took a quick shower. He admired his toenails as he rubbed the thick black towel down his legs. He had on a new polish—periwinkle. A nice break from the black. He wriggled his toes and grinned, then pulled on black leather pants, tied the vest's laces and walked out of the Room humming.

He came to a stop and stood in the hall. Bit his nail and glanced both ways, undecided where to go. Totally empty house. Empty and silent. He shivered and rubbed his bare arms. No Grant. No Jeffrey.

He hadn't seen any security guards—didn't go downstairs much. *Wonder if they're still here?* He went down to find out. The wide hall was empty. The kitchen. The parlor. "Hello?" His voice sounded echoey in the big emptiness.

His gaze fell on the door in the front corner. Grant's office. He suddenly remembered his dream. Or was it? Did he really see Grant get a key? "One way to find out."

He pushed on the door to Grant's rooms upstairs. It opened silently. *Everything was silent.* There was scarcely a sound through the whole house, except for the hum of the mini-fridge. Sebastian lay curled up asleep on the loveseat in Grant's sitting room, the cat's steady breathing audible.

Brian moved to the bedroom and opened the dresser drawer where he saw Grant get the key. Socks. And something else. He opened the small ivory box and grinned. He dumped the key onto his hand, put the box back exactly as he'd found it and closed the drawer.

He hurried downstairs. *This is perfect.* Matthew hardly ever came over here—just once a day to deliver the schedule, and Maria would be gone at least two hours.

He walked through the parlor and stood before the door to Grant's office, put the key in and turned. The door opened onto darkness. He swallowed and flipped on the light, half expecting an alarm to sound. Nothing. Silence.

He walked in and locked the door behind him, then leaned against it to survey the small room. The mysterious door behind the desk caught his eye; he'd always wondered where it led. He walked over and tried the key. It didn't work.

He gave up and sat in the leather chair at Grant's mahogany desk. Nothing on top of it, as usual. He tried the big bottom drawer. Locked. But the others weren't. Pencils, calculator, a pad of paper with a note scribbled on it in Grant's neat script. 'Call Bernie for lunch.'

He scrounged around, ran his hand along the sides. Moved to the next drawer. Blank paper. Envelopes. *Aha.* A small silver key on a hook toward the back. He put it into the lock for the bottom drawer and felt the bolt move. "Yes!" He pulled it open. Files. Lots of them.

He read one of the tabs, 'Parks, 02352,' and opened it. A photo of one of his clients was stapled to the first page. He scanned the information. Leland James Parks. Social security number. Birth date and place. Home address in Bel Air. All kinds of details about his business—his position, his salary, the hours he kept.

Brian turned the page. Another photo, a woman this time. All the same sort of information on his wife, Veronica Parks. Her maiden name. The clubs she belonged to. The next page had a photo of a little blond girl. Kathleen (Katie), nine years old. The address of her school, her ballet lessons, what time she was picked up.

He blinked. *Why would Grant need all this?* He imagined the answer. '*We're in the information business. We must protect ourselves.*' His mouth went dry as he forced himself to turn the next page. It took a moment to make sense of it. Medical records. Tests for venereal diseases. All negative.

He put the file back and pulled out the next one. Recognized the photo of another client. He gasped. 'Member of organized crime family. Exact position uncertain. Upper echelon.' He stared with round eyes. *I always thought he was harmless and sweet. Holy shit.*

He put it back in the drawer, not sure he wanted to see anymore. *Finish the job. This might be my only chance.* He pulled out Mr. Padrea's file and studied the photo. Padrea and Grant standing together in tuxedos. They looked much younger. Weird. Grant was so handsome, his ginger hair thick and full. *I wish I'd known him then.* He looked at the back of the photo. 'Bernie and Grant, 1971.'

There wasn't a lot of information on Bernard Padrea, just the usual statistics. Medical records. Something about a heart condition. He turned the page and stared into Leah's face. A candid shot on the street somewhere. His heart skipped as he read the information. The college she'd attended. Her parents' home address. Her father's business information. What time he left work. They had an Irish setter named Dale. *Jesus Christ.* He scanned the page for any reference to their friendship. Nothing.

He closed it and put it away. Tried not to think about what it all meant. He didn't want to go on, but he forced himself. Skipped Mr. Reynold's file. *Creepy Guy.* Couldn't bear to see the photo. He kept going, past files of men he didn't recognize. Discovered two of his regular clients were judges. One a detective on the police force, another the head of an oil company. Every file had recent medical test results for sexual diseases. He felt relieved. Not that he'd been worried, but still . . . .

He pulled out a thick file on Senator Jones. *This should be interesting.* He didn't understand much at first glance. He hated political stuff. But he forced himself to read it. It wasn't so boring once he grasped what it was about. Favors bought. Campaign money diverted. *Not to mention frequent visits to a brothel of boys. Where does the taxpayer's money go?*

A note was scribbled at the bottom of the page. 'Quite addicted to Brian.' He bit his lip. *With everything in this file plus the fact that he comes here, Grant has this guy totally in his pocket. A U.S. Senator. Jesus.* He'd never really thought about it before.

He shook his head and went through the rest of the files. Tried to memorize what he thought might be important. *I ought to know this stuff, too. They're my clients.*

He finally finished. Put everything back the way he found it, stood up and stretched. He'd been sitting a long time. *I wonder if Maria's back?* Nerves hit him again. *I could still get caught.* He turned off the light and listened at the door. Silence. He opened it a crack to peek out into the empty parlor. He stepped out quickly. Looked around again and locked the door.

He went upstairs to put the key back in the ivory box, then sat on Grant's bed and laughed. "I did it."

ಬಬಬ

Brian winced at the sharp pain as he sat at the desk in his room. He opened the prescription bottle and drank a pain pill down with water, then rubbed the muscle in his lower back. He didn't know exactly when he hurt it or how. Well, he knew how, but not who. *Doesn't matter.*

What mattered was it hurt like a motherfucker. *Don't be a baby. It's just a pulled muscle.* But it hurt every time he had a client—even the good ones. Even though he took a pill beforehand.

No clients today, but his back still hurt. Too much to go play the piano, though he needed to practice. He had a lesson tomorrow. God, he looked forward to Quinn's visits so much. His lessons took forever to get here, and then they were over. Made him feel even lonelier.

Just be glad you see them at all. Quinn in the morning and Leah tomorrow night. He smiled a little and clung to the thought. *Just make it till tomorrow.*

Ah, the pill was kicking in. He stared out the window, and his mind wandered. Landed on his mother's voice when she grabbed the phone. He reached for his journal.

> *She doesn't really want me back. She's just angry that she can't control me anymore. I don't know what I did to make her not want me.*

He buried his face in his hands and cried.

But he couldn't stand to think of her for long, and after a few minutes his mind sidetracked. Tried to escape the depression, but it was everywhere. Just one newspaper contained a whole world of pain and suffering. Eight-year-old girl raped by two men. Women mutilated in Africa. Famine and war. *The world is a sick place.*

If it weren't for River.... He wasn't sure he'd want to stay in this world. He scratched at his scars, rubbed his arms and rocked back and forth. Finally opened the box to pick up a joint. With the pill in his system, it would numb him. He fumbled with the lighter. Numb him from the pain.

He eased back against the leather couch, made sure the black silk robe covered him and grinned at Leah. "Thank you for the chocolate sauce idea. It was even better with River."

She shook her head and looked sad, then folded her arms and leaned against the stuffed chair. "I think I'm going to quit working for Mr. Padrea."

"What?" He sat up. Winced at his back.

She started to pace. "I can't stand what goes on here. I've played along, put it out of my mind. But by doing that I've become a party to it. Seeing you two together last time—I can't stop thinking about it." Her voice sank to a whisper. "It makes me sick."

He moved to stand before her. Blinked back tears as he stared into her eyes. "Do I disgust you so much?"

"No, Brian, I didn't mean it like that—"

"So much you have to run away and pretend I don't exist?" His chin trembled. "Leave me like everyone else?" The tears spilled over.

"Brian." Her fingers brushed the wetness on his cheeks.

"Don't leave me."

She looked like she might cry, too. She pulled him close and held his head against her neck. "Okay, I won't leave. I won't leave."

"Promise?"

"I promise."

He smiled through his tears and wiped his face. "Look what you did. Made me get all emotional." He laughed and moved away.

Leah followed him outside. He walked to the rail and stared out. "This view is so incredible. If I lived here I'd be on the balcony all the time." He breathed in the warm night air. "Except it smells like smog. Speaking of—" He reached into his robe pocket for a cigarette and leaned back against the wall to smoke.

Leah said, "What did you mean, leave you like everyone else? Who left you? Your parents?"

He gave a short laugh. "No. I left them." He shrugged. "I didn't mean anything. Just . . . everyone's out of town right now. River." He sighed and glanced down. "He's in Hawaii. I miss him a lot."

"I'm sorry. But you have other friends, right? Other boys where you live?"

"They live in the Other Wing. I'm in the Main House with Grant."

"Why don't you live with the other boys?"

He smiled at her. "Because I'm the Number One. Grant's Number One boy." He realized he was proud of it.

"Oh." She was quiet a moment. "So normally you only have Grant and River to keep you company?"

"River doesn't live with us. He just visits." He tried not to let bitterness into his voice. He took a deep drag on his cigarette. "But there's Jeffrey. Security guard," he explained.

"That's it? A security guard and the man you work for?"

"Well, there are servants." He almost said, *'Maria.'* But he felt he shouldn't give her any more names. She sure as hell shouldn't know Grant's. But stupid Padrea blurted it out in the very beginning. *I guess it doesn't matter. It's not like she could touch them.* "Grant's gone, too. He and Jeffrey went away on business."

"So you're all alone?"

He looked at the cement. "Yeah, pretty much. I've got a cat."

"And the boys next door, right?"

He shrugged.

"What does that mean?" she asked.

"I don't get along with the other boys, except one. But he lives in the Other Wing. He's busy."

"So you only have one friend, and you don't see him much. And you don't go out. Are your visits here the only time you leave Grant's?"

"We go to a club once in awhile. And I have guitar lessons."

"In a class with other kids?"

"No. At a studio near home."

Leah shook her head. "You're really isolated. And alone."

"No, it's okay." He frowned, then squatted to grind out his cigarette, careful not to use his back to stand up again. He threw the butt over the rail.

"Brian!"

He gave her a wicked smile and went back inside to sit at the kitchen table. She offered him a pastry, but he declined. Didn't have much of an appetite lately.

Her brow furrowed. "But I bought it just for you."

He smiled. "Okay." Once he started eating he forgot his objections. He licked his fingers and sat back. Winced.

"Are you hurt?" she asked.

"It's nothing. Just pulled my back."

"That could be serious. What happened? Maybe I can help."

He'd forgotten about her profession—physical therapist. "I think I pulled a muscle when I was with a client. It's no big deal. It'll heal." *Right?* The pain was making his upper lip sweat.

"What are you doing for it?"

"Pain pills. They help a little."

Her frown deepened. "Pain killers only mask the problem."

"They make it tolerable." Which it wasn't right now—he'd moved around too much with Padrea, and the pill didn't seem to be working. He pulled the prescription bottle out of his robe pocket and took another.

"Let me see that." She snatched the bottle from him to read the label. "Demerol? This is very powerful, especially for someone your age. Did a doctor prescribe this?"

"Yes." Although he knew there wasn't much information—no doctor or patient name listed. "I take it for my headaches."

"And now for your back. How often are you taking these?"

He shrugged and pain shot up his back. He bit his lip. "Before a client. And after sometimes."

"How often is that?"

He looked at her. Couldn't think well enough to determine if he should answer. *Doesn't matter.* "Two clients a day, usually."

"Two a day?" She closed her eyes, and he knew that bothered her. "You shouldn't take them before and after. That's too often. How long ago did you hurt your back?"

"I dunno . . . early last week."

"Brian, you can't take them like that, for so long. They're addictive."

"I'm not addicted. I'm just in pain." He felt desperate. "Every time I have sex—" He leaned his head back against the chair to stare at the ceiling. Said in a quiet voice, "It hurts a lot."

"Then you shouldn't have sex for awhile."

He snorted. "Yeah, right."

"Taking pain killers is not the answer. Let me work on it." She touched his arm. "I'll give you a massage. It's what I do."

"Okay." He got up carefully and followed her to the living room couch. The leather creaked as he lay on his stomach.

She sat on the edge of the couch. "Tell me when it hurts." She touched the silk on his back and pressed. Moved her hands down.

"Ah!" He flinched.

"Okay. Relax." She worked it gently. But she could tell even that hurt. "Hold on, Brian." She went to get her oils, then helped him pull the robe off his shoulders to uncover his back. So pale. Except for a red mark across it. She kept the oil away so it wouldn't sting and worked her way toward the pulled muscle. His breathing changed when she got to it. The only sign of pain. "I'm sorry if this hurts. But it'll help. I promise."

"'kay."

She finally left it to work the rest of his back, his arms, down to his fingers. He sighed—it felt wonderful. "Leah, why didn't we do this sooner?" Between the massage and the pills he was in heaven. It didn't even hurt much when she returned to that muscle on his back.

She stopped after a long time. "Better?"

He grunted. Didn't want to move. But he had to reciprocate. He pushed himself up, but she stopped him from pulling his robe up so he wouldn't get oil on the silk. "Your turn," he said.

"What?"

"You always do it for other people. Let me do you." He smiled. "I give good massages, too."

"Well, alright. But be careful with your back."

They switched places. She pulled her robe down carefully and hugged a pillow to her chest. He touched her warm skin and glided oiled hands over her back. She murmured, "Mmm, you *are* good."

Eventually he moved to her legs. Worked the oil into her thighs, down her calves. Spent time on her feet, each toe. He loved doing this. It gave the other person such pleasure. His fingers moved up her leg, and he bent to touch the back of her knee with his lips. Worked his way up.

"What are you doing?" She looked back at him.

"Using my mouth."

"Well, don't."

"Oh. Sorry. Your oil doesn't taste good, anyway. I should bring mine sometime." His hands moved up her thigh to caress her warm skin, and his groin tightened.

"Brian, what are you doing?"

"Just touching you." He lowered his voice. "I have female clients, too. I know what to do—believe me." He brought his lips to the back of her thigh.

"Brian!" She pulled her robe over her shoulders and sat up.

He knelt on the floor. "Come on, Leah. You'll have a good time. I guarantee it." He stroked her calf. "Please let me do this for you."

"I'm not having sex with you. Give it up." She removed his hand from her leg.

"But I'm not a kid anymore. I'm almost fifteen."

"That may seem old to you but not to me."

He sat beside her on the couch. "But listen to how low my voice is. I'm almost as tall as you." He took her hand and put it on his bare chest. "My body's growing up. I'm not a little boy."

She felt his heartbeat against her palm. He'd filled out and gotten more muscular in the time she'd known him. Almost a year. She didn't think of him as a child anymore. But that was more from talking to him than the physical changes. She moved her hand from his chest to stroke his hair. "I'm not saying you're a child. But I won't have sex with you. You can stop trying now."

He sat back and folded his arms. His forehead creased. "Really?"

"Really."

"That's the first time I've given a massage and not had sex." He laughed and indicated the lump in his robe. "You gave me a hard on."

She giggled and looked away. She felt like she was in high school again. He laughed, too, and leaned his head back against the couch. His eyelids drooped. Clearly drugged.

"Brian, you've got to stop taking those pills."

"Okay."

She hadn't expected him to give in so easily. She felt in her pocket. The bottle was still there. *And you're not getting it back.* "I should work on that muscle more. Come back in the next day or two."

"Okay. Sounds great." His eyes closed.

He settled in the breakfast nook, and Maria set a plate of unappetizing eggs before him. Breakfast and the newspaper. About the only time he came downstairs these days, except for his lessons.

Wish I could see Leah more. They had a great time last night, though it was kind of fuzzy. *Oh.* He clapped his hand over his mouth as he remembered the massage and what he tried to do. He shook his head. *I don't even want to have sex with her. Not really.* He frowned. *Guess I was pretty fucked up. The pills do that sometimes. Speaking of,* he hadn't taken one this morning. His back didn't hurt as much. He smiled. *Thanks, Leah.*

Though he felt a little sick. Achy. *I should take one so my back won't start hurting again.* He went up to his room and opened the bathroom cabinet. Not there. Walked over to the nightstand. Nope.

"Shit! Where are they?" He looked in all the likely places and a few that weren't, then thought back to the last time he had the bottle. He remembered taking it out at the kitchen table. *I must've left it at Padrea's.* "Fuck."

He picked up the phone to call Matthew. "I need them right away. I've got one of my bad headaches."

"We just got you a new bottle a few days ago."

"I lost it. *Really.* Please—I won't be able to see clients with this headache. But if I take a pill I'll be okay."

Silence. "Alright, we'll get them to you before your first client."

"I need time for it to kick in and to get ready and stuff."

"I'll call Dr. Griffin right now."

They hung up. Brian paced. Bit his nail and looked at the clock and wondered how long he would have to wait. He tried to relax, but he couldn't sit still, so he searched for the missing bottle again. Tore up his room. Looked in the same places three, four, five times. He finally gave up and sat at his desk. Lit a cigarette with shaking hands and stared at the clock.

Matthew brought the prescription over himself. Brian's room was a mess. *Weird, he's usually so tidy.* Matthew walked over to him where he sat at his desk. "I thought you'd be in bed."

Their eyes met. Brian didn't look so good. His coloring was off. *I guess he really is sick.* Matthew didn't care one way or the other. He handed over the bottle of pills. *Take as many as you want. Take them all.*

The next morning Brian went downstairs for breakfast and the newspaper, sat in the sun-filled nook and listened to the comforting sounds of Maria in the kitchen. His fingers reached into his robe pocket to feel the prescription bottle. That was comforting, too.

He picked at his waffles and glanced at the paper, not sure he wanted to read it. He was tired of being depressed. He pulled out the classified ads and flipped through them.

One caught his eye. 'Musicians wanted for Westwood Youth Band. Anyone aged 14 – 18 can tryout.' The list of desired instruments included flute. A phone number at the bottom offered more information.

His hand shook as he reached for his coffee. *Anyone fourteen to eighteen. Anyone. Can you imagine what that would be like? A whole band of people my age? Normal kids.* The thought terrified and beckoned him. Other musicians. *People. My age.*

He wanted it. Wanted it so bad it scared him. People to talk to, be with. People outside of this world. He lit a cigarette and smoked and drank his coffee. Stared out the window at the green lawn and let the idea soak in. *I need a change. Grant isn't here* to ask, so he can't say no.

He brought the paper to his room and dialed the number before he lost his nerve. A recording. "Tryouts close on September 4th at 4:30." *Shit, that's today.* He wrote down the address. Davis High School in Westwood.

He tapped the pencil against his teeth. He would have to sneak out—Matthew would stop him for sure. His heart beat faster. Would security realize he was gone?

He put on jeans and a tee shirt after his last client and waited twenty minutes to make sure security had left. Time to call a cab. He took a pill to soothe his nerves, then picked a number from the phonebook and explained to the dispatcher where the cab should wait down the road. The man said the taxi would be there in fifteen minutes.

He hung up and almost chickened out. "No. I'm going." He picked up the flute case and music folder. *Don't think; just do.* He hurried downstairs and out the back door, then around to the side toward the stables. He ducked off the trail into the trees—the same way he'd gone when he found Schnookie. Down to the front of the property. He walked along the fence until he reached the smaller gate. The cameras could see him, but security didn't watch all the images all the time. *Besides, I'm allowed to take a walk.*

He opened the gate and stepped out. Stayed near the trees as he hurried along, ready to hide if any cars drove by. Anyone on this road was probably headed to Grant's. But no one came. He made it to the appointed spot and stared anxiously down the road.

He bit his nail and went through a hundred reasons why this wasn't going to work. This was a stupid idea. He heard a car. A white taxi came around the corner and pulled to a stop. He waited a moment before he realized the guy wasn't going to open the door for him. He did it himself and slid in.

The car had a peculiar odor. He couldn't quite place the smell—and didn't want to. Clear plastic created a barrier between the front and backseat. He told the cabbie the address and stared out the window as they headed down into the city. They drove west on Sunset, past famous clubs and the giant Marlboro man, then left the cement world behind as they entered Beverly Hills. The trees increased in size and number as the road began to curve. The cab finally turned left and they drove past the Italianate buildings of UCLA.

A few minutes later they stopped by a grassy hill with a cluster of beige buildings at the top. Davis High School. His stomach turned. He ignored the nausea, got out of the cab and handed the driver a hundred dollar bill. "Keep the change. I'll give you another if you wait here for me. It won't be long."

"Sure." The man leaned back in the seat.

He turned toward the school and glanced at his note. The band room was in a separate building. M2. The recording said it was on the east side of the campus, near the soccer field. *Which way is east?*

He was sweating by the time he reached the top of the slope. He wandered around the deserted campus. Grey lockers lined the walls of the buildings. He couldn't remember how to open a locker. *I don't belong here.* He felt like a ghost.

A whistle blew off to his right. He squinted in the sun and saw people practicing some sport in a distant field. *Maybe that's the soccer field.* He headed in that direction and found a building at the edge of the campus marked M2. "This is it."

He pulled on the heavy double door and walked into a large room with a high ceiling. Rows of empty chairs and music stands formed a semi-circle facing a blackboard. No windows except one that looked into an office. He saw movement through it, and a man emerged and said hello.

Brian forced himself to speak. "I'm here for the youth band tryouts."

"Great. Come on in."

Brian followed him into the small office, crowded with a desk and a black music stand. The man sat behind the desk. "What's your name?"

"Brian."

The man wrote it down. "Last name?"

For a panicked moment he couldn't remember what he was supposed to say. Then it came to him. "O'Dell."

The man introduced himself. Mr. Williams, the band director. In his early thirties, Brian guessed. Not bad. He thought about what the man would be like in bed. It made him less nervous.

"Go ahead and play the piece you brought. Then I'll give you something to sight read."

"Okay."

He wasn't nervous while he played. It was talking to the guy that was scary. The man gave him the piece to sight read. It was pretty easy. When he finished, Mr. Williams leaned back and gestured to the only other chair in the office. Brian perched on the edge.

"Do you attend Davis High School?"

"No."

"I didn't think so—that's fine. Most of the kids do, but not all. How long have you been playing flute?"

"Since December. Almost a year."

"You sight read very well. You've been playing *something* longer than a year."

"I've played the piano since I was little."

"Ah." The man nodded. "Have you played in a band before, or with a group?"

He shook his head.

"Hmm. Well, Brian, you're in. Rehearsals are every Wednesday afternoon from three to four-thirty, starting September 21st. Good attendance is mandatory. And you'll need one of these." He dug around the papers on his desk.

Every Wednesday for an hour and a half? Plus travel time. Grant isn't gonna like that.

Mr. Williams handed him a piece of paper. "This is a permission slip for your parent or guardian to sign. You need to bring it with you to our first rehearsal."

Grant has to sign this? Shit. Maybe this wasn't such a good idea.

Mr. Williams was standing up. "Thanks for coming, Brian. We're glad to have you in the Westwood Youth Band."

He mumbled a thank you and walked out in a daze. *I did it.* By the time he got to the taxi he'd forgotten his worries. He sat in the backseat with a grin. He didn't feel like going home. "Take me to a phone booth. Please."

He got out the piece of paper he'd found tucked into his cigarette pack. From Leah. Her phone number and a note to call her. She wanted him to come back to work on his pulled muscle.

He borrowed a quarter from the cabbie and went into the phone booth. Her voice sounded different on the phone. He suddenly felt awkward calling her and almost hung up. *That would be rude.* "Hi, Leah. It's Brian."

She sounded enthusiastic. He relaxed a little. "You said to come over again. Is now a good time?"

"Yes—it's perfect. Mr. Padrea always takes a nap in the afternoon."

"Oh." He'd forgotten about him. "Did I wake him by calling?"

"No, my line's in my room. He can't hear it from his bedroom. Come on over."

"Okay!"

He gave the cabbie directions. He didn't know the address, but once they got on Wilshire he knew the way. He gathered his things and said goodbye to the driver. *I'll call another cab when I'm ready to leave.* He didn't want to feel rushed. He was excited to spend time with Leah in the afternoon instead of the middle of the night. Like a regular person.

The lobby seemed like a different place, full of people instead of deserted. Strange to walk among them with no bodyguard. He felt exposed. He stepped into the elevator. A different man operated the buttons than at night. *Good.*

He walked down the hall and knocked softly on the door. Leah answered. They grinned at each other. She put a finger to her lips, and he followed her to her bedroom full of white flowers.

He said, "I hardly recognize you in clothes." He'd only ever seen her in her robe. Her light ash brown hair was pulled back in a loose braid.

She laughed. "Me, too. Look at you, in jeans and a tee shirt. It's good to see." She indicated the thin black case. "What have you got there?"

"A flute." He sat on the bed and spilled the whole story about the youth band.

Her eyes widened. "Wow, Brian. I'm proud of you." She gave him a hug. "I'm so glad you'll be around people your own age."

"Me, too." He knew that was the real reason for his excitement. Not the music. It was the people.

She looked into his eyes and brushed the hair out of his face. "How are you doing?"

"Great. My back is a lot better."

"I should still work on that muscle, though. Take off your shirt. And those jeans are too high. Can you pull them down a bit?"

He gave her a little smile as he unfastened his pants. "I'm sorry about what happened last time."

She warmed the oil in her hands as he lay on his stomach. "I have to say I was surprised. I had no idea you have women clients, too. You're attracted to women?"

"Oh, *yeah*," he answered, his voice muffled by the pillow. "But I only have one female client. Guess there aren't as many women who like boys."

. . .

He snuck in the back door. No one confronted him. No one seemed to have noticed he was gone. He went up to his room and picked up the bottle of pills from his nightstand. It'd been a long,stressful day.

When he woke in the morning he took out a pill and noticed the bottle was almost half empty. *Shit.* He put the pill back in. *Better conserve. My back doesn't hurt anyway.* He stopped. "Why was I going to take it if my back doesn't hurt?" He remembered Leah saying, *'They're addictive.'* "Shit."

By the time he finished breakfast, he decided he should take a pill. He didn't want to risk hurting his back with his first client today. *That guy's kind of rough.*

In the afternoon he started feeling jittery, worried Grant wouldn't let him join the youth band. He figured he better take a pill so he'd be relaxed for his next client. *But I won't take anymore today.*

He lay in bed that night and stared into darkness. His eyes just wouldn't stay shut. *I need to be rested for tomorrow. I've got clients. Obligations.* He sat up to take a pill.

By the next afternoon he'd stopped making excuses. *Because I want it. I deserve it.* He shook the bottle and felt panic at how quickly it was becoming empty.

Leah had made him promise to come over one more time for his back. He called a taxi and made his way down to the road. He reached into his jeans pocket to wrap his fingers around the prescription bottle, nervous about sneaking out again. He took a pill to relax while he waited for the cab.

Forty minutes later he sat beside Leah on her bed and smiled at her.

"Are you okay?" she asked.

"Yeah, sure."

She held his chin and stared into his eyes. "No, you're not. You're still taking those pills, aren't you?"

He glanced away. "No."

"Don't lie."

He bit his lip. "I tried to stop. I really did. But I can't seem to do it." He looked at her and whispered, "I don't know what to do."

She held out her hand. "Give them to me."

He didn't move.

"Brian. You have to do this."

He reached into his pocket and pulled out the bottle. Stared at it. His hand shook as he held it out to her. He felt like he was watching from some great distance; he couldn't believe he was giving them to her, letting her pry the bottle out of his fingers. He watched it disappear into her pocket and felt like crying.

"Brian." She hugged him tight.

As soon as he walked into his bedroom, he remembered the two pills he'd tucked away for emergency. He went to his dresser to open the box. Still there. He paced and tried to reason with himself.

He couldn't stop thinking about them. *And I won't be able to until I take them. Just get rid of them.* He made up his mind and took one of the pills.

He kept pacing. *But there's still one left.* He couldn't stop obsessing. "Better just take it, too, to get rid of it." He did. As soon as it was down his throat he thought, *Shit. That was stupid. I should've cut them in half and made them last. Now I really don't have anymore. I really, really don't have anymore.*

He stared out the French doors and rubbed his arms. Pressed his forehead against the glass as tears streamed down his face. Time stretched before him. Tomorrow was Monday. Empty Monday. No River. No clients. No anybody. He felt a sudden heavy dizziness and release of tension—the double dose kicking in. He crawled into bed and fell asleep.

The next day he sat huddled on the bathroom floor. He laid his cheek against the cool tile wall as chills shook his aching body. A fine layer of sweat covered him.

He needed fresh air. His heart raced as he pulled himself up, stumbled downstairs and out the back door. Walked and walked until he came to a place that called to him. A little cave formed by bushes. Out of sight of everything. He sat on the dirt, surrounded by living walls.

He hugged his knees as nausea washed over him, his mind blank except for a stupid tune that kept running through it. Repeating endlessly. *Please stop.* He flashed on Creepy Guy and almost vomited.

Time stretched into eternity. Eventually the nausea subsided, left him weak and shaky. And down. So down. Alone in the empty world. He rubbed his arms and shivered. He tried to picture being in the youth band, surrounded by people his age, but he couldn't imagine it. It didn't seem real.

Do those people really exist? Does anyone? Is River coming back, or did I dream him up? How can I be so happy when I'm with him? Maybe it was all a dream, and I'll sit here in this garden alone forever. Because that's all there is. Alone forever.

He looked down and saw he'd been scratching the inside of his right forearm. Specks of blood oozed all the way from the scar on his wrist to his elbow. He hugged it against his chest and cried.

When dusk set in he made his way back to the house, slowly up the stairs to his room. So tired. Empty. A note was taped to the door. Maria's handwriting.

Message from Grant:

Hello, my dear boy. Good news—I'll be home tomorrow morning. We'll spend the day together. I miss you. See you soon.

Love,
Grant

He hugged the note to his chest and laughed as tears streamed down his face. He didn't go into his room, instead walked down the hall to Grant's. He removed the clothes he'd been wearing since yesterday, took a shower and lay down between the clean sheets. He wouldn't budge from this bed until Grant came home. He smiled through his tears and hugged the pillow to his chest.

A wonderful homecoming surprise, to find a lovely naked boy asleep in his bed. Grant climbed in beside him and kissed his forehead.

They spent hours in bed together. Brian was starving by the time they went downstairs.

Jeffrey joined them for lunch. Brian gave him a big hug. Jeffrey stroked his hair. "I think somebody missed us."

He held on tighter.

Maria brought the food, and they dug in. He hadn't been this hungry in weeks. He was already done with his second helping when Grant excused himself to answer a phone call. Brian turned to Jeffrey. "So. Give me the scoop."

Jeffrey always had a fun story. This time it was about a weird man on the airplane. Brian laughed, giddy. He couldn't believe his world could be so horrific yesterday and so great today. Or was about to be. River would be back in few days. He'd really be back.

"What's wrong with you? You ain't eatin your dessert."

"Just thinking about River. It's even harder to wait, now that he's almost home."

"You gotta distract you'self."

Brian gave him a coy smile. "Are you propositioning me?" He laughed at Jeffrey's expression and reached across the table to touch his hand. "I'm kidding."

Jeffrey took hold of his forearm and turned it up toward the light. "Whoa, boy, what happened to your arm?"

He pulled it back with a shrug. "I scraped it on something. I'm gonna go food shopping with Maria."

"You are?"

He grinned and nodded, then remembered he was supposed to call Leah yesterday. *She's worried.*

He excused himself to go up to his room and call her. Reassured her he was okay. "I was sick yesterday. But everything's fine now—Grant's back. And River will be back soon."

"show me sweetness, show me summer skies
show me how to make this wrong seem right
show me laughter in your pale blue eyes
tell me . . .

tell me, do we still have time?
to make this wrong some how be right"

- PJ Harvey (performed by Marianne Faithfull), "The Mystery of Love"

ᚾᚾ CHAPTER 26 ᚾᚾ

He raced downstairs as the front door opened, and River walked in. Glowing smile, tanned skin and hair bleached golden by the sun. Brian flew into his arms and held on tight. He couldn't stop the tears as he clung to River's neck.

They hurried up to his room to make love. The tears came again as River moved inside him. River kissed the wetness on his cheeks.

Afterward they lay quietly, and River held up Brian's arm. His lips brushed the pink skin at the edge of the long scab. "That looks sore, babe. What happened?"

"I don't know. I scraped it on something." He honestly didn't remember at that moment. His mind shied away from that eternity in the bushes. He breathed in River's scent and closed his eyes.

The next day he screwed up the courage to talk to Grant. His fingers clutched the permission slip as he approached Grant in his sitting room.

"Good morning, dear. Is something wrong?"

Brian sat on the edge of the loveseat, his heart beating hard. This was far more important to him than it should be. He cleared his throat and forced himself to speak. "I have a favor to ask. There's, uh, this band. The Westwood Youth Band. I want to join."

Grant lifted an eyebrow and frowned.

"Please." Brian's words spilled out in a jumble. "I've already been accepted. They only meet once a week. I'll make up the time, see extra clients—anything. *Please.*"

"Brian—" Grant shook his head. He was about to say no when he saw the panic in Brian's eyes, like something inside was breaking. He tempered his reply. "I don't think it's a good idea to associate with outsiders."

"I need this, Grant. *Please.*"

He stared into those deep eyes, afraid of what would happen if he denied him. *He's been so depressed lately.* "When do they meet? Where?"

"Davis High School in Westwood. Wednesdays from three to four-thirty."

Grant's frown deepened. He didn't want that much outside influence on him. But Brian seemed to be teetering on the edge of an abyss. "You would have to make sacrifices. You can't have a guitar lesson in the morning and then spend hours away at this youth band. You'd have to give up your guitar lessons."

Brian looked sad, but he said, "I will."

"Don't expect me to go easy on you. I'm not happy about this. I really don't approve."

"I'll work hard." He handed the crumpled permission slip to Grant and whispered, "I need this."

Grant studied the paper. "This mentions concerts outside the normal Wednesday rehearsal. I don't guarantee you'll be able to make any of those. I will give you Wednesday afternoons off, but that is all."

Brian nodded.

"You must remember to be careful what you say to these people. Can you do that?"

"Yes. I've been good with Quinn, haven't I?"

Grant hesitated a moment, then signed his name.

Brian hugged the flute case to his chest as he stared out the window of the Mercedes, so nervous he felt sick. *Wish I had a pill.* He'd thought about smoking pot to mellow out—he could act normal on that now. But then he remembered the paranoia factor and decided against it. *A pill would be better.* He sighed.

It'll be okay. They're just people. And I don't have to talk to them. He distracted himself with thoughts of tonight—River was staying over. Brian hadn't seen him since their anniversary on Saturday. River had seemed really glad about the youth band. Quinn and Leah were, too. Everyone was supportive. Except Grant. *But he's letting me do it. That's what counts.*

Jeffrey stopped the car in front of the school. Brian glanced at the clock on the dashboard. 2:52. Traffic had almost made them late. His heart picked up as Jeffrey opened the door for him. Then he had to convince Jeffrey not to come to the band room with him. "It's right up the hill. You can see the building from here."

"Alright, Mr. B. I'll be waitin right here if you need me."

Jeffrey gave him a hug, and Brian headed up the grassy slope. His eye started twitching as he reached the building. He stopped before the double doors. *I can't do this.*

The doors opened before he had a chance to make up his mind. Two tall boys emerged, laughing and talking. Didn't even notice him. He caught the door before it closed and walked in.

He stood there a moment in the noisy room. Kids warming up their instruments. Talking. Laughing. He swallowed hard and walked over to the flute section in the first row of the semi-circle.

The second seat was empty. The folder on the music stand had '1st Flute, Brian O'Dell' written on it in big black letters. He didn't look at anyone as he got out his flute, but he could feel the closeness of the girls on either side. To his left the first chair, the leader of the flute section. He would play the same parts as her—the first parts, but he was second chair. Second and third parts would be covered by the flutes to his right.

Mr. Williams took his place in front and tapped his baton. The kids fell silent. He welcomed them to a new season of the Westwood Youth Band. "We have a few new members." He mentioned several names. "And Brian O'Dell on second chair flute."

His ears grew hot as dozens of eyes turned toward him. Luckily it was brief. The band director got them started with a few scales. Then Mr. Williams named the first piece they would play. Through the rustle of forty kids searching their music folders, Brian heard a girl with long blond hair whispering from two chairs over. She caught him staring and smiled.

He glanced away and focused on the sheet music. A march—an unfamiliar style. The director lifted his hands, and they began. It was fast. And weird to play with so many other people. All the different parts. Fun, but distracting. It took all his concentration. He really had to remember to count the rests, or he wouldn't have a clue when to play. But he managed to get through it without getting lost.

He did fine while they were playing. But after forty-five minutes Mr. Williams called a break. *Shit. I can't sit here for ten minutes.* He went outside to sit on the short half-wall that ran in front of the building. He lit a cigarette and wished for shade, but there were no trees around.

He heard the door open. A few kids came out, including some of the other flutists. The girl with long blond hair. She giggled with her friends for a few minutes, then walked over to him with a smile. "I'm Claire."

"I'm Brian. Oh, I guess you know that already," he mumbled and felt like an idiot.

"You don't go to Davis High, do you? I haven't seen you before." Awkward pause. "What grade are you in?"

"Uh . . . ." He took a drag and hoped she didn't notice his hand shaking. "I'm not. I mean, I don't go to school. I've got a tutor."

"Oh." She looked a little surprised, then said, "I'm a sophomore."

He didn't know what that meant, so he just nodded and extended the pack of cigarettes to her.

"No, thanks. It's about time to go back anyway."

He felt relieved. But he couldn't help noticing how perky her little breasts were. He popped a mint into his mouth and offered her one.

"Thanks."

Her hand brushed his as she took one, and his pulse sped up. He watched her ass as he followed her back inside.

ꙮꙮꙮ

Brian got two of the special orange pills from Matthew and popped them into his mouth. He'd really been looking forward to the big party. And the pills. *I need to cut loose. It's been a hard summer.*

Too bad the party fell on Tuesday this year. *I'll be tired for band tomorrow. But it's totally worth it.* His pulse sped up as the pills kicked in. He wandered around the crowded courtyard, debating who he wanted first. *Aha.* Trevor stood near the fountain, surrounded by a group of Grant's boys. Brian didn't feel hurt or mad at him anymore. So much had happened in the two months since Trevor left.

He moved closer. Trevor was bragging about his new House. "Oh, yeah, I'll be Number One there soon enough." Trevor's confident voice missed a beat when he saw Brian.

They stared at each other. Brian didn't say a word. Just turned and walked away toward the woods. He knew Trevor would follow.

Brian wandered among the guests, searching for the one person he'd been longing to see. But the only woman he found was Pat. She wore a party mask, but he recognized her easily. He scanned the crowd for a glimpse of golden hair as she led him toward the house. But Michelle was nowhere to be found.

He asked Jeffrey about it after rejoining the party. "Is Michelle here?"

"No, don't think she made it this year."

"Why not?"

Jeffrey frowned. "People's got their reasons."

His eyes narrowed as he studied Jeffrey's face. *He knows something he's not telling.* But Jeffrey wouldn't say more, just reminded Brian he was on duty. Busy.

He gave up. *I hope she's alright.* He saw two older boys nearby and decided to drown his troubles with them. He took their hands to lead them into the woods. Didn't know their names or what House they were from. Didn't want to know. He didn't plan on talking.

The next day Brian stumbled out of the bathroom and headed back to bed, but a paper on the floor caught his eye. He picked it up. *What the hell?* Grant never scheduled clients the day after the big party. Brian was always completely wiped out. But here it was. A client at noon. Then band after that.

"Fuck." He looked at the clock. Already after eleven. *I can't believe I have to get up now.* He felt like he hadn't slept at all. His insides were sore from so much fucking. Hell, his whole body was sore. He remembered Grant's words. *'Don't expect me to go easy on you.'*

No shit. It's like he's punishing me. His jaw clenched as the paper crumpled in his fist. "I can take whatever he throws at me."

He trudged up the slope toward the band room. *At least I'm too tired to be nervous.* It always took a few days to recover from the big party; those pills left him shaky and exhausted. *They're worth it.*

He felt disconnected as he walked into the band room, like he was floating in a cushion. He sat down and got out his flute. Claire smiled at him across the empty chair between them, her yellow tee shirt snug across her chest. *Wish she weren't wearing a bra. Perky little breasts.* He had a sudden image of sucking on them.

The third chair flute took her seat between them and cut off his view.

The music kept him awake. He made it to break time and headed out, then slowed so Claire could catch up. He held the door for her and felt the closeness of her body as she moved past him. He was a couple of inches taller than her. *Nice for a change.*

He settled on the short cinder block wall and tried to keep his hands from shaking as he lit a cigarette. Wished it weren't so damn hot outside.

She leaned against the wall. "You look tired. Your eyes are red."

He smiled a little. "Yeah. Big party last night."

"Was it fun?"

"Yeah. What I remember." He gave a short laugh.

Her eyes widened, but then she smiled and started chatting, tossed her long, light hair over her shoulder. It glinted in the sun. He wanted to touch it. *She keeps talking to me. Does that mean she wants to have sex?*

He rested his elbows on the kitchen table and smiled at Leah. He was still tired out—and she noticed. He reassured her he was off the Demerol. "I can't get more, anyway. The doc won't give them to me again so soon." He hadn't asked for more; the doctor might say something to Grant. *I'm glad no one but Leah knows what happened.*

"Why are you here on a different night?" she asked. "I was worried when you didn't come on Tuesday."

"Sorry. Grant rescheduled cos he had his big party Tuesday night—that's why I'm tired."

"Big party? What's that?"

"Every year all the Houses come to this big party at Grant's. Well, not *all* the Houses." He wondered again about Michelle. "The Houses of boys, anyway. And a bunch of guests. Clients. It's a lot of fun." *The pills are fun.*

She frowned.

What is she thinking? He remembered the files and began to worry. "Leah." He put his hand on hers where it lay on the table. "Promise you'll never try to do anything against Grant. Never contact the authorities or whatever."

"I'm not sure how long I can stand knowing and *not* do anything about it."

His heart dropped, and he gripped her hand. "Leah, don't mess with these people. They could hurt you." He stared into her eyes. *How can I make you understand?* "They're powerful. And they'll protect themselves at any cost." He wasn't sure it was sinking in. "They have ties to the Mafia."

Her eyes grew round.

"Do you understand, Leah? You can't do anything. The only thing you could accomplish is get yourself—or your family—hurt."

She pulled her hand back and looked away.

He stared at the table. "You'd be better off without me. Maybe you *should* leave."

She whispered, "I'm not leaving."

He met her gaze again and saw tears in her eyes. His own filled in response. "Then promise."

She nodded. The movement sent tears down her cheeks. "I promise I won't try to do anything against Grant."

He got up to hug her.

"Brian." She pushed him back to look at his face. "Do you need help getting away from these people? Is Grant forcing you to do this?"

"No, no. It's voluntary. That's a Rule—the most important Rule. Grant believes in it. He enforces it."

"Are you sure?"

"Yes. Please don't worry about that—I do this because I want to, not because I'm forced. Okay?"

"Okay." She held him close.

ריריר

He squeezed into the phone booth with River and told him the number to dial, then chewed his nail and wondered who would answer. Couldn't risk hearing Mom's voice again.

River spoke into the receiver. "Hi, is Tanya there?" He mouthed to Brian, "It's a man." He paused. "Oh. Do you have her new number? I'm a friend from school. Wanted to tell her happy birthday." He wrote the number on his hand. "Thanks." He hung up the phone.

"She moved already? Geez, she didn't waste any time."

"Yeah. Your dad said she moved out today, into an apartment. He sounded kind of sad."

Brian's chest tightened. *Dad.* He took a deep breath and dialed the new number. A machine answered. *Damn.* Tanya and Vicky with a silly message. Then it beeped. "Oh. Hi. I, uh . . . wanted to wish you a happy birthday, but you're not there. I hope you're out having fun." He sang happy birthday to the machine. "God, I can't believe you're eighteen now and you've got your own place and everything. Don't work too hard. I'll try to call again soon." He whispered, "I miss you."

The tears started as he hung up. It was such a disappointment not to talk to her. River gave him a big hug and put his arm around his shoulders as they walked back to the car. Jeffrey ruffled his hair. They made it hurt a little less.

He lay on his back in the Room as sweat dried on his bare skin. His client was gone, but he didn't feel like moving. He stared up at the ornate medallion on the ceiling and remembered Grant's words from yesterday. *'It's not simply a decorative piece.'* Grant flipped a hidden switch. A piece of ceramic slid away and a pair of handcuffs lowered from a chain. It made him a little nervous at first. But it was okay—really fun, actually, once he got used to it. Different to be upright like that.

Grant was talkative afterward. Told him about the history of the House, how it was built for this specific purpose—a brothel for boys. At first they all lived in this building; that's why there were so many bedrooms. The Other Wing was added later. Brian wished there were still boys in those empty rooms down the hall.

His bedroom and this Sex Room had always been for the Number One. A tradition for over a hundred years. *How many boys have lain here and stared up at this ceiling?* He swore he could feel their presence, the echoes of their lives. Grant had also told him this House wasn't voluntary in the beginning. The thought made his stomach turn.

There's a lot of pain here. Over a hundred years. I wonder how many boys have been raped in this room? The intense emotions from the other boys surrounded him. His own were a part of it—*he* was a part of it, with the boys who had lain here before him. He was more comfortable in a room full of their echoes than in a room of real people his own age. Regular kids. They scared him.

He thought about what school had been like, so many years ago. Hadn't felt comfortable then, either. Childhood. His mother's voice shot through him. '*I can't stand to look at you,*' she screamed as she shoved him into the closet and locked him in.

"No. Go away." He blocked out her face with the fresh memory of his last client and the handcuffs suspended from the medallion. *I'm more at home in the bed where I have sex with strangers than I am with my own family.* He rolled onto his side and stared at nothing.

"I tried to call my sister again a few days later, but I got the machine again." He frowned into his bowl of ice cream. "I'm sure she's busy, with work and school and all."

Leah nodded. "That would be hard—to support yourself and go to high school."

"She can do it. She's strong."

"Must run in the family." She touched his hand and smiled. "I'm sure you'll get ahold of her soon."

"No, I won't. Grant said I can't call again for awhile. We have to be careful." His frown deepened. "I should've waited. Now I can't call her on my birthday. She'll be expecting it." *She'll worry.* He whispered, "I don't mean to cause them pain."

"You miss them a lot, don't you? Your family."

He crossed his arms over his chest. "I don't miss my parents. I don't want to be with them."

"Your sister."

He looked down and nodded. Leah leaned over to put her arm around his shoulders and kissed his forehead. He smiled at her, still surprised she cared about him. *Even though she knows what I am.*

"Brian, if you ever want to talk, I'm here for you. It's not good to pretend stuff didn't happen. Those feelings affect you—even more when you try to suppress them."

"You sound like a therapist."

"Have you had therapy?"

"Yeah, in the institute." He held up his wrists. "When I did this."

"Do you want to talk about it? About why you did that?"

He bit his lip and shook his head slowly. "I just . . . couldn't take it anymore. My mom—" His eyes stung. He shook his head again.

"Brian." She stroked his hair.

"She doesn't want me."

"I'm sure that's not true."

"Yes, it is." He looked her in the eye. "She doesn't want me. I don't know why."

The tears spilled over.

Leah stood and held his head against her warmth. "You are not responsible for anything your mother did or said to you. It wasn't your fault. Don't forget that." Her voice caught. "Many people love you. Don't forget that, either."

He pulled away and wiped his face. "I know. I'm lucky to have what I have."

She sat down again. "You mean at Grant's?"

"Yeah. But mostly I mean River." He hugged himself. "I wish I saw him more."

"Why do you stay with Grant?"

"It's my home. They're my family." He brightened. "I get to spend all day tomorrow with River. Except for band. I'm trying out for a piano-clarinet duet. I didn't join band to play piano, but I can't resist." He grinned. "I'm excited."

She couldn't help but smile back, even though it frustrated her when he steered the conversation away from personal issues. "I didn't know you play the piano. Are you good?"

His smile turned shy. "Yeah. I've played all my life."

"Really?" *That fits him somehow.* Another piece of the puzzle that was Brian clicked into place. *There must be some way I can help him.* She probed. "So you get to spend tomorrow with River?"

"Yeah, for my birthday."

"It's your birthday? Why didn't you say so?" She gave him a hug. "Happy birthday, Brian. It's after midnight. You're fifteen now, right?"

He laughed. "Yeah. Pretty weird."

"I would've gotten you something if I'd known. Hold on." She hurried off to her room and returned with a lovely bouquet of white flowers. "One of each kind."

A lump rose in his throat as he accepted the gift and whispered, "Thank you, Leah."

Time for band. He hated to leave River alone at their beach house. "Just for a few hours," Brian said. But he felt guilty; River was sad. He tried to hide it, but Brian could tell.

Oh, well. What can I do? he thought as he got into the limo. *I can't miss band.* Not after all he went through to be in it. He was surprised Grant hadn't scheduled any clients today—he always had a full load on Wednesdays now. That sucked when he'd been at Padrea's the night before. Grant used to give him a light schedule after his All Night sessions. But not anymore.

At least he didn't schedule any on my birthday. He and River had a wonderful day at the beach, and he was looking forward to band. He buttoned the cuffs of his purple silk shirt as Jeffrey stopped the car in front of the school.

Claire saw him come in. He wore black leather pants with his shirt tucked into the low waist. Sexy. Everything about him was sexy, even the way he moved. She felt weak—and a little scared of her reaction. She'd never felt this way before.

Their eyes met as he took his seat, and her heart did a little flip. He looked so incredible; his eyes glowed blue, and his cheeks had that gorgeous flush. *Is that from walking up the hill or from looking at me? I hope he likes me.*

They went outside together at break. His shirt rode up as he leaned back against the half wall. "Oh!" she said. "You have a belly ring." The words popped out of her mouth. Then she felt like an idiot.

He laughed a little. "Yeah."

She had to turn away, she was so overwhelmed. She composed herself while he lit a cigarette. "After band sometimes a bunch of us go out. Wanna come?" Her heart beat hard.

"Uh . . . today? I can't. I've got plans." He added quickly, "But that would be great. Maybe next week? If I don't have to work."

She grinned. "Okay. What are you doing tonight?"

"Oh, well, it's my birthday, so I've . . . got plans."

"Your birthday? Oh, my gosh, happy birthday!" She almost touched him but stopped herself. "How old are you?"

"Fifteen."

"Oh." Her eyes widened. "I thought you were older." She couldn't tell if he was pleased or not.

"How old are you?" he asked.

"I turned sixteen a few months ago. Got my license." She was surprised she could form coherent sentences. She felt so giddy talking to him. *He's going out with us next week. What should I wear?*

After band she hung around. Brian was waiting to try out for the piano-clarinet duet. He didn't seem to notice her, stood off by himself to watch the first guy try out. Then it was his turn.

He took a seat at the piano. Didn't have any music with him, just started playing. Claire's mouth fell open. *Oh, my God. How can he possibly hit all the right keys so fast?* Amazing. She'd never heard anyone play like that. She felt the emotions of the music as she watched his face. *I think . . . I'm in love with him.*

The other aspiring pianists quietly melted away. No one wanted to play after that. Mr. Williams asked him the name of the piece when he finished.

"Chopin's *Fantaisie Impromptu*. I like that one a lot."

"How long have you been playing the piano?"

"As long as I can remember." He shrugged. "As soon as I could reach the keys, I guess—before I could talk." His mother told him that once, then showed him a photo of her holding him up to the keys when he was a baby. A big grin stretched across his chubby cheeks.

He smiled a sad smile. *I wonder if she's thinking about me right now? It is my birthday.* He swallowed.

The director's voice intruded on his thoughts. "Here's the piece you'll be playing with Stuart."

He glanced at the sheet music. Easy.

A tall, gawky teenager approached the piano—the first chair clarinet who sat behind Brian in the second row of the band. Pale with messy dark hair and black-rimmed glasses. The thick lenses made his brown eyes seem bigger than they should be. "Hi." The guy smiled. "I'm Stuart."

Mr. Williams put a hand on each of their shoulders. "You two will need to put in extra practice together. You're welcome to stay after band, or you can meet on your own."

Stuart said, "We can do it at my house. If you want."

"Uh . . . ." He hadn't really thought this through. "I never know my schedule ahead of time. It's hard to plan." He rubbed his thigh. "Maybe you should get someone else . . . ."

"No, no," Mr. Williams said. "I'm sure we can work around your schedule, right, Stuart?"

"Sure. Do you want to start now? I can stay."

"Sorry, I can't. I've got plans."

Stuart handed him a piece of paper. "Here's my phone number. Call me when you have time to get together."

"Okay." *This is going to be weird.* He got up to leave and saw Claire watching from where she stood near the door.

They walked out together and down the slope. When she finished gushing about how amazing he was on the piano, she said, "I park down here, too, instead of the lot. It's easier to get to my house."

"Do you live around here?"

"Yeah, just up the street. Only takes five minutes to get home. Where do you live?"

"Oh, a lot farther."

They arrived at the waiting limo. She raised an eyebrow. "Nice car."

He shrugged. Didn't know what to say.

She leaned up close to whisper, "Happy birthday, Brian," and kissed his cheek.

His face was burning as he climbed into the car.

꣠꣠꣠

Brian got out the clarinetist's phone number. No more clients today, and Grant was playing golf at some country club. A perfect time to sneak out. It felt weird to talk to someone besides River on the phone. Luckily it was brief. Stuart sounded enthusiastic. They hung up, and he called a taxi.

Stuart answered the door. His dark hair stood out from his head in messy spikes. "Come in."

Brian peered inside. So long since he'd been in a regular house, where a regular family lived. The front door opened onto a small foyer, then the living room. He walked in and felt like he was in a cave, the ceiling was so low. He went to the spinet piano against the far wall and rested his fingers on the keys, then glanced around.

The room seemed small compared to Grant's but pleasant. Homey. An olive couch and loveseat squared off in front of a fireplace and large TV. A framed photograph hung over the mantel. Stuart and his family—a younger brother, mom and dad. He studied the man. *Nice. Very nice.*

"Aren't you glad it's Friday?"

Brian looked at him and shrugged.

"Want something to drink? Soda or juice?"

"Juice, thanks." He sat at the piano while Stuart went to the kitchen. Played around with it. It was in tune.

Stuart came back with their drinks and put his clarinet together. "You're really great on the piano. What school do you go to?"

"I don't. I've got a tutor." He rubbed his palms on his jeans. *He's just trying to be friendly.* But he wasn't used to idle talk. It was different with Claire—his physical attraction distracted him. "Ready?"

Stuart pushed up his glasses and nodded. They ran through the piece. It was so easy he didn't have to pay attention to what he was doing, so he listened to Stuart. *He's good. Guess that's why he's first chair.* When they finished Brian asked how long he'd been playing clarinet.

"Since seventh grade."

"What grade are you in now?"

"I'm a junior."

Claire said she was a sophomore. Brian shifted on the bench. "What does that mean, exactly?"

"Huh?"

"What grade is that?"

Stuart gave him a funny look. "Eleventh. How long since you were in school?"

"Not since sixth grade. Well, I started seventh, but only for a few weeks."

"How come?"

He shrugged and stared at his fingers where they rested on the keys. "That's when . . . I stopped living with my parents, and everything changed."

Stuart was silent a moment. "Oh."

"Let's play it again."

They worked for half an hour before Stuart suggested they take a break. "Let's go to my room."

Brian followed him down a hall lined with family photos. Stuart indicated a closed door on the left. "That's my brother's room. This one's mine." He passed the bathroom and opened the next door. "I need a bigger room."

Brian couldn't absorb everything at once. The room was stuffed. Overflowing and messy. Two posters dominated the walls. One of Flea playing bass onstage, and one of an attractive older man in an odd red and black outfit. *Posters of guys. I wonder if Stuart's gay?* "Who is that?"

"Captain Jean Luc Picard of the *U.S.S. Enterprise*, of course. Don't you ever watch *Star Trek: Next Generation?*"

"No, but I've seen some old *Star Treks*. They're pretty funny."

"This show is way better. You should watch it sometime. My mom bought me that poster. She thinks he's a good role model. And she says he's sexy." Stuart made a grossed out face.

He is. I wonder why I never put up any posters in my room? He'd loved his posters when he lived at home. *Not 'home.' That place I used to live.*

His attention moved to the bookcase. It was stuffed, with books stacked on top and on the floor beside it. "Guess you like to read." He glanced at the spines. Mostly science fiction. He pulled one out. "I read this. It was good."

"Which one? Oh, *Brave New World*. Yeah. Kinda scary though, in a way."

"Yeah." He put it back and pulled out another that caught his eye. It had a weird cover. A giant cartoon thumb and a round green face, featureless except for a big mouth with its tongue sticking out.

Stuart looked over his shoulder. "*Hitchhiker's Guide to the Galaxy*. That's really funny. Different. Want to borrow it?"

"Okay."

"It's the first in a series. If you like it you can borrow the rest." Stuart glanced at the clock. "Do you want to stay for dinner? My mom will be home soon. She's a good cook."

Your mom? "Uh, no . . . I—I've gotta go." He tried not to panic as he hurried out.

Stuart watched him get into the taxi that had waited by the curb this whole time and wondered what he'd done to make Brian leave.

Stuart approached him after band. "Do you have to work tonight?"

Brian shook his head.

"Want to stay and practice? Or we could go to my house."

"I can't. I've got plans." He watched Stuart's face fall. *He thinks I'm avoiding him.* "Hey, why don't you come? I'm going out with Claire and some people."

Stuart's face lit up. "I'll call my mom to see if it's okay." He borrowed the phone in the director's office and got permission. "Want to ride with me?"

"Uh, no, I'm riding with Claire."

Stuart's eyebrows shot up. "Oooh."

He grinned. "Yeah."

Brian walked with Claire to her silver BMW. He opened the passenger door and paused to look back at the black car waiting up the street. *Fuck it. I don't have a client. I'll do what I want.* He ducked inside and shut the door. *I work hard. I've earned it. Grant can kiss my ass.* He smiled. *Boy, can he.*

Hope he's not mad. Maybe he won't even know. He turned around and saw the Mercedes following them.

Claire turned up the radio while she drove. "I like this song."

It sounded stupid and commercial to him. He watched her move to the boppy music. Imagined her moving beneath him.

A few minutes later they pulled into a parking lot. He got out, and the Mercedes parked nearby. The driver stayed in the car. *I guess it's okay, or he'd come get me.*

He followed Claire into the fifties-themed diner. She led him to a big circular booth already full of teenagers. They made space for her, and he sat beside Claire on the end. Garden burger sounded great. He explained that he was a vegetarian.

"Really? For how long?"

"Three years."

"Wow. Neat." They grinned at each other.

He was quiet after they ordered. Listened to the other kids talk and laugh. He didn't know what to say, so he didn't say anything. But it felt great to be there. He spotted Stuart hovering awkwardly near the door and waved him over. Stuart sat at the end of the booth beside him.

Claire made a sarcastic comment, and everyone laughed. He liked her sense of humor. Of course, he'd like it no matter what. *God, I want her so bad.* He could feel her warmth even though they weren't quite touching. He was getting a hard on just sitting there.

He put his hand on her shoulder and whispered something stupid in her ear. It didn't matter what he said; it was an excuse to touch her. His fingers slid down the bare skin of her arm, and her breath sped up.

The food arrived. The French fries were crunchy and salty. "Yummy."

Claire giggled. He fed her one. Watched her lips as she sipped on her straw. *God.* His cheeks grew hot as his groin tightened. Stuart said something. Brian turned, grateful for the distraction. He was getting uncomfortably horny.

"Did you start that book yet? *Hitchhiker?*"

"Yeah—it's great. It makes me laugh out loud." They joked about the opening scene where a hungover Arthur tried to make sense of a bulldozer. "I'll definitely want to borrow the rest of the series."

Claire touched his arm. He and Stuart slid out of the booth so she could go to the restroom, then sat down again. The girl next to Brian smiled. He struggled to remember her name. Debbie, the flutist who sat between him and Claire in band.

"So, Brian, where do you work?"

"Uh . . . ." He realized the whole table was listening. *Don't panic. You rehearsed this.* "I work at home."

"Oh? Doing what?"

"I work for Grant. He owns an import-export business." *There. I did it without lying.*

"Who's Grant?"

"My guardian."

She seemed surprised. "You don't live with either of your parents?"

His heart started pounding. He looked at his plate and pushed it away. "No."

Stuart rescued him with a silly story about how his mom embarrassed him last week. *Thanks, Stuart.* Then Claire was back.

The waitress came to clear the plates away and set the bill on the table. Someone suggested the mall. Claire turned to him expectantly. He shook his head. "I better get home." Didn't want to push it *too* much with Grant. *I'm surprised I haven't already gotten in trouble. Is he just not paying attention?* All Grant seemed to do was schedule more clients.

He realized everyone was putting money on the table, so he pulled a bill out of his pocket and tossed it onto the pile. Stuart said, "Don't you have anything smaller?"

"No."

"I guess you get all the change then." Stuart pushed the money toward Brian.

He picked at the pile of bills. These weren't his tight pants, but there wasn't *that* much room. The front pockets already had his regular supply of condoms and lube. He took a couple of twenties for his back pocket. More than that would make a bulky spot.

He walked toward the door with Stuart and Claire. "Hey, Brian—" Debbie called. "Don't you want your change?"

He shook his head.

Debbie looked at Claire. "You're going to the mall, right?"

A look passed between them, and he had the feeling they'd be talking about him soon.

Stuart whispered to him as they stepped outside. "She *totally* likes you. It's so obvious." He said, "See ya," in a normal voice and left them alone.

She walked with Brian to the waiting Mercedes. He shoved his hands into his pockets and felt awkward. *We both want each other. So now what am I supposed to do?* He mumbled, "Um, maybe we should get together sometime."

"Yeah, I'd like that."

They grinned foolishly at each other. "Okay. I better go." His brain started working again as he was about to get in the car. "Oh, I should get your number."

"Sure!" She fumbled in her purse but couldn't find any paper. She did find a pen. "Can I have your number, too? Here, you can write it on my hand."

It was a great excuse to touch her. He cradled her delicate hand, turned it over and stroked the palm. Her breath caught. He wrote the number carefully.

She giggled. "That tickles. Hey, I thought you were left-handed."

"I'm ambidextrous. I use both hands—it depends on what I'm writing. Numbers are definitely my right hand."

"Oh. Wow." She smiled and took the pen. "My turn." She turned his hand over to write on his palm and gasped. She was staring at the scar.

Damn it. It's not fair something so personal is where everyone can see it.

She wrote her number. He avoided her eyes and mumbled a goodbye as he got into the car. *Now she thinks I'm a freak.* His finger rubbed the scar as the Mercedes pulled away. *I guess I am.* His lips tightened. He refused to think about the life that led to the scars. Focused instead on Stuart and his collection of books. And Claire. He held his palm open so he wouldn't sweat the ink off. *Hope she still likes me.*

He found something else to worry about as the Mercedes went up the curvy driveway. *I wonder if Grant noticed I'm late? I should talk to him.* They hadn't spent much time together lately. *I don't want him to be mad at me.*

He stopped in the kitchen to tell Maria he'd already eaten and wrote down Claire's number before it smeared. Maria told him Grant was in his office. He knocked softly and poked his head in. "Are you busy?"

Grant gave him a slight smile from behind the desk. "Not really. Come in, dear."

He moved to Grant's side of the desk and leaned back against it. "I, uh, I've made some friends and . . . . Is it okay if I go out with them once in awhile? I won't let it interfere with my duties here."

Grant leaned back with a sigh. He felt his control of Brian slipping more each day. *He's a teenager.* Brian looked worried at the moment, but he seemed happier in general. *Maybe this is what he needs.* "I'd like you to check with me first from now on, alright? And don't get too close to these people. Remember who you are. You must be careful what you say."

He let go his breath and smiled. "Thank you, Grant." He inched closer until his leg brushed Grant's. "I miss you."

"Brian." Grant's hand moved up his thigh. He pulled Brian down onto his lap—getting a bit heavy for that. *I should enjoy it while I still can.*

Naked in the Rain

. . .

The next morning Brian went to play his flute and realized he didn't have it. *Shit. I left it in Claire's car.* A good excuse to call her. He screwed up his courage and dialed the number. No answer. *Oh, she's at school.* He had no idea what time that got out. *If band starts at three, it must be around then.*

He called again at four o'clock. She sounded excited when she realized who it was. Then he felt awkward. "Uh, I left my stuff in your car."

"Yeah. I've got it right here."

"Um . . . ." *Just speak.* "We should get together. I need to get my stuff and . . . maybe we could hang out or something." *Why do I feel so stupid?*

"Okay!"

He grinned. *She still likes me.* "But I never know my schedule in advance. It's hard to plan anything."

"I'm free tonight . . . ."

"I can't. I've gotta work. Maybe this weekend?"

"Yeah—oh, no. We're going out of town. But I really ought to get your flute to you. Maybe I could just drop it by your house."

"Uh, yeah, okay." *We can meet down the road.* He gave her the complicated directions.

"Okay. I'll be there in about an hour."

He waited at his usual spot by the curve in the road. And waited. *Maybe she's not coming.* He pulled his watch out of his pocket. *If she doesn't get here soon, I'll have to go back.* Couldn't be late for his client. He heard a car.

Claire pulled her BMW onto the shoulder and got out. "Sorry it took so long—traffic." She handed him his flute and music folder.

"Thanks." He set them on the grass struggling back to life after the hot summer, and they smiled at each other. "Where are you going this weekend?"

"To Ventura to visit my grandparents. We try to go at least once a month. My grandma isn't doing well."

"I'm sorry." He touched her arm and stroked the bare skin. Watched her chest rise and fall in her snug top.

And they weren't thinking about grandparents anymore. He moved closer to smooth her hair away from her face. His lips moved on their own, toward hers. Brushed against them lightly.

He watched for her reaction. He didn't know how to treat a girl who wasn't a client or in the business. She gazed up into his eyes and put her hand in his hair, her soft lips open and waiting. He kissed her again. Not so gently this time. Their arms went around each other, bodies pressed tight. He sucked on her tongue. Her lower lip. Her neck. Lost himself in her scent and pushed her against the car. Rubbed his body against hers.

Almost forgot he had a client in twenty minutes. Almost, but not quite. He forced himself to back off and took a deep breath. "Claire."

Her palm rested on his chest. She could feel his heart pounding as hard as hers. She'd never been kissed like *that*. Her whole body felt warm and weak as she stared up into those gorgeous eyes.

He glanced away. "I—I have to get back. I can't be late."

She nodded. Rubbed her hand on his chest. Couldn't speak or move away from him.

"Call me when you get back into town, okay?"

She managed to whisper, "I will."

ಬಬಬ

He walked into Stuart's living room for another piano-clarinet rehearsal. The first thing he noticed was the sound of a video game. A boy sat on the floor in front of the TV, blowing up spaceships with a joystick. Stuart walked over to his brother. "You know what Mom said, Jacob. No more than an hour."

"Aw, come on. She'll never know."

"Yes, she will, cos I'll tell her."

"Stu!" Jacob threw him an angry look, and the screen flashed. "Look what you made me do."

Stuart turned off the TV. "Come on, Brian. Let's go to my room. I need to find my clarinet."

Brian smiled at the pouting kid on the floor and followed Stuart. "How old is Jacob?" he asked as they walked into Stuart's room. It was even messier than before.

"Twelve."

He blinked. "*Twelve?* But he's just a kid."

"Yeah." Stuart pulled dirty clothes off his bed. "I know it's here somewhere. I just practiced yesterday."

Brian barely heard him. *I was twelve when I met Grant. I never realized how young that is. I was a prostitute at that kid's age. Oh, my god.* He leaned back against the door. *Oh, my god.*

Something moved in front of his face. "Yoo-hoo, I found it." Stuart waved his hand. "Hello?"

Brian shook his head. His heart was beating too fast. He fumbled in his jeans for a cigarette. The first one he pulled out was broken. *Damn it.*

"Whoa. You can't smoke in here."

Brian stared at him.

"We can go out back."

He followed Stuart down the hall without a word. Didn't glance at the boy who hurried to turn off the video game. Stuart led him through the dining room to a sliding glass door, and they stepped onto a cement porch with an awning. Stuart sat at the patio table.

Brian leaned against a post and smoked and stared at nothing. *I didn't feel young when I was twelve. But I don't think I ever did.* He shook his head. *It doesn't matter. Doesn't matter anymore. Don't think about it.* He put on his sunglasses and turned to Stuart. "What time will your parents be home?"

"Around five."

Plenty of time. He sat at the table, put his boots up on another chair and took a long drag. Refused to think about the twelve-year-old on the other side of the wall. His gaze roamed over the freshly mown lawn surrounded by a tall wooden fence.

"It's nice out here." Private, yet he could hear sounds of the neighborhood. A car driving by, a dog barking. Reminded him there was a world out there.

"Dad's thinking about putting in a pool." Stuart watched him sit there in his dark Ray-bans and smoke. *Damn, he's so cool. And he's not even trying. Why can't I be like that?* He tried to figure out how Brian did it. *He's just wearing jeans and a tee shirt. Maybe it's the black nails and the earring. And the hair. Or maybe it's just him.*

Brian said, "I finished *Hitchhiker*. I loved it. Can I borrow the others?"

"Sure!"

"Oh, I left it in the car. Remind me to get it before I leave."

Stuart nodded. The Mercedes that sat parked on the street with a man in the driver's seat. *Just sitting there waiting for him. Weird.*

"Do you have an ashtray?" He lit a second cigarette from his first.

"No."

"'kay," he said with the cigarette dangling from his mouth. He stubbed the other one out on the sole of his boot and set the butt on the table's edge. "Remind me to throw that away."

Stuart nodded—definitely didn't want his dad to find that. He gestured at the boots. "Are those Doc Martens?"

"Nah. Those look stupid on me; they're too chunky. Or I'm too small."

"I like Docs."

"You should get some."

Stuart shrugged. *If they don't look good on him, they sure won't look good on a skinny geek like me.* "So how's it going with Claire?"

Brian grinned. "We kissed."

"Really?" Stuart leaned forward. "When?"

"Yesterday. She stopped by to give me stuff I left in her car. But now she's gone for the weekend." He hit his thigh with his fist. "It's driving me crazy."

"That's great, though. She's pretty." She'd never spoken one word to Stuart until the diner.

"Yeah." Brian sighed. "I can't wait to. . . . "

Stuart laughed.

Brian held the door open for Claire. Leah had told him to take her to a nice dinner. Claire picked Italian.

After they ordered he said, "Italian's my favorite." *Wish I could order wine.* He was nervous. *I guess this is my first real date.*

Claire sipped her iced tea. "Are you doing anything for Halloween?"

"Going to a party." *Michelle. God, I can't wait.*

"Oh?"

He realized she was waiting for him to invite her. "It's an adult party—" *That sounds bad.* "Sort of a business party. I can't invite anyone."

"Oh." Her disappointment vanished quickly. "There's a big party next Saturday night. Want to go?"

"Is that Halloween?"

"No, Halloween's this Monday."

Monday? Shit. River's not gonna like that.

"Do you want to come?" she asked.

"Yeah, sure. If I don't have to work."

He pushed up the sleeves of his black shirt. Her top looked like it had spandex in it, too. God, he wanted to touch those little breasts. Had trouble thinking about anything else. He remembered Leah's advice. *'She's only sixteen. You can't expect to have sex with her right away—if ever. You have to respect her limits.'* The *'if ever'* had him worried. *Who knows? Maybe we'll have sex tonight. We could go to a hotel or something.*

After dinner they went for a drive. Brian stared out the window. "I love the city lights. Can't see them from my house."

"Then I've got a great spot to show you." They drove up into the hills of Mulholland and followed the curvy road. She squinted into the darkness. "It's hard to see. Oh, there it is." She turned off onto a side road and slowed the BMW as the pavement turned to gravel. She pulled over when they reached a clear spot by a drop off.

He got out of the car with a big grin. "Wow. This is amazing!" The lights of the city spread before them in all directions, brilliant and clear. He took a deep breath of cool air. "Gorgeous."

"I like to come up here sometimes. When I want to get away."

He lit a cigarette and sat beside her on the warm hood. Brushed ashes off the silver paint. "Oops. Sorry."

"That's okay. I don't like this car, anyway. Mom's old castoff. She won't buy me a new one. But my dad might—if I don't get any tickets for six months. Of course Mom's mad. He always uses things like that to get at her." She frowned at the lights. "I never see him. He just buys me stuff."

He couldn't really imagine what her life was like. But she sounded sad. He took her hand and stroked it. "I'm sorry."

"Are your parents divorced, too?"

"No." But he didn't want to imply a huge lie. "But I don't live with them."

She nodded. "Debbie told me you live with a guardian. What's that like?"

"Uh, it's good. He's like a father to me." He finished his cigarette and popped a mint into his mouth, then offered her one.

She took it. "How come you always eat these?"

"I don't want to taste like an ashtray."

Her breath sped up. "Does that mean someone will be tasting you soon?"

His smile widened. "Oh, yeah." He stared at her and chewed the mint to bring that moment closer. "I can't decide if your eyes are blue or green."

"It depends on what I'm wearing."

"We could figure out their true color if you take your shirt off."

"Brian!" She pushed on his chest.

He kissed her. And kissed her. She tasted so sweet, *god.* She returned his passion and wrapped her arms around him. He pushed her down onto the hood of the car, felt the thrill he always got when he laid on top of a woman. His erection pushed against his leather pants. Against her.

His lips moved down her throat as his hand went to her breast. Damn bra was in the way. He cupped it anyway. Then he was lifting her shirt.

Naked in the Rain

"No." She put her hand on his. "Outside the clothes. It's only our first date."

He stared at her a moment, breathing hard. "Then will you do something for me? Take off your bra—I'm dying to see the shape of your breasts without that stupid thing in the way."

She gave an embarrassed laugh, then shrugged. "Okay. But stay outside the clothes." She sat up and reached behind her back to unhook it, then put her hand inside the sleeves to pull the straps down and pulled the bra out the end of her sleeve.

He'd never seen a woman do that. "That was amazing." All thought stopped. Small, perky breasts. Her nipples stood out against the spandex. His mouth went to them. He pushed her back again, sucked on her breast through her shirt. He stroked the other nipple with his fingers. Tugged on it gently. She gasped. Her legs spread and moved around him.

Next thing he knew he'd lifted her shirt. The pink nipple stood straight up. His mouth closed on it. She moaned and pushed her hips against him. He moved to the other, then down her soft stomach. He licked her navel, and his hand went between her legs. He groaned as he rubbed her heat through the cotton pants. He knew she was wet in there.

"No, no," she panted and pushed his hand away.

He pulled back and struggled to use his brain. *No. She said no. Have to stop.* He shook his head and stood up. Moved away from her. She sat up to pull her shirt down. "I'm sorry," he said. "I didn't mean to do what you said not to do. I just, I'm not used to stopping. I'm sorry."

"Not used to stopping?" Her eyes narrowed. "How many girlfriends do you have?"

Oops. Shit, I'm fucking this up. "None. Really." *Not girlfriends.* He sat beside her and smoothed blond hair away from her cheek. "I'm sorry," he whispered.

She smiled and touched his lips. "It's alright."

His gaze dropped. Her shirt was wet from his mouth. The way her nipple stood out against the damp fabric made him dizzy. He kissed her neck. "I'll try to behave."

She pushed him away. "Yes, you will." She didn't trust herself to stop him again. "It's not fair—you saw my chest, but I didn't see yours." *My gosh,* she thought. *I shouldn't be so forward.*

He raised a brow. "We can fix that." He pulled his shirt off over his head.

She touched him tentatively with her palm. Smooth and pale. Her hand moved up and down on its own. Grazed his nipple. His breath caught. But he held still—didn't touch her. "Want to see more?" he asked.

Her eyes widened. "No. This is enough for now."

They lay back against the hood of the car to cuddle. Her hand kept stroking his chest. Lovely and toned. Not skinny like she expected. "Do you play sports?"

"No, but I do yoga every day."

She kissed the flesh beside his nipple, then propped herself up to look at him. God, she wanted to eat him up. *Control yourself.* That belly ring was so sexy. And the hard muscle that ran down from it . . . down to the bulge in those tight leather pants. It seemed bigger than before. That was enough to cool her libido. Scary territory there.

She pulled on his hand, pulled him up. "Want to get ice cream or coffee or something?"

"Sure." He kissed her again.

They eventually made it back into the car.

*"I hold his head while he lies
and buries his face between my thighs"*

- Brian O'Kelly

ᚾᚾ CHAPTER 27 ᚾᚾ

"I'm sorry. I forgot to tell you."

"You forgot?" River paced the bedroom. "You forgot you made other plans on the one night we have together?"

"Michelle's party only comes once a year. It's not my fault it's on a Monday."

"Next thing I know you'll be hanging out with Stuart on Mondays, too."

"River! I would never do that. But I need to go tonight. I'm worried about Michelle—she didn't come to Gran'ts party."

River stood with his back to him, arms folded across his chest. "Fine. Go."

Brian touched his shoulder. "Please come with me. It's not just women—there are lots of men, too. You'll have fun."

He didn't answer. Brian rubbed his shoulder and kissed it. "River, you know you're more important to me than anything else. Please don't be mad."

"It's just—" He turned to face him. "I don't get to see you enough."

Brian gave him a sad smile. "I know." It was worse these days, with his schedule so full. "All the more reason for you to come to the party tonight. I promise you'll have fun."

"I don't like ties." Brian pulled the black silk from around his neck and tossed it onto the seat as he and River got out of the limo. Brian slipped into the tuxedo jacket, and they moved toward the crowd at Jasmine Lane. It felt like stepping into another time—this year's theme was a Southern ball during the Civil War era, with elegant ladies in hoop dresses and men in uniforms or tuxes.

He noticed River's breath pick up. Brian smiled and said, "Have fun."

River ignored him—still mad—and walked away toward a group of guys who looked like models. Brian wandered around, with Jeffrey close behind. Plenty of lovely men and women to choose from. But he only wanted to find one person tonight.

He finally saw her through a break in the crowd, lovely in dark green velvet, golden hair swept up to accent her graceful neck. She glanced toward him, then turned away abruptly and disappeared among the guests. "She saw me—I know she did. Why would she do that?"

Jeffrey frowned but kept silent.

Brian gulped the rest of his drink and strode after her through the crowd. He finally caught up with her in the hallway inside, rearranging flowers on a side table. She saw him and smiled—a forced smile.

He felt like he'd been punched in the stomach. *Why does she hate me now?* He blinked rapidly and found his voice. "I missed you at Grant's party."

She said nothing, glanced away with a strained look.

He took a step forward. "What is it? Why are you acting like this?"

Her head snapped back to focus on him, and her voice shook. "Did Grant send you here to try to convince me?"

"What? What are you talking about?"

She stared at him, and her anger melted away. She said softly, "You don't know." She grabbed his hand and glanced at Jeffrey who stood against the wall nearby. "Come upstairs with me, Brian."

He glanced over his shoulder. Jeffrey stayed where he was—the bedroom was about the only place security didn't follow. They hurried upstairs. Her wide skirts swooshed as she swept down the hall. She closed the bedroom door, then paced and wrung her hands. Finally blurted out, "Grant's trying to take my baby." Her face crumbled. She held it in her hands and sank onto the edge of the bed, sobbing.

Brian stood in shocked silence. *I don't understand.* Her sobs slowed, and she wiped her face. He asked, "What are you talking about? Tyler?"

She nodded. Bit her lip to stop the trembling.

"Grant's trying to take Tyler? But he's only two!"

"Three." She plucked at the comforter. "He's three. I really thought we had more time."

"I don't understand."

She reached out to stroke his hair. "There's nothin to understand. Grant wants my boy. My little Tyler." The tears came again.

He held her while she cried herself out, his mind reeling. *Why would Grant want a three-year-old boy? That was* much *too young for sex.*

She got up to splash water on her face and clean herself up, then came back to the bed where Brian sat, still bewildered. She took his hand and said, "Grant wants to raise him up there in that House. Thinks it's better for him than to be with his mama." Her lips tightened.

How can he think that? "You'll do the right thing. You're a good mother."

She hugged him and held him close. "Thank you."

He pulled back to look her in the eye. "Do you need money? I've got lots. Please—I want you to take it."

"Thank you, Brian, but no. I've been saving my money since I came here. I—" She cut herself off. "We'll be fine."

He knew she was holding back. *Of course she can't tell me her plans. I'm too close to Grant. And he's the Enemy to her.* He brought her hand to his lips. Kissed the back, the palm. She leaned over to meet his mouth.

She lay back and stretched her arms over her head. "I don't want to go back downstairs. Grace won't mind if we stay here awhile." She turned to look at him. "But I'm sure you wanna go have fun with some other women."

"No. I came here to see *you*, Michelle. I was worried about you."

She touched his chest. "You're so sweet. And here I was bein' rude to you. I'm sorry." A smile touched her lips. "I think you deserve a special treat." She picked up the phone from the bedside table. "Do you see Renee around? Could you send her to my room? Thanks."

She hung up and cuddled against him. Kissed his chest. "Look at you. You've grown so much. A year ago you were a boy. Now you're a young man." Her fingers traced the smooth skin, the toned muscles. "Bet you're gettin more female clients now."

He blushed and nodded. He'd gotten a new regular female client last week. Younger than Pat. *Maybe growing up isn't a bad thing.* He pulled Michelle closer to kiss her. Ran his hands over her soft skin. Kissed her harder and drew her down on top of him.

He heard the rustle of fabric and turned his head to see a dark-haired woman close the door. She sat on the edge of the bed and touched Michelle's bare back.

Michelle turned to unlace the woman's outer bodice, brushed her fingers along the exquisitely rounded flesh above the tight corset. The blood rushed to Brian's groin. The women's lips met, slow and long—the most beautiful thing. Michelle pulled the corset open to touch the nipple with her tongue.

He helped her pull off the rest of Renee's clothing. And then Michelle was on her back. Renee worked her way down. And stayed down as Michelle writhed and cried out.

Renee looked up at Brian and moved over to take him into her mouth. Michelle joined her, their tongues making patterns on his penis. His cock jerked, and he thought he would explode. Then Renee rolled a condom onto him and climbed on top. Slid him inside. Just for a moment. Just a taste.

Then she was off and Michelle took her place. He watched her lithe body arch as her warmth gripped him. Renee took Michelle's perfect breast into her mouth, and the waves crashed through his entire body.

And that was just the beginning.

Michelle tightened the laces of her corset. "I've been buggin' Grace to do the Southern ball theme for years. She always said no cos the clothes are so hard to get in and out of." She laughed as she struggled with the laces in the back. "I have to agree with that."

Brian tied them for her. It looked terribly uncomfortable, but he loved how the corsets pushed up their breasts. He watched the women touch as they helped each other dress. Beautiful. A most amazing night. Michelle took his hand. "I think we've stayed hidden up here long enough. Better get back to the party."

The three of them went downstairs together. Jeffrey still stood in the hallway. Brian couldn't keep the huge grin off his face. Jeffrey glanced at the two women and winked at him. "I see you been havin a good time."

"Oh, my god, Jeffrey. That was . . . *wow.*" Words could not describe it. "Wow."

Jeffrey's deep laugh filled the hall. "I'm with you on that." He put his arm around Brian's shoulders. "We better be goin. Mr. Grant wants you home early."

"Okay." He walked over to Michelle. Took her hand and whispered, "Give Tyler my love. I know you'll do the right thing." He ground his jaw to stop the tears. He had the distinct feeling he would never see her again. "Goodbye."

"You're quiet today," Leah said.

He shrugged and surveyed the condo from his seat on the couch. Weird to be there during the day. The living room seemed so bright. Mr. Padrea had fallen asleep right after their session, as usual. Gave Brian the chance to visit with Leah. It was good to see her outside his normal schedule; he was always glad when Grant gave him extra sessions here. *Grant.*

"Is something wrong?"

He looked down. "It's just . . . I love Grant, but sometimes I don't like him."

She held his chin. "What's he done?"

"I really can't talk about it." Leah looked worried. He explained, "He's not doing anything to *me*, but to someone I care about." He whispered, "Sometimes I really don't like him."

"Brian, I have something for you. Maybe this is a good time." She pulled a folded paper from the pocket of her chinos and handed it to him.

A phone number and a name.

"Emily Burns is a social worker. Please—hear me out," she said as he tried to hand the paper back. "I know you don't want to go back to your parents, and you probably have good reason. But Grant is not your only option. Mrs. Burns could set you up in a foster home. You could go to high school and live with a family. Be a normal kid. You don't have to stay with Grant."

He stared at the paper. *A foster home.* He'd never thought of that. But he couldn't imagine living with a family now. *It's too late. That's what I should've done when I got out of the institute. Maybe if I told the counselors about the knife thing they would have taken me away.* But he'd been too busy faking everything was fine so he could run away with River. *River. Things had to happen the way they did so we could be together. If I went to a social worker now, I'd not only risk being put back with my family, but losing River.* "I can't do that." He tried to give the paper to Leah.

She pushed his hand away gently. "Please, just keep it. Keep it and think about it."

He tucked it away to make her feel better.

He got home from Padrea's in time for dinner. He toyed with his lasagna and avoided looking across the table at Grant. But he had to when Grant put his hand on his.

Grant leaned forward. "How would you like a little brother?"

He blinked. "I would. But he should be with his mother."

Grant's eyebrows rose. He pursed his lips and pulled his hand away.

Brian blurted out, "He shouldn't be here. He's too young."

Grant's eyes turned cold. "Of course he's too young for sex. I want him here to bond with me—with *us*. With this House. We must plan for the future. There's no better way to ensure loyalty—just look at Matthew. He's lived in this House since he was five."

Brian kept his tone even and stared into Grant's eyes. "He should be with his mother."

"You're not with *your* mother."

His mouth fell open. "That's different. Michelle's a good mother."

"You really think a boy is better off surrounded by *women?*" His amber eyes flashed, and he took a deep breath. "That House is a brothel, too. How is that environment better?"

Brian leaned forward. "If Tyler is raised here, then he doesn't have a chance. He doesn't get a choice to do it or not to do it."

Grant's lips tightened. "You're letting your emotions cloud your judgment. You must learn to control that."

Brian clenched his fist. Nothing he could say would change Grant's mind. But he sure as hell wouldn't go along with it. *Wonder what he would do if he knew about the phone number in my pocket?* He stared into those cold eyes. *You don't know everything. You can't control everything.* He tried to keep the emotion out of his voice and spoke in a monotone. "May I be excused?" *I don't like you.*

ഇഇഇ

He sat on the short wall outside the band room with his arm around Claire. She said, "Come to the diner with us after band."

"Can't. I'm going to Stu's to practice."

"Oh." She pouted. "You're still coming to the party Saturday, right?"

"Yeah, if I can."

She leaned closer, so he kissed her. She jumped when Stuart's voice announced break was over, and her eyebrows lowered. "How long have you been standing there?"

"About two seconds."

"Oh." She brushed off her pants as she stood. "Well, you two have fun tonight," she said with an insincere tone. She stalked away into the band room alone.

"What's up with her?" Stuart asked.

Brian didn't know and didn't care. He couldn't get it out of his head—how Michelle had sobbed and sobbed. Because of Grant.

"You coming?"

Brian walked with him back inside. Walked with him again after band, to the parking lot. "I've never been over here." A large lot behind the soccer field, mostly empty. He climbed into Stuart's Pathfinder. "This is big."

"You like it?"

He looked down at the other cars. "Yeah. It's nice being up so high." That was the last thing he said until they reached Stuart's street.

"Something wrong, Brian?"

He shrugged.

"Wanna talk about it?"

Yes, but I can't. "Grant's being a dick."

"Parents suck sometimes. I mean, he's not really your parent, but—" Stuart stammered as he parked in front of the house.

"Yeah, parents suck," Brian said softly and got out of the car. He was relieved

Stuart's little brother wasn't around this time. Didn't want to deal with that.

They went to Stuart's room to get a new reed for his clarinet. Brian grimaced at the clothes and crap strewn around. "Hey, what's that?" The neck of a guitar poked up out of the mess. He made his way over to pull it out. It was bigger and heavier than his electric. "You play bass? I didn't know that. Play something." Brian handed it to him and sat on the bed. "Please?"

"Okay." Stuart moved a discarded pair of jeans to reveal an amplifier. He plugged in and tuned the strings, then played a phrase. A very familiar phrase.

Brian jumped up. "Joy Division—that's Joy Division! 'She's Lost Control.'"

"Yeah!" Stuart laughed.

"Oh, my god—I didn't know you like them." An epiphany struck him. A beautiful, crystalline idea, too exciting and delicate to share just yet.

He grinned as Stuart listed some of the groups he liked. Bowie, X, Concrete Blonde. "I like all of them, too!"

Stuart added, "And the Red Hot Chili Peppers—Flea is such an amazing bassist. He's my idol."

"What about The Cure?"

Stuart made a face. "Not really."

"What? How can you not like them? Where are your CDs?"

He pointed to a box. Brian sat on the floor to look through it. "Oh, I like this. And this." He picked up a CD case with two naked women on the cover. "Nice breasts."

"You like Jane's Addiction?"

"I don't know. Don't think I've heard them."

"They're on the radio all the time." Stuart dug through the box to find the other Jane's Addiction CD and slipped it into the stereo. He skipped to track six. "This is a great song."

Brian cleared a space on the floor, lay back and stared up at the ceiling. The music started slow with softly spoken words and a bass line for the melody. Built and changed and built again, swept him up in an emotional climax as he daydreamed about his new idea—forming a band with Stuart. He sat up when the song ended. "That was great! It's been so long since I heard new music I like."

"You can borrow it if you want."

"Thanks. I bet you can play that bass line, too. The one in the beginning."

Stuart played it.

Perfect. This is perfect. We could play this song. Cure songs. I could write songs. He was so thrilled he felt like he would burst.

Stuart held the bass guitar out to him. "Want to try it?"

"Sure." Brian played with it. The strings were much thicker than he was used to. But it was fun.

"You play guitar?"

He nodded and almost blurted out his idea. But not yet. He held it inside and savored it.

. . .

He felt like a kid as he walked up and down the aisles with Maria. He'd forgotten how many different kinds of cereal there were. He grabbed one that looked good. "Can we get this?"

He put it in the cart and followed her to another aisle. He grimaced as the chemical scent of cleansers hit him. "I'll wait over there."

He held his breath until he reached the end of the aisle where their driver stood. Brian watched the other shoppers. A woman struggling with three small children. An elderly couple. *I wonder if any of my clients shop here?*

A man caught his eye as Maria returned. Another of Grant's security. Brian pointed him out. She said, "Usually only one guard comes with me. Must be my special company." She squeezed his shoulder and smiled.

He smiled back. It felt good to be here, in a place where all kinds of people go. He glanced at the cart, and his heart skipped. "Bleach?" The blood drained from his face.

She patted his arm. "Don't worry, little niño, I know you are allergic. It is for the Wing, not the Main House."

But his heart was beating too fast, and his throat constricted. He backed away and turned to lean against the frozen food case.

Maria touched his shoulder. "Are you okay?"

He rested his forehead against the cool glass and struggled against the memory of his face plunged into a bucket of bleach. He tried to keep his eyes and mouth sealed shut against the burning liquid. But he ran out of air, and *I try to raise my head, but she's holding me down—I can't breathe—*

"Brian!"

He took a shaky breath and turned to see a worried face. Maria. He slowly remembered where he was. "I'm alright," he whispered.

She touched his cheek. "I'm so sorry." She turned to the guard. "Get rid of that bleach."

He wanted to tell her no, that's okay, but he couldn't bring himself to do it. He focused on the cool case against his back, the floor beneath his feet. Anchored himself in the present. "I'm okay." He pushed away from the glass door and shook his head. "Sorry."

"No, I'm sorry." She reached up to kiss his forehead. "I did not realize how sensitive your allergy is."

Me, neither. His heart pounded. *Don't think about it.* He looked for a distraction. "Oh, there's the liquor section." Claire had told him the party was 'byob,' then had to explain what that meant. *'Bring your own booze. Haven't you heard that? I thought you were a partier.'* He shrugged. *'I'm not a partier. But I can get the alcohol, no problem.'* She requested Miller beer in bottles. He picked up extra for Stuart, and selected vodka for himself. "Remind me to get cranberry juice to go with it."

Maria shook her head and muttered, "Little boys should not be putting vodka into the cart." She spoke louder. "Now you help me with the fruit." She led him to the produce section. "This is how you choose a grapefruit."

He picked one up and gave it a gentle squeeze. Hard but a little squishy, too. He held it to his nose. A faint sharp smell. A good smell. His fingers traced the slightly bumpy skin, so real and solid in his hands, and he smiled.

. . .

He stood in the dark waiting for Claire. No moon or stars tonight; smog or clouds obscured them. The air felt damp, finally getting cool now that it was November. He shivered as the breeze touched his bare stomach—he'd cut off the bottom of his Bauhaus tee shirt.

He lit a cigarette, as much for light and warmth as anything else. It glowed orangey red like a beacon in the darkness. He played with it, drew tracers in the air. Reminded him of acid. He wondered what drugs would be at the party.

He took a final drag and stubbed it out, then set the butt on a patch of dirt so he could pick it up later. Didn't like to litter out here among the grass and trees. The city was different—it was already dirty, was meant to be that way. But not here.

He heard a car and popped a mint into his mouth. Yep, her BMW. He picked up the grocery sacks of alcohol and got in. Claire looked great in a tight baby blue sweater. He kissed her, then sat back as they headed down the curves toward the city. "Stuart's excited about the party. Sorry I'm making you guys late."

He'd had an evening client—or rather, clients. Craig and Mary Andraide, a married couple. That was a bit weird. And quite gymnastic. It was great to have a female client, but it seemed a little twisted that a man wanted to watch another guy fuck his wife. Though Craig Andraide certainly did more than watch. *I do love the middle of the sandwich.*

A long, intense session. He'd accidentally fallen asleep afterward, but luckily woke up after twenty minutes. Bad timing for a session like that. It was still in his head every time he closed his eyes.

He watched Claire hum along to the radio, so opposite from what he'd been doing an hour ago. Innocent and pure. So different from all his clients. *And me.*

They pulled into the driveway of a house in Westwood, and a girl with long brown hair got in the backseat. Claire turned around. "Stuart, you know Debbie, don't you?"

"Sure. Third chair flute, right?"

"Yeah," said Debbie. "Are you the guy playing the duet with Brian?"

He nodded.

Claire said, "Nobody has a curfew, right, Stuart?"

"No. I don't think it occurred to my parents. They're just excited I'm going out."

She turned to Brian.

He shrugged. "As long as I'm not gone all night . . . ."

She smiled. "And I told my mom I'm spending the night at Debbie's. Which is true. I just didn't tell her I'm going to a party first." Claire pointed the car north on the freeway, crested the hill and headed down. "The party's at a house in the Valley."

Brian gazed at the new set of lights spread before him. "I've never been to the Valley."

"Really? How long have you lived here?"

"Three years, almost."

Debbie's indignant voice rose from the backseat. "Three years and you've never been to the Valley?"

Claire snorted. "I can hardly blame him. The Valley sucks."

"It does not!"

He said, "I went to San Marino once. Does that count?"

Claire glanced at him. "San Marino? That's the most expensive place to live in the whole country. What were you doing there?"

"I went to The Ritz-Carlton for tea." And to meet a prospective client. "That place is gorgeous. We should go sometime." He put his hand on her thigh. "Have dinner and get a suite for the night."

"Brian!" She sounded scandalized, but her warm hand rested on his.

Debbie cleared her throat. "Anyway, this party's a lot closer than that."

Fifteen minutes later they were looking for a place to park on the crowded street. It was easy to tell which house—the party spilled out onto the front lawn. Loud music and drunken voices greeted them as they walked up the street. They passed through the open door into a living room full of laughter and the smell of spilled beer. Clumps of teenagers stood around talking. Claire took Brian's arm. "Let's put the beer in the fridge."

Stuart and Debbie claimed the couch as a couple vacated it for the bedroom.

"I'm gonna get a refill." Brian stood. "Want anything?"

Stuart shook his head. Claire looked at the empty bottle in her hand. "I'm all out." She bounced up and leaned against him. "I'll come with you."

He put his arm around her waist, and they made their way to the kitchen. She watched him mix cranberry and vodka. "Can I try it?" She tasted it and made a face like she'd just bitten a lemon.

"Here, I'll make one with less vodka." He reached into the long cellophane bag on the counter for another Styrofoam cup. "You'll like it."

She sipped the new drink. "Mmm, that *is* good. Can't taste the alcohol at all!"

They returned to the couch where Debbie and Stuart were holding an awkward conversation. "Oh, I have something else." Brian reached into the purple velvet pouch he'd brought and pulled out three joints. He lit one and offered it to Claire.

She stared at it with wide eyes and shook her head. He held it up to Stuart, who said, "Naw, maybe next time."

Debbie also declined. Brian shrugged and passed it to the closest person, then lit the other two and did the same.

Debbie looked at Claire. "Come to the bathroom with me." The girls left.

Stuart said, "I think you shocked Claire."

"Huh?"

"The pot."

"But this is a party. Isn't that expected?"

Stuart shrugged. "I guess. But she seemed surprised."

One of the joints made its way back. Brian took a hit and held in the smoke. "Sure you don't want any?"

"Not now. I don't want my first time smoking pot to be at a party full of strangers."

He exhaled and nodded. "I can see that. Maybe some other time—just the two of us."

"Yeah, okay."

They grinned at each other. Brian took another hit before he passed the joint back into the crowd. "I still don't understand why Claire is upset. *Is* she upset? I'm confused." He covered his face with his hands and shook his head. Laughed at his dizziness.

"I think it's because she's *with* you, you know, but she didn't know you smoke that."

There's a lot she doesn't know. "Then I guess I shouldn't share this." He reached into the bag again to pull out a white ceramic cylinder with blue flowers painted on it. He unscrewed the lid and showed Stuart. "Coke."

Stuart's eyes got huge behind his glasses. "No, you definitely shouldn't let her see that."

"But it's a party." He screwed the lid back on. "Wanna do some? We could go in the bathroom or something."

"No. No, thanks." Stuart waved his hands. "Not interested."

He shrugged. "Okay." He put it back in the bag.

Silence settled between them. Stu took a swig of beer and said, "Why do you work such unpredictable hours?"

"Uh . . . ." His blurred mind struggled to come up with a safe answer. "We, uh, have to accommodate our clients' schedules."

"Clients?"

"Yeah . . . to buy the artwork and stuff." He bit his lip to stop his grimace at the lie.

"Oh. Sounds pretty cool."

He gave a short laugh. "It's fun sometimes."

"How's Grant? Is he still being a dick?"

Brian sipped his drink. "Haven't seen him much lately. He's busy a lot. But yeah, I'm still mad at him."

"Don't you hate that?"

"Yeah. I love him, but sometimes I don't *like* him."

Stuart nodded. "I know what you mean."

He does. They smiled at each other.

The girls returned. He put his arm around Claire and nuzzled into her neck. "Are you mad at me?"

"No, sweetie." She cupped his cheek in her hand and kissed him, then reached for her drink. "This is so good! Can I have another?"

"Sure." He got up and made eye contact with a cute guy on the way to the kitchen. A football player-type. *I'd swear that was a look.*

He smiled at the naked image in his mind as he mixed another drink for Claire. Made himself one, too. He carried them out of the kitchen but didn't see the football guy again. *Damn.* He made it back to the couch without spilling and sat down. Drained his old cup and grimaced. Mostly vodka at the bottom. "I gotta stir these better." He lit a cigarette.

Naked in the Rain

A loud voice rose above the noise of the party. "Yeah, he's some kind of Goth boy. Thinks he's so cool."

He looked up at the older teenager standing a few feet away. The football guy he'd just made eye contact with. Brian raised an eyebrow. *Guess I was wrong.*

The guy folded his arms across his chest, acting tough with his friends flanking him on either side. "That's *you* I'm talking about. Whatcha gonna do about it?"

Brian laughed and took a drag. "Do you really think you can intimidate me? Because you're wrong."

The guy seemed at a loss for a retort; then the party host ushered the troublemakers away. They grumbled but allowed themselves to be herded into another room. Brian shook his head. "What an idiot."

Claire huffed. "Jerk! I'd like to kick his ass."

They all laughed. Brian tapped cigarette ashes into his empty cup. "What did he mean, Goth boy? What is that?"

"Goth, you know," Stuart said. "Your black clothes and black nails and black hair. Don't people ever give you trouble?"

"No." *Why should they?* "People are weird."

"I'll drink to that." Stuart raised his bottle.

Claire drained her cup, then started in on Brian's drink. She leaned against him. "You really weren't afraid of those guys, were you?"

"No." It was true. *Guess it takes more to scare me these days.*

"You're so brave." She ran her hand down his chest. Her warm fingers touched his bare stomach, and she leaned closer to murmur, "I've never wanted anyone the way I want you."

He stared at her a moment in surprise, then kissed her. Her heated response got him hard fast. He whispered, "Have you ever had an orgasm?"

"Brian!" She sat back with big eyes and hissed, "I'm a virgin."

He smiled and touched her cheek. The thought of giving her her first orgasm made him dizzy. "Want to go to the bedroom?"

"We shouldn't."

"I won't do anything you don't want. I just want to be alone with you." He spoke in her ear. "I just want to touch you." He brushed his lips against her neck.

She stared into his eyes. "Promise we won't have sex."

I don't need to do that to make you come. His breath sped up. "I promise."

"Okay."

He took her hand and stood, then put his arm around her to steady her. Debbie looked up. "Where are you going?"

Claire said in a loud whisper, "To the bedroom."

Debbie stood up. "Oh, no, you're not. Brian O'Dell, you are *not* taking advantage of my best friend. She's drunk."

"I'm not taking advantage. We just want privacy."

They started to walk away, but Debbie held onto Claire's arm. "Please don't."

Claire shook free of her grip. "Leave me alone. I'm a big girl."

Debbie covered her face as they walked away. Stuart guided her back to the couch. "Don't worry, Brian's a good guy. He won't do anything Claire doesn't want."

"But she's drunk. She has a hard time saying no to him when she's sober. She's in love—that's a secret, by the way."

"Then what's the problem?"

"She's not ready! She shouldn't be drunk her first time." She shook her head. "I just know she's going to get hurt."

Brian reappeared and plopped down on the couch with a loud sigh.

"What happened?" they exclaimed.

His mouth twisted in a wry smile. "She passed out as soon as she hit the bed."

Debbie laughed. Stuart patted Brian's arm. "Bummer."

"Yeah."

Debbie stood up. "I'm gonna check on her."

Stuart waited until she was out of ear shot. "Guess things are going pretty well with you two."

"Yeah, but it's hard to wait. She wants to go so slow. Unless she's drunk."

"That's normal for girls." He snorted. "Or so I hear."

"Haven't you . . . ?"

Stuart glanced away with a frown. "I've never even been on a date."

"Have you kissed?"

He looked embarrassed. "I *want* to, but girls don't dig me."

"Maybe you just need to try harder."

Debbie reappeared and went to chat with another group of people. Stuart shook his head. "See what I mean? She's avoiding me like the plague."

"Do you like her?"

"Yeah. She's pretty. Don't you think so?"

"Sure, she's just not my type. Probably the brown hair—reminds me of my sister."

"You have a sister? I didn't know that."

He picked up his cup and stared into it. "Yeah."

Stuart asked gently, "Do you get to see her?"

"No."

"Not at all? Why not?"

He gulped the rest of his drink. "Because she's with my parents. I don't see them."

"Not at all since you stopped living with them? How long has it been?"

"Three years."

"Jesus, Brian. That's a long time."

He grimaced into his cup. Stared at the drops of dark red liquid at the bottom. *I wonder what she looks like now? She's eighteen.* He crushed the cup in his fist. *It's not fair—not fair I can't see my sister. Because of my fucking mother. I hate her.*

"You okay?"

He shrugged and struggled to keep the emotions at bay.

After a moment Stuart said, "Did you finish those *Hitchhiker* books?"

Brian smiled at the obvious change in subject and cleared his throat. "Yeah. They were fun. I like the first one best, though."

"Me, too."

"So you like Debbie?"

Stuart's lips curved in a shy smile. "Yeah. What do I do?"

"I dunno. Ask her out."

He shook his head. "I don't think she likes me."

Different music came on. They turned to each other and said simultaneously, "I love this song."

Brian leaned forward. "I had the best idea. We should form a band!"

"A band? With guitars and stuff?"

"Yeah."

"Yeah—that would be awesome! You on guitar, me on bass. Who'll sing?"

Brian shrugged. "I can sing. I mean, good enough, anyway."

"Great! This is gonna be great." Stu bounced on the couch. "What should our name be?"

"I don't know. We'll have to think about it."

They spent an hour talking about how soon they could start, what songs they would cover, coming up with silly ideas for a name. Debbie walked over and stood with her hands on her hips. "We should go soon. It's getting late."

"Okay." Stuart stood up. "I gotta use the bathroom first."

Debbie went back to her other friends, and the football player guy wandered through on his way to the kitchen. Brian got up, steadied himself against the couch and followed him, though he didn't know what he expected to accomplish. He found the guy alone getting a bottle of beer out of the fridge.

"Well, lookee here. Our own little Goth boy." His eyes flicked over Brian's body.

Brian didn't respond. *I swear he wants me. Am I just drunk and crazy?*

"What's the matter, cat got your tongue?"

Brian leaned back against the counter and gave him a slow smile.

The guy came closer and towered over him. "You wanna step outside?"

"Sure." *I hope he doesn't beat me up.*

They stepped out the back door into the cold dark. The yard was mostly deserted, just a few scattered drunks, the sound of retching in the bushes. The football guy staggered toward the side of the house, and Brian followed him around the corner.

The guy stopped suddenly and turned. Brian almost ran into him, came to a stop inches away and looked him up and down. Thick neck. Thick body.

"What're you doin'?" the guy slurred.

"Nothing." Brian laid his palm on the wide chest and slid his hand down.

"I'll show *you*."

"Mmm." He reached between the guy's legs and said in a low voice, "I bet you will."

The only response was heavy breathing. Brian unzipped the guy's pants and went down on his knees. Toyed with him a moment before he took the hard shaft into his mouth.

"Aaahhh." Beer spilled onto the wet grass as the bottle fell from his hand.

. . .

Brian stepped back inside and walked through the kitchen alone, into the living room.

Debbie was livid. "Where have you been?"

He stuck his hands in his pockets and shrugged. "Wanted some fresh air."

"Fresh air? We're trying to leave—you'll have plenty of fresh air." She hit his arm. "Come on, help us with her."

They managed to get Claire semi-conscious and walked her to the car. Stuart got behind the wheel. Brian fell into the front seat beside him. "How's Claire gonna get her car back?"

Stuart said, "She'll have to call me tomorrow, and we'll work something out. Debbie, I'll give you my number, okay?"

He and Brian exchanged looks. *Good move, Stu.*

Debbie leaned forward. "Are you sure you're okay to drive?"

"Yeah, I only had two beers. Besides, I'm the only one here with a license who's also conscious."

"Good point." Brian pointed at him. "God, I'm wasted." He leaned his head back, and the world spun.

They dropped the girls off at Debbie's house. Brian watched Claire stagger inside. "She's gonna be sick tomorrow. Hope she's not mad at me."

"Why would she be? It's not like you forced her to drink vodka."

Stuart aimed the BMW down Sunset Boulevard, mostly deserted at this hour. Brian showed him where to turn to head into the Hollywood Hills and guided him through the maze of turns. They reached the usual corner. "You can drop me off here."

"But there's no house."

"It's just up the hill."

"Why don't I drive you to it?"

"Well, there's gates . . . ."

"I could at least drive you that far. It's stupid to get out here."

He wracked his brain for a reason why Stuart shouldn't drop him at the gate. He couldn't come up with one. "Okay."

Stuart stopped the car in front of the huge wrought iron gate. "Wow." He squinted. "I can't see past it in the dark."

"You can't see anything in the daytime, either."

"Man, that must be some house in there. If Grant's so rich, why do you have to work?"

He shrugged and got out of the car. He really didn't have an answer for that.

"Tommy played piano like a kid out in the rain . . .

*I don't mind the sun sometimes
the images it shows
I can taste you on my lips and smell you in my clothes
Cinnamon and sugary and softly spoken lies"*

- Butthole Surfers, "Pepper"

ᚱᚢ CHAPTER 28 ᚱᚢ

Jeffrey held the car door open for him.

"No, I'll sit up front." Brian opened the door himself and got in. No outing after band today—he had a client. Just enough time to get home and shower. He fiddled with the radio as Jeffrey drove down Sunset Boulevard.

Jeffrey said, "You made an impression on Mr. Grant—he does listen to you. He sent a compromise over to Jasmine Lane."

Brian sat up. "What compromise?"

"He's offered for Ms. Michelle to come live with us—in the Other Wing, of course."

"Really? With Tyler?"

"No, Mr. Grant wants him in the Main House. But he ain't gonna have no woman livin that close."

"What about Maria?"

"That's different. She's a servant. He don't think of her as a woman."

He bit his nail. *It's not good enough.*

Jeffrey said, "That's a big deal, Mr. Grant offerin to let a woman into his House. She's been stubborn, and Jasmine Lane supports her. But he's real determined to have that boy."

I bet. But she doesn't want Tyler growing up here. I wouldn't either. "She'll do the right thing."

Jeffrey grunted and glanced at him. "And what *is* the right thing?"

He shrugged and stared out the window.

A bulging envelope caught Michelle's eye as she walked into her bedroom, her name written on the outside in unfamiliar handwriting. Her face drew down. *Grant again.* She ripped it open, and cash spilled out onto the bed. Anger surged through her as she picked up a five hundred dollar bill. *He can't buy my baby from me.*

Two pieces of paper lay folded among the bills. One was just a phone number and name. 'Emily Burns.' The other was a note. She glanced at the signature. Her anger drained away and left sadness in its place.

November 12*th*

Dearest Michelle,
I thought you might need this phone number more than I. She's a social worker. I hope she can help.
You're a good mother—I know you will do what's right. Please accept this money for little Tyler. I wish I could do more. Good luck.

Love,
Brian

She clutched the note to her chest and whispered, "Thank you, Brian."

ת ת ת

Claire settled on the hood of her BMW and shivered. Brian held her closer and tore his gaze from the city lights to brush his lips along her neck. He felt her intake of breath and worked his way up to her mouth. And they didn't feel the cold anymore. He lowered her onto the hood and rubbed his body against hers as they kissed harder. His crotch against hers. *God.*

His hands slid beneath her clothes to touch her breasts through the bra. He lifted her shirt, and she raised her arms to let it slide off. Then she took off her bra. Gorgeous, sweet little breasts. She reached up to unbutton his shirt, pushed it off his shoulder, and her warm fingers slid along his bicep.

He pulled it off the rest of the way, then touched her nipple with the palm of his hand to rub it back and forth. Her body arched. So small and lithe—reminded him of a cat.

His mouth moved to her other nipple. Played with it a long time. So wonderful in his mouth, he couldn't stop. His hand ran down her smooth stomach to slip beneath her pants. His fingers grazed curly hairs and kept going. Felt her wetness. He moaned and touched her clitoris. A beautiful sigh came from her throat. She gripped his arm, and her hips pushed against him.

He played with her awhile, then reached back further and slid inside. So warm and wet. She gasped and clutched his back as he moved in and out, pressing his hand against her clit with each stroke. She was moaning nonstop. He took her nipple into his mouth again. Then kissed her face. Watched her orgasm build. *Her first.* His groin tightened almost unbearably as she writhed beneath him, her cries loud in the stillness. He felt the muscle contractions around his finger as her hips lifted off the car.

He left his finger there while he kissed her, caught the stray pulse around it as she held onto him. His lips moved to her throat, her chin, her cheek.

She gazed up into his incredible eyes, scarcely able to form a thought, save one. *I love you, Brian O'Dell.* She didn't say it out loud—wanted him to say it first. *I know he does.*

She realized after a moment he was breathing harder than her. She trailed her hand down his chest, and her gaze followed. His thing was out—sticking straight out from his body. She blinked, too relaxed to feel alarmed. She'd never seen one in person before. It looked big. "Want me to . . . ?"

He nodded.

Her hand stopped at the hard muscle below his bellybutton. "I don't know what to do."

"I'll help you," he breathed and rolled onto his back.

Weird how it stood up so stiff. She let her hand move closer and touched the shaft with her fingertips. Warm, like the rest of him. She explored, traced her fingers down and around. Gripped it when he told her to. It felt strange in her hand. The skin was soft, yet so hard underneath. *How can it be so hard?*

She rubbed her thumb on the tip, where it was a different shape. His breath caught, and a little sound came from his throat. She liked that.

"Your hand should be wet. Here." He reached into his pocket, then pushed his jeans down farther.

He ripped open a little packet with his teeth and squeezed the contents onto her hand. Like moisturizer, but more slippery. Her brain was too full of other things to wonder about it for long. He lay back and put her hand on his penis. Showed her how to move it up and down, slick with the stuff from the packet. "Grip it harder. Yeah." He arched back. His breathing changed.

Wow.

"Twist your hand a little, like this." He covered her hand with his, made it go faster. Faster. "Aah." His back arched, and a stream of creamy liquid shot up into the air.

She jumped back, then giggled a little. "I wasn't expecting that."

He breathed a laugh and kept her hand going a moment longer, then pulled her down to kiss her. Murmured, "That was wonderful."

She cuddled against him, and her dazed mind replayed the last few minutes. *I never imagined anything like that.* She'd only let one other guy down her pants, and that had been totally different. Poor guy didn't know where anything was. Not like Brian—not like Brian at all. *Experienced.* She felt a jealous pang but dismissed it quickly. *Those girls are in his past. He's all mine now.*

Brian set his guitar on Stuart's bed and switched off the amp. "I gotta use the bathroom."

They'd been playing for hours, figuring out different songs—Joy Division, Bowie, he'd even convinced Stuart to play a Cure tune. It was incredible, like playing with Jeffrey, except it was the songs he'd loved for years. And it was Stuart. The bass guitar gave the music a different dynamic. Stuart was good. After the Bowie song they'd improvised and jammed for twenty minutes.

Brian smiled into the bathroom mirror as he washed his hands. *Next time I'll bring something I wrote.* He stepped into the hall, and a man's voice called out, "Stuart? Come here a minute, son."

Brian froze. *I'm not Stuart. Can I just ignore him?*

"Stu?"

That would be rude. He moved toward the voice and stopped at the end of the hall to stare at the man standing beside the dining room table. Their gaze met, and he melted into warm brown eyes. Dark hair and a bright, kind smile.

"You must be Brian." The man walked over to him. "I'm Ted, Stuart's father."

Brian shook his hand in a daze and tried to ignore the way his blood rushed from the touch. *He's Stuart's dad. Calm down. You can't have him.* He imagined running his lips over the rough skin of Ted's jaw.

"You two sound great in there. Are you having fun?"

He nodded.

"We'd love you to stay for dinner. I just started pasta."

Brian shook his head and found his voice. "I—I can't, thanks. I have to get home." He turned and raced back to Stuart's room. Started packing up his stuff.

"Hey, why are you leaving all of a sudden?"

"Sorry, I didn't realize how late it is. Grant . . . wants me home for dinner." *Lie. That's a lie. He doesn't care.*

"Oh. Too bad. Here, take this book." Stu shoved a thick paperback into his hand.

He muttered a thanks and headed out. Tried not to look at luscious Ted standing in the kitchen doorway.

Brian had an unexpected treat when he got home—River was sitting on his bed petting Schnookie. "River!" Brian threw himself on him and pushed him back against the bed. "If I'd known you were here," he said between kisses, "I would've come home sooner."

"I just got here." He sucked on Brian's tongue. "I can stay till midnight." Their deadline when River had a morning client. River's warm fingers reached under the sweater to pull it over Brian's head. The rest of their clothes followed as quickly as they could manage.

Afterward he lay in River's arms until his brain started working again. He sat up. "Did you hear what happened with Michelle?" He smiled. "She won. Jeffrey told me in the car on the way home. He said, 'Watch out for Mr. Grant. He's in a foul mood today.' Because Michelle left. She took Tyler and she left."

He didn't tell River the rest of the conversation. Brian had asked, '*Now what happens? Will Grant go after her?*'

'*Oh, no. It's over. Mr. Grant gotta obey the Voluntary Rule just like everybody else. If he breaks it, then other folks could, too. But he don't like losin. Ms. Michelle's outta reach now, but he'll take it out on someone. Jasmine Lane's got some tough times ahead of em.*'

She'll be alright. "I knew she would do the right thing."

Midnight came sooner than seemed possible, as it always did. He stood on the porch and watched River get into the car. Tried to ignore the soul-wrenching feeling he always got when River left.

He sighed and mounted the stairs slowly. When he reached the top he looked toward Grant's rooms. *I should see how he's doing. Maybe he could use some company.* He opened the door quietly and walked through to the bedroom.

He paused in the doorway and realized Grant wasn't alone—a naked boy slept in his arms. The kid was only vaguely familiar. *I don't even know who lives in the Other*

Wing anymore. He's so young. Probably new. It seemed weird, the young boy lying with the old man.

He thought of Stuart's brother and turned away. Stopped as it hit him—*Grant never initiates sex with me anymore.* He gripped the doorframe. *It's okay. He still loves you. He won't make you leave*—he promised.

He walked down the dark hallway. *He said my clientele would change, and it has. More women now. That's a good thing. It's good.* He crawled into bed and hugged Schnookie close.

He woke to a pounding headache. Nausea washed through him when he tried to sit up. He lay back and clutched his head. *Shit.* He managed to reach the intercom button.

Two minutes later Grant was sitting on the edge of his bed with a cold washcloth. "Where are your pills?"

"I don't have anymore. I ran out."

"I'll call Dr. Griffin."

"Wait." Brian grabbed his arm. "I don't want those pills—Demerol. Can I get a different kind? Please." *Please.*

"Alright, Brian. My poor boy." He leaned down to kiss his cheek. "I love you."

ಬಬಬ

The first thing he noticed when Claire answered the door was that she wasn't wearing a bra. He said, "Are you sure your mom won't catch me here?"

She took his hand and pulled him inside. "I'm sure."

She showed him around the house. Bigger than Stuart's. Clean and neat. Sterile. It didn't look lived in. *Must be lonely here by herself.* He followed her into the bedroom. Ah, this was better. A few posters, schoolbooks scattered on the floor. It smelled like her. He sat beside her on the bed and nuzzled into her hair.

She pushed him away. "Come on, you have to help me, or I'll never win."

"Is that really why you invited me over? I thought you wanted to mess around." He wouldn't see her again her for several days—she was spending Thanksgiving with her grandparents. He patted the comforter. "We've got a bed and everything."

She smiled. "We need to do this first. I want to win." She'd challenged Debbie for third chair flute. "Just help me for half an hour, okay? Then we'll have fun."

She got out her flute and ran through the piece. He let her finish, then pointed out her first mistake. "You're not hitting all the notes on that run."

She sighed.

"Go slow at first. Play it over and over until you get it right every time. It's not that hard."

"It's not hard for *you*. You're so talented, Brian. Why don't you challenge for first chair?"

"I don't want to be first chair. I don't have to always be Number One. I don't want the responsibility. Besides—" He smiled at her. "If you win the challenge, we'll get to sit next to each other."

She smiled back. "That's true." She turned to the music and played the run slowly, over and over until she got it down, then went on.

He stopped her. "You keep making the same mistake there."

She frowned. "I know."

"The problem is, the music's in your head with the mistake. You need to change the way you think about it. Hear it in your mind the right way. If you *think* you'll make a mistake, then you *will*. It's all mental. May I?" He borrowed her flute and played the phrase a few times. "Now keep that in your head when you play it—*don't* think about making a mistake."

It worked. She laughed and touched his arm. "You should be a teacher." She made it through the rest of the piece. "You were right. It's not really that hard—I just needed to practice more."

"That was good." He squeezed her hand and tried to sound casual. "Don't you think Debbie and Stuart would make a cute couple?"

"What?"

"Well, you know . . . they're both single. We could go on double dates."

She shook her head. "Oh, Brian. No."

"Why not?"

"Honey, Stuart's nice, but . . . he's kind of a geek."

"He is not!"

"You're a guy—I don't expect you to understand. But there's no way Debbie's gonna go out with him."

"Are you saying Stuart's not good enough for her?"

"No." She touched his cheek. "I didn't mean it like that. But trust me. It's not going to happen."

She kissed him until he forgot about being upset. He pushed her back against the bed.

"I brought you something." Brian opened the tinfoil.

"Ooo, chocolate chip cookies." Leah picked one out of the pile. "Who made these?"

"I did." He grinned. "With River yesterday—but he just watched."

"Mmm." Soft and chewy. "Great job. You made these without any help?"

He nodded. "First time by myself. But I knew what to do. I help Maria sometimes and . . . I used to help my mom. When I was little she'd set me up on the counter so I could reach. I held the eggs for her. I remember I tried to warm them up so they'd hatch. Never worked, of course." He laughed.

She gazed into those bright blue eyes with a touch of sadness behind the laughter and reached out to brush hair away from his face. "You're so sweet." It was almost unbearable when her brain put it together with what he did for a living. She had to look away.

"Leah, do you ever want to have kids?"

"Yes. Someday."

"That's good. You should."

A lump formed in her throat. She used his empty glass as an excuse to get up and took her time pouring more milk. Got her emotions under control. "So. How are things going with Claire?"

His eyebrow quirked as he took the glass. "*Great*. I think we'll have sex soon."

"Really?"

"Yeah. We've done just about everything else. And she let me into her bedroom today. We have hours before her mom gets home." He sipped his milk and looked thoughtful. "I think next time I'll go down on her."

Leah choked on her cookie.

"Sorry. Too much information?"

"No, that's okay." She cleared her throat. "I hope you're planning to use birth control when the time comes. Like condoms."

"Oh, I always use condoms. They work for birth control, too?"

"Yes, although nothing is a hundred percent." She studied him a moment. "Do you understand how women get pregnant?"

He shrugged. "Pretty much."

"That doesn't sound good enough."

"I stopped going to school before the sex ed stuff. But I know the basic idea. I know babies come from intercourse."

She nodded.

"But . . . I don't really understand how it happens."

"Would you like me to explain it to you?"

He gave her a shy smile and nodded.

"Come on, let's get more comfortable. Bring your delicious cookies." They settled on the couch, and she explained about the sperm in his semen, how they swim to fertilize an egg in the woman. How the comfy nest in a woman's body comes out every month if she doesn't get pregnant. She talked about some of the symptoms that come with it. "It's called a period or menstruating."

"Oooh. I've heard of that, but I never knew what it was." It clicked. "That's why Claire didn't want me to touch her last week. She said it was 'her time,' but I didn't know what she meant." He was thrilled to finally understand it.

Leah smiled. "I'll get you a book on all that stuff, okay? And how about a book on puberty, while we're at it?"

He smiled back. "Thanks."

"One more thing, Brian. Have you been with a virgin before?"

"I don't think so . . . oh, I was Brett's first—oops!" He covered his mouth with his hand, appalled he let a client's name slip.

But she didn't seem to notice. "I mean a *woman* who's a virgin."

He thought a moment. "No."

"The first time for a woman can be a little painful, and she'll probably bleed."

"What?"

She explained about the hymen and how it was different for each woman. "So don't expect her first time to be like what you're used to, okay? Be gentle with her."

He nodded, suddenly not quite so eager.

※ ※ ※

Brian laid his guitar down. "Are you sure your mom won't be home soon?"

Stuart nodded. "She'll be gone all day—she likes to hit the sales after Thanksgiving. Why does it matter?"

He shrugged. "Parents make me nervous."

That's why he freaks out and takes off sometimes, Stu realized. *It's not me. It's my parents.* "That's kind of sad, Brian. Not all parents are bad, you know."

Brian glanced at him, then looked away. Fiddled with the amp. "Did you find us a drummer?"

"Maybe. A drummer from the Youth Band, Roger. Do you know him?"

"Nope."

"Me neither, but he has a drum kit. We can talk to him at band on Wednesday."

"Yeah, okay," Brian said. "Then all we need is a mike. Maybe we could get one today. There's a music shop on Melrose—and you'll love the CD store."

"Phil's?"

"Yeah! I used to go there all the time."

Stuart grinned. "I love that place. Let's go." *I want to hear you sing—what if you're no good? What'll I say?*

They put the new microphone and CDs in the back of Stuart's Pathfinder. It was a lovely day—cool and breezy, but sunny. "I haven't been here in a long time," Brian said. "Let's walk around." He tucked his hands into the pockets of his leather pants and smiled. "Pretty Christmas decorations." Pine garlands with wreaths arched across the road.

"*Holiday* decorations, you mean."

"Huh?"

"I'm Jewish. We don't celebrate Christmas."

"Oh, right. Sorry."

"I don't really care." Stu smiled. "I just like to give you a hard time."

"I don't understand why it matters, anyway. I'm not a Christian, but I'm not offended by Christmas. I *like* Christmas."

Stuart laughed. "Good. Come on, let's go." He indicated the Dr. Martens store at the end of the block.

"Hold on." Brian went over to the large black man who followed at a short distance. "Jeffrey, do you have my sunglasses? Thanks." He put on the dark Ray-bans and walked back to Stuart.

Stu nodded toward the bodyguard. "He doesn't exactly blend in."

"He's not supposed to. Oh, that's pretty." He stopped to look in the window of a clothing shop.

Stuart pushed his glasses up and peered in. "I wonder if Debbie would like that. Should I get her a present?"

"Uh, no. I don't think you and Debbie are right for each other. She's kind of . . . shallow."

Stu grimaced. "She said something, didn't she."

"No!"

"Yes, she did. She thinks I'm a nerd. *Every*one thinks I'm a nerd." He stared at the gawky figure reflected in the window. "That's because I am."

"No, you're not."

"Brian, come on. Look at you in your leather pants and sunglasses. You're the epitome of cool. The two of us together must be a funny sight."

"Stop it. You're a great guy."

"You don't know what it's like to be an outcast, to have no friends."

"Yes, I do. Until I joined the band and met you I didn't have *any* friends. Except River."

"Really?" Stuart let that sink in. "River's a neat name. I bet he's a cool guy, too."

Brian smiled. "He's wonderful."

Stuart frowned at his reflection. "And then there's me." He leaned back against the glass with a sigh. "I'm hopeless."

"You are not."

"Then help me. What do I do to be like you?"

"You don't want to be like me. But . . . ." Brian paced and tapped his teeth with his fingernail, then stopped to face him. "It's the glasses. You've gotta get rid of those glasses."

"I know—I hate them! But my parents won't let me get new ones. They say it's a waste of money cos my eyes haven't changed."

"What about contacts?"

"Same thing."

"Why don't *you* pay for it, then?"

"They still won't let me."

"Why not? They're *your* eyes. Are they trying to torture you? Fuck that. That's ridiculous."

He stared at the sidewalk and shrugged. "Yeah."

"You should get contacts or new glasses or whatever you want. Fuck your parents."

Stu looked up with a fierce gaze. "Yeah. I *will* get contacts. Fuck my parents."

Brian laughed. "Good."

Stuart walked on with a new sense of freedom. His pace picked up as they approached the Dr. Martens store. Brian encouraged him to try on a pair of the big black boots and said, "They look good. They really do."

Stuart stared at the mirror, amazed that it was true. His face fell. "I can't. I need to save my money for contacts."

"I'll buy the boots for you."

"No, Brian. That's not right."

"Oh, come on." He tugged on Stuart's sweater. "They'll be my Christmas—I mean, Hanukkah—present to you. Please." Brian put his hands on his hips. "Don't make me beg."

Stuart wore them home.

Brian followed him in with the mike stand and heard a woman's voice say, "Oh, my, look at those boots."

Brian stopped in his tracks.

"I see you boys have been shopping, too. You must be Brian."

She left the kitchen doorway and loomed closer. Tall and thin with bushy dark hair and glasses. A kind smile. He tried to smile back. *She's just a person, like Leah.*

Just because she's Stuart's mom doesn't make her bad. He clutched the metal rod.

"Come on." Stuart pulled on his arm, and they made it to the bedroom. "Are you okay?"

"It's just . . . I haven't seen anyone's mom in a long time." He bit his lip and stared at the carpet. Fought the urge to leave—he really wanted to try out the mike.

Stuart squeezed Brian's shoulder.

Brian ground his jaw and tossed his head. "Let's get started." He set the mike stand on the floor. "We need to clear some space in here. Stuart, you are *so* messy. How can you stand it?"

"That's what my mom says."

Brian threw him a look with narrow eyes.

"Sorry."

He didn't say a word, just focused on setting up the mike. He held up a cord. "Where did he say this goes?"

Stuart helped him. They set the mike on the stand and flipped the switch. "Testing." Brian grinned. "Hey, it works! First try an' all."

Stuart grinned back. "What do you want to sing first?"

"Um, I have some lyrics for that song I wrote. I'd kinda like to sing that, even though it's not finished."

They picked up their instruments and launched into the intertwining notes. Brian let out a throaty growl that turned into a rich, ascending note, stretching the word,

"I . . . feel my face pulling me down.
See the blood on the carpet, blood on the door."

Stuart almost forgot to play. *And I was worried he couldn't sing.*

"I've made it an art
Not to think about it—
Think about what?
Does she even
think about me?
you hold me tighter, and I can't breathe
you . . . smother me."

Brian stopped. "I want to try something different. Let's start over."

"Your voice—you sound . . . like a black man."

"Really?" He grinned. "Thanks."

They started again. Worked on it for awhile, then Brian set the guitar against the bed and reached into his pocket to check his watch. "I've got a client later. I have to go soon."

"Why don't you just *wear* your watch?"

"It bothers my scar."

"What scar?"

Brian rolled his eyes. "The one time someone didn't notice I had to point it out." He shook his head. "I just assumed you'd seen them."

"What?"

"These." He held up his wrists.

Stuart's eyes bugged, his brain numb for a moment. His voice came out in a whisper. "When . . . ?"

"A long time ago. I was just a kid. I didn't know what life had to offer."

"Why?"

He avoided Stuart's gaze. "I couldn't . . . stand to live there anymore. I didn't know what else to do. I couldn't take it—" His voice caught. He turned abruptly and started putting his guitar away. "I should go. I can't be late."

"Brian—"

"I'll leave the mike here, if that's okay with you."

"*Brian.*" Their eyes finally met. Pain lurked behind that blue, deep inside. Reminded Stuart of a wounded animal. Stu took him into his arms and hugged him.

Brian and Stuart sat on the Berber carpet while their new drummer, Roger, went for a bathroom break. There was nowhere else to sit—no furniture. Roger's parents had been in the process of converting the detached garage into a guest house when they divorced. Now it stood empty, with carpet, painted walls and a sliding glass door, but nothing else. A perfect rehearsal space.

Brian said, "While he's gone, I thought of a name for the band—but if you don't like it, say so. We should agree."

"Okay. What is it?"

"Pandora's Box."

"Hmm." Stuart pulled on his lower lip. "I like that. Kinda mysterious." He stood and faced Brian with a solemn expression. "Welcome to the first rehearsal of Pandora's Box." He bowed.

Brian laughed and bowed to Stu as Roger came back in.

Roger's mother pointed to a small detached building. "In there."

Claire thanked her and headed across the neatly trimmed lawn. The sound of drums and guitar grew louder as she neared the building. And a voice. She opened the sliding glass door and watched Brian belt it out with all his heart. *I should have known he'd have a beautiful voice.*

His cheeks were flushed, eyes closed. So exciting, how he got completely lost in the music, the way his body moved, the way she could feel emotions emanate from him. Made her want him even more. His eyes opened, and he flashed her a smile. Her heart soared.

The song ended, and he came over to kiss her. "We just have one more to play. Then I'll be ready to go, okay?"

She grinned at him and nodded. Would've said yes to anything at that moment.

They played another song with blatantly sexual lyrics. He stared at her the whole time. Made her feel warm deep inside. He strummed the last chord and said into the mike, "Thus ends the first rehearsal of Pandora's Box." He and Stuart bowed to each other and laughed.

Fifteen minutes later, Claire and Brian walked into her bedroom. She said, "It was fun sitting next to you in band yesterday. Thank you for helping me win third chair."

"Mmm." His lips met hers.

He pushed her back against the bed. *Oh.* She loved the way it felt when he laid on top of her; he seemed so powerful. His mouth worked down from her breasts, down her stomach. He unfastened her pants and pulled them off. Her pulse raced. Her pants had never come all the way off before. But it was exciting to have his whole body between her thighs.

He nuzzled into her panties, scraped his teeth over the wet cotton. She wriggled—he was driving her crazy. Then she felt the material slide, and he was pulling them off. Her legs spread wider as his head sunk. "Aah!" Even better than when he used his hand. Her thighs trembled, and her orgasm snapped through her whole body, all the way to her fingers and toes.

But he kept at it. She hadn't realized she could have more than one, but she felt another on its way. Then he stopped. Moved to stare down into her eyes, his breath shaky. "I want to be inside you so bad. Please."

"Yes."

He looked so surprised she almost laughed, except her heart was beating too hard. "Really?" he said.

"Yes. I want you to make love to me, Brian. I want you to be my first."

"Are you sure? It—it might hurt . . . cos you're a virgin."

"That's okay. I'm ready. Do you have a condom?"

He nodded. "I've never been with a girl for her first time before." He looked scared. Almost as scared as she was. "I don't want to hurt you," he whispered.

She caressed his cheek, and he kissed her. His hand went between her legs and made her forget her nerves. His finger slipped inside. Familiar and lovely. Then something bigger. "It doesn't hurt."

"I haven't done it yet. I'm trying to stretch you out with my fingers."

"Oh." Her brain almost switched to panic mode, but the way he touched her kept it at bay. She'd almost forgotten her fear when something indescribably huge penetrated her. She gasped. It felt like her entire body was being impaled.

"God, I'm hurting you," he said and pulled out. "I'm sorry."

She smiled and put her fingers over his lips. *I love you, Brian. I know you love me, too. You'll say it when you're ready.*

He rolled onto his back and pulled off the condom. Held her as she snuggled against him. "I didn't want to hurt you." His voice was thick.

She kissed his chest. "It's alright." *Guess I'll get used to it.* She stroked his stomach, surprised to see his erection gone. "Oh. I was going to help you. You already . . . ?"

"No, I lost it. I don't like hurting people." He stared at the ceiling. "It isn't right that a woman's first time is painful. It's not fair."

She laid her cheek against his chest and closed her eyes. "Life isn't fair, Brian."

He heaved a sigh. "Yeah."

Naked in the Rain

༄༅༄

He waited by the gate beneath an overcast sky and climbed into the SUV that pulled to a stop. "Thanks for picking me up, Stu. But it would be easier for you if Jeffrey drove me to your house."

"I don't mind. I don't like those security guys following us around. It makes me nervous."

Stuart drove to Fairfax and Third and found a space in the crowded parking lot. "I think you'll like Farmer's Market. Tons of food and stuff to look at. Where did Claire say to meet?"

"By Starbucks." He followed Stuart to the coffee shop and scanned the crowds of people perusing the covered market enclosed by permanent buildings. "There she is, with Debbie and . . . ." A guy holding Debbie's hand. Brian touched Stu's shoulder. "Sorry."

He shrugged. "It's okay. I knew she didn't like me."

Brian kissed Claire hello. His arm slipped around her waist as they wandered through the stalls. The press of people didn't bother him like it used to. He liked it, actually, just being around people—even strangers. "There's a pet store. Let's go in."

He stuck his fingers through a wire cage. "Poor kitty. I wish I could take her home." The small grey cat sniffed his finger and rubbed it.

"Why don't you?" Stuart asked.

"I've already got a cat. And Grant barely let me keep him."

Stu frowned. "We can't have any pets. My mom's allergic."

"That's sad. River wasn't allowed to have pets, either." He moved to the next row. "What about something small, like a hamster? They don't have much fur."

Stuart pointed to a cage. "Or a rat."

"They're cute." White with long tails. "Holy shit—check out their balls! They're so huge they can barely walk. My god, the ratio is amazing."

They laughed and joked about elephantiasis. Stuart nodded toward the store entrance. The girls were leaving. "I think they're bored."

They followed them out. Stuart said quietly to Brian, "See those people over there? They're Goths."

"Oh. They look totally cool." Like Robert Smith. Ratted black hair, white faces and dark makeup. Even the guys had on makeup.

Debbie's boyfriend said, "You'd fit in with them."

Brian took it as a compliment even if it wasn't intended as one. He watched the Goths move through the crowd, past a familiar head of blond hair. His breath caught as the guy turned. *Brett.*

Brian took a step toward him and opened his mouth. Then clamped it shut. *I can't. Can't acknowledge him in public.* His hands tightened into fists at his sides. It felt so wrong to pretend he didn't know the man he had fantastic sex with once a week.

Brett saw him, and a grin lit his face. "Brian!" He walked over, with a woman trailing after. Brett touched his arm. "What're you doing here?"

He shrugged, though he knew his glowing face belied that indifference. *He didn't pretend I don't exist.* "Just hanging out. Christmas shopping."

"Me, too."

Claire moved to Brian's side and leaned into him. The woman with Brett did the same. Brian gazed up at him, and they gave each other knowing smiles as their arms slipped around their girlfriends' waists.

Brett said, "Have fun with your friends. See you around." He winked and moved away.

"Who was that?" Claire asked.

Brian caught a movement out of the corner of his eye and saw a man back into an empty corridor. But it was too late—Brian recognized him. Fury surged through him. He left his friends and strode over to the security guard hovering in the shadows. Brian kept his voice low. "How *dare* you? What are you doing here?"

"Just following orders."

"Orders?" Motherfucker. Brian turned abruptly and walked away. *Doesn't he trust me? After all these years? Damn him.* He kept going and found himself on the edge of the parking lot. He paced.

Stuart appeared. "What's going on? Who was that guy in the corridor?"

"Grant's security. I thought he trusted me."

He sought out Grant as soon as he got home, burst into his office without knocking. Grant looked up from his desk in surprise. Brian's voice shook. "How dare you have me followed?"

"Brian, calm down. Our men have never interfered with your activities, have they?"

"I thought you trusted me."

"I *do* trust you." Grant stood up. "It has nothing to do with trust. It's strictly for your protection."

"I'm not a baby. I can take care of myself."

Grant's voice remained calm. "What you don't understand is that power cuts both ways. It also makes you a target. Vulnerable. Makes *me* vulnerable." He leaned forward and held Brian's gaze. "I can protect you, but only if my men watch you every moment you are out of this House. Do you understand?"

He blinked. Nodded slowly as it sank in. He'd tried so hard to be a normal kid outside of these walls. *But I'm not. I was fooling myself.*

"They won't interfere with your activities. Alright?"

He felt numb. It had never occurred to him he might not be safe. He whispered, "Yes, Grant."

ഇഇഇ

He glanced around as he got out his flute. Their first concert was at a retirement home. A Christmas tree stood in the corner and swags of greenery lined the ceiling. *Nice place. I guess nursing homes aren't so bad if you've got money.*

Elderly people began to fill up the chairs. They looked excited. *I'm glad I made it.* The band director had been quite upset when Brian said he didn't know if he could make the concert. 'Can't you ask for time off? Where do you work?'

'I work at home. For Grant.'

'Well, then it shouldn't be a problem. I can call him if you want.'

'No. Grant doesn't want me in this band. If you tell him about the concert, he'll make sure I have to work.'

Mr. Williams had looked rather shocked. He smiled now at Brian as he took his place in front of the band. They played a few Christmas carols; then it was time for his duets with Stuart. They started with "A Charlie Brown Christmas"—it had a great piano part. The crowd gave them a standing ovation. He saw Stuart's parents and brother in the audience as they bowed.

One more duet, then the boys returned to their seats in the band for more holiday tunes. Brian watched the audience as they played. The old folks loved it—sang and clapped along. It felt wonderful to bring a little brightness into their lives.

He smiled as the band stood to receive the applause. Stuart's family made their way through the cheering audience, and his dad shook Brian's hand. "That was superb. How long have you been playing the piano?"

"All my life."

Stuart's mother gushed over both of them. "Brian, you really *must* join us for dinner."

"Uh . . . I'm a vegetarian."

"So I heard. I made a vegetable casserole especially for you. I won't take no for an answer."

He didn't want to, but it would be rude to decline. "Okay."

Then Claire was beside him. "Brian, I want you to meet my mother."

He managed to say hello to the lovely woman who looked so much like Claire. She seemed nice but . . . . He loosened the tie he had to wear for the performance and felt a little lightheaded. "It's hot in here. I'm going outside."

He hurried through the door and took in deep lungfuls of cool air, pleased to see his breath puff out into the night. He felt better and lit a cigarette.

"Brian?" Claire's voice called. "Are you okay?"

"Yeah, I just got a little hot. I hope I wasn't rude to your mother."

"Don't worry. She likes you, especially after hearing you on the piano." She kissed him. "Want to go for a drive?"

Yes. "I can't. Stuart's parents invited me for dinner."

Disappointment lined her pretty face.

"Maybe later? I could call you from Stuart's."

She grinned. "Okay. We can drive to the overlook."

His pulse picked up. Her second time had been quite an improvement over the first as her body got used to him. *Third and fourth will be even better.* "I can't wait." He gave her a deep kiss.

Stuart's voice carried from the doorway. "Hey, Brian, you left your stuff inside. Dad's got it."

"Oh, thanks."

He disengaged from Claire as Stuart's family approached with Claire's mother. She arched a brow. "I hope we didn't interrupt anything."

His face flushed with heat. Claire giggled and walked away with her mom.

He took a final drag on his cigarette and ground it into the cement. Ted frowned as he handed him his flute case. "Do your parents know you smoke?"

Brian looked up into his dark eyes. "Yes."

"Dad, Brian doesn't live with his parents."

Stuart explained about his guardian as they piled into the Saab. Twelve-year-old Jacob squeezed between the teenagers. Brian tried not to think about him. Or his father in the front seat. Or his mother, for that matter. *This is gonna be a blast.*

Actually it wasn't that bad. The food was good, and the adults did most of the talking. He and Stuart had a side conversation. Brian said, "I finished *Dune*. I need to borrow the rest of the series."

"That was quick—it's like 500 pages."

"I know, but it went by fast. It's such a great story."

"Yeah, it's my favorite."

Ted spoke up. "Brian, I understand you don't attend Davis High. Where do you go to school?"

Brian answered his questions—explained about his tutor, where he lived, how he heard about the Youth Band. He was too nervous to feel his usual attraction to Stuart's father. The conversation finally moved to someone else. Then the meal was over.

Stuart suggested Brian play something on the piano for his parents. That was much easier than being conversational. He chose the first thing that popped into his head. The Chopin *Impromptu* he played for the tryouts.

When they finished exclaiming over his talent, he escaped to Stuart's room to hang for a bit before he called Claire. *That wasn't so bad.* "Your parents are pretty nice."

ഇഇഇ

Brian watched Stuart move closer for the chorus, and they sang into the mike together. Strange to have their faces so close without kissing. *I wonder what he would do if I kissed him?* He imagined it. And realized he didn't want to. *That's weird—I'm not attracted to him.*

Stuart backed off when the harmony ended, and the song came to a close. Brian grinned. "I didn't think heavy metal would be so fun to play."

Roger the drummer had insisted they play a song he liked. Roger used a towel to wipe sweat from his brow and pushed brown hair out of his eyes. "It's weird watching you sing that kind of music. With your black clothes and black hair and black nails. What's up with that?"

"My hair isn't black. It's dark brown."

"Looks black to me. And what's with the nail polish? What is that supposed to mean?"

"It doesn't mean anything. It's just for the aesthetic."

"The what?"

"I just like the way it looks."

Roger shook his head. "You're weird."

Brian frowned at him, then shrugged. He glanced around the rehearsal space. "We need a piano. Is it okay if I buy one and have it shipped here?" He got a nod from Roger. "I'll bring a tape recorder next time, too. Be right back," he said on his way out the door.

Roger watched him leave. "I think he's gay."

Stuart snorted. "Hello, he's got a girlfriend."

"But did you hear those lyrics? He said 'he,' and it was about sex!"

"Maybe it's not literal. Or he could be singing from the other person's perspective. Who knows?" Stuart set his bass guitar on its stand and sat cross legged on the carpet.

Roger plopped down beside him. Brian returned a few minutes later, joined them on the floor and lit a cigarette. Stuart asked, "So what have you been up to?"

Fucking. Yesterday he only had one session—with two male clients—but it lasted all day. The three of them did ecstasy together and bondage stuff. It was a lot of fun, but he was completely exhausted afterward. Still tired, actually. "Just working."

"I heard Claire didn't come back to school Wednesday."

"Yeah." He'd met her at lunchtime. He'd never been on a high school campus during school hours before. All those kids made him nervous. But he didn't stick around long.

"So what happened?" Stuart pressed.

"We went to her house."

Roger grinned. "Did you nail her?"

Brian smoked in silence a moment. "You're not supposed to tell that stuff."

"No," Roger said. "It's *girls* who aren't supposed to tell. It's the opposite for guys."

He looked at Stuart for confirmation and got a nod. He smiled. "Yeah, well."

"Wow," Stuart breathed. "Is she your first?"

A short laugh popped out before he could stop it. "No."

Roger leaned forward. "How many girls have you been with?"

"Usually it's women, not girls."

"Really?" Stuart's eyes bugged behind his thick glasses. "How do you do that?"

Shit. Think. He tapped his cigarette in the ashtray to buy time. "Adult parties and stuff. There are women out there who like young guys."

Roger asked again how many women.

"Not that many."

"How many is not that many?"

"Uh . . . ." He tried to count them. "I don't know, like ten or eleven."

"Holy shit!" Roger said. "That's way more than me. And I thought you were gay." He laughed.

Stuart's eyes were huge. "Next time you go to one of those parties, can I come?"

Brian grimaced. "Sorry, I . . . can't invite people."

Stuart looked crestfallen. Brian touched his leg. "We'll figure something out, okay?"

He went without River this time—didn't want to spend the little time they had together traveling to a phone booth. Besides, there was no risk of his parents answering now that Tanya had moved out. But he didn't recognize the female voice that answered. "Is Tanya there?"

"She's at work. Can I take a message?"

"At work? But it's Christmas Eve day."

"Yeah, but the restaurant's open."

"Vicky? Is that you?"

"Yeah, who's this?"

"Brian." She didn't seem to get it. "Brian O'Kelly."

"*Oh!* My God, I didn't recognize your voice. It's so low."

"I'm not a kid anymore. I'm fifteen now."

"Not to us—you need to send more pictures. Or better yet, why don't you come home? It kills Tanya not knowing where you are, if you're safe."

"I'm safe. And happy. Everything's fine. Will you tell her that for me? How is she?"

"Besides the stress you cause her? She's good—super busy with her promotion and all. She's a manager now at Friendly's."

"That's great. She's still doing okay in school?"

"Listen to you—all concerned about her education, and you're not even in school. Yes, she's fine. But she has no time for fun anymore."

"That sucks." *Maybe I should send her money. But then she'll wonder where I got it.* "Will you tell her I love her?"

"Yeah, of course. Next time try calling late at night. She won't mind if you wake her up. You *better* take care of yourself."

"I will. Merry Christmas, Vicky."

He headed back through the drizzle to the waiting car. How strange to talk to someone else from back home. It was easier in a way—less emotional. But less fulfilling, too. He bit his lip. *Someday I'll catch up with her.*

ಌಌಌ

Brian sat up on his knees in bed at the beach house to gaze down at River's naked body. "I can't believe you're seventeen."

"I know!" He grinned. "It's so old."

"Exciting. You're turning into a man." Brian watched his body move as River joined him on his knees. He ran his palm over River's smooth, muscled chest, then up to graze the roughness where he shaved. "A wonderful, luscious man."

"So are you." River's gaze dropped down Brian's body. "Look at you. Your shoulders are broader. You're filling out." He reached down to take hold of Brian's penis. "And look how big you are."

He laughed and held River's face in his hands. Kissed him gently. "I love you more than chocolate."

River smiled.

"I love you more than ice cream. More than anything." He whispered, "More than myself."

"Brian." River kissed him. Sweet, tender kisses.

Brian sat back. "Let's open your present now." He reached for the large, flat box on the nightstand. "Happy birthday."

River ripped off the silver wrapping, lifted the lid and pulled out a thick sheet of paper. A pencil sketch of two hands, palms pressed together, fingers laced. Brian's hand and his own—he recognized them. "Brian, this is beautiful. You did this?"

He nodded. "Do you like it?"

"*Like* it?" His voice caught as his eyes filled. He wrapped his arms around Brian. "God, I love you so much. I miss you all the time."

They were in bed again after running around the beach naked. That hadn't lasted long—too cold this early in the morning. River scowled at the clock. His birthday was over, and their time was almost up. "So where were you Thursday? I had five hours between clients. I tried to call all afternoon."

"Oh, I wish I'd known. You should page me next time." Grant had given him a pager, now that he was away from home more.

"Where were you?"

"At Stuart's."

"Of course." His eyes narrowed. "In the bedroom, no doubt."

"That's where we practice."

"Yeah, right. Practice *what*?"

"River!" Brian pushed on his chest. "Are you jealous? That's ridiculous. You know you're everything to me. You should come to our next rehearsal. Pandora's Box is so. . . . " He struggled to find the words. "It's so amazing for me. Like the way I feel when I play the piano, but in a whole new way. I want to share it with you. Please come next time."

"Brian." He looked away, then sat up to stare at the wall. "You wanna know what John gave me for my birthday?"

Brian's heart dropped. He forced the words out. "You're going away again."

River turned to him in surprise. "You know?"

"I can always tell when you're going to say that." He steeled himself. "How long and where to?"

"Europe."

His eyes widened. God, Europe. He ached to go. "How long?" he whispered.

River turned away. Muttered, "A month."

"A *month?*" Brian got out of bed to stand by the window and stare at the grey ocean.

River came up behind him. "I'm sorry, babe." He wrapped his arms around him. "I almost don't even want to go. Whenever I travel I worry about you all the time."

"Grant will take care of me. You don't need to worry." He stroked River's arm and leaned his head back against him. "When are you leaving?"

"Day after tomorrow."

Brian closed his eyes. God. A *whole month without him*. Europe. *Damn, I want to go.*

Brian put on the blue silk robe he got for Christmas and sat on the bed. His last evening with River. "Where are you going?"

"John let me pick. Paris, Amsterdam, Greece—John says Mykonos is an international gay mecca." He grinned at the prospect of an entire island full of willing men.

"Oh—and Egypt." He grabbed Brian with excitement lighting up his eyes. "I'm gonna see the pyramids!"

"The pyramids. That's wonderful." He was truly glad for River, but he couldn't help feeling jealous, too.

"I wish you could come. John would let you."

"But Grant won't. No way—not for a whole month. But maybe . . . maybe I could come for part of it."

"You think?"

"It's worth a try. I'll ask him right now." He tightened his robe and strode down the hall before he lost his resolve.

He found Grant on the couch in his sitting room. Brian knelt before him and took his hand. "Grant, is there *any* way I can go to Europe with River? I know a month is too long. But maybe I could go for just *part* of it? Please."

"Brian." Grant cupped his cheek. "I wish I could say yes. But I can't let you go off with John. I don't trust him with you."

"You and Jeffrey could come."

"We can't drop everything and leave tomorrow. And I can't keep up with John. He'll be hopping all over the continent. I'm too old for that."

"You're not old." He moved to sit on Grant's lap. Let the silk robe fall open.

"I'm sorry, Brian. I have to say no."

He looked away to hide his tears. *Shouldn't have gotten my hopes up.*

"Brian." Grant's thumb stroked the wetness on his cheek. "We'll go sometime soon. Alright? With River."

"Really?"

"Yes. How about this summer? Does that make you happy?"

He breathed a laugh and nodded.

"But to one place only. I'll let you pick. It doesn't have to be in Europe. Anywhere in the world. Your choice."

Anywhere. So many places he wanted to see. But it was no contest. The country he'd longed for all his life, captivated by his grandparent's lilting voices. "Ireland."

Grant smiled. "Ireland it is."

Brian laughed and hugged him. "Thank you."

"Why don't you go tell River the news?"

He did.

"Awesome. I get to go to Europe again—with you!" They hugged each other tight. "But not this time." River squeezed his eyes shut. *God, I'll miss you so much.*

I'll miss you, too.

"I'm a man, a liar
guaranteed in your bed
I gotta place it on the rack
Got a place inside it"

- Brian Molko (Placebo), "Scared of Girls"

ᚾᚾ CHAPTER 29 ᚾᚾ

He watched Claire undress while he took off his shirt. He'd met her at lunchtime again to go back to her place. But thoughts of River kept creeping in. A *whole month.*

"Brian, are you okay? You seem sad today."

He shrugged. "I'm fine."

She frowned and wished he would talk to her. "Come here, you." She pulled him onto the bed and helped him forget his troubles. Clung to him as her orgasm took her. "Oh, Brian. I love you." The words were out before she could stop them.

She watched his face change. He looked like someone had just died. "But . . . you don't really know me. You don't know who I am."

She touched his cheek. "I know enough. You'll tell me the rest when you're ready. I'm in love with you. I want to know everything about you."

He rolled off her and stared at the ceiling, then sat up abruptly to pull on his clothes.

"Where are you going? We've got all afternoon. I'll skip class again—Brian!"

But he was already heading out the door. She threw on a robe to chase after him and tried to ignore the sick feeling in her stomach. *He loves me. I know he does. I just scared him.* "Brian, I'm sorry!"

She saw him at the front door with his hand on the knob, but he was looking the other way, at—"Mom! What are you doing here?" Claire clutched her robe closed.

Her mother folded her arms. "I might ask you the same thing. But it's quite obvious."

Brian yanked the door open and was gone.

He jumped when the phone rang. It was Stuart, thank goodness, not Claire. Stu told him his parents would be gone tonight. "It's their anniversary, so they're going to a fancy hotel."

"Tell them congratulations. How many years?"

"Nineteen."

"Wow. Next year's a biggie."

"Yeah—they're going to Hawaii for that one. Everybody thinks it's weird my parents are still married."

"I don't. So are mine."

"That's cool. I guess." Awkward silence. "So why don't you come over tonight, and we'll get stoned?"

"Yeah! But what about your brother?"

"He's spending the night at a friend's house. We've got the place to ourselves. Wanna stay over?"

"I can't. Grant would never allow that."

"Why not?"

"He's just . . . really protective. But we'll have fun anyway. I can stay late."

Brian made it to Stuart's before eight o'clock. He cleared a spot on the floor to set down his guitar case. "Sometimes life really sucks."

"Why?"

"River's gone and . . . ."

"Gone? What do you mean?"

"He's in Europe for a month. A fucking *month*. Grant wouldn't let me go." He sank onto the bed and put his head in his hands. "And Claire . . . I'm gonna have to break up with her."

"What? Why?"

"Because she's in love with me. And I'm not in love with her."

"You're not?"

"No. We have fun, but that's all it is for me." His voice grew thick. "I didn't mean to hurt her. Damn it—why did this have to happen?"

"You shouldn't be surprised. You're very loveable. And, you know, women tend to connect sex with love."

"They do?"

"Well, yeah. I can't believe I know more about it than you."

"I guess my education is . . . spotty. I don't know a lot of things people take for granted."

"Are you sure you don't love her? What about that song you wrote—I thought that was about her."

"No, it's not. But I never meant to hurt her. I wouldn't hurt her on purpose. I'm not that kind of person."

Stuart sat beside him on the bed and put his arm around Brian's shoulders. "I know you're not. And if you're really not in love, then you're doing the right thing by breaking up with her. Plenty of guys would go along with it for the sex. But you're better than that."

"I still feel terrible."

"You *should*—I mean, if you didn't care, that would be bad. You're a good person." Stuart gave his shoulders a squeeze, then let go. "Wait, but if that love song isn't about Claire, who is it about?"

"Someone else."

Stuart's eyebrows shot up. "There's someone else? Why didn't you tell me? Who is it—come on!"

Brian met his gaze. His heart pounded as he made the decision to tell him. "It's River."

Stuart looked confused. "River? I thought he was a guy."

"He is."

Naked in the Rain

"Oh." His brown eyes got huge behind his glasses. "But . . . Claire. I don't understand."

"I'm bisexual." *That's the first time I've said those words.* Brian searched his eyes as it sunk in. "Does that bother you?"

Stu blinked. "No. I'm just . . . surprised."

Brian looked away and watched his fingers fiddle with a thread from the bedding. He mumbled, "Bet you're not so eager for me to spend the night now."

"No. I mean, yes, I am." Stuart touched his arm. "This doesn't change anything. I'm glad you felt you could share with me."

A slight smile crossed his lips. "You're the first person I've ever told."

"I'm honored." Stuart gave him a fierce hug. "Now let's get stoned."

Brian laughed and nodded. He felt lighter as he packed the bowl, closer to Stuart now that he knew about the most important thing in his life. "River showed me how to do this years ago. It's great to be able to talk about him for real now."

"When do I meet him?"

"In a month. He said he'll come to a Pandora's rehearsal when he gets back." He sighed. "It's so hard when he's gone. I just try not to think about it, keep busy. Okay, the smoke will burn your throat—be prepared for that. Try to hold it in."

Stuart choked on the first hit.

"I did that, too, the first time. You'll get used to it." They passed the pipe back and forth a few times. "I'm definitely stoned. Are you sure you don't feel it?"

Stu shrugged. "My throat hurts, but that's it."

"Huh. Bummer."

Stuart turned on the radio and flipped through the stations. They made fun of the boppy music. Brian said, "Wait—go back."

Stuart stopped the dial on an old Fleetwood Mac song. Brian stared at the radio. "'The Chain.' I haven't heard this in ages. My parents used to listen to it." He sang along, surprised he remembered the words.

His mother filled his mind, her face and voice twisted with uncontrolled rage *as she screams, 'I can't stand to look at you!' She shoves me into the closet and slams the door shut. I hear the chair bump against the door so I can't get out. But that's okay. I like the closet. She can't get me in here. I try to forget her words while I hug my knees and wait. And wait.*

I'm thirsty, and I have to pee. I wait. All I can think about now is how bad I have to pee. It hurts. I drift into half-sleep. Visions of cool water fill my head, but I can't seem to drink it. So thirsty and hot.

And suddenly, Tanya's voice. The door swings open and cool air floods in. But it's too late. I'm so embarrassed I start to cry. Six is too old to wet my pants. I look at the clock as Tanya lifts me up. Almost three. It was morning when Mommy shut me in. What if Tanya hadn't found me? Would I be in there forever? My legs hurt.

"Brian!"

He jumped, jarred out of the memory by Stuart's hand shaking his knee. He blinked rapidly and tried to focus on where he was. "Sorry. That song . . . sent me—sent me back."

"You scared me. Your eyes—it's like you weren't there."

He shrugged. "Guess I wasn't, really. I get . . . lost sometimes."

Stuart met his gaze. "Your parents abused you, didn't they?"

He glanced down. "I guess she did, in a way. Dad . . . didn't do *any*thing. But she never hit me."

"Psychological abuse can be worse than physical abuse."

"I think it was both. I figured that out in the institution. But she never hit me."

Stuart sucked in his breath. "She molested you!"

"No, no." *God, I have to explain.* "Stuff like . . . she locked me in the closet for hours. Stuff like—like that." He stopped his brain from pulling up more examples. *Don't think about it.* His eye started twitching.

"Brian, I'm sorry."

He shrugged. "Doesn't matter anymore.".

"You were in an institution?"

"Yeah, after I cut my wrists. That's where I met River. He got me drunk for the first time on my birthday." He laughed. "I can't believe we didn't get caught."

"Are you still in therapy? My dad's a doctor—he could hook you up with someone good."

I never told them much anyway. "No, thanks. I'm alright."

Stuart shook his head and mumbled, "I'm not so sure."

Claire shut her bedroom door. "Mom came home early the other day cos she was sick. Not only did she see you—she *heard* us having sex! Oh, I'm so embarrassed." She giggled. "But she wasn't really mad. Just gave me the lecture about birth control and safe sex and all that." She moved closer and reached to unbutton his shirt.

"No, Claire, wait. We've gotta talk." He steeled himself. "I . . . I can't see you anymore."

"*What?*"

"I'm sorry. I never meant to hurt you."

"What do you think you're doing now?" Tears rolled down her stricken face. "Why?"

"Because I'm not in love with you."

She flinched.

"We have fun, and I like you. But that's all."

"But I love you. How can I feel this way about you if you don't love me back? It's not possible!"

"I'm sorry," he whispered and headed for the door.

"Is there someone else?"

He met her eyes. "Yes."

She gasped. "Who?"

"No one you know. It's someone I've been with a long time, who I love with all my heart. There's no room for anyone else."

"Someone you've *been* with—while we were together?" Her voice rose. "You cheated on me?"

"It wasn't cheating. I never said you were the only one."

She sputtered. "I just assumed! You wouldn't pursue me and make love to me if you were interested in someone else. How could you? How could you do that to me?"

"I never meant to mislead you, Claire. I'm—"

She hit his chest. "I *hate* you! How could I *ever* have thought you were a good person? Just get out. *Get out!*" She pushed at him until he was outside.

The door slammed. He stared at it a moment and whispered, "I'm sorry."

ഇഇഇ

Craig Andraide's pulse quickened as he aimed his white BMW up the long driveway. He scowled at the memory of Grant's snobbish voice. *'Brian is not available.'* Craig had been unable to convince him. *Damn it. I don't want another boy. I want him.* The memory of Brian's silky white flesh against his thighs flashed through his mind. Almost made him miss the final curve of the driveway.

He hit the brakes and stopped in front of the Wing. *Maybe I should give it another shot. That uptight asshole could change his mind.* Craig sniffed and paused to check his reflection in the rearview mirror. He wiped traces of cocaine from his nostrils. *I should stop doing blow in the car.*

He got out of the BMW, straightened his grey suit and walked toward the Main House. He hated being treated like an inferior. Hated Grant. But Grant had what he wanted. Brian's naked body filled his mind, the sounds he made while he was being fucked. The fusion of lust and anger blinded him a moment. He stumbled up the short flight of stairs and passed between white columns to pound on the doors. No answer. He tried the handle, pushed the heavy door inward and stepped inside.

The sound of a piano led him to the parlor. Fury raged through him. He strode over to the piano to grab Brian's arm. "What the hell is this? Grant said I couldn't have you today—you're too busy for me. And look at you! Playing the fucking piano?" He shook Brian's arm savagely.

"Fuck off!" Brian shouted.

Craig's eyes bulged and veins stood out in his neck. "How *dare* you speak to me like that." He yanked on Brian's arm and practically lifted him off his feet. The piano bench fell over.

Craig's fingers crushed his bicep. Brian tried to wrench himself free, but the man's grip tightened as he dragged him toward the stairs.

His heart beat so hard it hurt. "Grant!" They started up the stairs, and Brian hooked his arm around the railing. He held fast. "*Jeffrey!*"

A blow hit the side of his head, and the world reeled. He flashed back to when Alan hit him like that, lost his balance as panic filled him. He would've fallen if not for Craig's vice-grip. His arm felt like it was being yanked out of its socket. He struggled to get his feet under him as Craig pulled him up the stairs.

They turned down the hall that led to the Room, and Brian jerked and twisted. Almost broke free. Craig reached around his waist to lift him up. Brian's boots kicked at the wall as he struggled to get leverage. Craig carried him into the Room.

. . .

Jeffrey sat in the limo waiting for Brian. He checked the clock on the dashboard. *He's gonna be late for band.* Fuzz spat from his walkie talkie as he got out of the car.

Matthew. "Have you seen Craig Andraide? We let him in the gate, but he hasn't shown up here."

Jeffrey's brow furrowed. "His car's parked in front of the Wing. You sho' he ain't there?" He listened to the answer. "Alright. I'll check it out." He stepped into the House. "Mr. Andraide?" He paused in the doorway to the parlor and saw the piano bench on its side. "Mr. Brian?"

Craig threw him onto the bed. Brian crawled toward the headboard and reached for the panic button. His finger was inches away when Craig grabbed his leg to haul him down to the foot of the bed. He wrenched Brian's arm up behind his back. Brian cried out at the sharp pain.

"I'll teach you to disrespect me!"

He reached around Brian's waist, lifted him upright onto his knees and held him tight against his body. Craig's hand slipped under the sweater. Brian's stomach turned, and nausea rose in his throat.

Craig twisted his arm up farther, and Brian cried out. Craig moaned. *He likes that I'm in pain. Oh, god.* His gaze rose to the medallion on the ceiling as he tried to disconnect. He felt like he was going to puke. Craig's breath heaved in his ear as he unfastened Brian's jeans, then abruptly let go of him. Pushed him down.

Brian lay stunned a moment as pain lanced through his shoulder. He pushed himself up. *Panic button.* Craig's knee slammed into his back and pinned him to the bed. He pulled Brian's arms down to his sides and knelt over him, trapping Brian's wrists under his knees. Craig tugged on Brian's jeans, yanked them down to expose him.

Brian knew the pain he felt now was nothing compared to what he was about to feel. He tried to relax his body, but he couldn't do it. Couldn't get Alan out of his head. He smashed his face into the bed. *God, not again.* "Please," he begged.

"What's that?" Craig grabbed his hair to pull his head up.

"*Please.*" He gasped. Tears rolled down his face. "Don't!"

Craig let go of his hair. "Too late for that, boy."

He heard a zipper and buried his face into the bed.

The door flew open. Jeffrey grabbed Craig before he could react and hauled him away. Grant rushed in and touched Brian's shoulder.

Brian shrugged his hand off and turned away to pull up his jeans, then slid off the bed and stood on shaking legs. He backed up to lean against the wall. Stared at the carpet and tried to stop shaking.

Grant moved closer, but Brian slid away from him, still staring at the floor. "I'm alright." He wiped at his face. "I'm alright." He looked up at the ceiling, his breath coming hard, then pushed away from the wall toward the door. Mumbled, "I'm gonna be late."

"Surely you're not going to rehearsal now."

"Yes. Yes, I am."

"But—"

Naked in the Rain

"If I don't go, then he's won. I might as well have fucked him." He spit out the words and stalked out. Wiped his face on his sweater and gripped the banister tight.

There were men in the parlor—security. And *him*. Brian stared straight ahead, his jaw clenched, focused on getting out the door. On not losing it in front of all these people. Especially Craig.

The door to Grant's office opened, and security guards poured through it into the parlor. A small corner of his brain registered surprise. But the distraction only lasted a second. His voice rang out loud and sharp. "Jeffrey. Let's go!"

Jeffrey looked up to where Grant stood at the top of the stairs. Grant gave a reluctant nod. Jeffrey left Craig in the hands of the security team and followed Brian outside. "You sho' bout this?"

He nodded and got in the back of the limo. He pulled out a cigarette, but he was shaking so bad he couldn't light it. He finally got it, took a deep drag and stared out the window. The shakes were getting worse. He bent over and gasped convulsively. Began to sob.

Jeffrey's eyes filled as he glanced at the rearview mirror. He drove in silence.

Brian finally sat up to check their progress. *Shit.* They'd be at the school in a few minutes. *Pull yourself together.* He blew his nose, grabbed a water bottle from the mini-bar and splashed the contents onto his face. The cool water felt good on his flushed skin. He combed his fingers through his hair as best he could.

He closed his eyes and took deep breaths. *It's okay. It's okay. He didn't get you.* He bit his lip. Wrong thing to think about. *Don't think. Just breathe. Meadows. Trees. Schnookie.* He smiled as a tear slid down his cheek.

"We're there, Mr. B. You sho' bout this?"

He grabbed his things and got out of the car before he could change his mind. He managed not to think as he trudged up the hill. Music came from the other side of the door. Scales. They were warming up. *I'm late.*

He swung the door open and walked past Stuart without looking at him. Didn't look at anyone. He took his seat, and Claire edged away as much as she could. *God, I forgot about her. Lovely.* He grimaced. And winced—his cheek and jaw were sore. *Motherfucker.*

He had a terrible time focusing. Lost count of the rests and missed his entrance. He realized the band director was watching him. *Can't I have one bad day? Give me a break.*

As if on cue, Mr. Williams called for the break. Brian stood to go outside, but the director stopped him. "Are you okay, Brian?"

"I'm fine." *Leave me alone.* He turned and hurried away to sit on the short wall outside. He took deep drags on his cigarette.

"What happened?"

He turned toward Stuart's voice. "Nothing. I was late—what's the big deal?"

"There's a giant red mark on your face. Someone hit you."

He touched his cheek where it was sore. "Shit. I didn't realize you could see it." *No wonder everyone was looking at me.* "I shouldn't have come. I wasn't thinking."

"What *happened*?"

He whispered, "Nothing," and glanced at Stu's face. "I'm sorry. I just . . . don't want to talk about it, okay?" He stood up. "I should go."

"Where?"

Good question. Not home. "Wherever." He had the sudden urge to get drunk. Very drunk. He turned and walked away down the hill.

"Brian, wait." Stuart caught up with him. "I'm coming with you."

They reached the limo and piled into the back. Jeffrey turned around. "You okay, Mr. B?"

"I'm fine. We decided to leave band early." He opened the mini-bar and pulled out a bottle of vodka. "Ow." His wrists were sore from where Craig knelt on them. *Fucker.* "Can we just drive around or something?"

Jeffrey eyed the bottle. "Hold on." He picked up the phone. "Yessir, he's here in the car. Wants to drive around and drink vodka." Pause. "Yessir. I'll take care of him, Mr. Grant."

Jeffrey started the car and pulled out. Brian took a swig that warmed all the way down his throat to his belly.

Stuart's eyes widened. "Grant's letting you drink?"

"Sure." He took another gulp. "He treats me like an adult."

"That must be nice."

"I guess," he said softly. "Here." He passed the bottle to Stuart and fought the memories that kept surfacing. Craig's hands on his skin. The fear. He shook his head and shut down that part of his brain. *Nothing really happened.*

He turned on the radio, set at his favorite oldies station. "This music always cheers me up."

Stuart handed back the bottle and wiped his mouth.

Brian sang along. "'It's my party and I'll cry if I want to, cry if I want to.' I danced to this song with the first girl I ever made out with. Back at the institute."

"You had a girlfriend already? How old were you?"

"Eleven. No—twelve. I had my birthday there."

"It must've sucked to have your birthday at an institution."

"Not really. River got me drunk. He was my roommate."

"Were you guys a couple?"

"No. Though I can't believe I never jumped him—he's so hot. I *was* really attracted to him, but I hadn't admitted that to myself. I was confused cos I knew I liked girls. Didn't occur to me I could like both." He downed more vodka and felt dizzy and warm. "This stuff works fast." He pulled his sweater off—he had a tee shirt on underneath—and his head fell back against the seat. "Claire hates me now."

"What happened? She looked pretty upset at band."

"I told her I couldn't see her anymore, and I'm not in love with her."

"Ouch. But she shouldn't hate you for that."

"Well . . . then she asked if there was someone else."

"Did you tell her it's a guy?"

"No. She accused me of cheating. That's when she said she hates me. It was bad."

"Sorry. Shit—what is that?" He held up Brian's arm and turned it. Finger-shaped bruises were forming around his bicep. "Someone grabbed you hard. What happened?"

Brian looked away. "Stuart . . . I can't. I can't talk about it." He drank more vodka.

"I don't get you. You tell me all this personal stuff, but you won't tell me this?" He gasped. "Was it Grant?"

"No! No." He stared out the window and bit his lip. He couldn't bring himself to lie to his friend. *Distract him.* He turned back to Stu. "Claire's mom caught us last time."

"No way! What happened?"

He related the story. "Claire was embarrassed. Her mom *heard* us in the bedroom." He laughed. "I wonder if it turned her on? She's pretty hot."

"Brian!"

He laughed again. "Sorry. I'm kinda drunk."

Stuart looked at his watch. "I better call my mom at work." Brian handed him the phone built into the limo. Stuart dialed the number and waited. "Hey, Mom, is it okay if I go to the mall with Brian after band? We might catch a movie or something." Pause. "No, we'll get something to eat at the food court. Thanks, Mom." He handed the phone back.

"Wow, Stuart, I've never heard you lie before."

"You gotta do it sometimes. Parents."

"Yeah."

"Pass that vodka."

By the time night fell, the bottle was half empty. Brian realized how drunk he was when he could no longer feel the bruise on his cheek. *The bruise.* He stared at the empty seat in front of him. "There are bad people out there."

Stuart studied his face. "I know."

"I thought I knew that, too. But then you actually run into them, and you realize you never knew. Never really believed people can be evil." He was surprised to find himself thinking of Creepy Guy instead of Alan or Craig. "Some people feed off of fear." He twitched.

Stuart touched his arm, gripped it in silence.

Brian looked at him as tears ran down his face. He cupped Stu's cheek in his hand. "But not you. You're good. You're a good person."

Next thing he knew they were hugging. And he was crying. Crying hard. He sank down to lay his face against the cool leather seat. Tried to get that creepy feeling out of his body. Out of his mind. But all the showers in the world could never wash away the stink of Creepy Guy's soul. And it touched him. Too close, too often.

He covered his face with his hand. "Someday I'll be too old for him." His mantra—every time he had to go into the Room and face him.

"What?"

Brian shook his head. *Too drunk. Watch it.* He pushed himself up. "Nothing." It jarred him, changed his focus. He welcomed that, grabbed some tissues and tried to clean up. His eyes felt like swollen sandpaper.

He leaned back against the seat. "Sorry. I'm pretty drunk." He breathed a laugh and glanced at Stu. His face was white. So serious. Brian shook his knee and left his hand there. "Loosen up."

"Loosen up? You're the one who . . . ."

"Sorry. I just have to let it out sometimes. I've got a lot of stuff inside me." He wiped an errant tear. "I feel better now. Lighter." He laughed again. "Sorry. You must think I'm a nut."

"No."

"Good." His fingers slid up Stu's thigh.

"Brian!"

He jumped at the tone. "What?" He looked down and saw his hand inches away from his friend's crotch. He snatched it back into his own lap. "Oops—sorry. Habit."

Stuart shifted in his seat. He seemed nervous all of a sudden.

"What's wrong?"

Stuart blinked. "Are you serious? You just—was that a *pass?*"

"Uh . . . I guess. I didn't mean it though."

"Then why'd you do it?" His voice rose. "I'm straight, okay? I'm not interested."

Brian rolled his eyes. "Nobody's straight. They just *think* they are. But don't worry. I'm not attracted to you. Really."

"Then why'd you do it?"

"It's just habit—you're a guy, so part of me expects to have sex with you."

"Oh, come on, you have sex with every guy you meet?"

He leaned his head back. "Pretty much, yeah." He turned to look at Stuart. Had to laugh at the way his mouth hung open.

"What about River? I thought you were in love."

"I am. That doesn't mean I can't enjoy sex with other people—it has nothing to do with love. We have an open relationship." He grinned. "We've gotta stop talking about sex. It's making me horny."

Stuart's eyes bugged out even more.

He pulled at his jeans. He was getting a hard on. "Maybe I should go home." The thought was sobering. He sat up. "No, let's go to the beach. Jeffrey?"

"Yessir, Mr. Brian."

It didn't take long to get there. Brian gazed up at the whirling stars and fell onto the sand. Couldn't seem to get his feet under him. He laughed as Jeffrey picked him up. Put his arms around his thick neck and buried his face in the giant chest. "I love you, Jeffrey."

"I love you, too, Mr. B."

Jeffrey looked like he might cry as Stuart watched them. Stuart hadn't realized their relationship went deeper than business. Jeffrey sank onto the sand and set him on his knee. Brian looked so young and small as he stared out at the dark sea. Fragile.

Stuart sat beside them. Brian reached out to squeeze his hand and held onto it. They stayed like that a long time, until Jeffrey said, "We should be goin' home. It's gettin late."

Brian nodded, to Stuart's relief. He didn't want to be out too late on a school night. His parents might start inhibiting his freedom. *Hope they can't tell I've been drinking.*

Jeffrey insisted on calling another guard to drive Stuart's car home from school.

"You pretty drunk, too. I ain't lettin you drive."

Brian fell asleep after they dropped off Stuart. Jeffrey carried him upstairs and set him gently on the bed. Grant came in with Schnookie in his arms and set the cat down beside him, then helped undress Brian and tuck him in. Grant brushed the dark hair back and kissed his forehead. Straightened with a sigh. He felt old tonight. Old and tired.

Jeffrey put his arm around Grant's shoulders. "He'll be alright."

Nausea woke him early in the morning. And bad memories. *River. I need you.* "I wish you were here." He touched his bruised cheek. *No, I don't. Thank god he's not here. I can't put him through that again.*

The phone rang. "Hey, babe. I had a bad dream about you last night. Are you okay?"

"River!" He closed his eyes and swallowed his tears. "I'm—I'm fine. Just hung over. Got drunk with Stuart last night."

"Oh." His tone changed to annoyance.

"I miss you."

"Yeah."

Brian heard John's voice in the background.

"Look, I gotta go. We're flying to Paris tonight. I just wanted to make sure you're okay."

"I'm okay. Have fun in Paris. I love you."

He cried himself to sleep after they hung up. Woke up when Grant peeked in. Grant sat on the edge of the bed. "Are you alright?"

"Hung over." He pushed himself up, muttered, "Ow," and cradled his wrist.

Grant examined it. "Looks bruised."

"He—he knelt on my wrists."

"Oh, sweetheart." Grant held him close and kissed his hair. "I'll call Dr. Griffin. Perhaps we should cancel your piano lesson today."

No. But . . . the red mark on his cheek and jaw had turned into a bruise. He didn't want to explain that to Quinn. Plus he still felt like puking. "Yeah."

Grant looked him in the eye. "Do you want River to come home? I'll call John right now."

"No! No, don't. River mustn't know. I don't want *anyone* to know. It didn't happen—nothing happened." He gripped Grant's arm. "I don't want River to ever know. He doesn't need to be hurt like that again."

Grant searched his eyes. "Alright, Brian. We'll keep it quiet."

The phone rang again at three in the afternoon and woke him up. He reached for it carefully, his wrists wrapped in Ace bandages. Nothing serious, the doc had said, just sore.

Stuart asked, "You okay?"

"Yeah. Just a little hung over."

"Me, too. I think my parents know. They didn't say anything, but they're acting funny."

"Oh, I'm sorry. It's my fault." Never occurred to him to think about that stuff.

"Don't worry about it. Want to rehearse at Roger's tomorrow night?"

"Yeah. Bring your clarinet so we can practice that new duet." Mr. Williams had given them a jazzy piece. Lots of fun.

After they hung up he went downstairs and stared at the piano in the parlor. Finally walked over to finish the piece he'd been playing yesterday when that bastard prick interrupted. Then he moved on to something more aggressive. Didn't notice how sore his wrists were till he was done. He cradled them against his chest. *Fucking bastard.*

Maria's voice made him jump. "Would you like you some lunch, little niño?" She came closer to put her arm around his shoulders.

He leaned into her. Clutched her apron and buried his face in her bosom. "Okay."

He followed her to the table and toyed with his pasta. Wondered what to do the rest of the day. *I need to keep busy.* But the piano hurt his wrists. And he had no energy. He sighed and stared out the window at the green lawn. An idea struck him. He hurried up to his room to write out the parts to a Cure song for rehearsal tomorrow. That sparked an idea for a new song of his own. He wrote that down, too.

He stretched out on the bed when he was done. Next thing he knew it was dark, and Grant was sitting by him. "Do you want to be alone?"

He shook his head. They got under the covers, and Grant held him while Brian fell asleep again.

In the morning Grant said, "I'll cancel Brett today."

"No. Why?"

"I didn't think you'd want to see any clients."

"But I need to keep busy. And I like Brett. I *want* to see him. Just—don't tell him. Say I fell down or something. And I'm going to Roger's afterward to rehearse."

Grant kissed his forehead. "Whatever you want, dear."

The day went by quickly. He slept until it was time for Brett. That was fun, as always. Brett seemed concerned, but didn't comment on the bruises.

Later Jeffrey helped carry his equipment to Roger's converted garage, then excused himself and left the three boys alone. Brian reached into his bag. "Look what I brought." He held up a joint.

"Cool." Roger grinned. "I'm likin' you more and more."

Brian laughed and lit it.

"What happened to your wrists?" Stuart asked.

The Ace bandages. Brian looked at him a moment and shrugged. Stuart's frown deepened. Brian passed him the joint, then dug through sheets of handwritten music in his bag. "I want to play this. It's The Cure, but I think you'll like it. It's a great song."

Stuart and Roger looked over their parts.

Brian said, "Most of it's a guitar jam based around the theme. The vocals are only at the very end, but they're great lyrics."

Roger and Stuart messed with their parts while they passed the joint around. Brian stubbed it out when it got short. "Ready?"

He strapped on his guitar and began. They jammed while the emotion of the song built, and he lost himself in the music. So intense. Ten minutes in, he approached the mike.

> "Oh, kiss me, kiss me, kiss me
> Your tongue's like poison
> so swollen it fills up my mouth
> Just love me, love me, love me
> You nail me to the floor
> and push my guts all inside out
> Get it out, get it out, get it out,
> get your fucking voice
> out of my head
> I never wanted this
> never wanted any of this
> I wish you were dead
> I wish you were dead
> I wish you were dead"

He practically screamed the last part, drew out the word "dead." And it was over. His breath came hard as he wiped his face, surprised to find tears.

Stuart hugged him.

Brian cradled his throbbing wrists during the drive home. Jeffrey glanced over. "You gotta give those wrists a break. Stop workin em so hard."

"They didn't hurt while I was playing. Just after." *Maybe I should take a pain pill. I don't know . . . what if I can't stop?* He bit his lip and thought about something else that had been nagging him. The mysterious door behind Grant's desk. "Jeffrey, does that door in Grant's office lead to the Other Wing?"

Jeffrey looked surprised. Brian said, "When—when Craig was in the parlor, a bunch of security men came out of Grant's office."

Jeffrey chuckled. "Can't get nothin past you. Yessir, Mr. B. That's the only place where the two buildings connect. There's a tunnel. The main security station's at the other end, in the Wing."

"Hmm." *How many secret tunnels are there?* "I always wondered where that door went."

"Mystery solved. Maria's cookin up her famous cheese enchiladas for dinner."

"Yeah?" They grinned at each other.

Stuart walked into his house, and his father's voice called from the kitchen. "I've got a headache," Stu answered and made a beeline for his room. The marijuana had worked on him this time. It was great while they were playing, but he didn't want to face his dad like this.

"*In* the kitchen."

He sighed and went to his father.

"I want you to help with dinner." Ted looked at him more closely. "Your eyes are red. What have you been doing?"

"Nothing. I'm just tired."

"You were at rehearsal with Brian, weren't you? Brian and Roger."

"Yeah."

"Peel these potatoes." Ted watched him a few minutes, then went to the doorway. "Barbara! Come in here."

Stuart's mother appeared in the doorway. Ted crossed his arms and looked at him. "I think our son has been smoking marijuana."

"What?" Barbara and Stuart said simultaneously. She sputtered and pointed her finger. "And you were drinking the other night. I'm sure of it."

Ted nodded. "Are you smoking cigarettes, too, like your friend?"

"No!"

Barbara frowned. "We thought it was great you finally made a friend. But that Brian is a bad influence."

Stuart slammed his hand on the counter. "That's not true! Brian is a great person. With a lot of problems, but that's not his fault. His mother used to do terrible things to him. Did you know he cut his wrists when he was eleven? *Eleven*—that's younger than Jacob.

"And two days ago someone hit him, and he won't tell me who. Won't tell me what happened. He said some things—" *I don't understand, but they bother me. He's got secrets.*

Ted's eyes narrowed. "So you went out drinking with him."

"I'm worried about the best friend I've ever had, and that's all you can say? I thought you were better people than that." He pushed past them and stormed to his room.

Brian stared at the bottle of pills in his hand. *I am in pain. It would be legitimate to take one.* He rattled the plastic bottle and wondered how different these were from Demerol. He closed his eyes, then turned abruptly and walked out of the room.

He found Jeffrey in the kitchen teasing Maria. "Jeffrey," he said softly and pulled him into the hall for privacy. "Could you . . . could you hold onto these for me? For safe keeping." He put the bottle in Jeffrey's hand.

Jeffrey looked at it, then searched Brian's eyes. "Somethin you wanna tell me?"

"Just keep them for me, okay?" He turned to hurry upstairs before Jeffrey could question him further.

A few minutes later Grant knocked on his door. His heart skipped. *Did Jeffrey tell him?*

Grant sat beside him on the bed. "Tomorrow is Bernie Padrea's birthday. I planned to give him an extra night with you as our gift. But I don't think you want to spend the night after what happened. Would you feel comfortable with a short session, or should we cancel it altogether?"

Jeffrey didn't tell him. He tried to think past his relief and focus on what Grant said. *It would be nice to see Leah.* "I don't mind going. I'll spend the night."

"Are you sure? I don't want to push you."

"I want to go. I'm fine. Nothing happened—not really." He took Grant's hand. "Something *almost* happened, but it didn't. You and Jeffrey got there in time." Suddenly he was crying.

Grant held him.

Brian shivered on the balcony as he stared out at the lights. The cold wind went right through his net top. He took a sip of wine and drag on his cigarette to warm up, rubbed his bare thigh in a vain attempt to create heat. His boots were the only warm part of him. *Should've worn pants instead of a skirt.*

He turned to see Leah in the doorway. She stepped out to join him. "Mr. Padrea told me you were coming tonight. He was excited."

"Birthday present. So was the wine. Want some?"

"No, thanks. Red gives me a headache."

The city lights drew his gaze again. "Such a great view. Can't see shit at Grant's." He closed his eyes as the breeze blew his hair back. "It's like another world."

"Mmm. I bet."

"Thanks for the ashtray." He stubbed out his cigarette and shivered. "You put it here for me, didn't you?"

"Yeah. It's freezing out here. Let's go inside."

He followed her in and went to the side table to refill his drink, then steadied himself against the back of the couch. Wine sloshed out of his glass. "Oops." He wiped red liquid from his leather skirt and thigh. "Did I get it on the carpet?"

Leah turned on the light to check. "I don't think so." She felt the carpet. "Mr. Padrea isn't supposed to drink wine. And neither are you."

He laughed. "Yeah, right. Like that's a big deal."

She straightened up and gasped. Touched his cheek with her fingertips. "Someone hit you. Grant?"

"No." He pulled away. "Grant would never do that. Not even during sex." He picked up the almost-empty bottle and went to sit at the kitchen table.

She followed him. "Then who did?"

"Nobody. Nothing happened." He drained his glass and poured more. "Sure you don't want some? It's good."

She turned on the bright overhead light and sat down. "Don't you think you've had enough?"

"No."

"What is this?" She leaned across the table and pulled his hand closer to examine the bruises on his wrist. Her eyes moved to his other wrist. To the finger-shaped bruises around his bicep. "What the hell happened?"

He sighed. *I'm sick of having this conversation. I know how to distract her.* He got up and walked around the table to sit on the arm of her chair. Brushed her ash brown hair away from her neck and leaned in to nibble.

"Brian, stop it! You're not going to change the subject."

He stroked her hand. "How long since you had sex? Trapped up here all the time with Mr. P." He sat back with big eyes. "Or do you have sex with him?"

"No, Brian! That's gross. No offense."

He smiled and shook his head. Wobbled a little.

"I think you need to sit down—in your own chair," she added as he slid onto her lap. "You're heavy. Get up."

"Oh, Leah. You're no fun." He stood, then leaned down to kiss her on the lips. And felt nothing. "Let me know if you change your mind." He wandered back to his chair and flopped down. Sipped his wine.

"You're not getting out of this. How did you get those bruises? I won't stop asking until you tell me."

He rolled his eyes. "A client got out of hand, okay? But nothing happened."

"Doesn't look like nothing to me. How often does this sort of thing happen?"

"Not often."

"*How* often?"

He shrugged. "Twice in three years."

"One of these days it will go too far."

He glanced away. "Look, I answered your question. I don't want to talk about it." His voice trembled.

"It's a dangerous occupation you've chosen. A dangerous place."

"I'm happy there. It's where I belong. Those people are my family." He met her gaze, and his eye started twitching.

"Are you trying to convince me, or yourself?"

He leaned forward, suddenly angry. "What I do *helps* people."

"Oh, right," she said with sarcasm. "You relieve stress."

"I helped a girl who was raped. She couldn't let a man touch her." He tapped his chest. "I helped her. Now she can have a real life and get married and be happy. Because I helped her!"

"Well, good for you, Brian. But maybe you should start helping your*self*."

He pushed his chair back and stood up. "I don't need your pity, Leah. And I don't want it." He grabbed the bottle of wine and stalked away.

*"the moon is full, the stars are bright
and the sky is a poisonous garden tonight . . .*

and then came your sweet mouth"

- Concrete Blonde, "The Sky is a Poisonous Garden"

ඞඞ CHAPTER 30 ඞඞ

"Yeah, I think I can come." Brian moved the phone aside to take a long drag.

Stuart's voice sounded exasperated. "You *think* so? This is the performance we've been working toward all year."

"I know."

"We won't win unless you're there. Can't Grant let you have it off just this once?"

"No, but I've got a plan—cos I know my schedule in advance this time. I always have a client Tuesday afternoons. He's a regular. So . . . ." He lowered his voice. "Last time I saw him we made a deal. He agreed to cancel at the last minute." In exchange for a free session. Brian would meet him at a hotel after the youth band performance. "The only problem is if Grant schedules somebody else. So I'll need to leave right away."

"Sounds kind of risky."

"It should work." He traced the tip of his cigarette around the ashtray's rim. "But I wish River were here. He'd come up with a better plan. I'm not good at this sort of thing. Deception."

"Are you sure this guy will go through with his end and cancel?"

"Yeah—I promised him a free . . . a free piece of merchandise. In exchange."

Brian walked out the gate and strode through the tall grass beside the road. So far so good. Mr. Parks had called and canceled—told Grant there was an emergency at his business. Brian finished with his first and only client, then 'accidentally' left his pager in his room. *So Grant can't tell me if he books another client.*

But Grant's men would be following him. *They'll see me go to the hotel—but they won't know what I'm doing. Probably think I'm meeting Claire or something.* Mr. Parks would use the side entrance.

He heard Stu's SUV before it came around the corner. Right on time. They stopped for lunch on the way. Brian insisted on Ships. "You get to toast your own bread." He pointed to the dilapidated toaster at the end of the table.

"Uh huh. It's so cool we get outta class for this. No P.E."

Brian nodded. He'd always hated P.E., too.

"My parents are going to dinner with some friends tonight. Wanna come over?"

"I can't. I'm meeting with a client."

"How long will that take?"

"An hour."

"Why don't you come over after?"

"I don't know...."

"Come on. How often do we get the house to ourselves?"

Brian smiled. "Okay."

"Where's your meeting? I'll pick you up."

"No, that's okay. I'll take a cab."

"How much will that cost—fifty bucks? That's just stupid. I'll pick you up. What time?"

I guess it's okay. "Six forty-five." Brian gave him the name of the hotel.

"I'll meet you in the lobby."

"No, just pull up out front." He felt uncomfortable with Stuart going into the hotel. *I don't know why. It's not like he would see anything.* But the whole thing made him nervous. *Too late to back out now.*

The waitress brought their food, and Stu said, "What's in that duffel bag you brought?"

He opened his mouth, but nothing came out. He looked away. "Uh, paperwork. You know, for the . . . merchandise."

Brian put his bread into the toaster, then glanced at his friend. Stuart seemed a little upset. *Does he know I just lied?*

They arrived early at the Performing Arts Center. Another band was playing. Stuart checked the program. "Glendale Youth Band. They're the ones to beat."

They watched from the back of the audience. The band was good. Maybe too good. Stuart frowned. "Come on. We better check in."

They found the backstage area set aside for their group. Mr. Williams seemed relieved to see them. *He wasn't sure I'd make it. Me, neither.* Brian had asked him last week if any photos would be taken for the newspaper. Mr. Williams answered, 'If we win. With your duets, we've got a real chance to finally beat Glendale. They'll probably want a photo of you and Stuart.'

So Brian planned to leave before the winners were announced. He'd arranged for a cab to meet him at the Arts Center right after the performance. He had lots of time to get to the hotel—it wasn't far, but it would be rush hour.

God, I hope everything works. He tried not to think about what Grant would do if he found out. *Probably never let me see Stuart again. I shouldn't have done this.* He bit his lip. *Too late now.*

Stu said, "Let's see if my dad's here yet. He took the afternoon off to watch us perform."

They spotted Ted as he walked in the main entrance from the parking lot. Ted smiled. "Good to see you again, Brian." His gaze lingered on the faded bruise on his cheek. Brian frowned and wondered if Stu had told him anything.

Ted suggested they sit down and watch the next band. Somehow Brian ended up between Stuart and his father. He felt uncomfortable so close to Ted; they were almost touching. *He's so—*Brian closed his eyes. *Yummy.* He clenched his hands in his lap to keep them from accidentally straying. Kept repeating to himself, *He's Stuart's dad. He's Stuart's dad.* But it didn't stop his body's response.

Finally Stu said it was time to go backstage to warm up.

Thank god. "It was nice talking to you, Mr. Goldberg."

"Please, call me Ted."

Brian smiled at him. "Ted."

The performance went great. He and Stuart got a standing ovation. Mr. Williams was thrilled. Brian collected his things as soon as they left the stage and hurried outside to the cab before anyone could stop him.

He arrived in plenty of time, showered, then paced the hotel room in the tight leather skirt from the duffel bag. A soft knock at the door made him jump. He checked the peephole and saw the silver hair of his client, right on schedule.

Fifty minutes later Mr. Parks ran his fingertip up Brian's bare chest. "I like this discount. We'll have to do it again sometime."

Brian tossed the hundred dollar tip onto the nightstand. "I don't think so."

"Oh, I do. You'd be in big trouble with Grant if he knew what you've done here."

Brian met his gaze, and his voice turned cold. "And Veronica and little Katie would be a bit upset if they knew what *you've* done here."

Mr. Parks sucked in his breath, eyes round.

"Don't try to play games with me, Leland. I've seen your file." Brian got out of bed and tossed the man's clothes onto the rumpled sheets. "Time for you to go."

He lit a cigarette and watched Leland Parks get dressed. The man hurried out without a word. *I scared him. Good. Asshole.*

He rinsed off in the shower, put on his regular clothes and stuffed everything else into the duffel bag. He examined himself in the mirror for traces of what he'd been doing. Ten minutes until Stuart would arrive. It felt weird to see him so soon after a client. Mixing up his worlds.

He started to worry again about Grant. Picked up the phone and dialed. "Hi. I just realized I left my pager at home. I'm sorry."

Grant sighed. "You really should be more careful."

He didn't know I left it—he hasn't been trying to reach me. "I'm sorry. Is it alright if I go to Stuart's awhile, or do you need me to come home?"

"You've already been gone all day. But I suppose you can stay for a bit. I don't want you out late; you have a busy schedule tomorrow. I'll send a car for you at nine."

"Okay. Thanks—I'll see you tonight."

"Alright. Goodbye, dear."

Relief flooded him as he hung up. Grant sounded perfectly normal. *He doesn't know about Mr. Parks. I did it. I did it.* He felt giddy as he headed out the door and down the elevator.

Stuart's first words when Brian got in the car were, "We won!"

"Alright!"

They high-fived. "It didn't seem right that you weren't there. We all went onstage, and they handed Mr. Williams a trophy."

"I bet he's happy." Brian noticed Jacob in the backseat, and his heart thumped. *It's okay. They don't know what I've been doing.*

Stu said, "I couldn't leave him home alone. Anyway, they wanted you to play something on the piano, but you were gone."

"I'm glad we won. This turned out to be a really good day."

They ate dinner when they got to the house; then Jacob settled in front of the TV, and Brian and Stuart headed for the bedroom. They cleared a spot on the floor and sat down to look through Stu's CD collection. Stuart asked, "When are we gonna play a gig? Do you think we're ready?"

"Maybe . . . I hadn't really thought about it." He drained his glass of water. "I'm so thirsty." He knew why—nerves and sex. *But I can relax now.* "I'm gonna get more water. Want some?"

"No, thanks."

The duffel bag drew Stuart's gaze as soon as Brian left the room. *Why would he lie about what's in there?* He picked it up and stared at it on his lap. *I shouldn't.* But he unzipped it and peered inside. Something dark. Felt like leather. He pulled it out—a miniskirt. His brain made no sense of it.

He heard Brian go into the bathroom. *Hurry.* The next item was a see-through top. "What the hell?" Small packets littered the bottom of the bag. He grabbed a few and read the words printed on one. 'Mini Lube-Tube.' The others were condoms. His heart started pounding. He stared at the black clothes lying on the floor, the condoms in his hand.

He forced himself to look in the bag one more time. A long leather thing. He pulled it out and gasped. A riding crop. A hundred dollar bill fell onto his lap. Voices echoed through his stunned brain. *'Oh, come on, you have sex with every guy you meet?' 'Pretty much, yeah.' 'I had a client earlier. I'm tired.'* Brian's words clicked into place. *'I promised him a free . . . a free piece of merchandise.'* Stuart's throat caught. *And the merchandise was you.*

He heard the bathroom sink run and stuffed everything into the bag in a panic. He set it aside as Brian opened the door. His gaze rose to his friend's innocent face. *I can't believe it.*

"Stu, are you okay?"

"No. No."

Brian sank down before him. "What is it?"

"Are you . . . having sex with your clients—is that what you do? Is that what they pay you for?"

Brian's heart dropped, and his mouth fell open.

Stu said, "Can you look me in the eye and tell me it's not true? Tell me I'm wrong, and I'll believe you."

Brian stared into those big brown eyes and searched inside himself. *I could lie to you now.* But if he did, he knew something inside him would change forever. Tears stung his eyes. *I don't want to become that person.* He bit his lip and looked away.

"Oh, my God." Stuart's head sank into his hands, and his body trembled.

Brian rubbed Stuart's back, then pulled away. *Probably doesn't want me to touch* him. *My god, my god. I can't believe this.* He got up and started pacing. His impulse was to leave. *But I can't. I've got to deal with this.* "Stuart."

He looked up but couldn't see through his fogged glasses. "Damn it." He cleaned them with his shirt, then wiped his face and peered up at Brian. "Why?"

"Why?" He blinked. "It just . . . happened. It's not like I *planned* to become a prostitute. Great career goal, huh?" He shook his head. "Look, Stuart, you can't tell anyone. I mean it—not *anyone*."

Stuart was silent.

Brian knelt before him and met his gaze. "Stuart, listen to me. Your safety is at stake. These people have ties to the Mafia. And they will protect themselves at all costs. Do you understand?" He held Stuart's face between his hands. "You have to promise—I would *die* if I caused you to be hurt." Tears welled up. "Or your *family*, Stuart. No matter what you think of me—you have to promise."

Stuart's eyes were huge. "I promise."

"Not to tell anyone. Or do anything."

"Yes."

Brian nodded, then stood up and wiped his tears. "God, I hate this."

"Then why do you do it?"

"I mean I hate that I endanger the people I care about." He turned away and forced the words past the lump in his throat. "If you don't want to be friends anymore, I understand."

Stuart stood up. "I wouldn't just drop you—I *couldn't*. I love you."

Brian couldn't breathe for a moment. Stuart wrapped his arms around him and held him tight. Brian hugged him back. When he could speak, he said, "I love you, too." He looked up at Stuart's face. "But not in a sex way."

"Good."

He smiled at the relief in Stuart's 'good.' "I'm sorry."

"For what?"

"I don't know. For a lot of things." He sat on the bed, suddenly exhausted.

Stuart sat beside him in silence.

Brian asked, "What are you thinking?"

"I just . . . I can't believe it. I'm stunned."

He nodded. *Me, too.* "How did you know?"

"Your bag—I knew you lied about what was in it. So I looked. Sorry."

I knew something would go wrong today. "I need a cigarette." He rubbed his face and glanced at the clock. "God, look what time it is. Shit. I've gotta go." He stood and picked up his flute case, reached for the duffel bag and thought about what was in there. *That must've been quite a shock.* He looked at Stuart. "Are you going to be okay?"

"I was about to ask you the same thing."

"Oh." He didn't know what else to say. "I guess I'll see you at band tomorrow."

"Yeah. Brian—" Stuart stopped him on his way out the door. "I'll always be your friend."

. . .

Brian went outside at band break, sank down on the cement wall and lit his cigarette with a sigh. He'd hardly slept at all. Worrying about Stu. He closed his eyes, tired all the way through. Extra clients today, plus band. Grant was making up for yesterday.

He's annoyed I was out all day. I shouldn't have gone to Stu's. Then he wouldn't have found out. But he wasn't sure he wanted that, either. *Amazing how one little decision can change everything.*

"Hey, Brian."

They greeted each other with slight smiles that vanished quickly. Stuart sat near him on the wall. "I can't think about anything else."

"Me, neither."

"I didn't get any sleep."

"Yeah." Brian glanced around. "Let's walk."

They strolled away from the band room, across trodden dead grass between the buildings. Deserted. Brian stopped to face him. "You understand how important it is not to tell anyone? Not even your parents."

Stu nodded. "When someone says 'Mafia,' I get the message. I would never mess with those guys. You shouldn't be involved, either."

"I didn't mean to be. But there's no danger as long as you don't say anything."

"I won't. Even though what you're doing is wrong, and it upsets me." He laid his palm against Brian's heart. "You have to make me a promise in exchange. Promise you'll never lie to me again."

A lump formed in his throat. He put his hand over Stuart's and whispered, "I promise." He laughed a little and squeezed Stuart's hand. He felt lighter, like a weight had lifted that he didn't even known was there. He blinked back tears. "I *hated* lying to you. It felt so wrong."

"Well, don't do it again."

"I won't."

They settled on the ground. Stu said, "My head is spinning, I'm so full of questions. I don't know where to begin. So I'll just pick one. What happened with those bruises—who hit you?"

Brian glanced away. "A client. He was angry. I don't really know why."

"How did your wrists get hurt?"

"He . . . was kneeling on them." He ground his jaw to stop the tears. *I've cried enough over that.*

"I don't understand."

Brian looked up at the cloudy sky and took a drag on his cigarette. Distanced himself. "I tried to get away, so he pinned me down by kneeling on my wrists."

"Oh, my God."

He shrugged. "It's okay. That's as far as he got. Security took him away."

"That's terrible." Stuart hugged him. "No wonder you were so upset."

He leaned his head against Stu's shoulder and closed his eyes. "Thank you for holding me. River's not here to do it." He sat back suddenly. "Don't tell River—please. He worries about me enough as it is. I'm glad it happened while he was gone."

"I won't tell him."

Brian flipped on the bathroom light to examine his face closely in the mirror. All traces of the bruise were gone. *Good.* River would be back soon. He closed his eyes. *Soon.*

He stepped into the bedroom to pick up his schedule. *'Bernard Padrea, here at 1 p.m.'* "Here?"

He asked Grant about it over breakfast.

"Oh, yes. Bernie will be coming here for awhile; he's having his condo remodeled. That will be nice for you, won't it? You won't have to spend the night away."

"But . . . ." *Leah.* "How long will it be? Do they have a place to stay?"

"Bernie's booked a suite in a high-profile hotel, so he would rather come here. He doesn't want to get a reputation." He buttered his toast. "There's no telling how long the remodel will take. It's scheduled to be completed in two months, but it always takes longer than the estimates."

Brian stared at his eggs. He couldn't swallow. *Months? It'll be months before I see her again? And last time I was such a dick.* He excused himself so Grant wouldn't see his face.

He waited by the driveway in the warm afternoon sun and finally heard the sound he'd been waiting for. A black limo slowed to a stop in front of the Main House. His heart raced as the door swung open.

River emerged, his face aglow as their eyes met. They flew into each other's arms. He buried his face in River's neck and held on tight. Breathed in his scent.

They managed somehow to make it up to Brian's room and fell onto the bed. Made love over and over. Brian ran his fingers through River's hair and stared up into his eyes. "I missed you so much." His body pushed against River's. "My body missed you, too."

"Mmm." River turned him over. Bit his shoulder and took him again, hard and wild this time. He collapsed onto Brian's back. Panted into his ear, "I can never get enough of you."

River held him close against his chest and nuzzled into silky hair that smelled of roses. He felt Brian's breaths grow even as the room darkened. He loved holding Brian while he slept. It was one of the things he treasured most. He whispered, "Someday I will hold you like this every night."

"Seeing the pyramids was so unreal!" River grinned across the breakfast table. "I can't believe I touched them. But there's tons of beggers. Not like Paris. It's totally romantic. Made me miss you even more." He touched Brian's hand. "We have to go someday. But what about you? What happened while I was gone?"

"Uh . . . ." *Craig tried to rape me. Stuart found out what I do for a living. There's got to be something I can tell him.* "I had another famous client. A rock star who was passing through on tour."

"Who?"

He glanced around the empty room and leaned over the table to whisper in River's ear.

"Wow! What was he like?"

"Sweet. Gentle."

"Any other exciting clients?"

"No. Oh—remember the girl who was raped? She finally had an orgasm while I was inside her. I'm *so* glad. I think she's officially better now." *I helped her.*

"That's great, Brian." He squeezed his hand. "I know how important that was to you."

His smile turned into a grimace. "And I stopped seeing Claire. She was getting too serious. And my heart already belongs to someone else." He leaned across the table to give him a kiss.

ᛞᛞᛞ

Brian answered the door with a wide smile. *Oh, John.* John stroked Brian's arm and moved past him. Brian's smile returned. "River, there you are."

River stepped onto the porch. "What's this?" He pointed to a metal rectangle with a number pad beside the front door. "That's new."

"Grant had it installed so I can get in without a key. You know me; I'd never remember to bring a key with me."

"He's keeping it locked now? How come?"

He shrugged and pulled River inside to kiss him. "Come on. We don't have much time before we go out."

They passed Grant and John in the parlor and raced upstairs.

Grant sank into the soft cushions and ran fingers through his thinning hair. He rested his arm across the back of the couch with a frown. "Sometimes I think I'm losing my edge. Getting too old."

John folded his arms across his chest, leaned against the mantel and stared at him.

"In all my tenure as Head of this House," Grant said, "there's never been a serious incident. Now it's happened twice with Brian in the space of a few years."

"It was just a matter of time. Craig Andraide's a fuck-up. His coke habit went too far too long. And . . . ." He stroked his chin and paced. "Brian brings out extremes in people."

Grant lifted a brow. "Are you saying it's *Brian's* fault?"

"No, of course not. But . . . you've found an exceptional boy. Perhaps this is the price you pay."

"That doesn't sound logical. I'm surprised to hear it coming from you." One of the things he valued about John was his ability to view the world completely unclouded by emotions or moral inhibitions. *I know my emotions get in the way, especially with Brian.*

He stared into John's eyes. So cold and calculating. He wondered what was going on in that sharp mind. *I shouldn't have told him.*

John sat in the chair by the couch and rested his elbows on his knees. "I don't know why these things happen. No one does. But I do know you are *not* losing your edge." A slight smile flashed across his lips. "I wish you were." He sat back. "And I know you let that boy have too much power over you."

The limousine stopped in front of a brick building. Grant smoothed David's brown hair. "Remember to behave."

Brian got out of the limo and kissed Maria's cheek. "I'm glad you came." Two more cars pulled up, and men started unloading equipment—amps, two mikes, guitars. He tugged on River's hand. "Let's see if Stuart's here yet."

They went inside the deserted lobby, dim after the bright sun. "It's beautiful," Brian said. The walls were painted dark red, with ornate fixtures and decorative white molding along the ceiling and doorways.

Grant followed them in. "This building dates back to the twenties. One of the finest concert halls in its heyday. Gregory brought me here many times when I was a boy." His smile seemed a little sad. "Now it's used as a movie theater. But today we'll revive it a bit."

River paused at the glass counter. "Hope this candy hasn't been here since the twenties. Ooo, popcorn." But the popcorn maker was empty. "Bummer. We shoulda had em staff the place."

"River, you're always hungry. Come on."

Brian led him through to the auditorium, a large space full of empty theater chairs. A green velvet curtain hung at the back of the stage to hide the movie screen. Stuart was already there setting up. He waved and climbed down from the stage.

"Stuart, this is River."

Stuart held out his hand. "It's great to finally meet you."

River looked him up and down with narrow eyes, finally took the offered hand. "You're not what I expected."

Brian said, "Where's Roger?"

"He'll be here." Stuart glanced at the small crowd standing at the back of the hall. "I didn't know you were bringing so many people."

"They all wanted to see us play. And there's a bunch of guys here to help set up and stuff." Security.

The boys walked over so he could introduce Stuart around. John seemed a bit *too* friendly. Brian's heart pounded, and he gave John a hostile stare. *Keep away from my friend.*

Grant rested his hand on Brian's shoulder. "I'm glad we arranged this. I've been curious to hear your little project. Pandora's Box." He stroked Brian's hair. "An interesting name."

Stuart watched them—the way Grant looked at Brian, touched him. Not only sexual, but possessive. It clicked. *Oh, my God.* He hadn't made the connection before. *'I work for Grant.'* That wasn't a lie. Stuart's stomach lurched as he stared at Grant. *This is real. These people are bad. Are they* all *in on it?* He glanced at sweet-looking David. Didn't look much older than Stu's brother. He felt queasy.

"Oh, look! Quinn's here." Brian hurried over to him. "I'm so glad you made it."

"I wouldn't miss it."

"This is Stuart."

Stuart met his gaze as they shook hands. *What's your role in this?*

"Quinn's my piano teacher. He's *great*."

Stu nodded. *Maybe he's okay.*

Brian's voice lowered, like he was talking to himself. "And look who else is here." He strolled over to a guy with unnaturally bright red hair, loaded down with camera equipment.

"Let me help you with that." Brian's finger stroked Justin's as he took the bag out of his hand. Their eyes locked. Brian murmured, "I haven't seen you in a long time." He watched Justin's breath pick up and said in a louder voice, "I'll help you unload your car."

He led Justin into the empty lobby, glanced around and pulled him toward a door behind the counter. A storage closet. He pulled Justin in.

"What about Grant?"

"Shh." He touched Justin's lips with his fingertip. Then with his tongue.

Justin pushed him against the boxes.

"Where's Brian?" Roger asked as they finished setting up his drums.

Stuart straightened and pushed up his glasses. "I don't know. Oh, there he is."

Brian grinned and joined them onstage. "This is gonna be a blast."

Roger sat behind the drum kit and whacked the snare. "My mom wanted to come, but it was too short notice for work."

"Sorry. Maybe next time . . . ." Brian glanced at Stu.

Stuart hadn't even told his parents about this, at Brian's request. Brian said he didn't feel comfortable having Stuart's parents in the same room with Grant. Now Stu understood why. *How could I be so stupid? Of course it's Grant. The big gate. The busy schedule. He's a pimp. Jesus. How did I get involved in this?*

Brian tuned his guitar and grinned at the small audience, then spoke into the mike. "Welcome to the debut performance of Pandora's Box." He launched into the opening song.

River watched from his seat between John and Grant. "He looks great up there. I didn't know he could sing so good."

Grant smiled. "Brian has many talents."

Brian's voice filled the room.

> "I hold his head while he lies
> and buries his face between my thighs
> He fills me up—"

He breathed into the microphone. A shaky breath that reminded River of sex. Brian's eyes closed, his voice barely more than a whisper.

> "Oh, *yeah*.
> The taste of your skin."

He backed away from the mike as his guitar took over the song's climax. River squirmed in his seat. "Am I the only one with a hard on?"

"No," John answered without taking his eyes off the stage.

> "My hands held high
> in the perfect surrender
> Ties me down
> keeps me on the brink
> And let me tell you,
> I'm not really what you think."

The last line was spoken in a low monotone and ended the song. The small audience cheered wildly.

Grant murmured, "He's grown so much stronger."

River looked at Grant and wondered what prompted that comment. "He's always been strong. But now he's . . . less fragile."

Brian grinned at the audience. "Thank you. That was fun." He glanced around the big empty space and tried to imagine it filled with people in twenties fashions. But all he saw were security guards who dotted the walls. His gaze returned to the audience. *I've had sex with more than half of them—not counting security. I haven't had sex with any security guards.* He'd never realized that before. He smiled at Jeffrey and started the next song. A rolling, bluesy number. *He should play this with us. Maybe I'll write another part for him.*

Four more songs and then the closer. A slow one. Brian wove a melodic pattern with his classical guitar and gazed into River's eyes while he sang.

> "I see the sunrise over the mountain
> I see the sun rise in your eyes
> and I know
> I will always love you.
> The beauty of your soul shines through your skin,
> shines through my heart
> and I know
> I have always loved you."

Tears filled River's eyes. They smiled at each other when the song ended, and Brian spoke into the mike. "Okay. That's all we have for now."

They got a standing ovation. Brian said, "If you want to stick around, Stuart and I will play a piano-clarinet duet." He took a seat at the concert grand.

After the duet, he closed with two short solo works. Chopin's dramatic 'Revolutionary,' a showy piece that never let up, followed by Schumann's slow, dreamy 'The Child Falling Asleep'—he liked it as much for the title as the music. The innocence.

And then it was over. "Thank you all for coming." He hugged Stuart and stepped off the stage.

֍֍֍

Brian wandered through the flower shop. *I'm sure this is the one.* He'd wracked his brain to remember the name of the shop Leah told him she went to every morning. He'd been there almost an hour. He touched the velvet petal of a white rose and gave his money to the man with the lovely British accent.

He stepped outside, white flowers in hand. *I'll just wait a little longer.* He leaned against the building to gaze across the street at the tall palms that grew down the middle of Highland Avenue, then beyond them to the trees in someone's yard. Delicate new leaves reached toward the sun; spring had arrived, always early here. He smelled the sweet scent of roses and turned toward the waiting taxi, heavy with disappointment.

"Brian!"

He turned back and saw Leah rushing toward him. She wrapped her arms around him in a bear hug. He laughed and held her tight.

She brushed the hair out of his eyes. "What are you doing here? Did you come to see me?"

He nodded, unable to speak for a moment.

She took his hand. "How have you been? I was so sad when I realized I wouldn't see you."

"Me, too."

She nodded toward the café next door. "Let's get a treat and talk."

They sat down and ordered dessert and coffee. He grinned, excited to be able to share with her again. "River's back from Europe. He showed me his photos. Versailles is *so* gorgeous." He shook his head. "I can't believe how jealous I am. I feel terrible, but I can't help it."

"That's understandable. I'm jealous, too."

"But Grant promised to take us to Ireland this summer! I can't wait. And Pandora's Box had its first performance. It was a blast, even though it was a really small audience—I've had sex with more than half of them!" He laughed. "They say you should know your audience . . . ."

She smiled and shook her head.

"Leah." He touched her hand. "I'm sorry I was such a dick last time. I was upset. And kind of drunk."

"It's alright, Brian. I'm just glad you found me. I hope we can keep meeting here."

"Yes! Whenever I can."

"So how are things with Claire?"

"We broke up." He explained what happened. "I never meant to hurt her. I still feel awful. She hates me now, and I have to sit by her every week at band."

"I'm sorry, Brian. But I hope you learned from this. If you're going to have a relationship with someone, you need to let them know you're *already* in a serious relationship. So they know where they stand."

He frowned at the table. "Yeah, I guess. So what have you been up to? What's it like to live at a hotel?"

"It's okay. Room service is great. And I still buy my flowers every day. But it's not home, you know?"

He nodded and squeezed her hand.

Brian sat between River and Grant in their booth at The Lily, and it suddenly hit him. *Grant has me followed—he knows about Leah now.* His heart skipped. *Maybe the guard didn't see us. Maybe Grant doesn't care.*

Grant rested his arm along the back of the leather booth. "Do you know what Quinn told me the other day?"

Brian's breath caught.

"He said you're one of the best sight readers he's ever met."

The panic vanished. "He did?"

Grant nodded. "You really enjoy performing, don't you?"

"Yes." He watched stagehands set up for the blues singer. "It's like I get to share the music."

"You seem quite at home onstage. Watching you last week. . . . " Grant smiled. "Come with me."

He left River to follow Grant to the bar area. Grant shook hands with a stranger. "This is Brian."

A man with thick grey hair turned to offer his hand. "It's an honor to meet you."

He doesn't really think so. He saw distaste in the man's eyes.

"I'm Jack Peterson. I run this club."

"Oh! I love The Lily." Brian gave him a real smile.

Grant made small talk for a few minutes, then said, "Brian would love to play with the jazz group tonight. He's an excellent pianist."

Brian's eyes widened. Mr. Peterson couldn't quite hide his displeasure. "Perhaps he could join them during rehearsal."

"Brian, do you want to play tonight?"

He grinned and nodded.

Grant smiled at the owner. "It's settled then. Tonight."

Mr. Peterson stammered a protest.

Grant patted the man's arm. "No, really. I insist." He chuckled as he led Brian away. "He has no idea what you can do. Why don't you show him?"

They made their way to where the musicians were preparing to go onstage. Brian leaned up to whisper, "Thank you," in Grant's ear, then turned to the singer to tell her how much he loved her performances. "I've been coming here for years, watching you. I can't believe I get to play along! I'm so excited."

She gave him an uncertain smile.

Grant suggested he perform a solo piece first. The woman agreed. "Then we'll come onstage. Here's the sheet music."

Brian touched the dark, soft skin of her arm. "Don't worry."

The announcer walked onto the stage. "We have a special treat for you this evening. A young man is joining our band tonight. Brian, why don't you come up here?"

His pulse raced as he stepped onto the stage. The crowd was so polite. *They think I'm cute.* He'd put up with that all through his childhood performances.

He took a seat at the piano. All nervousness vanished as he touched the keys. He considered what to play—something to fit the evening. *I know.* He began with slow chords for eight bars that suddenly turned into rolling upward scales, intricate and fast. The audience seemed stunned at first, then burst into spontaneous applause. The pace never slowed. He imitated the great James P. Johnson's recording of "Liza" as closely as he could—he'd been working on it with Quinn. The 1940s jazz reminded him of Disneyland, so much fun to play it made him laugh out loud. Three minutes later it was over.

He took a bow and couldn't wipe the grin off his face. *Thank you, Grant.*

ⁿⁿⁿ

Brian surveyed the crowd as Stuart tuned his bass guitar. Grant had gotten them their first real gig—at The Lily. Stuart said, "I hope Roger gets here soon." He glanced at Brian and shook his head. "Is everything you own tight?"

He looked down at himself. Black leather pants and matching vest. "These pants aren't tight."

"Yes, they are."

"Not compared to the others. But these are more comfortable." He stared at Stuart. "I can't get used to you without glasses."

Stu grinned. "It's *great*. But I had a hell of a time putting them in. Almost made me late." He glanced around the full club. "God, I'm nervous."

"Why? You've performed before."

"Not with such a big audience."

"Once the music starts you'll be fine." He caught River's eye in the crowd and waved, then noticed a security guard making his way to the stage. Escorting Roger.

Roger checked out the drum kit and grinned. "This is so cool. Do we get beer after?"

"No," Brian said quickly. "Actually, you might not want to hang out here. It's, uh, kind of a gay club."

"What? We're surrounded by queers?"

Brian's jaw tightened. "They won't jump you. Grant got us this gig. He knows the manager. Just leave right after we're done—that way you won't see anything."

"Got it." He settled behind the drum kit, and Brian strapped on his guitar.

The announcer came onstage. "We have a special treat for you tonight—music of a different sort before our regular jazz. Perhaps some of you were here last week when Brian dazzled us with his phenomenal skill at the piano. Tonight we'll hear him sing with his group, Pandora's Box."

Polite applause. Brian walked up to the mike with a big smile. "Hi." He started the first song.

The audience responded well, especially the teenagers. Brian lost himself in the music. Yet he was still aware of the people around him, more so than when he played the piano. The music's raw energy mixed with the crowd's and surrounded him. Became a part of him. He'd never felt anything like it. *Like magic.* Before he knew it, their set was almost over.

Stuart said in his ear, "You should tell them the name of the band again."

"You do it. I feel stupid talking."

Stuart spoke into his mike. "We're Pandora's Box. And Brian wrote all these songs, by the way."

The crowd cheered louder. They closed with an upbeat, playful number about sex. He stared out at the audience as the final chord faded. He didn't want it to end.

He hugged Stuart and bounded off the stage, bursting with energy. River was waiting. And Grant and Jeffrey. He hugged them all. Within moments a couple of guards were ready to escort Stuart and Roger out of the club. Stuart got Brian's attention. "I want to hang out with you. I'm still all giddy."

"I know! Isn't it great? But you can't stay here." He pulled Stuart aside. "Grant doesn't want you here cos you might see something. He doesn't know you know."

"Oh. Right."

"Don't be sad." He reached up to ruffle Stu's dark hair. "I'm too wound up to stay inside. I need to do something with all this energy." He glanced at River. *Sex would be amazing right now. Next time.* "Let's go outside and run around or something."

Stu laughed. "Okay."

൰൰൰

Stuart leaned over the cake to blow out the tiny flames—barely got them all. "Too many candles."

His mother gave him a loving and slightly sad smile. "All seventeen."

Brian watched her cut the cake and put it onto plates. Neat and methodical. *Not like how Mom does it.* His throat tightened.

He distracted himself by staring at Ted. The top two buttons of his shirt were undone; dark hair curled on the exposed sliver of chest. Brian wanted to tug on it with his teeth. He jumped when Ted's wife handed him a plate. He stared at the chocolate cake in his hands instead of looking at her.

They settled in the living room. Brian chose a stuffed armchair—didn't want to sit on the couch by Ted. *We might touch.* The thought made his groin tighten. *Stop it.* He stuck his fork in the cake and tasted. "Mmm. This is great."

Ted leaned forward and rested his elbows on his knees. "So when do we get to see the famous Pandora's Box?"

"Uh . . . maybe you could come to rehearsal."

Barbara said, "But we want to see you perform in front of an audience. Stuart says the music really comes alive."

Ted shook his head. "I don't understand why we can't get into The Lily. I know it's a private club, but this is my son we're talking about."

"Sorry." *Grant will never let you in.*

Stuart pushed up his glasses. "Our gigs at The Lily are great, but when will we play somewhere else?"

Brian shrugged.

"We'll work something out." Ted finished his cake and stood up. "We should get a move on. I'm sure the hordes of spring breakers have already beaten us to the best rides."

Brian followed Stuart down the hall. "I thought you'd wear your contacts today."

"Shhh." Stuart pulled him into his room. "My parents don't know. They'd be pissed."

"Why?"

"Because they specifically said *no* contacts, that's why."

"Too bad your present isn't ready yet." Brian had gotten him new glasses for his birthday, but they were still at the shop.

"Yeah." Stuart put on the Dr. Martens boots he always wore, then rummaged through the clutter on his bureau. He found a few twenties and stuck them in the back pocket of his jeans.

Brian checked his own jeans to make sure he had money and smoothed his favorite tee shirt. "Bet you can't say you don't like The Cure now."

Stuart gave him a half smile. "They have a few good songs."

"A few?"

"So when will we play a gig somewhere else?"

"Never. I mean, not anytime soon."

His brow knit. "Why?"

"Stuart, remember what I do for a living?" *I can't let my parents find me.* "I have to keep a low profile. That club is a controlled environment. We can't play anywhere else. Not for now."

Stuart stared at him in silence.

"Don't be mad. Think of it as practice—it's our time to get better, get used to playing in front of an audience. Your parents can come to a rehearsal."

"Yeah, whatever." Stuart left the room.

"Alright boys—young men, excuse me—" Ted smiled. "Meet us in front of Pirates of the Caribbean at six. We've got dinner reservations at the Blue Bayou." He pointed as Stuart moved away. "Don't be late, son."

"We won't."

Brian and Stuart dodged through the crowds toward Space Mountain. The line was long, but it moved fast. Stuart touched the wall when they reached the interior. "I love how it's like you're going into space."

"Yeah. How many times have you been to Disneyland?"

Stu shrugged. "A bunch. We came a lot even before we moved to L.A. It's only two hours from San Diego."

"San Diego?"

"That's where I'm from. We moved to Westwood right before I started high school. Sucked."

Brian nodded. "We moved a lot. It's hard. But you like living here now, don't you?"

"Yeah, especially with our band and everything. And you. I didn't think you'd be able to come today."

He leaned back against the rail. "I convinced Grant. Told him I'd make up for it. And I will—don't expect to see me again for a few days."

"You'll be busy."

"And tired."

Stuart shook his head. "How can you do it—*why?*"

"You'll probably never understand."

"Well, at least *try* to explain. How did you . . . get into it?"

Brian glanced around. A woman with small children in line behind them. Giggly teenage girls in front. "This isn't the place."

After the ride they got a snack and settled on the curb by the motor car runway track. Brian hunted for crispy fries in the sack. Licked the salt from his fingers.

"So spill it. Tell me the whole story."

He stared at the pavement and wondered where to begin. "Well . . . I think you've already gathered I wasn't happy at home. So—" He turned to Stuart. "This is all secret, too. You can't tell anyone."

"I know. I won't."

"'kay." He sipped his Coke and stared into the blur of passing legs. "So I ran away. With River."

"Were you two a couple yet?"

"No. That came after Grant picked us up. We were really hungry. And cold. It was raining, and River had a cough. We had nowhere to go and no money—we'd been sleeping in parks." He looked down. "River had a cough."

"So . . . Grant offered you food? Money? In exchange for sex?"

"No, no—we weren't *that* desperate. He bought us dinner and convinced us to go home with him. I would never do that normally, but we didn't have many options. He didn't have sex with us right away. But when he did, it was wonderful—he's great at that." Brian lit a cigarette. "An expert."

Stuart tried not to visualize Grant in that light. "I still don't get how you became a . . . ."

"It was gradual. Grant started bringing in different men for sex, and before I knew it they were paying. Before I knew it. Huh. Literally."

"What do you mean?"

"Just . . . there were a few men who paid to be with me before I knew they were paying."

Stuart was quiet. *It's like he tricked you into it.*

"I found out because one of them tipped me." He gave a short laugh. "I wonder how long Grant would've waited before he finally told me."

Stuart shook his head. "Unbelievable."

"Is it?"

"Grant picked you up off the street cos you were hungry and homeless and desperate, and he turned you into a prostitute."

"That's about right, yeah."

"And you love this man? How can you? That's terrible, what he did."

"It's not terrible. I'm happy with my life." Leah's words rang in his head, *'Are you trying to convince me, or yourself?'* He frowned and flicked his ashes. "Sure as hell's better than living at home, anyway. Grant's like a father to me. He loves me."

"Doesn't he love all his boys?"

"Not all of them, no." He took a final drag. Crushed his cigarette on the pavement and stood up. "You don't understand."

"No, I guess I don't." Stuart followed him and threw his trash away. "Wait a minute. So River's a—" He grabbed Brian to whisper in his ear. "River's a prostitute, too?"

Brian's heart beat faster as he stared into his eyes. He gripped Stu's arm. "Remember, it's a secret."

"I know. I just didn't realize River is, too." He shook his head. "It's weird."

"But he doesn't live at Grant's. I wish he did." He was taken by surprise how much that still hurt. *I haven't gotten used to living apart from him—not really. I just push it out of my mind. But it's always there.* River's voice came back to him. *'I miss you all the time.'* Brian whispered, "Me, too."

ཀྐཀྐཀྐ

Brian touched River's hand and grinned at Stuart. "Isn't this great? We finally get to hang out here together." Grant couldn't make their performance at The Lily tonight. *So I'm in charge.* Roger had taken off right after their set, as usual. But Stuart got to stick around.

Wish I weren't so tired. The hectic schedule was taking its toll. Extra clients, all his lessons, rehearsals and performances. Grant had set him up with a few piano gigs at The Lily, too. But Brian was so tired he could barely enjoy them.

He leaned back against the padded leather with a sigh and glanced around the club. A client sat at a nearby table. *The mobster.* Brian had a session with him yesterday. The man walked into the House, and Jeffrey greeted him with, *'Hey, Frank. How ya doing?'* Frank had responded with equal friendliness. Brian was amazed—Jeffrey never addressed anyone without a 'Mr.' first. *Not even me.*

Brian asked him about it later. *'Oh, me and Frank go way back. We grew up together in New York—my father worked for his father.'*

So strange. Sweet, jolly Jeffrey had a past that connected him to the Mafia.

River's arm slipped around his waist and brought him back to the present. "What've you been up to?"

He shrugged. "Same ol'. Oh—" He spoke quietly so Stuart wouldn't hear. "Remember the girl who was raped? She's not a client anymore. She's got a boyfriend now, so she decided to stop seeing me." He smiled. "I'm so happy for her. But I'll miss her. She's sweet."

River kissed his forehead. Stuart watched Brian stroke his jaw, and their lips met softly. *Whoa.* He'd never seen two guys kiss before. And they kept on kissing. Stuart glanced away—out of politeness, not because it bothered him. It didn't. In fact, it seemed perfectly natural. *I thought it would gross me out.*

Brian finally pulled away and turned to smile at Stuart. "Sorry—not trying to make you feel left out. We just can't help it."

"That's okay. I don't wanna be included in that."

Brian laughed and kept looking at him, even though River was kissing his neck. "I'm still not used to you without your glasses. You don't look like Stuart."

"Good." He sipped his beer and felt terribly grown up. But his eyes burned. The contacts made them more sensitive. The club was smoky—*especially at this table. Maybe next time I'll bring my glasses.* His new ones from Brian weren't bad; he liked them, actually. He and Brian picked out the new frames together—still dark, but smaller and oblong. And even better, the lenses weren't as thick. *Maybe I won't look like a nerd anymore.*

The song "With or Without You" came on and Stuart said, "Did you know U2 did a cover of 'Unchained Melody?'"

"No way! Really? I love that song."

"I picked it up at Phil's the other day."

Brian and Stu talked for awhile about music. Stuart managed to ignore the way River kept nibbling on Brian. River touched his bare stomach, then rubbed the leather next to his crotch. Stu's eyes widened.

Brian trailed off mid-sentence. He turned and took River's face between his hands to kiss him long and deep. Whispered, "Maybe it's time to go."

River nodded and kissed him again.

Stuart cleared his throat. "When are they going to bring the bill?"

Brian blinked. "They never bring a bill."

"I think it goes onto an account or something." River drained his glass and pushed it away.

Brian's brows lowered. "I don't want someone else to pay for our drinks."

River shrugged. "Don't worry about it. Let's go."

Brian pulled out a couple of bills. "That should cover it." He slid out of the booth after River.

Stuart stared at the two hundred dollars on the table and shook his head.

Maria went into the Room to change the sheets and jumped, startled by the figure under the covers. She moved closer. Brian, sound asleep. She glanced at the clock and shook him gently. "Pequeño niño, you must wake. You will miss band."

He struggled toward the surface. Thought he opened his eyes but didn't. His brain refused to cooperate.

"Brian." She shook him harder.

He jumped, then glanced around in confusion. He sat up and rubbed his face. Couldn't force his groggy mind to think.

"My poor niño, you look so tired." She touched his cheek. "But it is almost time for band."

Band. Crap. He forced himself out of bed and stumbled into the shower. The water helped a little, but his limbs still felt like lead. Even his face felt heavy, like gravity was pulling it down.

He still felt that way as he climbed into the backseat of the Mercedes. Jeffrey looked at him in the rearview mirror. "You okay, Mr. B? You look pale."

"Just tired." He turned sideways to put his feet up on the seat. Smoked a cigarette. And another. Not sleepy now, but he felt like crying. *I don't want to go to band. I'm so tired.* He flicked his ashes toward the ashtray. *I never have time for myself anymore, to just sit. It's making me crazy. I haven't written a new song in ages.*

Fuck. He sat up and leaned into the front seat to check their progress. Still on

Sunset, where the trees got taller and the road started to curve—just entering Westwood. "Don't turn. Keep going."

"You sho'?"

"Yes, I'm sure." He closed his eyes and focused on breathing. No time for yoga lately, either. *I can't take it anymore.* "Bring me to the ocean."

When they arrived he walked toward the water until he reached wet sand. He gazed out at the sea, let the rhythm of the waves fill him, the lonely cries of the gulls. The warm salty wind blew against his face, and his mind cleared. Calmed. He bent to pull off his boots and socks. Wriggled his toes into the cool, wet sand. *This is life. This is real.*

How long since I stood and stared at the water? Too long. Something had to give. Last week the band director posted sign up sheets for next season. Brian knew now with sudden clarity. *I can't do it.* He bit his lip. *I'll miss it, but I got what I needed. Stuart. Pandora's Box. I never have time to feel lonely now, but I'm too tired to enjoy anything.*

But most important, the youth band cut into his time with River. *I hardly see him anymore.* His throat tightened at the thought, and he knew his decision was final. The season would be over soon. Then no more youth band.

A week later he was sitting beside Claire. Cold Claire. Mr. Williams had tried to talk him into signing up for next season. So did Stuart. Grant was the only one happy about it. *He thinks he won. Maybe he did.*

Brian stared at the writing on the chalkboard and remembered when he asked Claire about it months ago. *'We have a concert next week? I didn't know about that.' 'No, it's not for us. The stuff on the board's for the Davis High band.'* Made him feel sad and left out. She'd touched his knee and kissed his cheek.

Claire. I'm sorry I hurt you. I wish you could understand. He glanced at her—she was chatting with Debbie. Debbie saw him and glared. *Bet they're glad I'm quitting.* He turned back to read the chalkboard.

> *Countdown to graduation:*
> *Seniors: 18 days*
> *Juniors: 207 days*
> *Sophomores: 387 days*

I'd be a sophomore, wouldn't I? Fifteen, but I skipped a grade. If I were in high school. If I belonged here. He watched Mr. Williams study the sheet music. *I never even got to make a pass at you. You probably wouldn't go for it, anyway.* He was starting to get the idea that not *everyone* wanted to have sex with him. He sighed and finished reading the countdown on the chalkboard.

> *Frosh: ∞ + 1*

He laughed in surprise. The infinity symbol brought him back to when River carved into the tree with his pocketknife. 'River + Brian ∞'

River. I'll get to spend more time with you. That's worth everything.

Naked in the Rain

. . .

The Davis High auditorium filled with milling teenagers. No classes on the last day of school, just an all-day assembly. Stuart's parents took their seats, excited to finally see Pandora's Box perform. But first the youth band played. The proud parents weren't the only ones cheering loudly after the piano-clarinet duets. Ted squeezed Barbara's hand. "Our son's a natural."

The curtain closed for intermission; then Mr. Williams stepped up to the microphone and shushed the crowd. "Please take your seats. Thank you. And now for a change of pace, I'm proud to present a group consisting of three young men from the Westwood Youth Band. Please welcome Pandora's Box."

Barbara sat on the edge of her seat as the lights dimmed, and the curtain opened. "Look at him—he looks great. Where are his glasses?" She stopped thinking about that as the lyrics sunk in. "Oh, my."

Ted rubbed her back and spoke loudly into her ear. "Relax, honey. They're great. And look at the response."

The audience was on its feet, cheering and dancing. She shook her head. "But do you hear what he's saying? That Brian."

"He's incredibly talented—and talk about charisma. Not to mention our son chose him for a friend. Relax, Barb."

She did relax when the slow, quiet song took hold. Beautiful lyrics about love. The crowd was captivated. Ted put his arm around his wife, and she leaned against him.

The closer was a fun, bluesy number. Brian grinned at the audience. He'd never played for so many teenagers before. Their enthusiasm was exhilarating. But now it was over—they'd shortened the set list to exclude the really naughty songs.

The boys stepped off the stage, immediately surrounded by the excited crowd. "That was great! You guys rock! Play some more!"

Lots of girls touching him. He glanced at Stuart—he was getting the same thing. Stu met his gaze with wide eyes. Brian worked his way over and shoved a few condoms into his hand. Stuart's mouth fell open when he saw what he was holding. "That's not going to happen." He tried to give them back.

"No, keep them. Think of them as good luck."

Stuart tucked them out of sight. He pulled Brian aside. "What do I do?"

"Just go with it. It's your big chance."

"But I don't know what to do with a girl! Can't you give me some advice?"

Brian thought a moment. "Girls like softer touches than men. When you kiss, don't ram your tongue down her throat."

"Okay. What else about kissing?"

"Don't use your tongue right away. And don't think. Just let your body do what comes naturally. But make sure you hear her if she says no."

"Okay. Don't think. Not too much tongue. Listen to her."

"Yeah. Pay attention to how her body responds." He patted Stuart's arm. "Good luck."

"Wait—where are you going?"

He grinned. "I'm spending the rest of the day with River."

. . .

He wiped sweat from his lip as he put his flute down and scanned the audience seated at picnic benches, on blankets. No sign of him. Brian turned to the next piece, 'Deep River,' and sighed. River said he would try to be here. *He hasn't made it to any of our concerts. This is his last chance*—the last performance of the season. Brian's last time with the youth band.

He used clothespins to clip the sheet music to the stand. The wind had a tendency to kick up when they started playing—the only drawback to playing outside. But otherwise it was great. Sounded different, though. Like the music got swallowed up into the air. *A rather high ceiling,* he thought and gazed up at the hazy sky.

When he looked down again, he was staring into River's eyes—he was just taking a seat on a folding chair. They smiled at each other.

Claire saw the transformation in Brian's face. *He never smiled at me like that.* She couldn't believe how much it still hurt, five months after they broke up. She searched the crowd trying to figure out who made his face glow like that. It was no use. *It doesn't matter. He doesn't matter.*

But it ruined the rest of the concert for her. When it was over she put away her flute and walked to the picnic table laden with food for their farewell potluck. She didn't want to try the chocolate chip cookies Brian brought—but she had to. They were delicious, of course.

She heard him say he made them himself and looked toward his voice. Their eyes caught; then he glanced down.

When he looked again, she'd turned her back to him. He stared a moment at the blond hair shining in the sun. Shook himself and watched River load up his plate.

The band director came closer to shake his hand. "We'll miss you, Brian. If you change your mind, let me know."

He smiled. *I won't.*

Mr. Williams folded his arms over his chest. "A word of advice. If you continue to smoke as much as you do, it will affect your breath control and your voice."

Brian's brow lowered. *Fuck off.* He turned and strode away to stand by a picnic table apart from the others.

River and Stuart followed. River set down his paper plate and massaged Brian's shoulders. "Don't let him bother you. You know how adults are." He straddled the bench. "Always givin us a hard time."

"Yeah." He settled between River's legs.

River wrapped one arm around him and ate macaroni with the other. Brian faced the opposite end of the bench where Stuart sat. "So what happened after the assembly? Did you use the condoms?"

Stuart laughed. "No. But . . . I did get a little action."

"Tell me!"

"I met a great girl named Gina. We kissed."

"She wouldn't let you go farther?"

"I didn't try."

"*What?* How could you not?" Brian shook his head. "I don't understand you."

River glanced at Stuart. "Maybe he's gay."

"I am not! There's nothing wrong with going slow—"

"And there's nothing wrong with being gay."

"That's not what I meant. I was happy just to be kissing. Besides, I'll see her again."

Brian's eyebrows lifted. "Yeah?"

"She gave me her number."

"Stuart, that's great." He helped himself to a cookie from River's plate. "How old is she?"

"My age, I guess. She's a junior, too—or she *was*. I can't believe I'm a senior now. One more year in and out." His smile faded, and he mumbled, "Then what?" He shook his head and stood up. "I'm gonna get more punch." He left them alone.

Brian turned to River and touched his chest. "I'm so glad you made it."

River stroked his cheek. "I wish I coulda come to more."

River leaned down to brush his lips against Brian's. Soft, gentle kisses that warmed him all the way through.

The bench wiggled—Stuart was back, eating a brownie. Brian said, "Ooo, that looks good. Are there any left?"

He turned to see Claire standing a few feet away, hands on her hips. She glowered down at him, and her voice shook. "Are you trying to humiliate me? Haven't you done enough already?"

He said softly, "I don't know what you mean."

"Kissing a guy like that—in front of everyone?"

He blinked. He hadn't thought twice about kissing River. "That has nothing to do with you. I told you I was in love with someone else."

"What?"

"I was brought up differently—I didn't realize what I was doing would hurt you."

She looked away, but he saw her eyes fill.

"I don't expect you to forgive me. I just want you to know I didn't hurt you on purpose."

She covered her face as tears fell down her cheeks.

"I'm sorry, Claire."

She nodded, clearly unable to speak. She turned and hurried away.

He watched her leave, and his heart ached for her.

River rubbed his shoulder. Brian said, "Let's go. I don't belong here."

He saw Mr. Williams as they headed toward the parking lot. Brian stopped to say goodbye. He leaned up to kiss his cheek, then walked away.

*"in summer
cool slumber
my number
is up
there's peaches
in reaches
with leeches
at heart
I'm fakin'
and blinkin'
it's stingin' mine eyes
abhorring
he's gorging
still boring
on me"*

- Mark Linkous (Sparklehorse), "Cruel Sun"

CHAPTER 31

Grant was in his sitting room when his pager started beeping. He stared at it for a second. The blinking red light was reserved for emergencies—Brian's panic button. His heart thumped.

Grant was first to reach the Room. An old, naked man lay on top of Brian. Brian's hands were in cuffs over his head, his breath coming short and fast. Grant moved closer and realized the man was Bernie Padrea. It made no sense. Bernie would never hurt anyone.

"He—" Brian gasped. The man's weight on his chest made it hard to breathe. "He collapsed."

Jeffrey arrived as Grant turned Padrea's face toward him. His eyes were closed, skin damp. "Jeffrey, help me roll him off Brian."

Brian took in lungfuls of air as the weight lifted. "I think he had a heart attack."

Grant felt for a pulse. "He's alive." He left to call Dr. Griffin as more security poured into the Room.

Jeffrey told them to stand down and unfastened the leather cuffs. He squatted to look Brian in the eye. "You okay?"

He nodded as his eyes filled. Jeffrey's arm went around his shoulders. "Let's get you outta here." Jeffrey escorted him to his bedroom.

Brian couldn't stop shaking. "I hope he's okay."

He leaned against the wall of the rehearsal room as they waited for Roger to show up. "Have you called that girl from the assembly?"

Stuart grinned at him from his seat on the floor. "Gina. Yeah. We're going out Friday night."

"That's great."

Stuart tugged on the carpet. "I don't know . . . I've never been on a date."

"Your first date." He nodded. "Claire was mine."

"Give me some advice—*please*."

"Take her to dinner. Stop when she says no." He frowned at the lawn through the sliding glass door.

"Still feel bad about Claire?"

"No. I mean, yes. But that's not what I was thinking about. One of my clients—" He took a deep breath. "Had a heart attack. While we were having sex."

"Oh, my God."

"He was lying on me, and I didn't know if he was dead or not. He's a good guy. I've been seeing him for years. The hospital says he'll be okay."

"I'm sure he's in good hands."

He stared out the door again, at sunlight on green grass, green trees. And smiled. "There's good news, though. We're going to Ireland soon! I'm so excited. And when we get back we'll have another trip. An associate of Grant's just bought a club in San Francisco, and he wants Pandora's Box to perform there."

"Alright!" Stuart bounced to his feet and looked past Brian as the sliding glass door opened. "Hey, Roger the Shrubber—wanna go to San Francisco?"

"Why? Cos it's full of faggots?" He looked at Brian. "I saw you at the picnic. Kissing that guy. Disgusting. I *knew* you were a fag."

Brian stared at him a moment. He kept his voice low. "What's between River and me is the most beautiful thing in this world. If you look at us and all you see is ugliness, then I feel sorry for you." He walked out.

He peeked around the corner from the parlor to see who was at the door. John. His mood lifted when he saw River behind him. He laughed as River chased him up the stairs and into the bedroom.

Fifteen minutes later they lay side by side as sweat cooled his body. "I definitely want to spend time in the Galway area—that's where the O'Kelly's are from. My dad's parents came to America right after they got married."

"So you're half Irish?"

"No, three-quarters. My mom's half Irish, half English."

"Hm. No wonder you like the rain so much."

Brian smiled. "What are you? I mean, where's your family from?"

He sat up. "Fuck if I know."

"Deloy." He stroked River's arm. "Sounds kind of French. What about your mother's side? Didn't she ever say?"

"Naw. My grandparents grew up in the same shit-town we did. *That's* where we're from—Arizona." He lay back and folded his arms behind his head. "I think Grandpa missed it after he moved away. The desert's in our blood—that's what he used to say."

"Mm." He rested his cheek against River's stomach. "No wonder you like the sun so much." He felt River stroking his hair, and his eyelids drooped.

They both jumped when the door opened. John snapped, "River, get dressed. Time to go."

River pulled on his clothes and kissed Brian goodbye. "See you soon, babe."

After River left John came in again and closed the door. Brian felt very naked under the sheets.

John said, "I've got a problem—and you're going to help me." He crossed his arms and paced. "I don't want River to travel. He's just landed an important client; if he leaves now it will be ruined. But Grant refuses to postpone your trip. So you see ..." He turned to face Brian. "The solution is for you to go to Ireland without him."

"No."

"Are you sure? How do you feel when I say the name . . . Craig Andraide?"

He gasped. Flashed back to that moment with his face smashed into the sheets. Craig's knees grinding into his wrists.

"Oh, yes, I know all about how he hit you and came *this* close to raping you. Wouldn't River be interested in hearing about that?"

"You wouldn't do that to him!"

"Try me."

He stared into John's icy blue eyes and knew he would. *You're a horrible person.*

He wasn't sure River had ever truly gotten over what happened with Alan. He couldn't put River through that again. Nothing was worth that. His voice came out in a whisper. "What do you want?"

His lips curved in a cold smile. "I thought you'd see it my way. Your job is to come up with a credible story for Grant. Some reason why you'll go without River—or don't go at all. I don't care. Just make sure Grant buys it.

"Meanwhile, I'll tell River I stood up to Grant, and he backed down. That will be the story in my House. So not only do I win, but it boosts my power. Quite a satisfactory arrangement." He came closer, put his hands on the bed and leaned in. "Remember that, next time you think you can have your way over me. *I* have the power now." He closed his hand into a fist in front of Brian's face. "I have your secret." He turned abruptly and walked out.

Brian gave his prepared speech over breakfast after a sleepless night. "Grant, do you think we could wait to go to Ireland? Things are going so well with Pandora's Box; I don't want to be gone a whole month right now. I just wrote some new songs we need to learn and . . . ."

Grant stared at him, toast forgotten halfway to his mouth.

Brian stumbled on. "And . . . I'm excited to play Jim's club in San Francisco. I was hoping we could go sooner, when the new songs are ready."

"But you've waited all your life to visit your ancestral home." The lines on Grant's forehead deepened. "Does John have anything to do with this?"

"No!" *Shit. Don't panic.* He scrambled to think of something else. "It's just . . . Stuart's having problems at home. I don't want to leave him right now. I'm the closest friend he's got."

A warm smile touched Grant's face, and he rested his hand on Brian's. "You're the kind of boy people wish for."

He's buying it. Thank god. But why did you have to tell John? "Maybe we can go some other time." *I'll get there someday. I swear I will.*

. . .

River glared at John. "How *dare* you? This is going to crush Brian!"

"Calm yourself, River. It's business. We don't want to lose your new client."

"I can't believe Grant would let you cancel our trip." He headed for the door.

"Don't go to Grant about this. The decision is final."

"I'll talk to whoever I want!"

John folded his arms over his chest. "You won't breathe a word of this outside this House." A slight smile played on his lips. "I finally won over Grant. Let's not rub his nose in it."

"That's not what I'm trying to do." He met John's cold stare. "This isn't over yet."

"Oh, yes, it is. Remember who is Head of this House, River. Do not question my authority. If you talk to Grant, then I'll be having a little talk myself." He leaned back against the desk and cocked his head. "I wonder how sweet Brian would feel if he knew who was responsible for Alan's death?"

He felt like he'd been socked in the stomach. "You wouldn't."

John smiled.

"How could you do this?"

"Business, River. It's just business."

Brian hung up the phone. The most awkward, stilted conversation he'd ever had with River. *I hope he couldn't tell I'm hiding something.* The phone rang again. Stuart this time. Brian asked how his date went.

"Good, it was good. I was really nervous, though."

"Did she have to tell you to stop this time?"

Stuart laughed. "No. So when are you leaving for Ireland?"

Brian's lips tightened. "We're not. We're not going."

"What? Why not?"

"Uh . . . ." He curled the phone cord around his finger. "I don't know if I should say."

"What the hell does that mean?"

"I'll tell you later, okay? I don't want to talk about it over the phone. But listen, we're going to San Francisco soon. The problem is, Grant doesn't want you to come. He's afraid you'll see something."

"But how is it any different than playing The Lily? Security can spirit me away to the hotel right after the gig, where I'll be safe from all evils of the world."

"Yeah—that's a good point. It isn't any different than The Lily. I won't perform without you, Stuart. I'll convince him. But we need a new drummer. Roger is out."

A knock sounded at the door, and Grant's head peeked in.

"I gotta go." He hung up the phone and stood.

"How much rehearsal time will you need with the replacement musicians?"

Brian looked up at him, fists clenched at his sides. "We don't need a replacement for Stuart. I won't perform without him. He won't see anything—and even if he does, it won't matter."

His eyes narrowed. "And why is that?" Grant studied his face. "Is it because he already knows?"

Brian's mouth fell open. He couldn't get any words out.

"Damn it!" Grant's fist landed on the dresser and made everything bounce. "I knew I shouldn't let you join that band. I *trusted* you." Molten amber eyes bored into him. "How could you do that—tell someone our secret? *Why, Brian?*"

"I didn't." His voice was barely more than a whisper. "I didn't tell him—he figured it out. I guess I wasn't careful enough. I'm sorry!"

"To whom else have you *accidentally* let it slip?"

"*Nobody*. He's the only one."

"And what are we to do with dear Stuart now?"

"Nothing!" His heart pounded. "Grant, he's known for months. If he were going to do something, he would've done it already. He understands he can't tell. We can trust him."

"Like I trusted you?"

"Grant—" His eyes filled with tears.

Grant turned away. "Well, the damage is done. You'd best pray Stuart does understand, or *he* will be the one to pay for your indiscretion." He faced Brian again with eyes turned cold. "Stuart's young brother is quite lovely, isn't he? Don't worry—Jacob is perfectly safe. As long as Stuart keeps his mouth shut."

Brian couldn't speak. *My god, what have I done?*

"I found you a drummer." River sat on the bed. "Rick."

Brian tried to focus. *One of John's boys. And River's friend—he must be alright.* "He plays drums?"

"Yeah. Now you just need a bass player."

"No, Stuart's coming with us. Grant agreed."

"Really? How'd you convince him?"

"Uh . . . ." Brian paced, then turned to face him. "Stuart knows about us. About the Houses."

River stood up. "Are you fuckin serious? You *told* him? I can't believe you did that. Are you in love with him?"

"No! Of course not." He took River's face between his hands. "I couldn't be in love with him. You have my whole heart. There's no room for anyone else. Don't you know that?" He searched River's eyes.

River glanced down. "Yeah."

"Then why are you so jealous of Stuart?"

"I'm not!"

"River."

"You guys have so much in common. Your music . . . ."

"That doesn't matter. I love you because of who you are, not what we have in common. Stuart's my friend. You're my love." He touched his lips to River's.

They sat on the bed together, and River made him explain how Stuart found out. He listened intently as Brian told him about the client he met at the hotel. River was amazed. "I can't believe you pulled that off. You outwitted Grant. I'm proud of you, babe."

"No, it was stupid. Too risky—I shouldn't have done it." Brian told him the rest. "Grant was madder than I've ever seen him. He said some things—" He met River's eyes, and suddenly it was hard to speak. "Threatened Stuart's brother. I don't know if I'll ever feel the same about Grant again."

಄಄಄

Stuart followed him into the bedroom. "I never thought I'd get to see your room." He'd already gotten a tour of the Main House. He was as captivated by the ballroom as Brian, even though it wasn't empty—men were setting up a drum kit on the stage. Their new rehearsal space.

Stuart glanced around the bedroom. "No posters. I'm surprised."

"I used to have them, when I lived at . . . with my parents." He shrugged. "I need to write out a song for us to cover—Jim requested it. He's the owner of the club we'll be playing." Brian flashed on that afternoon in the hotel room. The whip in Jim's hands. "Stuart—" He met his eyes. *You're gonna see some things . . . .* "When River and I kiss, does it bother you?"

"No. It really doesn't. It seems totally natural."

He smiled. "You see more clearly than Roger. It'll be strange to play with a different drummer."

"Maybe he'll come around."

His lips pressed into a frown. "I don't know that I want him back." He sat on the carpet in front of the stereo. "Will you help me with this? Just pause the CD when I tell you."

Brian got out blank sheet music and wrote the notes as he listened. But he couldn't keep up. "Pause it."

Stuart watched him scribble with his left hand. "How do you do that? Write the music so easily?"

He shrugged. "I was reading music before I knew how to read. I guess that makes it easy for me."

Stuart pulled on his lower lip and nodded slowly. "My dad thinks you're so talented." *You are,* he thought.

Brian smiled. "He's a nice guy."

"Yeah. But I had to really fight for this trip to San Francisco. They—" *Think you're a bad influence.* "Didn't want us unsupervised. I reassured them Grant will be there. Isn't that a laugh? Knowing Grant will be there makes them feel *better.*" He shook his head.

"Stuart," he whispered. "The reason Grant's letting you come is because he knows. He knows about you."

Stuart's eyes got big.

"I didn't tell him—he figured it out. Damn it, I'm so bad at lying. Just remember your promise. You *can't* tell. He threatened your family." Tears fell down his face. "I'm so sorry." He bent over and sobbed.

Stuart hugged him. "It's not your fault you got mixed up in this. You're one of the good guys. One of the innocents."

"Not anymore." Brian stood abruptly and went to the bathroom to splash water on his face. He came back and took his seat on the floor by Stuart as if nothing had happened. "Let's finish that song." He picked up the pencil and hit the play button.

River stood before the closed door and braced himself for what he expected to see. He swung the door open without knocking and walked in. Brian and Stuart were sitting beside each other on the floor. But not touching. *Huh.* "What are you doin'?"

"Hey!" Brian stood and greeted him with a kiss. "I guess that means Rick's here. I'm not ready, though. I've got to finish this song."

"And say hello to me." River kissed him again.

Stuart excused himself and went into the bathroom to give them a moment alone. When he came out, River was on top of Brian on the bed. He'd pulled up Brian's shirt—they were really into it. Like they were about to have sex then and there. *That is what they do. They have sex.* It seemed weird, but only because he couldn't imagine it. Not even with a girl, let alone two guys.

Stuart gave a loud cough when River started unfastening Brian's jeans. Brian started and looked at him upside down. "Oh, sorry! I forgot about you."

River met his eyes with a smirk. Stuart had the distinct impression he'd done that on purpose. *It's not going to work. It doesn't bother me.*

Brian pulled his shirt down and scrambled off the bed. "Let's hurry up and finish that song."

Ten minutes later they made it up to the ballroom. Rick came out from behind the drum set as they approached the stage. Brian's eyes moved over Rick's tight tee shirt. "I haven't seen you in a long time." *Have we had sex?* It took a moment, but then he remembered. In the bushes with John at one of the first parties, long ago.

Brian mounted the stairs to the stage. *But I only sucked your cock.* He stepped close to Rick and looked up into dark blue eyes. Said in a low voice, "This is gonna be fun."

Rick's eyebrow quirked, and he smiled. "Oh, yeah."

Rehearsal went pretty well, considering it was their first time playing with Rick. Brian nodded. "We'll be ready." He stepped off the stage. "Come on, Stu. I'll show you the grounds. River, come with us." He tugged on River's arm.

"I can't, babe. I gotta go back."

Brian leaned close. "But we didn't even get to . . . ."

"I'll be back tonight."

"Okay." But it felt wrong to let River go without being with him first. Brian watched him walk away, then smiled at Stuart. "Come on—the grounds are the best part."

Stuart followed him down to the second floor and the long hall with closed doors on either side. Empty bedrooms, Brian had told him. Stuart peered down the short hall that branched off just past Brian's room. There was a door at the end, closed like all the others. The hair on Stuart's arms stood up. "What's in there?"

Brian paused. "It's—it's the Room. Where I have sex with my clients. You don't want to see it, do you?"

"No, no." Stuart walked on. The place was creepy. A beautiful, impressive house.

But so empty. He hated the thought of Brian alone here with Grant.

But the gardens were a different matter. Gorgeous. They entered a courtyard with a fountain. "Look—" Brian pointed. "There he is."

A fluffy orange and white cat balanced on the edge of the fountain; his pink tongue lapped delicately at the water. Brian walked over to pet him. The cat purred and pushed his head into Brian's stomach. "Stuart, this is my Schnookie. He keeps me company at night, so I don't have to sleep alone."

Stuart held out his hand for the cat to sniff. Schnookie gave him an uncertain look, then jumped off the fountain and trotted over to the edge of the courtyard. Stuart gasped. "A rabbit—he's going to get it!"

"No, it's okay. That's Oliver. They're friends."

Schnookie tapped the rabbit's back as he passed. Oliver gave chase. They dashed around the courtyard. Stuart laughed. "That's so cute."

"Yeah. They grew up together."

The cat and rabbit disappeared into the bushes. The boys walked on, along the wooded trail. Stuart said, "Are you sure you're in love with River—I mean, that it's not just lust? Dad told me sometimes people get that mixed up." *River's a jerk.*

Brian smiled. "I'm sure. I've been in love with him since I was eleven years old. Hey, how's it going with Gina? Did you call her?"

"Yeah. We're going on another date when I get back from San Francisco."

"That's great."

"Brian—" Stuart stopped to face him. "What is sex like?"

He was silent a moment. "Powerful. It's very powerful. And freeing." He watched the breeze flicker through leaves overhead. "And addictive."

ഇഇഇ

"This is your suite, Brian. And River, of course." Grant walked through the spacious living room with a view of the San Francisco skyline and indicated a closed door on the right. "Stuart will stay in the second bedroom."

"What?" River stopped in his tracks. "We have to share our room with *him?*" He glared at Stu.

Grant looked at Brian. "I want Stuart where you can keep an eye on him. He's *your* responsibility now."

He's still mad. He stared into Grant's cold eyes. *The feeling's mutual.*

"You boys settle in. I'll meet you downstairs in the restaurant at noon."

River started in as soon as the door closed behind Grant. "I can't believe we have to share our room with this—"

"River! It's no big deal. It's not like we're in the same bedroom." Brian pulled him closer and spoke into his ear. "Can't you be polite? For my sake?"

River glowered at Stuart but kept his mouth shut. Brian mouthed, "Sorry," to his friend.

Stuart shrugged and turned away to check out his room. Brian and River did the same. They emerged an hour later to find Stuart on the couch reading. Brian rubbed River's arm and smiled at Stu. "He's more relaxed now."

River said, "Let's go eat."

The three of them headed out. A security guard stood outside the door. The man escorted them down the hall to the elevator. "Does he have to stand so close?" Stuart murmured.

"We're in foreign territory now. Things are . . . different in San Francisco." Brian lowered his voice. "You're going to see stuff you haven't seen before. I'll be in work mode. Try not to let it bother you."

They arrived at the restaurant before Grant and sat at the reserved table. Stuart set his menu down. "When do we go sightseeing?"

Brian shrugged. "This is a business trip. But I'm sure we'll have time for fun, too. Have you been to San Francisco before?"

"Yeah. Just once, though."

"Me, too." He caught sight of Jeffrey emerging from the bar area with Grant. And close behind them—Brian sucked in his breath and stood.

A man with brown, slicked-back hair and a moustache strode over to the table. "Brian, my goodness, how you've grown." Jim took his hands and bent to kiss his cheek. "It's been *far* too long."

His heart pounded. Jim's voice, his scent, the tickle of his moustache, all brought him roaring back to their last encounter. The leather, the whips. His mouth went dry.

Stuart watched them and tried to piece together what wasn't being said. Brian seemed flustered, his cheeks flushed. Then the man turned to Stuart. "And who do we have here?"

Grant said, "This is Stuart, Brian's band mate."

Stuart didn't like the touch of Jim's hand. Didn't like the way he was looked at. *What the hell am I doing here?*

Stuart kept watching his friend during lunch. Brian hardly ate a thing. He acted nervous, kept glancing at Jim. The meal went by quickly. Jim seemed eager for it to be over.

They all stood to go and walked into the elegant hotel lobby together. Grant turned to Brian. "Why don't you show Jim the view from your suite?"

Brian moved to stand beside Jim and a security guard holding a black bag. Brian's eyes kept flicking to it. *What's going on?* Stu thought. *Why is he so nervous?*

Grant rested a hand on River's shoulder. The other landed on Stuart's and sent a creepy feeling through him. "Well, boys. Looks like we have the afternoon to ourselves. Why don't we do some sightseeing? Or perhaps we'll catch a movie."

Jim smiled. "Better make that a double feature."

"Three hours, Jim."

"Come now, I haven't seen Brian in almost two years. We need time to . . . catch up. Give me four."

"Three and a half."

Jim nodded. Grant steered the two boys in the other direction, toward the main doors.

"Wait—" Brian called out. He ran over to River and kissed his cheek. Stuart heard him whisper, "It's alright."

Are those tears in River's eyes? But River turned away before he could be sure.

Almost four hours later Stuart, River and Grant entered the suite. Jim was just coming out of the bedroom, black bag in hand. He shut the door gently. "He's asleep." He smiled at Grant. "Can I buy you a drink?"

The two men walked out and left River and Stuart alone. River ignored him and stood at the window, then turned abruptly to go into the bedroom.

Stu settled on the couch. He tried to read, but he couldn't concentrate. This was all so bizarre he didn't know what to think.

River finally emerged. He didn't even glance at Stuart. Went straight to the mini-bar and pulled out a bottle of Jack Daniels. He poured a glass and drank it down in a gulp. Poured another, then leaned against the wall and glanced around the room. He caught Stuart's gaze and looked away quickly. Stu's eyes widened. *He's been crying.*

"Crap. I forgot you were here." He gulped his second drink. Poured again.

Stuart didn't respond. River finally stumbled off to get ready for dinner. Stuart changed into his suit and walked out to find Grant on the couch. Stu leaned against the wall, and they waited in silence. So far this was hardly the trip he'd bargained for—spending the day alone with River and Grant, his two favorite people.

River came out of the bedroom. He'd managed to pull himself together. Grant stood to go. "What about Brian?" Stuart asked.

"We'll let him sleep."

Brian finally woke at ten o'clock that night, with River asleep beside him. Brian slipped into the blue silk robe that matched his eyes and tiptoed out. Stuart was on the couch in the dark, staring out at the city lights.

"Hey." Brian settled beside him. "I'm starved. Want anything?" He picked up the phone from the end table.

"No. I'm still full from dinner. Sorry we went without you."

"'s okay. I needed the sleep." He ordered pasta and hung up.

"What's going on? Does River always get upset when you have a client?"

"Jim's not a client." He lit a cigarette with shaking hands. "He owns the club where we're going to perform. And . . . ." It was hard to focus on the words. His mind kept returning to the image of Jim standing over him. The intense sensations that filled his whole body, took over his mind—pleasure and pain mixed together until he couldn't tell them apart.

"And what?"

He took a long drag and watched Stuart's face in the dim light. It helped anchor him in the present. "Jim's Head of the Number One House in San Francisco."

Stu's brow knit. "Number one house?"

"The top House. Like Grant's is the top House in L.A."

"Grant's . . . ." Stuart blinked and absorbed that in silence. He turned to stare out the window at the San Francisco skyline. *I can handle this—I have to if I'm going to be Brian's friend.* "So Jim's an important guy." *Like Grant. I knew I didn't like Jim.* "Then what's wrong with River? I'm still confused."

"River doesn't approve of . . . Jim's brand of sex. He's into a lot of bondage, S&M stuff."

Stuart remembered the riding crop in Brian's duffel bag that fateful night. Tried not to think about it too hard.

"It upsets River. I *hate* that." He rubbed his face.

"You look tired."

He nodded. A few minutes later a knock came at the door—the food had arrived. A guard brought it in and set it on a tray in front of Brian. "Thanks."

Brian reached over to the end table to switch on the lamp. The fork trembled in his hand. His silk sleeve fell back as he brought the food to his mouth, and Stuart saw a red mark around his wrist, a mark on the inside of his forearm. Stuart grabbed his arm to look closer. The red line went up past his elbow, with a bruise forming around it.

Brian whispered, "Now you know why River's upset."

Brian could barely get out of bed the next morning. Every muscle in his body screamed. Muscles he didn't even know he had, that had strained against the cuffs yesterday for hours. He soaked in the warm bathtub. It didn't help, just stung the millions of cuts. He gave up and dried off. Ignored his body and pulled on jeans.

They spent the morning wandering through the shops of Haight Ashbury, then walked along the wharf after lunch. The mild weather was a relief after the heat of L.A. They paused to look out over the grey ocean, the island of Alcatraz and the Golden Gate bridge beyond. River put his arm around Brian's waist. "You doin' okay?"

"Yeah. I'm sore, but it's better when we move around." He touched River's cheek. "Don't you love the smell of the sea?"

They smiled at each other.

Grant said it was time to head over to the club for their final rehearsal before the performance. "I hope Rick's there," Brian said, worried. Rick hadn't flown up with them—John wanted him to see a client last night. *John.* The thought brought a bitter taste to his mouth.

They walked into the deserted club half an hour later. The Iron Rod was ultramodern—nothing like The Lily's ambience. Strange to see a club void of people. He made his way around empty tables toward the stage. Rick leaned against the steel wall near it. Brian gave him a slow smile.

The three band members mounted the stage and looked out. Brian tried to get a feel for the place, but it was impossible, empty like that. Just Grant and a few security. And Jeffrey. "Hey, Stuart, Rick. Wanna play some blues tunes first?"

"Sure. You know, my name's Richard, not Rick—River's the only one who calls me that. I don't know why he refuses to use Richard."

Brian stared at him. "Because Richard is his stepfather's name."

Rick blinked. "Oh."

Brian met Stuart's eyes, then looked out again at the empty space as River appeared in the doorway. "River hates him." Brian turned on the mike. "Jeffrey? We thought it would be fun if you came up here and played some blues with us."

Jeffrey grinned. "Sho'." He borrowed Brian's electric guitar and told Stuart the key. "Slow and rhythmic."

Brian recognized the opening of "House Rent Boogie" and settled on the piano bench. He loved this song; it had a great piano part. And the lyrics always made him laugh when Jeffrey sang it—even though it was about being unemployed.

"Talkin about the back rent. She lucky she get any *front* rent."

Stuart laughed, too. Looked like he was having a great time. *We shoulda done this sooner.*

They got a smattering of applause from their tiny audience.

River watched Brian move the second mike to the piano for the next song, which Jeffrey announced as 'Ba-a-a-a-d Like Jessie James.' Brian took turns on the vocals and sang in a low voice about getting revenge. His sweet face didn't look like he meant it.

But Jeffrey's did. River suddenly felt uncomfortable as he listened to Jeffrey sing about hiring a hit man. Murder for vengeance.

Slight nausea washed through him, and River shifted in his seat. *Is Jeffrey looking at me? Is he suspicious about Alan?* He set his jaw. *I'm not sorry. I'm not sorry for what I did.*

River forgot to clap when the song ended.

Stuart's eyes bugged when Brian walked out of the bedroom. "That's what you're wearing to the club? Now I understand why you say your other pants aren't tight." The black leather looked like it was painted on.

His blue eyes glowed in amusement. "At least I'm not wearing a tiny skirt."

The long-sleeved purple silk would be normal, except for the way he wore it. Only two buttons fastened mid-way down his chest, with the silk pulled up and tied in a knot against his lower ribs. The gleam of the silver belly ring drew Stuart's eyes down to where the pants dipped low.

Brian laughed. "Don't look so shocked. This is nothing."

Stuart shook his head.

"I'll change for the performance, though. I don't want to sweat in silk—that's gross. Did you see the showers backstage?"

Brian donned a black blazer for the trip over, but handed it to Jeffrey when they arrived. He hooked his arm in Grant's as they walked into The Iron Rod. A different place than before—full of people and smoke and noise. It seemed a hush fell as they entered. Stuart heard a man say, "There's L.A.'s Number One boy."

Number one boy. Stuart felt light-headed as things fell into place, and he wondered again what he was doing here. *More importantly, what's Brian doing here?* Brian glowed, oblivious to the attention. *Or maybe he's used to it. Maybe he likes the power, the sex—he did say sex is addictive.*

Grant paused to kiss Brian on the lips. Stuart's stomach turned. He'd never seen them kiss before. Wished he still hadn't.

Brian's cheeks flushed when Jim appeared out of the crowd to greet them. He led them to a half-occupied corner booth. The young man on the end stood, and Jim introduced him as his Number One. The guy was in his early twenties, Stuart figured. *I guess the Houses aren't just boys.*

River, Grant and Brian slid into the booth, with Rick at the other end beside Jim's Number One. Stuart settled next to Brian, terribly uncomfortable and out of place. A waiter poured red wine, and Jim excused himself to greet another guest. Stuart gulped the wine. His glass was immediately refilled.

He glanced around the table. River was making eyes at the guy beside him. Grant had his arm around Brian and kissed his temple. "You look lovely tonight." He caressed Brian's bare waist. Stuart's skin crawled.

Brian reached for his glass and looked around the club. "It's so different with people in it. Oh!" He pushed on Stu to let him out of the booth.

Stuart watched him hurry over to a short, robust man with a grey beard. Brian greeted him with enthusiasm—too much enthusiasm. Stuart wanted to look away but couldn't. Like staring at a car wreck.

When Brian was done kissing the man, he led him to their table. "Look, Kristoff's here!" He introduced him as Head of another House from L.A. Stuart frowned.

Brian tugged on the man's hand and sat down. Stuart was forced to move over, next to Grant. He tried to keep a little distance between them and drank more wine.

Grant touched Stuart's hand. Stu almost spilled. Grant smiled. "Are you enjoying yourself?"

Stuart didn't answer. He tried not think about what a great lover Grant was supposed to be as Grant caressed his hand. *God, please help me through this.* Stuart pulled away and inched toward Brian.

Grant chuckled.

The evening crawled by miserably slowly, but finally it was time to get ready for the performance. Stu's head buzzed as he followed Brian away from the booth and Grant and all that was wrong in this world. *Let's just play our music.*

Brian changed into his black leather vest while Stuart put in his contacts. The audience cheered when they took the stage, captivated after the first few bars. *They love Brian. So do I. I wish he would leave these people. Why doesn't he see how wrong it is?* He stopped thinking as the music took over.

The next song was a new one. Brian played the piano with his left hand, picked the strings of his guitar with his right and sang into the mike.

Jim smiled. "How many things can that boy do at once?" He chuckled. "I'd like to find out." He tore his gaze from Brian to look at Grant. They were at a different table now, alone. "I wish you would consider my offer. Brian will be too old for your House soon." He leaned forward. "I want him. What can I do to convince you?"

Grant shook his head. "Nothing. Brian is not for sale—or trade. I would be a fool to give him up." He sipped his wine. "I'm not a fool."

"Of course not, Grant. But he's getting old for your House, and he would fit so perfectly here. The way he responds—there's so much I could teach him."

"I understand your desire. But the answer is no."

. . .

Stuart knocked on Brian's dressing room door. No answer. He went inside, heard the shower running and sat down to wait. A long wait. *What's he doing in there?* He thought he heard a voice when the water turned off. *Oh—maybe he's not alone.* He got up to leave.

The bathroom door burst open and Brian came out, naked and wet and giggling. He saw Stuart. "Oh, hi."

Rick came up behind Brian, naked, too. He rubbed Brian's arm with a smile.

Stu turned away. "Sorry. I didn't realize. . . ." *You're screwing our drummer.*

Brian seemed oblivious to his nakedness. He dried off, then pulled on a fresh pair of leather pants and tied the purple silk shirt. "Ready?"

Stuart followed him reluctantly back into the club. The noise and smoke assaulted his senses, and he almost bumped into Brian. Jim's Number One blocked their path, arms folded. "Don't even *think* about moving in on my turf."

"What?" Brian said.

"San Francisco's mine."

"Good for you. I'll be gone soon; what do you care?"

"That's not what I heard. Jim wants you. He's been talking to Grant about it all night."

"*What?*" Brian pushed past him through the crowd. His heart beat so fast he felt sick. He made it to the booth where Grant sat with Kristoff and leaned his hands on the table to steady himself. "You don't own me!"

Grant's eyebrows shot up. "Perhaps you should sit down."

He didn't. "You can't—you can't just *give* me to someone else."

"I'm not. Yes, Jim made an offer—quite a few offers. But I did not accept any of them. Don't worry. You're *not* for sale." He took Brian's hand and stroked it. "And I would never force you into anything. Remember, the Houses here are not entirely voluntary. Jim doesn't understand our ways."

His voice trembled. "You wouldn't—wouldn't do that. Give me away." Tears stung his eyes.

"No, Brian, of course not. I love you. Come here." Grant pulled him down beside him, stroked his hair and kissed his cheek. "I would never let someone else have you."

River glared at Stuart when they got back to their hotel suite. "Why are you even here? Brian doesn't need you—he's the one with all the talent."

"River!" Brian stared at him with round eyes.

Stuart went into his bedroom without a word and shut the door.

Brian's voice rose. "Stuart's talented, too. And I need him because he's my friend. Why do you have to be such a dick to him?"

"Because *he's* a dick."

"He is not! I don't understand what your problem is."

"At least I don't go around fucking your friends!"

River slammed the bedroom door and left Brian alone with his mouth hanging open.

Brian paced the living room and tried to cool down. It was no use talking to

River when they were both angry.

His silk robe lay draped over the back of the couch. He changed out of his tight clothes and put it on, smoked a cigarette and stared out the window at the lights of San Francisco. Felt lonely.

He opened the bedroom door and poked his head in. River was sitting on the edge of the bed with his back to the door. Brian moved toward him, his bare feet silent on the thick carpet, and sat on the bed to massage River's tight shoulders.

River let out his breath. "I'm sorry, babe. I'm just upset. I didn't mean to take it out on you." He glanced around the room. "I don't like this place."

Brian touched his lips to his shoulder, then River's mouth. Pulled him down onto the bed and wrapped his legs around him. River's hand slid up the silk on Brian's thigh.

Urgent and sweet at the same time—they were both brimming with so many emotions. They held onto each other tight.

Afterward Brian leaned back against the pillows and stared into space. "I miss Schnookie." *I want to go home. Thank god I can.* "If Grant *had* traded me to Jim, what would you have done?"

"I'd break you outta there. Or if you wanted to stay, I'd find a place to live nearby." He sat up. "You don't want to go to Jim's, do you?"

"No! He kind of scares me. And the whole idea of Involuntary—" He shivered. "I could never be a part of that."

The next day they all acted like nothing had happened and managed to enjoy their last day of sightseeing, for the most part. River ignored Stuart—an improvement overall.

Kristoff joined them for dinner at the hotel's restaurant. As if enough hadn't gone wrong already, he was coming on to Stuart during dessert. Brian frowned. *Poor Stu. Why doesn't Grant say something? 'He's your responsibility now.' I guess it's up to me.*

Brian cleared his throat and leaned toward Kristoff. "I'm sorry, Stuart is off-limits."

"Oh, is he? What a shame. Are you sure about that?" He touched Stuart's hair.

It was too much for Stu. He pushed back his chair and walked out of the restaurant.

Shit. "Excuse me, please."

Brian went after him and caught up at the elevator. A security guard squeezed in as the doors were closing. Stuart gave the man a sour look.

"I'm sorry, Stu. Kristoff's a nice guy. He doesn't know you're not in the business."

"And God forbid Grant should tell him."

"He's still mad. He said you're my responsibility, so I guess I should've told Kristoff. But I've never said 'no' to the Head of a House before."

"Listen to yourself. Doesn't that sound wrong to you?"

The elevator opened, and they walked down the hall to their room, the guard trailing a few steps behind. "Stuart, I'm sorry."

"Don't worry about it," he said as he opened the door. "I just want to get out of here. I'm glad we're going home tomorrow."

"Me, too." Brian followed him inside. The door shut behind him. A corner of his brain registered alarm. *I didn't shut the door.*

A burly arm reached out from behind to close around his waist. Pinned Brian's arms to his sides as a gloved hand clamped over his mouth. His heart thudded so hard he was dizzy. *Someone was behind the door.* A big someone. Time slowed as Brian was lifted off his feet.

Another man appeared as Stuart turned. A ski mask covered his face. He raised his hand to point a gun at Stuart. Brian's cry was muffled by the hand over his mouth. Stuart froze. The man said, "Don't move." He kept the gun trained on Stuart and backed toward the door.

Brian stared into Stu's shocked eyes, and then he was out the door. He watched surprise register on the face of the guard in the hallway. The man reached inside his jacket in slow motion. The ski masked man pointed at him with the long black gun. A small popping sound, and the guard was falling.

And they were turning, moving toward a closed door. The stairwell. Brian squirmed as they approached, but it was no use—the men were three times his size. *River!*

Stuart stuck his head out as the door to the stairwell was closing. A dinging sound came from the other direction, and the elevator opened. He ran toward Grant, almost tripped over the fallen guard. "*Brian!* They took Brian!"

"Where?" Jeffrey snapped.

He pointed to the stairwell. "They have guns."

Jeffrey took off running down the hall. River chased after him. Grant shouted, "River, no—stay with me."

But River didn't listen. He disappeared into the stairwell after Jeffrey.

Grant took the walkie talkie out of a guard's hand and turned back to the elevator. "Seal all exits—now!" He muttered under his breath, "Damn you, Jim."

River felt sick as he raced down the stairs after Jeffrey. Jeffrey's bulk moved faster than he thought possible, but not fast enough. Nothing could be fast enough. *Brian! God. I'm coming.*

"River," Jeffrey huffed. "The exits are sealed—they won't get away." He pressed on his earpiece. "We're almost there." They paused by the door at the bottom of the stairs, panting, and Jeffrey pulled out his gun. "Ready?"

They burst through the door to a storage area. A big space of concrete walls and floor, with large boxes scattered about. And two men with Brian—his Brian. The taller man had his arm around Brian's torso, holding him up off the ground. His other hand covered Brian's mouth.

A door on the far wall opened and at least twenty of Grant's men burst through to surround them with twenty pointed guns.

"Shoot them," River said.

Jeffrey shushed him. The man took his hand away from Brian's mouth. And then he was holding a gun to Brian's head. River fell to his knees. "No," he groaned.

Brian saw River's tortured face. Their eyes locked as cold metal pressed into his temple. Time stopped as his psyche prepared for the end. He felt his bond with River stronger than ever, a tangible presence connecting them. Like sparkling silver in the air.

And suddenly he wasn't in a cement room gazing into River's eyes; he was in a sunny meadow gazing into River's eyes. It didn't really look like River, but it was him. And they were happy. At peace. And so fully together.

Grant's calm, commanding voice brought him back to cement and echoes. "It's over. Let him go now."

Suddenly the cool metal was gone from his temple. He kept staring into River's eyes. *Is the ground coming up, or am I falling? Is this happening?* Everything was so slow. He wasn't sure his legs would hold him. He looked down at them and lost eye contact with River. His heart beat in his ears, the world suddenly very real.

His feet touched cement, solid beneath him, and he looked up at River's face. And then he was in River's arms. Lifted off the floor again. His arms locked around River's neck, his face buried in his scent. River's head sank against him as they knelt on the cold cement. Brian rested his cheek against his hair. Stroked him and murmured, "It's okay," as River shook.

Stuart watched them and sensed the bond between them. River's sobs echoed in the big space. Then another noise, the squeak of metal. Stu turned to see Jeffrey screw something onto the end of his gun. A silencer.

Jeffrey and several guards took the two men away. Stuart looked at Grant, numb. He thought he saw a flicker of emotion on Grant's face as he knelt down and touched Brian's back. Then all three of them were hugging. Grant said, "We need to get upstairs."

Guards helped them to their feet. River looked devastated, like he'd just been to hell and back. Stuart got into the elevator with them, crowded with security. Brian turned to him, his blue eyes huge, face pale and streaked with tears. He touched Stu's chest. "Are you okay? Did they hurt you?"

Stuart shook his head. "I'm okay."

They hugged. River's hand didn't move from Brian's shoulder. Didn't stop touching him for one second as they walked down the hall to Grant's suite. Brian and River sank onto the edge of the bed in shocked silence, staring at nothing.

Stuart hovered nearby and watched Grant sit at a small table and run fingers through his hair. One of the guards put a teacup in front of him. He sipped at it, but his hand shook so much the tea sloshed out and dripped over his pale fingers. He put the cup down with a clatter and reached into his jacket for a tiny box. Took out a small pill and put it in his mouth. He closed his eyes a long moment. The lines in his face seemed deeper. Stuart had never noticed how old he was until now.

Grant looked in Stuart's direction, and the vulnerability disappeared in an instant. Grant's eyes flicked to the boys on the bed. "There was never any real danger, Brian. We have security all over this hotel. And those men wouldn't have hurt you."

Brian's brow knit. "But they could've hurt Stuart. They pointed a gun at him!" Fresh tears fell down his face.

"Mmm."

Grant doesn't care, Stuart realized as he sat on the bed. Brian put his arm around Stuart and hugged him, then pulled River into the embrace. *Never thought I'd be hugging River.* Stuart almost laughed at his stray thoughts. Then he was crying.

Brian jerked awake and sat up to look around, disoriented. Grant was seated at a small table. Tons of security. It all flooded back. *It really happened.* He met Stu's gaze, then glanced toward the sound that had woken him—Jeffrey was back.

"Those men was just hired thugs. They don't know who was behind it, but we got some leads. We'll get the bastards."

"Yes, you will." Grant looked old and tired. "And I believe you'll find it's Emerson."

Jeffrey's eyebrows lifted. "Not Jim?"

"Jim was my first thought. But he's too smart to try something like this. No boy is worth the retribution forthcoming. I believe it's someone who *wants* us to go after Jim. The most logical answer is Emerson, Head of the second House in San Francisco. He always wanted to be Number One." Grant shrugged. "Whichever House it is will cease to exist shortly."

Jeffrey picked up the phone. "Frank, Jeffrey. We're gonna need your help. There's been an incident."

Frank—the Mafia guy. Brian swallowed hard.

ᚱᚱᚱ

Brian got out of bed while River was in the shower and padded down the familiar hall, safe now that they were home. He wanted to ask how the guard was doing—the one shot in the hallway. Last he knew the man was in intensive care.

The door to Grant's rooms was ajar. He paused at the sound of John's voice.

"What did I tell you? The boy attracts trouble."

"Please, John." Grant sounded irritated. "This had nothing to do with Brian—he was just a pawn. It's those damn feuding Houses."

"So you were right, it was the second House, Emerson."

"The *former* House, yes. I hope I've taught San Francisco to leave me out of their battles in the future."

John chuckled. "Indeed, I believe you have, Grant."

Brian went back down the hall to his room. *How many people have died over this?* He curled up on the bed and hugged Schnookie to his chest. *It's not my fault. It's not my fault people died.*

River came out of the shower with a towel wrapped around his waist and snuggled against Brian's back. Brian rubbed his damp arm, then turned over to bury his face in River's chest.

"Babe. How am I supposed to handle this? How can I ever let you out of my sight?"

"River." Brian stroked his face.

"I can't get that image out of my mind—the gun against your head." His voice caught, and he squeezed his eyes shut.

Brian brushed his lips against his eyelids. "Didn't you see more than that? When we were staring at each other, what did you feel?"

"Besides horror?" He blinked. "I don't know . . . for a minute it seemed like I wasn't really there. I can't explain it."

"Did you see a meadow?"

"No."

"I did. We were in a meadow—except you didn't look like you. But it was you. We were so happy. So together." He smiled. "One of the most beautiful moments of my life."

River searched his eyes. "I wish I'd seen it."

"You were there," he breathed and kissed him softly.

"You believe in reincarnation, right?" River asked.

"Yes. Do you?"

"I didn't used to. But . . . I'm sure we've known each other longer than four years. I think we've been together in another life—lots of other lives."

"Then you shouldn't worry." Brian smiled. "We'll always be together."

*"The boys stand in a crowd
all alone
Your boys are lost in the snow...."*

- Brian O'Kelly

ᛚᛚ CHAPTER 32 ᛚᛚ

David appeared out of the crowd at Grant's birthday with a wide smile. "I haven't seen you in so long. You're bigger." He laid his palm on the stretchy netting that covered Brian's chest.

"You look exactly the same."

"I know—I haven't started puberty yet. Isn't that great?"

He forced a smile. "I'm sure Grant's happy."

"Yeah." David picked up two drinks from a nearby table and handed one to Brian. "Did you hear? A boy at Mark's House got raped."

His heart skipped a beat.

"Oh—sorry, Brian."

He shrugged and sipped his drink. Avoided David's eyes. "Is he okay?"

"Yeah, Doc Griffin patched him up. It happens once in awhile in the Houses—but not nearly as much as on the street. I'm lucky. It totally could've happened when I was panhandling with my mom."

We're lucky it was Grant who picked us up.

"God was watching out for me—that's what Mommy used to say." David's face drew down. "I wish I could find out how she's doing. I mean, I don't want to live with her or anything. I just wonder sometimes . . . if she's okay."

"Maybe you could find out. Grant has resources."

"You don't think he'd be mad?"

"Not if you explain it. He trusts you. Besides, you're here voluntarily."

"I could at least try. Thank you." David gave him a fierce hug and ran off.

Brian watched him with a sad smile, then turned to see River enter the courtyard. Their eyes met, and he knew instantly something was wrong. Terribly wrong. He moved quickly to stand before River, afraid to ask.

"Babe." River's voice was thick.

In that one word he knew. "Schnookie."

He nodded.

"Is he dead?" Brian was already crying. He knew the answer.

River nodded.

He covered his mouth.

"I'm sorry, babe. He ran out in front of a car." River touched his arm. "He didn't suffer."

Brian moved blindly toward the house. River helped him get to his room, and he collapsed onto the bed sobbing. Sobbed and sobbed until he couldn't breathe.

My baby. My baby's gone.

River's hand on his shoulder was no comfort. There *was* no comfort. All the world had shrunk to that one fact, and nothing could change it.

A little later Grant sat on the bed and stroked Brian's back. "I'm so sorry, dear. These things . . . they happen. It's part of life we can't avoid." No response. "I know my words give you no comfort now. My poor boy." He took Brian's hand. "Do you want to see him?"

Brian lifted his head. "Is he . . . ."

"There's no blood."

"Yes, I'll see him."

Grant patted his leg. "Stay here. Jeffrey will bring him."

Jeffrey came in carrying a bundled up blanket, his face tight with sorrow. He laid his burden on the floor and pulled back a corner of the blanket. Brian looked down at Schnookie's still body. It looked normal—no trace of blood, no sign of anything. The cat looked like he was stretched out asleep.

He knelt to touch the fur. The cold rigidity of the body shocked him. *That's not Schnookie. Schnookie's gone.* What lay before him was only a body. Empty of what he had loved.

He turned away as fresh tears fell down his cheeks. River put his arm around him, and they took Schnookie away.

He kept waking up, despite his exhaustion. He felt so heavy and restless. *No Schnookie. No Schnookie tomorrow night when River isn't here.* He couldn't imagine how empty the bed would feel. He sat up and pulled on his robe.

River stirred. "Where you goin, babe?"

"I can't sleep. You don't have to get up."

But River already had his robe on. Brian wandered down to the parlor to look through the lace curtains onto the dark driveway. *That's where it happened.* He shivered and turned away. Touched the piano. "Did you see it?"

"Yeah."

His heart thumped. "Was it John who hit him?" *I could never believe that was an accident.*

"No. We were already out of the car. Schnookie just ran out—the guy had no chance to stop. It wasn't anybody's fault."

"No." His voice trembled. "It was mine. He was scared of all the people. I should've kept him in my room." Tears blurred his vision.

"Brian." River gripped his shoulders and held him at arm's length. "It is *not* your fault. We could go on all night—if only I'd done this or that. But it's not true. Do you really believe something as huge as death isn't fate? It was his time. His time to go."

He fell against River and sobbed. "Why? Why?"

River kissed his hair. "I don't know."

He cried himself out, then sank onto the piano bench. His fingers went to the keys and started playing. His mind escaped.

Next thing he knew Grant was standing nearby. "Have you been playing all night?"

Morning light streamed in the bay window. Brian looked the other way and saw River asleep on the couch.

"Maria's making your favorite breakfast. How do blueberry pancakes sound?"

"I'm not hungry."

"Please, Brian. Try to eat something." Grant stroked his hair. "It will make Maria feel better."

He looked down and whispered, "Okay."

He sat on his bed and watched the sun sink on the horizon, dreading the night. The empty bed. He opened his journal and wrote.

> *We buried Schnookie near where he and Oliver liked to play. Oliver will miss him.*

He started crying again. *Poor Oliver.* David brought the rabbit to the burial. David was miserable; he hugged Brian a long time and sobbed. Brian had just stared as Carl piled dirt onto the small box.

> *One second I'm numb; the next second I'm crying. He'll come back someday. I know he will. But I don't want another cat. I want* him.

He looked at Sebastian, sitting on the bed beside him. Grant had brought the Himalayan to Brian's room. *Sweet of him. He feels really bad.*

He stroked the long, soft fur. But it wasn't the same. *Why did it have to be Schnookie?* "Oh, that's a *terrible* thing to say. I'm so sorry." He buried his face in Sebastian's fur and cried.

Night came, and Brian crawled under the covers. He stared at the bright moon until Grant knocked on the door to ask if he wanted company.

"Yes."

Grant slipped under the sheets beside him. "My poor boy. I hate to see you in such pain." He stroked Brian's cheek. "You grew so attached. Perhaps I was wrong to let you keep him."

"No! It wasn't wrong. When I found him, I needed him as much as he needed me. My life is richer because he was in it."

Grant kissed his forehead. "Sometimes I think you are wiser than I."

I never thought Grant would walk down this hallway with me. Mr. Padrea's condo remodel was finally finished, and he was back from the hospital—and begging to see Brian.

Jeffrey followed them inside. Mr. Padrea looked healthy enough. Brian was relieved—last time he saw him, the man was pale and still as a corpse. *But not a corpse. I wouldn't think he was dead if that happened now. I know how a dead body feels.* Hard and empty.

The old man grinned at Grant and thanked him for coming. "Won't you sit down?"

"Thank you, Bernie, but I must be going. I just wanted to say hello."

Leah peered around the corner to study the big black man who stood by the door. Her eyes moved to the man in the expensive suit whose hand rested possessively on Brian's shoulder. She sucked in her breath. *Grant.*

"Now, Bernie, you let Brian do all the work. We don't want another episode."

"Oh, yes, yes. He'll do all the work."

She watched Padrea touch Brian's arm, his eyes frantic and hungry. *He's practically drooling.*

Grant glanced around the condo at new carpet and tiles, fresh paint. His cold eyes swept past Leah's hiding place. She froze.

Grant smiled. "I love what you've done with the place. Have fun—but not *too* much fun." He kissed Brian on the lips and disappeared out the door with the bodyguard.

Leah let go her breath and moved out of the shadows. Brian gave her a warm smile as he went with the old man to the bedroom.

She sat on the new leather couch and stared at the wall. Tried to get that kiss out of her head. Those cold eyes. *How can Brian live with that awful man?*

After awhile Brian emerged from the bedroom in a black silk robe. They hugged, and he said, "It's good to see you here again. Like normal. I want things to get back to normal."

They settled on the new leather couch. "What do you mean, back to normal? What's wrong? You look sad."

He heaved a long sigh and closed his eyes. "Bad things keep happening. I keep waiting for them to stop, but they *don't.*"

She touched his hand. "Bad things?"

"It started with Mr. Padrea's heart attack. Then our trip to Ireland got canceled. And San Francisco . . . ."

"What happened?"

"One of the other Houses tried to grab me. Grant said there was no real danger, but it was scary. They had guns." His voice trembled. "And last week—" He bit his lip and stared at his hands clenched in his lap. "My Schnookie died."

"Your cat?"

He nodded and tears slid down his cheeks. "He got hit by a car."

"Oh, Brian, I'm so sorry." She pulled him into her arms as her head spun. *Guns.* "That's a lot of awful, scary stuff. Maybe this bad streak is trying to tell you something."

"I don't know. I don't know," he said, his voice muffled in her bosom. "My Schnookie."

And he was crying harder. She held his head against her and stroked his back.

His mind pulled up a stray memory to distract him from the pain, and Pat's voice popped into his head. *'My young stud'*—what she said when she dug her nails into his back and wanted him to pound her harder. He suddenly noticed his face was on Leah's breast. He rubbed his cheek against it. Murmured, "You sure you don't want to have sex?"

She laughed and pushed him away. "I guess I'll never be a mother figure for you."

His face drew down and tightened. "You shouldn't want to be."

She took his hand. "Do you want to talk about it?"

"No." He gripped her hand. "It's just—" *How can I explain? I can't.* "My mother, she—she made me do this." He held up the scars on his wrists. "She made me run away and leave my sister. But . . . I shouldn't blame it all on her." He bit his lip. *Dad let it happen.* More tears slid down his face.

"Brian." Leah stroked his wet cheek and pulled him to her again.

He held on tight. Choked out, "I was just a little kid—*a baby*. What did I do to make her treat me like that?"

"Brian, you are not responsible for your parents' behavior. If they abused you, it was because of their own problems—not anything you did or deserved. Do you understand?"

He nodded. He knew that with his head but not inside. He sat back and wiped his face. "Sorry."

"For what?"

He whispered, "I don't know."

"Don't apologize for things you didn't do."

He nodded and fumbled with his cigarettes. Smoked in silence and thought of other things. His clients. Went through them in his head like counting sheep. Richie's earnest eyes. *'My reservoir of love.'* Brian laughed.

"What's so funny?"

"Nothing. Just something a client said once." He searched for something to tap his ashes into. Settled on an empty mug.

"There you go, avoiding the subject again."

He sighed. "I can only think about that stuff for so long. I don't want to go crazy."

"Brian, you won't go crazy by talking about it—more from *not* talking about it." She paused, but he didn't respond. "You were lucky to have your sister growing up."

He nodded. "I wouldn't have made it through childhood without her." He felt tired and sad. "I haven't talked to her in a long time. But I don't want to call her now, while everything's so bad. I'll wait until things get better. Then I'll call."

Leah brushed the hair out of his face. "And what if things don't get better?"

. . .

River's voice came through the phone. "How ya doin, babe?"

"I'm okay." *Lonely.*

"That's good. Good. Hey, do you think you could score me some coke?"

"What?"

"John won't give me anymore. He cut me off—bastard! Said I was doing too much. Bunch of bullshit."

A chill went through him. *If John cut you off, there's a reason.*

"So can you get me some?"

"I—I don't think Grant would let me have more." An outright lie. He didn't use it much.

"Oh. That's okay. I'm sure I can get it from someone else."

No, don't! But he didn't say it out loud. *River won't listen to that.* He sat in silence and tried not to cry.

"What's wrong?" Stuart asked.

Everything. Brian didn't answer. He walked through to Stu's bedroom without a word and settled on the floor. Avoided his eyes. "Are you going to see Gina again?"

"Nah. It isn't working."

"That's what I thought. Don't worry—you'll find a girlfriend someday. One who's smart enough for you." He tried to smile but ended up frowning at the floor.

"Brian, what's wrong? Your hand's shaking. Are you on something?"

"No. It's just . . . a client I had this morning. He gives me the creeps." He picked at the carpet and tried not to think about it. "Why couldn't I have a bad headache today instead of yesterday? Then I wouldn't have to see him."

"Is he that bad?"

He swallowed past nausea that threatened to rise up. "Yes." Creepy Guy was getting even worse. This time he wrapped his hands around Brian's throat while they were fucking. The memory sent shivers through him. *Please stop.*

Stuart touched his leg, and he flinched. Stu's voice was thick. "Brian, come live with us. Dad could set up another bed in here. *Please.*"

He blinked, shocked at the idea. "I'm sure your parents would be thrilled."

"I could convince them."

His heart skipped. "Don't tell them anything."

"If you lived here, you'd never have to see horrible clients again."

Lovely thought. But . . . . "It's not that simple." He tried to imagine living in this house. *I'd jump Ted for sure. No way I could stop myself if he were around all the time.*

"Brian?"

He shook his head. "Thanks. But it wouldn't work. That's not the answer."

৩৩৩

He clutched the phone to his ear. "River, are you sure you're okay?"

"Yeah, don't freak out. I'm just real tired. You know how paranoid they are about getting clients sick. So I gotta stay home and miss the big party. Fucking sucks."

"Yeah. I'll miss you tonight." Though truthfully they never saw much of each other during the all-Houses bash. The party was a few weeks early this year, so some special clients could attend. But not River. River had to stay home sick. *Are you still doing coke?* Brian couldn't bring himself to say it out loud.

"Have fun, babe. I'm gonna go lay down."

"Okay, River. I love you."

Brian walked over to where Matthew dispensed the special pills and realized he didn't want to get so fucked up this time. *I'm kind of tired of these parties.* He decided his goal was to remember getting to bed, so he didn't try to convince Matthew to give him his usual two pills. He just took one like everybody else, then strolled around and watched the guests.

Mr. Padrea never comes to these. I guess it would be too hard on his heart. He stopped short as he thought of Jean's French accent. *I haven't seen him in a long time. I hope he's okay.* He found Grant and asked.

"Oh, yes. Jean's fine. You're just a little old for his taste now, dear. That happens, though your clients are hanging on longer than usual. They all love you so. But don't worry—there are plenty who like older boys."

Who else am I getting too old for? Brett, Maurice? Creepy Guy? God, I hope so.

A few minutes later he spotted Jean, with David on his lap. Brian moved closer to give Jean a kiss on the cheek. *I'm glad you're okay.* He smiled at David and walked away without a word.

David caught up with him before he'd gone far. "Brian—wait. We found my mother. She's—" His eyes filled. "She's dead."

"Oh, my god." Brian wrapped his arms around him. "David, I'm so sorry."

"She overdosed on heroin a year after I . . . ." He whispered, "After she sold me."

Brian held him tighter. Didn't know what to say. "I love you."

Poor David. It's been a bad summer. That's what I thought at the party last year, too. "Summer is bad luck," he murmured and guided David to a chair. Got him a drink and sat with him until David said he should get back to Jean.

Brian left him, then caught Trevor's eye and headed into the woods to forget.

The next person he zeroed in on was Justin. He lured the photographer away, into the safety of the trees. Justin still worried. "Someone could see us." But he didn't stop Brian. Could never stop Brian. He clutched the warm skin. Tried to take his time. But he could never do that, either.

Brian gave Justin plenty of time to get back to the party first, then circled around so he'd enter the courtyard in a different spot. *Don't want to get him in trouble.*

He stepped onto the pavement. The party was raging. People kissing all over the place. Not just kissing. Jean had David bent over a chair, fucking him. Brian glanced away quickly. Little David. He felt vaguely disturbed.

Everywhere he looked people were fucking. An arm circled his waist from behind. *I'm next.* It was over quickly. He never even saw who it was. He hurried through the crowd and managed to get to Matthew before someone else grabbed him. *This is not the time to be sober.* He got his two orange pills and popped them into his mouth.

Seemed like everyone wanted the Number One boy. *Even though he's almost sixteen now.* Luckily the pills worked fast. He felt them kick in and started to enjoy himself. *I'm glad River isn't here.*

The sky was beginning to lighten. Most of the boys had gathered on the pavement near the fountain. Brian wandered through them. They all looked tired. He staggered and went sideways, bumped into the fountain. He leaned against it and stared into the water. He couldn't feel his feet on the ground. *How many pills did I have? Two, same as always. Oh—I had one before that. Oh.*

He glanced around the group of boys lounging on the cement. And there was Trevor, sitting on a chair like it was his throne. Watching him with burning eyes. Brian sauntered over. Straddled him and went to it.

They ended up on the ground. Brian didn't notice it was David who pulled his shirt off. David whose mouth closed around his cock while Trevor pulled Brian onto his lap.

By the time they finished, all the boys were going at it. Moving flesh surrounded him. He was hard again in minutes. His arms went around the closest body. He kissed the back of the neck and ran his fingers through soft brown hair.

David gasped as Brian gripped his chest. Sweet and slow, just like he'd known it would be. Even better than he imagined so many times. Afterward Brian licked the sweat on his shoulder. David turned to kiss him deeply. "I love you."

Brian smiled at him with a dreamy, hollow look and lay on his back. *He's really fucked up,* David thought and snuggled against him. Breathed him in while he had the chance.

David glanced up and noticed a circle of men standing around the boys. Most still had their own dicks in their hands, and they all had the same look in their eyes as they watched the orgy. David smiled and rested his cheek against Brian.

Brian woke up and glanced around in a daze. Grant's bed. David asleep on the other side of Grant. Brian lay back, shaky. Grant propped his head up and smiled at him. "That was one of the most successful parties we've ever had. Truly amazing. Thank you, Brian."

Brian stared at him. Didn't really know what he was talking about. Didn't remember much. Lots of men. *I was actually a little nervous before I got to the pills.*

Grant kissed his cheek, his mouth. Down his chest. *But I'm really tired.* He arched back. God, he'd forgotten how incredible it was—it'd been a long time since Grant gave him head. He didn't even care that David was watching. He was totally lost. Would have done anything at that moment for Grant. Anything.

. . .

He slept most of the day and went to Stuart's the next afternoon. He didn't feel like going, but he'd promised. Stuart's first words to him were, "Are you sick?"

"No. Just tired."

"What'd you do over the weekend?" Stu asked as they went into his room.

"Grant had a party."

"How was it?"

"Uh, okay I guess." He laughed a little. "I don't remember much. What did you do?"

"Shopping—back to school stuff. I'm a senior!" He grinned.

Brian gave him a weak smile and sat on the floor.

Stuart's brow furrowed. "You're shaking, and you're extra pale. Are you sure you're not sick?"

"Yeah. It's just . . . those parties are very physically demanding. I'm still recovering." His whole body ached—especially his insides. *Way too much fucking.*

"I don't get it."

He looked at Stuart and said matter-of-factly, "It was basically a big orgy all night. I guess. I don't remember much after the pills." *Until I woke up in bed with Grant and David. But I'm sure nothing happened—not with little David. I wouldn't do that.*

"Pills?"

"Yeah. Grant gives us these special pills once a year, at the big party. They're great, but . . . they'd be more fun if it were a small group." *It can get a little out of hand.* "They always leave me shaky for a few days. And tired—but wired, too." He shook his head. "It's hard to explain."

"Jesus, Brian. Sounds dangerous."

"Naw. I just think I took too many this time." His heart started racing all of a sudden. He held his head between his hands.

"You don't look so good."

"I've been getting these flashes. Since the party. Dizzy. It'll pass—I think it's just the drugs still in my system." He rested his head back against the wall and took deep breaths.

Stuart felt his forehead. "Have you been eating?"

"Well, no. Not much since the party."

"Maybe it's low blood sugar level. Hold on, I'll be right back." He returned with a glass of orange juice and insisted Brian drink it.

His hand shook so much he almost spilled all over the carpet. But it tasted good. The cold liquid hit his stomach, and the shakes started to abate almost immediately. "Wow, it *did* help. I just assumed it was residual speed or something. Maybe I'm dehydrated."

Stuart frowned. "I can't believe Grant makes you take drugs. Wait, yes, I can." He was silent a moment. "You keep saying you're happy, but you don't act like it."

"It's just lately I've been in this terrible bad streak. River . . . ."

"What?"

He looked away, and his throat tightened. "I think he's having a problem." He glanced at Stu. "A drug problem."

"Well, it's no wonder! Are you sure you don't want to come live here? Please think about it."

"No, Stuart."

"Then what are you going to do?"

"I don't know." Grant's words echoed in his head. *'Stuart's younger brother is quite lovely.'* Then he flashed on Grant's mouth on him yesterday morning. So good. "I don't know. I'll think about it later—when all the bad stuff stops."

Leah made the mistake of walking near Mr. Padrea's room while Brian was in there. She heard moaning, soon joined by another voice. Padrea's. Which meant the other sound was Brian. Heat rose in her face, and she hurried away before she heard more.

But she couldn't get it out of her head, compelled again to face up to what Brian did with that old man. She tried not to feel sick as she waited at the kitchen table.

Brian appeared soon after, cheeks flushed. He plopped down across from her and gave her a wan smile. His eyes flicked around the kitchen at the new appliances, new cabinets. She offered him cookies, but he shook his head. "Maybe later. I just want ice water now."

He drank half the glass, then untied the silk robe and let it slide off his shoulders. "I'm sorry, I know this is ugly—" He glanced at the strappy leather top. "But I'm hot." He held the ice water against his cheek.

He's really filling out, she thought. The strips of black leather stretched tight across his chest. She remembered the moans as a bead of sweat ran down his neck. She was feeling a little warm herself. Freaked out.

He said, "I usually wait longer to come out, but I was so thirsty. I think I'm dehydrated." He finished the water and caught her staring. "I don't choose to wear this, you know. It's ugly and a pain in the ass to take off. But it's requested sometimes." He cocked his head. "Tells me something about his mood. Though I'm not allowed to wear handcuffs since his heart attack."

Her eyes widened.

"Sorry. Is that too much information?"

Yes. "Don't edit yourself." She stood to get him more water—an excuse to leave the table. Sometimes it was overwhelming. That outfit. Hearing him have sex. She almost dropped the glass on the way back.

His hand trembled as he took it from her.

"Are you okay? You're shaking."

"Oh, that's probably just leftover from the party." He explained about the pills. "It's only once a year."

"What kind of pills?"

He shrugged. "Something Grant and the Doc cooked up. I took too many this time."

Her brow furrowed. *I can't tell you how appalled I am at these 'mystery' pills. You won't listen.* She pressed her fingers against her eyelids. *Time to pull out all the stops.* She met his gaze and steeled herself. "So. Is your sister a prostitute, too?"

His eyes flew open wide. "*What?* How dare you say that?"

"I'll take that as a no."

"Of course she isn't! Why would you even say that?"

She leaned forward. "Why does it upset you, if there's nothing wrong with it? How do you think she would feel if she knew?"

He glared at her and pushed his chair back. "Fuck off, Leah." He stormed away.

She watched him disappear into Padrea's room. *Please think about it, Brian. Think about it.*

He lay in River's arms on the deck of their beach house and tried to relax, but he couldn't. Not until he knew. *River seems okay . . . but he always does. I never even knew he had a problem. Don't let this ruin our anniversary.* He tried to sound casual. "So. Did you ever get more coke?"

"Naw. The boys all do what John says. Of course. No biggie."

Relief flooded him. He turned to nuzzle into River's neck. *Everything's going to be okay.*

They returned to the beach house for Brian's sixteenth birthday and went into town to buy his present. A leather jacket. River said, "I thought you should pick it out."

Brian walked into the shop and took a deep breath. "Mmm." The sharp smell was a turn on.

He picked out several things to try on. River said, "Too bad they don't have kinky stuff," and wiggled his eyebrows.

Brian smiled and leaned in close. "We've got plenty of that at home." He gave him a kiss, then looked in the mirror. "I like these pants, but not the jacket." He tried on another. The cut reminded him of Quinn's suit jacket. *God, he looked gorgeous the other night.* Quinn had given him a birthday present—tickets to a classical guitar performance featuring the Romeros. Quinn came, too, and brought a date. It was weird seeing him with another man. The guy was attractive, but nothing compared to Quinn. *Or my date.*

He smiled at River, then slipped the jacket off his shoulders. "It reminds me of Quinn, but that doesn't mean it looks good on me." He reached for another. "The Romeros were amazing, weren't they? I wish I could play like that. Maybe I can get my classical guitar lessons back." Now that he wasn't in the youth band anymore, it was much easier to get time off from Grant.

Especially since San Francisco. And the big party, too. *Grant seems really pleased since the party. I can get whatever I want from him again. Maybe my bad streak is over.* He was almost afraid to think it. "Oooo, I like this one." Plain black leather.

River nodded. "Classic James Dean look. But it's too big."

"It's big now, but I want to be able to wear it forever. I'll grow into it."

"Smart." River kissed his cheek. "Happy birthday, babe."

"Oh, my young *stud.*"

Pat's nails dug into his back. It felt good. He fucked her harder, felt her orgasm coming. And his own. She cried out loudly and gripped him until it faded.

He rolled off her, and they lit their cigarettes. They always had long sessions—

plenty of time for Pat to talk. He just listened, like a bartender or something.

And plenty of time for the kinky stuff and sex toys she loved. He pushed a vibrator out of the way and lay back. *'Is your sister a prostitute, too?'* The words kept popping into his head at odd times. Disturbing. Especially when he was with a client.

Pat distracted him by grabbing his penis. "Look at that magnificent cock of yours. It's already bigger than my husband's. And you certainly know how to use it better." She laughed.

Yeah, the senator's not exactly a good lover. I wonder if you two even have sex?

She traced her finger up his chest. "I'm so excited you've turned sixteen. That's the perfect age, you know. Sixteen, seventeen. *Perfect.*"

He smiled, glad to hear it—he had no idea anyone felt that way. All he knew was he was too old for many long-time clients. They kept dropping off the schedule. *At least someone's glad I'm growing up.*

ഇഇഇ

He sat in the back of the limo between River and Stuart and squeezed Stu's knee. "You'll have *so* much fun."

Stuart gave him a nervous smile.

River ran his fingers along the nape of Brian's neck. "Your hair looks good like that."

"Thanks." He'd pulled it back in a short ponytail. That and the puffy shirt were his concession to this year's theme for the Halloween party at Jasmine Lane. "Did pirates wear leather pants?"

"Probably." River kissed his neck.

"It'll be weird without Michelle. Sad. But maybe I can find out how she's doing." He turned to Stuart. "Remember, if any men approach you, just tell them you're not working."

"Got it." He fiddled with his suit jacket. "I don't know if I should do this. It seems wrong to go to a prostitute—no offense. I'd be perpetuating something I feel is wrong."

River rolled his eyes. "You wanna get laid, don'tcha?"

"Well, yeah . . . ."

"Stu, you're not *paying* them," Brian said. "So it's not prostitution. They're beautiful, experienced women willing to have sex with you. I don't see anything wrong with that."

"Yeah. You're right." Stuart's fingers tapped a nervous pattern on his knee.

"It'll be okay. They'll help you." He sat up. "We're here."

River left them immediately.

Brian touched Stu's arm. "Don't worry. I won't go off with anyone till we find the right woman for you."

Stuart's mouth hung open. "How do you choose? They're all so . . . ."

He laughed. "I know. Just take your time. Have a drink. One of them will catch your eye more than the others."

A lovely redhead came up to them and gave Brian a kiss on the cheek. "I almost didn't recognize you, you've grown so much! You're *sexy.*" She turned her attention to Stuart. "And who have we here?"

He'd never seen Stu blush before.

The woman wandered away after a moment, and Stuart leaned closer. "Have you been with her?"

"No. Not yet, anyway. But I'm sure they're all good at it."

"No, it's not that. I don't want someone you've been with. That would be too weird."

Why? "Okay."

They grabbed a couple of drinks and admired the scenery. "Oh, look at her," Stu said. "In the blue dress. Dark hair."

They made their way over to introduce themselves. Brian stood back a little so she would focus on Stuart. A hand stroked his ass, and he turned to see one of his regular clients.

"Brian, what a wonderful surprise to see you here. You look ravishing."

He smiled and leaned up to whisper in the man's ear. "I'm not working tonight."

He looked disappointed. "I see. I'm sorry."

Brian was relieved the man didn't get angry. He wasn't used to saying no to clients. In fact, he wasn't sure he wanted to say no. *He's fun.* Brian's body was automatically aroused by being near him. *What the hell?* "But we can go upstairs anyway."

The man's eyes lit up. "Lovely." He stroked Brian's back and nodded toward a woman. "Why don't we grab her on the way?"

"Yeah! And her." Brian pointed to the redhead.

The man laughed. "Let's."

Brian looked at Stuart. He was standing very close to the woman in the blue dress. She caressed his cheek.

"You alright if I go now?" He squeezed Stu's arm and grinned. "Have fun."

They piled into the limo. Brian laid his head back with a sigh. "I wish it were more than once a year."

"*Yeah,*" Stuart agreed. "Thank you for bringing me. I never imagined . . . ." He shook his head. "Wow."

They grinned at each other. *And Michelle's doing great.* He'd talked to the Head of the House and found out Michelle left L.A. to enroll in a community college somewhere—Grace wouldn't tell him where. He'd said, '*Give her and Tyler my best, if you talk to them.*' Grace answered, '*Yes, she always asks how you're doing, if you're still with Grant.*'

He stared out the dark window. *She wants to hear that I'm not.*

*"On candystripe legs the spiderman comes
softly through the shadows of the evening sun
stealing past the windows of the blissfully dead
looking for the victim shivering in bed
searching out fear in the gathering gloom and
suddenly! a movement in the corner of the room!
and there is nothing I can do as I realize with fright that
the spiderman is having me for dinner tonight!
quietly he laughs and shaking his head creeps
closer now closer to the foot of the bed and
softer than shadow and quicker than flies
his arms are all around me and his tongue in my eyes
'be still be calm be quiet now my precious boy
don't struggle like that or I will only love you more
for it's much too late to get away or turn on the light
the spiderman is having you for dinner tonight!'
and I feel like I'm being eaten by a thousand million shivering furry holes
and I know that in the morning I will wake up in the shivering cold
and the spiderman is always hungry . . . ."*

- Robert Smith (The Cure), "Lullaby"

ධධ CHAPTER 33 ධධ

Brett propped his head up and smiled at him. "I gave myself an all-nighter with you as a Christmas present to myself."

Brian kissed him. "Merry Christmas."

"I bet it'd be fun to smoke out with you."

"You mean pot? I've got some."

Brett grinned. "*Dude*, excellent."

"But I need to leave the Room to get it. May I?"

He seemed surprised. "Of course."

Brian considered inviting him along. *He's never seen my room, after almost four years. But no, he's a client. It wouldn't be right.* "I'll be back in less than a minute."

Two minutes later Brett was expertly rolling a joint. They passed it back and forth. Brian said, "You're one of the few clients I've had since the beginning who I'm still seeing. I've gotten too old for everyone else." He looked away, almost afraid to ask. "Am I getting too old for you?"

"No way!"

"Someday I will."

"No. Never." He turned Brian's face toward him. "You could never be too old for me. I love you."

Brian touched his cheek. "You're sweet."

Brett kissed him. Made him believe it was true.

Sometime during the night they fell asleep. Brett's eyes opened to gaze at the soft

453

light that edged the ceiling. A sound penetrated his consciousness. Not a good sound. He sat up, fully awake in an instant. Brian was choking. "Brian!" Adrenalin surged through him. *How could he choke on nothing? Does he have asthma?* Brett shook him hard.

Brian's eyes flew open, and he sat up into Brett's arms. Gasped for breath.

"Are you okay?"

He nodded as tears streamed down his face. He managed to say, "I'm fine. It was a dream. Just a dream."

"A pretty bad one." Brett stroked his hair. "Can I do anything? You want some water?"

He nodded. Not so much for the water, but for a moment to himself. He curled up on his side, lost in the old recurring nightmare from childhood. *Everybody has a monster under the bed.* His was a woman with long white hair and long white nails. Thin fingers like claws. She reached up to pull him off the bed, dragged him underneath with her. And then he couldn't breathe.

That's usually where the dream ended. But this time it went further. This time he remembered she put something over his face. To suffocate him. *Scary-lady-under-the-bed wants to kill me.* He shook his head. *It's just a dream.* But he hadn't had it in years. *Why now?*

River wrapped his arms around him as they soaked in the large bathtub at the beach house. Candles glowed all around; Pachelbel played softly from the next room. River spoke quietly. "I can't believe I'm eighteen."

"I know."

"Do you realize what that means? My parents can't touch me. They can't touch me."

Brian stroked his arm. Didn't know what to say to that. He turned around to gaze into River's eyes, then ran his palm up the slick wetness of his chest. "Remember the first time I touched you like this? Your shirt was wet."

River kissed him. Instant passion. Intense, but slow. River lifted him up into position on his lap. Murmured, "I like it best like this. So I can watch your face."

Brian kissed him harder and felt River slide inside. His head fell back. *Oh.* River always felt so sweet inside him. "*I love you.*"

Brian lay alone in his bed at home, caught in another dream.

I'm alone in a house. Something evil lurks outside, and it wants in. But the doors and windows are all locked—I made sure of that. I hear the chimes of an ice cream truck approaching. I peer around the corner and see it through the far window. It stops in front of the house. A man wearing a white uniform gets out and approaches slowly. I see him knocking through the distorted glass in the door. 'Do you want some ice cream?'

I shiver and cower against the wall. The man is evil.

The ice cream man walks along the front of the house, looks in each window as he passes. I know he'll go all the way around the house, checking for unlocked windows or doors. My heart's pounding so hard it hurts. *Did I leave anything unlocked?*

I dash to the bedroom when the man isn't looking and dig through the nightstand drawer, desperate to find my only weapon. Got it. I clutch the handcuffs to my chest and cram myself into the corner between the windows. I squeeze my eyes shut. He's peering into the window next to me. I try to disappear into the corner. But he knows I'm here!

Brian woke with a start, heart racing. He turned onto his side and hugged himself.

Not safe. Not safe.

Stuart cleared a space on the floor and sat with a grin. "It's fun being in charge while Mom and Dad are in Hawaii." For their twentieth wedding anniversary. "Except I miss good food."

Brian forced a smile. This ought to be the perfect time to party and let loose with Stuart. But he couldn't muster the energy or the desire.

Stuart put a CD in his stereo. "There's a new girl, Wendy, in my English class. She's so pretty. And mature—not like the other girls. I talked to her, and she didn't run in fear. She's new at Davis High, so she doesn't have me pegged as a nerd."

"Are you gonna ask her out?"

"Maybe. But not yet." He studied Brian's face. "You seem tired."

"Yeah. I can never sleep anymore. Bad dreams." He shook his head. "Let's go outside for a smoke. And you can tell me more about Wendy."

They walked into the living room and Jacob hurried to shut off his video game and switch it back to TV. Brian smiled a little at the vain attempt to fool Stuart.

A newscaster's voice blared from the television. "A man was arrested this morning on charges of sexual assault and murder of a twelve-year-old boy."

Brian's stomach twisted. His gaze was drawn to the TV. The screen showed a photo of an innocent-looking kid with dark hair.

"The boy's body was found last week in a dumpster in Hollywood. The suspect may be responsible for a string of unsolved murders over the last few months, all of young boys." The picture switched to a man being led into a building in handcuffs. The camera closed in on his face.

Brian gasped. Clutched his mouth and doubled over. He ran to the bathroom to puke and knelt in front of the toilet, shaking. *Creepy Guy. Creepy Guy killed a boy. Boys. Oh, my god. Oh, my god.* He rocked back and forth and sobbed.

"Brian!" Stuart's voice came through the door. "Are you okay?"

"Go away. Please." He tried to block the memory of Creepy Guy's hands on his throat. *I bet that's how he did it.* Nausea washed through him.

He managed to stand up after a few minutes and splashed cold water on his face. He stared into the mirror with puffy red eyes. *I look like someone just died. Someone did.* He gripped the counter and bit it down. *Don't think about it now. You've got to get out of here. Get out.* He steeled himself and opened the bathroom door.

Stuart stood there waiting. Brian swept by him. "I gotta go." He was out the front door before Stu could stop him.

He sat in Grant's office waiting for him to get off the phone.

"How long do we have before he goes to trial?" Pause. "Alright. We'll talk more later." Grant hung up.

Brian leaned forward. "Can I do anything to help? I could give a deposition or something. They can grant immunity, right?"

"That won't be necessary, dear. We have a judge on the case."

"Carmichael?"

Grant's eyebrows went up. He pursed his lips, silent a moment, then nodded. Brian realized he'd let it slip. *Yes, I've seen the files. Does it really matter now?*

Grant cleared his throat. "They have plenty of evidence. Mr. Reynolds was not so careful this last time. He left DNA behind."

"Was he . . . was the boy from a House?"

"Oh, no. That would've been too obvious. Reynolds didn't *want* to get caught. It was just a regular boy—all of them were."

He stepped into the Room and smiled at Jack; they always had fun together. But this time he felt nausea when the man touched him. The same nausea that hadn't left him since he found out about Creepy Guy. But it was worse now, with Jack caressing him.

Brian forced himself to press his palm against Jack's chest. But he didn't really want to. Didn't want to. *What's wrong with me? Jack's fun.*

But it wasn't.

He lay there afterward, long after Jack left. Stared at the medallion on the ceiling and felt the presence of all who had lain here before him. He tried to block out the echo of Creepy Guy's soul. Closed his eyes as it touched him. And suddenly he felt the boy. The boy who was dead. *It was supposed to be me.*

No, Brian. That man is evil. Don't ever blame yourself for that. Follow your soul. You will find your path.

Brian opened his eyes and stared at the medallion.

January 19th

> *Something strange happened today. For the first time ever I didn't want to be with a client—I mean, with a fun client. I just couldn't get into it.*
>
> *That boy spoke to me. He's right. Creepy Guy is evil. I've always known it, since the first time I laid eyes on him. When he was staring at me from the Other Wing. So long ago.*

He looked up from his journal and wished the nausea would go away. Wished River were here. *I seem to wish that a lot.*

> *I'm not with River enough. I feel like I hardly ever see him. And he's the most important thing in my life. That doesn't seem right, does it? Something isn't right.*

River leaned back against the pillows. "You're still upset about that guy, aren't you?"

He nodded and pushed himself up to look at River. "It's not going to just go away. Something—something has to change."

"What?"

"I don't know. I don't . . . I'm not happy here anymore. I want to leave." He didn't realize it until the words were out of his mouth.

River sat up and stared at him. "Are you sure?"

The immense relief flooding him silenced any doubts. He blinked back tears. "Absolutely."

"Okay. We'll go."

"No, just because I'm leaving doesn't mean you have to. You can stay with John if you want. I'll find a place nearby. Get an apartment or something—"

"No. We came here together, and we'll leave together. I never expected to stay *this* long." River smiled and shrugged. "We were just cruisin here for awhile. It was a fun ride." He glanced away. "Mostly. Now it's time to move on."

River pulled him close to rest his cheek against the top of Brian's head, quiet a few minutes. "Why do you really want to leave? Did something else happen?" He held Brian at arm's length and searched his eyes. His grip tightened. "Did something happen to you?"

"No, no, River." He touched River's cheek. "Ever since I found out what Creepy Guy did . . . ." He shivered. "I just can't—I don't want to do it anymore." A tear slid slowly down his cheek.

River said gently, "Then you don't have to."

"It's not just that. Things have been building up. San Francisco . . . ."

River squeezed his hand. "I know. It scared me worse than anything."

Brian held on tight and allowed himself to think it through for the first time. "You could have been killed."

"What?"

"If it was you instead of Stuart with me in the hotel room. Those men had guns." *You wouldn't have let them take me.* His mouth twitched, and he stopped the train of thought. That alone was reason enough to leave.

River touched his face. "I wouldn't have let them take you."

They were quiet a long time, until River finally spoke. "If your mind's made up, we need to do some serious planning."

"Yes."

"So . . . I guess we'll get an apartment. How do we do that?"

"I don't know. I've seen ads in the newspaper."

River rubbed his chin in thought. "We should set a time limit. Otherwise we might never go through with it. How long?"

Brian hugged the pillow to his chest. "Soon."

"Let's say no more than two weeks. Unless we can't find an apartment fast enough. Does that sound good?"

"Yeah," he whispered.

River touched his cheek. "You okay?"

Brian nodded. His lips trembled.

River held him tight. "You know we can't tell anyone—not *anyone*. Including Stuart."

"I know." Brian's fingers found the smooth round muscle of River's arm and held on.

Things seemed different after that. He looked at everything as though for the last time. The winter trees in the painting across the hall. The way the banister glided smooth under his hand. The sound of Maria's voice scolding the cat in Spanish. He clenched his jaw and moved slowly down the stairs.

Jeffrey walked in the front door with the newspaper and called up a cheerful greeting to him. Brian smiled, but tears stung his eyes. *Stop it. You've got to control yourself.*

Jeffrey joined him for breakfast. Brian read the paper as he ate but didn't turn to the part he really wanted to see. "Hey, look. Amelia's getting married."

Jeffrey sipped his coffee. "Who?"

"My former client. The one who was raped when she was fourteen. She's engaged."

"That's great, Mr. B."

"Yeah. It is." *I helped her.* "I'm going to take this to my room. I want to save that."

He sat in the privacy of his room to study the apartment ads. So many. *How do you choose?*

Someone knocked on the door. His heart thudded, and he closed the paper quickly. "Come in. River!"

River kissed him and sat on the bed.

"I was looking at apartment ads." He opened the paper to show him.

River browsed through them. "Hmm."

"How do we choose?"

"I guess by how much we want to spend and where we want to live. I wanna live by the beach. How much money do you have?"

"I don't know."

"You don't know? How can you not know?"

Brian shrugged. "I just stuff it in a box. It's pretty full." It was hard to get the bills in; they kept spilling out.

River shook his head. "I know exactly how much money I have at all times. Including stocks."

"Stocks?"

"Yeah. I've invested a lot. But I got plenty of cash. I bet you do, too. I can't believe you've just been stuffing your money into a box for four years."

Brian went to his dresser to get the blue ceramic box and brought it to the bed. It was overflowing with hundred and five hundred dollar bills. "Oh, wait. There's more." He opened the bottom dresser drawer. "I emptied the box into here a few times."

River helped him gather all the bills and dumped them onto the bed. "You sure that's all of it?"

He took all the photo envelopes out of the drawer. "Yep."

River sat on the bed and counted. It took a long time. "Add that to what I got, and we have plenty of money, babe. We can get whatever apartment we want."

"But we shouldn't go overboard. We need to make it last." He picked up the newspaper. "Look at how much some of these places cost." He shook his head. "I wish I knew Los Angeles better. Four years and I've hardly seen any of it. I don't know which areas are good. And how will we go look at apartments? Every time I leave here Grant has me followed."

"He does?"

"Yes. River—" Brian touched his arm. "We need someone to help us. Someone who knows L.A. Someone we can trust."

River's mouth tightened. "Stuart."

"He can keep a secret—god, he's known about me for a year and never told a soul. He can check out apartments for us. How else can we do it?"

Stuart answered the door. "Are you okay? Why do you look so happy?"

Brian laughed. "I've made a decision. I think you'll like it."

"*What?*"

"Come on." They went to Stuart's room, and he blurted, "River and I are moving out, into an apartment of our own."

"You're leaving Grant?"

He nodded.

"Oh, Brian." Stuart hugged him tight. "*God*, I'm so glad."

Brian touched his face. Stuart had tears in his eyes. "We need your help."

"Of course. Anything."

They sat on the bed, and Brian filled him in. "Where do you think we should go?"

"Maybe West L.A. or West Hollywood—that would be perfect for you. It's nice, *and* it's a gay area."

"Hmm. Maybe. Is it expensive?"

"Not too. Not as much as the coast. It's hard to even find an apartment near the beach. There's usually a waiting list."

"Oh. We can't do that. We need to go soon."

"Why did you decide to leave? Last time you were here . . . did you know that boy?"

"Not the boy." He tucked his knees up and wrapped his arms around them.

"Remember that client I told you about? The creepy one?"

"Yeah. The one who upset you so much."

"That was him on TV. He killed those boys." His voice caught and tears welled up.

"My God."

"He's evil." Brian shook his head and wiped his eyes. "But that's not the only reason. I've been ready to go for awhile. I just needed a push."

"That was quite a push."

"Yeah."

*"I see the sunrise over the mountain
I see the sun rise in your eyes
and I know
I will always love you*

*The beauty of your soul shines through your skin,
shines through my heart
and I know
I have always loved you"*

- Brian O'Kelly, "Eternity"

CHAPTER 34

Stuart picked them up in his SUV. "I think you'll like this first one—it's my favorite. Only drawback is it's a studio. But it's partially furnished and in West Hollywood. Close to everything—a bus line, grocery store, Laundromat."

"Laundromat?" Brian asked.

"Yeah. There's no onsite facility. I guess that's another drawback."

Brian stared out the windshield. *No more Maria.* The familiar lump caught in his throat. He bit his lip. *You'll be with River all the time. Don't think about the other stuff.*

He took a deep breath. Smoothed back his hair and tied it with an elastic. It was nice to get it out of his face. Made him feel older. Mature. *We are. We're getting an apartment. River's an adult for real—eighteen.*

River said from the backseat, "I guess we'll need the bus line. I was thinking about buying a car but . . . we should probably save the money."

Brian turned to look at him. "You don't know how to drive."

"Sure I do. John lets me drive the Jag sometimes."

"I didn't know that. Huh." He turned to watch eucalyptus trees sway in the breeze. They passed an old five-story building with gorgeous scrollwork, another with little ornamental turrets. *Nice area. And we'll be a part of it. Out here in the city with everyone else.* "You sure there's no 'For Rent' sign out front?"

"I'm sure."

Brian glanced over his shoulder. Somewhere back there one of Grant's men was following them. *They'll just think we're visiting a friend. Careful. We have to be careful.* He bit his nail. *Will he really let me go?*

Stuart turned off Fountain and drove down a street with nice homes and lots of trees—magnolias, palms, jacarandas. Less than a block later they stopped in front of a large Spanish-style house. "This is it. It used to be a house, but it was converted into apartments years ago."

Brian got out of the car and looked up at it. Off-white stucco walls, terracotta tile roof with matching trim. "Nice."

"The stairs to the studio are over here, on the right side. The landlady said she'll meet us up there."

They followed him up metal stairs painted cream to match the walls, to the top floor of the house. A white plastic chair sat on the small landing. Brian imagined himself sitting there with coffee. He turned to look around at the tops of trees and nearby hills sprinkled with a few houses. He took a breath of chilly air. "This is great."

River peered into the large window, but the curtains were shut. Stuart tried the door, and they walked in. A bare queen-sized bed jutted out from the wall on the left, taking up less than half the room. "Pretty spacious for a studio," Stuart said.

Brian opened the curtains. "That's better." Bright and airy with coved, high ceilings. Two more windows on the right-hand side showed trees out the back of the house. "Ooo, look." The kitchen area was opposite the door, separated by an archway. He ran his fingers along the cool plaster of the rounded opening. "I like this."

Stuart nodded. "I thought you would. The place has character. Not many amenities, though. No dishwasher or laundry. But it does have a microwave. And they installed an air conditioner—otherwise it'd be an oven up here in the summer."

"Oh." Brian's eyes widened. He hadn't considered that and wondered what else he was forgetting.

The door opened, and a woman stuck her head in. "Hello! You must be River and Brian." She stepped inside. A middle-aged, round woman in cheap-looking clothes. "I own the place here. Live downstairs on the ground floor. When are you thinking of moving?"

"As soon as possible," Brian said.

"Well, this studio's ready now. Great location. Utilities are included." She went on to list details Stuart had already told them.

Brian asked when it was built.

"In the twenties."

"Wow." He moved closer to River. "What do you think? I really like it." *And it's close to Stuart's.*

River shrugged. "Yeah, but it's a studio."

"I don't mind. And look—" Brian murmured in his ear, "The bed has a headboard."

River smiled. "True. That's an important detail." His arm slipped around Brian's waist.

The landlady said, "The bus line runs straight through West Hollywood to the beach."

River turned to look at her. "Really?"

Afterward Stuart showed them the area of Santa Monica Boulevard within easy walking distance. He pointed down the road, to the open west. "The ocean's right over there, not far at all. And Tower Records is north, up on Sunset. You could walk there."

The wide street, two-story buildings and small trees gave it an open feel. They walked around and saw coffeehouses, night clubs, restaurants. A sex shop and a bookstore. And two men holding hands on the sidewalk. Brian grinned. "This is great."

They forced themselves to look at another apartment before making up their minds. A big, modern complex with all the amenities. Low ceilings. Dark and depressing. "I couldn't live here." He touched River's arm. "I want the studio. *Please*."

He nodded. "Okay, babe."

Brian laughed and kissed him.

The next day they sat on folding chairs in the landlady's tiny office. She shuffled through scattered papers on her desk. "You need to fill these out." She handed over two credit applications. Brian stared at the blanks—social security number, current address, employment. *Shit*.

River folded the paper and put it in his pocket. "We'll fill these out later. In the meantime, we'd like to pay the first six months in advance." He pulled out a wad of cash.

Her eyes popped out, and she grabbed at it. "Yes—yes, great. Okay." She counted it quickly, then shoved it into a locked drawer. "Well, you boys can move in as soon as you want. Just sign the rental agreement." She pulled out another form and filled in the address. "No pets. No loud parties. The usual." She pushed it across the desk for them to sign.

River read it through, then signed his name at the bottom. 'River Deloy.' Brian's heart skipped. River whispered to him, "It's okay. I'm eighteen now."

Brian nodded and picked up the pen with his left hand. 'Brian O'—the rest was illegible.

The landlady stood and held out her hand. "Welcome to the neighborhood."

ധധധ

Brian sat on his bed, opened the old backpack and pulled out the jeans he wore when he walked out of his parents' home for the last time. The same jeans he wore when he first saw River again on New Year's Eve, and when they met Grant that rainy night. A lot of memories. He held them up, smiled and shook his head. "They're tiny."

He and River had slowly been giving clothes to Stuart to put in the apartment. But they had to be careful—didn't want to take so much that it was obvious to anyone who looked in the closet. He'd done the same with his CDs.

His amp and guitars would be easy. *I'll just bring them to Stuart's for rehearsal and leave them there. No one will know.*

I'll miss the pianos. No piano at the apartment. That's gonna be hard.

He jumped at a knock on the door. Crammed the jeans into the backpack and stuffed it under the bed. River poked his head in.

"Oh, you scared me—look what I found in the back of the closet." He showed him the backpack, then touched River's hand. "You know what I realized? I've never seen your room. Never been to John's. I feel bad I never saw where you live."

"Don't feel bad, Brian. You don't want to go there." His jaw clenched.

"What is it?"

River shook his head, and his voice trembled. "John. I saw him—I saw him beat one of the boys."

"What?"

"It was bad. Real bad." He was silent a moment. "You know, when Dick hit me, I hated him, but . . . at least I knew he wasn't in control. He'd get this crazy, hot look in his eyes. Like his instincts took over. But John—" His voice caught. "His eyes were so cold. He knew *exactly* what he was doing."

"River." Brian stroked his arm.

"I didn't do anything to help that boy. John saw me watching. He looked at me and . . . I was afraid."

Brian held him close. Kissed his hair. Stroked and soothed him like he used to with Schnookie. *He's afraid. My brave River's afraid.* "We'll be careful. John won't find out what we're planning."

River pulled away to look at him. "But what about after? Do you really think they'll let us go?"

He sat quietly a moment. "I believe Grant will honor the Voluntary Rule. It's so important to him—to all the Houses. He can't break it. And he'll keep John in line."

"John could sell us up to San Francisco."

Brian gripped his arm. Wanted to say, 'He wouldn't do that.' *But he would.* "Grant won't let him. He won't let anyone else have me. But still . . . it's a risk." He bit his lip. "Maybe we should leave L.A."

"But would that help?" River shook his head. "I don't want to spend my life running. I want to move into our little studio and be happy together." His voice wobbled.

"River."

"We might be safer *closer* to Grant, where he can protect us from the other Houses."

Brian nodded. "I don't want to leave L.A."

"Me, neither."

Leah rested her chin on her fist. "You're acting strange tonight, Brian."

"What? No. Just . . . ." He avoided her eyes. "Tired."

"What's going on?"

"I can't tell you, Leah. I promise you'll understand later. Soon."

He refused to discuss it further and pretended to be normal. But she could sense a mixture of sadness and nerves. Excitement.

In the morning when it was time to go he told her, "I've got a surprise for you."

"What?"

"I can't tell you now, or it won't be a surprise. But I'm sure you'll like it." He kissed her cheek. Whispered, "Goodbye, Leah."

He turned away quickly and went out the door.

. . .

Saying goodbye to Quinn was just as hard. Brian walked him to the door. "Quinn, I just want you to know . . . you're the best teacher I've ever had." He leaned up to kiss him on the lips. One sweet, gentle kiss.

Quinn looked confused.

Brian gave him a sad smile, then turned and hurried up to his room.

When he was done crying, he picked up his portable CD player. Time for another trip to Stuart's. He ran into Grant in the foyer. Grant's eyes moved to the stereo in Brian's hand. "Where are you going with that?"

Brian struggled to speak past the dryness in his mouth. "Stuart's borrowing it. His CD player broke."

"Oh." Grant kissed his forehead. "Have fun."

Brian nodded and walked out the door. *Grant.* He could barely see through the tears in his eyes.

ឃឃឃ

He went into the phone booth alone and glanced back at the security guard—the man had kept his distance. Brian stuck quarters into the slot. He'd picked a time when Tanya would be at school. He couldn't handle talking to her now. But he wanted to leave a message—just in case.

"Tanya! Hey. Sorry I haven't called in so long. I've been . . . really busy. I wanted to let you know—" He glanced around to make sure no one was in earshot. "I'm moving into an apartment with River. Leaving Grant. I figured you'll be happy about that—I know I am. I'm so excited to be with River. I'll call you once we get settled, okay? Tanya, I love you. I love you a lot. And tell Mom and Dad I love them, too."

ឃឃឃ

The day came. Brian had lain awake most of the night. *It won't be hard to pretend I'm sick.* The same ploy he used when he ran away four years ago. He took a deep breath and pressed the intercom button. "Jeffrey? Could you bring my pills? I've got a bad headache."

Jeffrey was there in thirty seconds. He stroked Brian's forehead. "Poor kid. Wish the doc could do more for you."

"It's alright," he whispered. *Don't think. Don't think about the fact that you'll never see him again.* A tear rolled down the side of his face when Jeffrey left him alone. *It isn't fair I always have to leave the people I love behind.*

He clutched the bottle of pills and got up to tuck them into the pocket of the jeans he would wear when he walked out of this room for the last time. He climbed back into bed. *This day is going to feel like an eternity.* An hour later the phone rang. River.

"We've got a problem. John changed my schedule. I can't come over."

"Shit."

"But we should still go through with it. Just have Stuart pick you up first. Then come get me. I'll meet you outside the gates at three o'clock. Grant will still be gone at his meeting, right?"

"Yes. But River, I don't even know where John's House is. I don't want to leave here without you. We should wait."

"No—I don't want to keep putting it off. We're doing it. It's easy to get to John's from there."

Brian scribbled the directions on a scrap of paper. "River, I'm scared."

"It'll be alright, babe. Just don't be late."

Jeffrey came in with a glass of juice around one o'clock. "I know you cain't eat much when you got your headaches, but maybe you could drink somethin."

Brian smiled. *It wasn't the last time I would see you.*

Grant walked in as Jeffrey was leaving. He stroked Brian's cheek. "My poor boy. Are you feeling any better?"

"A little."

"I'm sorry we have to go out. Will you be alright on your own?"

He nodded.

Grant kissed his forehead and started to move away.

"Grant—" Brian grabbed his hand. Squeezed it tight. *I love you.* But he couldn't say it. Couldn't speak.

Grant squeezed him back. Gave him a warm smile and left.

He tried to cry quietly.

February 5th

Dear Grant,

I'm sorry to do this in a note, but I don't think I could handle saying goodbye to you in person. I love you very much, and I always will. But it's time for me to move on with my life. And be with my love.

Please protect River from John.

Love,
Brian

P.S. John beats his boys.

Brian put on jeans and a tee shirt, tied his hair back and took a last look at the bedroom that had been his for four years. He tightened his jaw and walked out into the hallway. Glanced at the closed door of the Room as he passed. He had no desire to see it one more time.

His heart pounded as he laid the note on Grant's bed. *This is it. No turning back.* The dead boy's voice floated through his head. *'You will find your path.'*

Brian walked out.

He heard Maria in the kitchen as he reached the bottom of the stairs. Avoided her and headed toward the back. Out the French doors and into the magical grounds. *Goodbye.* He walked down the path toward the stable. Wished he could say goodbye to Glory. But the note was on Grant's bed. No time to dawdle.

He turned off the path and into the trees, down to the front of the house. He was shaking by the time he reached the gate. Hoped no one was watching the monitor as he hurried through. *Not that it matters. Grant will find us if he wants to.*

Stu's SUV was idling just down the hill. Brian broke into a run and opened the passenger door. Choked out a sob as he hugged Stuart.

Stuart put the car in gear.

"Turn left." *River. I don't like that he's still at John's.* "Hurry."

River checked his Rolex. 2:55. Time to go. He headed downstairs and muttered, "Shit." John was in the living room. *Maybe he won't notice me.*

"River. Come here."

Fuck. He walked over to John.

"I want you to meet our new boy, Toby."

River tried to hide his nervousness, his impatience at the chit-chat. *Come on. I gotta go.*

John said, "I was about to show Toby around the House. Why don't you join us?"

Fuck. River followed them around. Kept glancing at his watch. 3:10. He knew where the tour would end—in the bedroom.

He hung back. Waited until John and the boy disappeared around a corner. River turned and ran the other way. Down the stairs to the front door.

Grant walked into his bedroom, home earlier than expected—the meeting had run short. He picked up the note on his bed. His heart thudded as the words hit him. He closed his eyes and reached into his pocket for a pill.

Brian stared at the gate seventy feet behind them. *Come on, River.* He checked the clock on the dash for the hundredth time. 3:12. "Where the hell is he?"

"Don't worry."

"How can I not worry? You don't know what John's like. If he's found out somehow—" He couldn't finish the sentence.

John's frown deepened. *How dare River disappear like that? Especially in front of a new boy. Makes me look like a fool.* A guard hurried up to him. "Sir, Mr. Nesbit is on the phone." John picked it up.

Grant's voice sounded shaky. "Do you know where River is?"

"As a matter of fact, he's just disappeared on me."

"Yes, he has. Brian's gone. They've left us."

"*What?*" He shouted to a security guard down the hall. "Seal the House!"

. . .

River had almost reached the gate when he heard someone yell. He glanced over his shoulder. Two security guards were racing toward him. He ran faster and slammed into the gate. Yanked on the handle, but it didn't open. He stared at it for a second in disbelief. Tried again, but it still wouldn't budge. Adrenalin surged through him. He jumped up, grabbed the metal bars and climbed with all his will.

Brian gasped. "Oh, my god!" He opened his car door. Stuart reached across him to pull it shut.

"I've gotta help him!"

Stuart grabbed his arm and held fast. "You can't help him."

Brian looked back. River was almost to the top. But the men were getting closer. River hooked his leg over and hung down on their side of the fence, then jumped and landed on his feet. He sprinted toward the car as the security guards went through the gate.

Stuart reached into the backseat and pushed the door open. But the guards were too close. River wasn't going to make it. Stuart slammed the car into reverse.

River dove in. "Go!"

Stuart floored it.

They watched the security guards grow smaller and disappear as they rounded a corner.

"River!" Brian reached into the backseat and clutched him tight.

They heard a car as they climbed the stairs to the apartment. A black BMW slid to a stop across the street. River kept his voice level. "That's one of John's cars."

Brian pushed on him. "Keep going. Go up."

Stuart followed, and they went into the studio. River stood in the open doorway to keep an eye on the car out front. "It's just sitting there. No one's getting out. Yet."

Brian's grip tightened on River's hand. *Grant, please help us.*

Grant sat on the couch in the parlor and watched John pace. "John, call off your men. The boys will come back on their own."

"You really believe that?"

"Yes, I do. *I* will handle this. Don't ruin things." He leaned forward. "Call off your men, John. You know the rules. If you go anywhere near those boys, I will take you down."

John stared at him a moment. Turned away and reached for the phone.

. . .

River craned his neck. "They're leaving!"

Brian peeked around the corner. The black car was gone. He laughed in relief and hugged River, then moved to hug Stuart as tears stung his eyes. "Thank you."

River touched Brian's shoulder. Brian turned, and they were holding each other tight. And kissing. Kissing as if they'd never kissed before. With all their pent up fear and sorrow.

And joy.

To be continued . . .

Information on the sequel available at www.crookedhills.com

Acknowledgments

My sincere gratitude goes out to everyone who volunteered to read this story before it was published; your feedback was invaluable. Thanks especially to those early readers who slogged through the gargantuan mass of the first draft. Combined with the sequel, it was well over 2,000 pages.

Thank you also to the musical artists and their publishers for allowing the use of their lyrics to enrich this story. And thanks to Crooked Hills Publishing and Willamette Writers for their support.

But most of all, I thank my mother, whose help and encouragement mean so much to me. And thank you to Brian, who helped me find myself.

About the Author

Naked in the Rain is the debut novel from Eowyn Wood. In addition to her work as an author, she performs editing for Crooked Hills Publishing and works at a non-profit AIDS organization. She has lived in many areas of the United States. After five years in Los Angeles, Wood relocated to the Pacific Northwest, where she now resides happily with her cats.

For additional information go to

www.crookedhills.com